Once in a Million Years is p   to
storyline, names of businesses, characters,   es.
Any comparison to real persons, dead or alive, o. any
business, would simply be a coincident and not intentionally
applied by the author.

Historical events and persons within the historical events,
are for the most correct, though mixed with parts of fiction
to fit the storyline set by the author.

Geographic locations are not meant to imply places or areas
associated with specific persons, dead or alive, but solely to
lend ambiance and setting to the story. For the most the
locations are correct, but at times adjusted by the author to
fit the storyline.

Please acknowledge that this is my first attempt at creating a
novel and my first attempt publishing. A lot of time was
spent proof-reading, editing and correcting. I have gone
through these check-points many times, but I am sure that I
could continue to do this till the end of time (and further)
and still not be satisfied. So please accept the small leftover
hick-ups that might have gone undetected (spelling,
grammatical errors, etc.) and if you find any, I beg your
forgiveness. If the errors in your opinion are too blatant,
please let me know (Web-Site: petersteiness.com) so I can
make the corrections.

I do hope that you will enjoy reading this story as much as I
enjoyed writing it. Thanks for your time and interest.

Sincerely,

Peter B. Steiness
Author

To my best friend ever

ONCE IN A MILLION YEARS

By
Peter B. Steiness

INITIATORY

"Once upon a time" is the universal key that unlocks doors to stories and fairytales, to the worlds of kings and queens, princes and princesses, heroes and villains. We experience horrors and happiness, confusions and solutions. We enjoy those emotional rollercoaster rides; we treasure being told stories, so we turn the pages as fast as we can. When it looks the bleakest for our heroes and heroines, we wish in our hearts that it will all be solved, and end with the proverbial: "Happily ever after" - well, *proverbial* for the most.

Events are tearing at us from beginning to end, but we still come back for more. Happy endings in stories and fairytales make us feel safe and comfortable, no matter how much controversy we are dragged through; it's just like life! Okay, maybe not precisely, but pretty darn close.

For the most, fairytales imitate life as life imitates fairytales. Look around, notice what you see and then compare. If you are as average as I, not many kings or queens or emperors come knocking, but when we do compare fairytales with the real thing, real life, we are actually able to find more similarities than we expect. We have heroes and heroines in real life; we face challenges, and for the most we find solutions. We deal with anxieties, frustrations, stress, hope, danger, life and death, love and hate; the rollercoaster ride is long. We can decide where we want to go, what we want to achieve and for the most figure out how to get there. But we can also fail and do nothing about it. What we do and what we want is for the most controlled by ourselves; we can pretty much choose our own destiny; within reason and reality, of course - or can we?

Real life can also have a life of its own; that is the part which is uncontrollable, also known as *fate*. Fate can be cruel and utterly devastating, but also utterly wonderful. Whatever fate dishes out, good or bad, we find a way to adjust, and when challenged again, we find ways to readjust. These diverse challenges change us and for the most they make us stronger - just like in fairytales.

The following is a fairytale about real life mixed with a bit of fate; or is it real life about a fairytale? That will be for you to decide. Whatever it is, the key unlocking the doors to all the magic will always be "Once upon a time"; so that is how we start.

****

Georgi's father was carving a pretty good life for himself. Being a lawyer in Russia in early nineteen hundred was a fine and revered occupation; in that respect he considered himself fortunate as well as somewhat lucky. He lived in a small, but very functional, apartment in the better outskirts of Kazan, one of the country's larger cities, located about 800 kilometers east of Moscow. The two main features in his office was the big, old and heavy mahogany desk, and the young, light and beautifully shaped secretary; she was twenty years his junior. Her name was Agnessa Tumanov; *Agnessa* fittingly meaning *pure*. She was always willing to work late hours for Georgi's father. Also employed were two boringly dry law-assistants; they had absolutely no interest in staying beyond the end of the workday.

Asking Georgi's father, he would in a conceding way inform you that he had a grand social life. It consisted of large quantities and a broad variety of female companions, lots of so-called friends, too many parties, seven-course dinners and an excessive consumption of alcohol. He attended concerts, the theatre, gallery openings and was often found strolling the halls of Kazan's many museums and parks. Most women found him handsome, charming, interesting and engaging; and he did too. Everybody thought him a connoisseur of culture, therefore trusting him to be a true intellectual and a genuine gentleman. But Georgi's father knew better. The truth was that he was as shallow as a human could possibly get. He knew he was shallow, but he also knew he was good at it. His sole existence was planned, scheduled and executed for three reasons only: Hunt, Gather & Conquer. He was constantly looking for new, exciting and willing overnight bed-partners and nothing else. He didn't care if they were married, divorced, or in any way attached, as long as they had somewhat pleasant looks and grand bedroom talents; and conquer he did. The only rule Georgi's father had, however shallow, was that the very moment conversation turned to hints of commitment, the affair ended. Surprisingly enough, he never experienced any irate or angry or jealous husbands or boyfriends or parents; he was very lucky that way. Life was shallow for Georgi's father, but that was the kind of life he wanted, so that was the life he lived. Fedyenka Milkovich was indeed a very happy camper. Ironically, *Fedyenka* means *God's Gift;* but his mistresses didn't find it ironic at all. Unfortunate for *God's Gift,* things would soon change and dramatically so.

The first of two lifestyle altering events for Milkovich materialized in early 1917 and was labeled *The February Revolution;* ruthless Czar Nicholas II was forced to abdicate. Later on Nick, his wife, their many children, as well as the cook, the valet and God knows who, were all unceremoniously *abdicated* forever - but seriously, why the *cook*? The second of these two lifestyle interruptions, was the *Red October Revolution of 1917. Abolishing private ownership and seeking to create a classless society* was not what Milkovich really wanted to hear, but that was what the Bolshevik Revolutionaries told every Russian, and quickly followed up with thousands of even more suppressing rules in the name of Communism. The brutal control of the Russian people was obviously not going to die with Czar Nicholas II – nor the death of his cook. The *Union of Soviet Socialist Republics*, aka USSR, was born; and Georgi's father didn't like that one bit. But he quickly understood that it would be in his own interest, and rather essential to stay alive, that his mouth stayed closed and his more liberal opinions kept to himself. Admittedly, Milkovich was shallow, but he was far from stupid.

Things were progressing okay the following years; Milkovich adjusted quickly. He was adamant about not giving up his pre-revolution lifestyle without a fight. Some former convenient and available items and services were now neither convenient nor available; at least for the masses. But with his vast and willing connections, and sponsored by a lot of cash, he didn't experience too great of interruptions concerning consumer goods and luxury items for himself. It was also helped by the fact that as Russia turned red, his legal services turned even more profitable. Sure, his clientele had changed, but demands, actually *commands*, for his services from city government and the local Communist Party's rulers, kept him busier than ever. The under-the-table legal advice many in government and the party needed, but couldn't go public with, was paid to Milkovich in large quantities of cash. It could have been risky work, but he made sure that all these *desperate* clients knew that if anything ever happened to him, their careers and possibly their lives would end rather abruptly; he covered himself well that way, and it would later on come in rather handy. This was the sleazy part of the workday, but the cash did not smell bad at all. Milkovich really loved Russia and he loved his Russian people, but he despised Communism and the direction the common Russian was forced to take; he despised it with a passion. Milkovich was shallow, but had been quick enough to see, that if he didn't play along on all levels, he would soon be eliminated as the Czar had been, as many millions of his beloved true Russians in the years to follow would be.

His social circles had quickly evaporated as so-called friends were now busy trying to make up their minds what side to join. The options were few and soon many were spying for the communist dictatorship. Nobody could admit associations with free-thinkers, liberals, suspect individuals or loose cannons. Even though Milkovich had always been charmingly diplomatic and exceedingly careful, he *was* considered to belong in at least one of those four danger zones; actually most people felt he was a perfect fit for all four, so they avoided him like the plague. His amorous affairs had dwindled a bit in quantity, but he made sure he didn't miss much; he just had to work a little harder in that department. So all said when the revolutionary dust settled a bit, Milkovich was back on track enjoying his shallow lifestyle, while consistently trying to ignore the loud realities going on around him.

By mid 1918, he employed four new, though still boringly dry law-office clerks; these *Motherland Patriots* had come highly *recommended* by the party. By rule, party *recommendations* should be followed to the letter – or else. He was fine with that, and adjusted the way he did business accordingly. The secrets he had were secrets he kept. He had enough dirt on his under-the-table clients to keep him alive; but of course there was always a risk.

His beautiful secretary Agnessa Tumanov was still employed by him. The pregnancy fully agreed with her, and made her glow so beautifully. And that was how Milkovich actually became Georgi's father. Miss Tumanov knew Mr. Milkovich was the father, as she had been faithful to her adulterous lover through the years. He had been her first lover and would also be her last. They married without delay, as that was the decent thing to do. Okay, so Milkovich was shallow but not *that* shallow. Days after returning from their honeymoon, he also returned to his exploration of available temptations and was soon again in full stride. Agnessa Milkovich was okay with that, but had instantaneously applied two non-negotiable rules: Her husband should always spend the nights at home and was to fully stop any extramarital affairs from the very moment their child was born. If he violated either rule, he would be barred from taking part in their child's life. Georgi's father needed only a short moment of consideration before he signed on the dotted line; and this he actually did with a smile. Admittedly, he had always liked her, had always enjoyed her company, her intellect and humor; and maybe he even loved her! For the record, Georgi's father stayed faithful to Georgi's mother from the second he had signed the agreement, which was approximate seven months before their child was born. Georgi's mother was most certainly not a stupid woman; not at all - and neither was Georgi's father.

Georgi Milkovich was born a lively bunch of baby. He would never become the social dynamo as his father, but he was energetic in many other areas. The gentle soft looks and personality he definitely had from his mother. From early on Georgi kept busy learning to read and write;

everything he could get his hands on he would read and then write down – whole novels and many of them. He especially enjoyed the authors from Russian literature's golden age, including Chekhov, Dostoyevsky, Tolstoy and Pushkin. When not spending time with these authors, he would spend the time with his mother, who read to him while he wrote it down – word by word. By the time Georgi was seven he was very advanced in the Russian language.

As he became dissatisfied with only reading and writing Russian, he made up his own strange foreign languages and constantly tried to communicate these to his mother; of course she didn't understand a word of what he said. One day she brought home a worn-out English dictionary. Georgi eagerly read the thousands upon thousands of words again and again. Though he was simply guessing the pronunciations, he later realized that he had been very close to what English really sounded like. His mother enjoyed this new eagerness and soon found more books in English. A good friend of hers, who spoke and wrote English well, would often come by to help Georgi by reading English for him and listen to him reading English back. Soon they only chatted in English when she visited. She had obtained some American magazines via the black market, and Georgi quickly considered them his holy shrine. The pictures and words told him about a land of milk and honey. He was eagerly impressed with America from that very moment. The interest in the English language and in America kept Georgi very busy; he soon had a plan, but not a lot of patience.

By the time he was 15, he fully controlled a highly sophisticated level of English, as well as his Russian was far beyond the level of even Russian language experts. The teachers at school suggested the next academic move for Georgi should be to a much higher educational institution; due to his massive talent, his young age would not be a hindrance. His proud parents fully agreed and Georgi was more than eager to forge ahead.

It so happened, that Moscow State University was founded by the linguist Mikhail Lomonosov back in seventeen hundred-something, and through the years the language departments had developed to be the best in Russia. Though barely a teenager, Georgi was granted special acceptance. Soon it was *goodbye Kazan* and *hello Moscow* for the young boy. He couldn't be more excited; neither could his parents, though with moist eyes and heavy hearts. They had send him on his way, but they had no idea how far he would go; no idea at all.

Shortly after his arrival to MSU, two serious looking government officials contacted him. They explained that they were determinedly looking for students with extraordinary language talents to do work for the government. They had been watching him for a while, actually since elementary school, and their comrade superiors were very impressed. Georgi initially thought he had a choice in the matter, but the tone of their request gave him the irksome feeling that there would only be one correct answer; the sheer mentioning of *The Kremlin* confirmed this sentiment.

Georgi's father had nodded oh so gently when told about the meeting with the two Kremlin officials. He had for years encouraged his son to find a way out of the Communist Soviet Union, just find a way to get the hell out, no matter how, when or to where; just get out. Georgi had already decided *where* he wanted to go; to the land of milk and honey. What he had gathered and learned from all the magazines and books he had read through the years, he knew that America would be the place. But he hadn't told his father as his father did not want to know – just in case somebody was listening – which of course they were. The demand of his services within the Kremlin would fit in perfectly with his plans, might open up chances to get out, chances he might otherwise not get. So he accepted the position (like if he had a choice) and comforted himself that it would only be for a short time; the money and the experience would come in handy.

Life at the university was hectic and fun. Socially he lived a little like his father, but was only a tiny bit shallow and certainly not as sexually active – he didn't have the time. It was the language studies he really had his interests glued to; that was his passion. The attention to women faded in comparison.

By the end of August 1939, he was the proud owner of a Masters Degree in Russian and English. Georgi had passed every course and finals with top grades, highest honors and in record time. To celebrate these achievements with his parents, he had spent hours on the train from Moscow to Kazan. It was late morning of September 1st when he rolled into Kazan Train Station. As he walked down platform 6 and into the warm, loving and teary-eyed embrace of his mother and father, Adolf Hitler rolled into Poland, starting his vicious Blitz Krieg. A few days later, France and England declared war on Germany and Georgi was immediately called back to Moscow to do his job: translate and interpret foreign documents. His celebratory visit with his parents was cut rather short – actually less than eight hours.

Georgi's workload grew in relation to the flow of the war. He had been security cleared to handle the most sensitive top-secret document translations and interpretations in Russian as well as in English. He had an extreme gift for reading between the lines, but most of this *gift* he kept to himself. His office was big but his staff was small. More staff would be added as his need for help increased, as the war seemingly was not going to slow down. The huge window behind his desk had the perfect view of Kremlin's gray walls. He felt he was in jail and desperately wanted to get out; the sooner the better.

Georgi had worked for the government over the last 4 years in a part-time capacity – whenever they needed him. From just a few documents here and there, it had soon escalated to more and more. He translated documents from English to Russian and from Russian to English; he was swiftly acknowledged for the excellence of his work. First the documents had been more of cultural and diplomatic nature, but during the last few years they had turned to full military and political contents. This started to include top-secret documents addressed to Stalin's office inside the Kremlin, as well as many translations were headed to party officials, specific political and military leaders, NKVD departments, as well as high-up commanders. The originations of the documents varied, but it had quickly turned to documents *acquired* by the Soviet's Secret Police, the NKVD and other *spy-clubs*, as he called them. They arrived from the Soviet embassies in England, America,

Germany and many other countries. Georgi was assigned to translate and then analyze. He felt that some of these documents were *acquired* in conspicuous ways. *Aren't they supposed to be Allies?* He'd often think; but he kept his mouth shut. At times he found fake documents. He knew he was constantly being tested for reliability by factions of the State's Secret Police. Georgi laughed every time, as all the attempts, in his opinion, were idiotic and naïve. They never challenged him, but he didn't tell anybody; that would be another of his many small well-kept secrets.

Besides his work with foreign and domestic documents, Georgi was also engaged as a translator in the Kremlin. This brought him in contact with many of the English, American and other foreign diplomats meeting Soviet government officials during their visits to Moscow. These same diplomats realized Georgi's work knowledge was extremely unique, especially for somebody so young. They never discussed their possible plans with neither Georgi nor with any of the other diplomats – that would stay their own little secret till the time was right. All of them would naively try to get on Georgi's good side with small hints, a lot of presents and friendship. He simply said *thank you* with a big smile, feeling that it was all going his way - hopefully.

One day Georgi was called up to Stalin's offices in the Kremlin. He had always been curious about the Soviet leader. Through one-sided and heavy propaganda he was depicted as a nice, warm and caring man, but some of the documents Georgi had been exposed to the last few years, told a rather different story; an extremely dark and very gruesome tale. But here he was in Stalin's offices and he soon after became one of the lead translators and interpreters for Stalin, his staff, party officials and top military brass. He kind of laughed at this predicament, still wanting to get the hell out of the Soviet Union and would now at times be working in the ruthless dictator's offices. Georgi was eagerly hopeful as well as thankful, that nobody could read his mind; if anybody could, he would quickly be extremely dead – and that was the very severe reality of his situation. And time went by and work was all Georgi did – still looking for a way out.

Vadim Petrov, Georgi's best friend from MSU and a supreme language expert in Russian as well as fluent in German, was working in the same capacity as Georgi. Vadim had asked him for a *casual* meeting that morning. *Casual* for Georgi and Vadim was code for *extremely important*. Neither of the young men trusted anybody, but they did trust each other with their lives. They had agreed to meet in the middle of Izmailovsky Park; one of their usual spots for these gatherings. Even a slight fraction of the information they had shared over time, would be more than plenty to get them executed; they were both fully aware of that. But they had found that they needed to do this, as it was an essential tool with respect to their official work, their clandestine efforts and their sanity. The additional knowledge they shared made their intelligence results more valid, fuller and further essential; more importantly, they would also know what to manipulate, which was basically anything they felt would be damaging to innocent entities; that had been their mission from the day they met, and being extremely cautious was the part that kept them alive. One hiccup and they would be dead.

Izmailovsky Park had enough corners and bushes and benches and buildings and trees and lakes and monuments to walk amongst undisturbed. As they had become rather good at keeping look-out over the years, another necessity concerning staying alive, they felt very comfortable here.

"*Operation Barbarossa*", was the first thing his friend whispered that morning.

"What do you mean *Operation Barbarossa*?" Georgi asked, fully aware what he meant.

"The German's are planning an attack on Russia in June, is what it means."

"That's insane, Vadim. There's a Treaty of Non-Aggression in place. You were there when it was signed." He giggled, "together with your pals Ribbentrop and Molotov – back in August of '39, I recall…"

"I know, but Hitler is going to attack anyway."

"How do you know this?" Georgi asked, pretty sure that he knew the answer. He had picked up many signs through his work as well as several commanders had mentioned it, when they didn't think he knew what they were talking about.

Stalin had been advised of the possibility a number of times, but had brushed it aside.

"That I prefer not to tell you; you know, just in case; better that you don't know, okay?"

"It sounds unrealistic," Georgi continued, testing the knowledge his friend had. "Why would they set a date this far in advance; that doesn't make sense at all. That information got to be wrong, my friend." Georgi smiled a bit, but saw seriousness in Vadim's face. "But you are sure about this; you truly trust that this is correct?"

"Yes, I'm very sure." He paused. "Why do you think Hitler is attacking?" Georgi smiled.

"You recall that Great Purge Stalin executed back in the thirties, you know where he incarcerated and killed millions…"

"Unfortunately, *yes*…"

"Would you say that there were thousands of otherwise good military leaders in that bunch?"

"*Yes* and your point is?"

"Adolf hates Communism, Bolshevism as well as Slaves, Jews or what have you. And when you remove leadership of your soldiers, wouldn't they run around like headless chicken?" Vadim started to see the point.

"So the Red Army is in a sad situation, is what you say…"

"And you have a moronic dictator with grandiose ideas of a world conquered, Adolf's World… So what better idea to knock the shit out of a weakened country that is also sitting on a lot of good stuff you want; actually what you need to build Adolf's World…"

"Oil, food, labor… I got it – but it's still a stupid attempt…"

"Coming from a disturbed man, it's not stupid – to us normal humans, it's insane." Vadim smiled and looked at his friend.

"You already knew about Barbarossa, didn't you?"

"You will never know, will you?" They kept walking through the rose-gardens.

"You have access to Stalin and those moronic gangsters of his; and they all trust and love you, Georgi." Georgi laughed out loud; to both of them, this was a sick joke.

"Yes, Dear Mr. Petrov, they trust and adore me because they are stupid, dangerous and ignorant moronic morons, whom I have trustfully fed a lot of made-up shit over time. But don't be naïve, my delusional comrade; the second they become displeased with me over anything, like burping, passing gas, wearing the wrong tie and especially for coming up with some shit prediction called *Barbarossa*, they'll all shoot me at the same time. Don't ever think that could not happen; they would even blow me away without a reason, just for the sheer sadistic fun factor." He continued to laugh. "And by the way, have you turned legally insane? What the heck, do you think I can just walk into the Kremlin, slap Stalin on his ass and go: Hey Uncle Joe, the Krauts are coming for a visit; what do you think about that, Old Pal," Georgi kept laughing.

"*Uncle Joe?*"

"Yeah, *Uncle Joe*; that's what Churchill's calling Stalin these days. Kind of trying to soften the image for the Brits of his favorite Allied Russian, our beloved tyrant and insane dictator, the murderer of millions; yeah, *that* Uncle Joe."

"You're crazy, Georgi, real crazy."

"I know and I'll have to do something about that as well." Georgi suddenly realized he had to stop right there. Wanting to get the hell out of Russia was *his* secret; it would never be shared, not even with his best friend."

"Yeah, you gotta tell *somebody*, Georgi"

"Why? But much more important: Why *me*?"

"Because I can't; I know the source of the information and you don't"

"I know from where, but that's not the point. The thing is that if the Krauts don't attack I'll soon be vacationing in a Siberian Gulag & Death Spa. The winters are rather chilly there; I might be wrong, but at least that's what I hear."

"You got to warn them, Georgi, please! It could save millions of lives."

"But Dear Friend, if I do I will no doubt have a few intimate meetings with the supporting cast from the NKVD, you know those brass-knuckle no brains guys from the People's Commissariat for Internal Affairs, AKA secret bloody state police, the ones who believe torture is some kind of therapeutic application; do you remember those guys?" Georgi didn't laugh. "Remember, that to them, *softening up* a fellow comrade means breaking every bloody bone in his body. I'm not sure I'm up for that; I like me too much for that kind of bodily adjustment, if you know what I mean."

"Georgi, you'll find a way that leaves you out. You have done this so many times before; you can do it again. Think of the lives it could spare - be a hero."

"If I'm going to be a hero, being a dead hero with a severely mutilated body is not the image that comes to mind, thank you." Georgi paused, and then continued: "But seriously, let me chew it over a few times and see what I can come up with. You must realize that I need to cover my cute butt big time. This would not be the time to do a screw up, okay?" He took a deep breath and grinned: "So when are they supposed to attack again?"

"It's scheduled for June 22nd this very year of 1941, early dawn with over four million troops, massive quantities of equipment and that Blitz Krieg approach; everything on a very huge scale. They have already started stacking numerous divisions up and down the borders." He paused. "And by the way, your butt is not really that cute." Georgi ignored the last remark and thought for a moment.

"I'll try to come up with something, but you'll have to do some magic as well." Vadim nodded in agreement. They both looked further down the path at the same time. Georgi continued: "And talking about magic, here's Vadim's girlfriend and right on time."

As the young woman slowly pushed the stroller along the path, she kept reaching for the cooing baby inside. Her sweet smiles caused even more cooing. She had of course noticed the two young men coming towards her. They were walking tightly side by side, involved in hushed conversation. As the baby interrupted her again, she reached inside the stroller, pretending to care for its needs. But this time her hand quickly found the small switch. As the young men were close enough, her index finger slowly squeezed and held. Nobody else could hear the film-camera's stealthy humming. Unfortunately the young men had acknowledged her; they both smiled while expressing their greetings: "dobroe utro", but since they had otherwise stopped talking, that was the only thing the high powered microphone picked up. "Good morning!" yeah, her boss would surely be impressed with that audio clip.

"What a lovely baby," they both expressed as they had stopped and looked inside the stroller. The young woman was blushing, but solely from irritation, not from shyness.

"Is this your baby?" Vadim teasingly asked. She responded a bit too fast.

"No it's my sister's baby." Vadim smiled.

"Oh, that's good. Have a lovely morning, Miss." Flustered she answered:

"Thank you and you as well." She hurriedly scampered along. Vadim and Georgi were holding back boyish giggles.

"You are one smooth operator, aren't you Petrov. *Is this your baby*, how vague but loud is that! Are you trying to pick up an NKVD agent and get us both turned in because you are sweet on her? If you are just trying to get laid, I'll let you borrow my little black book for a peek and choose." Vadim changed the subject real fast due to slight embarrassment.

"Wouldn't that baby make the list for the youngest NKVD agent ever?"

"Nice try, lover-boy." Georgi and Vadim kept giggling as they continued down the path. They had seen her several times before, and not only in this park. Based on their *spy* experiences, they had already voted her *the top clumsiest not-so-secret agent of all times*. They had even talked about conversing with her beyond daily pleasantries as she actually was rather elegant, but they felt that too much conversation might cause her early unemployment; so they let her do her thing, no matter how badly she seemed to do it. They were still trying to figure out exactly what agency she worked for, but it really didn't matter at all. They both felt secure concerning their own behavior and felt that nobody would ever be able to charge them with anything; and they were both right about that. But Vadim did have many pleasant dreams about this, for him, perfect secret agent.

Back in the office Georgi thought about, researched and looked for specks of related information that would confirm any hints about Barbarossa; slowly bits and pieces appeared. Based on what he found, he finally came up with a way to communicate the Barbarossa information to Stalin and his moronic puppets in a way that would cut the risk of losing his own life, and perhaps save millions. On the other hand, rumors had floated around the Kremlin for a while. He was fully aware that Stalin had been informed of the Barbarossa possibilities, but he still didn't believe Hitler would attack. Stalin also had a problem making up his mind, more so repairing instead of preventing. Georgi shook his head. He really needed to get the hell out of this land.

He made up a genuine looking intercepted document *originating* from the Germans, where it would signify that it had been in contact with and/or approved by Adolf himself, though he never signed anything, just in case. Vadim's German expertise had delicately created a Germanic translation in a believable Adolf henchmen's style; Georgi carefully put it all together.

Finally he had the finished report on his desk; he was utterly impressed with their work. He placed it in the middle of the stack of documents for that morning's security briefing. He would casually bring it out during the presentation; the top brass and some of Stalin's assistants would be there. Georgi would just melt it into his daily *believe it or not* category. If there was no reaction at first, he would make sure to give it another go the next morning. Maybe the morons didn't love him, but they did actually trust him. He had been correct and foreseeing on many other important *predictions* to big applauds. But this was an extremely different situation, much bigger in scope. This Barbarossa thing could be rather dangerous to suggest. But now Georgi Milkovich suddenly found it important to get across.

He tried to stay calm as he presented the made-up *intercepted* Barbarossa document. At first, everybody in the meeting-room laughed. They truly felt it was just another diversionary document. At times, the German's would test their ability to decipher secret messages and hope their Russian friends would react accordingly, which would prove their point. Georgi showed them comparative likeness this document had with previously proven documents. He showed them similar structure in wording, paragraph and language organization. He was a good salesman and he knew very well what he was selling. They all began to acknowledge that maybe this could be the real stuff. Georgi still wanted to cover his cute butt, so for the record he finished the presentation by clearly stating: *I could of course be very wrong*. But nobody in the room could see how he could possibly be wrong at all; the proof was right in front of them. It was too important to ignore, so one of Stalin's assistants wanted to bring the situation to the boss' immediate attention, so he raced out of the room with a copy of the Operation Barbarossa confirmation document flapping in his sweaty hands.

Later that day, Georgi was called to Stalin's office. This would be the ultimate test for his inventive creation. Stalin was standing by the large window as Georgi entered. "Young comrade," he mumbled, "I am impressed by your work. I read the document concerning Operation Barbarossa and I appreciate your eagerness for us to consider its validity." Georgi swallowed hard. Stalin continued: "Hitler is preparing to attack Russia in June, it says. Young man, that's the silliest thing I have ever heard. We have a Non-Aggression treaty, signed, sealed and delivered. They would not dare to attack." Stalin smiled broader now. "They are trying to find out if we can dissect their documents and their stupid made-up secrets. And we can do that because of comrades like yourself; you have done excellent work again. Keep up this level of production and you will go far, I promise you that." Stalin motioned Georgi to leave. As he was on his way out the door, Stalin added: "Milkovich, I'll give Comrade Adolf a call, you know, see what's up. Would that make you feel better?" His big moustache was sarcastically grinning.

"It would probably help, Sir; but are you sure Herr Hitler will tell you the truth?" Now Stalin had to laugh out loud.

"Probably not, young man, probably not." Georgi rushed away from Stalin's office as fast and as calmly as he could. He pretty much flew down the halls of the Kremlin, shaking and sweating like an airborne pig. He felt relieved as it didn't look like he was going to die today after all. Safely back in his office looking out at the Kremlin walls, he quietly moved the Lenin bust on the windowsill a couple of feet to the left. During his daily stroll inside the walls that afternoon, Vadim Petrov looked up at his friend's office window and knew it had been done. It was all about building trust with the morons for future action and results. And by-the-way, Stalin forgot to call Hitler concerning Operation Barbarossa.

At 0600 the following day, Georgi's apartment, office, car, and other facilities used by him, was heavily bugged and put under constant surveillance and extreme observation; this by courtesy of NKVD and due to the gruesome fact that Stalin didn't trust anybody what-so-ever. Also at 0600 that same morning, Georgi was fully aware of his situation. As he had been on his careful toes since day one, he didn't need to change anything, routines, or ways he normally did his daily mechanics. The morons from NKVD would find nothing on him. But the unfortunate reality that they executed peasants for things they had *not* done was also feared. So from that day forward, Georgi was extra careful.

It was in the evening of June 22nd, 1941 that a courier brought a letter for Georgi. At dawn the combined German forces had attacked Russia and Operation Barbarossa was now a gruesome reality. The letter was from Stalin's office. He acknowledged Georgi's work from a few weeks back, and wanted him to be closer attached to the core offices of the Soviet Intelligence. If he ever heard other like *rumors*, he should make sure to contact Stalin's office directly and at once. Georgi had actually expected his death sentence; he was receiving extended life on a much higher level instead; *go figure,* he thought. This didn't change anything concerning Georgi Milkovich's plans to flee the Soviet Union and hopefully land safely on both feet in America. He kept waiting for the right moment to show up; and he was still sure that nobody knew about his plan.

The first NKVD report on Suspect Georgi Milkovich was clean as a whistle. No matter how deep they dug, the agents did not find a single hick-up and declared him a true, dedicated and hard-working patriot and comrade. They also found that he had been a valued member of the Communist Party from early Pioneer days on; in this specific case they were pathetically misinformed. Georgi was most certainly not a member, but the fake document he had produced as well as his worn and forged membership card, said that he was. They also found that their suspect liked sex a bit beyond the norm; Georgi never figured out how they came to that conclusion, but as things unfolded, he really didn't care. In their ignorant wisdom they applied the old and tried interrogation method of *information through sex.* Soon, nice looking female agents were sent Georgi's way. He appreciated the efforts and immediately spotted every single attempt. He tried not to disappoint them. They eagerly tested everything in the book to please him in exchange for possible information – but he never leaked a single word; also because he was too busy enjoying being interrogated this way. All Vadim Petrov could do was laugh and shake his head, trying not to appear too envious.

The head of the local NKVD department was the one reporting and Stalin was extremely glad to hear the non-news about Milkovich; in some strange way he was extremely fond of this talented young man. But his final order was: *Stay on him and dig much deeper!* Which they did, and Georgi knew right away that they did. However sure he was about his own little secrets, he was also starting to get more concerned. Maybe there was a small crack in his armor that he had overlooked. Georgi didn't enjoy this new concern at all – far from.

The deeply secret actions Georgi Milkovich was also engaged in, was only known by a very small and tight group within the Kremlin. They were all silent and threats of torture and death would never make them talk. At this point, the NKVD knew nothing about their existence; the chance that they would and possibly could at any moment was realistic. One slip-up and hundreds of additional people would die.

Georgi was an expert translator and a superb interpreter of what he read and translated. He purposely under-covered and manipulated a lot of information to save lives; nobody knew about this, except Vadim. Georgi's responsibility within the organization was to point out people who should be evaluated for importance and for levels of threat. Then it was up to other members of the group to decide what process should be used to fix the issue. Numerous situations during Georgi's watch had been solved successfully, though he never personally dealt with the *solutions* himself. Only Georgi and Vadim knew of each other's involvement and though he trusted him with his life, it was still not a good thing. The members of the organization communicated through a system where they would never find out the other member's identities; it had to be this kind of ultimate clandestine protection if they wanted to stay alive. What they dealt with would hopefully within a nearby future, bring Communism and the Soviet Union to a halt and free the Russian people. It was something Georgi only talked about twice, but many years later and just before he died.

Working life within the Kremlin was tolerable. The horrific reports of atrocities from the battlefields and especially from behind the fronts, was bringing Georgi to a point of terrifying despair; a place he did not like. The horrendous murders and inhumane treatment of prisoners as well as civilians were committed by the Germans as well as soldiers of the Red Army. NKVD murdered Russians for the slightest reasons. Defectors and traitors was shut on the spot, no trials, just because and swift. Though he did all he could from where he was, the painful feeling that grew stronger every day was nearly killing him. But he stayed strong, at least on the surface. He felt growing guilt that he wanted to escape, but rationalized that he had wanted to do so from the time he was a little boy. The situation was rather different now, so he felt he was letting his people down.

As the German armies flooded eastward, many of Soviet Union's industrial factories, manufacturing military necessities, had to be relocated beyond the reach of enemy bombers. A big portion of these facilities settled in Kazan, about 500 miles east of Moscow. Some of Georgi's work responsibilities included translation and understanding of secretive military equipment manufacturing manuals, so he often traveled to his home town. This was a thrill as he could visit his parents. They always looked and acted like newlyweds; so much in love. In spite of being 20 years younger than her husband, she had obviously been able to help Georgi's father find his true self. He had quickly become a satisfied, healthy and happy individual. The way he kept looking at her, touching her and kissing her, underlined how much he was in love. Georgi shook his head with a smile and could seriously not see himself become smitten and puppy-love gooey eyed like that. No way - that was not his style; but of course Georgi couldn't look into the future – as far as we know, nobody can.

After the Sunday morning attack on Pearl Harbor December 7th 1941, the Americans were finally in the war, busy chasing Japs in the Pacific. Hitler declared war on

America a few days later. Though the battle at Midway and the hard fought victory on Guadalcanal had been promising turning points, 1943 didn't look too promising on the fields of war for the Allies. But still, through the haze of battle, small specks of light started to become visible.

As they held up their champagne glasses in Kazan that last evening of 1942, toasting to life, health, happiness and possible peace, in spite of a world in turmoil, they couldn't know that this was the last time they would ever see each other. Georgi's chance to escape would soon present itself and when it did, he had no intention of letting it slip away. He loved his parents, but that was never going to hold him back when it was about his very own life, health, happiness, peace and especially about freedom. Georgi's parents fully understood and accepted that. They had anticipated the moment to come sooner or later and they would never stand in the way of their son's dreams.

The package from Stalin's office arrived by courier January 2nd, 1943. It was a rather thick brown canvas envelope, weighing at least 2 kilos. He signed the receipt and immediately put it on his desk to uncover the content. After the wrapping disappeared, he found a rather deep stack of documents. Just reading a few lines of the cover page made him shake and sweat and feel dizzy. He quickly waved his two secretaries out of the office. The cover page spelled: SYMBOL. Georgi knew immediately what that meant, but not the meaning for him personally. He would soon understand how important this was; how important indeed.

He had been attached to Stalin's staff for the trip to Casablanca. He would be part of working the conference between Stalin, Roosevelt and Churchill, code-named SYMBOL. He had been given the responsibilities of coordinating translators and interpreters and he only had a few days to get ready before leaving. He was soon fully involved with all the preparations, finding and deciding on the staff he wanted with him. He knew the department's employees better than they thought he did; he knew their strengths and weaknesses. He finally settled on the group he felt confident would do a satisfying job. It was utterly important for Georgi to succeed, and he suddenly found that it was more important to him than he would ever realize.

That Stalin called off his own participation at SYMBOL due to the situation at Stalingrad didn't matter much to Georgi; the excitement of getting to meet Roosevelt and Churchill was more important. The commandant from Stalin's office had insisted that the assigned Soviet delegation should still travel to Casablanca to observe the conference' progress and keep a direct and active line of communication with the Kremlin. Georgi was more than fine with that. He was soon on the plane to Morocco.

After arriving in Casablanca, situated in the French Protectorate of Morocco, North Africa, he was assigned a small room at the Anfa Hotel. The rest of the staff was quartered elsewhere. He couldn't believe that he was actually going to meet Franklin Delano Roosevelt as well as his top hero, Winston Leonard Spencer Churchill. But he had to stay focused, get the job done without mistakes. He was sure that Stalin was expecting the very best, and Georgi was going to make sure that's what Stalin would get; but of course only what Georgi wanted to give him. Considering the end result, Stalin became *very* disappointed and angered; but that was due to something very different.

Those ten days in January 1943 were utterly exhausting for Georgi. He worked 18 to 20 hours every day, making sure his responsibilities looked like perfection. He held numerous daily meetings with his staff and they were all giving their very best, days and nights. Even though he had been cleared security-wise and selected especially for this mission, it proved obvious that he was constantly followed and observed. He was tempted to approach his tails and tell them how bad of a job they were doing, but he decided against it. He did his job and he let them do theirs.

Between the many meetings of the Allied leaders, Georgi reconnected with several of the foreign officials he had met in Moscow. Two American diplomats he had spent a lot of time with during their last visit, had gone out of their way to get together with him in Casablanca. It had been in a bar, heavily protected, and over several glasses of Moroccan wine. The chit chat had been rather informal and involved a lot of laughter. After a couple of hours it seemed to be time to break up. They all stood up, and that was when the taller of them whispered in Georgi's ear:

"Georgi, we want you to meet with one of our guys; his name is Hamilton. He's kind of running our Special Operations. He'd like to talk with you, okay?" Georgi nodded somewhat puzzled, though excited.

"Okay. I'm scheduled to fly back to Moscow the day after tomorrow." He whispered back.

"Then let's set it up for tomorrow evening; let's say about 22:00 hours and here, okay?" Georgi nodded again. "And Georgi, come alone, okay?" This had all been on the level, just social chit chat, some jokes, view of the war and stuff like that. But this *invitation* excited him. "You know you're being followed, don't you?"

"Yeah, I know." He smiled. "They are actually not that good, so it will not be a problem shaking them off. I mean, I got rid of them tonight"

"Good boy. See you tomorrow."

Through the days in Casablanca, Georgi had had numerous conversations during work situations with Roosevelt and Churchill. He had especially fancied a couple of conversations alone with Churchill. One morning he was called over to Churchill's breakfast table and they had chatted away like two blokes of a long friendship; it had been a lovely time. Georgi was in seventh heaven and as his responsibilities had come off close to perfection; he couldn't be happier. So the next to last evening he invited his staff to a four course dinner with all the wine they wanted. It had been a good evening and his speech of thanks and appreciation had been inspiring and a tear-jerker for most.

Later that evening, a bit before 22:00 hours, Georgi had quietly sneaked through the large kitchen and out the back of the Anfa Hotel. Losing his tails had been a piece of cake; they would never find out. A few moments later he arrived at the bar. The second he walked through the door and into the smoke, noise and darkness, firm hands grabbed his arms and quickly steered him through the maze of people, tables and chairs. A door opened and he found himself in a long dark hallway. The grips on his arms had disappeared and as he turned around, he only found an empty and nearly black space. In front of him, he saw a bit of light through a half open door; he soon stood in front of it.

A large framed man sat on a wide sofa. On the table in front of him was a bottle of bourbon, as well as a couple of glasses, a bucket of ice and a big brown envelope.

"Hey, Georgi, come on in." His deep American voice was friendly and smiling as he stood up. "Very nice to finally meet you in person" he held out his right hand. "I assume that you didn't bring any friends along! I'm Hamilton, by the way." Georgi shook Hamilton's big hand.

"Nice to meet you; I'm Georgi, and *no* I didn't bring any friends along." After a few more pleasantries Georgi sat down, now with a half-full glass in his hand; he seriously didn't like bourbon. Hamilton talked about the nearly finished conference and about how well everything had gone. They sipped a bit from their drinks.

"You look even younger in person; very impressive," he noted as he started to open the large envelope. "Georgi, what I'm about to tell you will stay between the two of us. Besides you, only two other people know about the contents of this envelope and our little get-together here." Hamilton smiled. "If you decide to decline our offer, then this meeting never took place. Are you okay with that?" Georgi nodded slowly. Hamilton started to remove some documents from the envelope. "What we want to offer you is a one-way ticket to the United States of America." Georgi looked somewhat stunned.

"Meaning what?" He said quietly.

"Meaning that we want you to switch over and work for us, and do pretty much what you are doing now, but in reverse, of course." Hamilton kept smiling, "that's about it in a nutshell". Georgi went slightly dizzy. Was he hearing this right: *They wanted him to come to America?*

"I don't understand," was all he could mutter. Hamilton smiled.

"The deal is, that our guys, the ones you met a couple of times in Moscow, were very impressed with your abilities. We did some observation of you, and found that you know a heck of a lot more than you have ever communicated and for a young guy like you, you show a vast amount of additional potential that would blossom in the right environment. When they came back from Moscow, they begged us to do something about bringing you over to our side. So here we are. What do you think?"

"I don't know. All I do is translating documents. How could you be interested in that?" Hamilton laughed out loud, and poured himself more bourbon. "What's so funny?" Georgi asked puzzled.

"Comrade, we know a bit more about you than you think we do. I actually think we know more about you than your Soviet pals do."

"Meaning what?" Georgi was all of a sudden on guard.

"Well, we have found that you are extremely sharp concerning reading between the lines of those *documents*, as you call them." Hamilton was leaning back in the sofa. "We even tested your abilities, just to make sure that you were actually that sharp and especially that quiet about it."

"Tested my abilities? I'm not sure I understand." Hamilton smiled.

"You know precisely what I mean, Georgi." He offered Georgi a cigarette; he waved it off. "But there is one thing that we have been very puzzled about, and that is why you haven't communicated *all* your findings to your comrades." Georgi all of a sudden froze. He knew precisely what Hamilton meant. But if the Americans knew what he knew, then they would also know in the Kremlin; wouldn't they? But then again, if Kremlin knew, wouldn't they have disposed of him by now? He started to feel extremely uncomfortable. Hamilton was studying his face, smiling a tiny bit. "So you are wondering why we know and they don't; or maybe they actually do know already!"

"Yeah, I sure do; but I don't know about them."

"I'm positive that we are the only ones who figured you out so far. And we also assume that all the *extra* information you obtained and kept more or less for yourself, were just an extra challenge for you. Why you kept *some* of that stuff to yourself, we are somewhat puzzled about. I mean, we even wrote certain *secret* documents with a lot of hidden meanings between the lines, documents we knew the Russians would get their little dirty hands on, and they would eventually end up on your desk; and you passed the test, comrade." Georgi smiled nervously. "We figured that you withheld certain information to protect certain people?"

"Yeah I remember that one. I also remember that I felt it was a clumsy attempt of code-manipulation. I wasn't sure if it was to test me; maybe somebody else, but not me. I never communicated the additional information I found, just gave them what the lines said." Georgi exposed a slight smile. "And by the way, I did all the *for me only* stuff to do precisely what you assumed."

"Why?" Hamilton asked.

"It has always been a combination of things. Not happy with life in Russia and leaning towards a possible life somewhere else. England, France, America, just somewhere else. Also a lot of those documents would get some good people in bad trouble, so I lightened the load a bit." Hamilton smiled and nodded.

"So let's see if we can work something out for us, you and America. As we didn't find any reaction to those fake documents, we were pretty sure that you had some personal agenda for not communicating all the additional stuff you decoded. It was actually rather intriguing, really, so we had to approach you and test the waters." Hamilton smiled again, "so that's why we are here."

"Interesting, because I *did* have a very slight feeling of something like this, but I never wanted to rely on it. It was wishing too high, and I didn't want my hopes shot down."

"Yeah, and you have been good at keeping your mouth shut; very impressive." He took a sip from his glass. "You *must* come and play with us, Georgi. You really must. I seriously do not think that you are fully safe in Moscow anymore. I'm afraid that they'll soon figure you out. I mean *we* did and from far away." Georgi looked thoughtful and agreed. Hamilton took another sip of the Bourbon followed with a smirk.

"Oh by the way, did you hear about that so-called *Kremlin Angel of Death* who gave out orders concerning people who should be eliminated or whatever you'll call it; he worked around Stalin's offices," Georgi tried to look casual.

"I'm not sure I do; what about him?"

"Somebody popped him the other day in a bathroom not far from Uncle Joe's office. They found him with one huge hole in the back of his head; his face was pretty much gone, you know a big crater where the nose used to be." Georgi tried desperately to look surprised.

"That's amazing; inside the Kremlin, you say?"

"Yeah, inside the Kremlin and it happened just before you left for the airport and your trip to Casablanca." Georgi felt

shaken inside; looking at him would never give him away, but he was in the middle of an internal turmoil. Hamilton smiled. "Relax Georgi, there is nowhere in hell or on earth anybody else know about your little club, and the saint who popped the Angel will never be found; so don't worry, okay?" Georgi tried to look casual again, but this time it didn't work.
"How do you know?"
"Your comrade: Vadim Petrov."
"He told you?"
"No, we planted him there; he's one of the good guys. He's the one who started that club and we control the action more or less from Washington. Of course your participation has been utterly important; a really great job on your part, Georgi, really great and very much appreciated." Georgi was now really sweating inside. So his pal was the guy; he would never have guessed, not in a million years.
"Wow," was all he could say. Hamilton smiled and continued:
"So you want to come and play?"
"I need to think about it," he said quietly.
"Well, you see, that's the problem. We don't have time for that, really. It's one of those *decide now either way* things. You see, we have the whole plan ready to go; all we need is for you to say *yes*".
"You don't even know if I want to go to America or anywhere else, for that matter."
"I think we had a pretty good idea, otherwise we wouldn't have asked you. We have followed you around Moscow and on your trips to Kazan the last 6 months, and according to our experts, you are not a happy Kremlin camper."
"What do you mean *followed me around*?"
"You know, the usual stuff, bugged office, telephones, apartment, girlfriend's living quarters. And your roommate: working for us, but you didn't give him much of a chat either, did you, Georgi?"
"I didn't know." Georgi was puzzled yet again. How could they have covered him without his knowledge? He thought he was much smarter than that; but at least he had been right about his roommate *spying for one side or the other*.
"Doesn't matter; we were not out for evil, we only wanted to find out where you stood, that's all" Hamilton smiled. "So

where *do* you stand, comrade?" Georgi leaned back in his chair. It was all happening so fast, and though he had prepared himself mentally for this precise moment for many years, it still came up confusing. He knew he had to make a quick decision; but in reality, he had already made that *quick* decision years ago.

"Okay, so if I say yes, what will happen next? I mean, I do believe that Stalin and his comrades would be a bit against me disappearing all of a sudden. You know, they do like me, the work I do, you know, basic stuff like that." Hamilton laughed.

"Well put, Milkovich, and you are right. So what we have prepared is a disappearing act, Hollywood style. You'll leave as is. You can't go back to the hotel, no personal stuff, no check out and mushy goodbyes to dear friends and colleagues. The farewell hug for Uncle Joe is not in the script either; you got that?" Hamilton handed over some of the documents for Georgi to look at. "What we'll do with you, is ship you to America; departure within the hour. You'll fly to England, refuel; then off to the good old USA. We'll set you up in Washington D.C. There's an apartment waiting for you, new I.D.'s, an automobile, a bank account and a job with your own staff, basically the works; any questions?" This was going a bit fast for Georgi, but he started to understand what was going on. His mind was finally working at full capacity, though he still had a hard time grasping the enormity of the situation. Hamilton smiled: "But we do not supply any female companions; you are on your own in that department."

"What will it look like, you know, me disappearing?"

"With your hotel room left as is, whatever you left there, in whatever order, it will look like you have been a victim of foul play. The normal investigations and proverbial searches will be done by all secret service attachments from the conference. It's all pretty much a routine act of *pretending*. The Russian delegation will issue a statement that one of their staff members has mysteriously disappeared. Representatives from the U.S., England and France will condemn the perpetrators and we'll all look sad, angry and surprised." Hamilton stopped - Georgi continued.

"Will the Kremlin buy that story?" Hamilton smiled.

"Not for a blooming second. And nobody else will either. They'll all know we whisked you out of here, but by the time it all becomes an issue, you'll be safely tucked away in Washington D.C. – Nobody will admit it happened as it would be embarrassing to do so."

"Will they try to get to me or my parents?" Georgi asked quietly.

"I don't think so. Through the years of your father's law-practice, he collected so many secrets about so many high-ups in the party and within the Kremlin that they wouldn't dare touch him, less kill him. He has his butt covered all over the place. Also, we know who you really are, what you can do and what you have done; but your comrades don't know that - yet. They might suspect that you were much better than they thought you were, but that will be it, and too late. So to them it's just the loss of a translator, no matter how blooming nice you are. But to be fully safe, we have you covered from head to toe and beyond. If anybody, and I do mean *anybody,* ever try to figure it out, they will have absolutely no chance in hell to get within a million miles of you. I can promise you that. You have already existed in D.C. as a director for over six months – social life and all, by somebody who looks very much like you. It is all set, everything is ready to go." Hamilton leaned over and showed Georgi a page from the stack of documents. "And here is your new name." Georgi read his new ID and liked it immediately. Then Hamilton's face turned serious. "As part of covering your butt, Georgi, you will not have any form of contact with your parents or Vadim or anybody else, for a long, long time and possibly forever. The war has to be over and old wounds healed; and even then only maybe. You fully understand that?" It had to sink in a bit, but he had also covered that aspect over the years. He knew his parents would fully understand, and he also believed that they would know that all was okay with Georgi, even when they got the letter from the Kremlin that their son had gone missing. He would also miss his closest friend Vadim Petrov.

"I do," he answered softly.

"I'll do you a favor, my friend. In one month I'll make sure your parents will be notified that you are doing well. Basics, that you are alive, satisfied and happy; nothing else. I assume that we can trust them?"

"You can trust them, and thanks," he responded somewhat relieved. He already missed them, but now he had to apply himself to his immediate future. He realized that he had seen his parents for the last time.

"What about Petrov?"

"He'll know by tomorrow morning," Hamilton said matter-of-fact – Georgi nodded softly and looked at the document in his hands.

"I do like my new name. Who came up with it?" Hamilton smiled and pointed at his own chest.

"I did, and I was sure you'd especially like the middle name, considering your hero." Georgi was impressed. Hamilton had done his homework, that was for sure; but how could he know? "When you arrive in D.C. you'll find your new name on everything; it's already done."

"You were sure I would sign up!"

"Yes, Georgi, you would sign up because you are not a stupid man." Hamilton stretched his hand out towards Georgi; they shook warmly to seal the deal. "You will become a very happy camper; I will make sure of that." Georgi nodded with a smile. He was finally getting excited about the whole thing. This was what he had wanted for so long, and it had finally landed in his fortunate lap. Yes, he was indeed going to be a happy camper, an extremely happy American camper. "Do you have any last concerns or questions?" They had both gotten up.

"You said that you pretty much know everything about me." Hamilton smiled and nodded.

"That's pretty much true."

"Well Mr. Pretty-Much-Know-It-All, for you information, I *hate* bourbon," Georgi stuck it to Hamilton - Hamilton just laughed.

"We couldn't find a single bottle of Pshenichnaya, so I grabbed a bottle of bourbon instead." Now it was Georgi's turn to laugh.

"Okay *now* I'm impressed; you can't find better vodka. I think we'll get along rather well, don't you, Mr. Hamilton?" They kept laughing and shook hands again.

"We will, and it's John, from now on. Not any more of that *Hamilton* shit." John and Georgi quickly became close friends.

He was rushed out the back door and into a powerful sounding dark blue sedan. He was asked to curl down on the back seat and was immediately covered with a blanket. The ride to the air strip through the blackness of the night was dusty, bumpy but fast. Still hidden by the blanket, he was swiftly hoisted on board the waiting plane. Somebody kept him covered up and it was not before the plane roared into the air that the blanket was removed.

"Welcome on board, Sir." She was a friendly looking brunette with a wide smile. The US military uniform fit her well and clearly stated the shapes it was trying to cover. "What can I get you: food, beverage, pillow, a blanket?"

"What about your hand in marriage, Miss?" She rolled her eyes and smiled.

"That's the third offer today, sorry!" She giggled and continued: "Let's just start with a real nice cocktail, okay Sir? Then we'll get back to that question of yours and discuss the possibilities." Georgi smiled back; she had a sense of humor.

"What's your name, Miss?" He asked when she returned.

"Irene," she answered. "Irene Samson - and what's yours?"

"My name is George Winston Miller." He said it with the greatest conviction for the very first time, and he would never be called anything else.

"Nice meeting you, George Winston Miller; I think I might get both of us a cocktail. I'm kind of off duty till we get to London. Do you like vodka?"

Irene stayed on all the way to Washington D.C. She served the few other passengers their food, drinks and other conveniences as well as she casually chatted with each of them. But she spent most of her time in the seat next to George Winston Miller. He found her engaging and funny. He had never met a woman like her. Irene found him a fun conversation, very interesting in a cynical and sarcastic way. He seemed rough on the social edges, and she wondered why. Some day she'd find out, but by then it had no meaning at all. Though Irene at this point had only known of George Winston Miller 14 hours, she already decided that he was the one she'd spend the rest of her life with – however long, however short.

He had Irene's naked body in bed with him, just the way he always looked at women he met. But that picture faded away. Maybe he wasn't as shallow as he thought! George felt she had figured him out really fast and surprisingly, he was okay with that, because she seemed okay with what she found. As they landed near D.C., she had given George her phone number. He promised to call her when things settled. She knew he would, and he knew it too. They gave each other a light kiss and a warm hug, and their deal was sealed. This was the second deal he had sealed within the last 48 hours, and he was rather pleased with himself. Though they didn't verbally express it, they were in silent agreement of what was going to happen next; a decision they were happy with. George Winston Miller's new life in America already looked fabulous; and he had barely landed.

Hectic weeks followed his arrival to Washington D.C. He moved into an apartment with a well-stocked kitchen, given an automobile, with a driver for the first month or so, a bank account, identification cards, drivers license, passport, a wardrobe and a small library of books about life in America; George knew most of them already. In a quick closed-door session he denounced his Russian citizenship to instantly become a citizen of the United States of America; retroactively with no possibilities of tracing. Birth-certificate showed George Winston Miller was born in Bozeman, Montana in 1920. His parents were listed as 3rd generation Russians. Hair and eyebrows were colored dark brown to match his new ID photos as well as several silver framed photos displayed in his apartment of him and his *birth* parents. Later George was allowed to let his hair's true color return, but by then it was a becoming gray. And Irene? He called her as promised.

The following morning he was introduced to his new employment where he met the staff and was shown to his office. As Hamilton had said, he would be doing the same here as he had done in Moscow, only in a somewhat reverse way. He quickly settled in and showed his immense knack for this type of work, far beyond what Hamilton and his people could have imagined. New challenges, more sensitive and top-secret documents and situations were added to his responsibilities. George's vast talent in reading between the lines of documents traveling through his fingers and his superior interpretations soon created an enormous leap forward for all the intelligence factions within the U.S. government. Though George was soon admired for his keen insights by his staff and colleagues from top to bottom, he stayed quietly humble. He absolutely loved what he was doing, and that was enough reward for him for now. And this time around, he didn't keep much to himself.

The masses of Russian and English communications the Americans were able to consistently supply his department with, were simply breathtaking for George. The vast quantity of intercepted messages and recorded conversations was an additional workload he eagerly attacked. He had been promised a challenging job, and that was precisely what he got; and George didn't want it any other way. One thing that often popped into his head was the fact that none of the Allied trusted each other at all. Hamilton gave him the professional and clinical explanation: "Everybody cover their asses; it's as simple as that. And on top of that, we all pretend none of the above is taking place – at all."
"And we are all adults!" George added.
"That's debatable! Let's just say dangerously *silly* adults and leave it at that." George was soon doing 12-14 hour days, 5-6 days a week in his office. Things were going well at work and life at home was quickly creating a superb balance for George.

Irene and George married in September 1943. It was a simple, but very romantic outing. The quick ceremony was conducted by a city clerk. Hamilton was best man and a couple of Irene's military girl friends and Hamilton's wife, had eagerly lined up as bridesmaids. Irene was as family-less as George; her parents had died when she was a little girl. But that did not put a damper on the festive occasion, nor did it obstruct their obvious happiness. Irene moved in with George; his apartment was bigger and more central. They quickly found that their life together was easy, fun and constantly romantic; they expected nothing else. They could not keep their hands off each other and every single possible moment they could be together, they would and they were.

But some nights for George were painfully sad and horrific in scope. The feeling of guilt leaving his true Russians behind was excruciating. He felt as a traitor would feel, but possibly worse. The nights of torture and interrogations by vicious and malicious NKVD agents who had tracked him down and had found him in his apartment, awoke him in cold sweat and no desire to go back to sleep. Getting up at all hours of the night was not uncommon. Holding George was all Irene could do.

World War II finally ended, but the Cold War started up soon after. George was asked to expand the department, as new military and political confrontations created massive new responsibilities; more than anybody could ever have imagined. This time around the urgency of his work seemed even more pressing. Irene stayed with her military job at the Pentagon. Whenever she was offered a promotion, including better pay, but outside the D.C. area, she declined. Being away from her husband was not an option she considered. George never advised Irene one way or another about her job; he fully appreciated her choices. Spending as much possible time together was an utmost priority for both of them.

Their income made for a comfortable lifestyle. High on money, but low on time to spend it; whatever time available, included traveling. One of the destinations was Canada, exploring the vast and beautifully majestic wilderness by wagon, by horseback and hiking. The simplicity and the restfulness was the balance they needed. The moonlit nights, the silence of nature, the singing and sounds by local wildlife, was refreshing, recharging, as well as utterly romantic. But they found the ultimate place in the South of France, a place where they had the best romantically rewarding times together. It was a small, old walled-in village purged on the peaks of a mountain, Saint Paul-de-Vence. That was the place they would travel to as often as they could get away from D.C. Many of those visits were aligned with George's government travels.

But back home, everyday life wasn't bad either. Candlelit dinners were the norm of their routine, as well as just being together, reading, listening to music and making love. Life was good for Irene and George - very good indeed. But unfortunately, that life would change.

In early 1949 Irene started experiencing slight headaches. At first she ignored them, so no need to tell George. As the headaches persisted and got more severe, she finally consulted a doctor. At first he had prescribed a more potent medication than she could purchase over the counter. The headaches would disappear for weeks, but on their unwelcomed return, they were more vicious and prolonged. Her condition started to interfere with her job and she finally asked George if he was okay if she took a break from work - just for awhile; he agreed at once since having Irene at home would be wonderful. She never told him the real reason.

George worked hard as responsibilities in his department kept growing. But by the end of the work day, nothing could keep him from racing home to Irene. He had started getting to his office around 4 in the morning so he could be home around 4 in the afternoon whenever possible. He had supportive and efficient staff and they had no problems running the show when George was absent; so spending time with Irene had no stress attached.

As he returned home one afternoon, she was sleeping on the couch. He gently kissed her, but she didn't open her eyes as she normally did from just the slightest touch. He fixed himself a drink and sat down with the paper. An hour went by and Irene was still sleeping which puzzled him. He gently woke her up and she seemed confused and disoriented.

"Where were you, sweetheart?" He kissed her forehead.

"I don't know. What time is it?"

"A bit after 6," he answered.

"Oh, I got to get some dinner together,"

"Don't worry; I'll take care of it." George got up and headed for the kitchen. Irene slowly sat up and then headed for the bathroom. The vomiting was violent and the blood was a clear red. This she didn't tell George either.

During the next weeks, George found Irene sleeping either in their bed or on the couch as he returned home from work. She kept insisting that nothing was wrong. Though George trusted her, he figured that something was not right.

By now the headaches had become unbearable. The doctor ran many tests and sent Irene to several specialists. One evening after dinner, a dinner that had been especially romantic, they were lying in bed, both glowing in the aftermath of their intimacy. Irene turned and looked at George as he looked at her. She was especially beautiful this evening; so wonderfully soft and happy, he thought.

"George, I have been thinking that since I'm home these days that we should make a baby." She smiled and snuggled closer to her husband. "What do you think?" George was not unprepared at all. He had anticipated this question, but always wanted it to come from Irene.

"Okay," he said with a straight face, turning his back with a big teasing smile. "Shouldn't we get some sleep now?" Irene looked shocked, grabbed and pulled his arm.

"Hey, what do you mean *okay*?" George giggled as he faced her.

"I mean *okay, let's make a baby*, that's what I mean." Irene sat up, smiling.

"You really mean that?"

"You know I do, so let's get started. We might need to practice a bit first, you know, figure out how to do it." Irene laughed the way he loved hearing her laugh; it was deep, exotic and utterly sexy. He grabbed her waist with both hands and pulled her closer to him. "Let's do a couple of run-throughs right now, just in case..." Irene giggled and was soon in the warmness of his embrace. Four weeks later she was pregnant. The conception took place in Saint Paul-de-Vence, in their favorite bed, in their favorite room.

George worked even harder to spend more time at home. She started to take naps in the afternoon, but it didn't take long before George also found her sleeping in their bed more often. She kept assuring him that all was fine and it was due to the pregnancy that she was so tired. The truth was that Irene was constantly exhausted. Her migraines became more and more painful, but fortunately she did get breaks in between. Those were the times when she wanted to be with George. Pain-killing medication was not an option she allowed, as that would possibly harm the unborn baby. The doctors had finally been able to tell her what she was suffering from and what would happen if she didn't seek treatment at once. But since the treatments would harm the baby, and her condition only had a fatal outcome, she firmly declined. So she suffered through her headaches and migraines without any form of help and without showing or telling anybody; especially George. All she hoped to have enough strength for was to give George their child.

It was an immensely painful pregnancy for her. She had valiantly pretended normalcy around George, but when she was alone, she suffered and cried. The friendship she had formed with one of the doctors, Colleen Ryan, was tremendously helpful and supportive. Colleen was a rock for Irene, though she constantly urged her to tell George about the situation. She also found comfort talking to the baby. She would read, listen to music and whenever possible, take short walks for the exercise and fresh air for the both of them. She would rest as much as possible before George returned home, so she could be as awake as expected of a tired, pregnant woman. But George started to see beyond her brave facade. He tried to find out what was going on, but Irene kept insisting that all was as normal as one could expect.

About the time of full term, Irene's water broke and contractions began immediately. George rushed her to the hospital. They were met by several physicians plus Doctor Ryan; George noted that as a bit peculiar. Irene was rushed to a delivery room, where she was stabilized by efficient nurses. As George was brought in, standing by the bed, he found an even higher love for her than he would have ever thought possible. Her face was red and sweaty, but with a wonderful glow, beyond the way she had been glowing the last few months. He held her hands with tears in his eyes.

"George," she said, suddenly squeezing his hand as she looked at him. "Promise me that you will take good care of our child, will you?"

"Sweetheart, we'll *both* do that and we'll do a terrific job, really."

"You are an angel, dear. Just promise me, that whatever happens, you'll be the best father for our child; can you promise me that?" Her grip was getting tighter and her face started to show the pain and tension.

"Of course I will, dear, but you'll be there." George bent over and gave her a kiss on the forehead. "I love you so much, Irene, and thanks so much for this miracle." The tears were now rolling freely. Irene looked at him, tears on her cheeks as well.

"Thanks for letting me have such a wonderful life, George. I have always loved you so much, my Dear George." Her face now twisted in suffering. One of the nurses gently grabbed George's arm and softly pulled him away from the bed and from Irene.

"Sir, you'll have to wait outside, okay? It's better that way." George didn't hear her at first. He looked into Irene's eyes, got caught and finally he knew. "Please, Sir, let me take you to the waiting area." She led him out while his eyes were still on Irene. She had turned her head, and the nurses and doctors hurriedly started their work. He finally knew and as he sat down, he broke into a sorrowful understanding of what Irene had tried to tell him for the longest time, but had not wanted him to know; she simply wanted to protect him and their baby. His body was shaking and he was beyond devastated for the love of his life, for his dear Irene.

The following hours seemed like days; whenever somebody passed by the waiting area, George jumped. A door would open or close and George's heart skipped. The two doctors who finally entered the waiting area looked tired and sad; they sat down in front of George.

"Mr. Miller, I'm Doctor Colleen Ryan and this is Doctor Lance. We are so terribly sorry to tell you, that your wife passed away a few minutes ago. She died from complications that she has suffered from for some time." There were tears in her eyes as she quietly reached over for his hand. George heard what she had said, but didn't grasp the meaning at all. Things around him became slow and foggy, and the dizziness only got worse. The other doctor started to speak; he also had teary eyes. George was floating in a narrow and clouded space, he couldn't feel any gravity pull, just the roaring silence.

"We did save the baby, and he is 100% healthy boy." He cleared his throat. "You have a son, Mr. Miller, and a very noisy one." The smile didn't make it. Doctor Ryan squeezed George's hand and moved a bit closer.

"We have some people here who can help you with the baby and they can stay with you when needed. Are there anybody you want us to call?" George's body had stopped shaking, but the tears kept rolling.

"Irene had so much life to live," he said quietly. "Oh my God, what could I have done; why didn't I do something? Why didn't she tell me?"

"There was nothing you could have done; nothing anybody could have done at all. I was Irene's doctor through these last 10 months, and she begged me not to tell you anything. She wanted you to be happy and she wanted you to have hers and your child," she paused, then continued: "She loved you so much, Mr. Miller. You were all she ever talked about. I heard about how you met, how much romance she got from you, from your friendship," she had to stop as George was weeping.

"But we weren't finished with our lives together. There was so much more." Through his tears he asked. "We have a baby boy?" The male doctor got up.

"Yes you do. Let me take you to him. Come with me." George got up slowly. Doctor Ryan kept her hand on George's arm for support - for both of them, it seemed.

"He's a beautiful boy, really beautiful." Her smile was honest, deep and warm.

The room was sterile and cold. The two nurses stepped aside as he and Doctor Ryan entered. George was led to one of the cribs. The baby boy had a reddish face, a little bit of sprouting hair on top and was packed in a white blanket. George looked at him with teary eyes.

"He's beautiful, just beautiful." One of the nurses picked up the baby and held him out towards George.

"Say *hello* to your son, Mr. Miller." George carefully took the baby and gently placed him in the nook of his left arm, cuddled against his chest.

"Hello little one; you are the cutest thing aren't you!" Everybody in the room smiled bravely. They all felt an instant bonding between this devastated husband and his new son. The feeling was unusual and strong.

"Do you have a name for him?" Doctor Ryan asked softly. George looked at her with a faint smile; then looked at the baby boy.

"We decided it should be Jack Winston Miller." He kissed his son on the forehead, "yeah, that's what it is."

As he saw her, he broke down and both doctors held him up. Irene looked at peace and beautiful; her eyes were closed with arms crossed over her chest. George sat down next to the bed and put his right hand on Irene's, while still holding Jack in his left arm.

"Jack, this is your mother. She was the best thing that ever happened to me, the very best thing." Through the tears he continued: "She loved you very much, Jack, and she would have kept loving you more and more. She would have been the best mother." He quietly handed Jack to one of the nurses and everybody backed out of the room. George leaned over and rested his head on Irene's chest. It was quiet and cold. He closed his eyes and slowly started to realize the sudden finality of his life with her; at the same time recognizing the enormity of their short life together. Nobody would ever be able to take that away from George; neither from George nor from Irene. He thanked her again and again and through the last tears, he repeated how much he loved her and how much he would love her forever. He told her that they would always live on in his heart. Though he wasn't a man of faith, he did trust and hoped that some day they would meet again. He slowly got up, leaned over and kissed her eyes, her lips and her forehead for the very last time. "Goodbye my Dearest Irene. You will always be part of me and Jack, I can promise you that." George slowly backed away from the bed and finally she was gone from his view - but never from his heart.

*****

It was a dramatically different life for George after the death of his wife and the birth of his son. Mourning death and celebrating life was emotionally an exhausting rollercoaster ride. Becoming an instant single parent was at first challenging, but only concerning the practical aspects. Bonding with Jack had started immediately. It was the mechanical parts of feeding, diaper changing, washing, napping, play-time and other baby essentials, that just needed a bit of scheduling. But George was an expert in that area, so by applying adjustments, being a single father was not that hard – kind of.

Newborn father and son received many offers of help and support. Doctor Ryan, or Colleen as it now was, had offered her time right away, and she had been instrumental in helping George fight the emotional imbalance he scattered through the first few months. Colleen organized shifts between two willing nurses from the hospital and herself. John Hamilton and his wife had also been supportive for George and Jack.

From the day Jack was born, Colleen had been a tremendous help. She quickly found that George was a well suited parent and he quickly adapted to a balance of child rearing and government responsibilities; both at the highest level. Colleen's husband Charles had been smitten by Jack and quickly became a good friend of George's. Colleen and Charles looked after Jack when George was traveling; those were times they treasured. George knew that Jack was in good hands as he trusted the Ryans with no reservations. As Colleen and Charles didn't have children of their own, they quickly became Jack's substitute parents which he fully embraced. Sure his father was number one on the parent list, but Colleen and Charles were right up there. The Millers and the Ryans lived only a few blocks from each other, which worked out well – especially for Jack.

Jack's childhood was safe and secure. His father was home as much as he could manage, but traveling and staying late at the office due to his job, became more extensive. But Colleen and Charles were readily available any time George wasn't. Besides Jack's two male influences, an extremely motherly mother in Colleen gave Jack a fine balance as he grew up. He didn't miss much; in the matter of fact, he later on admitted that he had been spoiled rotten, something he never took advantage of – well, at least not *full* advantage of; and the years rolled along.

Academically Jack was about average. He did not have talents that made him fly through school – far from. But he had a knack of applying himself, work hard and study for long hours; the results showed accordingly. He had a few friends from school and from his neighborhood, but for the most he kept to himself, spending time reading, writing, studying and cooking. Yes, food preparation was an interest he had acquired from Colleen who had always solicited his help, from cleaning, laundry, ironing and especially cooking. Jack was very comfortable in the kitchen at the Ryan's and at home. But he never told his friends about this, as he was a bit embarrassed having this kind of interest, as it was not really the image he was aiming for.

George had at least one Special Service Agent nearby at all times. Several were on duty in and around the office; normally two tagged along on trips, depending on where he traveled. Though George was against it, agents would also keep watch on the exterior of his house when he was home and later on when Jack was old enough to be home alone. George never felt this *protection* was necessary; he wasn't really that important, he argued. Hamilton, being the boss, insisted that he was – and underlined that he was far beyond important. But stubbornly he kept nagging Hamilton. He pleaded to be left alone at home and on his personal journeys with or without his son. There had never been an incident of any threats on his life or that of his son's. The constant begging and whining finally made Hamilton give in. The SSD adamantly disagreed and denounced any responsibility if anything happened to either George or Jack Miller during these exceptions. Due to the agreement and pointedly demanded by SSD, George was issued a side arm. To get comfortable with the weapon's mechanics and extreme power, several hours of instruction and target practice was mandatory. The Remington Rand US Army 45 Colt accompanied by five full clips, was now securely under lock in the right desk drawer in his bedroom; he was never comfortable with this weapon in his house.

Hamilton and George shook hands on the new deal and the second George was out of the office, Hamilton sat down with some of the agents and quickly came up with the undercover game-plan. *Watch George, but don't let him know*. Two hours after the plan was implemented, George was fully aware of the watchful eyes. It was flashbacks to his life in Moscow. He never told Hamilton – but then again, Hamilton knew that George knew, because George was really that good at his job. But it was only four weeks later that the SSD was beaten by a better foe.

It was deep into a dark and dreary night. The rain was mercilessly hammering on the windows. George was preparing for bed and hoped he could sleep through the storm. He was alone in the house, as Jack was spending a few days with Colleen and Charles at their beach house in North Carolina. He had worked late at the office and felt tired and worn out as he got home. He blew out the last candles and was on his way to the second floor and his bed when the doorbell sounded. He looked at his watch and thought it was strange with visitors at this hour. Keeping the security bolt and chain solidly engaged, he firmly asked who it was.

"Special Service Agent Bigalow, Sir. Some documents Mr. Hamilton wants you to read." George knew Bigalow from the department, but why Hamilton wanted him to read something at this hour puzzled him; he had never done that before. He deactivated the security bolts and it was by the first crack of the door opening, that he knew he had made a huge mistake. The hard and very cold barrel of a large pistol leaned confidently against his forehead. The deep rusty voice was now accented in heavy Russian. It was eerily controlled, and effectively broke the frightening silence.

"Open door and quietly step back Comrade Milkovich." George's heart stopped as it immediately froze. Was this what he thought it was? Had the NKVD or what was now KGB finally found him? His mind turned to empty. He stepped back and a large man with a hat covering his forehead pushed in and grabbed George's shoulder. The sun glasses were out of place on a black night as it was. The wide Stalin-like moustache covered his upper lip and most of his mouth. The full length double-breasted black leather coat looked as heavy as it was; typical GESTAPO/KGB issue. But it was the huge pistol still resting on his forehead that he paid the most attention to. The woman, who had quietly entered and securely closed the door, was also wearing leather, but more elegant than the man's. The scarf around her head and face encircled her sunglasses. She moved as a shadow and after she had scanned the interior of the house, upstairs and downstairs, she placed herself behind George.

"All clear," her voice was harshly soft.

"Comrade Milkovich, please move in to living area." George followed the order. He was pushed into a large chair. The woman was still behind him and the impressive man sat down on a chair facing him. The heavy Russian accented voice continued: "Vee have looking for you very long time, you traitor! Vee vondered vhat happened to Milkovich. Didn't like kommunist Soviet – go to kapitalistic Amerika to vork for enemy government! Milkovich big traitor! Our boss told us find and destroy traitor. That's vhy vee here, understand? Vee find you." George's heart stopped even more, if possible – he fully understood. So this was it, this was what he had been troubled about for so many years. It was part guilt and also the part about not getting a chance to die from old age. George nervously thought that a large caliber bullet through his head would definitely ruin his plans about that *die from old age* wish. The man looked around the living room.

"Very nice large area! Many patriotic communist family can live here; at least seven, don't you agree Comrade Alena Smirnova?"

"Da; many needing and suffering families," her voice was husky but her English clear. "Comrade Milkovich, how many kapitalistic families live here?"

"Only one."

"You say only one? How many members of family? Twelve – or perhaps more?"

"Just me and my…" George stopped himself, the woman continued:

"… And your son Jack Winston, we assume – correct?" She had put her hand on his right shoulder. "Correct, Comrade Milkovich?" How did they know!

"My name is Miller, not that other name you keep calling me." He felt it was a feeble attempt, but he gave it a go. He felt he was going to die soon anyway, so why not. The large man got up.

"You better not lie, you kapitalistic dog, or vee vill smash your nose and pull all your finger-nails out very slowly one by one. Vould you like that?" George shook his head violently. "Vell, do you have drinks in house. Vee'll have drink before vee do the *destroy traitor* part, understand?" George understood too well. "Comrade Alena, look in traitor's freezer, maybe he hide secret Russian favorite vodka." The woman went into the kitchen. George could hear the freezer door open and close. She returned with the frost covered bottle and three ice-cold shot-glasses. The man spoke again. "Let me guess vhat kind, Comrade Alena." He pretended to think hard. "Ah, but of course it must be Pshenichnaya vodka if I'm not so wrong." He laughed hard when the woman showed him the bottle. "Vell of course – I could not possibly be wrong. Give traitor a glass of his favorite vodka, please." The woman moved in front of George's chair and poured the cold beverage into a glass. This could be the last drink he would ever taste, he thought sadly. The woman stayed in front of him, and started to remove her scarf – very slowly.

"It is warm in capitalistic dog's house." Her hair was blond as could be, and as she also removed her sunglasses, George could see that she was not the stereotypical mustached female NKVD agent from the past – far from. Her eyes were of the clearest blue, and her complexion was clean and smooth. As she unbuttoned her leather coat and placed it on a chair, she exposed a gently curved body packed in a below the knees length tight black skirt and a shiny white shirt-like blouse. She crossed her legs as she sat down next to the large man; he was smiling.

"I see you still like good looking Russian voman, huh?" The man said. "This one look familiar to you, Milkovich?" George's mind spun a million miles. Could this possibly be one of his former conquests and her husband seeking revenge! He desperately looked at the woman again. Many faces were eagerly tumbling by in his mind, trying to remember, trying to find out if this was the reason. Nothing came up. "Had too many Russian beauties to remember, Comrade?" The man laughed. "No memory?" Suddenly George saw something. Yeah, she did look somewhat familiar, but he couldn't place her yet. The faces kept swirling by. The woman lifted her glass:

"Vhat should we toast to?" She asked.

"Freedom, vhy not?" The man answered. George thought that was ironic for two KGB agents to toast to freedom. "Freedom from traitor's like Georgi, of course." The man laughed and inhaled the contents of his glass. George quickly gobbled his down as the woman did the same. She got up and poured them all another round – again they all emptied their glasses and they were filled up again and emptied and filled up. The large man was laughing and moved closer to George's chair. He noticed that the pistol was now resting on a side table. Maybe this would be his chance to fight them off – but he doubted if he could.

"So dear Georgi, you don't recognize Alena at all?" Suddenly his English was fluent with just a slight accent. "Now think back, old pal. Nothing here sounds or looks familiar?" George's mind was again racing wildly; suddenly he saw her. She was in the park; she was pushing a stroller coming towards them – *them* being himself and? - *Vadim*?

"My dear God, Barbarossa?" The man smiled big as he carefully pulled off the large moustache, "Vadim - you shithead!"

"The one and only Russian shithead you love." And they embraced for the longest time. Alena was smiling with tears streaming down her face. "How are you doing, Georgi old pal?" This had gone from one of the worst moments to one of the best moments in George's life; good old Vadim Petrov was back and with that former NKVD agent – *what a silly world we live in*, he thought.

"Did Hamilton know about this?" George asked and Vadim laughed.

"Hamilton who?" George just shook his head and smiled.

The reunion lasted till early morning. Alena held on for several hours and then retired to one of the upstairs guestrooms. Vadim and George talked all night and during breakfast for three. The vodka shots had followed them the whole way – just like their Kremlin days so many years ago.

George told his story, from departing Moscow, through Casablanca, meeting Irene, Jack's birth and Irene's death, through a very non-informative description of his work. Even best friends would never know what George did and what he was responsible for – too sensitive and for his eyes only.

Vadim had continued his work at the Kremlin after George had *disappeared*. The NKVD had summoned him for interviews, more so interrogations, as he was a known best friend of the traitor Georgi Milkovich. In one of the last so-called interviews, they had brought in an additional agent, Alena Smirnova. Vadim had recognized her immediately, but didn't show it. Alena had also stayed neutral during those first moments and had done her part of the interrogation with a straight and business-like face. The NKVD found that Vadim had not been aware of Georgi's plans of leaving the Soviet Union, which of course was the truth as George had never told him anything.

It was several weeks after the last interview when agent Smirnova was ordered to befriend Vadim Petrov. She was ordered to implement a romantic approach to be able to soften him up. Alena could hardly believe her luck, as she had been attracted to Vadim from the first assignment of shadowing him and Milkovich. She was not keen of Georgi as she found that he was somewhat of an active woman chaser and rather successful at it. When female NKVD agents were asked to go after him, she had declined. Her colleagues though, would come back and tell stories about their sexual encounters with Georgi, and how much they felt they should go back and do some more *interrogating*. But Alena was not interested in Georgi one bit – no, it was Vadim she wanted.

One evening Alena positioned herself in a restaurant near the Kremlin that Vadim frequented; she thought that *casually* bumping in to him would work. It turned out to be the best day of her life. Vadim genuinely got ecstatic when, during dinner, she whispered in his ear that she had been assigned to romantically squeeze information out of him concerning Georgi Milkovich. They soon did a lot of squeezing, but nothing that brought out any information about Georgi; Georgi who? Alena soon told Vadim that she did not want to live in the Soviet Union anymore; from that very moment Vadim was sure that she could read his mind. They quickly worked out a plan of action; it would take time to implement, as it was intricate and utterly dangerous. Finally they made their move with help from the British Embassy in Moscow. British Intelligence had for a long time been interested in Vadim's services through his language talents, as well as his work experience from inside the Kremlin. They also had a deep interest in Alena's knowledge about the inner workings of the NKVD. So for the British it was a two-for-one deal, and everybody was happy; well, not the Kremlin, of course. When the British had asked for Hamilton's blessing as Petrov was still attached to his department and the U.S. Secret Service, he was willing to give it; he didn't want to stay in the way of Petrov's happiness, and Petrov's role in Moscow was also running thin; it was time to get him out before it was too late.

From the moment Vadim met up with Alena, he realized that she was not the clumsiest agent ever, as he and Georgi had named her a long time ago - far from. She was intelligent and street smart, but had purposely as an agent acted naïve and gullible, but only to the point where her bosses didn't think she was useless. That would have dissolved her right away. So she played on the edge, and had survived in fine style. For her it was a matter of scanning the field for her next move – getting out of the Soviet Union.

Alena and Vadim were smuggled out of Russia via a divided Berlin about six months after the war had ended. They were given a small apartment in Kensington, West London, and started work right away. They soon married which worked perfect with the establishment of their new identity, and their life together was more than they could have ever asked for; they were very happy.

Many years later, Vadim was asked if he would be interested in working at the British Embassy in Washington D.C. for a while. Alena was ecstatic as she had always wanted to try out America. She contacted the person in charge of the decisions concerning the move, and quickly got herself a job at the embassy as well.

Vadim always had a sixth sense about Georgi's whereabouts, but had not felt it safe to explore his thoughts for Georgi's sake. So he put it on the back burner for some other time. He only mentioned this to Alena once, and only in passing. But sitting on the plane midway to their adventure in America, Alena handed him a folder, smiled and said: *You might be interested in this. Might be somebody you want to look up.* It contained the full life-story, photos included, of an American citizen named George Winston Miller, from the day he was born in Bozeman, Montana till just a few weeks ago in Washington D.C. When Vadim had finished reading the folder, he looked at Alena with teary eyes: *Thank you so much Dear Alena – thank you.* The planning of the gag surprise reunion had been Alena's as well. Vadim had laughed and then hoped that good old

Georgi, or George, would not croak from a massive heart attack; Alena had laughed off his concern.

"Well, I have heard from several female NKVD agents that he is a terrific kisser, so in case of an emergency I guess I'll just have to volunteer CPR on him." She smiled teasingly at the thought.

"No you won't. I'll do the CPR myself, no matter how bad *that* picture might look." So here they were with their pal George, everybody feeling mighty happy; and no heart attacks.

Alena and Vadim worked in D.C. for 12 months before returning to London. George had fully enjoyed hooking up with Vadim and now Alena. In the years forward they stayed in contact and visited each other in the U.K. as well as in D.C. *It's great having them back in my life*, George thought with a big smile. But the eerie feeling that KGB might still be looking for him was not pleasant and didn't go away. Vadim had informed him, that according to his findings before leaving Moscow, KGB, or NKVD as it was at that time, had lost interest – but George never felt sure at all; in the eyes of the Soviet Union, he was a traitor. That was something he had to live with and something he had to die with. But for now, life moved on.

In early 1963, at the age of 13, Jack had found an interest in the Civil Rights Movement. At first he had kept this to himself. Interest came from discussions and debates in school, newspaper articles, radio and television. The topic was brought up more often. As with all his school-work, Jack wanted to be sure that he fully understood the issues concerning equal rights before he expressed his own opinions in public. In his heart he thought that segregation of any kind was wrong. He did not understand racial diversity based on one color or race or beliefs being superior to another. Many of his opinions were based on his father's views. He had talked with Jack about the unfairness of the issues and emphasized that it was against the ideals of America's founders. The Declaration of Independence clearly said: *We hold these truths to be self-evident, that all men are created equal, that they are endowed by their Creator with certain unalienable Rights that among these are Life, Liberty and the pursuit of Happiness*. They had risked their own lives to create this, one of the most important documents in history and even now, it should be respected as written, nearly two hundred years later; it was as true now as it was true then. George was adamant about this and so was Jack.

At school the discussions had started out quietly, but as opinions on both sides of the issue heated up, the communication at times turned ugly. A lot of passion took the place of common sense. There were neither black students nor black teachers in Jack's private school and the more Jack got involved, the more uncomfortable he began to feel about that. It was like *he* was deliberately trying to segregate himself, by his choosing. He felt that the school he attended was a statement that though he was all for equal rights, the issue didn't really apply to him; Jack didn't like that thought very much.

His father had helped him along, discussed the issues, by playing the devil's advocate, challenging Jack's opinions and passions. It had made Jack think hard and logical and had brought him closer to not just talk about the practical fairness of equality, but the full meaning of it as well. His conclusion was that something had to be done and that he would be willing to support his convictions. His first serious commitment to this cause took place on August 28th, 1963. The event faded a bit in comparison to something else that happened that day. But he wouldn't know the effect of it for many years.

The March on Washington for Jobs and Freedom took place on a Wednesday. The march itself started at the Washington Monument and finished at the Lincoln Memorial. It was later estimated that over 250,000 people, mostly blacks, participated. Passionate speeches were held by many, even Josephin Baker, the only female speaker, got the crowd going. Bob Dylan showed his support with a few songs. Jack felt an enormous positive energy among all these people. He was in awe of the power; it was refreshing, eye-opening and breathtaking.

George looked at his son as he saw him in the middle of the masses of people; he felt proud and humbled. His son was a good kid, he thought and having watched him grow up had so far been a tremendous kick and immense privilege; George was indeed a lucky father; he thanked Irene many times every single day.

Jack kept busy looking around, listening to the music and especially to the speeches. At one point he felt somebody was staring at him; the feeling that makes the hair on the back of the head tingle a bit. He didn't want to turn around, so he tried to concentrate on what was in front of him. But the tingling didn't go away. A few moments later he slowly turned his head. The first thing he saw was her eyes. They were large, deep and beautiful. Her big smile created distinct dimples on both sides of her shiny white teethes. She was saying something, but he couldn't hear from all the noise around them. He turned forward again and tried to concentrate. The back of his head kept tingling, so he turned around yet again. She had moved closer; maybe just a few feet. Her right hand was extended.

"Hi, my name is Nora." She smiled as she spoke through the noise. "What's your name?" Jack was a bit puzzled, but shook her hand.

"Jack Miller," he responded, also trying to fight the crowd noise. Nora moved closer to him.

"What made you come here, Mr. Miller?"

"To correct injustice," his answer sounded more like a question. Nora smiled even more.

"Advise from your father?" She nodded towards George who was engaged in listening to the music. "Or are you here on your own behalf and convictions?"

"A mixture of the two, I guess."

"You guess; you don't know?"

"I'm sure it's the *mixture*." Jack giggled as he did feel he sounded more like his father than himself: "Why are you here?"

"Same as you, pretty much; and my father," she nodded towards a tall, young looking man, "he suggested that I should come along, so here I am." Nora moved closer to Jack and put a hand on his arm, like the most natural thing to do. Jack was immediately taken by her straightforwardness; she oozed self-confidence. Most of what she said was on the edge between sarcasm and cynicism. Jack found it charming, besides very funny as their conversation took off in all directions. The only time they kept quiet was during a speech by Martin Luther King, Jr. Nora had grabbed Jack's hand and held on to it. Again Jack found it surprisingly natural, and he felt a genuine warmness from her. As Doctor King finished: *Free at last! Free at last! Thank God Almighty, we are free at last*, the crowd, including Nora and Jack, erupted in thunderous applauds in a show of deep appreciation.

Jack introduced Nora to his father as well as Nora introduced her father to Jack and George. They only exchanged a few words as the crowd-noise was getting even louder. It had been a superb day for Jack. The only bad thing was that when he and Nora said their goodbyes, he forgot to get her address or phone-number or something. Nora had given him a quick hug and as she waved from a distance, she shouted: "We'll meet again some other time, Mr. Miller, I'm sure we will." But Jack wasn't so sure at all; and life continued.

Jack had reached 15. So far, his life had been a mixture of richness and excitement, in a kind of bland and boring way; the bland and boring stemming from Jack's lack of social skills. He had three loving parents, no siblings to cause friction or jealousy, so he was somewhat over-stimulated being an only child. He had his own room at home as well as one in the Ryan's house. Colleen and Charles were his normality of a full home-life, where life with his father was consistently sporadic. The frequency of George's travels had increased and had become more involved. But he made sure that whatever limited free time at home in Washington, was all about his son. They had great times together and felt very close to each other. Jack never complained about the lack of time with his father; he more so valued the time they did have together. George often realized how time was moving along as he had watched this boy becoming a young teenager and growing into a young man too fast. He was sure Irene was observing with pride from above; he didn't doubt that at all.

Jack was doing okay academically. Most of the time he spent by himself was with his nose in the schoolbooks. He still had to work hard for his grades, but also found it a legit way to avoid socializing. He was an observer more than a participant, but he felt comfort and balance in who he was – at least at that time in his life. He always trusted that one day he would evolve, become more social. But for now he really didn't care, other than the usual teenage fear of pimples and the starting interest in the other gender – *that* way... His love-life was non-existing other than the puppy-eyed dreamy one, where juicy fantasies ran extreme, while his body was staying still – well, still to some extent.

When that pre-adult attraction to the opposite gender started, it was a mixture of lust, love and curiosity – not particularly in that order. He talked with his father about it as well as discussed same thoughts and feelings with Colleen and Charles. There had always been a free flowing communication between Jack and his three parents, so even this was easy to talk about. Colleen was the technical advisor, being a doctor and all, and Jack's father was the strategist, and to some extent, the common sense provider. Charles just smiled and rolled his eyes, putting all the trust in Colleen and George's advise. He didn't feel he had the experience or the technical know-how to guide Jack. So it was also for those reasons that it was Father George who had the *talk* with his son.

"So what is it that you don't know about sex?" He asked Jack one evening. After the initial surprise, Jack was ready to talk.

"Okay, so I know all the technical stuff, not that I done any, of course"

"Well, good; of course you know that I have all the information you need; don't you?"

"Oh, I'm sure you have been around before you met Mom and that's according to what you have told me."

"I wasn't bragging, you know." George made sure.

"Yes Dad, you were just being *informative*." Jack was laughing.

"So let's see; to start with, it is utterly important that you are respectful to anybody. Never treat a girl or a woman with disrespect…"

"… And that was what you did in…"

"Jack," George tried to look serious, "let's *learn* from my experiences, mistakes as well as successes, okay? I can't go back and erase, can I?"

"Sorry Dad; please continue - talking about respect."

"When you meet somebody or you are approaching somebody that you like, that might be for her looks or her personality or the mixture of both, the more respect you show, the better chances are that she'll create an interest in you."

"But how do I start talking with somebody I like?"

"The basic approach is to simply walk up and start talking."

"That's the hard part, Dad; that's the worst part."

"There's nothing to it, Jack, nothing at all. The surest way is to bring the conversation in her direction, give her a chance to talk about herself. That's what most people like to do anyway - really."

"So I shouldn't bring *me* up at all?"

"Try it out the other way first. You'll see that it works really well," he paused, "and Jack, here's another advice: never be guided by your genitals, 'cause your common sense and brains will be left behind and you'll only do stupid stuff…"

"Dad, come on, that's silly."

"I hope you won't let that happen, but you're a teenage boy and as far as I remember it is part of the package, part of the experiences you are heading for. But don't you worry about that, it's rather normal, even for you, Son."

It was the next day in school that Jack pulled himself together. He had been infatuated with a senior for the longest time. Her name was Victoria Grant and she was a couple of years older. At first he had been taken by her budding body, her curves more distinct than most other girl's her age, and long shapely legs. She looked like the girls in the Playboy Magazines he kept hidden under a dresser drawer in his room. He had fantasized about Victoria for the longest time. Kissing her, touching her, caressing her; actually more like *fondling* her. He imagined what she looked like naked, how he would touch her and feel her skin. Jack would shake his head at this point and be embarrassed about the obvious excitement from the wild thoughts about Victoria. *Do not be guided by your genitals*, his father had told him, but it was hard not to be – very tough indeed.

But today was the day he would finally talk to her, as he had planned so many times before. And again, this *would* be the day he would *really* do it. He knew where she would be at recess and at what time. He knew that her girlfriends would be there as well, but that didn't bother Jack at all - it brutally horrified him. He nervously crossed the school yard and was soon in Victoria's territory. She was only 10 yards from him and getting closer very fast. It was approximate at the 5 yard line that Jack lost his guts; he could actually hear them hit the ground. He froze, and then half thawed, turned around and was in the process of a speedy retreat when he heard her commanding voice:

"Hey you," was the first Victoria ever communicated to Jack. "Come back." Jack froze yet again, turned slowly as if he was going to be hurt or something. He stuttered:

"Mmee?"

"Yeah, *youyouyou*," she imitated. "What do you want?"

"Eh, nothing," he blushed and felt utterly uncomfortable. But he knew what he wanted, but he couldn't tell her, could he?

"You want *nothing*? You have been hanging around spying on me for so long; you finally get your guts gathered and now you are telling me that you want *nothing*! That doesn't make sense, boy." Her voice was sarcastic and sharp. For some reason that didn't make Jack feel bad. In the matter of fact, it made him feel rather excited. Did she like him already? Was her sarcasm a way of telling him that it was okay? Or was he being too optimistic? Jack's brain went to work. He suddenly had a brilliant idea; even his father would think so. But Jack would have to tell a lie and that part would not please his father at all.

"I'm trying to find a math tutor and I was told that you might be able to help me." This was for the most a lie; but the part about her math skills, were true. He had overheard a teacher praising Victoria's math, and now that information came in very handy, very handy indeed. Victoria looked curious.

"Are you serious?"

"Yes I am," his voice was getting calmer, though still shaking violently inside. Jack simply hated lying. "You are good at it; I mean the math stuff."

"What else would you mean?" Jack blushed deeply.

"I meant the math thing." Victoria laughed and the other girls giggled. Jack hadn't paid attention to the other girls so far, but now they were certainly there, in his face, giggling loudly – at him.

"He's cute" one of them said: "Your new *boyfriend*, Vicky?" Victoria snarled.

"You must be joking. He's barely potty-trained. What are you, boy?"

"I'm a sophomore."

"Oh how adorable is that?" She sounded sarcastic again, but Jack only heard it as increased interest; his mind teasing him. The recess bell rang and the yard started to empty. Victoria and her cohorts moved as one giggling group. Jack was left alone in despair and embarrassment. As the group reached the main building, Victoria slowly turned around, smiled directly at Jack, and said:

"You *are* cute – for a sophomore that is." This time she didn't laugh at all; she just kept smiling at him. Jack had never been in seventh heaven before, but he felt that this was it. Walking on air was even better than he had been told.

A few days later, Victoria stopped Jack in the hallway outside his classroom. She was wearing a tight fitting white V-neck cashmere sweater and a …, well Jack didn't notice anything else. Her breasts were beautifully framed and that was the only area Jack noticed.

"Are you still looking for a math tutor, sophomore?" This time she didn't smile at all. Jack looked up fast. He was actually doing well in math, so the initial approach had been rather weak; he quickly switched to plan B.

"I'm thinking of taking an honors class next semester. I'm sure I will need some help to prepare for the class." The uneasiness of lying was painful.

"What do you pay?"

"I don't know what the rate is. Do you?"

"I'm good, so I'm expensive."

"That's fair enough, but you have to talk with my dad about the money thing. Is that okay with you?"

"When would that be?"

"Tomorrow is Saturday; around three? Would that work? He should be home."

"Okay, I'll meet you at three." Jack gave her the address. She turned around and walked away. He was shaking as he watched her skirt swing sexily from side to side. He was sure she did it on purpose; it was like she fished for stares from any boys nearby. And stares she got, as well as the normal animalistic preadolescent male sounds of approval. Jack could only imagine her smile above it all. Victoria always smiled above it all; she knew precisely the affect she had on boys, as well as the jealous stares from the girls.

Saturday morning the 5 minute shower took more than 15. He used more cologne than usual and in places he had never applied the smelly stuff before. His father was reading the paper in the kitchen with his second cup of coffee.
"Dad, remember that I want to take an honors class in math next semester?" George didn't move an inch.
"Not really, but go on...?"
"Well, I think I will do okay, but I'm also wondering if I could have a tutor to make sure I'm well prepared." Jack was cringing through the lie. He had never lied to his father before – ever. Starting now was not what he really wanted to do, and especially not about something this banal and self-serving.
"Who is she, Jack?" He asked without looking up from the paper.
"Who says she is a *her*?"
"I can literally smell it, Son. Any cologne left?" Jack blushed immediately.
"What I meant to say was..." George laughed and put the paper down.
"If I'm not totally off the track, she's good looking, well-shaped and rather beautiful, huh?" Jack didn't think he could blush more than he already did, but he found that he could.
"*Dad,*" George laughed again.
"Come on Jack, I'm only kidding. When do I get to meet this voluptuous tutor prospect?"
"This afternoon a bit after three; would that work for you?"
"I'll even take a shower." George went back to reading the paper.
"Thanks Dad." Jack was dizzy and happy, extremely excited and horrifyingly nervous. This afternoon would never come, he thought; but eventually it did.

Victoria rang the doorbell three o'clock sharp. She was wearing the tight white V-neck cashmere again and long black pants. Her lips were red as could be and her skin-tone un-seasonally tanned.

George was a true gentleman when he met Victoria; very cordial. They agreed on a price per session and two sessions per week. After Victoria left, George smiled at Jack as he shook his head slowly. Jack knew precisely what he meant, and didn't like it; he knew his father had figured him out. However irritating that was, it still left a faint smile on his face. Jack was very excited, not so much about the math, but more about other possibilities.

"Nice tutor, Son," his father said with a smirk, grabbing his briefcase and went into the office in the back of the house, "And by the way, don't ever lie to me again." His voice was sharp and demanding.

Victoria was smiling as she left the Miller's house. Tutoring and the money was all fine, but what about that boy? He was actually very cute, not the most handsome, but charming in that awkward boyish way. She knew she could correct the boyish part, make him more sure of himself; as sure as she thought he could be and as sure as she wanted him to be. He had a cute body and though her girlfriends laughed when she talked about him, she also sensed that they were all a bit jealous. There was a certain class about him and that made him a bit sexy as well; in a very innocent way of course.

Most of Victoria's sporadic boyfriends had been one-nighters more than anything else. She tired of them quickly, as she cruelly and ignorantly rejected them when they returned, stupidly expecting more than she had already allowed. She was always in full control, just the way she liked to be. Victoria knew what she had, how she could use it to drive them to the point where they became pathetic puppy-dogs begging for scraps, but she was the one calling the shots. Now, this new *project* would probably not be a challenge at all, but seducing a younger boy would be something new and perhaps refreshing, even exciting? Victoria kept smiling as she continued walking. *Oh yeah*, she thought, *this will be fun*. She couldn't know that the fun would suddenly stop and become something she would not be able to control at all, no matter how hard she tried. This realization would be a bitter pill for her to swallow and impossible to accept.

The first few tutoring sessions had been just that: tutoring. Jack had faked his semi lack of math knowledge, which she found flattering. There were other intentions on Jack's mind; he was a male after all. In this case the feeling of excitement was close to equal her usually controlling, conquering and manipulating *what else is new?* attitude. During the first sessions she found it hard to concentrate, which was also a new feeling. There was something about Jack that she actually liked. He had an awkward charm and he was funny in a cynically sarcastic way. These were new aspects Victoria had never been exposed to. She had to admit that Jack was not that dumb little kid after all; far from.

"How's the tutoring going, Son?"
"Fine Dad, just fine, thanks!"
"Learn anything, I mean math-wise?" George smiled away from Jack.
"Nice Dad, real nice." For some reason he was only a little annoyed, as he knew his father wasn't being demeaning.
"Are you staying cool, Jack?"
"I believe so if we are talking about the same thing."
"I'm sure we are," George sat down at the kitchen table. "So since we are, I can only suggest that you stay cool and slow and respectful. Don't hurry anything, just stay respectful. And don't go where you shouldn't go, okay Jack?" Jack nodded. He fully understood what his father was saying, and he appreciated his advice, as he had always done. He had talked with Colleen and Charles about Victoria and what he felt about her; well, some stuff he had left out. But he also knew that Colleen and Charles were not fooled. They had both smiled and told Jack that they trusted he would always behave like a perfect gentleman. Jack wanted to behave like one, that was for sure, but these days he was consistently challenged by a multitude of raging hormones that didn't seem to want to go the *perfect gentleman* way at all. It was a very confusing and utterly exciting time for Jack.

Victoria soon found herself thinking about Jack more often than she wast comfortable with; she had never experienced this kind of emotions before. But every morning she shook off those feelings before she headed to school. This way she would, as usual, arrive in full control, the way the boys and the girls expected her to. The only irritation concerning her arrivals and departures was that she had to drag her little sister Sara along; *Little Miss Perfect*, as she called her. She was only a freshman and was not one Victoria wanted to be seen with. But her parents insisted; Victoria was defiantl, but did it. Sara was fine with that, as she had never found her older sister much of a sister. They had always upheld a diplomatic relationship and avoided confrontations.

"Jack, you are doing it again," her voice was teasingly stern. Jack's eyes pulled up at once.

"Doing what?" His feeble defense sounded.

"You keep staring at my breasts,"

"No I don't," he stuttered too fast.

"Yes you do. Your eyes are going from side to side. Have you decided which one is your favorite?" Jack was blushing as never before. He quickly felt a bit of excitement and hoped Victoria didn't notice, but she knew what aroused boys and she knew what little it took to get them going. The controlling aspect of her game surfaced with satisfaction, but as she looked at Jack's red face, there was something different about it this time around; she had to find out what it was. "Jack, just relax, though at this point I don't think you are completely relaxed, are you?" She smiled as she looked towards jack's lap. He was twisting on her hook trying to use the notebook as a shield. "Oh Jackie-Boy," she giggled, as she fully enjoyed the moment. "Okay, let me see the notes you made concerning problem 52." She grabbed the notebook from Jack's lap, and the sensation he felt as her fingers slightly, slowly and deliberately touched his pants, was extraordinary and much more exciting than when he did the touching himself. Victoria gave Jack a wicked smile. "Oops, sorry about that," he swallowed wildly and tried to control himself, but that did not work at all. Victoria kept giggling: "Let's go on, well, I mean with the math, okay?" Jack tried to speak, but a gurgling sound was all he could muster.

The next few weeks the world of sexual awareness opened up for Jack. Victoria gently guided him through the jungle of awkwardness. Though Jack had started out as an experiment for Victoria, she soon found that the way he caressed her, the way he would gently kiss her, the sensitive and caring touches of her body, had given her an excitement she had never experienced before. Jack had quickly evolved from a too eager and utterly curious and clumsy novice lover, to a patient and respectful partner; Victoria guiding and showing him the way. But most of what Jack did as the weeks went by, seemed to come naturally, she thought. They would lie on his bed talking. They would hold hands and softly explore each other, physically and mentally; and Victoria stayed emotionally confused.

It was one such afternoon Victoria experienced her first fulfillment. It was something she had only fantasized about, something she had not even been able to reach by her own doing, not with this deep intensity. Jack had been gentle and loving in the glowing aftermath, a maturity Victoria had never experienced with anybody else; only with him. She felt she was losing more of the control she had enjoyed for the longest time. In spite of this curious dilemma she never-the-less felt delighted; and more and more so. All this in spite of Jack just being another project for her; *or was he?*

Jack was delighted with his life at this point. He felt calm about himself and found that he could concentrate a lot more efficiently about school, and *yes* his math skills had also improved. Victoria was math-smart and had a talent communicating that knowledge. *But not only math*, Jack thought with a shy, though satisfied smile. George recognized a change in his son's demeanor. He seemed happier than usual. He was also sure that Jack was learning something more than math, but he kept quiet about it. If Jack wanted to talk, he would no doubt come forward; it was on a Sunday morning when Jack wanted to come forward.

"Math is going really well, Dad," he started. "I mean, really well."

"That's good. Money well spent, huh?"

"Yeah, and there is another thing and that is that I think Victoria is kind of my girlfriend now." Jack looked like a question mark after that statement.

"You *think*! Does Victoria by any chance know that she *might* be your girlfriend? And will there be some kind of follow-up explanation?" George smiled a bit, as his son did sound rather confused. After a short pause Jack slowly tried to sort things out.

"Victoria seems fine when she tutors me here…"

"Math or…"

"That and the *or*…" Jack stated blushing. "But in school she acts like she doesn't know me, you know; she does *see* me, but she doesn't really *see* me and certainly not when her girlfriends are around."

"What do you think the problem is?"

"That she's embarrassed to have anything to do with a sophomore or something like that? Maybe she's not up to admitting the relationship with me to her friends?"

"Could possibly be; did you ask her?"

"No, but I will. You see, Dad, she seems fine here, but she isn't keen on doing anything other than meeting here; no movies, no walks, no dinners with me, with you or with Colleen and Charles – nothing, just us here, in my room."

"Is there some kind of a complaint in this?"

"I don't think so. She started out really tough and cold, but now she's really sweet and nice, and she's smart like heck," He paused, and then continued: "I think she really likes me."

"Are you in love with her?"

"I wouldn't know; I don't know what that is."

"Are you guided by you-know-what?"

"I was in the beginning, but not anymore."

"Are you and Victoria, you know…."

"*Dad;* no, we're not."

"Good, let it stay that way" George was relieved. "Well, if it's all that important to you, I suggest that you ask her where she stands relationship-wise." Jack agreed and Sunday morning continued.

But Jack did not ask Victoria; he was afraid of ruining what they had, or at least what *he* thought they had, so why take a chance! It was rather confusing for him; he felt such a warm closeness from her and not just from the sex-stuff. She bloomed during their times together in his room, twice weekly. The hardness of her attitude in school totally melted in Jacks room. *Oh well,* Jack thought, *no need to rock the bed,* so he didn't.

Victoria had slowly gotten used to her thoughts about Jack. At first they had disturbed her tremendously, as she had never felt like this about anybody. But she had found that her thoughts about him, the *Little Kid Sophomore Project,* had taken a turn into another world, one she liked more and more. Jack was sweet, innocent and lovely; *yeah, lovely,* she thought. She began to look forward to the tutoring sessions. Her time together with him had turned in to warm and semi romantic moments, where she found that she received an innocent love, packaged in a lot of respect. And she did like it, which was also a problem. She started to feel vulnerable, slightly out of control, and it was putting cracks in her armor, something she was not ready for at all – *ever*, she thought.

Over a short period of time Victoria had built her reputation ground up. She had always known what she wanted, when she wanted it and how to get it; she rarely failed. She found most boys to be stupid and guided by their raging hormones, more so than by their brains or any expected quantity of common sense. She became a pure *boy-hater* after Kevin had loved her, at least she thought he did and then he dumped her. She was in love from the second she saw Kevin and had eagerly welcomed him onto her open arms. He had taken full advantage of her infatuation, but after three weeks and finding that Victoria wouldn't go all the way, he unceremoniously dumped her. In his rejected spiced anger he had scolded her with name-calling. Every name in the book he used hit Victoria deeply as evil and unfair; she had loved him – where was the fault in that? Kevin told everybody about Victoria, from minute details of his *conquest*, the *easy lay*, to other outright cruel lies about her. He had used vicious language about Victoria's eagerness to have sex with anybody any time. He verbally tore her apart. Due to Kevin's angered outbursts from rejection, Victoria's peers had started to stare and giggle and point at her. She was hurt and angered beyond description. It had taken devastating months of trying to ignore her surroundings and move forward; she found that the longer it took, the more revengeful she got; not forgiving. Her hatred of boys, their immaturity and their stupidity, finally reached an ultimate boiling point and it was at that time she decided what to do and she would never look back, she promised herself that.

She would punish as many stupid boys as possible. She would take her anger out on any boy who was naive enough to think he would get in her pants; and with the false rumors about her sexual promiscuity, every single boy was ripe for the taking, all lined up; she would simply pick, choose, use and discard. Even before she had met Kevin, Victoria had been any boy's sexual fantasy. Her curved body underlined the way she dressed, but she never dressed with the intentions other than wearing clothes she felt comfortable in; but now she did so with intentions. Her white and wide smile had always been surrounded by red and full lips; one of those smiles that you simply had to smile back at. In her anger-filled and revengeful mode, she would now use all those tools, plus apply whatever else was needed for her quest; catching those stupid boys was going to be a piece of cake. Victoria decided that after they were hooked, she would tease them to the point where they would beg for more and in the process belittle themselves to whimpering nothings; and then she would dump them. None of them would ever hit a home-run with her; she would never let that happen – ever. She was physically a virgin and she would stay that way. Boys were stupid and none of them would ever be worthy of breaking that last barrier of innocence.

   She worried about the person she had become. She realized that in some ways she did fit the cold, calculating and heartless bitch, as she sarcastically called herself; but that was not who she wanted to be. She found herself confused and concerned about where this would all end up. And then Victoria had in a disturbingly surprising way found that Jack Winston Miller was not from the *stupid boy's* category – not at all. This was the admission that scared her. She shook her head and repeated her promise not to go anywhere near falling in love again – ever. Got hurt once – don't get hurt again. But what Victoria didn't know was that no matter how much she fought against it, this was a battle she was not going to win.

   Encouraged by her math tutoring, Jack decided to take honors classes the next semester. He was excited about that, but he also felt a bit sad that Victoria would be off to college at the same time. He wouldn't see her that often, but her departure was still far away. At this point his everyday life was pretty much occupied with school and studying. To keep a decent grade level, decent for him, he still had to study hours on end; but the report cards showed a nice payoff. He talked with his father about future goals, and somewhat inspired by Charles, Jack was looking towards a business degree at some point. Charles had already offered him a position with his company whenever he was ready. Charles was a builder and owner of CR Constructions; a solid business with a good group of long time employees. Jack had made a bit of cash helping out on construction sites during school-breaks. It had been exhaustingly hard work, but fun. He felt Charles was pushing him harder than the other workers, but he was fine with that. He knew what Charles was doing and that he only meant the best.

Math tutoring with Victoria finally ended. The sessions had actually taken math preference, though they did find time for romance. She was still holding her true emotions back, but Jack felt she was giving in bit by bit. It wasn't that he wanted her to change, far from, as he was happy with their relationship as it was. But he did notice an increased warmness from her. They had finally started to go for walks around D.C., had shared popcorn and sodas in the nearby movie theater, but at school, Victoria kept her distance. She never gave Jack a logical explanation and he never asked.

The first time they had dinner together was at Colleen and Charles'. Colleen and Jack had prepared the dinner. Victoria had laughed all evening as Jack had never seen her laugh before; he found that he couldn't take his eyes off her. George had a late meeting at his office right after dinner, so Victoria and Jack took a taxi to bring her home.

"That was a lot of fun, Jack," her head resting on his shoulder and her hands holding his. "Thanks for inviting me."

"You're welcome," Jack smiled; it had been a grand evening.

"And the food, oh my God; how did you achieve such talent?"

"I told you, Colleen is the master chef. She hauled me into her kitchen when I could barely stand."

"But such talent; nobody can teach talent like that; wow!" She reached up and kissed him. "My Jack: *Culinary genius.*" The very second she said *My Jack,* she froze. *That should not have come out*, she thought, fearing that Jack had heard it and taken it for something more than it was. *Yes* it was getting close to how she felt about Jack, but that was nothing she wanted out there for anybody else to know, not at all, that was only for her.

"I'm glad you liked it," Jack responded, pretending he hadn't heard what she just said; but he heard it loud and clear. He blamed the euphoria of the evening, but at the same time sensed something more. They were good friends and were also physically romantic, and though it would have been nice some time back to have a more committed relationship, at least Jack had wanted one, those two words suddenly sounded unwelcome. It was confusing and he decided to deal with it some other time – very soon; but he never did.

As they arrived at Victoria's house, Jack gallantly jumped out, opened the door for her, embraced her and kissed her goodnight. As the house-door had closed, Victoria safe inside, Jack got back in the taxi and was soon home. It took a while for him to finally fall asleep. As thoughts flew around in his head, he decided to do a bit of inventory. The point was that he had liked Victoria for the physical part to start with. It had been exciting exploration and he knew it had been so for both of them. Victoria had been rather mechanical in the beginning, but as time went by, they became more romantic, more caring beyond the sex. The sex became the lesser part of their time together. It had been more about holding hands and great conversations. *She is a smart girl*, he always thought and just lying around doing home-work, listening to records, reading, walks, museum visits, a few movies, were things friends did together. Sure their physical togetherness was nice, but he found lately that he was not as romantically engaged as he had been at one point. He was concerned, as it seemed Victoria was getting more and more into the romance and maybe commitment? That made it uncomfortable for him – very much so. Jack decided that he would talk with her about it – but he never did.

As Victoria prepared for bed that night, she felt fantastic. Jack had been such a sweetheart. The food had been great, the company entertaining and fun, and Jack's father had been a riot. The many stories about his life in Russia, meeting Churchill, Roosevelt and Stalin, were all fun and exciting. She absolutely adored Colleen and Charles; how fortunate Jack was with three such caring parents. She had felt Jack's eyes on her all night and it had made her feel very special and tingly all over. She asked herself if this was more than she would admit to, but it had already reached that point for her, no matter how much she fought it. She loved him – the feeling that scared her. Her head found the pillow and the darkness of the room embraced her. She could feel Jack's hands and kisses all over her body; being close, engulfed in such warmness. It was then she decided that Jack was going to be the one; with Jack it would be beautiful. Her dreams were full of love and gentle lust; the two of them –together on a fluffy bed of clouds, losing their virginities.

The day was sunny and warm, laced with the proverbial D.C. humidity. Jack had been in the pool the last few hours; try-outs for the school's swim-team. The co-ed prospects were now hanging around for the results. The coaches said that it would only take a few moments. Jack didn't know any of the students here, so he sat by himself with his feet dangling in the cool pool water. He thought he had done well and though he was in no sharp shape fitness-wise, he thought he'd make the team.

"You did well." The voice was clear and direct. He turned around, but couldn't see much of the person talking; the sun was right behind her head.

"Thanks; you did too." She giggled lightly.

"You didn't really watch me swim, did you?" Jack smiled a bit.

"I sure didn't."

"Well, hoorah for honesty," she smiled as she moved a bit away from the sun and proceeded to sit next to him on the edge of the pool. "Do you mind?" She asked.

"Not at all; I was getting worried that nobody would come sit next to me and here you are. Thank you." He smiled as he turned his head towards her. The feeling that went through his body was enormous, something he had never ever experienced before; and this reaction from just looking for one split second. It didn't feel real at all. His throat tied a knot which made breathing near impossible. Next to him was the most beautiful young goddess he had ever seen and now he was going to die. *That was not fair at all*, he desperately thought.

"Are you okay? You look kind of weird." She seemed puzzled, but with a smile. "You look like you can't breathe – something wrong?" Jack turned towards her again. No, she was still stunningly beautiful. But that wasn't it; there was something very extraordinary about her – something he could not put a finger on.

"No I'm fine, thank you," the words struggled to pass the huge knot in his throat; and that was precisely what it sounded like.

"I'm sorry, what did you say?" Jack tried again, but failed. She smiled even more. "Well I thought I would come over and talk with you, but at the moment it seems like you are not capable of talking at all. Is that about right?" Jack nodded wildly as he eagerly pointed at his throat. "Well, maybe we can try this some other time when you are a bit more capable beyond nodding, pointing and shaking your head, okay?" Jack nodded wildly again. He didn't want her to leave; but she was already gone.

"What's up Jack, you haven't said a word all evening." George was rinsing the dinner dishes, "what's on your mind, Son?"

"I met this amazing girl in school, at the try-outs," he had to swallow. "She was absolutely beautiful, in a kind of not totally beautiful way, but ..."

"That's a clear picture, Jack."

"No, but it was the reaction I felt just *looking* at her. It was amazing – it *is* amazing. I have thought about her all day. She just came over and said: *Hi, can I sit here?* Just like that – like she knows me."

"Maybe she does?" George smiled. He remembered the first time he had looked at Irene. He remembered it vividly – was it only yesterday? George smiled even more. He looked at his son and saw himself, recognizing that same glow, that same smile, that same acknowledgement of his future. But Jack didn't know it yet; it would take time, but then he would know – and then he would be very sure about what he knew and what to do about it; or maybe not!

Victoria had been over in the early evening and they had just talked, but nothing about the girl he had met. It would only be a short while before the spring semester was over and Victoria would be off to California and USC. He was neither saddened nor worried when Victoria reminded him. His lack of reaction had upset her, but she kept that to herself. George drove Victoria home and on the way back, Jack had been silent and in deep thoughts; he couldn't sleep that night.

He was out of bed earlier than his father, who normally got up at 4:30; breakfast on the table and the coffee brewing.
"Morning, Jack,"
"Morning, Dad." He gave his father a kiss on the cheek.
"Did you sleep well?"
"Thanks and you didn't sleep at all, did you?"
"Not a blooming wink." George smiled and thought back. He hadn't slept well either after he met Irene the first time.
"Enjoy, Son. It only happens to a few of us."
"What do you mean?"
"I'm not telling. If you are where I think you are, just enjoy." He looked directly at Jack. "It's a terrific ride, if that *is* the ride you are on now. And remember, Son, it's like a rollercoaster and all you have to do is hold on for dear life." As George poured the coffee he saw Irene across the table; it felt good that he did – very good indeed.

Jack did not see the girl in school the next day. He checked the list of the swimmers who had made the team. He didn't know her name, so he looked for anything that might look like a name she would have. He was not on the list, but that didn't matter now. She wasn't on the list either, he felt. He found a classmate who had been watching the try-outs, but he didn't have a clue who Jack was talking about. He asked several others, but no one knew or had seen anything or anybody of that description. Jack thought that maybe he wouldn't even be able to recognize her because he had only seen her in a tightly wrapped towel and wet blond hair; but he kept looking.

After several weeks of no luck, Jack decided that maybe it had been a hallucination, a mirage or something even more exotic, or horrific! He thought that maybe he had gone a bit nutty, but he reasoned that it was just bad luck and a blown chance. *Oh well*, he sighed, but not giving up just yet. How could he! Her image was burned on his mind, etched in his heart and constantly in his thoughts.

His times with Victoria had started to be a bit strained. She was getting clingier, as he was backing off. It was a strange situation as the table seemed to have turned; something Jack never imagined could have happened. It was also strange since Victoria still didn't acknowledge their relationship officially in school. The few times they had met her friends outside the school, she had immediately let go of Jack's hand or closeness. That was one thing he resented. Even if they were not *officially* a couple, he did think they were at least really good friends. Did Victoria still consider him an *embarrassment* in public? Jack had known Victoria for a long time it seemed and though he thoroughly had enjoyed her friendship both physically and mentally, it was beginning to unravel for him, but firming up for her. Anyway, it would only be a few more weeks and she would be off to Europe with her parents for a long time and then she would return home, pack and be off to California. So Jack let it be, and for now he was okay with that.

Victoria had felt Jack's enthusiasm concerning their relationship fade a bit. He was not the eager lover as often as she expected him to be, but she was sure it had nothing to do with her efforts and skills nor her body; she especially kept that part in shape. He had learned everything from her, but he had also accumulated his own skills and a tenderness she absolutely adored. He knew how to make her explode, and he knew how to hold the embrace afterwards. But lately Jack had not been Jack. *I just have to try harder, and all will be back to normal,* she wrongly thought.

"So you are leaving tomorrow evening!" Jack was cleaning off the dinner table as Victoria sipped from a small glass of wine they had shared for the occasion: *their last evening together*, as she called it.
"Yeah, all packed and exited," she said with a sad smile. "I'll really miss you, Jack – a lot."
"Ah, you'll forget all about me," he teased. But her eyes were now filled with tears, and though Jack had slowly reclined from their relationship the last couple of months, he saw softness and vulnerability on her face that confirmed that to her, they were much more than friends; something he

would eagerly have embraced many months ago. He did like her, had loved her, but now it wasn't so. Her tears were rolling freely now and she was very far from the tough person she wanted to be, pretended to be for the longest time. Jack kneeled in front of her and put his head in her lap. She caressed his hair as she wiped tears off her face.

"I love you, Jack," she said quietly. "I really love you." Jack didn't know what to say. He moved up and found her lips. They were soft and eager and the kiss lasted a long glowing time. He did like her, especially when she let her guards down. That was when she became tender and loving, sweet and soft. "Let's go upstairs, Jack." They both got up and slowly moved to his room. Jack lit a candle and got up on the bed. Victoria stood beside the bed and slowly undressed; something she had never done in front of Jack. He was mesmerized because what he saw had such innocence, a sweetness and calm. He had never seen Victoria fully naked, but there she was. She was simply beautiful; her hair over her shoulders and her head facing down as if embarrassed.

"You are very, very beautiful, Victoria." He reached for her hand and gently pulled her to him. Her nakedness was intoxicating. He slowly moved his hands over her, feeling the softness of her skin, the warmth. Her eyes were closed as her hands guided his, helping exploring her body. Victoria had never felt this close to any human being.

"I want you to make love to me, Jack."

"I am – I will." He could hardly speak.

"No Jack, I mean *really* make love to me." Her voice was shaking. Jack sat up a bit. Did she mean? - There was a long pause. He was hoping his interior turmoil didn't show. This was crazy. A few months ago he would have welcomed the request, the opportunity, with all he got, but now it seemed terribly wrong. He didn't want to make love to her under these conditions. He didn't want to take advantage of her vulnerability to any extent. He could never do that to her, to anybody.

"Victoria, we really don't have to do this, no matter how much we would want to. It doesn't seem like the right thing to do, though I'm sure it would be absolutely wonderful, really. Don't get me wrong." Her hands stopped moving his. She stretched out next to him, pressing herself against him.

"Jack, I really want you to, from my heart. I have wanted to for so long – this is the perfect time." She kissed him and led his hands exploring again. Jack had the hardest time resisting, but it didn't feel right.

"Let's just snuggle for a bit and let's see what happens, okay?" He rolled over on his side, found her lips and gently kissed her. She responded with eagerness and her hands started to undress him. Jack quietly slowed her down, but kept kissing her. With his eyes closed he could concentrate better, enjoy the closeness; but this time it didn't work at all. Suddenly a lightning flash went off in his head and unexpectedly the image of the girl by the pool appeared. He thought she whispered: *What are you doing Jack?* Her voice was teasing him in a sad and disappointed tone. *Do you really know what you are doing?* Her smile was faint and then she disappeared.

"No I don't." The loud outburst stunned him; Victoria pulled back.

"What?" She asked with an edge of surprise, "*No,* you don't what?"

"Oh, I'm sorry." His response was confused; he tried to continue kissing, but Victoria gently pushed him off her lips.

"What's going on?" She asked in a calm voice with a small smile; her right hand still resting on his chest.

"Going on what?"

"What's the matter Jack; just tell me, okay?" But he was not sure what was going on. Whatever it was, even if it had an explanation, one thing was for sure: he had to be truthful to Victoria, no matter how mad or disappointed she would get; he certainly owed her that much. But he didn't know what had just happened. He had seen a clear picture, or was it a vision? It was the girl from the pool. She had looked directly into his eyes with such gentle strength, something he had never felt before. The most confusing part was that he had not thought about her for the longest time; he had simply given up on ever seeing her again; and there she was, right in front of him asking what he was doing. Jack pulled Victoria closer to him, nestled her head on his shoulder; he kept his eyes open. The flickering candle sent smooth shadows dancing on the wall, as Jack desperately tried to find some meaning to it all.

"Are you okay Jack?" Her voice was sweet and warm again, with hands embracing his back.

"I'm fine," he lied as his hands slowly caressed her shoulders; but he was not fine. All *this* suddenly felt very uncomfortable. How could this possibly be changing in just seconds? He gently pushed her away, looked at her face and found her welcoming lips; he had to find out. Victoria kissed him with a passion he had never experienced; but now he didn't feel a thing, no matter how hard he tried.

"Make love to me, Jack," her eyes were moist with tears, "I want you to make love to me." Her hands were fumbling, while trying unbuckling his belt. Instead of becoming more excited, Jack froze. *What are you doing?* There she was again; this time clearer than before. He could feel her sparkling blue eyes driving into his soul. *Should you really be doing what you are doing?* Jack all of a sudden realized that he should not be doing what he was doing – it wasn't right; it *dramatically* did not feel right at all.

Victoria's heart rate had increased steadily from the time she and Jack had planned this evening. She would be off to Europe the next day and it would be an awful long time before they could be together again. She even thought about asking her parents if she could stay home or at least shorten the trip; but she never asked. Lately she felt that the closeness and intimacy with Jack had become more intense. First she worried that it was all her own imagination, but then she convinced herself that Jack was with her. The decision to finally fully be with him was made several weeks ago, so the time from then on, the excitement and the expectations, had been a time of extreme euphoria. She fantasized about their night of perfect passion, over and over. This was not a matter of just losing her virginity; it was a matter of giving herself fully to Jack. She was convinced that he would give himself fully to her and not just that night, but forever.

Jack suddenly pulled away from the naked body next to him. Her face immediately showed confusion; her eyes wide open and her face a big question mark.

"What's the matter?" Her voice shaking slightly, "Did I do anything wrong?" Her mind was already racing at this point. She reached out for Jack's hands. The second he felt her touch, that insignificant physical contact that a few moments ago would have excited him, he now found invading and wrong. He never figured out why, but what he said next was an evolution and a shock he could never have prepared for.

"I'm in love; I think I'm in love," his voice was quiet but controlled as he more so spoke to himself. "I really think I'm in love." Tears immediately welled up in Victoria's eyes as she started to float.

"Oh Jack, that is wonderful, so wonderful." She hurriedly pressed her body against his. "I love you too, Dear Jack, oh so much." Her sobbing stopped abruptly as Jack pushed her away.

"No Victoria, I'm not in love with you – I'm in love with someone else." His voice was purely matter-of-fact, but not intentionally. "I am so sorry, but I just realized that I love somebody else; I'm in love with somebody else." Victoria violently pushed Jack off her. She did not believe what she had just heard. It couldn't be true, not at all; her world was imploding.

"Jack, what are you telling me?" Her voice shook off key. "Do you know what you're saying?" Jack's face was trembling.

"Oh my God, Victoria, I am so sorry, oh my God," he sat up on the bed. This had become surreal; this was beyond belief.

"Are you telling me that you love somebody else while we are together here? Is that what you are trying to tell me Jack?"

"I am so sorry, Victoria. I really don't know what has happened, oh God." Victoria got off the bed and covered herself with the sheets.

"Who is she?" her face getting very red.

"I don't know."

"What do you mean you don't know? If you are in love with somebody don't you think knowing her name would be a bleeding factor?" Jack's head snapped up, staring at Victoria's face. It was showing a vile look, her eyes rolling.

"I don't know her name; I don't even know where I can find her." Victoria's stare was ice-cold. Her body had stiffened, but her mind was churning. Deep in Victoria's heart, she had always been prepared to handle any form of rejection from Jack – she thought. When she finally admitted to herself that she loved him, she still savored that small possibility that

Jack wouldn't meet her expectations. But the way Jack had treated her the last few months, had made her believe that he was in love with her as well; nothing he had done had been contrary to that. In her heart she had hoped for them to be together. She had offered herself fully to him and he had ruthlessly turned her down. Nobody would ever get away with that alive, she assured herself. Her anger was now fierce and would get even uglier.

"Let me get this straight," her voice was now clear, sharp and freezing. "You are telling me that you are throwing me out for some slut you don't even know the fucking name of; is that what you a telling me?" The outburst again took Jack by utter surprise; the clarity as well as the vicious delivery. He was all of a sudden scared of Victoria.

"I didn't mean it to happen, Victoria; I had no control over it."

"But tonight you were ready to screw me in more than one way, weren't you? And think about *her* at the same time. What an idiot you are and what an idiot you must think I am."

"Not at all - it was never going to happen; oh God, I am so sorry." Victoria was hurriedly getting dressed. She snapped on her bra, ripped her arms through the blouse, fastened most of the buttons, pulled her underwear and skirt on in one move, stepped into her shoes and then grabbed her jacket and purse. Her body quickly turned and headed for the door.

"Victoria, please understand." Jack's voice was pleading and shaking. "Please let me explain." Victoria stopped in her tracks, turned around and faced Jack. Her voice was sharp, slow, controlled and hurtful:

"No Jack, let *me* explain something to *you*." Jack recoiled, expecting the attack. He saw pure anger as he had never seen anger before. "I picked you up from your little miserable pathetic life. You stalked me, followed me every God damn where. You thought you were invisible? You were just a little prick trying to find a way into some girl's pants. I made you my boy-project and damn well taught you all you know. I guided you through everything, every bloody thing you can do now. And how do you repay me? You fucking dump me! Who the hell do you think you are? Oh, I'll tell you who you are, just another little shit, that's what you really are!" Jack was stunned and shocked. He would never have imagined this side of Victoria.

"I'm so sorry. I know you probably are as confused as I am…" She quickly interrupted.

"Don't assume shit about me, Jack. You obviously don't know me at all, and I was right about you all along. Just another stupid prick of a boy! You are all the bloody same – all of you. All you stupid little horny boys believe your genitals are your main organ; how pathetic is that!" She turned and walked towards the door yet again. As she walked into the hallway, she slowly twisted her body around one last time, looking violently at Jack and sneered. "One last thing, you stupid jerk. Don't you ever try to get hold of me, contact me or in any other way communicate any of your sweet-boy shit to me, because we are done, over with, finished!" She let a small smile slip through. "And oh-by-the-way: I will make your pathetic life so extremely miserable from now on, and whoever the bitch is that you think you're in love with, I will make sure she knows all about you and me and every little bloody detail we ever did and I'll even tell her stuff we didn't do. I'm glad you didn't get to screw me, Jack, because now I'm so sure that no boy or man will ever get that pleasure. Have a nice day, you jerk."

Tears were streaming down Victoria's face as she hailed a cab. She was shaking uncontrollably and wept as never before. Her anger was boiling and her disappointment painfully severe; she would make him pay with all her might. She knew he would suffer and she wanted him to suffer for the rest of his miserable life. How could he do this to her – do this to them? Didn't he know that she loved him? They had been best friends for the longest time. Didn't that mean something to him? He was going to pay, that she was sure of and he was going to pay big.

Close to home she had started to calm down, but was still furiously angry and trembling. How could he? Millions of questions were swirling in her head. Her very best friend had dumped her for somebody he didn't even know. How cruel and insensitive was that?

As she undressed and crept in to bed, her crying had turned to whimpers. Victoria knew what she was going to do. She had decided on a plan of revenge. She felt calmer now and she comforted herself that on the plane to Paris the next morning, she would purposely have forgotten all about Jack. *Screw Jack Winston Miller, that pathetic boy*, she thought out loud. But on the inside she had already started to regret all the things she had called him. She was hurt in mind and heart. She knew she had learned so much from him, about respect and consideration, about the true friendship they had both enjoyed; it had been a special friendship, one she had never had with anybody else and would probably never find again. Victoria was quietly crying as she now realized the most disturbing feeling: she was still in love with Jack and perhaps even more so now than before. She didn't have a single idea how she was going to handle that part – none what-so-ever. All Victoria knew was that she had always been strong, that she would get back up and that she would survive it all, and that she would make Jack pay for his cruelty. Luckily she had never talked much about Jack at home. Her parents were oblivious to any romantic link between them. He was just somebody she tutored. Her stupid kid sister knew less than her parents, so Victoria didn't have to explain anything to anybody.

Victoria's eyes finally became heavy and just as she approached a peaceful sleep, she found Jack's loving and sweet smile in front of her. She could hear him whisper quietly: "I'm so sorry, my darling." An exhausted smile formed on her face. "Goodnight my sweet Jack; remember that this is not the end, this is just a new beginning." The kiss was long, warm and tender.

The days and nights following that fatal evening, Jack stayed in his room. He was depressed and confused as well as he felt anger towards himself for being such a hideous friend. How could he have been so insensitive? Victoria had truly been his best friend and he had discarded her like garbage. How could she ever forgive him? She had called him many names that evening and he had to admit, that his behavior called for all of them. But no matter how much guilt he admitted to, it still hurt him that his stupidity had upset her so much. She had cut him off for good, so he wouldn't be able to seek her forgiveness. He would still try to explain to her what it was all about. It was at that point Jack suddenly realized that he actually didn't understand it himself. What was really going on with him? He had to find out and that he would.

He looked utterly cute when she saw him sitting on the edge of the pool, dangling his feet in the water. There was a certain satisfied look on his face. She had watched him from afar, from behind the group of try-out swimmers. He hadn't seen her; she was sure of that. And this was all new to her. She had never had any special interest in boys the way her girlfriends had begun to explore that area. *Boys* was pretty much all they talked and giggled about these days. How could they all of a sudden become so shallow when school-work demanded their full attention? She was the only one left behind to do what she knew was much more important – academics and working on the future. Her goals were already carved in stone; *rock solid*, as her teachers said and she knew precisely what it would take to get there. Boy-distractions were not part of the plan. But there had been something about that boy on the edge of the pool; even thinking and feeling what she thought and felt, puzzled her in curious ways. But it was her spontaneous reaction that puzzled her even more. She had walked over to him and as calmly and as controlled as she normally was, she talked to him. Granted, he hadn't said much, but it had been an extraordinary experience and however short a communication it was, she was totally mesmerized concerning her response from such a short moment. The fact that she had thought of nothing else for weeks afterwards, placed a question mark on any logic. She had purposely not looked for him in school, as she was somewhat hoping that it would all go away, that it had just been one of those fluke moments, a bit out of control; and being out of control was something she was not familiar with at all. But he had not disappeared; it had been quite the opposite. Now there was just one thing left for her to do: sort it all out, rationalize facts versus fiction, advantages and disadvantages, negatives versus positives. After she reached a decision, she would move on to the planning stage. When all was lined up and if it spelled *go*, she would implement a plan of action and would of course achieve the purpose of her efforts; there were never any doubts about that last part. This way of operation had made her a top student. She knew she would succeed, because she had never failed in anything. Of course *boys,* so far, were unexplored entities, but that was a reality she considered utterly insignificant.

George was busy with work and as he had spent most of the summer away from home, Jack had pretty much been on his own, but under the loving and watchful eyes and care of Colleen and Charles. School would start soon and he was looking forward to his last high school year and then it would be off to college. He was still dabbling in thoughts of a business major. Charles had hinted that if he went in that direction he would have the door open for Jack's employment. Though it was a well meaning offer, Jack also felt like *creating* something on his own from the bottom up. But there was still plenty of time for decisions.

His thoughts had partially lingered on Victoria and the way they had parted. His massive guilt, mixed with his total lack of appreciation of their friendship, was something he struggled with for months on end. But now as the closure of the summer break was near, he had thought less about it; he only randomly felt sad that she wasn't around. With his new driver's license and father's very available car, he had purposely cruised by where she lived several times. The house had looked dark and empty. He knew that Victoria's parents were going to stay in Europe longer than her and figured that she would probably return home earlier and then be off to California. Maybe she would call him while passing through D.C.; but she never did. So he had fully accepted that he would never get a chance to explain how sorry he was.

Jack was a couple of months into his senior year and had aggressively applied himself academically from day one. He became friendly with a classmate who was new to the school. William Baxter was on the shorter side physically, but a giant academically. His constant dry comments and remarks through their classes made even the teachers giggle. They rarely had to tell William to be quiet, as he also had a knack of knowing when enough was enough. Jack found him to be a very entertaining, interesting and fun person to be around; they soon started spending more and more time together, and they both felt a warm friendship developing.

"So it's William and not Bill, huh?" Jack asked his new friend.

"Yup, that's correct. I don't like abbreviations, so William it is, please."

"And Baxter is from where?"

"My mother's maiden name; they divorced when I was 2 and my mother was so pissed about the whole thing, that she didn't want to have anything to do with my dad at all - ever." William was very matter of fact.

"Do you see your dad?"

"Never met the guy; only saw a single photo of him before she threw it in the fireplace. I don't even know if he's dead or alive – don't really care. I never mention my dad to my mother because it still upsets her." William smiled, "well on to something a bit lighter, okay?" Jack smiled back.

It was during the final recess that Friday when they had chatted away. Suddenly a flyer was handed to William. The voice delivering the flyer was clear and direct.

"This is a meeting you must not miss." William looked up, as Jack looked at the flyer.

"Young lady, is that an order or a warning?" William responded with a smile.

"Whichever will get you there;" the answer was cut and dry. She had already moved on when Jack froze. It was *her*; it was the girl from the pool. He turned around fast, but she was gone – yet again.

"William, what did she look like? That was her, the one I told you about; the one from the pool." His voice was fast and eager.

"Oh the girl of your hallucinations; yeah I remember. So maybe she is real after all, huh Jack?"

"Where did she go; where is she." Jack got up and looked around, but she was nowhere to be seen.

"Not to worry, you puppy-eyed-lover-boy; we'll just have to go to the meeting. Let's see what it's about and when." William looked at his new friend and smiled. "Wow, she's really got a good bit of you, hasn't she!"

"I don't care what the meeting is about, I'm going."

"And I'll go with you as moral support, reality provider, but for the most out of morbid curiosity."

The meeting was arranged by SDS, Students for a Democratic Society. They were coming to the school the following day to talk about their position concerning the Civil Rights issues and information about the March on Pentagon a week later, October 21st.

"It's just a bunch of hippies flying high, heating it up with free love and draft-card burnings; your cup of tea, old chap?" William was not an ignorant individual, but he was set in his ways and strong about his convictions and for the most he'd win any debate coming his way. In the beginning of their relationship, Jack had found that irritating, but now he found their *debates* fun and challenging. Many hours were spent with arguments about all kinds of issues and though they differed on many occasions, the arguments had hardened their friendship more so than softened it.

"I'm going. I don't care what it is, where or when; I'm going to be there."

"Oh I get it; not for the hippies, the free love and the under-the-counter drugs, but for the goddess of your illicit dreams, you sly devil you." William was shaking his smiling head. "Okay Jack, I'll go but only if the free love bit is readily available, both at the meeting *and* at the Pentagon."

"You are going for whatever reason, William. I need your help."

"Help with what again?"

"That moral support thing, okay?" William laughed, but agreed.

"What a lusty old dreamer you are, Mr. Miller!"

She was sitting at the table by the door to the gym. There were sign-in sheets as well as flyers with the meeting's agenda. Buttons and T-shirts with V-fingers of peace in red, white and blue were displayed for sale. Jack started to sweat as he saw her. Though he had practiced what to say many times over since yesterday, he was sure that it would yet again come out as a bunch of nondescript gurgling sounds.

"There she is, old chap," William was pointing as they were standing in line.

"Don't point;" Jack's words came whistling through his teethes. "Act normal, William." His friend turned and smiled.

"You are kidding me, aren't you; or are you just legally insane? Gotta be one of the two or possibly both?" William was laughing, but he did behave.

"Name here and address there, please." William finished quickly and Jack was next. He looked at her; well actually he stared at her with clear and obvious fixation. She hurriedly pointed at the spaces to be filled out; she didn't look up. Jack wrote with a shaking hand. As he walked away he damned himself for not being more assertive. Then he heard that clear and direct voice as she read from the sign-in sheet:

"Excuse me! So you are *Pool-Boy* with no address and just a phone number!" She still didn't look up. "What about an address?"

"That's all the information you'll need," Jack replied as he turned towards the table with a smile; but she was already helping the next in line.

"That was really truly smooth, *Pool-Boy*." William's voice was filled with teasing sarcasm. "If I ever get in a similar situation, please don't advise me, okay?" Jack had giggled a bit nervously, but inside he was outraged concerning his feeble attempt of communicating with her; had he screwed up yet again? Going back was not an option due to the embarrassment factor.

She had prepared herself for the moment when she would reconnect with the boy from the pool. The specific time and place had to be determined by feasibility, so when she was handing out flyers for the SDS meeting, the opportunity had presented itself. She had been calm and collected as she was with anything she did. He was sitting on the bench next to another boy. She assumed he was a friend, as she had often seen them together. She was also sure that the boy from the pool didn't have a girlfriend, at least from school. But a *girlfriend* would not be an issue of concern – just a distraction to deal with. When she reached the bench, she had on purpose handed the other boy the flyer. There was a short exchange of words between him and her and she quickly moved on. She had done and seen what she needed to do and see. His body language told her all she wanted to hear. He had recognized her voice, but not reacted fast enough. She figured that he had to process the situation and that was why he hadn't jumped up or at least turned to see if he was right; but then again, she had not allowed him much time to do so.

Saturday afternoon she insisted to help out at the sign-in table. He arrived and had performed beyond her expectations. His *Pool-Boy* and phone number bit was inventive and funny. He had charmingly opened the door so she could walk through. No matter how well she had trusted her planning, *Pool-Boy* had cut the process a bit shorter and she was fine with that. The target was now within sight and a simple phone call should seal the deal. It was all going very well, thank you. But what she didn't know, what she couldn't be prepared for, was that a much bigger challenge was not so far away. Her decision abilities would be tested to the utmost and the choice she made, would either give her a future of happiness or one of cruel disappointment. It was a decision she would have to make from her heart; something she had never done before in her young life.

"She'll call; just you wait." Jack's voice was excited, but doubting.
"I know she will, my friend, I'm positive she will." William was smiling a bit envious. He hadn't seen Jack this happy since they hooked up some months back. He had found a true friend in Jack and had not spent many waking hours apart. They quickly found that even though they did not agree on everything, actually far from, they had established a respect for each other that made their friendship unique and warm. He was living with his mother; he had no siblings and had no social life to write home about, but then he met Jack. He felt rather quickly that not only had he gained a terrific friend, but he had also been embraced by Jack's father, as well as Jack's *other* parents, Colleen and Charles. It had all happened so fast, but it had all been good. His mother was pleased to see a much happier and more energized son. She had met George a couple of times in passing, as she picked up William or brought Jack home. George was fun and charming; very much like his son and they had all enjoyed some entertaining dinners together, as one big happy family of friends.

"So *Pool-Boy*, when do you think she'll call?

"I have no clue, but it'll be soon; that I know." He was overly eager and had a hard time controlling that eagerness.
"Are you jealous, William?" It suddenly occurred to Jack.
"Yep, that I am; as you know several times over, I have never pleasured from the company of a representative from the other gender group in any capacity of *girlfriend*, sorry to say." William smiled: "But I am now observing you to learn about the intricate roads of romance, learning from either your success or your failure. I am taking mental notes, so thank you and please forge ahead, young lad." Jack laughed.
"And if she has a sister, I'm readily available to fall in love."
"You are so weird." William didn't know that Jack had been through the *gender-connection* before. He had not talked to anybody about his relationship with Victoria other than to his father and the Ryan's. He was still awkwardly embarrassed of the way he had disrespected their friendship and certainly in the brutal way it had ended. Those old wounds were painfully torn open again and again, guided by massive guilt; Jack had accepted that as punishment for his ignorance. But he had no clue that it would soon rip wide open again, becoming a rather decisive issue concerning the happiness of his future; he had no clue at all.

He answered the phone on the second ring. His father would normally call around this time when he was out of town, so Jack was casual based on this assumption.
"Hello Dad!" A bit of silence followed.
"Impossible; as far as I know I don't have any children at *this* point." Her voice was the same on the phone. "Can I assume that you expected this to be your father calling, or did confusion set in while you patiently waited for me to call?" Jack giggled.
"*Yes* to the first part, and *no* to the second; *patiently* most certainly had nothing to do with the waiting part at all."
"Good. We should never take anything for granted, should we?"
"I fully agree." Jack found himself surprisingly calm. Her voice was sharp in a controlled way and laced with a distinct sound of a tongue-in-cheek sarcasm.
"So what's the deal?" Jack asked.

"Well, *the deal* is that we should go to the rally on Saturday. I suggest that we meet at the bottom of the stairs to the right, facing Abe. Let's say around ten!"

"The Lincoln Memorial?"

"That's the one. You read the flyer, obviously."

"I sure did, several times."

"Bring your friend. There'll be someone he should meet."

"Not meeting you, I hope!"

"No, *Pool-Boy*, I'm already taken." By those words Jack froze and felt silent. "Are you still there?"

"I believe so." His voice was not so eager anymore.

"Good, so I'll see you and your friend on Saturday at ten, bottom of the stairs, Lincoln Memorial. Remember, we are hiking to the Pentagon, so wear comfy shoes, okay?" Jack smiled a bit from her motherly advice, but also thought: *What the heck is going on?*

"We'll be there," he briefly paused. "Can I ask you a question, just out of basic curiosity?"

"For the most, questions come from basic curiosity. Go ahead." He took a deep breath; maybe this would kill his hopes, but he had to ask.

"So you said earlier that you are *already taken*, does that mean you are bringing a boyfriend on Saturday?"

"That's correct. You already confirmed that you'll be there, so that's what it means." Jack paused.

"Sorry, but maybe I'm a bit slow…"

"Noted…"

"If I understand you correctly, it sounds very much like that *I'm* that boyfriend you are bringing along."

"Not fully correct" Her tone was matter of fact. "You *are* my boyfriend, but I am not *bringing you along* to the rally. You are getting there by yourself. I have to go with my aunt and uncle, as my parents are out of town, so we'll meet you there, okay?" Jack smiled in surprise.

"I'm not sure I fully understand this one either, but at what point did I become your boyfriend."

"The day I saw you by the pool." Her voice was flowing in a very straight line.

"If I may ask: when were you going to tell me that I'm your new boyfriend?" Jack shook his head with a silent giggle.

"Not *new* boyfriend, just *boyfriend*. I have never had a boyfriend before, so you'll be my first and of course my last; any more questions?"

"Well of course," Jack was giggling a bit more.

"What's so funny?"

"I'd say that your approach is unique, utterly surprising, but yet refreshing in an out-of-this-world kind of way."

"And your point is?"

"I really don't think I have a point at this time. This is all so, well, sudden."

"I know it appears a bit sudden, but I'm sure my choice is right; I *am* sorry about the suddenness, but I truly trust that the two of us will work out really well. What do you think?"

"With the time you have allotted for a response, I must say that my initial reaction is covered with confusion."

"I expected nothing less."

"On the other hand, I have thought of nothing else but *you* since the pool-day."

"I know that."

"How do you know that?"

"Gut feeling and a lot of hope. I went through the same thing."

"Interesting; so on Saturday, are we going to discuss the relationship you have planned for us in detail, so that we'll both end up on the same track?"

"Come to think about it, Saturday is not good; too many people, as well as my aunt and uncle will be there. Why don't we meet before Saturday?"

"That might be a good thing, no doubt. Have you selected a specific accommodation and time?"

"Is this an attempt in humor?"

"Admittedly *yes*."

"Okay. I, seriously, suggest we meet at your house after school, if that'll work."

"That'll work, and when?"

"What about tomorrow?"

"As good a day as any; I walk home from school, so maybe we can walk together, okay?"

"No, that's not good. I'll meet you at your house a bit after school."

"Why?"

"I prefer not to be seen with you until we have agreed on the details of our future relationship." Jack was confusingly impressed, and laughed.

"Wow, you sure have it all figured out."

"It saves a lot of time." She still sounded matter of fact.

"It sure does, seriously. I have another important question: In these plans of yours…"

"That would be *our* plans," she interrupted.

"Okay, in these plans of *ours,* are we going to be happy?"

"Jack, we are going to be extremely happy – otherwise I wouldn't have approached you; it wouldn't have been worth our time." Now he smiled even wider.

"It all sounds very nice indeed - however weird." This time Jack was dead serious.

"I'm glad you like our plan." Jack already liked the use of *our* in her voice.

"No offense, but this isn't really romantic in the old-fashioned romantic kind of way, is it?"

"No it's not, but I figured that we could save a lot of time up front, not doing a lot of dancing around the issues, therefore have much more time for romance when we know precisely where we stand with each other. Don't you agree?"

"You mean not have to go through the agony of maybe *you* liking me and maybe *me* liking *you* kind of issues?"

"Precisely…"

"But isn't that part of it, that whole insecurity thing, the agony of wondering, the suspense, all that stuff?"

"It's an option we have. This way we are going in the right direction from the start. I already like you and you already like me, so all we have to do is solidifying that by getting together, plan and then move forward. Don't you see that we bypass all the games other people play; this way we are saving a bunch of time. " Now Jack was laughing.

"You are already amazing to listen to, wow. How old are you again?"

"17…"

"Probably going on 30…"

"At some point, I hope." Jack could hear her smile. He gave her his address information and she sounded like she was ready to end the call; Jack didn't want to end it at all. He suddenly realized something he had forgotten all about.

"One last thing: now since you are possibly going to be my girlfriend, I think it would be appropriate if I at least know your name."

"Jack, you cannot use the term *possibly*, since I *am* going to be your girlfriend. That has already been established; has it not?"

"I believe that to be true, whatever intricate realities prevail." She spelled her name and the line went dead.

Jack didn't need to look up the meaning of *euphoria*. He was sure that he felt the fullest explanation of it. That was the most interesting conversation he had enjoyed with just about anybody. He absolutely adored her voice, the sharpness in the way she communicated and though it sounded so organized and controlled, it was also laced with a subtle sense of humor. He was on a great white cloud and nothing would be able to push him off. It was all so excitingly surreal.

He called his father in London. It was 0300 GMT, so a sleeping voice answered. The conversation had been short, but exciting. Then he had called Colleen and Charles and they had all three been on the line. Then it had been William's turn. William even had his mother listen in. When Jack told William about a friend she wanted him to meet, he simply responded with a *wow!* Jack was so overly excited, that falling asleep was a struggle; but he didn't care at all. So tomorrow he was really going to see her, the girl he had thought, fantasized and dreamt about for so long. He liked the name, too; it was perfect – maybe too perfect?

Though Jack had expected the doorbell to sound around this time, it still sent a shockwave through his body. He was nervous in a surprisingly calm way. She had smiled when he opened the door and soon they sat in the living room across from each other. It was the first time Jack really saw her. The previous times had been short blurs. Her hair was in a ponytail, her eyes round and warm; her lips rosy and naturally so. Her clothes looked a bit on the conservative side, matching in colors and well-kept. Jack couldn't keep his eyes off her. As she sat in the sofa, she looked confident and seemingly at ease with herself and her surroundings.

"Nice place."

"Thanks."

"So have you thought about our conversation?"

"Thought of nothing else," he smiled, "and you?"

"Pretty much the same," she answered, smiling back. Her smile made Jack melt even more.

"So what's the plan?"

"Well, I thought we should talk about our future relationship, how to approach it and also what we should expect from each other on several levels." She was trying to read Jack's expression. He was smiling a bit, which she found encouraging.

"Okay, we can do that." He paused and continued: "Is it just me or does this all sound a bit cut and dry, somewhat business like?"

"This is the first and last relationship I'm going to be involved with, Jack, so I don't want to take any chances wasting time fumbling around for answers, playing silly games with my time and my feelings, what I like and what I don't like. When I know what I like, why not go for it?"

"Indeed; why not? Seems like a rational way to approach things."

"I'm glad you agree", her smile was relaxed and sweet. "If you don't mind, I'll tell you about me and after that you can tell me about you. And we can finish with questions and answers…"

"Just like the good old debate routine…"

"Yeah, just like that, okay?"

"I'm all ears."

She was very well-spoken for her age, Jack admitted. She could sound a bit too organized at times, a bit business-like, too matter of fact and maybe even conceited. But she got to the core of the issues extremely fast, wasting no time. Jack found her very refreshing.

During her first seventeen years, she had concentrated on her education and *knowledge beyond*, as she called it. Her GPA was impressive, much better than Jack's, and she already knew what she wanted to do professionally; she was going to be an attorney, with corporate law as her specialty. Jack was sure that failing was not a possibility she considered; she would no doubt do well.

So far she had not had any interest in boys. The only contact with members of the other gender had been through groups in class with respect to school assignments. Another area of contact was through her participation on the school's debate-team; she was the school's first female debate team captain, a fact that didn't surprise Jack. Her girlfriends had started that *boys* thing a few years back and as they spent more time on that issue, the less time she spent with them. She soon found herself with just a couple of true friends left. But she was doing what *she* wanted to do, so everything was fine. A few years earlier she had thought through the *boys* issue and had determined that she was not going to waste time on boys, but was just going to find the one she'd spend the rest of her life with. She knew she was going to find a boyfriend who would be a great husband and friend, as well as a great father. She wanted four children, just for the record. After deciding on this part of her future, she had left the subject alone to concentrate on her academics. So how was she going to find that person? In this case and this case only, she decided to let her intuition do the initial work. Leaving anything to chance was not the way she conducted business with her life, but in this case she felt it was the right way to approach it – intuition should lead the way, but only this once.

Her *intuition* had sprung into action the second she saw him at the pool. She was not looking, had not thought about and had not to any extent searched for that specific boyfriend at that specific time; it just happened. She knew the moment this new exciting feeling invaded her body, that he was the one. Getting over and communicate with him had been as natural as anything. She found herself calm and in control, which of course was nothing new. She also knew that the moment she had established contact with him, she had made the right choice. The rest was just patience, planning and scheduling.

Jack smiled as she talked. The way the words came out, so smooth and coherent, all breaks so fitting; it all sounded logical, though he also knew that nobody would believe him if he told them about her plans. Her body language was subtle and determined and Jack was seriously falling in love. Though he had never been in a state of love before, he was very sure that this was it – and big time. He wasn't even surprised when he politely interrupted her.

"Sorry, this might sound a bit sudden, but I do believe that I'm already falling in love with you." She looked at him, smiled and responded:
"I fell in love with you at the pool. What took *you* so long?" They both laughed. She continued a bit further, but not much about her family; and then it was Jack's turn.

He went back to his Russian grandparents and his father arriving in America in 1943. He talked a little about his father's involvement in the war, but also told her that he wanted his father to tell her in his own words. He quietly talked about his mother's death the day he was born and how Colleen and Charles had become part of his and his father's lives. Sara was watching how Jack had shown an honesty of emotions, but she wasn't surprised. He finished with his everyday life, school and plans for the future.
"Business or construction, you say?"
"Yeah that's the general direction. Would that be a good fit? I mean, I could change to whatever you have planned, couldn't I?" She smiled and raised a finger.
"Now let's not get on my case because I seem to have it all figured out. I'm sure we'll agree that the direction is defined, but the *how to get there* no doubt needs a bit of flexibility and work... And business or construction is all fine, but only if that's what you will be happy with; otherwise it shouldn't be considered at all." Jack had to smile again; this still felt rather surreal, but it was also taking form of something looking extremely promising.
"This all sounds wonderful and organized, but will we also venture into romance and silly spur-of-the-moment stuff at times?" Jack's face was showing a big question-mark.
"It will be a major part of our relationship, Jack. With the romance, you must help me along as I have no experience besides hugs from my parents."
"I'll do the very best I can; but not that I know it all. Both of us helping out will no doubt be the way to approach it." Jack smiled; now *he* sounded business-like.
"And talking about romance, what about a former girlfriend or girlfriends, Jack?" He had hoped that subject would have been swept under the carpet; but here it was, dangling in front of him. There was no doubt in his mind that he would be honest with her about everything; that was not the question. But he did feel uncomfortable to have to talk about

it, so hopefully she would accept wide generalities; but that wouldn't be so. "You seem uncomfortable."

"I do feel uncomfortable because here you are with no experience in the *boyfriend* department, so I'm on a limp as I have no idea what you really want to know and why?"

"Would it be easier if I just ask questions?" She smiled gently.

"That might be the way to do it. Okay, let me have it." Jack took a deep breath.

"You don't have a girlfriend now!"

"That's correct." One down; *but how many more to go?* Jack wondered.

"But you had a girlfriend?"

"That is also correct."

"How long did the relationship last?"

"I'd say about a year." No, he did not like this at all; this was all something that had nothing to do with the two of them; it really didn't.

"Were you ever in love with her during that time?"

"I can truly say that I was not. I loved her more like a friend." He moved nervously in his seat. "Do we have to do this?"

"Were you physically involved with her?"

"Please, come on; isn't this a bit too personal?"

"I guess, but I would feel better if I knew your background, whatever there is. Don't worry about it; it will not alter our plans to any extent – seriously."

"Yes, I was physically involved."

"How physically?"

"This is not fair, not fair at all." His heart was pumping faster now and he felt very uncomfortable.

"I'm sorry Jack; *no* this *is* not fair - I'm sorry. I just feel I need to know our starting point; but if it makes you that uncomfortable, we can drop it, okay? "

"Thanks for understanding," Jack felt relieved. He felt fine telling her about his past, including *girlfriend*. The embarrassing part was to have to reveal the details; that didn't seem fair to him and he couldn't see the reason why he had to unravel such personal stuff. But he also understood what she had said about it, so he felt that he should.

"What if I ask you just one more question, and then done, okay?" She leaned over and put her hand on his. "Okay Jack?" Her touch was calming.

"Sure, just one more," he caressed her hand.

"Are you a virgin?" He sucked in a big relieved breath.

"If we are talking within the physical and technical sense, I can proudly confirm that I am most certainly one of those."

"I'm glad to hear that." She squeezed his hand a few seconds. "Well, I think we have a good start already; so next is the rally on Saturday. I'm looking forward to that." She leaned over and kissed his cheek. "See you then."

"But we'll see each other in school tomorrow, won't we?" He had opened the front door.

"Of course we will. Our relationship is at least official what you and I are concerned. Everybody else can figure it out by themselves – if they want to." She gave him a warm hug and a kiss on his lips; a light friendship kiss. "And then we'll start serious work on all that kissing stuff. Remember, you'll have to help me out on that one, okay?" Jack smiled a big okay.

"I'll be more than happy to; but the way you *do* things as far as I have noticed, I'm sure you'll learn rather quickly and even be able to teach *me* something." They were now outside the house. She smiled back at him as she approached her uncle's car; he had arrived to pick her up just a few moments earlier. As she proceeded to open the car-door, she turned one last time.

"Okay, just one more question!" She said while smiling a bit sheepish.

"Come on Sara, we have already done all that."

"Please Jack, just one more and I really promise you I'm done." Jack smiled and nodded.

"Okay, just one more."

"What was your girlfriend's name?" Jack was puzzled why she would ask that.

"Victoria," he answered. He was glad the questions were now done with, but he quickly noted that Sara's face had turned white - very white. Her hand dropped off the car-door handle.

"Victoria Grant?" She asked quietly. Jack nodded and smiled.

"Yeah, Victoria Grant; do you know her?" Sara's voice was small and shaking. She had to support her body against the car as her knees gave in. This she had not expected; this she had not even considered; this was a horrid shock. She had no reason to even add this possibility into the equation. Her research concerning Jack and his background, had not found even the smallest hint that he had had a girlfriend. That he had freely volunteered the information had not surprised her. How could she have been so blind? This was a devastatingly huge shock and one she didn't feel could be solved. Sara felt the tears fall from her eyes and saw Jack in a blur coming towards her. He reached out to hold her, but she instinctively pulled away from him.

"My God, what's the matter Sara?" She pulled further away as he tried to approach her again. She spoke through her tears.

"Victoria Grant; she tutored you?"

"Yes; Sara, please tell me what's the matter?"

"I'm sorry, but this will never work." Her body was now shaking violently. "Victoria is my sister." She quickly opened the car-door, got in and the car pulled away. Jack was left on the sidewalk stunned and devastated as he realized what had just happened. A few minutes ago he had been in heaven, but now he was surrounded by hell.

The house was dead quiet as Jack stumbled back in through the door. He was in a daze, soon finding the seat on the sofa where Sara had been sitting; it was still warm. The wires in his head were all severed; no logical thoughts could be formulated. This was insane. He told himself that he could not have had any idea that Sara and Victoria were sisters. Victoria had only mentioned her sister, *a* sister, very briefly and not kindly. She had not mentioned her since; not with a single word and Jack had never had a reason to talk about her. She had only been an instance and then immediately forgotten – until now. Sara had simply not existed until the day at the pool and most certainly not as Victoria's sister. During her visit today, she had not mentioned her last name; he would have remembered. Sara didn't look like her sister at all, no resemblance what so ever. He would have picked up on that immediately. She didn't have any of her sister's mannerisms or looks. Jack couldn't find anything that would have made a connection. But here he was with a tremendously broken heart. This was the most devastating moment in his life, and he was positive that he would never get over it – there was no way this would be forgotten or forgiven. Deep into the night he finally fell asleep on the sofa, totally exhausted. He would skip school the next couple of days, as he mentally, emotionally and physically felt utterly sick.

Sara's uncle was wise enough not to ask any questions on the way home. He knew her very well and if she wanted to talk, she would; but she didn't. The silent trip was only supported by Sara's sniffling whimpers. He offered her a handkerchief and she quickly put it to good use. Her aunt had given her an understanding and caring hug and Sara was soon tucked under the covers in the guestroom.

She desperately wanted to sort all this out; and as quickly as possible. This was the essential center for her happiness. She knew the vast implications involved, so she had to handle this with the utmost consideration. First, Victoria had only briefly mentioned the boy she tutored; never given his name. Sara wondered if even their parents knew; maybe they did, maybe they didn't. She had done the tutoring for the longest time and Sara knew she had also spent time with *this boy* beyond the tutoring. She was pretty sure that there was more than tutoring math going on. She had never dwelled on these possibilities at all, as she did not get along with her sister. Any interest in what Victoria did with her life was a mute point for Sara. They pretty much stayed out of each other's way. Victoria's values, her boy-hating attitude and other boy issues, never had Sara's interest. She leaned heavily on her academic challenges; Victoria didn't seem to lean on hers. The difference between Victoria's and Sara's academic approach was that Victoria had it easy absorbing knowledge, whereas Sara had to work hard and long hours for her grades.

But Jack had been Victoria's boyfriend, she had kissed him as well as he had kissed her and God knows what else they had done. This was beyond what Sara could comprehend at the moment. She knew she really loved Jack; she had no doubts about that. He was even sweeter and more adorable than she could have hoped for. This new situation changed everything. But she had to sort it out; she had to find a solution, if finding a solution was even possible at this point.

The emotional rollercoaster ride drained Sara dry. It was just a bit past midnight when she finally could close her crying eyes to find some rest. The last image she saw before she fell asleep was of Jack as he stood alone on the sidewalk. He had looked terrified and devastated; a vast sadness was painted on his face and his body seemed collapsed. Her heart stood still and she tried to reach out to him, but it was too late. He soon disappeared and Sara was alone again.

It was late Friday evening. William had just left; he'd visited Jack as moral support. He tried to find a phone number where Jack could reach Sara, but he didn't have enough information to do so. He only found Sara's parents phone number, but no answer. Then he suggested sending her a letter, but Jack shook his head in response. William looked for Sara at school, but didn't see her anywhere. He found a girl he had seen with Sara. She had told him that Sara hadn't been in school the last few days, which was very unusual, she added. So all William could do was comfort his friend and that he did.

Jack was lying on the sofa across from where Sara sat such a long time ago it seemed. Their life together had been in the starting-blocks, but then it all went black. He choked up just thinking about it. It was close to eleven when he turned off the lights. As his father would return home after midnight, so the light in the hall was left on. He was halfway in bed when the doorbell rang. He looked at the clock and it was just after midnight. So his father had forgotten his keys, which was nothing unusual. He grabbed his bathrobe and went downstairs. The bell sounded again; this time longer.

"Hold your horses, Dad, I'm coming, I'm coming." He reached the door, unlocked and swung it open. It was not his father; it was Sara.

"Sara, is something wrong?" She looked miserable, cold, wet and crying.

"Everything is wrong."

"Come in." He reached for her hand and she grabbed it.

"How did you get over here? It's after midnight."

"I ran."

"You ran; are you crazy?"

"Yes I am."

"Does your aunt or uncle know where you are?"

"No, I didn't tell them."

"You *are* crazy. Call them now, okay?" He led her in to the living room and the phone.

"Later?"

"No Sara, right now." She looked at him and immediately saw his utmost concern. She quickly told her uncle where she was and that she was fine. "Give them my phone number, okay?" which she did. After the call Sara sat down on the sofa across from Jack. She wiped the rain and tears off her face with the towel Jack had rushed to her; then she spoke.

"How have you been?" Jack melted by the shear sound of her voice.

"Not okay at all, just miserable and sad; how about you, Sara?"

"Same as you; I just lost it, Jack. I was not in control of me. That was the first time ever. I really didn't know what to do, when to do or if I should do anything at all. It was miserable, really miserable; it still is." She tried to smile.

"Are we going to find a solution; are we going to talk it all out, clear the plate and start over fresh?" Waiting the few seconds for the answer seemed like hours.

"I want to, Jack, yes I really want to."

"So what do we do next?"

"I need to learn not to think about you and Victoria together when you and I are together. I need to forget any pictures of you kissing her, her kissing you and whatever you did with each other. I don't know how I can do that!" She paused. "It's that image of you kissing my sister that haunts me."

"Doesn't make it sound very romantic now, does it."

"I'm sorry; I didn't want to belittle the relationship you had. That was wrong."

"Sara, I can't say I'm sorry because I'm not. Victoria and I had a good friendship, and another thing: I can't un-kiss her to erase that image you are talking about."

"I know. But I don't know what to do about it." She looked straight at him.

"I don't know either, Sara, I really don't. Maybe time will help us out or maybe not. Maybe it takes something else, but I don't know what that might be, not now at least." He took a deep breath. "Maybe we should just forget about all that stuff for now and see what happens. I want to be with you, Sara, more than anything else in this world. If it includes kissing and stuff or not, is not important at all at this point." She was observing how his lips moved and treasured his words. He was the boy for her; no doubts about that.

"So you don't want to kiss me, is that it?" Jack giggled.

"Maybe deep down, that might be the truth." They both laughed. "Nah Sara, that is so far from the truth. But it must be on your terms and in due time for *you*. If it helps you, I know that I will only think of you when the kissing thing is going on." He smiled as he felt it had sounded silly; but he tried to bring it all to a lighter level. Sara smiled back. She got up and sat next to Jack, finding his hand, wiping tears from her face.

"I feel a little bit better now, really. The last few days have been hell. It was the Sara-out-of-control thing that I couldn't understand, didn't know how to deal with; and then I didn't want to lose you either."

"So it had nothing to do with me or us; it was all about that control bit, huh?"

"No, it had everything to do with you; it was just that I couldn't fix *us* as I have always been able to fix everything else. It was such an enormous issue, so very important to me – important to us."

"So are you getting back to normal again?"

"I'm trying; with your help I'm going to be fine, hopefully."

"Well thanks for the warning." She looked at him, smiled a little and shook her head.

"Admit it; you wouldn't like me any other way, would you."

"No I wouldn't." And that was the truth. They heard the front door being unlocked, opened and closed.

"And now you can meet your future father-in-law." She gleefully smiled.

"Can't wait." She liked the sound of what Jack had just said; it sounded so right.

"Honey I'm home," was the routine silly entrance by Jack's father. He was soon in the living room and smiled widely.

"So what are you two night-owls up to?"

"Dad I want you to meet your future daughter-in-law Sara Grant. Sara this is my father George Winston Miller." George moved towards Sara with open arms. She moved towards him and they soon embraced.

"Welcome to the family, Sara. It's a pleasure to meet you."

"Thanks Mr. Miller." It felt good in his arms; warm and safe.

"And since you are now part of our little family, it's George, not that Miller stuff, okay?"

"Okay", she smiled back. "*Winston*, would that be in honor of Churchill by any chance?" She pointed towards the black and white photo on the wall with a younger George standing next to a cigar smoking Churchill.

"Smart girl, Jack," he laughed. "Sure you can live up to that?"

"I'll do my very best, Dad." And that he would.

Getting to the bottom of the stairs at the Lincoln Memorial had been a rather interesting task for William and Jack. They later learned that the March on Pentagon was made by over 100,000 people, but they did make it to the stairs in time. Sara arrived with her aunt, uncle and girlfriend Alice at 10:00 sharp. She introduced everybody to everybody, and William was quickly engaged in a lively conversation with Alice; Sara and Jack pretty much didn't see them the rest of the day; and what a day it was. As the rally started moving towards the Pentagon, Sara held on to Jack as he held on to her. She had quickly slipped her hand into his and it was the most natural and the most comfortable feeling ever; it just felt right.

They were in deep conversation when Jack heard a voice he recognized immediately; his heart jumped as he turned.

"Well, if it isn't Mister Miller." Nora smiled from ear to ear. "What an extreme pleasure." They rushed towards each other and the hug was warm and long.

"I really missed you and I thought a lot about you and I'm sorry I didn't get your phone number. Wow, it is so great to see you again." And for both, that was the truth. Jack quickly grabbed Nora's hand and went over to Sara.

"Nora, I want you to meet my girlfriend Sara; Sara this is Nora." Nora and Sara shook hands.

"Hi Sara, so nice meeting you; I don't really know much about Jack, but what I do know makes you a lucky girl." Sara smiled and nodded.

"I know."

"How long have you been going together?" She asked both of them.

"Since last night," was Sara's answer. "And so far, it's going extremely well." Nora laughed.

"Sara, you and I will get along just fine." And that they would. They stayed together all the way to the Pentagon and deep into the evening.

Sara was ecstatic as everything had materialized beyond her expectations. She felt a bit embarrassed about the way she had planned and executed the whole boyfriend thing, feeling rather immature and childish. She reasoned from the way Jack responded, it had been the right way. But childish she felt, though Jack, sweet Jack, had just smiled and kissed her with the calm assurance, that no matter how crazy and insane her actions had been, no matter how crazy and insane she was, the result was a happy one; nothing else mattered.

It was early afternoon between classes. Victoria had initially just scanned through the letter from Sara. As far as she recalled, this was the first letter she had received from her sister. She acknowledged the neatness of the writing as well as the grammar, the organized sentences and the well phrased paragraphs. But Victoria was not at all impressed with the content. The moment she realized what Sara was telling her, she got physically ill and had to quickly sit down in a wasted effort of letting the horrific feelings of deceit and betrayal pass; but nothing passed and nothing ever had and it never would. She thought she had moved forward, but the memories of those last moments with Jack on his bed ripped her wide open again – and again. She could still feel her warm and naked body eagerly craving him, to fully commit *till death do us part*. But then the total shock of his hideous and sudden callousness, claiming love for somebody else. It had been devastatingly embarrassing and had ripped her heart out; and now this? His love had been for her stupid kid sister Sara! That little bitch of a sister! And what a traitor Jack had turned out to be. Had they been sneaking around behind her back, laughing hysterically as they were screwing each other and thereby screwing her? Had Sara pursued Jack because Jack belonged to Victoria? Was it some kind of sister revenge shit? The many questions tore vividly around in her head, but none came up with solutions that calmed her down. And what could Jack possibly find in Sara that she couldn't offer him! She was taller than Sara with longer legs and a much better body; her breasts were full and certainly didn't need a bra to stay in place; she had everything any sane male fantasized about, any sane male wanted. But insane Jack had chosen her no-chest no-body sister and that made it even more sickening. *Sara, you little bitch of a sister; don't you ever think you'll get away with this. That will not happen – ever*, she irately thought. It was severely hard for her to feel revengeful towards somebody she still loved. Deep inside she had not fully given up on Jack and that was a very confusing feeling and a disturbing scenario; but her sister? That was something totally different. Some day she would let Sara know that she shouldn't have crossed that line; she would make her pay dearly for that massive mistake.

Dear Sara.
I'm in between classes, so just a quick note. Thanks for your letter. I appreciate your concern with respect to my feelings. That was very sweet of you. Of course you and Jack have my blessings. I had a naïve school-girl's crush on him and it was just a fling – nothing else. Jack is a nice boy and I had my fun, but also had to move on. I do hope you will be happy as long as it lasts. Just a sisterly advice: remember that there are so many frogs to be kissed before you finally settle down with the right one.
Love Always, Victoria

Sara had read it out loud, a bit slower the second time and looked at Jack as she finished. His facial expression looked puzzled with a slight smile.
"So what are you thinking, Jack!" She handed him the letter.
"I think it smells a bit – stinks a lot, actually."
"Why?"
"Well, first of all it was not a school-girl's crush, far from. I know she liked me beyond *liking* me, and I also had feelings

for her beyond a crush." Jack wondered if he should go further than that, but Sara didn't seem to be bothered. "So I'm not sure what to read from this. My initial thought is that she doesn't mean a bit of what's in the letter. My guess is that she's up to something."

"This is the only letter I have ever gotten from her and as I know that I'm more of a pain to her than a loving sibling, I agree that this is not the Victoria I learned to ignore. You are probably right; she might be up to something."

"So the plan would be what?"

"Deal with it if anything comes up, I guess."

"Sounds good to me," Jack smiled, trying to look unconcerned. The Victoria issue could be something they would have to deal with down the road, and though he was still worried deep inside, a worry based on Victoria's violent reaction that night, he tried to push it off his plate; but didn't succeed. Sara looked speculative and concerned. Victoria is up to something, was her last thought that moment.

"But what am I going to do about that *kissing many frogs* stuff she suggested?" Sara moved closer to Jack. "Do you think I should follow her advice and kiss more than one?"

"Well, Sara darling, there is only *one* for you," pointing at himself, "and this toad will always be more than willing, able and ready."

"That's good news, because you *are* the only toad I ever want to kiss; so pucker up *Frog-Boy*," and he did – as the fairytale continued!

With Sara's inherent lust for planning, they stated in front of their parents that they would get married the day after Sara's 18th birthday. She would apply for admission to Georgetown University, pursuing a law degree. With her top grades and her parent's financial support, being accepted looked very realistic. Jack would work for Charles and CR Constructions until he could start at Georgetown the same semester as Sara. He would apply for admission to the school's business program and George would be his financial support, as well as he would work part-time, as long as it didn't get in the way of school.

Sara also informed their parents that they wanted to have children; four was the number she mentioned. They would find a small apartment close to the school; she already knew a few they were considering. The parents uniformly agreed to help the young couple financially beyond the academic expenses. Several other issues were brought up by Sara, and as she finished by closing her notebook, she smiled and said: "So that's the plan". The silence in the room was nervous, as Jack and Sara's parents were eagerly trying to digest what they had just heard, and were desperately trying to come up with a positive response. Inside their collective heads they now realized what the *deer-in-the-headlight* meant. Sure they supported these two youngster's relationship, but marriage so soon, before they finished their education, before they had jobs? And having children while they attended school? Planning was good, they all agreed, but certainly not this fast…

Sara beamed with happiness, while Jack's smile seemed a bit shaky. He was in love and had the greatest respect for Sara's judgment. The way she had animatedly told him about their future, had all sounded so wonderful, so fairytale-like; but looking at their parent's lack of immediate reaction, suddenly confused him. Then he looked at Sara and felt all would be fine – actually beyond fine; but some doubt was lingering, no matter how hard he tried to shake that feeling out of his head.

After Victoria ended the call from her mother, she was shaking. Her game plan would not be altered to any extent by what her mother had told her, quite the opposite; it would be implemented even sooner. She would make sure that Sara and Jack's fairytale would become a horror-story. Victoria was patiently waiting in the shadows; waiting for her turn.

As Sara and Victoria suddenly found themselves in a relationship that seemed at least diplomatically friendly, Sara had asked her sister to be her maid of honor, and Jack asked his father to be best man; William fully understood. George had reacted rather emotionally when Jack asked him for the honor. Sara's parents, Jack's father, Colleen and Charles had all agreed to give the newlyweds a practical gift. With both of them starting at Georgetown and the cost of the small apartment as well as food and other daily necessities, the gift was the promise of their financial support.

And then there was this *new* Victoria, Jack thought. She had embraced him warmly before the wedding and whispered in his ear that all was fine between them – she had moved on. Jack had thanked her, but didn't believe a word she said. There had been something in her attack on him that night, something in her eyes and in her voice that he was not able to erase. He stayed cautious as well as suspicious concerning what Victoria had on her mind. He was positive she had not moved on - not one bit.

Sara & Jack Miller it said on the brass plate to their apartment building. It wasn't big at all, but it was enough for now. They had enjoyed shopping for the many things needed for their new household and the three main purchases had been the two large desks and a new bed. Not much else was actually needed. The happiness of being together had not diminished at all, quite the opposite. They found themselves compatible even within these small quarters and rarely had any form of arguments built on anger, stress or frustration. It was always easy for them to make choices and decisions. Jack found that many of the basic issues were more important to Sara than to him, so never a reason to argue. If Sara was happy, Jack was happy – a rather simple situation, and one that worked well.

Everything was going according to schedule. They decided the birth of their first child to take place during the following summer break, and Michael arrived as planned. Two years later it was Jasper's turn and five years after Jasper the blessed arrival of Caroline. Sara made time in her busy daily schedule, mixing school, studies, home, Jack and time with baby Michael. And a few years later, Jasper became part of that equation. Jack was helping along in the same fashion, tending school and part-time work at CR Constructions. But after a while, Sara found for the first time that academically she was not on top. She was playing catch-up in most classes and her grades confirmed this decline.

Jack found his classes to be tough and needed a tremendous amount of studying from him; he felt bad that he couldn't help more at home as he did. And now with two children it was an even more stressful situation. Sara kept assuring him her full support. But the stress increased and for the first time, he had to make a huge life-altering decision. He had of course discussed this with Sara, had also talked numerous times with his father, as well as with

Colleen and Charles and his good buddy William. After many days and sleepless nights he had come to a decision, however hard it was.

"I'm quitting school, Sara." His eyes red and tired and showed a sad disappointment with himself. "It's too much and this last semester I have really struggled; you already know that. Doesn't matter how much time I have poured in to studying, I can't get ahead; I don't even seem to be able to keep up. It's frustrating and I really hate to give up, but I can't see what else I can do." Sara was holding his hands, patiently listening to what he said. "It's not that I don't want to finish school, but at this point it's just too hard."

"I know, Jack, and I think you are making a good decision."

"You really do?"

"Of course I do. You can always go back to school. I mean you have decent grades as it is, so talk with them and see how you could come back – if that's what you want to do later on. Just see what options are available."

"I already did and it looks feasible, so we'll see."

"So what's the plan?"

"Well, I want to take care of the boys; I'll do all the daily stuff with them so you can concentrate on school. You know house-stuff, shopping, cooking, you know, stuff to make your day easier." Sara looked at him with loving eyes.

"What about money?"

"Meaning what?"

"Money we are getting from your dad, Colleen and Charles for school? Do we need to look for loans?"

"No, Sweetheart, they are okay with whatever we do, so they are not going to change anything. I have already talked with them, but of course I would talk with you about it before we decide anything. Charles has offered me a job with a lot of flexibility. The money I can make there is fine, but won't be able to support us *including* school. But they are all fine with continuing paying what they told us they would; so we should be okay." He paused as Sara squeezed his hand. "So if this all pans out, my priority will be to spend time with the boys, look after the house, make your day less stressful and bring in a bit of money while I try to figure out what's next; if that is getting back to school or finding a solid job, whatever." Sara looked at him with teary eyes.

"You are okay with all this?"

"I am if you are!" Sara gave him a deep embrace and a warm kiss. "So you are going to cook a lot more, huh?" She whispered in his ear; Jack finally smiled.

"Yeah, I thought that would be the part I would pay the second most attention to."

"Sounds good to me; whatever you want, sweetheart, really – you know that. And I can get my grades up with all that additional help and support at home from you. It will really be a big huge help." And they kissed some more, and their new plan went in to action.

For Jack, quitting school was a huge failure. Not going to school he could accept, but it was the feeling of being forced to quit something he had started that bothered him more than he imagined it would. He felt he had failed Sara, failed their plans; accordingly, his self-confidence plummeted. But he never told anybody about it.

Life with Michael and Jasper as well as running their small household very quickly occupied every waking moment of his day. Sara spent more and more time at school, the law library, classes and studying. She tried hard to come home when she didn't have a lot of work pending, when she didn't have to ask for peace and quiet. She was the happiest with Jack and the boys; those were her most favorite moments. But it didn't take long for all of them to realize that the arrangement worked out very well, no matter how tired they all were by the end of the day. They tried to sneak in romantic moments here and there, most of them hurried to the tunes of crying babies, diaper changes and feedings. *Now, where were we?* was used often, but the follow-up giggles put it all in perspective. Life was hectic for Sara, Michael, Jasper and Jack, but they agreed that it was a good life – at least for now. But he kept struggling with the feeling of personal failure, not contributing according to plan. But no matter what, life kept rolling along. Sara finished her years at Georgetown and finished very well. She took a job in a small D.C. firm that specialized in corporate law. She was now in training, as she called it and after passing the BAR exam, she had officially been hired in her new legal capacity; Sara Miller was the first female lawyer in the firm's long history.

So Jack worked part-time for Charles and full time at home, it seemed. The first few months he was able to bring work home; papers and documents to sort through and deal with. This way he learned about many aspects of CR Constructions. It also gave him time to look after the boys, keep the apartment clean, grocery shopping, and have dinner ready when Sara got home. Colleen had cut down her hours at the hospital as part of easing into retirement, so she gladly and willingly, looked after the boys so Jack could go to work. He learned to like the business of creating things; the planning, the scheduling and then erecting the buildings from the ground up. Charles didn't spare him to any extent; he actually pushed Jack to do more than any of his other employees. But that was okay with Jack; he liked working hard. As Charles was contemplating retirement within the near future, several hints during conversations with Jack had been about *taking over* and run the company. But Jack was hesitant, as he didn't feel he had the business savvy to be successful, at least not yet. He felt he was too young and inexperienced. Sure he could swing a hammer with the best of them, and in most cases better than most, but the whole thing about accumulating work and maintaining a profit, being responsible for so many people's livelihood! That was something totally different. Skating on very thin ice was the thought that came to mind. So he didn't feel he was ready to *take over* and still believed he needed to do his own thing. But sometimes life doesn't pan out as planned; those are the moments where fate rules.

The phone rang in the middle of dinner.
"Jack here…"
"And it's Nora here." Jack nearly fell down.
"Nora! How the heck have you been? Wow, what a surprise! We haven't heard from you in years. When we tried calling you, the number was disconnected or something."
"Yeah, I'm terribly sorry. How are you and Sara doing?"
"We are just fine. We got married, two kids, Sara is a lawyer now; you know, just stuff like that." Nora laughed. "And what the heck have you been up to?"

Nora had started an education in business administration. She struggled and fought to get accepted to any university, and finally prevailed. She had been one of only two females in a class of 58 males. Nora had found the studies tough and the rules even tougher, but she didn't tell Jack that. She did, though, with bragging rights and great pride tell him that due to her GPA, third best score at graduation and honor student, she did just fine, no matter how much crap she endured in the process. Her father had been shipped to Vietnam and was killed only three days after his arrival. She was not sure how, as the State Department had not issued a detailed explanation; and she would never get one. She was ready to look for a job in business administration.

She had experienced an extraordinary quantity of job interviews and though her papers were superb, she had consistently been turned down. She acknowledged the reasons why, one of them being a woman, but she never dwelled on that or to any extent pitied herself. Luckily her father had left her enough funds to survive.

After too many interviews and too many rejections, she decided to look for another solution, and soon contemplated starting her own company. She knew it would be a struggle, but she also knew she could fight, and fight even harder than she fought in school. As she was listening to Jack's story, she suddenly saw a small light at the end of the tunnel. Nora hated to ask friends for favors, but all of a sudden she sensed a possibility. Nora's stubbornness and determination would move her forward ones again – but this time she could possibly have a good friend by her side. The initial thought excited her.

"Jack, when can we get together?" Her voice was eager and excited.

"Any time; just let me know."

"What about tomorrow?"

"Fine, when and where?"

"What about your office around noon?" Jack gave her the address and hung up. Sara looked at Jack's puzzled face with a smile.

"So that was Nora, wow; great to hear from her, huh?"

"Yeah, that was really great." Jack sat down and slowly finished his dinner; "yeah, really interesting."

The next morning he told Charles about Nora's call and that she was going to come by.

"That's wonderful; we haven't seen her in such a long time. What's she up to these days?"

"I guess we'll find out in a minute." Looking out the window, Jack saw Nora walking towards the entrance. She was as tall and elegant as ever, maybe even more so since he had seen her last. Her clothes were business-like and her briefcase had not been cheap. He rushed downstairs and greeted her in the lobby. The embrace was warm.

"Wow, you look stunning; I am so happy to see you again." Nora smiled.

"You mean stunning for a black woman or just simply adorably stunning overall?"

"Not the silly part, but the last part; wow, it's so good to see you. Come on up. Charles is looking forward to see you again." They were soon in Charles' office with fresh coffee in front of them. Charles was staring at Nora for the longest time, smiling.

"Nora, so glad you found your way back to us. Colleen will be so excited when I tell her. You got to come by for a visit, okay?" Nora smiled. This was what she had needed for the longest time; good friends who seriously cared for her. After her father's death, every day had been a struggle. She fought for everything and anything she wanted to accomplish. She had been an emotional wreck for such a long time. School had pretty much been hell, but in spite of it all, the thought of giving up was never an option.

"So what've you been up to, Nora?" Charles asked leaning back in his chair, ready to listen. And Nora told both Jack and Charles her story, including the struggle through the last several years, school, the job-search, all the failed interviews followed by the equally many heart-breaking rejections. She kept everything in a tone of matter of fact; nothing was expressed with emotions and she was not whining nor was she complaining. It had obviously not been easy, but that was not the point Nora made at all. After half an hour she had gone through the last 4 years of her life. Both Jack and Charles were exhausted.

"Wow, Nora, that's quite a story. So what are you plans?" Charles asked.

"I've decided that I want to build my own company. Nobody has hired me, so it seems to be the only way to get myself a job. I have a nose for business, at least in theory, and I do like people a lot. I have a bit of money, not millions, but I should have enough to start something." Charles glanced at Jack, then at Nora.

"What kind of business are you looking for?"

"Well, the entity doesn't matter at all; I mean it could be anything, like this type of business, contractor, construction, and building stuff – anything. My father left me a bit of property outside Houston, not much, but enough to do something with some day – or perhaps sell it." She paused for a second looking thoughtful: "Yeah, something I can build from." At this point Jack's mind was going fast. Charles had wanted Jack to take over his business for the longest time, and Jack had been thankful for the offer, but also wanted to do something himself. Sara had gently questioned his reasoning for not accepting Charles' generosity, but had not pushed the issue. With their two jobs, Sara bringing in the majority of their income, they would be fine with a few lean years if Jack's potential pursuit didn't pay off immediately. They were both in agreement on that. His next words came out in a calm and controlled manner, which actually took even him by surprise.

"Interesting enough, I have also had these *thoughts* about finding something to get involved in, something to build and create myself. I believe it's for the excitement of just doing that; at least that's the only explanation I can muster." Nora interrupted him:

"Me too…"

"So here you are telling us what you are looking for, and I'm looking for the exact same thing." Jack smiled and continued: "So what about looking at this company, CR Constructions? Sure it's not building from the foundation up, but there's a lot we could do." Charles' eye size doubled and his mouth fell open.

"We?" Nora uttered.

"Yes Nora, *we* and why not *we?* I've been here many years and Charles has taught me beyond what this business *is* doing to the vast spectrum of what it *can* do; it has tremendous possibilities; huge potential. Charles' brought the business to this stage and at some point soon, he wants to get out." Charles smiled and nodded. "I have years of experience working the sites and working with the crews. I've been out there hammering, pouring cement, and the list is long; a ton of hands-on. With your business administration diploma and my experience in the field, we could possibly make a good team." Nora smiled.

"*Partnership*, I do like the sound of that. But Charles! Is Jack really worth anything around here?" Charles laughed.

"I'm rather bias, Nora, but cutting to the bone of the matter, if I was in your shoes, only in a matter of speaking of course, I would partner with him in a second." Nora smiled.

"I have the same feeling about him." She winked at Jack and Charles continued.

"Let's put some cards on the table and see if we can find a way to play." Eight hours, a large pizza and a lot of coffee later, they had drafted an idea that they would all consider over the next few days and then get together and discuss the following weekend.

When Jack enthusiastically told Sara about the day's exciting development, she had nearly squeezed the life out of him with tears of relief. She had wanted this day for Jack, for them, for so long. She felt that he had always regretted dropping out of school and though he had been and was the greatest help to her, the kids and their home, as well as working for Charles, she knew that he still didn't think he was pulling his share. But sharing for Sara was precisely what he had always done and more. She loved him dearly and simply wanted him to be as happy as possible. He had always gone out of his way to make her happy and she always tried to do the same for him. So here he was in front of her, flustered and laughing, explaining the initial plan of Nora and Jack buying in and taking over. Charles had been even more excited and Colleen had shed some tears as he had told her about what could possibly happen very soon; and it didn't take long to get rolling.

Nora spent the following two weeks in CR Constructions' offices, going through documents and accounts together with Jack, the company's CPA and Sara, who was making sure all the legal aspects were in place. Then it was time to meet with the staff of 45 employees, crew and office. Charles opened the meeting with confirmation of the random rumors concerning a change in ownership. He acknowledged that Jack had been around for some years and everybody knew him well and that Nora had the skill and talent to run the business through continuing success. Jack introduced Nora as a long time friend and respected professional. After a brief hug and kiss, the podium was left to her.

"Good afternoon. My name is Nora Clark. I am pleased to be here and very excited about what we are all going to experience with the continuation of our company, CR Constructions. It is utterly important for both Jack and I that we are all on the same track from the start. We want to secure your employment with us by aggressively finding and providing continuous work. We want to bring you further into our company and will soon present you with several profitable options. We want to continue the benefits you are already enjoying, but we will also go through them all, to look for ways to improve. This is all extremely new to both Jack and I. It's also going to be new to Charles who has built this company from the ground up to what it is today. For a smoother transition, Charles has agreed to hang around for some time, but more so at home or on travels with Colleen, but never the less, he has agreed to help us out and be available when unfamiliar situations arise. His expertise will of course be highly appreciated." Sporadic applauds quickly brought everybody to their feet. Nora smiled as she bowed towards Charles. When all were sitting down again she continued: "As for the future of CR and about where Jack and I will fit in, we have decided the following: First of all, we want you to know everything that is going on with CR, so never hesitate to ask, really! Jack and I have invested in an equal share partnership. Charles has not expressed interest in keeping any shares of the business, so we have agreed on a full buy-out with cash up front and the rest to be paid over the next 10 years. Jack and I have already decided that if we work hard and efficient enough, Charles will be paid in full within 5 years – with your help, of course. Even though Jack and I have an equal partnership, equal in investment and ownership, my official title will be president. I will be in charge of the business' administration and financial. Jack will be vice-president and in charge of sales as well as he will be working closely with the crew managers, site-work planning and work execution. Please be aware that to Jack and I, these titles mean nothing and you should ignore them as well; they are just that: silly labels.

We are simply Jack and Nora, to ourselves as well as to you – nothing else. The titles are for our suppliers, clients and customers." Lots of smiles lit up the room. They liked what they heard so far. Nora continued: "Jack and I expect only the very best from ourselves. We will work extremely hard for all of us to succeed, for all of us to have fun and to be engaged in our jobs and in our work - together. That's what you can expect from us, and that is what you should expect from yourselves – that is what we *must* expect from each other." Again applauds and smiles. "So let's start moving forward Monday morning." Nora paused and took a visible deeper breath. "And finally, there are two important things I want to address. First, you all have a copy of my resume, which is the same resume I distributed to numerous companies over the last six months with no results. I want you to know where I'm coming from and what I have done so far. I especially want you to know and I want to clearly emphasize, that the opportunity I am facing now, with you and Jack and CR, is what I have always been looking for; it has always been my first choice. Thanks to Jack and Charles and all of you, that dream is now a reality; I feel blessed and I am thankful." She swallowed visibly. "The second and last thing is the following: As Jack knows, I have always been a stout and firm believer in any and all forms of racial and human equality. I firmly believe that all men, as well as all women are created equal. You might have noticed that I am a woman of color, a black woman, a Negro woman, and…" Some smiles and giggles interrupted her flow, but Nora didn't smile back, "… and it is of the utmost importance that while being employed here, that you fully accept and respect that, as you respect yourself and your colleagues and any diversity we no doubt will meet in the future. I firmly believe that when each of us respect diversity, we will all get stronger - together. As we fully trust that we will all succeed in reaching the goals we set, we must also understand that to do so, the need for additional staff will arise, and in all of those cases we will *only* look at experience and talent; we will never look at what color or gender this experience or talent comes in. If this is an issue that you know you can't or won't deal with, you do have the choice of leaving. If you choose to leave, which we seriously do not wish you do, we will fully support your record with CR as well as supplying you with the appropriate letter of recommendation, not acknowledging the reason you resigned. Your decision to leave due to this issue will not be questioned as it is fully a choice you make based on your convictions. Do you all fully understand that?" Though a bit stunned by the reality and honesty of Nora's remarks, they all nodded in understanding. Nora rounded up her presentation with thanks and gratitude. Monday morning, four employees resigned.

After the meeting, Jack, Sara, Nora, Colleen and Charles mixed with the employees around the caterer's huge spread in the boardroom. There was a lot of laughter and smiles. By the end of the evening, Nora, Sara and Jack walked Colleen and Charles to their car. He had turned and smiled, now looking straight at Nora and Jack: "You know, you are already a success." - So far, the *once upon a time*, was going well.

*****

The next years were filled with family, school, work, new home, some leisure time and just a few vacations. Many of life's challenges can tear families apart. Sara and Jack met their challenges head on. Overcoming challenges brought them even closer. Sara was the most determined of the two; failure to her was never an option. She excelled in her work and was made partner in the law firm after just a few years. She was adamant about her dedication to work as she was adamant about her role with her family. She ran her office and staff with an iron fist and utmost efficiency and had only lost two cases of the many she had presented in court. She was somewhat pleasant to work with, but stubborn and never satisfied before everything was on track and beyond. The office staff respected her and her work ethics, but didn't particularly find some of her ways very charming. Sara knew how the staff felt, but didn't care too much about it, as long as the job got done. And then she broke away and started her own firm.

But at home she was the relaxed and nurturing mother of two sons and a daughter, the loving wife and romantic partner to her husband. Sure she had control of the home as well, but it was on another level than the one at the office. She assigned daily mechanics to the children according to age and ability and this added to the wholeness of *family*. Sara and Jack would often sneak away for romantic overnights and trips by themselves, with George, Colleen and Charles ever so ready and available to look after the kids.

Jack quickly learned what real business was also about. The partner purchase of CR Constructions with Nora had been scary for both of them. Now he could somewhat smile when he thought about the first day in Nora's office. Charles decided to make a getaway immediately, and had left on a cruise with Colleen. So there they were all alone, Nora and Jack, new owners of a situation that employed a total of 41 people, enormous responsibilities and not a lot of experience. Sure Jack knew about the business, but now he didn't have the security blanket called Charles – and now *he* was the one residing in Charles office. It did comfort him a lot that Nora was close by and the door connecting their offices was always open.

"It's a good start." Nora was smiling a bit nervously.
"What do you mean *a good start*?" Jack asked.
"I mean the coffee isn't bad." They both giggled.
"Sure isn't; but minor detail: What's next?" That first Monday they went through all the individual employee interviews. Though they had worked on the questions and the order of same, it had still been a bit of an eye-opener as they also realized that the staff was much older than the two new owners. The only same-age employees were Nora's assistant and just one of the field-crew – that was it. But the interviews had taught them a lot and as they both had taken notes like crazy, the collected information helped them mold at least the immediate future of the business. It had been a good experience and one they would do once every quarter to learn more and to make sure the staff had a loud voice in the interest of their own place of employment. But it was that next morning Nora and Jack had nervously contemplated the next important moves. The pending work and work in progress was keeping them afloat for the next 180 days, but they had nothing after that, so additional contracts were necessary and as fast as possible.

They needed work, so they needed sales. That was Jack's responsibility. In the past he listened in on Charles who had closed all the deals. Jack thought he learned a lot, but now it was his turn without Charles holding his hand! This was quite a different story. Picking up the phone to dial that first sales-call had been awful; but he survived and quickly moved on to the next call on the list. That one was not as bad as the first one, the third not as bad as the second and soon, okay, after about forty calls, Jack started to formulate an approach and attitude that he began to feel comfortable with. He remembered Charles kept telling him that in sales *always ask for the money*, which meant *always ask for the order*. Nora had been listening in on those first forty calls, primarily for moral support, but also to help getting a sales concept together that would be efficient and something that would relate to Jack's comfort-zone and personality. It had been a great help for Jack's self-esteem and he slowly started to feel more relaxed, after about a hundred calls, the nervousness and insecurities had faded - but sales did not materialize.

Nora dived right into the business and was working long hours to get everything on track as soon as possible. She had rented a small apartment and as she didn't have much of a social life as in boyfriend or nearby family, work for her was the thing to do. After several weeks with no sales accumulating, she started to worry a bit as the bank balance was decreasing rapidly paying salaries and benefits. Nora and Jack couldn't take any wages for themselves, as the staff had priority. Jack also started to worry, but he worked long hard hours to make something happen – anything. Sara had noticed his anxieties, of course, but Jack hadn't volunteered anything yet. She wanted him to figure it out, work on it himself, though she knew that he knew she was always available with big ears and support – always; but he just got worse.

"I know I'm asking for the orders, trying to get some work and I know they are okay with me and the company. I don't know if they are afraid of dealing with CR without Charles at the wheel; I really don't know." He looked miserable and tired.

"Dear Jack, we'll get it going – I know we will." Nora had a wild hope in her heart. She was not concerned about the money she had invested or the job; she was more concerned about her friend sitting there in front of her. She wanted fun and happy Jack back, *the one we all love and treasure*, she thought. But there he was, a near beaten man, slumping in the chair and wondering what was going to happen next.

Sara was pouring more wine in their glasses. It had been a nice dinner and the kids were in their rooms playing or doing homework. Michael, Jasper and Caroline had their own rooms located on the east side of the second floor, far away from Sara and Jack's bedroom which was on the west side of the first floor. She gently touched his hand.
"Jack, let's move on, okay?" He looked up. "I can't have you mope around here like a grumpy old man. The kids are scared as they can't find their happy daddy, so let's see if we can find him for them and for me, okay?" Jack didn't know if he should laugh or keep moping; he settled for a giggle and squeezed Sara's hand.
"I'm sorry Sara, but it's not going as I want it to go. It's tough with all the responsibilities at work and here at home; it's very tough at the moment."
"Jack, don't worry about here at home, you know I make plenty to support all of us and then some, so don't worry about that. The kids are old enough to feed themselves and do the stuff they have to do."
"But it doesn't feel right that I'm not financially doing my share."
"Please, Jack, that's silly. It all goes into the same pot. It's not *me* or *you;* it's all about *us*, you and I, and of course the three monsters." She smiled at him.
"I know, Sara, I do know. I just have to really convince myself of that - again."
"Precisely; so get started." She slid onto his lap and wrapped her arms around his shoulders and kissed him; he smiled. "First we have to recognize the problem," she continued. "Then we'll agree on a common and logical goal, we'll look at the options, decide how to pursue all of them, choose and then establish a plan of action and voila: solved. That's how we have always done it, Mr. Miller and as we have always succeeded, we will succeed in this case as well." She gave him a big wet kiss and continued: "As your legal advisor, I will take your case pro bono, or you can pay me with

intimate physical flavors." She kissed his neck and raked her fingers through his hair. "What do you think, Mr. Client?"

"I think I'm worried if this is how you start all your new cases!" Sara giggled.

"Not *all* of them," her teasing comment made Jack laugh.

"If this *is* your standard starting point of taking cases, I'm very willing to become a client real fast. What's next?"

"Let's wait till the kids are quietly in bed and I'll show you." They finished their wine and a bit later that they were in a warm, exciting and loving embrace, tucked away in their spacious retreat, far away from the children.

At breakfast Sara talked things out with Jack. She asked questions about what he had done sales-wise, his approach, his feelings and emotions about rejections and what kind of follow-up did he do after his initial communications. She was *in court* now and ripped through Jack in a constructive and energetic way.

"Jack, at times I have to sacrifice my ethics, my *normal* style of dealing with clients and situations to reach the results I want. I have to sacrifice ways I normally feel comfortable about, leave the zone I perceive as being fair, honest and ethical. Not that I prostitute my own rules; but at times I am dancing around them a bit. That might sound cold to some, but we have to push our clients and customers to do what we know is best for them, decide for them, because most of the time they seriously don't really know what is up and what is down. And as long as we can push them in a direction that makes them fully believe was their *own* choice, it's a win-win scenario. Well, you have to be right, of course." Jack smiled and looked at Sara with admiring eyes.

"You are ruthless, aren't you, my little deal-maker."

"One of the best," she teased back.

"Yeah, especially last night, huh?" Sara did blush a little, but smiled. Jack was feeling rather good this morning. Talking and sharing issues and concerns with Sara had that positive influence on him. She could always calm him down and charge him up with new energy. He was looking very much forward to go to work the next morning to apply all they had talked about. He looked at Sara and asked himself as he had done a thousand times before: *What would I do without her?* She was his life and she had always been.

Jack forged ahead with his refreshed energized attitude the following day, and the next, and the next. Weeks passed and he had yet to make a sale. The bank account reached a zero balance. Nora talked about selling her property in Texas and a friend had started the process. The cash from the sale would only carry them over a few months at the very most. Nora and Jack had a meeting with the bank concerning a line of credit, but they were denied. They had enough equipment for collateral, but for some reason the bank said they were sorry, but no deal. In his disappointment Jack was wondering if it had anything to do with Nora being a woman, being black or both; a thought that bothered him, not that she was black, of course, but the possible lack of lending equality from the banks. Approaching other financial institutions produced the same lack of results. They kept the staff informed as they had promised, so everybody was aware of the situation the company was in. Some had volunteered to take unpaid leave of absence, and were promised that as soon as things turned around, they would be back at work again. It wasn't just CR Constructions who suffered, as it seemed that new business was down for everybody, especially for the smaller companies. It was just so much harder for Nora and Jack, as they weren't in possession of a lot of reserve cash and would falter much quicker then more established companies. Even Charles had helped out by contacting his old friends to drum up any form of jobs, any form of work, no matter how small, but no bites at all. Charles was feeling guilty depressed about it all, but Nora and Jack kept trying comforting him that he couldn't possibly have known – nobody could. The situation looked bleaker and bleaker. It was at this lowest point of despair, that Jack got the call.

"Jack, there's a Victoria Grant on line one for you." It was Karen Lee's voice on the intercom. She was the youngest employee now, Jack's assistant and newest member of the team. She had overwhelmed Nora and Jack during her initial job interview. Karen's pure energy, attitude and optimism was beyond the norm, and though she barely had a high school diploma, Nora and Jack had no problem hiring her ahead of many applicants with academically better credentials. She was working out far beyond expectations. She soon became a popular employee, as she treated all with charm, concern and efficient work ethics – she always *got the job done*. Unfortunately it was just a few months later that the business did not do well at all. At that time she told Nora and Jack that she would hang in there with them and if it came to not being able to get paid, her parents would take care of her. She was already living at home, and her parents could easily support her financially. Nora had shed a few tears in her office after the short get together with Karen and Jack had also felt moist eyes. Karen's optimistic attitude had encouraged him even more to make it all work out. Here she was, believing more so than Jack, that it would all get solved. Just like Sara, she had pumped some energy into him. "Jack, are you there?" Karen's voice sounded again. "A Victoria Clark on line one, please." Jack froze and his mind went twirling. *Victoria! What the heck did she want?* He thought. Sara had not heard anything from Victoria for years. She had no idea what she was doing, where she was – nothing. Jack had not thought about her a single moment in ages, as he finally had been able to eliminate her from his mind - erased her from memory. The last time he saw her, he had apologized for his innate, immature and rude way of causing the end of their friendship. Victoria had told him that everything was fine and that she had finally gotten over it, so no need for Jack to worry. She had sounded and acted sincere, which made Jack feel a lot better – finally. Sara had smiled when Jack told her, but she also thought that she knew Victoria better than he did; she felt that *sincere* applied to Victoria like water to a duck. *Sincere* was not the correct term – *scheming* was a much better fit. But Sara didn't tell Jack that; she kept staying cautious.

      He was pausing for the longest time. Suddenly Karen was by his side whispering quietly near his left ear:
"Earth to Mister Miller - Victoria Grant is impatiently waiting on line one." Jack smiled nervously and reached for the phone.
"You are a persistent little bugger, aren't you?"
"You trained me well, Jack." She made a silly face at him and left the office.
"This is Jack Miller."

"Well Mr. Jack Miller, this is Victoria Grant, if we have to be formal." She laughed a little. "How the heck is my brother-in-law?" Her voice certainly hadn't changed.

"Well! And how are you?"

"Moving along and working hard."

"So what are you up to these days?"

"The short version: finished school, finished short internship with an architectural firm in Los Angeles; worked a couple of fairly good jobs in New York and ended up with a much more challenging one here in D.C." She was very matter-of-fact.

"So you are an architect?"

"No, not my cup of tea, Jack; I got my masters in business administration and now I'm a project management specialist for the Anchor Corporation." Jack knew exactly who that was; the most aggressive building planners on the east-coast, from Maine to Florida and beyond. They were known for their tough ways of doing business and several sub-contractors got burned by not finishing contracted projects on time; several had been forced into bankruptcy and many within the industry would not take contracts from Anchor at all – for the most because they were scared. But they were still the biggest suppliers of work, by far. Jack had been considering contacting them, but Charles had discouraged Nora and Jack to sign any contracts with Anchor. So far they had followed his advice. Since CR was near faltering, Jack had several times been tempted to dial Anchor, but had not done it. Now that Victoria worked for them, would that be a way out of CR's downfall? Would Victoria come to their rescue? *I mean we are family*, Jack fleetingly thought.

"Well, Victoria, that's impressive, congratulations."

"Thanks Jack, that's very sweet of you." Her voice sounding soft and appreciative; she asked about Sara, the kids, George, Colleen and Charles, Nora and CR. Then she talked about her social life, no husband, just a few boyfriends – nothing serious; all her time dedicated to her career and work; bought a house using one of the bonuses she had received for finishing projects before due date. Very little leisure time spent on traveling, fitness and *yes* most of her *leisure time* was spent at work. Jack was drained just listening to her. She sounded balanced and as together as ever, and it reminded Jack of the beginning of their relationship, when he wanted her more than she wanted him. She sounded very self-assured, confident to the point of cocky and smart – yeah, that was the dominant sound from her, *smart*. Jack remembered that was the side of her that really intimidated him as a boy; to his frightened surprise, that feeling of intimidation was suddenly as powerful now as it had been so many years ago; he started to sweat a bit.

"Quite a life, Victoria," he stated nervously.

"Yeah, I know. Well Jack, the reason I'm calling you, actually CR Constructions, is to see if we might be able to do some future business together, you know look at your capabilities, manpower, equipment, possible available time and all that. We have a couple of local projects, in Virginia actually, that we need help with. There's a small one, only three or four million plus, which might actually be too small for you. But it's the one closer to six mill I really need help with. Do you think you have time to take a meeting and chat about it? I mean if you are interested and you could find room on your project-schedule?" He swallowed big time. The biggest project CR had tackled with Nora and Jack at the wheel had been smaller than the *smallest* project Victoria had mentioned. A fraction of that project alone could save CR – that was the terrifying reality. But Jack also saw red lights popping up in front of him. There were so many warning signs Jack had to deal with, but if it all panned out, the signature on a contract with Anchor could be the resurrection of their company, but it could also become the signature on CR's death certificate. No matter how you looked at it, it could be a huge gamble.

"Yeah, that sounds like something we could get together about." Victoria gave him a day and time and finished the call.

"Jack, please send my love to Sara and the kids from me, okay! Since I'm back in D.C., maybe we could all get together again soon?" And she hung up. Jack was left sitting stiff and contemplating. It all sounded great and hopeful, but with an edge he didn't feel good about.

"Nice look, boss." Karen was standing in the doorway.

"What do you mean?"

"You look pale, white and sweaty."

"Thanks *so* much Karen; don't you have something important to do?"

"Of course I do; coffee anybody?" Jack smiled, but not for long. His thoughts were back to the conversation with Victoria, word for word. He would do that many times before he moved on – very cautiously.

Victoria was smirking as she ended the call. On her desk was a detailed report concerning the turmoil CR Constructions were in; it seemed as the folder was smiling at her - at least that's what she imagined it did. CR was in a dire situation and on its way down the toilet; a single courtesy flush would end it. She'd already crushed two other sub-contractors, put them out of business; it had been a piece of cake. The process itself had been very enjoyable in a strange kind of tingling way. Both of them had crossed her. They naively believed that just because she was a young woman she could be pushed around and manipulated. How wrong they had been. She had played them in a scheming and controlled manner from the moment negotiations started. She was excellent at her job, the best in the business according to her – and not far from the truth. They had been eating out of her hands after she reeled them in by acting naïve and vulnerable and played the new girl on the block in this self-prescribed man's world. She had teased them with promises of big contracts, tight fitting and revealing clothes, brushing up against them during meetings and business dinners, leaning over while smiling with some slight touching. Their eyes, their crotches and their feeble efforts of charm and seduction had reduced them to wimpy fools. All males were bleeding pathetic and stupid that way – nothing had changed, so Victoria kept playing her game. Jack was one of those pathetic boys who had crossed her and now it was time for him to pay – and pay he would.

She had worked hard in school, mowed all competition down during job-interviews and powered her way into corporations that she knew would benefit her career and bank account. She used all her weapons; she had teased the tougher ones with sex to the point where they squirmed on a hook, pleaded and begged. As she had come to expect, they always gave her what she wanted. Victoria called it *convincing somebody*, everybody else called it *blackmail*. But Victoria didn't care about anybody else. Though she implemented sex when needed, nobody had ever *had* her *that* way; she was still a virgin, of course more so technically. She was saving her virginity for just one man – the only man she would finally and truly give herself fully to – heart, body and soul.

"So how do you feel about it?" He was clearing the breakfast table. Sara and Jack was talking about the upcoming meeting with Victoria at Anchor that afternoon.
"Well, we are in dire need of work, actually in dire need for work to survive, so I have to listen to any offers coming our way. But as you, I'm also wary about your sister. I'm not sure what this is all about." Sara smiled in a teasing manner.
"I think she still got the hots for you, sweetie!"
"Sara, please! You know I don't like it when you make fun of me like that. I'm so sure she was over me a very long time ago. She sounded friendly and business like, so I believe that this is all on the up and up."
"I'm sorry, Jack, but you just get even more adorable when you blush a bit." She grabbed him and they were soon in a loving embrace. "Maybe I can get you to blush a lot more tonight, if you know what I mean." Jack smiled.
"Maybe I'll let you do just that." He pushed away from her with one last and wet kiss, grabbed his briefcase and went out the door. She was smiling one of those loving smiles. It had been an amazing life so far. He had turned out to be the most perfect partner for her and her for him. He was loving and giving and funny, a great husband and a terrific father and friend. He was passionate about what he did and about his position in life, in their lives, except for the way CR was going at the moment. The kids adored him and when he came home from work all three kids would rush to the front door and great him with smiling faces, kisses and hugs, as if he had been gone for years. Caroline was especially clingy and rarely left her father's side. He would often tease her by asking: *who are you gonna marry?* She would giggle and blush and scream: *Daddy, of course.* They would kiss and hug and she would be smiling from ear to ear – in daddy's arms, of course.

From the kitchen window she saw the next-door girl race across the front lawn towards Jack, who had just reached his car. She flew into his waiting arms; he swung her around several times, sat her down and gave her a kiss on the forehead. She happily waved to Jack as he drove off, turned and waved to Sara who waved back and with a big smile ran back to the neighboring house.

Anna and Harry West, the next-door neighbors, had recently lost their son and daughter in-law. They were both killed in a horrific auto accident in Los Angeles. It had of course been a devastating shock, a gruesome loss and something they had the hardest time conceiving as reality. Sara and Jack had in the past been more so casual neighbors with the proverbial over-the-fence chats, but after the accident, they had welcomed them into their home whenever they wanted to talk, grieve, cry and mourn. Sara and Jack would extend sympathetic ears, embraces, friendship and whatever they could do to ease the pain and the sorrow.

Anna and Harry had flown to Los Angeles immediately after they received the tragic news. Their daughter in-law was from Huntington Beach where her parents still lived, and they had asked if it was possible to have the children buried there. The West's had agreed. After the funeral they spent every waking moment in the hospital by the bed where their only grandchild was fighting for her life.

She was in the backseat when the car was hit. As the rescue units arrived on the scene of the accident, they shook their heads as they saw a totally crumbled vehicle. They were sure nobody could have survived that crash. It had been an unusual long and tough job to cut the car open, but they were finally able to remove the two bodies in the front. They were both killed on impact, nobody doubted that. One of the rescuers searched the leftovers of the car for personal items to identify the victims. It was then he had found a little girl unnaturally folded on the floor behind the front seats. The tangled body of the demolished car had barely missed cutting her in half. He twisted an arm through the wreckage to reach her and when he finally did, he couldn't find a pulse; he rightly assumed she was dead. But as the rescuers worked on cutting the metal to free the small body, they suddenly found a vague pulse. The effort of getting her out went frantic, fueled by a sliver of hope; finally she was freed. Under all the blood, the medics found numerous lacerations and broken bones. The damages to this little girl were massive. As the rescuer carefully carried her to the waiting ambulance, he looked at her bloodied face. He had a daughter about her age and this was the only thing he didn't like about his job – seeing innocent children being mangled up for no reason at all. He saw peacefulness in her face, as if she had already been welcomed by the good Lord above – in spite of the blood and the many injuries, she still looked like an angel in his eyes. He gently put her down on the gurney and as naturally as anything, bent down and kissed her forehead while quietly whispering: *God Bless you, little girl*.

Anna and Harry learned the waiting game very fast. Several operations were essential for their grandchild's beginning recovery. From the time she was rolled into OR and until the surgeons came out bloodied and exhausted, explaining how things were going, was the longest time for them both. It helped them cope better when they saw the dedication and energy in every nurse and doctor's face. They felt that there would be hope for their grandchild and they would do everything in their powers to save her – anything.

Two weeks later, Molly had finally been able to utter a few sounds; it was a heavenly moment for her grandparents. The next scary step would be to find out how much brain damage was done. Molly's head had been battered around violently as well as her body had been twisted and turned, so they were prepared for the eventuality of extended damage. When Molly opened her eyes, her grandmother had cried and cried. It had been so exhausting not knowing, all the nights and days of waiting and the constant agonizing. The relief was finally streaming down his face as well. Molly had looked at them for a moment and was soon back asleep. The next morning she had opened her eyes again and this time she had looked directly at her grandparents with a very tiny smile. From then on she recovered bit by bit and then faster and faster. The surgeon had looked in on Molly during his rounds; he'd always ask her: *how's my favorite girl today?* never expecting an answer.

"I feel better." Everybody in the room froze.

"You can actually talk, huh Molly!" She smiled a small but significant smile.

"I can talk a little." Her grandparents were by her side at once.
"Welcome back, Molly." And they were swept away by tears of joy.

It was determined that Molly had not suffered any form of damage to her brains as far as they could tell at this time, but she should continue to see a specialist in Washington D.C. just to make sure that all was going well. She was discharged and flew back with her grandparents. Anna and Harry had agreed with their son's in-law's that Molly should live with them in Washington. They promised Molly would come and visit them in California often. The promise was kept as Molly visited Huntington Beach many times over the years, her grandparents as well as her parent's graves.

The West's had kept in contact with Sara and Jack while in Los Angeles, so they knew what was going on. They had been looking after their neighbor's house and now it would be nice to finally welcome Anna and Harry back home and meet Molly for the first time. An ambulance had picked them up in the airport. Sara, Jack, Michael, Jasper and newborn baby Caroline had all been home when they arrived. There were a lot of hugs and warm embraces, and everybody met Molly. She had her left arm in a cast as well as her right leg. The cuts and bruises on her face had healed well over the many weeks and the accident had certainly not ruined her smile. They all went into the West's house and were soon chatting away. Anna and Harry smiled as they saw how the two boys were so eagerly attentive to Molly. When Molly turned and softly looked at her grandparents with a heartwarming smile, they knew that she would do just grand and very much so. In the midst of all the sorrow and sadness, they had finally found a small flake of happiness again.

It took Molly about a year to fully recover. She had approached getting better with a very mature energy, lots of smiles and even though some of the physical therapy had been painful and exhausting, she never whined and she never complained nor did she feel sorry for herself. Molly did what Molly had to do. The loss of her parents was another thing. Though she handled her physical recovery well, the mental anguish and confusion was not that easy for her at all. She had loved her parents and been a fortunate child receiving so much parental love in return. But they were not here anymore, and that she couldn't fully comprehend. Being only six years old, some of the more abstract issues did not register yet; but some day they would.

She spent a lot of time with the Miller's next door. She was six years older than Caroline, and a bit younger than Michael and Jasper. Caroline had immediately adopted Molly as her best friend ever, and Molly was very fine with that. They did everything together and there was always a vast quantity of giggles and laughter from Caroline's room when Molly was visiting. And the *visiting* quickly became semi living with the Miller's.

Anna and Harry worked with UNICEF, helping out and financially supported projects for orphaned children in Africa. Their foundation was located in Washington D.C., but they also had an office in New York City. This forced them to travel quite a lot, and on most of these trips they were not able to bring Molly along. Sara and Jack had offered to look after Molly and she would of course stay with them while Anna and Harry were out of town. It had been very tough on Molly in the beginning, but she did finally settle in with the Miller's. It was all about the horrific fear that she would lose her grandparents as she had lost her parents. At least when they were home, she could keep an eye on them and be comforted by their presence.

They put an extra bed in Caroline's room for her. Caroline had eagerly made room for Molly's stuff and clothes in drawers and closet space. There were many places Molly could do home work and there was always one of the guestrooms if she wanted to be alone, on her own – which she wanted to at times. The Miller's had all fallen in love with Molly, and she was soon considered a member of the family. She participated in everything the Miller's did, and it was a given that when they talked about *we* and *us* and *the kids*, that Molly was included. Even when Anna and Harry were home, Molly spent most of her time at the Miller's. Anna and Harry were fine with that, as they saw Molly bonding with a family, with a new set of parents and three siblings. It was all working out very well.

"So our planning ended up correct!"

"What do you mean?" Sara was looking at Molly helping Caroline with her homework on the living room floor.

"It seems we finally got it right, that four-kids thing." Jack smiled. "The positive side of it is that we didn't have to do that naughty bit a fourth time. And you didn't have to go through all the pain and I didn't have to listen to you screaming in agony." Sara smiled and shook her head.

"The screaming in agony, was that during conception or during delivery?" Jack had to laugh.

"Actually both, as far as I recall."

"She's a smart kid, isn't she?"

"She sure is; as well as she is very determined and rather stubborn, in a charming kind of annoying way."

"Have you ever thought about adopting her?" Sara looked at Jack.

"No, I never had and I never will."

"Why not?"

"First of all because she is being lovingly cared for by her next of kin, the extremely capable set of grandparents. And even if Molly was *up for adoption*, I would not do it. Don't get me wrong, I love her dearly and will do anything for her, but adoption, no that part I have a bit of a problem with."

"I don't understand why, besides the grandparents bit."

"I don't know Sara. There is something about it that I don't understand either. You know the other day Molly straight out asked me if she was a daughter to me, I mean she put me on the spot."

"What was your answer?"

"I told her that biologically she was not my daughter, that I didn't look at her as my daughter, but also that I didn't see that to be so important. To me she was something beyond being a daughter: she was one of my very best friends in the whole world ever." He grinned.

"How did she respond to that?"

"She said that if it was better to be one of my best friends in the whole world ever that was what she would prefer to be." Jack smiled. "And I have never been crushed by a hug as I was crushed by Molly's. She's a strong little bugger." Sara smiled. That Jack didn't want to adopt Molly was okay with her, though she had hoped he would.

Jack waved to Molly as she raced across the lawn returning to her grandparent's house. She also waved to Sara watching from the kitchen window. As he drove to work, he realized how fortunate and lucky they all were with Molly in their lives. She was a bunch of energy, positive and smart for her age. Michael and Jasper loved her and were very protective of her as they had always protected Caroline. Of course to Caroline, Molly was enormous. She was the older sister now and she took very good care of Caroline in play and especially in academics. She kept pushing Caroline to do her very best and then some, but she did it in a way Caroline found fun and challenging. And talking about best friends, Molly and Caroline were most certainly that.

"So today is the day, huh?" Nora's greeting was serious. Jack kissed her on the cheek and sat down in front of her desk.
"Yeah; and a good, lovely morning to you as well, Dear Nora."
"What's the plan?" They had talked about this so many times since Jack had gotten the appointment with Victoria at Anchor. They still needed any sale on the table, so this afternoon's get-together loomed utterly huge, actually: extremely enormous.
"For the fiftieth time within the last 24 hours: I will listen and not speak. I will gather pertinent information, will no doubt be issued specs, budget and date of delivery and I will come back home and maybe weep from either joy or agony in your impatiently caring and waiting arms."
"And that is as dramatic as this can get, huh?" Nora was smiling, but Jack did notice the slight shiver at the corners of her mouth spelling concern and anxiety. Well, he wasn't doing too good himself, but he thought he was covering it up a bit better – he hoped. After lunch Nora walked Jack to his car; she walked with her arm in his, leaning against each other.
"Jack, remember that this is important, this is something that could save our collective butts, but there is something that is much more important and that is that I love you and you are my best friend together with Sara, the kids and all the rest of you. That's the most important bit to me, as it should be to

you. So you go in there and you do the best damn job you can do, and that's all you can expect from yourself, and if it doesn't go our way today, it will some other day, I promise you that. We'll survive because we can and because we want to. Nobody is going to get in the way of that, okay?"

"Wow, Nora, you *are* amazing."

"For a black woman or a rather wonderful human being?"

"Both! But especially that last bit." Nora planted a big wet kiss on Jack's lips.

"And that's from me to you and good luck to us. Now go kick some serious ass, boy, and don't fuck up!" She laughed.

The Anchor building was impressive and intimidating. The huge chandeliers reflected thousands of sparkling stars on the shiny marble floor in the huge lobby. Jack thought it actually smelled of money to some extent.

"Can I help you, Sir?" Jack told the uniform about his appointment as he handed him a business card. After a short phone call he turned to Jack again.

"Miss Grant's office is on the twelfth floor. Her assistant will be waiting for you." He turned to another visitor's needs. On the way up in the elevator Jack made sure his tie was straight and his zipper in the *up* position – some nervous routine he always went through. He grinned as he thought about how silly *that* was. The assistant was a heavier set woman, probably around 40-plus. Her smile was canned, not sincere at all.

"Mr. Miller! This way, if you please!" They walked by several large windowed offices. When they reached the first corner office, she stopped. "Here we are. Miss Grant will see you shortly." She turned around and left him standing there by himself. The brass sign on the door read *Victoria Grant, Project Specialist*. Rather impressive he thought. A few minutes later the door swung open.

She wore a well fitting and expensive looking business suit over a white blouse. The cuffs were slightly exposed by the end of each sleeve. Her face was smiling, her lips red and her eyes shining. She walked towards Jack with outstretched arms.

"Jack, this is most certainly a treat to see you again." Her embrace felt sincere.

"Good to see you too, Victoria. It's been a long time, years, actually." She stood back still holding on to Jack's hands looking him over.

"Wow, you are as cute as ever," which made Jack's face a bit redder. "And you can still blush," she teased him, "so adorable." After Jack had admired the view with the Washington Monument gracing the horizon, he sat down in front of Victoria's desk; she placed herself on a chair next to him. Jack had hoped he would be a lot calmer by now, but no such luck. He felt that this was all way above his head, over CR's probabilities; that didn't help much on the nerves either. The feeling of small and very uncomfortable raced in his mind – and they hadn't even started.

Victoria looked at Jack. She knew precisely how uncomfortable he was, from the way he talked and the way he moved. She knew him that well. It reminded her of the first few times they had been together, the way he had looked at her, studied her curves, the way he blushed and sweat a little when he got caught staring at her breasts. She liked it because she had excited him. He had been like a little puppy-dog in the beginning, and now she saw that same sad little puppy-dog next to her here in her office so many years later. She was positive that he didn't want her body today, but was after something else that she had available: money and lots of it. But she wouldn't fight him off if he decided that he wanted her body; he could have that anytime he wanted and he could have her heart as well, she fantasized. Victoria smiled at the prospects but was also soon reminded of the pain he had brought upon her, the agony, the embarrassment and the devastation he had thrown in her face, while ripping out her heart. She smiled at her Jack, and knew that pay-back time was getting close. Victoria looked at her watch.

"We better get going. The meeting will start in a few minutes."

"What meeting? I thought it was just you and I to start with!" Jack was confused.

"I always bring in some people from the departments involved so we can do a good job presenting the situation to you, okay?"

"Well of course." They left her office and went up a few floors. The conference room was enormous. The huge and heavy mahogany table with the large high backed leather chairs filled up the room.

"Impressive," Jack mumbled. Four men in expensive suits and two women with note-pads were already there. Jack was placed in front of them, with Victoria next to him. He placed his leather briefcase on the table to his right. It was a gift his father had brought home from Italy.

Victoria started the meeting by introducing Jack and CR Constructions, told them about Nora and Jack's buy-in some time back and that within the industry, CR was known for exquisite quality on the higher end of cost, but also that CR had a reputation for punctuality, meeting deadlines, and finalizing jobs to everybody's satisfaction. She mentioned two projects and slid one folder to each of the men in suits. None of them opened them, but kept listening to Victoria as she presented her opinions as well as the rough specs of each job. After 30 minutes she rounded up the presentation and allowed for questions.

"The Virginia job, I believe the 45009," he had opened the folder and shuffled some papers around, "you have the budget at $4,250,000. Is this low-ball and if it is, what about room for add-ons? If not, it doesn't look feasible at all." The man on the left was talking. Victoria responded immediately.

"Assuming materials will stay the same for another 120 days and we can come to a cost-friendly agreement with Jack and CR or another builder with respect to labor, I am sure the figures will stand. The second part of your concern: I have not allowed many add-ons for this project. I have actually padded the initial budget and will reward the builders for early finish and a lower labor cost. Our client has agreed on total cost so we have free hands within that budget." Victoria smiled – the man didn't. "It's rather feasible." He had another question.

"You truly believe it can be built for this amount? It seems low, actually very low. The Peterson Building was smaller than this and ran over 6 million. It's pretty much the same structural entity, so I'm concerned that the funds you are allowing are much below reality."

"Now let's all remember that it was your group who handled the Peterson project and not mine. I had said again and again that its budget was inflated, but even so the profit margin was insignificant to the point that we nearly lost money on the deal. I unsolicited submitted an estimate report to your team that clearly specified where you were over-calculating and where your numbers were way too low. It could have been built for 13% less and even more efficient and we would have profited accordingly." As Victoria paused all four men were fuming. Then she continued: "I highly suggest that you go through the specs folder today and you'll see how it all fits together," Victoria's response was presented in a cold voice. "But we need to get going with this project a.s.a.p. so get back to me by tomorrow morning with other questions or concerns." They all stared at her, but not in a kind way. There was a long uncomfortable silence. The man on the left spoke:

"Jack – it is Jack!" Jack nodded. "What's your take on this?" All eyes pointed at him. Thoughts flew through his head. He couldn't figure what was going on in this room, but whatever it was, it wasn't pleasant. He had to be careful.

"I met up with Victoria just an hour or so ago and I haven't had an opportunity to study this proposal, the specs, timeline, etc. at all, so at this point I can't possibly have much of an opinion. But what I'll do is discuss the project with Victoria, run my office through it and look at how we possibly could be involved – or not."

"Can your company handle projects this size and have you in the past?"

"*Yes* to the first part and *no* to the last. But don't get me wrong, there are of course ways to make things happen, get it done according to specs and time and within budget."

"How does the budget for this project look to you?"

"Again I haven't looked through any info, so I can't really comment on that at this time. Victoria has no doubt considered all the facts to be considered arriving at this figure, but as I said, I need to look it over myself and together with my staff." A few more questions and the meeting ended. A few moments later they were back in Victoria's office.

"What's the deal, Victoria? Aren't you guys on the same team?" He looked straight at her.

"What deal? What team?" She sounded innocent and sarcastic.

"Your colleagues; what's going on?"

"Our way of approaching new clients and new projects is that we look at the other team's estimations, just to check for profitability and approach. Will the project fly money-wise, time-wise and so on; so we bounce numbers around to make sure the projects are healthy so we can move on. So this afternoon I was presenting my team's new projects to the other team's leaders."

"But they all seemed so hostile; is that normal?"

"Unfortunately *yes;* but Jack it's nothing. The hostility comes from the fact that they are resentful I'm half their age and make twice their money. I don't really care; I mean it doesn't bother me." Jack looked at her.

"Yes it does. Remember that I know you well, and I can see that it does bother you."

"Maybe you're right, but it's not cramping my style or work. I won't let it. Also, they are just a bunch of spoiled jerks in middle management, and they are pissed that my results are much more profitable than any of theirs, so my superiors are giving me the bigger and more important jobs, the top clients, and my *in name only colleagues* don't like that at all. I also came off the street so to speak and within a couple of months got the much bigger office." She smiled a bit. "This is boring stuff, Jack, I'm a bit business burned out for today." She looked at her watch. "Let's go out and eat a nice meal with a nice bottle of wine or two – how about that?"

Jack looked at his watch, he had looked forward to get back to the office, talk with Nora, and let her know what was going on. But he also felt it was important to get along with Victoria to find out how feasible this project really was.

"Sounds good to me," he said with caution on his mind.

"Do you need to call Sara?"

"No. She left for New York this morning and won't be back for a couple of days."

"So is your dad looking after the kids?"

"No Colleen is."

"Say *hi* to all of them from me, okay?"

"Why don't you come by and say that *hi* thing yourself? The kids are actually wondering whatever happened to Aunt Vicky."

"Yeah right, Aunt Vicky!" She giggled "I'll come by soon, I promise."

She gave him two full copies of the project package which he placed in his briefcase; as he did, he also flipped a small switch to the *off* position. She grabbed her coat and purse and they were soon down on the street.

"Let's walk. The place I really like is not far from here and I need some fresh air. I hope you like good Italian food; this place is the best pasta joint in D.C. and nobody knows about it." She tucked herself closer to Jack as she put her arm in his and about ten minutes later they were in front of Piatti di Nonna. From the outside the restaurant looked tiny though cozy. Jack smiled a bit as he saw the red and white checkered tablecloths. He smiled even more spotting the empty basked Chianti bottles with the proverbial dripping candle on each table. Oh well, the food might be terrific as Victoria said and it sure smelled like it would be. They were immediately greeted by a large man.

"Bella Victoria; so very nice to see you again," his accent was definitely pure Italian; nobody could fake it that well. "So vonderful to see you." He grabbed her in a full embrace and kissed one cheek after the other. Victoria smiled big and turned towards Jack.

"Romano, I want you to meet my old friend Jack Miller. Jack this is Romano Rossi, the owner of this fine establishment." Rossi grabbed Jack's hand.

"It's pleasure meeting you, Jack Miller. Are you Miss Victoria's boyfriend perhaps?" Jack smiled as Victoria answered.

"I wish he was, Romano, I really do. He's my brother-in-law and very yummy." She grabbed Jack's hand, "and he's mine tonight," she added as she kissed his cheek. Jack smiled as he was still shaking Rossi's big hand.

"Welcome to Piatti di Nonna, Jack."

The restaurant was more than half full; mostly couples but also a table with an energetic family, kids and adults alike. The first bottle of Chianti was near empty as the appetizers arrived. Victoria took care of the major part of the wine. Jack was not a big drinker, so he timed himself accordingly. The conversation had been all about business to this point and Jack sensed some bitterness in her tone of voice, or was it something else? Though she had already told him the abbreviated story of her life the last few years, this was the detailed version. He listened as he sipped the wine and kept Victoria's glass full; another bottle arrived automatically.

The food was simply heaven. She was right, this was the best Italian he had ever tasted, and decided to bring Sara and the kids here as well as everybody else, as soon as possible. After finishing the second bottle, it was dessert, coffee and a large snifter of Grand Marnier. They chatted, laughed and giggled about stories from school, remembering many of their fellow students. A classmate Victoria kept in contact with supplied many juicy rumors, so she had many stories to tell; they were actually having a very entertaining time, supported by Chianti and Grand Marnier. It had a feeling of the good times in his room so many years ago. As Victoria left for the restroom, Rossi came over to the table.
"Jack, you like the food?"
"It was absolutely marvelous; very delicious. I'll bring you a bunch of new customers, that's for sure."
"That would be nice, Jack." Rossi paused; he looked towards the restrooms. "Can I say something in confidence to you?" Jack looked up at him.
"Of course you can!" Rossi sat down on Victoria's chair.
"Jack, I like Victoria, no I mean I love her, no not love her more than my wife, but like a daughter. I think Victoria is a good person. She doesn't let that show much, but I see it in her. She come here often, with people, you know – business, but mostly she come alone." He pads the table in front of him, "this is her table, this is where she sits all the time. You know Jack, I see that she is lonely and she look sad a lot. Sure she smile, but I see sadness behind the smile. I have no idea what it is, but sadness does not become her. She should be happy. What you think, Jack? Am I right?" All of a sudden Jack knew what it was he had sensed earlier. *Yes* he felt he knew what it was, and it made some kind of sense. Victoria should be happy, and he actually felt that from his heart.
"Rossi you are so right, really. I can see that now, yeah, you might be very correct."
"Good, Jack, I thought maybe only something I see. You see it too?"
"Yes I do; now I do." Rossi looked up as Victoria came towards the table. Rossi got up and pulled the chair out for Victoria.

"I'll bring more coffee and more Grand Marnier, on the house, of course." Jack could surely feel the alcohol he had already consumed, but it felt good. Victoria had consumed much more and appeared rather tipsy, but in a cute way, Jack thought. So far it had been a nice and fun evening, just what he needed.

They had hugged Rossi goodbye and was standing outside the restaurant. Jack looked at the sign above the sidewalk window.

"So what does Piatti di Nonna actually mean?" He asked in a slurred voice. Victoria was holding on to him.

"I think it means grandma's dishes or something like that." She kissed Jack on the cheek: "You are a lovely man, Jack." He heard it but continued.

"He doesn't look much like a grandma, does he now?" Victoria was laughing.

"You never know about them Italians, do you?"

"I guess not; so what now, Aunt Vicky?" She faced Jack and put her arms on his shoulders. She looked very relaxed, Jack thought, and pretty as ever. She smiled.

"Jack, it's so great to see you again, being with you. It makes me very happy." She kissed him on the lips and Jack kissed her back, but hesitantly so. There were no flashing warning signs. "What now! I only live four blocks from here, so I would appreciate if you would walk me home safely, please." She kissed him again; he didn't mind this time, so he kissed her back again.

"Of course I will, so let's go." They walked calmly arm in arm and they both enjoyed the coolness of the night. The fresh air didn't decrease their spirits, the ones sponsored by alcohol and they soon arrived in front of Victoria's apartment building.

"Jack, I expect you come up for a nightcap and then I want you to put me to bed and tuck me in before you leave, okay?" Jack even surprised himself.

"Whatever you want, I'm here to help."

"Whatever I want; ooh Jack that was a risky statement." She kissed him again and giggled. The doorman had opened the door from inside and they were soon in the elevator to the sixth floor. On the way up Victoria had rested her head on Jack's shoulder while embracing him with her arms; it felt good to Jack.

Her apartment was big, bigger than he had thought it would be. It was tastefully decorated with lots of seemingly original art on the walls. He took his time in front of every painting, inhaling the impressions he got from most of them. Quite a collection, that was for sure. Victoria had given him a gin and tonic before she disappeared in to her bedroom. When she reappeared he nearly lost his breath. When he was able to speak, he stumbled out:
"As they say in the movies, you have slipped into something more comfortable." He swallowed deeply. Victoria blushed as she stood in the doorway to the bedroom; being supported by the door-frame was a necessity. The light from behind emphasized her still beautifully curved body through the thin fabric of her gown. She was most certainly naked underneath. She walked to the bar and poured herself a large brandy, and then walked over and sat down in a big soft sofa. She had removed her make-up; to Jack that made her look even more beautiful. Her head was tilted a bit downwards, her eyes focused on nothing. She looked very vulnerable all of a sudden. Jack's heart was saddened as he looked at her. The candles flickered in her hair sending soft and gentle shadows dancing on the walls. The classical music was sweet and flowing as the softest pillow. Victoria was slowly twirling her brandy around in the glass, inhaling the aroma, wetting her lips with the liquid and slowly licking it off. She didn't do it with purpose, Jack thought in a haze. He found a seat in a soft armchair; he just wanted to sit here for a while and look at her. Victoria's head moved only when she sipped her brandy, and she didn't look up at all. The way her bare legs were tucked under her on the sofa with the gown barely covering; the way her breasts were slightly touching the thin fabric, a picture of pure innocence filled Jack's mind. It was a very special moment of something that could never had been planned or arranged and it would not be something that could be explained to anybody else. Jack was holding his breath and was afraid to move. The image in front of him was burning unto to his mind.

This was too easy, she thought. Sure she was in the middle of an Oscar moment, but still. Had he learned nothing since he was 15? To her, he was seemingly still guided by his genitals, and now he was dangling helpless in front of her. It was too easy, but still a lot of fun. She smiled inside as she imagined how her stupid sister Sara would react to the news – and she would make sure Sara was fed all the information about her husband's infidelity. What a sweet moment that would be. But onward, she thought; time for the kill.

Victoria slowly raised her head and a small smile appeared as she looked at Jack. She didn't say anything; she just kept looking at him. Jack looked back, into her eyes and into her smile. He sat the glass down on the table and knelt in front of the sofa and Victoria. As he put his head on her lap and his hands around her hips, she softly caressed his hair. As their lips met, the kisses started gently, but it slowly became more and more passionate. Her body felt exciting and her reaction to his touches were immediate and soon turned eager. She pressed herself against him as he pressed against her and for the longest moment they were locked in the warmest of embraces.

"You feel so good." She whispered. "So very good, and I have missed this for so many years."

"You feel good too, Victoria." He gently pulled away from her and looked into her eyes as he grabbed both her hands; with a soft and gentle voice he continued: "You are an extraordinarily beautiful woman, Victoria, and I do love you dearly, because I know what you can be and I know who you really are. I think about the times we were together so many years ago, and in spite that I failed you as a friend, I only have good memories." Victoria tried to speak. "Please let me finish. Tonight has been wonderful, it really has and I'm glad we got a chance to spend some time together besides the business stuff. It has been wonderful, really wonderful." Tears started rolling down Victoria's face. "If I hadn't met Sara, I seriously would have pursued you, I really would, because I know who you really are deep inside, but I'm not sure you know yourself."

"So who am I, Jack?" She asked softly.

"You are smart, rather brainy, actually, which to me is very sexy. You are also compassionate, which for the most is about your success in business, about what you do and what you make. But I also see that you could be as compassionate about other things and especially about people. But you keep up this tough guy image of not caring, where I trust that you actually do. I think it's just difficult for you to change lanes after so many years, to be the nice guy. I don't know what it is you want to prove, what you have to prove."

"I don't know either; at least for now."

"Victoria, the most compassionate part about us humans is how we handle our vulnerabilities, our insecurities. We all know that we are imperfect, so when we try so hard to be perfect, we are pushing away what we seriously crave more than anything: other people's respect, other people's love. That's not a good life. We are frail to some extent; that's a simple reality, but we also have stronger sides that easily make up for our frailties and insecurities, and the sooner we acknowledge this, the faster we can learn to live with it." She looked at him.

"You are right, Jack. The sad fact is that I know all that; but it's hard for me to fix it."

"Which I fully believe and trust that you can and that you will." He gave her a kiss on the cheek and got up. "Let me tuck you in as I promised." She got up slowly. Her face showed tired and sleepy. They walked in to the bedroom where Jack pulled the bedspread off, and fluffed the pillows. Victoria came back from the bathroom and slid in to bed. Jack pulled the covers up and sat on the edge. She looked at him as she took his hand.

"I assume that you are not staying?" Her voice was a little sad.

"That is a correct assumption."

"Are you sorry that we kissed a bit tonight?

"No Victoria, I am not. That was just you and I and nobody else. I will deal with the guilt tomorrow, but not tonight."

"Are you going to tell Sara?"

"*Yes* that I have to do. If she'll understand, forgive and forget is of course another issue; but I'm not going to lie to her – that I can never do, so I'll have to accept whatever consequences are coming my way."

"You're good man, Jack. I'm sorry that I didn't hold on to you – very sorry."

"You'll find the right man, Victoria, the one who as I will find the real you., and I bet you will be very happy." He smiled and kissed her on the forehead. "Remember that I do

love you, Aunt Vicky, and I do hope that we are good pals again."
"That we are, Jack, and it's nice to have you back, it really is; it really, really is." A final embrace and Jack got up and left.

As the front door closed Victoria sat up in the bed. "What have I done?" She panicked. "Oh my God, what have I done?" It wasn't about the evening with Jack. It had been romantic and fun and just what she had needed so much. Sure she wouldn't have minded if Jack had spent the night – forever, but she also knew the score that Jack would never leave Sara. It was her plan of revenge that suddenly loomed gigantic. What had she done! She left the bed and paced up and down the floor. This was terrible; this was all of a sudden a huge mistake. How could she ever had let it go this far? Had she really hated Jack this much? He loved her; he said he did and she could also feel that he did. The way he treated her, the way he kissed her. He wanted them to be friends again and she had welcomed it, no questions asked, because she wanted to be friends with Jack very much; but what now? How could she fix it all to be right? She couldn't hurt Jack, not now, not when they were friends again. How could she have been so utterly dumb and angry! She desperately had to find a way to fix it – but at the moment, she didn't know how to do that, as the ball was already in play.

It was late into the following day when Nora, Jack, Karen and two crew-managers found themselves exhausted from going over the project specs from Anchor time after time. Initially it had looked feasible, actually rather good, but as they did a couple of run-throughs, they started to see some small holes here and there that didn't add up. They decided to take a break and Jack got on the phone.
"William, old chap, it's your best buddy in the whole world."
"Oh, hi Mom..." William sounded as cheery as always. "What can I do you for, Mr. Miller?" Jack explained the situation and asked for his advice.
"I'll be in your office within 30 minutes; how is *that* for service?" Due to William's math skills and overall having

lots of fun with numbers, he had decided to become an accountant. With his own business, small office and small staff, he had done well for himself. When CR's accountant had decided to retire, Nora and Jack acquired William's services right away – which he was more than happy to supply. He had been a big help through the recent lean and fragile times, and did all he could to make CR hobble through this nerve-racking period without folding.

William had sifted through the numbers from the Anchor specs several times. He looked puzzled as he finally presented his findings.

"I'm not sure what's going on here, but to me it looks like that whoever takes this project will be on a very shaky edge. If I read the contract correctly, it could nail any smaller company to the cross; but let Sara look at that part. I'm not the legal eagle she is. I'm more like an illegal turkey at best," he giggled. Nora, Jack and the rest agreed; also concerning the turkey bit. They had all sensed something didn't add up. The strange thing was that in the first couple of reads, it all looked good, legit and profitable, but with a fine tooth comb it started to fall apart, and looked extremely risky. They agreed that the proposal was well written, *if* it was written to fool somebody, but the monies allotted for the project looked like it was at least undercut by half a million; and that might only be a conservative estimate. It did not make sense at all.

Jack had thought about last night and in a strange way he didn't feel the kind of guilt he expected. It wasn't this excruciatingly devastating feeling of guilt as in movies and books. He was not trying to justify his infidelity by any means, as infidelity was just that. Now it was a matter of Sara's understanding and acceptance or not, as Jack also knew in his heart that this had been a one-time-only thing; he was fully sure of that. But it was the way the proposal was written that he was much more concerned about. He was puzzled why it didn't add up, very puzzled indeed. Did Victoria know? Had *she* composed it and missed some essential numbers? Could she possibly have made such big mistakes? That didn't sound right at all as she had a very impressive track record with Anchor and wherever else she had worked. Had somebody misled or misinformed her? Jack was reaching for his coffee when Karen came in to the office; she walked over to his desk and gave him a kiss on the cheek.

"Go home Mr. Miller. You look exhausted." Jack smiled and nodded as she left. "And there is a Mr. Fielder on line one for you."

"Thanks Karen, go home and goodnight and thanks for all your help." He reached for the phone.

"Mr. Miller, or Jack, this is Richard Fielder from Anchor. Sorry to call this late, but I was wondering if we could get together with you tomorrow morning."

"*We* as you and Victoria and …"

"Victoria is in Virginia tomorrow, so it'll be you and the four of us from yesterday." Hesitantly Jack responded.

"Okay, I'll make time to come by; how about ten-ish?"

"We'll see you then. Thanks Jack." He slowly put the phone down, wondering what was going on. Jack asked Nora and William to come along – just in case.

The collective faces of all four men fell as Jack, Nora and William entered the conference room.

"We were kind of expecting just you, Jack." Fielder stuttered.

"I'm sorry, but I hope this is okay. Nora Clark is my partner and the president of CR and William Baxter is our accountant." They all shook hands with Jack and William and just nodded towards Nora, though she had her hand out. Jack saw her knowing smile, the one nobody else could see but him.

"Well, it's a very delicate matter, and we wanted to keep it limited."

"Mr. Fielder, please know that whatever is expressed in this room this morning and as well at any other time or meeting stays within full confidentiality." Jack lied a very rare time. "We don't have any reason to share whatever it is with anybody else."

"Okay then," Fielder responded hesitantly. Jack put his briefcase on the table, opened it and pulled out a legal pad; he also flipped the small switch to *on*. Fiedler started nervously:

"Did you get a chance to go through the Virginia proposal?"

Nora answered:

"Yes, we ran through it a couple of times."

"So are you comfortable with what it says?"

"Please define *comfortable*, Sir." Nora was already in her business groove. Fielder looked puzzled.

"Is there anything in the proposal that you cannot accept?"

"We still need a day or so to run through all the numbers a bit more. We also need our corporate attorney to look at the fine print." Fielder was now visibly nervous.

"Your *attorney*?"

"Of course, to make sure we are on the right page, so to speak." There was a long silence. Fielder picked it up again.

"We went through the Virginia proposal yesterday and all last night. We are concerned about some of the numbers. To us it didn't add up in some areas, whereas some of the more obvious areas look fine and profitable. But some of the underlying, more hidden cost factors could be conceived as either calculated incorrectly or applied on purpose." Nora looked directly at Fielder.

"Please define your understanding of *applied on purpose*." Fielder swallowed hard as the other three men moved a bit in their chairs.

"Maybe the numbers were purposely applied that way to force the contractor to fail on the project?" Nora looked at him coldly.

"What would that achieve?"

"That's what we are trying to figure out. I mean, it might just be a mistake, but one that has to be corrected if that's what it is." Jack spoke:

"Who put this project proposal together?"

"Virginia Grant – and her team, of course." To Jack it sounded to have come out too eagerly.

"So why are we not seeing Miss Grant this morning?" Nora asked.

"She's out of the office today."

"Couldn't this have waited till she got back?"

"We all thought it was important to figure out what's going on, so we felt we should look into it right away." Nora looked straight at Fielder.

"But obviously not important enough to wait for Miss Grant!" She looked at each of the four men and continued. "I suggest that we meet again when Victoria can join us; that way we'll know from her what might just be a simple explanation." Fielder smiled a bit.

"Listen very carefully, young lady" he leaned towards Nora. "Victoria Grant and her so-called team have in the last 6 months implemented two projects where the contractors got screwed and they both had to close shop because a few so-called details in the contract were not fulfilled. Sure the stupid contractors should have read the bleeding fine print, but they didn't. They were so blinded by the work and the *profit margin* they thought they would collect. But they were wrong, because of a few hidden conditions that dear Miss Grant *forgot* to highlight."

"And this is brought up because of what?" Nora asked.

"Anchor cannot allow screw-ups. It cuts down on profit and reputation. We can't afford that. So we are chatting with you to make sure that it's all on the up and up and to make sure that a third tragic event is *not* going to take place, not with the Anchor brand attached to it. We wanted to see if you found what we found, and seemingly you did."

"We still have some looking to do, but we found a few things that could be a concern if not adjusted." Jack lied again. He was not sure what was going on. He looked at William who had been taking notes. "If we find issues, we will of course bring them up for discussion, and for adjustments fitting a sound proposal. If we find everything to our satisfaction we will of course consider accepting the contract, but if anything is amiss and can't be agreed upon, we'll of course decline." Nora leaned over and looked straight at Fielder:

"Listen very carefully, *sir*. You no doubt know that CR as a business is skating on extremely thin ice these days. That is not a big secret. But we also want you to know, that we are not going to prostitute ourselves into a contract that we *might* be able to fulfill. That is not who we are and that is not who we want to be and that is not what we do. We *only* do quality work, we finish on time and we are expensive. Now if that's what you are looking for, we can certainly help." Nora's voice got colder: "If you have some in-house issues and concerns that is not any of our business, we do not appreciate being brought to the table to discuss any such situations to any extent." While Nora spoke, Jack slowly put his legal pad back in the briefcase, closed and locked it and placed it on the chair next to him under the table. Nora continued: "So for all practical purposes, I think we'll leave and if you feel that we should continue our chats to find solutions with Miss Grant present, please give us a call. We'll certainly work with you as long as we keep moving forward. If you already have decided that we are not a match, we expect to hear that from Victoria, not from you, as we understand that this is not your project." Nora smiled and got up. "Have a nice day, Gentlemen, you hear!" Jack and William filed out the door together with Nora. Jack didn't carry his briefcase, but nobody noticed.

It had been the most somber conversation between Sara and Jack. He had told her moment for moment what he had done and what he had thought the day he met with Victoria at Anchor as well as the dinner at the Italian restaurant. He told her about the several bottles of wine they had gone through as well as after dinner drinks on top. Sara heard the conversations Victoria and Jack had during the rest of the evening and into the night. Jack didn't spare a description and he was fully honest about what he had seen in Victoria, her vulnerability and her loneliness. She had looked sad and depressed. Jack didn't use any excuses, didn't tell anything untrue – simply told Sara what it was, what it had been and how he felt then and how he felt now. He had cried, but not for himself, but for them, for Sara and Jack.

Sara's face was never filled with shock or disgust. Her heart was cracked but not broken; she knew it could be repaired because she wanted it to be whole again. She had listened to Jack and she understood the honesty he showed had been as brutal to express as it was brutal to listen to. Though Jack had not been unfaithful in the full sense of being unfaithful, he had bruised trust and respect, but not severed it. They both knew it would take time to heal, but they also felt in their hearts that as long as they worked on the repair, forgiveness could be forthcoming. Sara knew that Jack was suffering from guilt and regrets and also believed that he should. She was not going to tell him that all was okay, because it was not. He had honestly expressed how he had felt for Victoria those moments and in a small way she understood his compassion for another human being; but compassion had moral limits. He knew he had broken those limits, as well as she knew. The rest of the evening they

talked about the children, other things, just for a moment to push away the thoughts and feelings of Jack's indiscretion. Later in bed Jack embraced Sara and whispered more apologies. They had been silent for a while when Sara quietly said:
"At least you found a great Italian restaurant!"
"I sure did." Jack let out a deep breath. "If nothing else, I sure did that." They had turned away from each other to finally go to sleep. They had both smiled to themselves and they knew that the repair had already started.

The phone call Jack expected came early the next morning. It was Karen and her *line one* that made Jack giggle.
"Good morning Jack. This is Linda Cann from Anchor; I'm Victoria Grant's secretary. I believe you forgot your briefcase here yesterday. I have it in my office. Do you want me to send it over or will you pick it up?"
"Thanks Linda, it was silly of me to be so forgetful. I'll be by shortly. Thanks again Linda." And Jack hung up. His smile was broad, but in a way that was not fully on the level. His father had put him up to it. He called Anchor back and asked for Victoria's extension. He was told that she was still in Virginia, but that she would be back in the office that afternoon. He left a message for her to call him at work or at home – he marked it *urgent*.

"So what have you done, Dear Jack? Have you joined the ranks of sleazy spies, shady characters by somewhat not playing nicely with the other children?" Jack felt embarrassed. This had all been his father's idea from the get go. George had the whole situation explained several times over concerning CR's financial problems. He had offered Nora and Jack a loan that could easily carry them through many months and hopefully within that time they'd create sales and profits and get back on track. Colleen and Charles had also offered financial support, but they had gratefully said no thanks to them as well. When the meeting with Anchor had materialized and Jack had talked with George about how Anchor and especially Victoria could be rather brutal in the way they treated sub-contractors, George immediately saw several red flags pop up. He knew that Jack liked Victoria and they had been friends, but also that Victoria had felt rejected some years back; he had an inclination that she had not fully forgiven Jack at all. This he didn't communicate to Jack. His son was an adult and should deal with his feelings on his own. No need of help from daddy – only maybe just a little.

George's concern was that Nora and Jack needed to keep their collective butts above water – they needed to know what was going on. If anybody was going to blow them out of the water for whatever reason, it would be nice to know when, so lifesavers could be applied in a timely manner. So he had borrowed Jack's briefcase and some of the boys from the office made a few *adjustments* for that butt-covering thing. At first Jack had said *no* on the top of his voice and refined moral ethics, but the more George had talked and explained the more he thought it would be necessary. So he had finally walked out the door, briefcase in hand and knew how to use it – still feeling a bit awkward, but calmer to some extent.

So he had done the first part and was now sitting in front of his father in the kitchen. If there was any form of ammunition from the recordings, he would be the only one who had the gun to use it so far. George was working the screwdriver and seemingly enjoyed every moment of it.

"What's with the grin, Dad; back in the Soviet Union outsmarting KGB again?"

"Back then it was the NKVD, son; get the facts straight." He finally had the recorder free and soon the small silver-colored disc popped out. "Now, you know this is the newest CIA and FBI technology, and if you ever tell anybody about this, I'll seriously have to spank you."

"That's a pretty picture, Dad." George snapped the disc into the player in front of them.

"Let's take a listen, comrade spy." For some reason they leaned towards the player, but didn't need to as the voices from the tiny speakers were as clear as could be. What the voices were saying was even clearer and frightening so. The next part would be very tricky indeed and would no doubt leave some bloodied casualties on the playing field.

George had gone to bed and Jack had listened to the disk several times. The only voice he could connect with a name was Fielder's, and of course Nora and his own. As a side-thought, he smiled as he listened to Nora's way of communicating. She was good, he thought - very good indeed. She had been diplomatic and very firm. But it was all the other stuff that was recorded after they had left that blew him away. It had saddened and infuriated him. If this was the way people did business, he was seriously in the wrong field of work. He listened yet one more time and then made two phone calls. Sara was still up and he would be on the way home soon. She asked if he was going to tuck his father in; he giggled and declined to answer. The next call was to Karen; her voice was very sleepy.

"What's your problem, Miller? I'm sure you know what time it is, but you really don't care, huh? What's the emergency?" Jack told her and he would pick her up at 5 AM later that morning. They would go to George's house where Karen would type everything down from the disc.

"Is your father going to be home?"

"Yeah; why?"

"I like him – a lot."

"Karen, this is serious stuff."

"You mean your dad and me?"

"He's a million years older than you?"

"And your point is?"

"Forget it – 5 sharp. Get some sleep." Jack was soon in bed next to Sara.

Karen was physically disturbed from the contents on the recording. It had taken her about two hours to get it all down. George had supplied the coffee on the way and when she was done, he had made her breakfast. Jack grabbed the copies and was fast on his way to the office.

"Don't be too late, Karen. You'll be needed." He gave her a hug and a kiss on the forehead. "Thanks so much for your help and remember: Nobody must know any of this from you, okay?" and he was gone. Karen turned to George:

"I love it when Jack tells me that I'm needed. My imagination runs wild every time, but then the image of Sara gets in the way." She leaned closer to George over the pancakes, smiling sweetly: "So George, any girlfriends I should be worried about?" George laughed. He liked Karen. She was funny and quick and not that bad looking at all.

Very charming and straight forward – just like Irene had been.
"How old are you again?"
"How old do you want me to be, Mr. Miller?" He shook his head and rolled his eyes. Yeah, she was definitely cute. There was eternal sparks in her eyes that said she had a lot of fun – and for the most on your behalf, like it or not. George, as everybody else, liked it plenty.

Jack had given Sara a hardcopy of the recording. He wanted her input and her evaluation.
"Jack, first of all you must realize that this has been obtained illegally. It is not something the courts look on lightly. If you even mention the fact that you have recorded these people's voices without their knowledge, you are going to be knee-deep in manure; I mean we are talking serious jail-time." Jack was listening to what he already knew, but he needed to be reminded. Maybe he was already in too deep, but there had to be a way out. This was too important. Both Nora and Sara's first reaction had been extreme, but also a somewhat *yes it might work if played to perfection.* Of course they could also drop the whole thing here and now, but that would for sure ruin Victoria, though she seemed to have dug her own grave already. Sara was agreeing with Jack concerning her sister, but Jack's plan of getting her to pay the piper and then rectifying herself and get back on track, was a risky proposition. Of course there was that Plan B thing, which would have CR walk away from Anchor, a possibly good future account, and let them fight their own internal battle; what would he really care! But he did care about Victoria, in spite of her possible plans of ruining him for whatever pathetic reason. Later in the morning Nora, Sara, William and Karen had decided a direction and a first plan of action. It was then Victoria finally called.
"We need to talk." The sound of his voice was cold and demanding; immediately her body started to shake. There was no way Jack could have found out – no way what so ever, as she had not told anybody.
"I'll pick you up in front of Anchor in 30 minutes." No goodbyes, just the two firm orders. She took a couple of deep breaths, sat down behind her desk and tried to figure out what Jack was up to and tried to find answers to solve

the situation. Maybe it was something totally different – maybe, she hoped.

Jack pulled to the curb and popped the passenger door open.
"Get in." and she did. As she saw Jack she was shocked. He did not look like normal charming Jack. He looked furious. He drove in silence for awhile and finally parked in a fairly empty parking lot near the Washington Monument. He killed the engine and turned towards Victoria.
"So the question is: Why the hell have you waited all these many years to force this vicious revenge on me, to ruin me; and not just me, but all the people I love. Did I really hurt you that much so long ago, that it has made you such a bitter, lonely and pathetic person? Is that what this is all about? Or are you just that hollow and vicious by nature?" His eyes bore into her. He had played his hand and her reaction would tell him if he had guessed right or wrong.
"What do you mean, Jack?" Her voice was desperately trying to sound in control.
"You know precisely what I mean. Don't play fucking games with me anymore, Victoria. I seriously thought we had finally renewed our friendship; that we had made up and moved forward – acting like adults. But it was all a game to you, wasn't it? Just a fucking game; and what really pisses me off is that I fell for all your pathetic crap which makes *me* feel utterly pathetic. So I ask you again: Why now?" Tears were flooding from her eyes. So he did know, but how? There was no way he would explode like that for anything less. He was the calmest person she knew; and now he hated her with a passion, brutally despised her. How could she have been so stupid? Her body was shaking as she wiped her face with her sleeve. "I'm not buying any of your crying shit, Victoria. Start explaining." He hadn't heard the confirmation from her yet, so he was getting anxious. Losing face now, was not an option. As much as he wanted to embrace her and tell her that all would be okay, he was more so furious and deeply disappointed with his own stupidity. Victoria's red eyes stared at him as if she didn't know who he was. Her mouth was quivering and Jack got his confirmation.

"How did you find out? Did you guess?" The words came out in a quiet staccato.

"I'm not telling you how, I just want to know why – and I want to know that *now*, Victoria."

The next half hour Victoria opened up. She knew she loved Jack and that was never going to go away. She also knew the pain that had kept growing inside her from the moment he had rejected her. To start with, it had been a natural reaction from being pushed aside by somebody you were in love with and had been ready to fully give yourself to, become part of him, become them – become us. But the pain had not gone away; it had grown and worked its way in to every fiber of her being. It had finally become an obsession that had eaten her heart and had effectively chewed away all common sense. She had planned and thought of many ways to have Jack pay for what he had done to her, because it was fully his fault; he was the only one to blame, and he should pay. She moved back to D.C. with a plan she felt would ruin Jack. She heard about his purchase of CR Constructions, so she had unsolicited applied for a job with the biggest builder on the east coast, Anchor. She had no doubts they would hire her. Though she was very young she already had a superb track record and showed even more promise for the future. Anchor had hired her on the spot.

Now she was near Jack so she would patiently wait for her chance to snap the trap. All she had to do was to wait for the mouse to get real hungry. Weekly she had her assistant produce an update on CR Constructions as well as other sub contractors, as not to create suspicion about her special interest. When she saw that CR was scraping the bottom, she brought out the cheese and called Jack. The trap was soon ready to snap and Jack would be extremely dead. The revenge would be sweet and according to Victoria: Justified. She kept wiping tears from her face as she was talking. Jack looked at her with sadness. Understanding how a person could be so evil, so obsessed with another human being didn't make sense to him at all. Victoria continued. A couple of building projects had surfaced and she picked one to use. As she worked the budget she had low-balled materials by using faulty pricing. She had on purpose calculated shorter building time and labor estimates. She had done everything possible to create a project that had no possibility to be finished within the time-line. The attached contract would in not so clear terms specify the penalties for not finishing on time, and the penalties were fierce. It would simply devastate any smaller sub contractor such as CR – and with it, Jack. She had worked the project estimates to the extent that the shortcomings were hidden so well, that only very few people would ever find them – and if they did, they would be so deep into the contract that it would be impossible to turn around – they would falter and they would die. When she talked with Jack she saw that he was very hungry. She didn't pity him at all, didn't feel sorry or any *oh poor thing*. She fully enjoyed watching him eying the cheese as he had slowly moved towards the trap. Sweet revenge was near.

The dinner with Jack at Piatti di Nonna had been lovely, really. He was easily pulled in to her web as they got to her apartment. She gave him the whole repertoire of sexy seduction, yet another thing she was so perfect at. With a body like hers and the way she could put it to good use, she knew that any man would desire her. But it was a bit more difficult with Jack. She realized that he knew her too well already, so sultry eyes and see-through nightgowns revealing her soft curves didn't do the trick. She had actually planned for Jack to finally break her virginity that evening, but it had not happened. If it had, she would have made sure that Sara knew about it the very next morning. What they had ended up doing wasn't enough to make her stupid sister get rid of him. So she would just have to break him on the contract and she was fine with that.

"How did you find out? And what do we do now?" Victoria had slumped deep into the seat. Her face was swollen and she hadn't stopped crying. Jack wasn't sure if she felt any regrets; he didn't read that at all. But he was sure that she had told the full truth as she looked relieved – an enormous pressure had evaporated. But she also looked miserable. Jack didn't find any signs of remorse on her face – at least not yet, he thought.

"At this point I can't tell you how we found out."

"*We*? Who else knows about this?" Victoria's voice was shaking.

"Well Nora, William, Karen, she's my assistant, Sara and my dad; but only us – nobody else at this point." Victoria looked shocked.

"Oh my God – what have I done?" She sniffled a bit and tears started to show again. "Oh my God, this is not good, not good at all. What do we do?" Jack started to see the fear in her face now, and Jack being Jack, started to feel sorry for her.

"It's not that *we* are going to do something about it, Victoria, it's what *you* are going to do; and going to do fast, very fast." He looked into her red eyes. "Your pathetic scheme is nothing compared to the real and immediate problems you have." She shook more.

"What do you mean?"

"You are on the edge of losing your job, your reputation and no doubt your level of lifestyle; pretty much everything you have worked for. It's not that we only found out about your wishes to destroy me, this other thing is about some of your colleagues at Anchor who wants to kill you off really bad – and believe me, they have the ammunition." Victoria's face went very white; she quickly opened the door, leaned out and violently threw up.

"Have a nice day, Gentlemen, you hear!" It was Nora's voice through the tiny speakers. The sound of a heavy door closing came next.

Voice one: "What the hell was that all about? And what's with the black bitch? She's actually president of that little shit company? I'm not dealing with any bleeding *Negros*; that will not happen."

Voice two: "Come on, it's not a fucking color problem we are facing. It's more like a white trailer-bitch issue we need to deal with and fast."

Voice three: "If she was a man we'd have her by the balls on this one."

Voice one: "We already have her over a barrel on the other two deals. She purposely led them fail. That was her goal the whole fucking way. I don't know why she did it; can't figure a reason."

Voice three: "Maybe she's just perverted and sick!"

Voice four: "Or maybe you are all jealous of her, you envy the results she's accomplished so fast!"

Voice One: "What side are you on? You're the one who wanted to nail her; you're the one who started all this shit, so where the hell did that come from?"

Voice four: "I've been watching you and been listening to your ranting and it started to sound like it was a case of extreme jealousy. Here she arrives, a terrific looking sexy broad that anybody was immediately drooling over and fantasizing about. You all looked like pathetic horny little bastards ready to jump her bones if she would through you one. But she played you the whole way. You are all three times older than her, but all you could see was tits, ass and long legs you wanted so badly around your neck. You guys are pathetic."

Voice three: "Well, well, what have the dog dragged in? Why the bloody change? What happened to *get the bitch*? Are you going to let her sit around and out-sell you, making four times your salary - our salaries? She's stealing all the best clients and all the best deals away from you, away from us. Shit, we have been here over 20 years and this young woman bitch struts in and out-smarts all of us? And you are just going to let that happen?"

Voice one: "She's got to go. I want the bitch out of here, I want her destroyed and I want my territory back, so let's find a way to get rid of her – and fast."

There was a pause in the recording.

Voice three: "Do we have enough on her as is?"

Voice four: "If you can nail her on anything from the two contracts that caused the subs to close shop, then you are a fucking genius. She wrote those things to perfection – she is that good and you know it."

Voice one: "We can't find the smoking gun. We know she did it, so we should be able to find the shit she played."

Voice four: "Well, be my guest, play genius and if you succeed, I'll kiss your ass forever."

Voice one: "Not the picture I'm interested in, thanks. So what would be the alternative, Gentlemen? Eliminate her the old fashioned way?" Some giggling could be heard.

Voice three: "Not a bad idea. But look at the Virginia project she's aiming at the little shit company. There is no way in hell that they can fill that contract within time or within budget – no way in bloody hell. We should be able to sit back and watch her drown."

Voice four: "You don't think that Miller guy will figure it out?"

Voice three: "He looks too bloody stupid to figure anything out. And the black bitch seems to have the mouth, but not the brains. They'll sign and they'll drown together with Victoria – no doubts about that."

Voice two: "So, all we have to do, is sit back and watch; is that it?"

Voice three: "That's about it and if it doesn't materialize, we'll go to plan B."

Voice four: "And plan B is what again?"

Voice three: "Our lovely and brainy Miss Grant will no doubt have an unfortunate accident; you know, shit like that happens and nobody will know where it came from."

Voice two, giggling: "You know, I wouldn't mind banging her before she has to go." The other voices were laughing.

Voice one: "You are a sick bastard, but I'm with you, banging her would no doubt be awesome. I wonder how many of the board members she has screwed!"

Voice four: "With the clients and projects she's getting, I can imagine all of them – and several times over." They all laughed again.

Voice one: "Hey shit, look here. The little jerk forgot his briefcase. Let's see what inside – just a little peek." There were some bumps and noises. "Oh, the little boy has locked his toy."

Victoria had listened with a white face and got physically sick. Jack had put his coat around her shoulders. They were all sitting in his office at the conference table. After the player went silent, there was an eerie quietness in the room. Sara, who purposely sat the farthest away from her sister, spoke first.

"Just to make totally sure that you all understand the legalities; there is nothing on this recording that can be used in a legal capacity. It's up to you to act and react to what you have heard and have learned, but there is nothing you can bring up about this with anybody without breaking the law. Are we all on the same page about that?" They all nodded in agreement.

"Vicky!" It was Karen who spoke next. "What's your relationship with upper management at Anchor?"

"I think it's good," she answered with a shaky voice. "But after this, I don't know, I really don't know. This is so, well unbelievable."

"Did you purposely bring down those two sub contractors?" William asked. Victoria looked up with a frightened face, as she shook her head.

"No, I didn't, no not at all. If you go through the project, check work-orders, time-lines and all documentation, you'll see that they broke the contract, and not just broke it, they smashed the agreement and I really tried to rescue the situation for them."

"Can you get us all the documentation and paperwork from those cases?" Jack asked.

"I can get them, but it won't be easy."

"We need to know that you are telling the truth."

"You don't trust me?" Victoria realized what she had said. "I'm sorry, of course you don't." Her whole body slumped deep in to the chair. "How stupid I have been."

"Would it be possible to find anything incriminating on Fielder and his friends?" Karen asked.

"I doubt it. They have been with the company a long time and had up till my arrival been the only kings of the hill. I'm sure they wouldn't be around if they'd screwed up at any point. Richards always speaks highly of them."

"*Richards*, being who?"

"The CEO; very nice guy, really; I have always got along well with him. He hired me just 15 minutes into the interview." She dried off more tears. Looking around from face to face, she took a deep breath: "You all really hate me, don't you? I understand, I would hate me too, and trust me, I really do hate me. This is…" Jack interrupted.

"Victoria, stop it; we don't have time for self-pitying crap. You screwed up really bad and now we are trying to save your sorry ass as well as we want CR to come out of this with some form of redemption."

"What do you mean? You have a plan?" She looked puzzled. "You are going to help me after all this?" Jack looked straight at her.

"Get this very straight, Victoria: First of all we are going to help ourselves first, help CR. You are a very distant second on our list of priorities. In the process of helping ourselves, we need your full cooperation and you need to do precisely what we tell you to do, as well as do it at the time we tell you to do it. If you agree, you might help yourself out of this crap. But you have to be honest with us and with yourself, and if you are not honest with us, we are all royally screwed. So what do you think?" They all stared at her.

"I don't understand why you are doing this, trying to help me, but of course I'm on board. I'll do anything to save my sorry ass. Thank you so much." More tears were wiped from her face. Sara was thinking that she still had a long way to go to ever be able to forgive her sister. She didn't trust her and she probably never would. William was looking at Victoria with wondering eyes. For a *sorry ass*, it was one of the nicest looking sorry asses he had ever seen. Jack disturbingly read his friend's face, and shook his head accordingly – he would deal with that later.

"We want to go ahead and sign the Virginia contract and get going with the work." Victoria's face went white.

"I'm sorry, but are you insane? You'll falter, Jack. It can't be done; no way can it be done. I worked that contract to fail with perfection." Jack looked at Victoria. "Nobody can find out how and why – nobody. You can't build that project on the money I allowed."

"We know all that, Victoria. We saw that on our first read-through; it was in the small print well hidden, we admit. Our plan could work, but it's all up to the way we execute it that will show us if we are right in our assumptions," Jack smiled, actually grinned: "That last bit is the part that will be rather tricky. Those four musketeers at Anchor are dangerous, Victoria, and we decided that by going through with the Virginia project, you could actually nail them to the cross." He looked at all the faces around him: "So let's get going, Ladies and Gentlemen." The meeting was over a couple of hours later.

William was the only one left in Jack's office. He was finishing collecting some papers from the table, when he looked at Jack's smirking face and the question mark so visible on his forehead.

"What?" William asked his friend.

"*What* meaning what?" Jack answered.

"That smirk on your otherwise lovely face *what*."

"Oh, that one! That's the one that says that William has the hots for Aunt Vicky; that's the one." William was smiling sheepishly.

"Oh, you noticed. I thought I was smooth and cool."

"Neither; it was as blatant as could be. I think that Victoria was the only one who ignored you."

"I'm sorry to hear that."

"Watch your steps, my friend. She'll play with you, break your heart, chew you up and spitefully spit you out like you were nothing; just something stuck between her teethes for a short moment."

"Thanks for the warning. I'm sure she'd still be worth it, though." Jack smiled.

"Yeah, and you are certifiably weird. It's people like you I hope will never reproduce..." And they left the office laughing, walked out of the building and went home; but still very concerned.

The next morning Victoria entered Fielder's office.

"Here's a copy of the signed Virginia Project contract. I have submitted the first payment check request. They are starting as soon as they have the money in their account." Fielder looked at her. She looked stunning as ever. A pity he had to destroy her; what a waste, he thought.

"Thanks Victoria; and congratulations - I guess." She smiled wide.

"Thanks Fielder." She turned and walked back out. She was tempted to smash his ugly face, but she had also promised Jack to play along to perfection; *follow the script word by word.* It felt horrific knowing what Fielder and the three other jerks had said about her, were planning against her; the only positive thing was that she knew about it. If Jack hadn't picked it up, they would have been successful in eliminating her forever. At least for now, she had a chance to fight back – and hopefully succeed with a little help from some friends, though she wasn't sure if she could call them that. She had pretty much tried to screw all of them over, especially Jack, and here they were still willing to help save her butt. She really didn't know why they were doing that for her, but had an inclination that it was more so self-serving, which was fine with her. The next move was together with Jack and a meeting with the Virginia Project clients. That would be interesting, weird, scary, but still interesting. It all depended on the outcome of that meeting.

Through Jack's half hour presentation, the two owners of the Virginia Project had listened in surprise and somewhat in awe. Jack had been straight forward, but weaved fiction with non-fiction; not his favorite thing to do. He explained that from suspicion, a gut feeling, and evolving from the fact that the budget for the upcoming project was about half a million off, he felt somebody wanted to destroy CR, but he didn't know who. If he had signed the contract and tried to do the work according to the way it was worded, he would have been ruined. Asking for additional funds to finish the project would of course be too late, and it would surely be turned down - and CR Constructions would crash.

"So according to your estimate here, you are pretty much going to be half a mill in the red when done with this?" One of the owners underlined. "So how are you going to handle that? And isn't this package prepared by you, Victoria?" Jack took a deep breath.

"Yes, it's from Victoria's team, but she has been fed invalid cost information and didn't double check it; her fault. But somebody within Anchor wants to get rid of her; not top-management, but somebody else. We don't know who – yet. You have worked with Victoria on several projects and have received excellent work as well as on time delivery. So what we are offering is an even higher quality of work to carry us all into the future hand-in-hand. We are extremely organized, we do only top quality work and *yes* we are more expensive up front and only with minor follow-up corrections. But we need your help; we need your help really bad."

"So why haven't you had any major projects lately?"

"Sir, we have not had *any* projects lately. Right now we are skating on very thin ice with respect to surviving, and even though my father, actually both my father's have offered financial help and support, Nora and I want to fix it ourselves or we'll have to close the doors. But we have a tremendous responsibility to our employees and their families, and we'll do whatever it takes to live up to the promises we have given them. So that's why we are talking with you today, actually begging you to consider our outline." The two owners glanced at each other.

"So Jack, you are how old again?" Jack smiled; he had heard that a lot.

"Hopefully old enough that you want to help us!"

"Let's hear your plan and we'll see what we can do." Jack looked at Victoria as she passed a folder to both of the owners. Then she started to talk.

"You have four more projects beyond Virginia; four projects you have already asked me to look at and you want them started and finished within the next few years. I have already done pre-calculations as you asked me to do, and when we hand those projects to CR, you'll pay more up front on each project as Jack mentioned, but you'll get a superb quality project done, and just very minor after-market added cost, if any. That is the proven track record for CR Constructions the last 25 years, and something Nora and Jack have continued and will continue to do as long as they are at the wheel." Jack started speaking:

"We have gone through the numbers, the expected increases of materials and labor costs, considering all factors for the next seven years and covering all eventualities. We can give you the cost of building each of the four projects within only a 10% variation…"

"What do you mean *variation*?" One of the owners asked.

"We want a buffer on either side."

"You mean it might cost 10% less as well as it might cost up to 10% more?"

"Precisely'"

"I'm a bit confused; but you'll charge us less if you are expending less?"

"Of course."

"How would we know?"

"You'll have full access to our accounting on these projects and we'll present you with monthly progress reports including all invoices, labor cost, including benefits, etc.; the whole deal from our side will be accessible to you at any time. This way you are on top of what we are doing and how much it's costing us. It'll all be on the level."

"We have never heard of a situation like this."

"Well, Gentlemen, now you have. As long as you provide us with projects, we will always conduct wide open business with you. We won't do that with anybody else, mind you – just you. You can actually consider us you own builders – but without the headaches."

"Why?"

"We want to do your projects, but as we have already established, we'll be approximately half a mill in the red when done. If you give us just two of the next four projects you already have on the plate, we will charge you using the same cost factor we always use. We will work really hard at producing the quality product you expect and with the help from our material suppliers, support from our employees applying even more effectiveness and efficiency we should be able to regain some if not all of the loss we'll take on Virginia. And we are also calculating that we can decrease the loss from the Virginia site to less than half of the estimated loss. And the last factor is our possible rewards-money from finishing the jobs earlier than due date; that could flip the whole picture into a slight profit." Jack was exhausted. He looked from one owner to the other.

"It's a big bite to swallow, Jack, so we need a few days to chew and digest."

"That's understandable. We didn't expect anything less."

"Where does Victoria fit in to this picture?"

"For now I'm staying with Anchor. As we talked about before, it's Fielder and his three henchmen I have a situation with, but Richards so far seems on the level, at least with me."

"Are the two of you talking about bringing you to CR at some point?" Victoria looked at Jack; he spoke first.

"It's a possibility, but I haven't discussed it with Victoria."

"I can't even see why Jack would consider that." She looked at him and saw that little boy she met so many years ago. How could he be so nice! For now it didn't make much sense to her.

"Victoria, if you at some point consider moving on, how about coming over to us? We could surely benefit from your talents."

"Are you serious? You want me to come and work for you? Even after all this?"

"That would be a consideration – so if you feel like a change at some point, we could at least talk about it." Victoria was screaming inside. This was a lot more than she could ever have imagined. She had felt she was ruined, but all of a sudden heaven opened up instead of her spinning towards hell. She composed herself and smiled an honest smile.

"I will certainly keep that in mind."

"Well, Victoria, Jack, it has been rather interesting and we have a bit to think over and talk about. We do need stuff built and we are known for our ethically high quality, but we also know that applying just two projects your way, we are seriously helping you get out of the fire." Jack cringed as that was pretty much the gist of it. Both the owners smiled at Jack's physical change.

"Don't worry Jack, we are never going to do anything that wouldn't profit us, and though your suggestions are life-saving attempts for CR, they could also be good business for us. We have dealt with Charles and CR for years, and CR has never let us down; actually the opposite, as we always received a better product than we paid for. So hopefully this would be on the same level."

"We will not disappoint you." Jack tried to smile.

"I hope not. We'll call you tomorrow Jack, Okay?"

As Victoria and Jack stood outside the building she gently embraced him.

"Thanks so much, Jack. I really appreciate all you are doing. I still don't know why you want to have anything to do with me after all this." He gently pushed her away.

"Victoria, for the last time: You are a good human being. I believe I can see that more than anybody else. I believe that I can see that more than you can see it yourself. You've just acted like a real bitch for a long time to prove some stupid point. You are smart and you are nice and lovely deep inside your heart; I have seen all that. Now bring it to good use, because what I'm concerned, this is the last chance I can offer you. If you screw up again, you'll be on your own." Victoria looked at Jack with tears in her eyes.

"I won't screw up again; I promise." And that came from deep inside her heart.

That very moment Fielder and the three henchmen were sitting cozily in his office. The brandy had been shared plentiful as a congratulatory liquid. They had agreed that all they had to do now was just patiently wait for CR to default on the contract and Victoria Grant would be history – eliminated for good. They would finally be the kings of the hill again – sole rulers and much richer.

Karen was leaning against the door frame to Jack's office. He was deep in thought, so he jumped when she spoke.
"I get that reaction from most men I meet."
"I'm sure you do, Karen." Jack smiled.
"But unfortunately not from George." Jack looked up and shook his head.
"You are so weird. What do you want with my father anyway?" Karen smiled sweetly – but in a mocking manner.
"Oh, he is just so dreamy, so mature, so… Well, experienced." Jack looked at her.
"And he is also so... Well, a million years older than you, and especially when you act like a four year old." Karen giggled.
"So you don't see me having any chances with your dad?"
"If you fully understand the meaning of *NO*, you truly understand my answer. And I would never have called you *mother* anyway – so take that, Karen." She pouted.
"You are absolutely not helping. Well, then I suggest you answer line one." And she went back to her office. After he finished the call, he ran in to Nora's office; she looked up as he raced through the door.
"Better be good news, Jackie Boy."
"We're on. They will use us for at least the next two projects and if we do well, they'll stay with us until we screw up." Nora got out of her chair and embraced him.
"We will *never* screw up, Jack. It's not an option." Karen came rushing in; she had heard the news.
"Can I join in?" Nora and Jack reached out for her and the group-hug was long and warm. Soon the news had spread to every single employee and Karen was quickly on the phone to the workers who had been temporarily laid off. Soon they would all be back at full strength and for now CR Constructions would be very busy indeed.

The Virginia Project didn't particularly go smoothly the last few weeks of construction. It seemed that every time a problem had been solved, a new one showed up. Jack had been suspicious the last few days. With the early finish compensation deadline coming up, he suspected foul play, with Fielder and his buddies as the culprits. He suggested to Victoria that she kept an eye open at Anchor. Jack fully trusted his crew and everybody they had brought in from outside. He could not see why their suppliers would fiddle with delayed deliveries, defective materials or in any way risk losing CR, Virginia Project or Anchor as major clients. That was not where the problems came from, he was sure of that. Everything had otherwise gone smoothly, but not the last few weeks.

It was when the scaffold on the east side of the nearly finished building had collapsed that Jack got very nervous and violently angry. Two of CR's crew members had been standing on the lower level as it happened. If the scaffold had collapsed a few minutes later, it could have been horrific, as they had been on their way up. They were raced to the hospital and were both treated for deep cuts and many bruises. They would not be able to help finish the job. Jack had found a couple of available bodies and they had started that same afternoon. Everybody worked on the scaffold and had re-erected it in record time. Though progress on the site was lost for the day, Jack offered double pay to those who would stay longer and help catching up. He was impressed, but not surprised, when most of the crew worked deep into the night; they all knew the score.

Victoria had nearly given up when she heard about the scaffold's mysterious break-down. She sat for a while at her desk, trying to collect herself. There had been too many setbacks on this project lately and it seemed very suspicious to her. She had not brought any of this up at Anchor and whenever Fielder asked how things were going, Victoria always told him that everything was running along just fine, thank you. She could see that he got more and more aggravated as the project progressed according to schedule. He had not closed any deals of any big value the last six months, and he didn't like that at all. The day Victoria had been praised for her additional four contracts from her Virginia clients, Fielder had rushed out of the boardroom. All of management had been present and Richards had underlined that those four contracts were the biggest project totals that Anchor had ever received. Victoria had been asked to say a few words. She had praised Richards in his foresight of letting her entertain the Virginia account and also letting her sign CR Constructions to the project. She mentioned the tremendous job CR was currently doing and was looking forward to many more projects and years with their partnership. Everybody had given her a standing ovation – except absentees Fielder and his three pals; they had other things to think about.

"Vicky, could you come up to my office in about 15?" Richards had smiled as he left. Victoria wasn't sure what that was about.
"Let's cut the bull. I have looked over the statements concerning the present Virginia Project and I want you to explain to me what's going on." Victoria knew precisely what he wanted to know. She had dreaded this moment, but she knew he was not stupid, so it had to come up.
"Meaning what, Sir?"
"Vicky, like I said, no bullshit, please. Don't insult me by pretending that you don't know why you are here and what we have to chat about, okay?"
"I'm sorry, Sir. I know it doesn't look profitable for CR and only a thin profit for us."
"Looks to me like CR will not be doing business with anybody in the future, wouldn't you say?"
"Yes Sir, it looks that way, but let me tell you the story behind it all and about the whys and the solutions." Richards leaned back in his large leather chair.
"Please do Miss Grant, and it better be something I'll get very excited about." Victoria didn't know if he would, so she mentally started to update her resume.

   It was about thirty minutes later that Victoria had told Mr. Richards the whole story, the truth and nothing but the truth - and very detailed. She had not left anything out. Her feelings about Fielder and his buddies came out, the loss on the present Virginia project and the way she and CR had negotiated future projects and contracts with the Virginia people, how CR was putting everything on the line to make it work, as well as the recent *mishaps* on site and Victoria's suspicions concerning who could be the background culprit. When she was done talking there was a long eerie silence.

Richards had twirled his chair and was sitting looking towards the Washington Monument pointing towards a bluish evening sky. He twirled back to face Victoria. He looked at her with concerned eyes; then he leaned towards her. She was getting very small in her chair and was ready to run out of his office as fast she could, but she couldn't move. He pointed at her with a stern and cold voice.

"Listen here young lady. Don't you ever do a deal or anything close to a deal like that again, ever; you got that?" Victoria couldn't get any smaller.

"Yes Sir" she whispered.

"You not only put Anchor at risk for your own revenge crap, but didn't consider the devastating situation you could have put all of CR's employees and owners in."

"I know Sir."

"You jeopardized Anchor's integrity, the one I have worked the last 35 years to shine beyond everybody else's. You were willing to shoot that down for your own bleeding reasons. How ignorant and stupid is that?"

"Very ignorant and very stupid, Sir; I'm very sorry."

"What the hell were you thinking?"

"I obviously wasn't."

"Do you believe that I should keep you employed here?"

"No Sir."

"Do you think that I have enough shit on you that I can through you out on your butt with no regrets?"

"You have plenty, Sir." He paused, shaking his head. His voice had changed to another, it was soft and direct.

"So you fully agree that you really fucked up by using Anchor's resources for you own crusade?"

"I fully agree, Sir"

"So since we are in agreement of the past situation, you hereby promise not to do anything, not even close like that, without consulting me. Is that fully understood?" Victoria was stunned; did this mean that she would still be alive, actually even have a job?

"Fully understood, Sir."

"So now we will be moving forward, won't we, Vicky?"

"Yes Sir, we will."

"Anything you want to add?" Victoria paused; a small smile appeared on her face.

"Thank you for not killing me," she paused again: "and my name is Victoria, not Vicky."

"Don't push your luck, young lady," Richards said with a small smile as he continued: "And talking about fucking up, *Vicky*, and just between us; please help me keep an eye on Fielder, and while you are at it, keep an eye on those other three asshole buddies of his. Jack Miller came by the other day and he had some rather disturbing information about them."

"He did?"

"Yeah and recorded; no doubts about the direction they are going." He looked out the window again. "So Vicky, help me nail them, would you please?"

"I sure will." Her voice sounded more at ease now, but only a bit. So Richards knew about Fielder and the gang of three as Jack had told him about them. Next step was to get rid of those four pests. Richards had sounded disappointed when he asked her to help. Those four were supposed to be trusted employees and they had been with Anchor for so many years. But greed changes human beings, unfortunately. Now their demise was near, she thought and hoped, but it would have its problems.

When she moved a bit closer to the vent in the wall by the copy machine, she could hear what was going on in Mr. Richards' office. Today had been no different. But the contents of Mr. Richards and Miss Grant's conversation had been very different and vey intriguing indeed. After Miss Grant left, Mr. Richards' *trusted* secretary sent an unsigned memo to Fielder's office; *we need to talk*, was all it said.

Jack was on the phone: "We are ready for the walk-through." Victoria smiled. They had finished the Virginia Project three weeks ahead of time. The initial loss would not be as much as they had calculated. She was nearly out of the hole she had tried to dig herself into. CR had started the second Virginia Project three months earlier and it was rolling along according to schedule. Jack and Nora's people were doing a terrific job and when the second project would hit the halfway mark of completion, CR would finally start to make a bit of profit from that point on; Victoria couldn't be happier.

"We'll see you tomorrow morning. I promised to tell Richards 'cause he wants to come along." Jack could hear her smile.

"Sounds like a deal." Jack paused. "We are still keeping the security folks on site. The Virginia people want them to do their thing until a few weeks after we have finished. They are not interested in any more acts of vandalism or sabotage."

"Sounds like a good plan. See you tomorrow."

The four men were sitting in silence. It had not been a good day and the last 12 months had not lived up to their expectations to any extent, quite the opposite. They could feel their jobs slipping away bit by bit. The clients they were handed had been puny and the projects had not generated the type of income they were used to. Victoria Grant had out-raced them on all fronts. She brought in big time clients and the multi-contract deal with the Virginia people had smashed all records. Now it seemed as the relationship the bitch had with CR Constructions was a huge success in efficiency and looked like it would accumulate big time profits and massive bonuses for her now as well as deep into the future. Richards had only given them the scraps of projects, but all the meaty stuff went to her. They were sure Victoria was banging her way to the top, with Richards riding her hard whenever he wanted. There was no doubt in their feeble minds that she was banging her way to success, the success *they* should have had. But they could not prove any of that. Secretly each of them would not have minded the possibility of getting to know her that way themselves, no matter how much each of them despised her. She was after all an extremely hot woman, and sexy as hell. All four fantasized about her constantly; but that was something they never told each other about either.

"So they are actually finishing Virginia tomorrow." Fielder's voice was defeated as his body slumped in the chair. "The bleeding bitch beat us again, gentlemen; she bloody well fucking slaughtered us." He took another big gulp of his brandy. After only 30 minutes they were deep into the second bottle. "And from a dependable source I also found out that Richards have forgiven the bitch for all the shit she pulled trying to crush CR. Can you fucking believe that?" Another gulp went down.

"Un-be-fucking-lievable!" The other three men kept pace with Fielder in the brandy department. "You got that info from your Richards spy?" Fielder made a disgusted face.

"Don't even go there."

"And what do you have to do for secret CEO information these days, Mr. Fielder." His voice was sarcastic and rude. "You have to supply physical flavors or something like that?"

"Shut up, you ignorant asshole."

"So that's what it is," he smiled, "Now tell me how you can possibly do that at all, I mean bloody technically wouldn't that be an impossibility? I mean she's not your typical hot choice, actually far from. So what does she look like naked?"

"Just shut the hell up."

"All in the line of duty, I assume." He paused. "I must give you credit, I couldn't get it up for her with a gun to my head; so good for you." Fielder looked at him with disgust.

"Just shut up, will you! We have more important things to deal with, like our bloody jobs and a bitch named Victoria." Another gulp of brandy went down his throat and into his blood. "So what are you pathetic assholes gonna do about that?" He looked at his three vastly intoxicated colleagues; they had no answers, other than gulping more brandy. "It's come to the point, in case you haven't noticed, that either she has to fully disappear or we will automatically be eliminated and lose our formerly cozy and profitable jobs, the jobs she has ripped away from under us. So the fucking question again, gentlemen: What are you gonna do about it? Just bloody sit around and do nothing and take it up your collective fat rear ends?" His voice had become blurrier. The three men didn't respond. They knew what the situation was and they never really believed that Fielder's plan would work in saving their collective rear ends. The three of them more or less accepted the fact that they had been squeezed to the present point because they simply were not good enough. They had been outmuscled by a better brain, much younger and a bloody female to boot; she had beaten all four of them for good. How embarrassing was that? But they never communicated that between themselves. Fielder emptied the second bottle and opened number three. After a refill and a large gulp, he continued: "Well, my pathetic musketeers, I don't know about you, but I'm going to do something about it, so if you want revenge, if you want your fucking jobs back, you stick with me." None of them moved. It was getting clear that Fielder was getting revved up and uncontrollably drunk. Then one by one they got up, put down their glasses and went for the door. "That's right, just escape and do nothing. You are all pathetic and now you're running home to your mommies to cry and feel bloody pity for yourself. What a bloody joke you all are." And the door closed, leaving Fielder by himself, all alone and utterly intoxicated; but he was far from done.

It had been a good day, Victoria thought; an extremely good day. She had taken a long bath surrounded by massive quantities of lit candles, her favorite Chopin piano pieces playing in the background and a glass of Merlot. Richards had been stern and firm and she knew that he would be watching her work very closely in the future. She was paying for her stupidities and that was as fair as it could be. She dried off and was sitting by the desk in her fluffy robe, opening the day's mail. Jack had been so much more than a friend. That he had helped her out instead of discarding her as old trash was still beyond her comprehension. He was still the man for her, but it had come to the respect and understanding that he would never be, no matter how hard and how much she tried – it would never happen. She loved him dearly, but he loved Sara and he was never going to change nor jeopardize that, she finally understood. But she also accepted that in spite of it all, she would never give up on having him; a reality she would always keep to herself.

Sara was still suspicious; she had no doubts. She told her that after what she tried to do, it would take a long time for her to get back to a *normal* relationship with her, whatever that was, Victoria accepted that. Sara always stated that she liked people until they proved her wrong. Her view of Victoria at this time was reversed: She didn't care too much for Victoria; *she* had to prove she could be trusted and then possibly liked. She had been at Sara and Jack's house several times over the last months to dinners and the kids' birthdays. Her role as Aunt Vicky to the kids was something she found to be fun and honest for her. She really liked Michael, Jasper, Caroline and of course Molly, the neighbor kid. Molly was actually a mouthful all by herself. Victoria saw a lot of herself in Molly, but only the better of her, not the crap and…, oh well, let's not go there tonight, she thought. Jack had told her several times that the children loved and adored her. She wasn't sure why, but he had said that kids are not stupid to any extent, quite the opposite. They sensed honesty from her and accepted that as a sign of respect. She had dried a few tears off her face as Jack told her.

She poured a little more Merlot and moved towards the bedroom. It was close to midnight and it was time to get some sleep to prepare for the most important day tomorrow. It was when she had draped the robe over the chair near the window that she heard the knock on the front door. She looked at the wall clock. It was now a few minutes past midnight. She picked up the phone and dialed the security desk in the lobby. Nobody picked up. She let it ring another three times when another series on knocks sounded on the front door; this time the knocks were louder and more demanding. She slipped on her robe and as she looked through the eye in the door, she saw the doorman's hat.

"Hold on," she said as she unlocked the deadbolt, the main lock and slid the massive safety chain off its track. She had barely turned the door-handle half way down when the door sprung open with a massive bang. The solid edge of the heavy steel hit Victoria on the side of her head with horrific devastation. As she tumbled backwards, blood was already streaming down her face from the wide open cut; she was unconscious before the back of her head hit the carpeted floor.

As he dragged her further into the apartment, masses of blood left an eerie trail. He closed the front door and looked around. So this was how the queen of the hill lived, he thought. He spotted the bar-table with the many bottles, found a fine cognac, popped the cork and took a large gulp. He grabbed a towel and pressed it against the flow of blood on her face. As he was holding the towel as firm as he could he looked at her body which for the most was exposed and near naked, as the robe had fallen aside. He let his free hand open the robe even more and was instantly further intoxicated from what he saw. It was the most beautiful shape, and even though she was lying on her back, her breasts were standing up, reaching for his touch, he thought. Her stomach was flat and strong and her legs long and shapely. She was more beautiful than his fantasies about her had ever mustered. He had made love to her many times in his mind, and there she was in front of him, finally; the real thing. Sure she was a bitch and she had purposely ruined his already miserable life, but in spite of that, he desperately desired her.

She groaned some and he got up and got another towel from the bathroom. It smelled good around here he thought as he took one more large gulp of cognac. Everything was getting blurrier and he giggled as he acknowledged that he was not exactly steady on his feet anymore. He returned to Victoria's body and found that it wasn't bleeding as fast from her wound anymore. He wondered why; he giggled again, as he thought it had stopped because she was dead - maybe? Is the witch dead? He leaned closer to her mouth, wiped away some of the blood oozing from the corners and put his ear close to her lips. He thought he heard faint breathing, but he wasn't sure at all. He had been close enough to where her lips had touched his ear; they had left bloody marks on him. He looked down her body again and his excitement kept rising. His right hand roughly touched her skin and was soon fondling her breasts. He was squeezing and fumbling and soon engaged both hands. The feeling was accelerating. He had never felt this sexually aroused before – ever. He was close to explode as he moved forward. Now lying next to her, his hands became even busier. He tried to unzip his pants, but his intoxication had diminished his motor-skills. Then he tried to unbuckle his belt and then worked the zipper again. This time he succeeded. He looked at her and knew he would reach the highest form of ecstasy ever. He struggled pulling his pants down, and hoped that in spite of his drunken persistence that he would soon be in heaven and his dreams would become reality as he had always hoped. He struggled up on his knees and was now ready to begin to make it all happen. Victoria groaned blood, so he hit her hard with a clinched fits – again and again. The groaning eventually stopped.

"George? It's Bernie." George immediately sat up in his bed. "What's up, Bernie?"
"We have a bit of a situation. Target One left the office a minute ago, but it doesn't seem like he's heading home. It seems as he is heading towards you-know-who's place. We are tailing and on him. What do you want us to do?"
"Stay close, Bernie. I'll be right there." George hung up and jumped out of bed. He was in his sweat-suit within seconds and out the door. As he arrived at the apartment building, he spotted Bernie and his partner right away.
"We lost him on the way, and can't find his car, so maybe he didn't head for here. Maybe he was drunk or something and was just cruising around."
"Thanks Bernie, I'll go check on Victoria, just to make sure she's alright. Stay here and call me if he shows up, okay?"
"We'll do, George!" Nobody answered the bell. After a short moment, George negotiated the lock and was quickly inside; the doorman was nowhere to be found. He rang the bell several times but nothing happened. He was just about to call Victoria's apartment when he saw a pair of shoes attached to legs behind the counter. It was Chuck and he was not conscious, far from; and he was without his proverbial hat. George raced out in front and flagged Bernie and his pal over. They both jumped out of the car and were in the lobby within seconds.
"Bernie, come with me, and Gene, take care of Chuck. Call an ambulance, make sure he's handled. Call the cops in about 15 minutes – not before…" Gene nodded and went over to Chuck's lifeless body. George and Bernie raced up the stairs, bypassing the elevator. On the sixth floor they became stealth. George motioned hand signals to Bernie and he knew precisely what he wanted him to do – guard the outside of the door to the apartment. They were ready.

This was going to be heaven, Fielder thought as he straddled Victoria's body. He had covered her face up, as all the blood was becoming nauseating to look at. But the rest of her body made up for it plentiful. He felt that she was waiting for him, was ready to make her own fantasies come true. She was calling him, begging him to excite her and bring her the ultimate reward. He grabbed her hips, spread her legs wide and pulled her closer to him; he was ready.

"Here comes big daddy, you little bitch." But his hands froze fumbling her breasts as he suddenly felt something cold and hard pressing into the back of his head. His feeble mind tried to process what it could possibly be; but in his condition, it came up with no information what-so-ever. The voice he heard was cold, calm and scary.

"Just in case you wonder, asshole, this is a 357 Magnum. My advice to you at this very moment is that you put your happy stick back in your pants as fast as you can. If you don't, I can inform you that the hole this sidearm will make in the back of your skull is rather small compared to the crater it makes on your forehead where the bullet exits and where your so-called brains used to be. Are we talking the same language?" Fielder started convulsing immediately. All he could do was nodding and that he did. "Now I suggest that you get off Victoria by not touching her again." Fielder swung from side to side, his intoxication working overtime. He stupidly pushed off her body supported by his right on her stomach with his left hand flat on the floor. He soon acknowledged the move had been a huge mistake. "I told you not to touch her again." George's voice was calm and controlled. The butt of his 357 Magnum hit Fielder's left hand so hard that most of the 27 bones splintered or broke on impact. His scream was horrific. He had never felt this type of pain before, this kind of devastating agony. "I'm sorry, did that hurt real bad?" George was not in a good mood. He grabbed Fielder's broken hand, twisted it several times as he dragged his limp body away from Victoria. Bernie had called for an additional ambulance and attended to her immediately.

"She's alive, but barely. You want me to call the cops?" George shook his head.

"Not yet. Give me a couple of minutes, please." Bernie knew why. He had worked so often with George that he knew the way he functioned. He knew he wasn't too happy with Fielder, and he was going to let Fielder know first-hand, no pun intended, he thought. He flipped her eyes open and checked her pupils. The pulse was weak and her breathing shallow, noisy and labored as could be expected. Overall

Bernie marked her okay till she would get help from the medics and soon after in ER. It was the big gash running from her temple to her jaw and the amount of lost blood that he was concerned about, as well as he should be.

After George had closed the door to the bathroom, he turned his full attention to Fielder. He had shoved him into the bathtub and now sat on the edge and looked at this miserable excuse of a human being.

"So Mr. Fielder, you were going to have a bit of fun in there, weren't you? You were going to make your sleazy fantasies about Victoria come true, weren't you? You couldn't keep your hands off her, which reminds me: Let me see your right hand?" George had to grab the hand himself as Fielder at this point was not responsive. The butt of the 357 came down hard and also rendered that part of Fielder's body inactive. George felt absolutely nothing mentally, emotionally or physically. He could not relate anything to a piece of human garbage like Fielder – he had never been able to do that. Fielder started subbing as George finally left him alone.

As the police officers removed Fielder in cuffs and Victoria had been rushed to the hospital, George was sitting next to Bernie on the couch, both with a gin and tonic in hand. George had surrendered his weapon as part of the investigation, but as the detectives checked the column of numbers on the handle with their office, they quickly handed it back to George.

"Sorry about that. Not used to that code; they told us all is fine."

The detectives had left him pretty much alone after his *adjusted* version of what had happened. It was written down, and as he showed them his identification card, they respectfully and quickly backed off from any further interrogation. The report would be precisely what George said happened – case closed. Fielder would be looking for many years in the slammer and with non-functional hands. As the two detectives had shared a couple of drinks and a bit of chit-chat with George and Bernie, they finally got up. On the way out the door, one of them turned towards George.

"Just for my own curiosity, totally off the record, you explained that the damage to the guy's hands was what again?" George smiled.

"Oh, unfortunately both Bernie and I accidentally stepped on those hands of his. We did tell him that we were very sorry."

"Well, then, that wraps it all up; thanks." The detective smirked and shook his head. "But that long gash, the cut on the face from his temple and all the way down to his lower jaw, what was that from again? You know the one that looked very similar to the damage on the victim's face."

"Oh, that one; yeah you see, he was bleeding from his hands so as I took him out to the bathroom to get cleaned up, the weirdest thing happened; he ran smack into the door – wham and there was more blood everywhere." Both detectives shook their heads this time, smirking away.

"Well, goodnight gentlemen. We might stay in touch." And they were gone.

"Thanks for the help Bernie."

"You're welcome – anytime."

As George was heading for the hospital, he started to shake. He never liked this kind of action. Unfortunately this time anger had guided him; he had not been in full control, and that was something he was not happy about. Smashing Fielder's hands was his way of saying *hands off* and that should have been it, or it shouldn't even have been *it* at all. He opened up Fielder's face with his weapon, so he was reminded about what he had done to Victoria every time he saw himself in a mirror. In an awfully strange way, he was okay with that and didn't feel any emotions from it. A piece of human garbage deserved nothing less; he deserved quite a bit more, actually.

He was relaxed again and back to good old loveable George as he parked his car in the hospital's garage. A deep and invigorating breath quickly erased the last three hours from his life's memory-bank. He had always been very good at doing that. George would now have to dig really deep to recall anything. His partner Bernie would remember every single minute detail of the evening's action; he was extremely good at that. Bernie was also very good at keeping this information to himself. Nobody other than Bernie, Gene and George would ever know the correct details of what had taken place that night. What they were concerned, they had not been there and that was also the strict orders the detectives received from higher ups. It had not happened, they were told.

It seemed as everybody were hanging around in the waiting area. Sara and Jack with the kids in colorful pajamas and fluffy slippers; Colleen and Charles looked worried; William was quietly chatting with Nora. George thought *the gang is all here,* as Jack approached him.

"Hi Dad, you heard?" George nodded. "I called you the second the hospital called us, but you didn't answer."

"Sorry I was out late."

"In your sweat-suit?"

"Rather casual situation."

"The police was here to see if Victoria could give them any information, but she hasn't been able to; still unconscious. But the doctor told us all vital signs are good, so they expect full recovery, though it might take some time. The cops also told us that the guy who attacked Victoria, had two broken hands and a smashed up face. Didn't know who came to her rescue." George nodded as if the information was new to him. He left for a moment, made a call and the police never came back.

"How's Victoria's face doing?"

"They told us that she might end up with a scar, but that it had not severed any ligaments or muscles, you know, not any of the big important stuff." George was relieved to hear that.

"That's good news, Jack." He lifted his arm up to pad Jack's back. It was just a split second, but enough for his son to figure it out, he thought, but maybe not; the arm came down really fast. Jack grabbed his father and pulled him out of the waiting area, far away from everybody; he looked angry now.

"How did you know about the injury to Victoria's face?"

"You mentioned it, I think."

"You think very wrong and don't start lying to me now; I'm a bit too old for that."

"Somebody must have mentioned it!" George was on thin ice. He normally didn't make mistakes like that, but it had been an exhausting night and he was getting older.

"You only talked with me Dad. And just as a silly by-the-way question, is that blood all over the underside of your right sleeve or should I be naïve enough to believe it when you tell me it's ketchup?" George turned his sleeve and looked.

"Oh shit," was all he said.

"No Dad, *shit* it is not, so let's get the truth; you know that father/son bonding thing." Jack didn't look happy. They found a bench by the entrance to the hospital. George looked at his son and started.

"After you told me about the problems Victoria had at work, the four guys not precisely loving her, the problems she'd gotten herself in and all that stuff, I called her and asked a few questions. She came over one evening and I got all the nitty gritty details. She sounded scared, so I told her that I would look into the situation and come up with something to help her feel safer. As you were close to finish the project in Virginia and the vandalism became more frequent, I asked a friend of mine to look after Victoria from where she wouldn't know. He did that since last week, and called me around midnight and the show was on." Then George told Jack nearly everything from that night and made Jack promise never to tell anybody else, not Sara, not Victoria, not anybody; Jack kept that promise.

"You are bleeding crazy, Dad. What could have happened to you? You could have been hurt or worse." Jack was shaking his head.

"Son, I know what I'm doing, and I know how to do these things without getting a scratch. And this is the last we talk about it." Jack embraced his father.

"Thanks Dad." He was still totally confused, but he also realized that his father had probably saved Victoria's life – that part was not confusing at all.

It took several days for Victoria to gain consciousness. As she fought her way back, family and friends were constantly by her side. Sara and Jack visited several times daily, and when she had a bit more strength, they brought the kids along, with Molly, of course. Everybody had by now fully embraced Molly as part of the family, so seeing her everywhere was as normal as seeing the other Miller kids. George had been busy with work and travel, but when he finally returned to D.C., he felt a need to go check on Victoria. Colleen and Charles were on their way out of the room as George entered. They chatted a bit and soon George was alone with Victoria. Even with the bandages on her face, hospital hair and no make-up, she still had this classic beauty look, he thought. She grabbed his hand as he placed himself on the edge of the bed. Her eyes looked deep into his. It made him uncomfortable, so he looked around the room.

"Nice digs, Vicky." She smiled and squeezed both his hands. Her eyes had turned moist with tears.

"Thanks George," was all she said; he twisted in his seat.

"Thanks for what?"

"Thanks for being there for me."

"Being where for you?"

"George, please. One of the medics came by the other day to see how I was doing and we got to talk. He was very vague and sketchy about what he had seen in the apartment when they picked me up."

"So what has that to do with me? I was out of town that day or night."

"He told me that a certain government agency had informed him that nothing had happened and that he should pretty much keep his mouth shot."

"Again, Victoria, what does that have to do with me?"

"He told me that another ambulance had picked up an older man and that this older man had two terribly crushed hands and a large bloody cut down the side of his face very similar to mine." George didn't blink. "I also found out that the attacker was Fielder." She caressed his arm. "George, I'm not going to tell anybody that you were involved, that you saved my life, saved me from being raped and beaten up or whatever that psychopath would have done. I will not tell anybody, all I want to do, Dear George, is thank you with all my heart. Please let me do that and then we'll never talk about it again." George looked at the floor. His mind was running fast. For something that was supposed to be non-existing, as something that had never happened, action he could not officially be engaged in, this was pretty much all out there. Jack had been lucky guessing, but now this medic and now Victoria; and only God knew who else. "The medic knew you from some incident at the Pentagon. He knows who you are." He gently took her hand, looked in to her eyes and gave her a soft smile. His voice was only a whisper.

"You are welcome, Victoria." She cried for a few minutes and they sat quietly in a long embrace. She had no idea that anybody in the whole world would have risked their own life to save hers. But here he was, this sweet, loveable man. She really didn't have words to describe the gratitude and how fortunate she was with a friend like George Winston Miller - her gentle hero.

Sara and Jack's life rolled along. Michael was now 15, Jasper 12, Caroline 5 and Molly 11. Sara was deeply involved with her corporate law practice, a firm she started up with two other women. Jack had plenty to look after at CR, and Nora had proven herself a solid administrator. The long term business from the Virginia Project and several additional referrals, all brought plenty of work and profits. They were treating the employees like family and when things were going very well, everybody would participate in bonuses and other rewards. But it took lots of hours of work, so Nora and Jack spent large quantities of time together, slaving away at all hours.

Victoria recuperated satisfactory, though the pale scar down the side of her face was the best the dermatologists' could do. She accepted that and after her lengthy hospital stay, she was soon back in action. Three new employees had replaced Fielder and his whipping boys, but she stayed the highest producer of sales the company had ever had. Mentally she was fighting nightmares and a phobia of being alone in her apartment; but it was getting better as the days and nights slipped by. Her relationship with Sara and Jack had improved, and she felt she had finally found her sister as her sister had found her. Jack, as always, was, well Jack. Victoria had neither been dating nor seeking any male companionships; work was her fulltime drug, with the occasional interlude of dreamy fantasies with her and Jack making love. She accepted that she was still very much hooked on him, but she would never again let that get in the way of their friendship; and that was more than okay, as some-Jack was better than no-Jack. *Go figure*, she often said to herself. Life was rolling along, precisely as it was supposed to.

"Good morning, Sara."
"Yeah! And the same to you, Buster!" She responded with a jab to his chest.
"Oh I see it's beating up the spouse day today; long night?"
"Got home around eleven and it was a very long day too; thank you. How about you?"
"Rolled in around nine; thought that I would spent time with the kids." Sara looked surprised in a mocking way.
"Kids? We have kids? How many?"
"I believe three or four."
"What do you know, you turn your back for a day or so, and *wham* you have kids." Jack smiled.
"Yeah, funny the way that happens."
"Do we know who the mother is?"
"They are still working on it."
"Well good; keep me informed."
"Will do; coffee?"
"It's a two morning."
"Two cups coming up." And Jack started the coffeemaker and proceeded to make breakfast. He moved closer to Sara as she was inhaling her daily multi vitamin.
"I think we better get this out of the way before the kids get here." He grabbed Sara around the waist and pulled her close." She was fighting it a bit.
"Who are you? And be aware that my husband will be back from bowling real soon, so hurry up." She lifted herself up on her toes and a moist kiss was exchanged.
"Wow, Miss; you are rather good at this thing."
"From years of intense training; let's try it again, maybe it was just luck." They kissed again and finished with a tender embrace.
"Get a room." Jasper entered the kitchen and was shaking his head.
"Good morning to you as well, Dear Jasper." Jack tried to grab his younger son.
"Get a room? That sounds like a good idea; what do you think, Jack?" He reached for Sara's hand. "We'll be back in ten minutes. Watch the pancakes, Jasper."
"You guys are disgusting."

"So they are at it again, huh?" Michael had picked up the paper from the porch and was scanning the front page. Without looking up he continued: "What about taking a break once in a while?" Now he was also shaking his head. Jasper was flipping pancakes, one of his favorite things to do for breakfast.

"They never do; it's an ongoing annoyance, and in front of innocent children."

"When are we eating?" Michael asked.

"Twenty minutes with your help." He put the paper down and started to set the table.

"I'm hungry!" Caroline was wearing a pajama many sizes too big. Her feet stuck into huge fluffy bunnies. Jack looked at her and smiled.

"And you need to eat a lot more to fill that thing out. Is that Molly's discarded nightwear?" He lifted Caroline up. She eagerly nodded.

"Yes it is and it's my favorite." She hugged her father tightly.

"So how's the most favorite daughter of mine, the pick of the litter doing this morning?"

"I'm your only daughter, Dad."

"Yes, as far as I know; but that makes you even more special." He gave her a kiss and put her back down on the floor. Michael didn't look up.

"That's favoritism at work. You never pick me up anymore, Dad, and why is that?"

"Very strict orders from my chiropractor; it's nothing personal, Michael."

"He doesn't have a chiropractor." Sara whispered loudly in her son's ear.

"But if I did, that is what he would say."

"Assuming it was a *he* and not a s*he*." Sara smiled as she scrambled some eggs.

"Oh, you female evangelizers!" Sara laughed.

"Women evangelizers? What the heck does that mean?" Jack pouted.

"I'm not telling…" Jack smiled and sipped some life-giving caffeinated morning liquid.

"So how old is grandpa today?" Jasper was asking.

"Good memory, son. He'll hit the ripe age of approximately 162, give or take, a lot."

"Dad!" Caroline was hitting his leg.

"Okay, my little litter pick, it's actually 114."

"Mom, tell Dad to be normal."

"Sweetheart, I have told him so many times and this is what we get, sorry."

"Nice choice, Mom." Jasper was rolling his eyes, "real nice selection."

"Princess C, my dear father will be 63 today."

"So when you add it all up, Grandpa had Dad when he was ten." Sara was laughing at Michael's comment.

"Well, that explains a lot." She said while kissing Jack's cheek. Caroline looked puzzled.

"Is that true, Dad?"

"No, my slightly confused child, Dad was actually 12." Caroline still looked puzzled at the same time Molly entered the kitchen with a cup in her hand.

"We ran out of sugar." Her smile was wide and white. Jack bent down towards her.

"I know you: you are that Molly West person from next door. You can't fool me, hiding behind an empty cup. So how's my favorite neighbor girl this morning?" Molly laughed as she swung her arms around Jack's neck and squeezed hard.

"Now I'm really fine." Jack held her tight for a moment. Sara was next to them.

"And what about me?" Molly let free of Jack and was quickly in a bear-hug with Sara. She continued hugging everybody, finishing with Caroline.

"You know where the sugar is," and she did.

"Hey so are you all having breakfast?" Jasper tickled her.

"Yes Molly, that's normally the meal we eat at this time."

"It looks yummy." Molly moistened her lips.

"Grab a chair, girl." And she did. They were all gathered around the kitchen table and loud busy chatter soon filled the room.

It was not often that they were all together at meals. Either Jack was missing or Sara and in many cases both. They did reserve one full day a week, all five, actually all six, to do fun things and spend time together. Often they left D.C. for day trips and at times overnighters. Molly's grandparents felt very happy for Molly that the Miller's had somewhat adopted and included her in all their activities.

When they were out traveling, Molly stayed with the Millers and though she had the guest room to herself, she still preferred to stay with Caroline in her room. Michael and Jasper protected her as a sister; Caroline was positive that she *was* her sister and knew she was her best friend in the whole world. Molly, on the other hand, though only 11, for some reason didn't see herself as a sister or belonging to the Millers other than being a family friend. There had always been some form of independence about her, especially after her parents died. Not in her younger years, but as she had gotten older; this independent side grew stronger and stronger as the years rolled along. Every time her grandparents uttered: *But they are like family to you*, she adamantly underlined that they were not and would embrace them and sweetly say: ***You** are my only family and the only family I'll ever need.* There was no bitterness, disappointment or sadness in that statement; it was just the way Molly felt about it. The only other person who fully agreed with her was Jack. She loved Jack for that and for so many other reasons, of course. He was funny and silly and at times rather weird, but he was also thoughtful and very generous to her as well as he was to his family. Molly saw the relationship between Sara and Jack was filled with fun and love and respect. She was treated with the same fun, love and respect from them, as well as Michael, Jasper and Caroline were.

      She had her own key to the Miller house, so she could pop in anytime at all. When she was younger she had gone through a long period of vicious nightmares and many times she had sneaked over to the Miller house in the middle of the night and found comfort in Sara and Jack's bed. She had seen a psychiatrist about her violent dreams and after many tests, trials and errors, they found the only remedy that really helped her, was the comfort and safety she found sleeping between Sara and Jack. It had been a long spell of three months. One night Molly knocked on their bedroom door; Sara knew who it was right away and Molly had raced in and jumped up in the bed.

"Bad dreams?" Molly was grinning from ear to ear.

"No bad dreams anymore; they are gone." Sara had hugged her and Jack smiled big.

"Good Golly Miss Molly; you got rid of them, huh?" He also gave her a hug. She looked at both of them:
"Can I stay with you tonight even though I don't have bad dreams anymore, please?" That was the last night she ever spent between Sara and Jack in their bed.

Look up *tomboy* in the dictionary, and it will no doubt include Molly West. It wasn't that she was boyish to any extremes or not girlish enough; it was somewhat of a confusing mix of the two, but a mix Molly juggled very well. Her social life was pretty much non-existent. She didn't feel she was on the same level with other kids, so for the most she kept to herself. She was a top student, but often extremely bored which brought her in trouble with teachers and caused many visits to the principal's office. The teachers kept encouraging Molly to read books beyond her maturity level. It was more so to keep her occupied and quiet, and Molly knew that. For the most the subjects were boring and uninteresting for her, until she found books about Africa in her grandparent's house.

Anna and Harry West were deeply involved with UNICEF and dedicated to helping unfortunate children through this international organization. Due to their financial status, they had helped set up kindergartens, elementary schools and health care centers in Africa. Their many travels were dedicated to whatever they could do to help and wherever they were needed. They had established offices in Casablanca, Morocco, from where a small staff managed their numerous projects. They had named it The West Foundation. Besides their own money, donations from friends and solicited participation from several corporations in America, kept the help expanding. Molly had been on one of their many trips, but she had only been seven and had not fully grasped what was going on, other than she had a lot of new kids to play with every day for months.

Now, though only eleven, she had decided what direction her future was heading. When Molly explained her plans to Sara, she could only smile as she saw herself at eleven when she had already been ready to implement the route towards her goals; as Molly, she knew precisely what she wanted. Molly was a carbon copy of Sara in that respect, but she had never been as eccentric as Molly, she thought with a big smile. The maturity level was far beyond her age and at times that part was very challenging, not just for Molly, but also for her surroundings. Did you talk with an eleven year old girl or a thirty-two year old woman? But you never doubted who Molly was when she spent time with Caroline. The six year difference was not obvious when you saw them together. Caroline was very attentive to what Molly did, what Molly said and how Molly acted; she was the tutor with Caroline as the willing student. After just a few years of their friendship, it was easy to see that Caroline had jumped ahead academically on all levels. She was an advanced reader, very good in pre-math and her writing was extraordinary. Molly also encouraged her to go jogging with her, Sara and Jack once in a while, and Caroline's legs moved as fast as such small legs could carry her; she wanted to be as fast as Molly. Their friendship was obvious to anybody who saw them and very clear to the girls. And life kept rolling along, one day after the other.

Michael and Jasper were brothers and not much more than that in their relationship. It wasn't that they just tolerated each other as such, but their personalities were worlds apart. Michael was outgoing, a bit cynical, though not in a bitter way, where Jasper pretty much spent most of the time by himself, though his relationship with his mother was exceptional. Sara and Jasper had long conversations filled with common interests, humor and lots of love. Sara sought Jasper's company as he sought hers just as often. They went jogging together whenever possible, drank buckets of tea, movies, museums and through it all chatted away big time. Jasper's relationship with his father was a bit more reserved; it wasn't that he didn't like his father; it was just that the relationship with his mother was so much stronger.

Michael was more of an equal opportunity child: loved Mom and Dad the same. He was a very diplomatic soul and good at pleasing everybody around him. But one strong bond the two brothers had in common was their innate love for Caroline as well as for Molly. They were extremely protective of the girls and made sure they were treated nicely and were safe. The first time they met Molly, she had raced straight into their hearts and they immediately adopted her as their sister on the same scale as Caroline was.

The times the boys and the girls were together, were the times when Sara and Jack would observe in awe. The four children would laugh and play and interact with love and respect. Those were the times that especially Jasper opened up and was as engaged as any of them. *The Four Musketeers*, as Jack called them.

Romano Rossi was scanning the crowd with a satisfied look on his face. The evening was already buzzing as the guests were eating, drinking, smiling and laughing between lots of chatter. He had at first wanted Piatti di Nonna to be a family style restaurant, but quickly realized that for him to survive in Washington D.C. most of his customers would predominantly be wearing suits and carry briefcases. But since he still dreamed *family restaurant*, tonight was very special; it was George Miller's birthday party and every time the Millers made reservations, they would bring all the kids along and Romano adored those evenings. The noise from the mixture of adults and bambinos brought him straight back to Mirandola Bassa where he grew up.

Mirandola was located in the Province of Verona in Northern Italy, not far from the river. As a young boy his grandmother insisted that her only grandchild learned to cook; it was her passion so she thought he should make it his passion as well. Cooking with his grandmother had quickly become an obsession with him. Many hours were spent in the kitchen preparing traditional Italian meals and creating new versions of old recipes. It had quickly become a big part of his being; not only did he learn to cook, he also learned about life from an old and very wise woman. When his Nonna died, he was only 16 and devastated – but he kept on cooking.

His grandmother had often joked, that some day he should go to America to open a restaurant and serve original Italian food, the kind of food they had cooked together so many years. They would laugh and hug and he would whisper his promise in her ear, the promise that he would do precisely that for her.

The day after his 18th birthday, Romano was on his way to America, sponsored by his aunt and uncle who lived in Virginia. By the time he was 24 he had barely scraped enough money together, but forged ahead anyway, made his dream come true and delivered what he had promised; he named the restaurant *Piatti di Nonna* in memory of his grandmother. He thought about naming it *Grandma's Dishes*, but the Italian version was after all more appropriate.

The first many months were scary with only few customers; he kept losing money he didn't have. In spite of that he felt that someday his luck would turn; and he was right. It all turned for the better when the people from Anchor, the big corporation located just a few blocks away, had started coming to the restaurant. Employees started arrive by themselves, then in groups, then with clients and then with families and friends; the proverbial meatball started to roll. It all began when a young executive from Anchor, Victoria Grant, had visited the restaurant with a colleague. She had enjoyed the food and the atmosphere so much that she had returned the next night and the next and the next. She had been a Godsend for Romano and business started to grow. Politicians, government officials and workers also started to show up, so it was often extremely lively and very loud; just what Nonna would have loved. Romano did believe in his heart that she was looking down from above and approved everything she saw. He always missed her, and at times painfully so. The big picture of his smiling grandmother on the wall did ease the pain somewhat. But no sorrow and sadness tonight, he thought; tonight was going to be fun and family.

Sara, Jack and the kids had arrived first. Romano received hugs from everybody and still got a giggle when the kids called him *Uncle Roma*, something they had done from the first time they visited the restaurant. Colleen and Charles showed up, as well as Nora and an apparent boyfriend. William arrived together with his mother and Victoria. Romano wondered if there was something going on as he had never seen them arrive together. He did notice the way William kept looking at Victoria with those big puppy eyes; he smiled at the thought. William was such a nice man and Romano felt that maybe a connection between him and Victoria was developing. He absolutely adored Victoria. She had become a close friend and he pretended in secret that she was his daughter. Many times she would come to the restaurant by herself. She would look tired, but he also saw loneliness and a bit of sadness. Most of those nights he would sit at her table and they would have long conversations about work, about life, about Italy and just about anything. After she was done eating he would walk her home; she only lived a few blocks from the restaurant. As they walked, she would snuggle up to him with her arm in his and in front of her building they would double cheek kiss and he would wait till she was safe inside the lobby. If only he had been a lot younger, he sighed.

    George and William's mother came in often, but Romano didn't really know if their relationship was more than friends. George was such a gentleman and William's mother had the loveliest laughter and George could sure make her use it again and again. Over the years George had been eating with many different women, and he pretty much made them all laugh; Romano thought that William's mother would be the perfect fit. But he also knew from the way George told him about how he had met Irene and how much he still loved her, that another romance in George's life seemed impossible. It was a pity, he thought, as George obviously had so much to give. His grandchildren adored him and the way he interacted with them, he clearly adored them back. It had taken Romano a few visits from the Millers to find out that Molly was not their daughter. Jack had told him that, on the side, kind of. But they all treated her as a family member. She was energetic and seemingly beyond her age on many levels. Romano loved it when she would come and sit on his lap and just listen to the chatter, participating, laughing and enjoying herself. He often saw her glued to Sara as well as she seemed to have a special love for Jack. He'd always tease her and make her laugh. Romano knew her sad story and was happy to see how she, over the years, had become a solid part of this family. Michael, Jasper, Caroline and Molly were always bouncing around from one person to another, having a great time. When the meals were served, Jack would ask them the sit down, and they would all do so immediately.

    Tonight William was sitting next to Victoria and he could sure entertain her, which warmed Romano's heart, but with a bit of fatherly jealousy. Nora was sitting between Jack and her male companion and having a good time. Nora and Jack came to the restaurant several times a week. They seemed to be doing well with their business and well in their relationship. At times they'd run in to Victoria and they would quickly gather at one table chatting away. Romano had noticed early on that she looked at Jack very differently than she looked at anybody else. She would often reach across the table and touch his hands or his arms. He would to some extend do the same, but the way Victoria did it, told Romano that there had to be more to it than met the eye. One evening, as he walked Victoria home, she had unsolicited talked about her past relationship with Jack, sparing no details. She also admitted to him, that she was still in love with him, but that she would never let that interfere with their friendship. To Romano it was a little sad, as she was a beautiful and vibrant young woman, successful and headstrong. There had to be somebody else out there for her; and if she ever found that someone, he would be an extremely fortunate man indeed. But she was not looking. Sure she had lots of *wannabe boyfriends*, but obviously not any prospects she showed the slightest interest in. Was it different with William? She did look at him with wider smiles and lots of laughter and she did touch his arm at times, or was it just something Romano observed with hope? She deserved to be happy, she really did.

He remembered the first evening Jack had visited the restaurant. Victoria and Jack had been laughing and smiling and chatting and eating as well as a bit of drinking; well, actually a lot of drinking, certainly more than Victoria would normally consume. It was the first time Victoria had brought a male friend with her. Romano was immediately curious as to who he was. He seemed nice and was very attentive to Vicky and she seemed extremely relaxed in his company. It warmed Romano's heart to see her so happy.

Jack had come in a week later with his wife Sara. A few days after that, Jack had brought the black woman by and he learned that she was Jack's partner Nora. He had been invited to join them after their meal, and Romano found that Nora was funny and sharp. It didn't take him long to fall in love with her as well, in that kind of parental way. She left before Jack, so Jack and Romano went through a bottle of Chianti and conversation. From that evening on, their friendship had grown steadily. Sure they had all started out as customers, but now they were family. Life was good for Romano and it would have been perfect if his Nonna could have been here.

The evening had gone well and parting was as usual Romano's worst part. He wanted them to stay forever, all these wonderful people. Hugs and embraces plentiful and soon he were sitting at a table with his staff, sharing a glass of vino to let the evening wind down and out. As he walked around in the empty restaurant and turned off the lights, he blew a kiss towards the picture of his grandmother. He smiled with eyes getting moist.
"Grazie, Nonna!" As he was locking and securing the front door, an arm snuggled into his. He knew who it was right away; she had been waiting for him.
"Feel like walking me home, Valentino?" Victoria went straight to the point, as she always did: "What do you think about William?" Romano smiled. So he hadn't been wrong in his assumption.
"Besides that he looks at you with puppy eyes, yes?" Victoria laughed.
"Roma, they all do – haven't you noticed?"
"I have noticed plenty."
"William is a smart man, very smart and I really find that appealing."
"*Smarter than you* kind of appealing?" Victoria laughed again.
"Nobody's smarter than me; you should know that by now?"
"I do."
"He's also funny and tentative, well funny with a lot of sarcasm attached."
"Does that bother you?"
"Not really, but at times it sounds cynical, like he has an axe to grind."
"Maybe he does?"
"I don't know." There was a pause as they strolled along.
"Vicky, I believe that when we have to deal with shyness and insecurities, we tend to cover it up by using sarcasm or cynicism and especially humor. We feel that by doing so we are maybe not leaving ourselves so open – perhaps." Victoria smiled.
"I thought about that. But to me William seems too smart to have to cover anything up."

"So maybe he is just a funny guy, huh?"

"I'd like to think so." They were now in front of Victoria's apartment building. Romano faced her and grabbed her hands.

"Vicky, you are one of the most competent, charming, beautiful and intelligent women any man could ever wish for." Victoria actually blushed. "The man you will hopefully meet some day will have a lot to live up to, but I know there got to be one out there for you. I would never ask you to lower your expectations, but I would ask you to keep looking if they are not met. Now, William might be it, and since you asked me about him, I think you ought to explore a bit more. I would hate to see you get burned..."

"Like Jack?"

"Like Jack; but let's not bring him along. Don't compare Jack with any likeable prospects. Nobody can beat the Jack you have on your mind and in your heart, so don't make it an unfair contest."

"I'm sorry. I'll keep him out." They kissed and Victoria was soon safe in the lobby. Before the door closed she smiled. "Why couldn't you be a lot younger, Roma?" And she waved. *Yes, why not indeed,* he thought as he walked home to his wife.

His mother had been talking the whole way home. George's birthday party had been loud and fun. He had enjoyed observing his mother having a good time next to George. He knew they saw each other often, but he wasn't really sure what kind of relationship they had, and he also knew that it was not any of his business. His mother was old enough to take care of herself. Victoria had been lovely, absolutely lovely all evening. Admittedly he was falling for her big time, but didn't have a clue as to what she felt about him. Sure he was neither Adonis nor Freud or any combination of the two and being an accountant removed all possibilities of being considered a stud-muffin; so was that *strike three and out*? He had talked with Jack about her, but Jack had not taken him serious, so he was on his own. Victoria had the last few times they met, casually as it was, been very personal, asking a lot of questions about him. He had felt relaxed and comfortable with the interrogation, but never considered it a possible boyfriend research approach.

She had sounded genuinely interested in him and about what he had been up to in his life. She had also asked questions about his future plans and again, he had been straight forward and honest. He never sugarcoated or bloated his thoughts and feelings and maybe Victoria had sensed that. If she was going to like him, it was going to be him she would like, not a pretend William, no Sir, not his style. He was careful concerning calling her for no other reason than to chat. He knew she was often tired and worn down, so he refrained from bothering her at those times. But then Victoria had started calling him late nights when they had both turned in or were close to. At first it had been a couple of times a week, but now it was more often. As they said goodnight she would always ask if it was okay to call him again some other night. He never said no. And then he called her once and she had sounded very tired, but he sensed that she was happy that he'd called. If nothing else, William felt they were becoming friends, and if that was all he could get out of his relationship with Victoria, that would be more than fine with him. He also felt that maybe it would develop to more than that, but as status quo, this was pretty great.

Shortly after William had brought his mother home, he entered his own apartment, undressed, brushed his teeth, tucked himself in and dialed Victoria's number.

"What took you so long, Billy-Boy?" Her voice was a bit sleepy, but sounded glad. Billy-Boy smiled. *Lovely*, he thought.

"Vicky-Baby, you are way too impatient." A short pause occurred. "But I agree, it's been too long. I missed you." Victoria was giggling sleepily.

"I missed you too, William."

*****

The early parole hearing had been allowed due to exemplary good behavior by the prisoner. As he explained to the board, he had found God in Christianity and he had fully repented his crimes. It was with great sorrow he realized that what he had done was so terribly wrong and was also punishable in the eyes of the Good Lord above. But he had found forgiveness from God and was now looking for forgiveness from the victim and pleading his case for an early release.

To the commissioners, the prisoner's demeanor had appeared soft and quiet. They felt he was honest concerning his regrets and that he would more than likely be able to refit himself into society and become a law-abiding and productive citizen again. They all seemed to be in agreement at this point.

As he was removed from his cell, he had been told that the hearing was open, so he expected to see her again. As he entered the room, he looked around, but only saw an older grey haired man sitting in the back, leaning his chair against the wall. He had just finished his plea and felt that the commissioners were in favor of releasing him. At that moment a clerk entered the room and handed a note to the commissioner placed in the middle. She immediately called for a short recess and he was quickly led out by the guards.

The commissioners had each been given a letter which they opened and read. They conversed for a short moment, heads together and quickly nodded in agreement. The prisoner was brought back in and was not asked to sit down. One of the board members spoke immediately. It was in a cold and hard tone that *parole was denied.* He froze instantly as the hammer came down hard. Had they just refused his parole? Was that what he just heard? His head was spinning. How could they deny his release? He had done everything he was supposed to do to get the hell out of prison. He had even played the *I found God* - shit. He had done everything possible and they fucking denied his release! What was going on here? The guard's hands had a solid hold of his upper arms and were firmly guiding him out of the room. It was then he got another glimpse of the old man. He was sitting in the same position as he had all through the hearing, arms stretched out and legs crossed. Suddenly he knew who he was. Both of his mangled and cuffed hands shot up to his face and his deformed fingers ran along the severe scar tracking from his temple to his jaw. Now he knew who he was and he realized in horror why he was here. *Just you wait you prick, I'll pay you back one of these days.* He was screaming out loud; but fortunately for him, it could only be heard inside his own sick head.

Life for the Millers, their families and their friends rolled along. For the most they were functional and happy lives, mixed with the normal controversies and obstacles to be solved and overcome. The whole gang pretty much got along and they tested that as often as possible. Any reason to get together was utilized and even if they didn't have a specific reason, just getting together would be reason enough.

Sara and Jack's life was not fully based on the planned and scheduled ideas of the younger Sara anymore. Though she was still stubbornly headstrong and knew precisely what she wanted, when she wanted it and why she wanted it, she had also come to realize that dealing with a husband, bringing up three plus one kids, a home, two business' and all the additional trimmings, sure called for more flexibility than planning; even perfect predetermined plans and schedules could not win that battle. Sara was more than fine with that. Sure their daily lives had to be organized, so Sara had everybody meet once every weekend, when they were actually all together in one place at the same time, which was often a problem. They added their schedules to the master schedule, which was the large calendar in the kitchen. This way everybody would somewhat know where most were at all times – at least that was the plan. As Molly spent more time with the Millers than with her grandparents, she was as much part of the kitchen calendar and the household as anybody else.

Sara, now 39, was very involved with her law firm. It was long hours, constant court appearances, travel and many conferences; she was on the go most of the time from early morning to early evening. She rarely brought work home as the time there was for Jack and her, as well as for the kids – nothing else. That was a rule Jack and Sara had agreed on a long time ago and a rule they rarely broke.

Jack adored Sara. When they were together, a lot of the same feelings persisted from that first time they had met so many years ago; they literally couldn't keep their hands off. The kid's stable comment was the old and reliable *Get a room!* Molly was the only one who never used that phrase. Jack and Sara would travel on getaway trips to find romantic places on the Atlantic coast, New England in the fall and the

Florida beaches in the summer. Their conversations were at times heated and stubborn, at times silly and funny, serious and direct. When they were lying in bed holding hands, the glow on their faces would tell the full story. Happiness comes in many packages, Sara and Jack's happiness came in a huge gift-wrapped box, filled to the top.

Jack, Nora and the rest of the CR family of employees felt fortunate as the business had stayed profitable. They were still the Virginia Project's main contractor and that didn't seem to be ending any time soon. CR had first right of refusal to any new proposals, which was an option they never used. Whenever the jobs were bigger than they could manage with their core staff, they would hire additional help. Nora kept proving her abilities running a tight ship. Jack had improved his marketing skills, but with stable clients like the Virginia Group and Anchor, *selling* was not something he had to do often. His focus was on getting the jobs done efficiently and on time.

Jack and Nora's relationship beyond work had solidified their good friendship. They liked spending time together at work, the occasional lunches and dinners, or just productive walks around town, discussing business. Nora was a big part of the Millers life and she especially loved the kids. For some reason she related more so to Molly than to the others. Molly consistently surprised her with her thoughts, her mature, though at times, very eccentric ideas. It was as if Molly spent a lot of time in another place, on another planet. Nora had discussed this with her many times and they always ended up laughing about it.

Nora had not been dating much; didn't seem to be something that was on top of her list of priorities. Early on she had spent a few months together with William in a short term relationship that had been fun, interesting and intimate, in an exciting and satisfying way. But after a while they agreed to go back to friends again; friends without the commitment. And they did just that. They had continued the occasional intimate moments for a while, but found that the sex was not as much fun anymore and not as intense as it had been in the beginning, so that stopped as well. They had never told Jack or Sara about this *interlude*, this intimate relationship of theirs, but Jack and Sara had known about it from the day it started. They had silently wanted Nora and William to become more committed than dating, so not to jinks their hopes, they had kept quiet; obviously that did not work at all.

It was shortly after William and Nora had called it quits when William was sitting next to Victoria at a CR company picnic. It had been more or less by chance, as he always believed that Victoria was so out of his league for him to even be considered any form of potential dating material. So it wasn't that he had avoided her, but more so that he had written her off his list of hopefuls and moved her directly into his fantasies. But they had started talking and Victoria had taken the lead, which totally surprised him. He had been nervous and uncomfortable in the beginning, but he found her easy to converse with, as she was a terrific listener. It was a few weeks later that they hooked up again at a dinner at Colleen and Charles' house. It seemed by sheer coincident they ended up next to each other, but neither of them was against that at all. William had told Victoria that he had thought a lot about her since the picnic. She had laughed and William was sure any further positive development between them had just been shot out of the water in one swell swoop. But she had touched his hand and smiled at him. With a little squeeze she told him that she had also thought about him a bit and in a good way. So they had slowly started with the late night phone conversations, filling each other in on the day's highlights. It morphed into relaxed lunches at Nonna's, then dinners, a few short hikes on weekends, a movie and constantly long chats. Victoria seemed to enjoy herself and he knew that though she was a tough nail to do business with, from his capacity as CR's accountant, she was sweet and thoughtful on the other side, the side of her that he was seriously falling in love with. They were not intimate, only with a bit of handholding and a few light kisses here and there. But he was in no hurry.

The dinner had been long and as usual vivid and entertaining. William was clearing the table as Victoria sat and sipped more wine. She had laughed a lot, something he adored and could listen to forever. But now she was all of a sudden quiet and seemed thoughtful.

"William, come and sit here, please." She had moved over to the couch near the window. He did. Victoria held his hand and looked at him.

"I really like you; I like you very much."

"I like you too, Victoria." She smiled.

"No William, you are in love with me; see that's the difference." He nodded in agreement. "I love you too, but I'm not *in love* with you and that makes me sad."

"What do you mean?"

"What I mean is that I really want to be in love with you, I really do, but it's not a feeling I can force or fake. You are such a wonderful man, you are funny, you are smart and charming and I could go on..."

"Please do!" She smiled.

"But in spite of all these great things about you, I can't seem to fall in love with you.

"It's because I'm an accountant, isn't it?" He tried with a bit of humor; Victoria smiled.

"No, because this accountant is sexy and funny, so that's not it." She paused and turned serious again. "Trust me William, I have tried so hard to find a way, but so far I have not succeeded. And it has nothing to do with you; it's all coming from me." William was going to be very careful with the next question.

"I'll sound a bit paranoid and naïve, but is there somebody else?" The answer could be his kiss of death – and he knew it. Victoria's eyes slowly became moist and then the tears started down her face. The grip on his hands became tighter.

"I have really tried. I really want to fall in love with you, but I haven't found the way yet, but maybe someday. Would you be patient with me?" She looked straight at him.

"I have to think about that, Victoria, but you didn't answer my question." His voice was quiet and soft. She looked down.

"No, there is nobody else. It's all me." William was disappointed as she had not answered the question honestly. He knew the score, but he wanted Victoria to face up to it and in some way handle it, if she possible could.

"Victoria, please don't lie to me. I don't deal with lies very well. I'm a heck of a lot better at handling truth and honesty. At least I know where I stand. So please be a pal and don't take me for a fool; I deserve better than that." She froze at his words. They sounded bitter and distraught. How could he know? Was it that obvious?

"What do you mean?"

"Victoria Grant, please stop right now, okay?" Her tears flowed freely. He pulled her into his arms and he knew he would have a very hard time letting her go. Her head was resting on his chest.

"How do you know?"

"From the first time I saw you and Jack in the same room, same space, it was bleeding obvious that you were so much in love with him. That hasn't changed a bit. Maybe it has even gotten stronger. The way you look at him, the way you touch him, the more extended embraces and hugs; much more for him, much less for others. The kisses lingering longer on his lips than on others." He paused. "Should I go on?" She was whimpering quietly.

"I'm sorry; I'm so sorry." William gently pushed her away and held her in arms length. His voice was firm and clear.

"Don't feel sorry for me. I knew what I was competing against but I kept quiet about it. I didn't want to rock *our* love boat. I am not a stupid man, Victoria, but I was naïve in believing that through my wit, charm and stunningly good looks, I could eliminate your innate obsession with a man who will never be yours in any shape or form, other than being a good friend. But I can assure you that if you don't play that friendship part correctly, he will drop you like a hot potato – I know him that well and better than you'll ever know him." Victoria had never seen that side of William. He took a deep breath and continued. "I assume you agree, as you don't say anything". She nodded quietly. "Now since I'm on a roll: *Yes* I am in love with you, but it's wearing off bit by bit as I normally restrain myself from engaging in impossible battles. But this is not a war against Jack, as he is not the enemy. It's a war against your pathetic obsession with this fantasy person, this impossible quest of yours, to finally win him over, making him yours and only yours. Earth to Victoria: It will never happen - ever." Her tears were rolling and dripping on to her blouse.

"I'm sorry, William." He shook his head and let out a deep breath.

"At this point, I don't think I give a damn, seriously. I'm giving up. I have tried to accept the score and I knew it was an uphill battle I couldn't win. And I think that even if I did win, I probably wouldn't want to keep the trophy for very long. You would no doubt fall back to the pathetic obsession bit, and I'd be left rejected again. I don't want to put myself in that situation. There are many other fish in the water and I'm a patient man, so someday I'll catch the one that's meant for me." William got up from the couch and grabbed his jacket. Victoria looked up at him.

"I'm not the one for you?"

"Frankly me dear, at this point you are not. I did my bit, but you couldn't do yours. That's not a combination that will go anywhere." He walked towards the front door and turned. "It really is a great loss for both of us, Victoria. We like each other, we are compatible, we have fun, great moments of togetherness and I'm convinced that the sex would have been out of this world. But you couldn't do your part, or *wouldn't* do your part. What a terrible waste that is." He turned towards the door again, but William didn't feel he had finished. He came back and sat on the armrest of a chair in front of Victoria. She was clinching a little as it looked like more would be coming her way. He made a grimace before he continued. "Isn't it ironic that here you are telling me that you are in love with somebody else and I get up and leave? Doesn't that remind you of something similar, so many years ago?" Victoria knew precisely what he was talking about. She had never thought that Jack would have told anybody about that night. "So now you are doing precisely to me what Jack did to you, with the only difference that I won't dwell on the bloody possibilities of *what ifs*. I'm forty years old and I don't have the time. Besides that, fanatic obsessions about something or somebody impossible and unrealistic, is not my cup of tea and that'll never ever change." He went over to the dinner table and poured a glass full of wine, took a sip and sat back down. Victoria froze and knew he was right about everything he had said.

"But Jack deceived me, he threw me out." She stuttered. "He broke our love."

"Please grow up, Victoria. You are such a wizard concerning the business you're in. You are assertive, aggressive, organized and you get things done to perfection. You are a true master in your field, probably one of the best in the country. You are in control of every bloody detail of every project I have been privileged to be involved in with you at the wheel. You make people jump through flaming hoops again and again, and though they know you are pushing them hard for the results that *you* want, that *you* must have, they all come back for more because they know they are dealing with one of the best, namely Victoria Grant. But when you cannot figure out how to rid yourself from this pathetic, immature and utterly boring self destruction of believing that you are so much in love with Jack, this phantom image, a fixation of love that will never ever be returned the way you wish it would, then the majestic picture of the business genius falls apart. You become this little whimpering and idiotic piece of human being who has determined never to be happy without him; the *him,* who will never want you the way you want him - ever." Tears rolled down Victoria's face. He sipped more wine. "And for your information, Jack never loved you. He had a crush on you and was sexually inexperienced when you took him on as this little boy-project of yours and that made you interesting and exciting for him - in the beginning. He never loved you, because he had no bleeding clue what being in love was. But the funny thing is, if I'm not totally off track here, that suddenly *you* knew what it was to be in love – to be loved and respected, to have somebody genuinely like you for who you really are. You had screwed around with so many other boys, played with them and made them eat out of your hands and then discarded them when you got bored. But here comes a decent bloke who went from sexual interest to actually finding that Victoria wasn't such a bitch after all – the rumors were incorrect. She was actually warm and loving and gentle and smart, very smart, but obviously not smart enough to accept the score. Jack fell in love with somebody else. That was the part you absolutely couldn't handle, so you went through all this crap, all these plans of revenge and then even tried to seduce him years later when you knew he was married with kids and all. Rather pathetic, don't you think?" William's face had turned a bit red; he took another sip of wine.

"But he wanted me that night." She mumbled quietly. William laughed out loud.

"You got to be kidding. If you believe that, you are more naïve and delusional than I thought you were. Jack is a fucking pushover, Victoria, haven't you noticed?" She looked up and shook her head.

"What do you mean *pushover*?" He laughed even more.

"Don't get me wrong, I love Jack as if he was my most favorite brother, but the fact is that he's constantly been lead by others."

"What do you mean?"

"His father, dear George, has been the grand protector of Jack to make up for the fact that Jack's mother died when he was born. Jack's extra set of parents could not do enough for the boy. Sure it hasn't ruined him, but he was guided and handheld all through his childhood, even into adulthood." He took another sip. "Then you came along and he ate out of your hands immediately as you taught him many new intricate things. Then Sara took over where you left off and she pretty much told Jack how things were going to be from then on and way into the future. He wanted badly to finish school, but due to Sara's income, the kids and all the supporting duties that had to be kept going, he quit; he fucking quit. How do you like that?"

"But wasn't that his choice?"

"Believe what you want, but in my book he still regrets his *choice*, but in retrospect it wasn't his choice really – Sara supported this somewhat vague decision of not continuing school and that was enough for him to quit. Then Uncle Charles quickly presented Jack with a fat paycheck and the whole bloody business of CR Constructions on a silver plate. And guess who shows up next to hold Jack's hand? Jack's business solution and rescuer: Nora."

"You sound bitter concerning Jack."

"Victoria, you are lot listening. I love the guy. The question is that he is a pushover. He has had people around him forever who literally have shaped his life and guided him to where he is today."

"But he's very good at what he's doing; you know the father thing, work..." William scoffed.

"Pay attention and you'll learn. It's not a question if he is good or not; the question is that he was easily manipulated when he was younger. Today is another story, another Jack, but he's still guided by others. But mark my words, it's in his blood and might turn up again and again. I wouldn't be surprised." William was exhausted in a way, maybe more so bored and tired of this stupid conversation. He looked at Victoria and saw a miserably pathetic figure, locked in her own miserable world of make-believe. He felt that he didn't really desire her anymore. What a difference an hour makes, he thought with sadness.

He went over and picked up Victoria's wine glass, brought it into the kitchen and filled it halfway up. Her wet eyes followed his moves. She knew she was losing him, yet another man she loved, because she did love William. He looked beaten as he poured the wine, his shoulders slumped and his face sad. He handed her the glass and sat down on the very edge of the armrest. It looked like he was getting ready to leave; she really didn't want him to.

"What do you want me to do, William?" He looked at her.
"*Do,* concerning what?"
"About *us*."
"What about *us*? As far as I know there never was an *us*, so I have a problem seeing where that question is going."
"Aren't we friends?" William shook his head slowly.
"I don't know Victoria, not now. I'll have to think about that for some time and see if I can figure it out." She visually sank deeper into the sofa, took a labored breath and looked at him. Maybe she shouldn't tell him.
"You know what's even more pathetic?" She giggled tiredly, talking more so to herself.
"I can't wait to hear this one." His voice was cynical.
"I'm still a virgin." The words came out slowly but quietly. William's head snapped up.
"What? You gotta be kidding me!"
"I'm not kidding you. I have never slept with any man that way."
"You're 42 and you have never had intercourse?"
"Nope, never; well, sex all other ways, but not that one." His head was spinning as the answer to his next question would either make Victoria a total moron or a rare angel; he formulated the question very slowly.
"I'm afraid to ask, but all this time, have you been saving yourself for Jack?" His eyes got wider, as he didn't want to miss the answer. Victoria nodded slowly up and down; her voice was just a whisper.

"Yes." William didn't know if he should laugh or cry. So she was a total moron, not a title he could fall in love with. How crazy could she be? She was crying now, shoulders shaking, breathing forced and uneven. She had pulled a pillow up to her face, as to dampen the sounds of her confusion and despair. William went over and sat next to her. She rushed into his embrace, resting her head on his chest. The crying didn't stop for a long time. He stayed with her till she calmed down.

"You understand why I can't be with you, don't you?" She nodded. "You have a great deal of superb things going for you Victoria and we have already gone through those attributes of yours several times tonight. But you more so have some huge issues that *you* have to fix, *you* have to figure out, as nobody else can. But I cannot and I will not be part of the solution; that has to fully come from you alone. You understand that?" She nodded again. He kissed her forehead and got up.

"Fortunately it is Sunday tomorrow, so maybe a good long rest will help a bit."

He left her apartment in bitterness and was on the way to his car. The night was beautifully black and after a few deep intakes of the fresh and cool air, William felt a bit better, actually he felt rather relieved. He had wanted to confront Victoria with that Jack situation; he was tired of tiptoeing around the fire. That it could cost the possibilities for them, he was very saddened about. He also thought that if he hadn't told her, nobody else would have. But it was at a high cost, and that was not good, but it was something he could find a way to live with. Tomorrow he would call Nora. She was good at giving advice and a terrific listener and that was what he really needed.

Victoria emptied the bottle of wine and was soon tucked in. She left the light on, something she had done since the attack. Being alone was still very uncomfortable for her. After that night, George had some of his people install security equipment all over the place. If anything ever happened again, he would be the first to be called. He also had the doorman exchanged with one of his retired agents who needed a cushy job. How he had done that, she never figured out.

But now it was William who was on her mind. What he had said to her was devastating and though she was against admitting he was right, it was losing him that pained her the most. There were a lot of issues she had to deal with; she had to resolve her obsession and move free from Jack and then see where that would take her. She knew in her heart that she wanted William, but being with him and seeing images of Jack would never work. He was right: she would never catch Jack, so she had to let Jack go, now and forever. She was waiting hours for William to call, but it seemed the call never came.

When she teary-eyed finally fell asleep, the foul smelling man was on top of her within seconds, forcing his mouth against hers, ripping her nightgown to pieces with his deformed hands, groping her viciously, trying frantically and roughly to invade her body. She screamed and fought, she kicked and scratched. Minutes seemed like hours and the pain was horrific. Then everything went black and quiet; it had all ended in a flash of thunder as sudden as it had started. When she finally and hesitantly opened her eyes again, she saw that his face had exploded and felt brain matter and blood dripping down on her neck. She couldn't scream anymore, no matter how much she tried. Her throat was bone-dry and hurting. The scar had ripped open, wide from her temple to the jaw and the blood wouldn't stop running.

She sat up in the bed; her face wet from sweat and angst, her hands were shaking, her body trembling. The nightmares had gone on for so many years, but she had never told anybody. George was the only one who could read her; when he asked how she was doing, he knew she wasn't telling the truth. Though he knew she was lying, he never called her on it.

She washed her face and hands, drank some water and went back to bed. She cautiously picked up the phone and dialed the number. She heard the phone being picked up. Victoria's voice was trembling, weak and quietly pleading.
"I am so lost; oh God, I'm so lost. Will you please help me?" she listened for a moment, nodded her head and then listened again. "Yes, I know, sweetheart." She fell quiet as she dried more tears off her face. "I love you too." And she hung up.

"Good morning, Michael." He was scooping up breakfast cereal from a blue bowl in front of him.

"Morning, Dad." He kept eating and sipping orange juice.

"What's up, Son?"

"Not much."

"How's the *catch-a-thief* training going?"

"I assume you are referring to the Police Academy!"

"A very correct assumption." Jack started the coffeemaker.

"It's going very well, thanks."

"Good morning, Michael." Sara went over and kissed her son.

"Morning, Mom." He didn't look up, just kept eating.

"He's very informative this morning," Jack said to Sara while pointing at Michael.

"Just leave him alone, Jack," Sara teased. "Maybe he doesn't like you anymore."

"There could be some truth in that." He turned towards footsteps behind him and quickly swooped Caroline off the floor.

"Dad, stop it. I'm too old for this." Jack laughed.

"No my little sourpuss, you will never be. 12 isn't old." He planted a big wet kiss on her cheek and put her down.

"Mom, you got to talk to him about that picking up stuff."

"Sorry, can't do. He's still bigger than me." Sara gave Caroline a hug. "Let's concentrate on breakfast and packing your lunch, okay?" The morning moved along and the everyday kitchen traffic in the Miller's house was noisy and busy as ever. Jasper had come down and joined them and finally a worn out Molly showed up.

"Good morning, you'all." Nobody turned, but everybody answered.

"Mornin' Molly."

"So how's everybody this lovely morning?" Nobody answered.

"Well, I'm doing grand, thanks so much for asking." She went over to the coffeepot and poured a mug – black. "Yummy, smells so good." She grabbed a piece of toast, placed a bit of jam on top and sat down next to Michael.

"So what's up, Mikey?" She put an arm around him and gave his cheek a kiss.

"Not much. What's up with you?"

"Off to classes, debate club and studying. A day made in heaven. Two tests tomorrow that I'm planning on acing; soccer practice and back to the library, then home, more studying for the tests and hopefully a few Z's if possible. I'll also try hard to take a few breaths in between as well as find some food I can inhale on the run to keep me alive." She drank more coffee and finished her toast. She looked at Michael with a question-mark on her face.

"So what's going on, Michael?" She smiled. "I see something in your face, Dear Boy. Tell Aunt Molly what it is, please." She turned towards him, as he took a deeper breath.

"I'm pregnant." At first it didn't hit correctly. Molly was good at staying in control. Michael was not the most humorous guy on the block, but he could be cynical, though he called it sarcasm for the most. Molly didn't blink.

"You mean you personally or somebody you know?" The kitchen went silent; even Caroline stood still.

"Me and Linda; we got pregnant." He kept eating, scraping the last few pieces of cereal off the edge of the bowl, got up, rinsed the bowl and stuck it in the dishwasher. "Well, gotta go." Jack stepped in front of him as he tried to leave the kitchen.

"Sorry Buddy; but you just said what?" Michael looked casually at Jack.

"Linda and I got pregnant, that's what I said." Jack was visibly surprised by this information.

"How did that happen?" Michael looked at his father and shook his head a bit.

"You want the detailed technicalities of making babies or are you fine with *what are we going to do next* department?" Jack sat down as Sara placed herself next to him. She looked at Michael with large eyes; Molly grabbed Michael in a big hug.

"Congratulations Michael, that sounds lovely." Michael smiled.

"Well, at least one can speak." Caroline looked at her mother.

"Does that mean I'm going to be some kind of aunt or something?" Sara smiled nervously.

"Yes, you'll be Aunt Caroline; how about that?" Caroline's face turned strange.

"I'm too young to be an aunt." She said pouting. Jack reached out for Michael.

"Wow, Michael that is quite some news. Does Linda know?" Michael's face turned a smile.

"Yes, Dad, I'm sure she does; if not, I'll be sure to tell her." He laughed and shook his head. Sara finally spoke.

"Yes, Michael that is some news. So what's the plan or is this part of the plan?"

"No, Mom, it was a slight hiccup, but we'll make it all work. Linda will finish the first two semesters at the academy, take maternity leave and go back when she feels comfortable with the baby in day-care or some other caretaking situation."

"Like grandparents?" Jack was asking.

"Whatever we can figure out, yes."

"When is the baby due?"

"In June; so about six months from now." Molly spoke more to herself.

"Wow, and she doesn't really show yet, does she?" Sara agreed.

"When were you going to tell us this great news, Michael?"

"A few minutes ago; Mom, we wanted to make sure we had the plan ready, had decided how we were actually going to swing this baby thing. We hoped that we would both be finished with the academy and then I would carry the bacon part while Linda would do the baby bit till we felt that she could go back to work. But that didn't materialize. So here we are and we know what we want to do and we feel that we will do okay on most fronts. We'll be a bit strapped financially, but should be able to wobble through that part as well." Sara interfered.

"Don't worry about that; we'll help you out, of course."

"Thanks Mom. But if we can, we'll try to do it on our own first, but I do appreciate the offer." Molly went over and hugged Michael again.

"I'm so happy for you guys, I really am. Linda is such a great person and you are going to be fantastic parents, I have no doubts at all. Well, gotta go; see you all later." As Molly was on the way out the door, Caroline turned to her mother.

"Is Molly going to be an aunt as well?" Jack answered.

"No, Honey, remember that she's not Michael's sister."

"Yes she is," Caroline insisted.

"No I'm not; I'm a best friend, but not a sister. See you later Aunt Caroline." Molly smiled and winked at Jack; he smiled back and understood. After some more chatter about babies and related issues, the family spread out to work and school and all the stuff in between. The day had started in its normal manner, and then another branch on the family tree had just sprouted and the day had become utterly wonderful.

"See you later, Grandpa," Sara teasingly shouted as she backed out of the driveway. Jack shook a fist at her, screaming.

"Don't you ever call me that in public - I have an image to protect. Besides, I'm way too young to be called one of those things – so take that, Grandma Miller."

Michael and Linda were friends from elementary school; actually sat next to each other in many of the same classes, but rarely spoke. As they continued with junior high and high school, they still stuck together and finally started to communicate little by little, then more and more. When high school was over, they decided to backpack Europe during that summer within a group of other friends. As Michael wasn't particularly verbal with Linda or her with him during all these childhood school years, friends and family who observed them constantly shook their heads in amazement as they couldn't understand why they even wanted to spend time together; what could they possibly have in common, as they didn't show any direction in this strange relationship. But Michael knew what was going on as well as Linda knew where it was all heading and that was the only important part.

After landing in Heathrow (London), they traveled across the English Channel, went through Normandy, Paris and down to Arles, Nice and Cannes. They bussed through Monte Carlo, crossing the border into Italy and spent many days in San Remo splashing around in the Mediterranean and then it was by train to Venice for a few nights. Linda and Michael had been museum hopping all day and by mid evening they had ended up on Ponte degli Scalzi, one of the four bridges spanning the Grand Canal.

"Why are you removing your shoes, Mike?"

"This is the Bridge of the Barefoot, my bewildered tourist." Linda removed her shoes as well.

"Does this have any significant meaning of any sort?" Michael laughed.

"I'm not sure. I only know my sightseeing stuff to a certain artificial level." He looked at Linda. She was perfectly backed by the setting sun. The smells and sounds around them were intoxicating. It had been such a grand trip, so many experiences, all the people they had met, the country sites, the cities and villages; but tomorrow they would fly back home. They were looking forward to that, but they were also sad about leaving. *We'll come back*, they promised each other.

Linda was quietly inhaling the moment in the middle of the Barefoot Bridge here in Venice in Italy in Europe. Michael had been a joy to travel with and a gentleman as they shared the same rooms in hotels and youth-hostels. They had traveled as platonic best friends and sharing beds on the way had not been a problem for either of them. So here they were, last night in Europe and Linda couldn't imagine a better ending to a perfect trip. Michael looked happy as he stood there, leaning against the railing. He slowly turned towards her.

"You know what they say…"

"Who are *they*?"

"Haven't got a clue, but they say it anyway." He smiled as he grabbed one of Linda's hands. "People, who travel well together, live well together. Did you know that?"

"Now I do. And this is going where again?" Michael had put his arm around Linda's shoulder as they faced the sunset.

"I think it's time, on this very bridge, here in lovely and romantic Venice, barefooted and all, that we declare our future union as officially being boyfriend and girlfriend from this day forward, later to get engaged, and then do that husband and wife thing. Do you agree?" Linda was hopping up and down inside, but looking at her, you wouldn't know; exteriorly she stayed cool, calm and very collected. Still looking at the sunset, she smiled slyly and said:

"Only if I can have my way with you tonight." Michael laughed out loud.

"That's a deal I can live with."

Linda and Michael never officially told anybody about their plans. Not because they didn't want to, but just because, well, that was pretty much who they were. So it was some years later they got married as they had gotten pregnant; a bit off schedule, but they dealt with it in their own well-mannered and relaxed way. Michael continued his police training and Linda did the taking care of the babies. It was a set of twins, therefore *babies*. They were both overjoyed and extremely happy, and no matter how challenging this whole school, babies, financial situation would become, they were together, so all would be well. Sara and Jack helped them out when needed, so Linda could stay home while Michael continued at the police academy.

It had been one of the happiest days for everybody in *and* surrounding the Miller family. The hospital staff had tried hard to make some form of order of the chaos all these people made. Balloons and flowers were everywhere, as well as very excited grandparents. It had been a festive day. The girl was named Nicole after Linda's grandmother. The boy was named Frank – nobody knew why, not even his parents.

It took several hours after returning home before he could finally put it all in some kind of perspective. He had always been a big picture kind of guy and though he praised himself as being calm in all forms of pressure situations, he was seriously disappointed that he hadn't stayed as cool and calm as he should have. Yes, there were issues and personality flaws, but he reminded himself, that perfection was never 100% no matter how hard one tried. But it was the extremes of illogical situations, thoughts and mental blindness he had a hard time understanding and therefore accept. It made him angry that he couldn't be more compassionate and supportive. She had expressed an honest vulnerability, had trusted him by showing how gravely lost she was. It would take enormous strength from any human being to be so brutally willing to rip so open for all to see. But she had chosen him; she had decided to risk it all for him and for them, their relationship and their friendship. Was she taking such risk because she loved him? That was the one thing that especially pained him. Had she asked him to be patient, to help her, to help them find a way from being so split to be together? It pained him because he loved her. If nothing else would have come out of this terrible evening, it would be that he was in love with her. It was no longer the infatuation, the *in awe* of who she was when he first saw her. He had initially been reeled in by her looks; he was impressed by the way she carried herself and the much assured self-confidence. The sexiest part about her was her smarts. He soon found that the person, the woman behind all that glitter, was sweet and romantic, sensuous and caring and the utmost you could possibly want in any close friend – and that was what he quickly had fallen in love with. There were just a few issues in the way, issues he now realized he would jump off a cliff to help her solve - only in a matter of speaking, of course.

He was in bed and nearly asleep when the phone rang. He listened with tears in his eyes and his heart beating faster. He nodded a few times, with a small smile, but his *yes sweetheart, of course I will*, was filled with loving concern. He had finished the short call with a soft: *Remember that I do love you*. She had answered just as softly: *I love you too*, and the phones went silent.

Victoria and William married a few months later. It was a small romantic affair with Sara as the bridesmaid and Jack as William's best man. They flew to Hawaii for the proverbial honeymoon. It had been a wonderful time and Victoria only saw a few, though strong images of Jack during her many intimate moments with William. She didn't tell him about that. But William soon found that vicious nightmares often plagued Victoria. She would scream and toss, bringing her body in to contortions of horrific pain. At times she would fight William, hit him, scratch and bite him, as he tried to calm her down. In the aftermath, she was crying in his arms with her head on his chest, weeping loud and uncontrollable. It took time to finally hear normal breathing again, and then she would fall asleep. She never remembered any of these episodes, and William rarely spoke of them. When suggesting professional help, she would softly decline – never explaining why. The scar was running from her temple to her jaw; it was clearly visible, but when she had those nightmares, it lit up in the most red of colors. William, as anybody else, didn't really acknowledge that thin line on the side of her face anymore, but to Victoria, it was a vicious and horrific reminder of that horrid man on that awful night. She was positive that one day or one night he would come back and finish his crime – and she knew she wouldn't survive that. They told her she had been lucky, but if what she saw in the mirror had anything to do with luck, she was not sure at all what luck was. But she knew he would be back and when he did, whatever luck she had left would run out; she never told anybody about these fears.

Jasper finished high school and was off to Georgetown University and law studies. His mother had sponsored him, but his GPA was tops, so he could have made it on his own. Sara's and Jasper's friendship was getting stronger and stronger and she was looking forward to welcome him into her law firm.

Jasper was a serious individual, not many friends and for the most just studying at home or at the library. He would often get together with Molly concerning certain subject matters, and she would support and help him if he had any problems understanding or solving. They were close friends, as Molly was with any member of the Millers. They would visit the many museums in D.C. again and again, dinner and lunches, and they would especially hang out at Nonna's, inhaling their favorite Italian dishes. Romano, the old romantic, always wanted them to become more than friends, but he knew that Jasper considered Molly his sister, so that fantasy stayed impossible.

And then there was Molly. Her grandparents was spending most of their time in Casablanca and traveling around Africa tending to their various humanitarian projects. That left Molly home alone for the most, but fortunately for her and also the way the Millers looked at it, she pretty much lived with them. A few nights she would sleep in her own house, but for the most she stayed next door. Jack was adamant about Molly rooming with them when her grandparents were away. He had Victoria's senseless attack in constant and clear memory, but never mentioned that to anyone as the reason.

She had fought her way out of boring high school, and was finally approved to leave in the middle of her sophomore year. Her *dismissal* was based on grade points beyond her age, her level of academic maturity and performance bypassing basic curriculum; several of her teachers had labeled Molly a genius. Though they were impressed with her time in school, they were also very glad to see her leave. This student had not been the easiest to deal with. As she was obviously extremely uninterested, she made up for the boredom by challenging and arguing just about anything possible. She was stubborn as could be and rarely lost any form of confrontation; she had to win and she did for the most – even when she was wrong.

She had been tested again and again and passed anything thrown at her with max points; in the process it was confirmed that her I.Q. was comfortably far beyond average. Georgetown University had quickly picked her up, based on her impressive resume and test results; and Molly had barely reached the age of 15. She started with advanced G.E. as well as intensive sociology studies. Her results consistently exceeded expectations. Unfortunately, as in high school, she quickly got bored with the *slow* progress of her classes. As faculty watched her closely, she was quickly moved to advanced levels; but the same thing happened. Molly finally decided to advance on her own by staying within her selected classes, and finding resources beyond what the school could offer. In addition, her grandparents encouraged her to apply for educational programs offered by UNICEF (United Nation's International Children's Fund). This was something that she had always wanted, something that was part of her plan for the future – a vision she had at the age of 12 – she wanted to continue her grandparents work; she wanted especially to work helping orphaned children, just like they were doing.

As Molly was now being celebrated at her 18th birthday party, it was obvious to those close to her, that she was rather exceptional concerning her academics and where she was going with her life. But when you came from the outside heading in, Molly was so basically bland, not purely in a negative way, but bland anyhow. Seeing her and just meeting her, you would have absolutely no idea what she was, where she was, who, why and how. She still dressed in a *tomboyish* fashion, and it was rumored that only Caroline had ever seen Molly with her hair down, literally; ponytails were her favorites and didn't consider any other hairstyle valid or practical. For those who knew her, that was the Molly they all loved and accepted. Those who didn't know

Molly would first see her as rude, as well as seemingly aloof and ignorant. But she never recognized those signs herself, not because she felt beyond everybody else, but simply because anybody else's thoughts about her never registered. The Millers thought highly of Molly, not all the academic trophies she kept collecting, but just Molly - just the way she was.

Romano was in heaven yet again. It was Molly's birthday party and the gang was all there. He had set up the tables to accommodate everybody. Jack had *ordered* him be a guest tonight, not the host. Romano was flattered, but had declined, as he wanted all to be prefect – and it was. Several speeches had been made and Molly, who had been rather intimidated by the attention, had laughed nervously, but seemed to have a great time. Jasper was sitting next to her, and she had never seen him enjoying himself as much as he did that evening. He ranked highly with Molly. She saw a sweet innocence about him and somewhat envied his relationship with Sara. He was for the most thoughtful and quiet, but she could challenge him in loud debates and heated conversation and he never backed down from his convictions – she liked that about him as well. Some of the best times with Jasper were the spirited and massive conversations they both had with Sara. All three would be in each other's faces and loudly trying to convince them of their supreme point. Jack would quickly leave the area when those explosive battles started, shaking his head – Caroline would be right behind him on the way out.

Though Molly had never entertained the somewhat common notion that she was more like a sister and daughter to the Miller family, Michael was the one she felt the most sibling-like attachment to. She didn't know what a brother was supposed to be like, but as she didn't have friends beyond the Millers, she only assumed that Michael was it. There was a protectiveness about him that made her feel very comfortable and safe. Michael rarely showed any feelings towards others and only occasionally, birthdays and Christmases, distributed kisses and hugs. But that was so totally opposite when it had to do with Linda. He would constantly be by her side and it looked wrong if he didn't hold her hand, hugged or kissed her. Often the old and tried *get a room* would be thrown at them. Linda would just smile and give him another kiss, just to spite the perpetrators. They looked very much like Sara and Jack in that department, Molly thought with a smile of envy.

Sara had swiftly taken over from the mother she had lost; but she was also an incredible friend on top of that. Her support of all that Molly had ever done, what Molly did and what Molly was planning to do, was constant. Sara would challenge some of Molly's decisions, but she would never tell her right or wrong – she left that up to Molly to figure out. She wanted to drag Molly along when shopping with Caroline, but in spite of how much Molly loved to spent time with the two of them, she would rarely go. According to Molly, clothes were something you bought from necessity, not something you shopped for. On the few occasions Molly did go along to the mall, she would for the most spent in the bookstores, while the *girls* went shopping.

Caroline and Molly's relationship stayed strong. They bonded from the very moment they had met and it kept growing. Caroline had looked up to Molly the first few years, but as Molly had always treated her on an even field, never talked down to her or teased her about the age difference of six years, she ended up looking at Molly as her even friend on all levels.

Caroline had learned a lot from Molly, as she had consistently as well as patiently encouraged her to study more and more. It had helped enormously with respect to her academics and gave her some of the self-assuredness Molly had. But though they seemed equal concerning interest in learning, they were rather different in many other areas. Caroline had not picked up Molly's hairstyle or manner of dressing and though *tomboyish* was okay for Molly, Caroline didn't embrace that direction, no matter how much she loved and respected her best pal. She had from a little girl stayed with the girlish look, and now at age 12, she was pretty, in good shape and the boys had started to pay attention. Molly would at times tease her about that; Caroline would just smile shyly and blush.

They spent as much time together as they could and it was common to see them, noses deep in books, in the libraries at Georgetown University. Most people were sure they were sisters, which was okay with Molly – that way she did not have to constantly correct the misconception.

Caroline bloomed every time somebody thought she was Molly's kid sister – she liked that a lot.

"Have you ever had a boyfriend?" She was whispering across the table. Molly looked up.
"No! Have you?"
"Don't be silly, I'm only 12."
"In some countries they are married at your age." Molly continued reading.
"Don't you want a boyfriend?"
"Why?"
"You know; somebody to marry someday."
"I repeat: Why?"
"That's what you do."
"Who do?"
"Everybody does."
"Not I; so the argument *everybody does* is very incorrect." Caroline smiled.
"But you will get married some day, won't you?"
"Are you legally irritating or are you just freelancing?" Molly kept reading.
"The second one; so are you or aren't you?"
"The second one; and what does it matter?" Molly had taught Caroline to be persistent.
"So I'll never be your bridesmaid?"
"You got that one right, Carl." Caroline made a face.
"But don't you have some kind of boy in mind that could be your husband?" Molly looked up and whispered slowly and clearly across the heavy library table.
"I will never get married; I have no reason to and I don't think I would ever be able to find a man that would fit the marriage bill what I'm concerned. Can we concentrate on stuff way more important than this idiotic conversation? Let's go and eat; that's far more exciting." Molly started collecting her books and stuffed them into her backpack. Caroline wasn't giving up.
"But there got to be somebody that you'd marry?"
"Caroline Miller, you are so utterly impossible. Okay, I'll go for your father, he would fit the bill." Molly thought that would end the topic; Caroline froze.
"Not my dad, are you insane?"

"One of many charming sides of me; let's go eat." She got up, grabbed her backpack, pushed the chair under the table and headed for the exit. Caroline frantically stuffed her stuff into her backpack and caught up by the exit.

"Don't even be kidding about that." She caught up with Molly.

"Oh I see; that's the one *you* want to marry." She laughed. Caroline was shaking her head wildly.

"Stop it. You can't say things like that. It's too weird and icky."

"I fully concur; and now let's do the eating bit." Caroline swung her arm in to Molly's as that was the way they always walked side by side. "I'll never mention it again; and I am really sorry about that bridesmaid thing, I really am." Caroline smiled and squeezed Molly's arm; she knew she was kidding.

"I might forgive you someday." And the two best pals were soon doing that eating bit and eagerly chatting about so many other things.

For Molly, boyfriends and even the thought of a longer male relationship other than friendships with Michael, Jasper, Jack, George and her grandfather was out of bounce; in the female department, well, that was the same deal. Besides the Miller clan, she really didn't have any relationships other than sporadic debate and study groups at school. She never got involved beyond the task at hand; she showed up, stayed the time, did the work and left. To some it made her look aloof, unfriendly, arrogant and rude; but she didn't take the time to care one bit. It wasn't that she lacked offers of dates, coffee, movies and picnics; but they were all turned down and at times not in the most charming way. Pretty much for all interested in that side of Molly, it was a first and last offer, all in one. They comforted themselves by reasoning that she wasn't that hot looking anyway and her attitude sucked – or perhaps she was a lesbian; yes of course.

She had started jogging with Sara and Jack whenever she was around. It had started with twenty minutes and it had soon reached a level of an hour and then an hour and a half. It had become a drug for Molly and she couldn't seem to get through the day without a jog around the neighborhood. Caroline had joined them in the beginning, but she quickly lost interest. Sara had difficulties finding time on her schedule, so it had ended up being Jack and Molly who did the running. Molly would often drive from Georgetown between classes to Jack's office. They would be in their running outfits in seconds and off they went. Many times they wouldn't say much on the way, but sometimes they would save the world or at least gallantly try. Afterwards she would take a quick shower at the office and soon be back in class.

Molly loved Jack as she loved the rest of the family. He was fun to be around and though he didn't have the same seriousness about him as Sara did, he could still be drawn into heavy debates, and often apply and hold on to his opinions with great argumentation. She found he was very passionate about his family, and he was never going to let anything bad happen to any of them – he would make sure of that. She knew that he had felt some guilt with respect to the vicious attack on Victoria due to things he had done; but everybody involved kept assuring him that he had nothing to do with it. But it was the lingering feeling of guilt he had talked with Molly about. He was very open and easy to talk with. Jack's favorite topic was Sara; Molly was okay with that, of course, as she also loved her. Though she had decided that boyfriends and marriage were not on the schedule, she did acknowledge that if she ever tied any knots, that if she would only experience half the dedication, half the respect, half the love and passion Sara and Jack had for each other, she would be an extremely fortunate person. She had always been in awe of what those two had.

But for now it was school only, actually *schools* only. She would take the train to New York and attend classes and conferences offered by UNICEF during weekends and weekdays when she was available with respect to her Georgetown schedule. She had committed herself to advance as fast as she could by educating herself with the policies and functions needed to join her grandparents and their work in Africa. She had four more semesters left at Georgetown to get her Master's degree. If she worked and studied hard, she would be able to apply for a position with UNICEF that would put her in the proximity of where her grandparents spend most of their time. That would give them a chance to see each other on a regular basis again, and that she wanted more than anything; she did miss them terribly. But in spite of that, life was grand, though very busy, Molly West thought with a smile.

It was a rather normal morning in Sara and Jack's home. Just about everybody was running amok, which was part of the normality. At one precious moment, all were in the kitchen at the same time. Michael, Jasper, Molly and Caroline were sitting around the table while Jack was finishing his coffee by the sink, with Sara lovingly leaning up against him, cup of tea in hand.

"Listen up!" Her voice was loud and demanding. "It's George's 70th birthday today, so don't forget the party at Nonna's, okay?" Everybody mumbled okay in response; nobody was looking up. Sara looked up at Jack: "They are so attentive, don't you think?" He smiled and kissed her forehead.

"Let's make some more of them, huh?"

"Don't get a room," was Michael's dry request.

"So I'm driving you to work this morning?" Sara confirmed with Jack.

"That would be lovely. I'm ready in five minutes." He placed the cup in the sink and left the kitchen. One by one the kids kissed their mother goodbye and she got an especially big hug from Molly.

"See you tonight, Sara." She smiled as she squeezed Molly's hand. As she looked into her eyes, she thought she saw a glimpse of sadness; but she quickly shook it off. A few minutes later, she was waiting for Jack in the driveway.

"Are you going to make it on time?" She asked.

"I'll be fine; no need to rush. I called Nora and told her I'll be a few minutes late for the meeting. No need to hurry."

"But not the scenic route, I assume?"

"Not the scenic route, no matter how tempting that sounds." They drove in silence for a moment.

"Did you get a chance to call George?"

"I did and he's all set for the party – rather excited, actually." Jack giggled.

"Rather excited? That doesn't sound like your father. Are you sure you spoke with the right person?"

"It sounded like him; you know all excited in that whiny voice of his." Jack was mocking his father: *If I really have to be there I guess I really have to be there.* You know; that kind of excitement." Sara smiled.

"Well, at least he's consistent."

"Yeah, he's consistently whiny, cynical and sarcastic; just what you want from a 70 year old man." They followed the slow traffic in silence. Jack was looking at Sara's silhouette. Her features were smooth and beautiful in a gentle flow. Her short hair outlining her face and her cute mouth and lips showed a tiny smile.

"What are you doing, Jack?" She asked slowly and without turning; he smiled big.

"I'm just thinking how lucky I am that you found me all those years ago."

"We found each other, as far as I remember."

"Sara, I really love you very much." His hand rested on her thigh.

"And you love me in spite that I'm a married woman?"

"Especially because you are a married woman; makes it more exciting, if you know what I mean."

"That I do; very clearly indeed." She caressed his hand. After a bit more driving they finally got away from the stop and go traffic.

"By the way, Molly told me yesterday that she has somewhat of a date for next Saturday..." Sara was smiling and Jack was giggling.

"... And she told me this morning that she had cancelled it."

"Oh my God, what's her problem? As far as you know, has she ever had a date or even been interested in a boy or man or whatever?"

"Not even a *whatever*. She's not interested; I guess that's fair enough. She obviously has other things that are more important to her. Okay, she is not a stunning beauty in a way…"

"…Jack, that's rude; she's, well nice looking, but dresses in somewhat of an attitude."

"What I mean is that she's lovely, but she doesn't have this real female thing. Even at 18 she's still kind of tomboyish, wouldn't you say?" Sara nodded.

"I agree, but if you tart her up a bit in a dress and all, she surely has the body for it, she'd look smashing."

"Tart her up a bit? That's a charming way to put it. But you know, she is smart and really funny in that weird kind of

way of hers and we all love her dearly – all of us. I for one think she is rather beautiful in that kind of special way. I don't think she's lacking dating offers, but I can also see that her intellect can be intimidating."
"Does she intimidate you?" Jack smiled.
"Sara, we know her, and we love her, so I am not intimidated one bit; okay a bit at times, but I can see how she would push many a suitor away by simply being who she is; even without herself knowing what she's doing – that kind of situation."
"I do love her like my own child."
"Dear Sara, I know what you mean, but she is not. That doesn't mean we love her less, far from." Jack giggled again: "And we wanted four kids, we had three and here comes Molly. However sad the circumstances, she was a Godsend for all of us." He smiled as Sara did the same. But she didn't mention the sadness she had seen in Molly's eyes that morning.

They reached the CR building and Sara stopped the car in front of the main entrance. Jack leaned over and kissed her. She smiled as he started to open the passenger door, grabbed his arm and pulled him back in.
"Not so fast Pool Boy. I'm for a bit more of that stuff you just did." She planted a big wet kiss on Jack's lips. "That's how it's done, don't you think?" Jack nodded eagerly.
"Yes Mrs. Miller, it sure is." He kissed her again and proceeded to exit. As he stood outside the car, he leaned in again.
"Thanks for giving me a ride this morning, Sara. Make it a good day and I'll see you tonight at Nonna's." He blew an air kiss. "And remember that I love you very much, will you do that?" Sara smiled and nodded her head. She waved and soon turned left towards her office.

Molly sat on a bench outside the classroom building. There was something dizzying going on inside her head and she didn't know what it was, other than a feeling she had felt before, many years ago. She was just a kid, that much she knew; but how old had she been? Her brains worked overtime, swirling and turning, trying to pin down the time and day, figure out what that feeling was associated with.

She sipped some water from her bottle and slowly screwed the cap back on. Nothing came up, no information what-so-ever. As it was time to go back to class, she grabbed her backpack, got up and entered the red brick building – but the dizzying feeling didn't go away, and it didn't decrease, it only increased.

"Good morning Miss President." Nora was standing by her desk as Jack walked in. He gave her a light kiss and sat down. Karen came in with a cup of coffee and handed it to Jack. "How's my superb support system this morning?" He asked. Karen put the mug in front of him and smiled.
"Just dandy my fearless slave driver." She sat down next to Jack and placed a brown folder on the table as well as pen and pad. Nora pulled a chair out as William and two of the crew foremen entered the office and the morning briefing started; it was already a productive day.

"Good morning Sara," her assistant greeted. He was a 24 year old who she had hired several years ago. He hadn't had the academic background or experience she was looking for, but she saw something she didn't see in any of the other applicants; he had turned out to be a good choice. After inspiring him to go back to law school, he now worked as many hours as he possibly could during the week, took evening classes, studied hard on the weekends and any other chance he got.
"So what kind of fun are we having today?" She asked as she sat down, looking at the messages and folders on the desk.
"We have to finalize the Carlton documents, wrap up the Singleman contract proposal this morning and do lunch with Colleen at noon. She called and told me she'll pick you up. Court is at 2:30 and after that you are a free woman." Sara smiled at Mr. Efficiency.
"So what you are saying is that the only fun starts at noon!" He smiled.
"I am sorry, but I guess that's pretty much it." He sat down at the oval conference table in front of the floor–to-ceiling window. If you strained yourself dramatically to the left, it was rumored that you could see a bit of the Treasury Building.

"But I will also have fun tonight as my father-in-law will be celebrated for 70 years of stamina." Sara smiled at the thought and was looking forward to the evening as they would all be there. She got up with folders in hand, a pen and a pad and sat down across from her assistant; soon after the two partners arrived, as well as their assistants. She looked up and smiled good mornings, and soon all sat around the oval table. The daily briefing could begin. They looked forward to a productive day.

A sharp and eerie pain sprang through her head. All of a sudden she knew where the feeling came from. Yes, it was a long time ago, a very long time ago. But how could she possibly remember that? She had only been six years old. She never questioned her abilities to call up anything from her memory bank and from her experiences; actually she took it for granted and perhaps ignorantly so. But this was extraordinarily strange. In a daze she stuffed her books into her backpack, noisily pushed the chair back; everybody in the classroom turned. She nodded towards the professor and mumbled: *I'll be back in a few minutes*. He nodded back in no surprise as he had found her to be an eccentric and complicated individual. But in spite of personality traits of that kind and similar, she was the best student in the 20-some years at his job; but he never told her that – he was sure she already knew. He nodded again as she hurried out the door. *Take your time Miss West; take your time.* But she was far gone.

She ran with a determination she didn't pay attention to. What was it she had seen? The look in Sara's eyes had been new to her; frightening new actually. It had been a moment of severe sadness for her. But it had also been the invisible sorrow she felt from everybody in the kitchen that morning; but Sara had looked the saddest. Now she remembered when she saw that same look so many years ago. She was lying in the backseat of the car; her mother kept turning to make sure she was alright. Every time she turned, Molly sensed it before she had actually turned, so she met her mother's smiling face with an even bigger smile in return. She loved her mother. They were best friends and buddies and did everything together. Her father would always laugh from sheer happiness when he saw his two favorite girls in their world of whisper and laughs and giggles wherever they were. But the last time her mother had turned around, she had seen the same glimpse of sadness in her eyes as she had seen in Sara's this morning, again and again. And then she recalled that her father had turned around with a big smile. *I love you, Princess,* he had said. It was with the same sadness as in her mother's eyes; that precise same sadness. Then he had violently turned his attention back on the freeway in front of them, but it had been too late – after the explosion everything went black and silent. Molly started to shake. She found a phone and dialed Sara's office. Asking for Sara she was told that she would be occupied in meetings and couldn't be disturbed. Molly asked the receptionist to give Sara an urgent note from her. The shaking wouldn't stop and she hung up.

Sara read the note and smiled. Molly would often leave notes with hearts and small drawings for her, something she had started early on and not only with Sara but with everybody. *Dearest Sara, make it a safe day, with all my love, Molly. PS. we must talk; it's urgent.* Sara read it again, shook her head and smiled even more. *Aren't you a sweetheart!* She thought tenderly. Looking at the clock on the wall; it would soon be lunch with Colleen, something she always enjoyed.

A few minutes before noon, Sara wrapped up the meeting and was in the elevator heading for the lobby. She felt good this morning, in spite of the sharp and sporadic pain-like jolts in her head. This one was a bit sharper than the ones before. But as unscheduled as they appeared, as quickly they disappeared. As this had gone on for about a week, she made a mental note to bring it up with Colleen. Though she had retired from the hospital, she might still be able to apply some of her medical knowledge - even during a friendly lunch. Sara and Colleen were soon in a warm embrace and off to lunch they went.

As the bell rang, Molly was out of the classroom in a second. She dialed Sara's number again and was told she had left for lunch with Colleen; they didn't know what restaurant. Molly called Romano at Nonna's, but they were not there and were not expected until tonight. Molly dialed

Jack's number, but he was at a building site and couldn't be reached. She dialed Victoria's number and her secretary informed her that Victoria was in Los Angeles the next few days. She started to tremble even more. The sweat had drenched the top of her T-shirt. Her mind was painfully wrenched, trying to solve whatever it was that needed solved. She dialed Colleen and Charles house, but Charles didn't know where they had gone. He did suggest that they might have gone to Bernie's. *Are you okay Molly?* The unanswered question was left hanging as the line went dead. Molly grabbed her backpack and ran to her car. She knew Bernie's Cafe and could be there within 20 minutes if she hurried. The moment her seatbelt clicked in place, the car's engine roared and she was racing out of Georgetown towards D.C. As she ran red lights and made unsafe passes, she already felt it was too late, but she had to try, she had to get hold of Sara.

Jack had returned from the morning's visits to two of CR's building sites. Things were going well and though one site was behind schedule, it wasn't anything dramatic. Some materials had arrived later than anticipated, but Jack just added a few more bodies for a week or two. With the adjustments they should catch up within three weeks and be back on track. Karen greeted him by the entrance to the building as she had seen him arrive and parked his car. She looked frazzled as she ran towards him; he wondered what could be wrong.

"Jack, Molly is trying to get hold of you. She has called several times and wanted to know if you have any idea where Sara went for lunch today. She sounded really frantic." Jack stopped and looked at her. She certainly didn't look right; she looked very scared.

"Molly probably is in one of her moods, you know *eccentric Miss Molly*." Karen didn't think so.

"No Jack, she really sounded concerned."

"Did she say about what?"

"No, she just asked for you and also if I knew where Sara might have gone." Jack paused a bit, then he walked over to Karen, put his arm around her shoulders and they walked through the lobby together and up the stairs to second floor and their offices.

"Let's see what we can do." Jack was on the phone the next many minutes and finally got hold of Sara as she arrived at Bernie's Café.

"Hey Sara; Molly for some reason is desperately trying to get hold of you, and according to Charles, he believes that she is on her way to Bernie's." Sara smiled on the other end of the line.

"I wonder what's up. I got a somewhat strange note from her at the office this morning; oh well, I'll see her soon, I guess."

"Okay honey, just wanted to let you know. See you tonight; love you."

"I love you too, Jack," and they hung up.

Traffic was a *pisser,* Molly thought. It was slow and erratic, no flow what-so-ever. The traffic lights did not cooperate either. The 20 minute ride had passed 25 minutes and she wasn't even halfway there. Her trembling had increased and the sweat was now pouring off her. *What the hell is going on?* She thought with fear. She decided to stop and make another call to Bernie's. Her cut-offs of other drivers quickly engaged angry horns; she didn't notice them at all.

"I must speak to Sara Miller immediately." Her voice was demanding and cold.

"She is having lunch at the moment. Do you want to leave a number where she can reach you?" Molly was steaming.

"No, I don't want to leave a fucking number; I want to speak with her now – you got it?" Her voice was now loud, rude and hard.

"Please wait." The line clicked to bland holding music. A minute later Molly breathed a sigh of relief; Sara's voice had never sounded better.

"Hey what's up, sweetheart?"

"God, I am so happy to hear your voice. I just had this insane vision of something bad happening to you, so I desperately wanted to get hold of you to see if you were okay, and you are."

"Yes I am, sweet Molly; I'm more than okay, having a great time lunching with Colleen. Hey, if you are in the neighborhood, come by and join us – that would be wonderful." Molly smiled with tears in her eyes; the weight off her shoulders was tremendous.

"That's nice of you, Sara, but I'll head back to school. I think I can make my next class, though traffic really sucks at the moment. Enjoy, and kiss Colleen from me." There was a brief pause: "I love you, Sara."

"I love you too, Molly – a whole lot. See you tonight." And Molly couldn't wait.

Sara was smiling as she returned to Colleen and their lunch. The sharp pain had returned. It was lingering a bit longer yet again and now she also felt a slight numbness of the left side of her face.

"That was dear Molly. She had some vision or something that I was in danger or something." Sara smiled. She adored Molly and was appreciative of her concern, no matter how silly it was. "Which reminds me, Doctor Colleen; I want to ask you about these headaches I've had the last few days. But first on to much more important stuff: deciding what kind of dessert to feel guilty about. So what are we going to have?" Colleen scanned the menu and smiled; there were too many yummy choices.

Brain aneurysms, also known as cerebral aneurysms, can attack anybody at any time, at any age. A weak or *thin* spot on a blood vessel wall can fill up with blood in a balloon like way. When rupturing (hemorrhaging), the blood seeps into the brain causing massive destruction like strokes, permanent brain damage, disabilities and very possibly death. People between the age of thirty and sixty are at a higher risk and the risk is somewhat more elevated for women than it is for men. There are certain life-styles that might promote aneurysms more so, but anybody within the risk group can be affected, even fit and healthy individuals. Among the symptoms are pain behind the eyes, severe headaches, paralysis on either side of the face, vomiting and loss of consciousness. Unfortunately there are not any known ways to prevent brain aneurysms to form. Smaller aneurysms can be present through your whole life, never causing any form of problem; but when the aneurysms get bigger and start to gather large quantities of blood within, it is sadly another end result. The aneurysm located in Sara's skull was unusually large. The walls had stretched to their utmost; it was only a matter of time.

The dessert had arrived and two good friends were going at it. Colleen was eagerly concentrating on digging in for that first bite, so she didn't catch the severe pain and surreal shock Sara's face momentarily expressed. When she looked up, Sara's body had already slumped into the chair. Her eyes were glazed and lifeless, her face pale as a sheet. Her hands seemed to be trying to reach up towards her face, but the shaking was too brutal for seconds; her arms quickly fell down along her body, as if paralyzed. The breathing was violently loud and fighting for any amount of needed oxygen, but the flow was by now cut off for good; her body stiffened and fell to the floor. After one final convulsion, Sara Miller's body and soul had fully closed down. In morbid grace, her death had been swift and painless; she never knew what happened.

Within seconds Colleen was giving Sara's unresponsive body CPR. She screamed out orders to the people who had come to help. Two other doctors were at her side immediately and all three worked hard to find some form of pulse, a heartbeat, anything; but found none. Colleen slaved hard and furious, counting out loud, breathing air into the body's lungs; but that was the only reason the chest moved.

"Come on Sara, don't do this to me. Come on, girlfriend, you gotta snap out of this." And she blew more air into the lifeless body, pressed the chest one hand over the other, counting out loud, again and again. The two doctors had to physically pull her away, as the medics had arrived and taken over. Colleen's world was foggy, dizzying and devastated. She cried and cried and screamed for Sara in an eerie pitch of total despair. The two doctors sat with her, one on each side. They were gently, but firmly holding her back as she tried to reach Sara's body again and again. The medics tried all they could, but they were fighting a battle that was lost before they had arrived. There was a sad and withdrawn look on their faces as they quickly placed the body on the gurney, while still applying CPR. The guests in the restaurant had stayed in their seats in stunned and shocked conditions; some had finally found enough strength to get up and slowly exit. Police had arrived and were quietly talking with the staff and guests; everybody shaking their heads in disbelief. The medics calmly and efficiently continued the resuscitation as they rolled Sara out to the waiting ambulance. Seconds later it was blaring off to the emergency room.

Colleen was in total shock. It had all gone so fast. One second they had been laughing and giggling; the next thing she knew was that Sara was dying right in front of her. *Sara dead?* She thought again and again. It could not be right; it couldn't be true; it couldn't be real. One of the doctors gently grabbed her arm and offered to get her to the hospital. She nodded, picked up her purse as well as Sara's and they were soon on their way. The 10 minute drive seemed like hours and all in a daze, a slow-motion so unclear and so violently unreal. Would this horrific nightmare ever end?

The ER doctors and nurses had continued the resuscitation, checked for any vital signs again and again: pulse, heartbeat, pupils; again and again. Finally they knew that nothing could be done. The doctor in charge declared Sara Miller dead as he signed her death certificate. Colleen had been in the room during the whole process. He came over and sat down next to her.

"Colleen, I know that you are a friend of the Millers, so if you want to call next of kin, it would be okay with me. You know it's a bit off the procedure, but if you feel up to it, you can do that." He paused. "And if you need help calling anybody about this, I am here, of course." Colleen froze.

"Oh my God, oh God, yes I must call Jack." The doctor put his arm around her shoulders.

"Again, if you want me to, I can make the calls."

"No, I have to do that; it must come from me." She looked at this gentle man with her tearful eyes. "I must do this - thanks."

"You can use the phone in my office – I'll come with you." She nodded and cried in silence as they walked down the corridors.

The phone was sitting right in front of her like a horrifying hurdle. She had made so many calls to mothers and fathers, sisters and brothers, husbands and wives, children and friends, informing them of the unfortunate passing of loved ones. But *this* was not familiar to her at all.

Her hands were shaking as she picked up the receiver and desperately tried to dial the number. She missed numbers a couple of times before she finally got the right connection.

"Good afternoon, CR Constructions; this is Karen. How may I direct your call?" Her voice was cheery and energetic, but Colleen didn't hear it.

"Jack, please."

"Can I tell him who is calling?"

"It's Colleen. I need to speak with Jack." Karen heard something in Colleen's voice that stunned her. Her fingers immediately jumped over the switches.

"Right away Colleen," she heard a click and the extension ringing. The phone was picked up before the second ring.

"This is Jack." His voice was also cheerful and energetic. Colleen was not prepared for what she said next.

"Jack," her voice broke down and she shook and could hardly speak: "Jack; Sara is dead." The words came out uncontrollable. "Sara is dead," she tried to say again. The line was quiet for a moment.

"What are you saying?"

"Sara died, Jack. She's dead." Her voice was crumbling. "She died right in front of me." Jack did not understand what Colleen was saying; everything went still.

"Sara died? What do you mean Sara died?" He fell back in his chair. Karen was immediately standing in the doorway to his office, pale and shaking; she could not fathom what was going on other than what Jack was stuttering. She ran in to Nora's office, screaming:

"Nora, I think something terrible has happened; come, hurry up." Nora looked up and saw a wrenched look on Karen's face: "Come on, hurry up." Nora dropped what she had been reading and raced after Karen. Jack was white as snow, shaking and whimpering in disbelief. His gut curling moaning and cries went through the building as a sharp knife. The phone was lying on the table in front of him. He looked up and saw Nora. She saw a lost man in agonizing pain; he looked directly at her.

"Sara died; she's dead." He couldn't say more as his throat twisted and turned. Nora picked up the phone.

"Hello?" Karen came to her side, tears rolling down her face.

"It was Colleen who called."

"Colleen?" She asked; a man's voice came on the line.
"I'm Doctor Arlone, a colleague of Colleen. We are in the emergency room and we think it is best that Jack is brought down here right away, okay?" Nora paused in total confusion; but within a moment she shifted to a full control mode. Nora would deal with the devastating news at a later point. The priority now was to take care of Jack and whatever needed to be handled. Tears were for later; people needed Nora to be solid as a rock.
"I'll get him over there within half an hour. I'm Nora, by the way, Jack's business partner and friend." Their goodbyes were short; Nora had Jack in the car within minutes. Before she left, Karen picked up the phone and dialed Linda's extension.
"What happened?" Linda automatically asked.
"Be in charge; I'll call you later." She hung up and raced down the stairs, out the front door and towards Nora's car. Jack and Nora were sitting in the backseat, Jack with his head in his hands visibly trembling. Karen was soon racing towards D.C. center.

She was serene as she was lying in front of Jack. Colleen was holding him up on one side and Nora on the other. She looked a bit pale, he thought, but nevertheless she looked so beautiful and restful. Jack had been given a tranquilizer a few minutes after he had arrived at the coroner's office. They had asked him if she was his wife Sara Miller, and he had signed the papers to confirm the identification. His hand was shaking, but the signature was clear. He asked to spend a few minutes alone with her and after twenty minutes he slowly got up, held her hands, kissed her lips and her forehead. There were no more tears left and he exited the room a broken man. Jack's world had crumbled in a horrific way and was beyond repair. His life ended a few moments ago. He could not to any extent imagine going on without his Sara – life without her was not an option, that he was sure of, and he knew what he had to do to be with her again. Those were the only thoughts calming him. He smiled a hopeful smile within; and then he fell to the floor - unconscious.

Nora had made the calls and painfully delivered the devastating news to Michael, Jasper and Caroline. Jack,

Colleen, Charles and George had been there to help out with embraces and holding hands, but it was Nora who was strong for all of them. The children were in total disbelief and their violent grief was heart-wrenching. Michael had cried in convulsions and Caroline was hanging on to her father, crying and crying and screaming for her mother. Jasper was sitting in a corner chair alone. His stare was ghostly, his body shaking and he pushed anybody off who wanted to comfort him; no tears had flowed from Jasper.

Nora had finally found Victoria by phone in Los Angeles and she would get on the next flight out and be in D.C. the following day. She had sounded in control on the phone, but the second the call had ended, she fell to the floor in agony and tears. She had to call her parents in Europe to tell them the terrible news. Like Nora, Victoria quickly took control of her actions; the emotional stuff would be dealt with later – and that they would. Nora had left it to Victoria to call William. He was in Florida on business. He would be on the next flight out and go directly to Sara and Jack's house. But it wasn't Sara and Jack's house anymore, he thought with a broken heart.

Nora had not been able to find Molly. It was now early evening and she had not come home. Nora would check her house later and also leave a note on the door. Karen had been on Nora's side constantly, helping out wherever she could. Her face was wet from tears and they had flowed without borders. But she was the support Nora needed to get everything done as right and as comforting as possible, no matter how impossible the situation was. Karen showed her strength as a human being and deep under it all, Nora was truly appreciative and impressed. Karen did what Karen was good at: being a true friend and as she loved all the people gathered here, to her it was the most natural thing to do.
"Nora, I'll call the library at Georgetown, see if I can find Molly there."
"Good idea, Karen. Use one of the phones upstairs."And Karen disappeared.

Molly had turned the car around with a smile of relief. How silly could she be, *feeling* that something was going to happen to Sara? She had sounded like same old lovely Sara, giggling when Molly had asked if she was okay. Molly had also heard a lot of love in her voice. She was never her substitute mother, but she was such a dear friend. She had always treated and understood Molly with the greatest respect, and she had felt that from the first time they met. She smiled again as she parked the car in front of the library back at Georgetown University; she felt much better now. But a few hours later, she would feel an excruciating pain of loss and disbelief.

It only took Nora's few sentences on the other end of the line for Molly's world to explode, causing massive destruction of who she was, who she had been and crushed her trust in any form of future happiness in her life. She had loved her parents and they were ripped away from her in a senseless accident. She had loved Sara with all her heart and soul, and she had died right in front of her, a death she could have prevented, perhaps? The doubts in Molly's being were already gnawing at her. She had smiled to her mother and smiled to her father as they had turned their attention to her in the backseat instead of the road in front of them; she knew she had caused their deaths. This morning she felt something was wrong with Sara and she had not persisted trying to rescue her; she believed she really could have. So Sara had died and Molly had done nothing – absolutely nothing. Her world had exploded once again, and this time she knew there was no way to believe that it would ever heal – it would not happen, so why even bother anymore?

She had tried hard to keep the people around her at an emotional distance, but Sara, Jack, Michael, Jasper, George and lovely Caroline, her best little buddy ever, had marched straight into her heart and sat up camp. But now she had ruined it all again and it had disappeared because she had failed. She should have protected herself and kept everybody at a distance, but she negated to do so. For Molly *failing* had never been an option to even consider. But now failure was sitting heavy on top of her again, smashing her deep into the ground, smothering her soul and stopping her heart. As she sat in her car with tears flowing, she felt eerily empty and sadly dead.

Jack sat very still as the information was communicated to him. He didn't really hear much of what was said, if anything at all; Colleen was next to him with her arm around his shoulders. The coroner had explained that by law they were obligated to perform a thorough autopsy when the cause of death was not clearly apparent. Due to Doctor Ryan's description of the situation in the restaurant, it was pre-assumed that an aneurysm could have been the possible cause; they soon found that to be true. In his naïve belief that it would comfort Mr. Miller, the coroner explained to him that Sara had died in an instance. She would not have known what happened – that would have been impossible. Cause of death: A ruptured cerebral aneurysm.

*****

"She was the best friend I ever had – I will ever have. Her genuine kindness, love, respect and concern for others was unique and exciting to watch, fortunate to be part of. The center of Sara's life was about her family. It was all about Michael, Jasper, Caroline and Molly. They were her lifeline, they were the energy that powered her to greatness as a mother, as a wife, as a lawyer and the good friend she was to so many. Sara will be missed for that as well. Did she have faults? Of course she did. She was stubborn, heavily assertive and believed that for the most, actually all the time, that her opinions, her ideas, her way of thinking was *it*, was the only way. I also loved her for that. She was the master planner. I still, as if it was yesterday, remember how she, on our first day of meeting, spelled out our life together. From becoming girlfriend and boyfriend, our educations, getting married and having four children. It all materialized as she had predicted, as she had planned - except her own death and the two of us growing old together." Jack wiped tears with his hand. He saw so many familiar faces, the many hearts and souls Sara had touched. "We made three of the four children. But the plan had called for four and that was when we were all blessed as Molly entered our lives." Jack looked up and found Molly sitting stiffly between Caroline and Jasper. She was dressed in all black, a black scarf around her head as well as large, dark sunglasses, covering most of her face. She was sitting very still, only looking straight ahead, looking at nobody, looking at nothing. It had pained Jack to see how she had detached herself from everything and everybody; nobody had been able to penetrate the wall she had put in place since Sara's death – she had only said very few words since that day. Caroline had tried, Jasper had tried and Michael had been the most persistent, but Molly had pushed everybody away. She had stayed in her grandparent's house, curtains closed and the blinds shut. She didn't answer phone calls and didn't respond to knocks on the door, notes placed in the mailbox - nothing. The only thing she did was drive to school, spent the day and evening there, come home late and shut down until the next morning – and then repeating the same routine. Jack was bewildered and sad that he couldn't get through to her. At least she had showed up for the funeral, but had left immediately afterwards. The reception had been empty without her, in spite of the hundreds of other guests. Caroline was crushed as Molly did not acknowledge her anymore. Sitting between Jasper and Caroline had been Nora's firm order to Molly; she had resentfully obliged.

"I am deeply saddened that Sara did not get the full life she deserved, the full life she had planned." Jack smiled a bit. "She had so much to live for and so many to live for. But now *we* have to live that life for Sara instead. We have to live life for her as she would have lived it with us. I know in my heart that the rest of my life here on earth will continue with Sara in it. I will always love her and always respect and treasure the many years we did have together, the wonderful children she left behind and the extraordinary memories we will always visit." Jack pointed with both hands toward the sky. "She is watching us from above and she will continue to send us the love and respect she blessed us with here on earth." The hall was silent as Jack stepped down from the podium. Caroline had stood up and was soon in his arms. Michael and Jasper followed and they embraced for a long moment. Molly had quietly left through a side door without a word; Caroline's saddened eyes had followed her every step. She had lost her mother, but she had also lost her best friend and she didn't understand why.

Jack took another sip of wine; his teary eyes red and sad. The images on the screen of the people at the reception blurred a bit. The somberness on their faces when passing the casket was heartbreaking. Michael and Caroline were clinging to each other and Jasper stood silently a few feet from Jack. Colleen had her arm around his shoulder and Charles was on Jasper's other side. Nora and Karen stood together, hand in hand; Victoria was sitting down with William standing behind the chair. She had become physically ill from the moment she was informed of Sara's death. Her normal cool leveled head, her innate way of always dealing with situations and decisions, had suffered an extraordinary meltdown. William had struggled comforting her, but decided to let the emotions run their cause. George could not fathom what had happened. He had lost Irene so early on and now he saw his son buried in the same sorrow, the same devastating loss of the one he truly loved the most. It ripped open emotions he did not want to revisit. His efforts of comforting Jack had been futile, as he couldn't even comfort himself. It was all so senseless and it was so very unfair.

Jack poured a bit more wine. The bottle was nearly empty and the video cassette had finally played out. He must have seen the two hour tape hundreds of times over the years. He especially liked the collage of photos and video clips of Sara from a baby, through the life of teenager, meeting Jack, into adulthood, marrying Jack, having the children: one two three and then Molly's arrival. And there were Michael and Linda getting married and having the twins, and then her death, her funeral and then nothing; it had been precisely ten years now, ten long and sad years. Jack opened another bottle of wine, poured the glass full, rewound the cassette, leaned back in the sofa and watched it again.

George was now 80. He was in good health, mentally as well as physically. He had retired from his government position and pursued hiking in the wilderness, especially in the north-western parts of Canada and anywhere in Alaska. Charles had died from a massive heart attack just a year after Sara's death. Colleen had found George an immense comfort through her grief and after several years of hiking together as well as many trips abroad, they had decided that Irene and Charles would approve of their cohabitating, meaning that Colleen had moved in with George, thereby made their relationship *official*. Maybe a bit naïve, as everybody around George and Colleen had quickly realized that their friendship was more than a friendship. They had decided not to get married, respecting their late spouses. *Living in lusty unmarried sin is much more exciting*, was the way George referred to the situation; Colleen agreed with a satisfied glance.

Michael was now 30. He graduated the police academy and had done the uniform bit without any incidents. Linda liked him in uniform, tongue in cheek, but she liked him even better out of it. He had studied hard beyond what was expected to quickly and efficiently to become a homicide detective. At times it had caused a bit of a struggle at home as he constantly had his nose in various books, but as he was promoted to detective early on, rather young actually, all the hard work had paid off. He was soon known as an aggressive and clever investigator. His main strength had been his intimate knowledge of what computers could do for him and his department. He was adamant about his department having the most updated and newest software available.

Linda had taken a break from the police academy to deliver the twins. The academy had let her participate in classes up till a day before her water broke and credited her academic records accordingly. After 4 months of solid baby-caring, she went back to the academy and quickly caught up with the training. Michael had helped out with the kids at home so Linda could do what she also wanted to do, become a homicide detective. They shared the children's upbringing and maintenance. At times they ran a bit tight – but they had endured. Linda finally worked cold cases, something she had a passion for and was quickly getting good at. Her persuasion was that no proven criminal would run free.

Nicole and Frank had been very cooperative from birth. Linda would never be able to tell long tales of extended delivery, suffering and pain. Nicole and Frank had pretty much *popped out* and in that order – ten minutes between each *pop*. They were now 10 years old and very close. Nicole was the sweet, nurturing friend to Frank. She acted more like a support group for him then an equal sibling. She mastered rolling her eyes, as it was something she felt should be applied to a lot of what Frank did and even more so to most of what Frank said and/or expressed. She loved him very much and they rarely spent time apart.

And Frank was something else. Well, not in a bad way at all, but he was one of those few people you meet in your life who totally impress you. It was not charm or wit, though some would categorize him as cynically funny, and it wasn't good looks as he was a bit, okay a lot, on the nerdy side. But when Frank spoke, you'd forget all that. Early on, he had shown signs of knowledge accumulation beyond his age and maturity level. *Photographic memory* had been a label stuck on him from the age of three. He started formulating words and sentences by the time he was barely 8 months old. Granted that many of them were a bit incoherent, but the fact that he tried speaking was fascinating to his parents. To outsiders, Frank could be rather annoying, actually extremely so. He had a very hard time keeping his mouth shut, as he commented on anything anybody said wrong or even said right. Though he was only ten, his knowledge of the English language was extreme. That caused him a bit of trouble at times. His reading level was high and his academic interests so varied. But it was the English language that he had the most fun with – some wouldn't agree with the *fun* part, especially when the fun was made on their behalf. His great-grandfather George had often told him about *his* language skills back in Russia.

As Linda, Michael and the kids only lived a few blocks away, grandpa Jack was often utilized as the sitter. Nicole was in love with her grandfather and Frank had a good relationship with Jack. He knew Jack liked him for the kid he was and had never been one of those *in awe of his gifts* kind of adult; Frank loved being treated as a regular kid and besides his parents and Nicole, Jack was one of the few who did. For some reason, Frank had always called Jack *Jack*, never grandpa or grandfather; nobody had bothered asking *why*.

Jasper struggled through a long devastating sense of total loss after his mother died. He had locked himself in his room for days and refused to come out. He hadn't eaten, had not had any water and kept silent, no matter how much everybody pleaded with him. Jack reached the point where breaking down the door was eminent, but Michael had begged him to hold off and instead get hold of Molly. They hadn't seen or heard from her since the funeral, and weren't even sure if she was still around. Jack had desperately tried to find her, but it was Michael who had camped out on the porch of her grandparent's house for hours on end; waiting and hoping. He was rolled up in a sleeping-bag trying to stay warm, when Molly finally showed up; it was past midnight. He begged and pleaded with her to come and talk to Jasper. He was afraid that Jasper was reaching a point where he would hurt himself; even consider suicide. Molly showed no emotions as she nodded and followed Michael to the Miller's house. She knocked on Jasper's door, first politely, but when she didn't get the answer she wanted, she knocked loud enough to wake everybody up, which they did. But they all stayed where they were – in their rooms; they didn't feel they should disturb the situation to any extent. If anybody could talk any sense into Jasper besides his mother, it was Molly. Her voice was firm and demanding.

"Jasper, can you hear me?" No answer.

"Jasper, I can't really stand here and waste my time if you don't want to talk. So I suggest that you let me know if you want to listen. A basic yes or no will suffice." Jasper's voice was weak and trembling.

"Okay."

"Okay what?" She shot back.

"Yes." His voice slightly irritated.

"So you listen well: Why have you locked everybody out, Jasper? Why are you punishing everybody around you with your sorrow? Don't you think they are suffering too, or do you think it's only you who's going through a really shitty time concerning your mother's death?" Jack heard every word as did everybody else in the house; he coiled by the directness in her voice. "Do you hear me?" She demanded.

"Yes!" was his timid response.

"You are not alone about this, so I advise you to come out and open your arms to help others through their pain and loss. Don't be such a selfish twit and think it's all about you and all about how *you* feel. This is about all of us, every single one of us, so don't be so bloody selfish." Jack was wondering why she would say that to Jasper, as *she* most certainly had not shared *her* sorrow with anybody but herself; *she* was the one being selfish, he thought. But if it would force Jasper to come out, he didn't care at all. "I lost both my parents when I was six, and I still miss them. I also lost Sara and I miss her terribly and that will never change. I always envied the relationship you had with your mother, as you had a closeness I have never seen before and probably will never see again; or experience myself, for that matter. Don't disrespect that special relationship by feeling so utterly sorry for yourself. You respected your mother in life Jasper, I know that. So for crying out loud, respect your mother in her death as well. She would be extremely disappointed if you didn't. You must continue your plans, the plans you made together with Sara. You want to be a lawyer like your mother and she was so proud of you. So my suggestion is that you get off your ass and become an even better lawyer than she was. She will be following your every move as she is watching you, so don't fuck all that up and disappoint her; just get the hell going." She paused. Her facial expression was tense and tight; it showed an inner anger and sense of loss that she tried to keep to herself. "And you have a terrific father who loves you more than anything on this earth. He needs you very much, especially now. And you have a loving brother who cares so much about you and a sister who looks up to you like nothing I have ever seen before. So are you going to ignore their needs and their sorrows so that you can dwell on your own misery? Is that what you are all about now? If that's the way, Jasper, then you have turned pathetic and extremely egocentric. But I don't think that's you, because I know you better than most, because I knew your mother better than most, but not better than your father, your brother or your sister. I just knew her in a very special way, and you did too. So don't sit in there and pity yourself; don't fuck up by making the wrong decision." She paused. Michael was sitting on the floor a few feet from Molly. He had tears in his eyes and looked at her in awe, with love and respect. "I have to go now, Jasper. I'm not wasting any more of my time on this, so now it's completely up to you. Remember, don't disappoint your mother, but much more importantly, don't fucking disappoint yourself. Get your shit together, Jasper." Her face had turned red in anger, but as she turned towards Michael, she quickly returned to no emotions at all. "He'll come out soon; he'll be alright." She turned and walked down the hall and down the stairs. Jack saw her only as a blur passing by his bedroom door; that was the last he saw of Molly. A few minutes later Jasper came out of his room, exhausted, pale and crying. They all embraced in a warm and loving hug; Jack, Jasper, Michael and Caroline; finally they could comfort each other in their saddened sorrow. *Where's Molly?* Jasper had asked, but nobody knew.

Jasper was 27 now. A few months after his mother's death, he continued his law studies at Georgetown University. The fact that his mother had graduated from the law department and had been one of the more dynamic alumni's had of course helped. But the more important deal was that he was a 4.0 plus honor student from an academically tough and prestigious private school. Jasper worked night and day on his studies; he also took extra classes and whatever else he could to advance quicker. He was a superb debater and communicator who rarely lost a case in class; he was as stubborn as his mother, if not more so. By the time he was a year from graduating, he had seven solid offers for employment from seven of the better law firms in the Washington D.C. area. Jasper gracefully declined seven times. His mother had always wanted him to join her firm and Sara's two partners made sure that offer was on the table as he left school. Both partners had kept in contact with him and had also solicited his help whenever he could find time to do so. He passed the bar as one of the youngest applicants and impressively nailed what had to be nailed.

Two days after law school was done with, he was sitting in Sara's old office. The partners had removed cases and case files, but left everything else where it was for Jasper to take over. But they hadn't told Jasper, and when they presented the office to him and explained why they thought he would like it, there had been a bit of hesitation from his side. He had asked for a moment alone, entered his mother's office and sat down in her chair for several quiet minutes. With closed eyes, he could see and hear his mother do her business. He could clearly sense her presence and found it very strong, and surprisingly more pleasant than sad. It would be okay, he thought with a smile. The partners came in quietly with question marks on their faces. They were nice women, the same age as his mother had been. He had always liked them and through the years he had found a terrific zone of comfort with them. He answered their question marks.

"This feels right, you know. It feels really good. I was afraid that I would freak out and see my mother's ghost or something. But this feels really good, it really does." Both women smiled big from relief.

"We are very happy that you like it." They exchanged quick glances with each other. "There is another matter that we want to bring up now. The tradition, if we can call it that, is that a new partner has to earn his or her marks. But since we have followed you very closely in school and your overall progress, we have found that you are way beyond the new legal counselor status, but still can't title you full fletched partner, so please accept this little token till the time you have earned full partnership." She handed Jasper a name plaque; it read: Jasper Miller, Honorary Partner. He laughed out loud, got up and gave them both a hug.

"I am seriously honored and will do my utmost to live up to your expectations as well as to your high standards." They opened a bottle of champagne and the whole office had now joined them in a toast for their new member. Jasper was in seventh heaven and he wished that Molly could have been next to him sharing this special moment. He wanted to thank her for kicking his butt when his butt needed kicking. But nobody had heard anything from Molly for many years; he realized again that he missed her tremendously.

She had softly melted her way into the welcome party in Jasper's new office. Though the room was packed with laughter and lots of smiles and energy, she caught Jasper's attention at once. No, he was not your average Don Juan, the farthest from and had only had two girlfriends since puberty – one of them rather platonic. But there was something fascinating about this young woman, but he had no idea what it was that hit him so strongly. She was nice looking with soft and gentle features. She wasn't a stunning looking woman like Aunt Vicky, but what he saw that afternoon made his heart beat fast and he had to admit, wobbled his knees. Maybe it was the euphoria of his career start or the champagne; either way he excused himself and walked over to her.

"Hi, I'm Jasper. I'm neither drunk nor weird, but I felt a force pulling at me to meet you." She smiled and giggled a little bit.

"I must say; a rather unusual pick-up line." He blushed very reddish.

"Oh God no, that's not what I meant, oh no. I mean, I had to come over and introduce myself. I must sound like a strange person. I'm sorry." She kept smiling.

"I already know who you are. For the record, I'm Ella, by the way." She stretched out her hand; he grabbed it and mumbled.

"Fitzgerald?" She laughed out loud - in a quiet way.

"That was random, but you are right. My parents are great fans, believe me. Not much else is heard at home."

"I'm sorry; that came out a bit wrong, but thanks for playing along."

"No really Jasper, it's the truth." He was relieved.

"What do you do here, I mean work wise?"

"I'm freelancing when I have time."

"Meaning what?"

"I'm called when needed."

"What do you do in between?"

"Go to school." Jasper saw an opening.

"Where?"

"Georgetown Law."

"No kidding!"

"No kidding!" Jasper looked relieved again. Stuff he could talk about.

"Now this might sound very forward, extremely weird and you can hit me if you feel threatened."

"So which one of the three is it most likely to be? Oh, that even rhymed." She giggled.

"All three, I'm sure, rhyme or no reason." She smiled.

"Okay Jasper, try me."

"If you go to school and you are only helping out here when needed, you would not legally be an employee of this firm, correct?" She felt she knew where this was going.

"I would consider that a correct statement."

"So if you find this legally and ethically correct, you should be able to go out to dinner or on a date or something with me, without breaking company policies?" She looked speculative.

"I should be able to do one or all three if I so desired; but that might be the question, of course. I'm not fully sure of the legality of such proposal, though."

"How about desiring all three if the coast is legally clear and any unethical fog has been lifted?" She smiled and moved closer to him and whispered in his ear.

"How poetic; but why don't we get a second opinion concerning this intriguing, though sordid proposal?" Jasper looked confused. "I mean, let's ask my mother." Now he was even more confused. She grabbed his hand and pulled him along; a short moment later they were in front of one of Jasper's new partners.

"Mom, Mr. Miller has asked me out on a date, or something," she giggled the last part, "so the question was brought up if that would be ethically, morally..." Jasper interrupted.

"The *morally* part was never brought up, Ella."

"I'm sorry, counselor. The question was if it would be legally and/or ethically within the rules of this firm's policies for such a proposition to be activated." They were met with laughter.

"I fully trust that the rules do not hinder such a union, but of course it must be considered on a trial basis only, at least during the first ten dates." Ella had not released her grip of Jasper's hand, which he of course had nothing against; he was holding on as well.

"Okay, it's all settled then. Would tomorrow evening at my favorite restaurant work for you?" She smiled at Jasper and squeezed his hand as confirmation.

The next evening they spent four and a half hours at Nonna's. Romano was so happy to see Jasper with a girlfriend. Jasper was in high heavens and Ella was right there next to him, hand in hand. Life had turned out to be just fine and Jasper could feel his mother's approval and love coming from above and right smack down into the middle of it all; and there was nothing wrong with that.

Caroline left Washington D.C. after she finished high school. She had accumulated an interest in chemistry. One of her favorite teachers had suggested that with her academic talents, as well as the interest that was driving her, Michigan State University had a tremendous forensic science program, specializing in deoxyribonucleic acid research, better known as, and easier to pronounce: DNA. Caroline was 22 years old at this point and deep into the Master's Program with a few more years and additional options left at MSU. Though she hesitated or more so had a lot of doubt concerning this field in the beginning, she quickly found great excitement and many superb challenges that made her a true believer in the line of work she had chosen.

She had learned a lot from Molly when she was younger. Study habits, priorities, organized life-style, friendship and purpose from the time she'd get up till going to bed at night – boys were not part of the plan. She wanted to get her education, be able to fully take care of herself financially as well as intellectually – and she was on the right track. She constantly sent a lot of thanks and gratitude Molly's way, but would like to deliver those appreciations in person – face to face. But she had finally accepted that Molly was gone forever.

Molly had been a huge part of her growing up. She had been her best friend and role model, as well as mentor and teacher. She had never talked down to Caroline, had never treated her as *that little kid*, but had always shown her equality, respect and lots of love. And then one day she was gone, had disappeared without a word, without a goodbye. It had taken Caroline several years to recognize that it was not her doing that Molly vanished, but it was something Molly had to figure out alone. Caroline had a very hard time forgiving her for not saying proper goodbyes and explaining why.

Oh yes, Caroline was still her daddy's little girl. Jack would often visit her at MSU as well as she would spend all breaks and many weekends in Washington. Summer breaks she traveled; Caroline and Jack were travel buddies, visiting Asia, Australia, New Zealand, and most of Europe.

Jack saw a lot of Sara in his daughter, but she was still much more Caroline than Sara. She had developed into a bright, funny and entertaining young woman, and though Jack felt it a bit odd that she didn't have an interest in men, in dating and those sort of things, he did appreciate the time with her. *I'll get there*; she said when that topic came up in conversation. Jack was selfish and didn't press the issue. He would gladly take as much time with Caroline he could get. And then there was Jack.

He had reached 50 and the ten years that had passed since Sara's death had been horrendous and horrible for him. The first many months he had not been able to function at home or at work. Nora had taken care of the business end of his demise, but at home it had pretty much been Caroline's responsibility to keep her father alive. Jasper and Michael had purposely fled the nest as soon as it was possible, which stranded their sister to fend for herself – and her dad. Jack had been pathetically weak, and had at times dragged Caroline with him on his tours of deep depression. If anything positive came out of those first few years, it was that Caroline had matured and grown up tremendously fast. As a 14 year old she acted more like she was 40, and a very mature 40 at that; Jack had stayed the baby – (no disrespect to babies).

Days and nights, weeks, months and years, all blurred together in sorrow and sadness. Every waking hour filled with mourning and self-pity. He would lie on his bed, holding on to a sweater or a blouse or a pair of Sara's pants, pretending he could still smell her. He didn't date or socialize; the only stimulation from other human beings would be when the kids came by. His father would spend some time with him, as well as Nora and William would drop by from time to time and discuss business. In the beginning it had been to support Jack in his grief, but after a year, it became too much and much more of a joke; everybody getting rather bored and in some cases rather pissed about his pathetic behavior, and the visits started to stop. But his depressing behavior, self-destruction and extremely tedious being had not just lasted that one year, it kept going full speed, and finally nobody other than Jack wanted to be on that ride.

Victoria had been one of the last survivors, as she had hoped to salvage whatever was left of Jack. Sure she had thought about trying to make him love her, thought about seducing him in his weakness of suffering, but as she had looked at him, sitting deep into the sofa with the saddest *and most pathetic* puppy face, she actually felt turned off;

something she never thought would have happened. She was finally over Jack, and William smiled big.

Karen had given it one last shot. She reasoned that so many other family members and friends had *tried* their healing luck on him, so a measly assistant probably shouldn't add her few words of condolences. But Nora had actually asked if she felt like going. Karen had been a bit puzzled, but was laughing hard as Nora explained the reason why she thought it would be a good idea.

"You are just about the most straight forward person I know." Karen looked for more of an explanation.

"Is that good or bad, Nora?"

"That's very good. You always speak your mind..."

"... and get in trouble doing so." Karen smiled.

"No really, Karen. You are just my kind of pal, and if you can apply your no shit attitude to Jack, maybe it could shake him up."

"But what's the deal with him?"

"He's been oh so depressed and sad and shit like that for way too long."

"It has been close to ten years now, hasn't it?"

"Precisely!"

"Has he dated or something like that, you know, socialized any?"

"Not a bit, nada - nothing."

"So he obviously needs to get laid, if I'm not totally wrong."

"Maybe a bit harsh Dear Karen, but correct just the same." They both smiled and Karen drove off to conquer the saddened.

"Hi, Karen, it's so nice of you to come by." Jack greeted her in a happy and somewhat energetic voice; but from that moment on, it went downhill very fast. After 45 long minutes Karen had had enough. She had with pain stayed beyond normal courtesy and politeness, but she did not want to be exposed to this boring and depressing shit one more second.

"Jack I like you, I actually *loved* you, you know, good old Jack. But this person you have turned into is self-centered, pathetic, a bore and not fun to be with. You need to get your shit together, go out and find some women, get laid, anything to help knock you out of this cocoon-like crap you have spun yourself into. This is not the Jack I want to remember, so I'm getting my cute and well-shaped butt out of here and if you don't re-invent the old you very soon, I'm not going to be around. I like working for positive people, not self-centered pathetic shelves of human beings. I'm sure you'll understand." He nodded and wanted to confirm and explain, but Karen didn't see or hear it as she was already the heck out of there, mad as hell. Karen felt she had done her share concerning dealing with Jack through his depression over the years, and though she for the most worked with Nora, he was still a partner – something she had never understood. But enough was enough; this was the excuse she needed.

It was just a few days later Karen gave Nora her letter of resignation. Through the years she had received several job-offers from suppliers and customers of CR Constructions, and she had finally decided to move on. It had been an extremely interesting and challenging job being Jack Miller's assistant, but Jack Miller had left the building and was now a boring imposter. Karen disliked the imposter, so she found no reason to stay. At her age, she also felt that with her talents, people skills and experience, she wanted to get up higher in the ranks and challenges, be more of a decision maker. *Yes* she was a bit young for that, had no academic training beyond high school, but she had a lot of great work experience; she knew she was good and most people around her fully agreed.

Nora read the letter a couple of times. She adored Karen. She was a tremendous individual, utterly efficient in everything she did, precise, never late with anything and a swirling brain with so many ideas and comments and suggestions – and most of them inventive as well as progressive. It was especially Karen's outstanding relations with her fellow employees that were so unique. She could get anybody to do anything at any time, and on schedule. For many reasons everybody respected Karen and could not resist her (or her wishes). It was a brilliant talent for this type of time sensitive business. Now they were going to lose her due to Jack's consistent pathetic absence; but Nora was not going to let that happen.

Her own personal assistant, Alice, was very good. Her office organization skills superb, her dedication unquestionable, but people skills did not exist with her at all. She played by the book-of-rules, but didn't gain any great groups of supporters from that, as she also lacked charm and humor; Karen didn't. Nora could not lay her off as she certainly had done nothing wrong and there was plenty of business and work to be done through the next many years. Nora was saddened by that, but had to bite her lip and stay the course with Alice. But fate plays many mysterious tricks on us at times, in real life as in fairytales - even if we don't deserve it.

Alice looked miserable as she entered Nora's office. Her face was white and she had obviously been crying. Her father had offered her a job with his company for a lot of money and needed her there. Alice had told him that she was happy where she was. But her father had hooked her with an even fatter pay-check, so *family business & much more money* won her over. Nora had pretended to be sad and worried, but comforted Alice that she should be able to find a replacement, and perhaps two would be needed. They had hugged and Alice left. Nora waved goodbye with one hand, as the other hand was busy fumbling for the phone to make that all important call to Karen.

Karen had explained the Jack thing to Nora as somewhat the sole reason for her resignation. Nora fully understood that reason and had seriously contemplated a similar move herself, though a fleeting thought of that. Nora dialed Karen's number, mumbling to herself: *Here comes the tricky bit.*

"So that's the situation, Karen. Alice left and that leaves a position open for you."
"Nora, thank you so much. You know that I love you and I have always been very impressed with the way you function; I pretty much look at you as my role-model concerning work. But I have a great offer sitting here that I will accept because I need to move on."
"Karen, I know that and that's why I want to bring you back to much more responsibility, more decision making, fully supporting *me*. I want you to take an active part in the future of CR. I also want you to develop our marketing department more effectively. I want you to travel with me and

participate in conferences and trade-shows; pretty much be my Siamese twin." Karen giggled.

"So I would be the white version of the twins, huh?" Nora giggled too. "But they have offered me a lot of money, Nora."

" I know, dear. We'll do the same and also put you on our management bonus program." Karen knew how huge those checks had been the last few years – and they were getting bigger.

"It's very tempting, Nora."

"But listen, there's more: You have mentioned that you are looking for your own place, you know, you living with your folks and all."

"That's true." Karen's interest was peaking.

"I moved out of my apartment a few months ago and haven't sold it, so I came up with the brilliant idea that you might want to live there. You know it's a great neighborhood and just a short bus-ride from CR." Karen loved Nora's old place; two rooms, large bathroom and a delightful kitchen, plus an attached garage.

"But I can't afford to live there or buy it or anything, really."

"Here's the deal…" and fifteen minutes later it was all settled and they were both satisfied and happy.

"Nora, this is all so generous, I don't even have to think about it. Can I start tomorrow?"

"Now remember, that I will make you earn your salary. Working with me is a lot tougher than working with Jack, and I'll never consider you a charity case, Karen; please remember that. I'll see you tomorrow."

"I'm on board; see you tomorrow." When Nora told Jack that CR had been very close losing Karen because of his behavior, he just rolled his eyes and slummed further back into the sofa. It would take a long time for Jack to get better – too much time already, Nora thought.

Jack remembered when William had stopped by with some paperwork from the office. It had been the last time he had seen him. They had talked about business, but at some point, like clockwork, Jack had mentioned something about Sara. Jack couldn't remember precisely what he had said about her or his loss, but William had quickly gathered all the papers and stuffed them into his briefcase. He rolled his eyes and shook his head as he went for the door as fast as he could and then turned towards Jack.

"You know Jack, you really piss me off and not just me, but everybody who loved you a long time ago. You are so fucking pathetic that it makes me sick just being in the same room with you. It is constantly about Sara and your bloody misery being alone, her leaving you; for the most it's all about you, not her. She's the one who missed out, Jack. You have a life to live and you have done absolutely nothing to honor her, like living a respectful life, like caring for your children, nurturing your family and friends. All you have done for so many years is just bloody sit there pitying yourself and linger in this self-fabricated misery. All this spells a weak human being. You have been hand-carried through life by your father, Colleen and Charles, Victoria, Sara and now finally Nora; it's been a free ride, buddy. And this is the result: a pathetic and sorry excuse of a man, whimpering tears of *why me*?" Jack sat frozen in the chair, staring at William. "So the question is: Will Jack do something about it or is he going to stay the course and keep racing to the bottom of the land of *patheticness*? You know, what I'm concerned, you are too weak to do anything for your children and your family, so I'm positive that the latter is your choice, because you are too petty to do anything constructive. I have two options now: one is sticking with my friend who turned pathetic or simply twirl around, leave and not come back because my former friend *did* leave the building a long fucking time ago. At this point Dear Jack, I choose to leave, because I have had enough of your mourning shit." William stormed out the door and didn't look back. Jack was left sitting stiff as a board with a lot to think about.

It was a while after William's final visit that George made his last appearance. Jack had teary-eyed told his father what William had thrown at him. George had laughed and giggled, while shaking his head.

"Well good for William. I've always liked his forthrightness. He has always been a superb friend of yours, Jack, but he got fed up, like the rest of us."

"But you don't understand…"

"Listen to yourself, son, you are still whimpering *your* own misery, *your* loss, how the world has mistreated *you*. It's all about you, and that got old years ago. You let your children fend for themselves; your friends finally run as far away from you as possible; your partner-in-business keep carrying *your* share, *your* responsibilities on *her* shoulders – and keeps paying you. And you do absolutely nothing to earn it. This kind of behavior actually makes stupidity sound fascinating." He paused. "So here's the deal, Jack: I'm also out of here and will stay out of your life until you make an effort to change things around. You might ask yourself how you'd do that. My very last suggestion: grab a firm hold of your balls, if you still have them; decide where you would like to be within a foreseeable future, what you want to do for your lost children, your family, your friends and your business partner. When you realize how stupid you have been these many years, I'm sure there might still be some brain cells left to find the correct way for you to amend and move forward – and hopefully fast. So give those balls a tight grip and work them hard. We all *loved* you, Jack, but you successfully pushed us all away and you have nobody left other than yourself. And that is very sad." Jack was stunned and his mind went all over the place. This was his father who had said all these terrible things, his father who he had been sure would stick with him through thick and thin. Obviously it had become much too thick for anybody; even his dad.

Nora and Karen paid one final visit that day too and it had not been a happy one for Jack. He had ignorantly thought *compassion*, but suddenly that had been painful to even expect anymore. They had not been their own charming selves, far from. They had arrived with a mission, and they stuck to the agenda, which left Jack in confused turmoil. He had noticed how Karen had matured under the tutelage of Nora. For a split second he was impressed, but it quickly turned to jealousy and loss.

Nora and Karen painted a situation for Jack that clearly spelled that he either pulled himself together or Nora would use a clause in their contract through which she could buy out an inactive partner – and she would do so very fast. She told Jack that since he was absent and only sporadically participated in the business, Karen had taken control of his responsibilities and was doing a tremendous job, and had already achieved higher profit margins among other things.

The site crews respected her directions, efficiency and common sense, and as she worked very close with the crew bosses, she had in spite of her young age reached surprising results. Jack fully understood why Nora told him this, as it was the nicer way of saying that life at CR was not interrupted by his absence anymore - far from. So if he wanted to join the team again was fully up to him. If he decided not to join by staying pathetic within his own world of stupidity, he would be kicked out – and fast.

Nora had already talked with Jasper about the legality of dissolving the partnership. She was a bit hesitant approaching CR's new legal advisor about this issue, due to the blood line, but Jasper, who was also tired of his father's state of mind, had no qualms being involved what so ever. He had actually brought Nora's attention to that specific clause in the contract that stated if one partner did not produce and/or did not perform to expected levels or standards, based on the company's recent profitability; did not participate reasonably, equal in time spent with the company, such partner could be forced to sell shares and/or dissolve his/her full share of partnership, determined and agreed upon by legal advice from both sides of negotiations. Nora knew she could get rid of Jack in a second if she so wished. When they had formulated the contract before entering the partnership, they had both giggled concerning this issue and Jack had uttered that such situation would of course never happen, but what the heck, let's stick it in there to satisfy the attorneys. Now he realized that Sara had been extremely adamant about adding this clause, as both Nora and Jack's legal adviser. Could some kind of irony be found in this?

Karen had presented the future plans of the company. She was fluent and energetic in her delivery and anybody listening would certainly be drawn in. Jack had been good at stuff like that, but now he knew he could never be as good as Karen. She was charming as well as pleasing to the eye, but besides that she had sternness in her verbal skills that made you pay attention to whatever she communicated. Jack knew she could replace him without any hiccups, and seemingly already had; a thought that depressed him even more.

Nicole and Frank had been listening from the family room. After Nora and Karen left they did a soft high five between and smiled. Nicole looked at her watch and started packing her stuff; Frank did the same. Their father picked them up a few minutes later.

"Hi Dad," Michael saw his father still stunned in the chair. He had passed Nora and Karen on their way out, so he figured something did not fit into the *happy department.* Jack didn't react.

"Hi kids. How was your day?" Both Nicole and Frank smiled big.

"It was superb, Dad." Nicole said in her father's hug.

"Yeah - just superb." All three turned towards Jack; he didn't look up.

"Bye Dad," Michael had the kids by their hands and they were soon in the car and on their way home. "You okay?" Michael was asking the twins. "You think this will work?" Nicole and Frank were sitting in the backseat; they both nodded with sad eyes. Jack was left behind in total silence, in a shattered world that he only vaguely felt could be repaired. Of course there was still that last option, but he sadly felt that he was too much of a stinking coward to do even that.

The loud banging startled him. At first he was confused as to where it came from. The alarm clock told him 2:45 AM; the outside darkness confirmed it. The banging persisted, this time even more demanding. Jack swung out of bed, grabbed his robe and went downstairs. The noise came from the kitchen entrance. Without thinking, he pulled out a knife from the block and was soon searching for a peep-hole that was not there.

"Who is it?"

"Never mind who it is – open up." The voice was female and slurry. "Open up or I'll break it down." The body attached to the seemingly drunken voice sounded as it was in no condition to even break an egg. "Let me in." The slurry voice had gotten blurrier and more pleading. "Please." Jack carefully slid the deadbolt to the left and cranked the door handle lock to slowly open the door. He was not to any extend prepared for what he found outside his kitchen door that dark and dreary night.

He did a quick scan of the female person in front of him. She was dressed in an oversized men's pajama, extremely unruly hair, a multicolored blotchy face and large fluffy slippers with worn-out bunny ears. She had a bottle of some kind of alcohol in each hand and supported her balance with the use of the doorframe; but she still swung from side to side. Drunken eyes slowly reached Jack's face; she took a big swig from the bottle in her left hand and quickly followed up with the one in the right. He was wondering if this was one of the new neighbors who'd moved in across the street a few weeks ago.

"Equal opportunity, hah?" She tried to laugh as she held up the bottles, but it only materialized in slight drooling and a wrenched facial expression. "How you been, ole buddy?" Her speech was near impossible to understand, but Jack got the essence of what she was trying to say.

"I've been fine, thank you. Who are you and whoever you are, what are you doing here?" She took a few more swigs and tried to catch Jack's eyes.

"Who'm I? But Jackie-Baby, it's moi." She unsuccessfully pointed at herself, nearly hitting her left eye with an unsteady finger; but Jack was still perplexed.

"Me who?"

"But don't you reacaglize me, Jackie-Baby. It's me, the Molly next door person." Jack stepped back with a jerk. He leaned forward a bit and looked more concentrated at her.

"You are Molly?" Now he was totally confused.

"That's se troooth; at least lassed I shecked." She giggled as a drunkard. "Lassed I shecked, hows about that…" She made the mistake of letting go of the doorframe and fell into Jack's arms. He grabbed her before she would have smashed her face against the tile floor.

"Nice catch, Jackie-Boy." She was hanging onto Jack trying to look up at his face. She held up one of the bottles.

"Hey big boy, why don't you join me and Jack and Johnny for a bit of some fun?" She paused. "Hey it's two of them Jack boys and then Johnny and Molly. Let's party smarty." And she swigged some more.

"Molly, this is really you?" He asked in disbelief. "Where have you been all these years?" He supported her weight on the way to the couch in the family room; her drunken look staring at him all the way.

"From blooming hell and back, that's what I'm whered." She slumped fully onto the couch as if she was boneless. Her head slowly swung to the side and the rest of her alcohol numbed body followed willingly. "God I'm so schleepy." And she fell over. Miraculously neither of the two bottles spilled a drop. Drunks seem to have a bit of luck with that. "I'll schleepy forever now, I don't mind if I do – sank yuoo." Jack carefully wrestled the bottles out of her tight grips and sat them on the sofa table. He gently lifted the two boneless legs up on the couch and stretched them for comfort. He grabbed a pillow and placed it under her head. She looked awful. Her face was a mess and her hair like a rain-storm ridden haystack. She had already started a very loud and disturbingly nasty snoring. Saliva was freely flowing from each side of her mouth, landing on the already soaked pillow. The stench of her breath was a terrifying mixture of alcohol on top of even more alcohol; it was nauseating and tickled his gagging-reflexes - he could barely keep them under control. He got up and grabbed a blanket from a closet. As he placed it on top of her, he saw a disturbed peace on her face; an extremely tense peace at that. He pulled a chair closer to her as he decided to make sure she was okay. A few minutes later her breathing was regular and consistent, but the snoring had not lost any volume – quite the opposite. To cool her off a bit, Jack gently wiped her face with a moist washcloth. Before he went up to bed, he placed a large bucket on the floor right below her head – just in case.

It had been the most horrific day for Jack. The final visits from people he loved, but who didn't love him anymore had been eye opening. Nora had looked frustrated, disappointed and angry as she and Karen had left. Frank and Nicole, no matter how young they were, had nailed him to the cross and pretty much discarded him from their lives. Michael had looked over his shoulder one last time as they left and had glanced at him with whatever little hope he had. It all hit Jack in the heart with excruciating pain; it pretty much knocked him over. He was not able to fall asleep, and when he finally did, he had only slept a few hours before the banging had started.

He couldn't believe Molly had all of a sudden showed up. It was exactly ten years ago they saw her last.

She had disappeared without a word, and not communicated since. After a few years nobody asked about her anymore; seemed like she was finally forgotten. Caroline was the only one who at times would bring Molly's name up with her father. Whenever she did, it was about how much she missed her, stories from the past, things they did together and thoughts of what could have been. Caroline was most disappointed that her best buddy in the world had just left her guessing what had happened and why she could not have been respectful enough to explain and say goodbye. She still felt hurt and unjustly discarded. Even a few months ago, when she was home from school for the weekend and they had dinner at Nonna's, Molly's name had popped up. Jack could easily hear the lingering disappointment in her voice even after ten years. But she told a story about her and Molly that made them both laugh, and the subject of Molly that evening had ended with a smile. Jack appreciated the memories Caroline had of Molly. They were all fond and fun, never negative. Molly had been an energetic addition to the Miller family, no matter how eccentric she was or perhaps because of. And now she all of a sudden was downstairs, drunk as a skunk, snoring away like a boozed up sailor on leave, and ten years later. Jack finally fell asleep.

Sara snuggled up and put her arms around him. She liked to do that and he had nothing against it. The feeling was always heaven and made his heart beat faster, no matter how tired he was. He found her hands around his chest and quickly covered them with his. They felt a little different tonight, but they were still soft and sweet and searching. He backed up closer to her and she responded by pressing her body even tighter to his. They had always been a terrific fit and they were fitting especially well tonight. He gave her hands a tender squeeze and got a caressing squeeze right back; he smiled and soon found himself floating around in sleep-land on the whitest cloud, making love to Sara again and again; his very lovely and sexy Sara.

Victoria had also given up on Jack. He had become a shell of something she didn't care for anymore. His quiet sexiness had evaporated, his charm and wit disappeared and his sense of humor had left him, no doubt from sheer boredom. She spent many hours and an enormous amount of effort to entice him to love her, make love to her, because she still had the obsessive urges to let it happen. *If he would just do it and get it over with,* she thought in desperation, but quickly regretted her animalistic instincts. Though Jack had not yet officially deflowered her, a technicality not realistic anymore, of course, she was still hoping, however naïve that thought was.

But something positive had come out of this. Since Jack was now turning her off sexually, she took that frustration out on William. She had become an aggressive lover more so and pushed William to places in their sex life they had never visited before. She was eager and warm-blooded and couldn't get enough; William was not a bad partner at all, so he had found this new sex drive of his wife's to be the hottest thing ever and was right there with her all the way and beyond. More and more became better and better. What William didn't know, of course, was that she was having sex with Jack most of the times she was intimate with him; but it was oh so great that maybe he wouldn't even have cared if he had known?

But slowly, all of Victoria's attention swung to William. She had finally seriously falling in love with him and the thoughts of lusty moments with Jack had disappeared; and for that she was more than grateful. Life had finally opened up for her and she felt the relief from her own pathetic obsession enormously gratifying; William did too…

Far from Washington D.C. inmate Fielder had escaped. Due to his well behaved prisoner status, he had been assigned work at the laundry facilities. The guards had over the last few years started to like Fielder. He was an intelligent man, charming and well spoken. They knew about the violent crime he was in for, but as they got to know him better, they started to feel that he had been applied too long of a sentence. He often talked about how he truly regretted what he had done, how much he wanted to undo it, but knew of course that he couldn't. They would find him weeping in his cell, banging hard on his bed for consolation. Whenever the guards asked him to help out, he was more than willing, always polite and never whined about anything.

A couple of the guards started to feel sorry for him, a feeling they had never applied to any of the other prisoners; Fielder seemed like a really decent man, who had just lost it for a split second and was now paying dearly with too many years.

The guards were big stupid assholes, he thought. He played them like violins and they ate it all up. Fucking assholes, that's what they were. It had been way too many bloody years. He started working on a plan to get out of this awful place the second he was denied parole for the fourth time. The parole hearing had gone well until that old fuck-head had showed up again. He had been at the previous three hearings and here he was again – and again *parole denied. What the fuck does he want, and why keep punishing me?* He thought aggressively angry.

But the plan was now in place. He had buttered up the stupid guards and they even felt a bit sorry for him; what ignorant idiots. He was assigned laundry detail and that would be his way out. Only well behaved inmates would be allowed to work the loading docks, so when the trucks rolled in and out, Fielder would help load and unload the laundry. He patiently made acquaintances with some of the drivers and over the next year, he became closely acquainted with Gordon James, a veteran driver. Gordon was friendly as well as greedy; Fielder knew that right away and that was why he zeroed in on him. It had been a cat and mouse game as Fielder couldn't show preference to specific drivers; that would have caused immediate suspicion. So he spread out his *friendliness* to several, but slowly and surely reeled Gordon James in specifically.

The final stage of Fielder's escape was set in motion. It was not going to be quick, but Fielder had all the time on earth. Another ten years had been added to his sentence some eight years back from a failed escape attempt.

One day he had with teary eyes asked if Gordon could do him a great favor. He needed him to go to Pensacola, Florida, and give some money to his cousin. It didn't matter what it was for, really, and Fielder told him that it was nothing illegal, not really. All Gordon had to do was pick up the money from Fielder's attorney in Washington D.C., fly down to Pensacola, visit his cousin and hand over the cash. Fielder's cousin was bedridden and he had no way of getting the money any other way. Fielder whispered in Gordon's ear: *and it's a bit of money the IRS don't know about.* Gordon had nodded in understanding. For the two days work, Fielder paid him $1,000.00 cash plus expenses – he was hooked and was now being reeled in.

Everything went the way Fielder told Gordon it should go. The attorney met him in the airport as scheduled and Fielder's cousin had a nurse open the door when he arrived in Pensacola. The poor sap was strapped to the hospital bed and looked miserable, so Gordon felt good about helping out, but felt even better with the big pay-off. The moment the door to the cousin's house closed behind him on his way out, the *cousin* jumped out of bed, threw the packet that was supposed to be cash in the trashcan and started to remove the nurse's uniform, one button at a time. She didn't mind at all and they were soon rumbling around in the rented hospital bed. The so-called attorney Gordon received the money packet from as well as the $1,000.00 cash payment for services to be rendered, left the airport in his dry-cleaning delivery van, $500.00 richer.

Fielder had a few more *please help me out Gordon* scenarios. Gordon carried every one out to perfection and within 3 months he had made more money than he could scrape together in a year; and tax-free. Fielder left him alone for a while, but kept his eye on him. Then he started feeding him with hints about something big coming up. He asked if Gordon knew anybody who he thought could help him with that. Gordon had been curious as to why Fielder would ask somebody else; actually he became a bit annoyed about it. Fielder told him that he was considering paying somebody $10,000.00; it would be risky, but less than 3 hours of work. Fielder didn't tell Gordon what it was. He wanted him to chew on what he could spent the $10,000.00 on; tax-free. Fielder had plenty of time. As he predicted, Gordon finally gave in and brought up the *big job* proposal again. He was wondering why Fielder didn't consider him for the job. He had already done several for him to perfection, so why not this one? Fielder had pretended to fumble around with an answer, and finally told Gordon that he really liked him and considered him a true friend, a friend he obviously could trust with large amounts of money and do what he asked him to do. But the *big job* was risky, and he did not want to lose his best buddy by letting him take any big chances. Though the job was easy, it also had some risks. But they would continue to do the smaller jobs together; that was all fine, but that *big job* could be too dangerous. Gordon had pouted and shown irritation, signs Fielder knew what meant. He was reeling him in and Gordon had not disappointed him yet. Next time around would be the catch and cook.

Fielder purposely avoided Gordon the next few weeks. He wanted him ready and eager; greedy, actually. It was Gordon who approached Fielder one morning as he had just backed his truck up to the dock. He had jumped out of his cab a bit fast and was in front of Fielder in an instant.
"I'll do it." He spat out. "I know I can do it." His face was glazed with sweat.
"Do what?" Fielder asked.
"The *big job*; I know I can do it." Fielder looked at this piece of shit in front of him and spitefully pitied him.
"But you have no idea what it's all about."
"No matter fucking what, I know I'm your man."

Fielder explained the drill, when and what to do, and Gordon's eager response was nodding in agreement and understanding. The plan was executed to perfection six days later; Fielder's plan, that is.

Gordon's van had been unloaded and then re-loaded with rolling bins full of dirty laundry. The dirty bins were constantly checked for possible escapees. A few had been caught over the years and nobody had succeeded an escape that way. Fielder had for a long time practiced flexibility of his limbs. He also lowered his weight and after the loss of 32 pounds, he felt he was ready. It had taken him many months, but he was finally able to fit into an extremely small space, as on the floor under the bench in the cab, covered by the legs of the truck's driver - hidden from view. When the driver went through the final checkpoint, where mirrors were applied for searches underneath the trucks, Fielder noticed that the guards paid little to no attention to the driver's side of the trucks. He had yet to see a guard stepping up on the running boards to look into the cab on that side. So Fielder pressed himself as deep under the driver's seat as human possible; even Gordon was impressed as he placed his legs over Fielder's body. The truck was quickly cleared and the last several bumps over the final security grid told Fielder that he was very close to freedom and his plan would continue uninterrupted. *The dumb-ass guards would be chewed up by their superiors in a big way; stupid assholes,* Fielder grinned.

Gordon stuck to his normal route and, as usual, stopped at Annie's Café. It was lunchtime and that was what he did. He swung out of the cab and wobbled over to Annie's. He didn't notice Fielder get out of the truck and quickly disappear into a waiting van. If he had turned around, he might have recognized Fielder's *cousin* and *lawyer*. The van didn't move as it was waiting for Gordon to return from his lunch. Fielder was now in civilian clothes, beard shaven off and hair in a crew cut. The non-prescription glasses made him look like a professor of some sort, and a gentle demeanor was obvious. He appeared as a kind, elderly gentleman if anybody looked at him, not the psychotic human being he was underneath the suit. The apparent scar running from his temple to his jaw was red from the excitement and his deformed hands shook just a little.

Gordon came out of Annie's. It was obvious that he had inhaled more liquid lunch than solid; there were ten thousand reasons to celebrate. His steps were not fully synchronized and every time he lost a bit of balance, he giggled happily. Finally sitting behind the wheel again, fumbling the key into the ignition, the nice looking gentleman politely tapped on the passenger window. He motioned with his one hand to roll down the window and Gordon did just that. The nice looking gentleman had a fat white envelope in his gloved hand, which he held out for Gordon to take.

"I think I owe you this, Mr. James." He smiled. Gordon was puzzled due to his intoxication, but he soon connected the dots; the red scar was the clue.

"You gotta be fucking kidding me; Fielder old pal. You look great and so totally different." Fielder smiled as Gordon's fingers greedily started to curl around the envelope. But what Gordon didn't pay attention to, blinded by greediness, was the large Pistol, caliber .45, automatic, M1911A1 with a long black silencer attached; it was pointing directly at the middle of his forehead. There was an uncanny and eerie moment of slow-motion as the bullet left the muzzle, spun violently on the way from the sidearm towards Gordon; he literally saw it coming. The only dampened sounds to be heard was a pop and a splash; the pop from the pistol being fired and the splash from Gordon's brains and pieces of his skull hitting the driver-side window and part of the cab's ceiling. But Gordon had heard absolutely nothing; he was pretty much dead before the .45 caliber bullet had made it all the way through his head.

Fielder took a satisfied last look of the damage as he ran his crippled gloved fingers along his facial scar. Very methodically he pulled the envelope out of Gordon's hand, picked up the empty cartridge from the passenger seat and made sure the bullet had gone fully through Gordon as well as through the ceiling. He pulled out a soft cleaning rag and wiped both doors and part of the dashboard clean; no prints would be found. He felt good and knew that the police would not be able to find evidence pointing towards him what-so-ever. One last look around, he smiled and headed for the waiting van.

"All's well, boss?" Fielder smiled as he laboriously pulled off the latex cloves and dropped them into the large black trash bag his *cousin* held open for him. They landed unceremoniously on top of his prison clothes, everything he had worn for so many years, including his watch, shoes and glasses. He took one last look around the quiet parking lot, glanced towards Annie's with a bit of a smile and was soon sitting in the passenger seat. Nobody was around; it had been perfect. Going east on the near empty highway felt like heaven.

"All's very well, thank you." The road to the Victoria bitch was now wide open for business and he knew precisely what to do; she had no idea what was heading her way.

Sara's arms were still embracing him; her hands firmly holding on to his chest. His soft awakening also took place on that white cloud he had spent the whole night on. He so enjoyed her warmness; felt her comfortable and sexily curved body perfectly fitting his. He smiled and slowly started to turn his body to the left to face her; he teasingly kept his eyes closed. He felt very amorous and most certainly excited. He moved his right hand over Sara's hip and then up her back. He had expected her naked body, but she must have spent the night in one of his pajamas'; she'd do that ones in awhile. The rougher material was in a silly way inspiring as he caressed her back, slowly up and down. The moaning was a bit different. He never seemed to fully know his Sara; she constantly surprised him. Her right hand had also found Jack's back and was slowly moving up and down as well; her moaning slowly became louder as she pressed herself against him. This was most certainly new and very exciting for him. He inched his face toward hers as he was eager to kiss her. She felt his move and seemed to have the same thought. Her lips parted as they were eagerly reaching for his.

The brutal shock of the horrid stench that violently invaded Jack's nostrils had an instantaneous effect. He hurriedly pulled back, eyes wide open. The face in front of him did not belong to Sara – far from; its blotchiness, the utterly messed and dirty hair. This was certainly not his Sara. He jumped out of bed, stopped and stared. What was that thing in his bed, in his and Sara's bed? It was female, no doubt about that – he hoped. It had a small satisfied smile curling around the mouth while her hair was busy covering just about all facial features. She didn't move for a moment. Then her left hand slowly started to pad the side Jack had just evacuated. It was searching, but didn't find anything. She mumbled a bit and tried desperately to open her eyes. Jack looked closer and suddenly it blew his mind: It was Molly – from last night. He remembered that he had tugged her in on the couch in the family room, so what the hell was she doing in his and Sara's bed, cuddling up to him. What had happened? Had he… and her? Jack shook his head in a feeble attempt to clear it for morning cobwebs and unthinkable thoughts. He took a step back and fell into a chair just a few feet from the bed. He sat there staring in wild disbelief. Molly's hand was still searching, but it had lost a bit of the energy. Soon she was snoring loudly again, yet still with that little satisfied smile going on. Jack hoped and prayed that it was not one of those *after satisfying sex* smiles. Oh my God, please don't let it be, he begged. He did his own physical exploration as to that possibility, but couldn't really tell. He knew in his dreams that he had made love to Sara several times during the night, but that had only been a dream – hadn't it?

He would not be able to tell you how long he had been sitting staring at loudly snoring Molly. Time was irrelevant; but Molly's body in his and Sara's bed was very relevant. After the longest time Molly started to move and that was when the sounds of the morning after having *tried-to-kill-one-self-with-alcohol* started. First it was the small hiccup whimpers, then the guttural animalistic groans, followed by volcanic rumblings from the deepest part of the stomach; then came the wide open eyes of pain and surprise, realizing too late what would come next. The loud gagging and the expected spastic jerks of mouth and body were finally followed by the extremely violent projectile vomiting – again and again and again. It was that very moment Jack found that he was sitting in the wrong spot at the wrong time – again and again and again.

Molly convulsed eerily on the bed. Her utterance of pain and illness was loud and frightening. Jack was busy with his own dilemma of dealing with several layers of vomit on his pajama and body, face and hair. But Molly's obvious excruciating pain quickly made him forget about his own dilemma. He hurried to the bed and tried to at least stabilize her violent seizure-like jerks. Her face was red and covered in a mess of vomit, blood and hair; her eyes wild and scared. After a minute of no changes, he grabbed the phone from his night stand and dialed 9-1-1. The medics were on Molly's side within eleven minutes and she was soon after being handled in the emergency room. Jack had whipped off his soiled pajama and cranked on sweat pants, a T-shirt, socks and sneakers. As he was sitting in the ER's waiting room, he realized the smell coming from him was sickening and had not decreased a bit by the change of clothes. Luckily there were not many people waiting around – so far so good.

After about an hour the on-call doctor sat next to Jack; he quickly moved a couple of chairs away from him, and Jack appreciated why.

"Interesting choice of cologne you splashed on this morning." The doctor thought that was funny; Jack didn't.

"How's Molly?" He was eager to know.

"Well, she had a bit of alcohol poisoning, so we pumped her stomach. We didn't find any food, so the massive quantity of alcohol had room to roam." He looked down at some papers in his hands. "Did she eat anything yesterday?"

"I have no idea. But she didn't eat anything at my house last night; I know that for sure."

"Can you tell me what happened?" And Jack told the doctor precisely what had happened. When he was done, the doctor had a bit of a problem holding back a sly smile. He wasn't sure if this older man told the truth about this much younger woman and their *relationship;* but he kept those images to himself. "Miss West had a rather large quantity of alcohol in her system. It bordered very close to a lethal dose." Jack looked uninformed so the doctor explained: "If she had negated eating anything for a day or two, her stomach was readily available for the alcohol to do its utmost damage. You informed us that she had irregular breathing and seizure-like convulsions; those are all indicators of poisoning. The blood sugar level falls dramatically and seizures take over. It can actually be fatal if not treated at once. Miss West was lucky to have you react as you did." The doctor's sly smile disappeared: "You probably saved her life." Jack's mind twirled frantically.

"I probably saved her life?"

"Yeah, you probably did." Jack thought for a moment. He put his hand on the doctor's shoulder.

"Please do not tell her that, okay?"

"My lips are sealed."

"Thanks."

The nurse informed him that Molly was sleeping at the moment and figured she'd stay in that condition the next seven to eight hours. She was plugged in to several machines and IV's and was stabilized to the point where she was safe and would soon be sound again. Jack saw an opportunity to flee the hospital in a cab. The driver immediately asked if it was okay to drive with all the windows opened; Jack insisted.

The stench occupied the whole house; it was big time nauseating. Before the long shower, he ripped off the sheets, comforters and pillows and soon the washer and dryer were working overtime. For some reason none of Molly's hurl had hit the carpet or the chair. He grimaced as he realized that it had all landed on the bed and more so on him. Finally in clean and fresh clothes he dialed his maid-service and asked for emergency action. He figured that with a thorough cleaning of the whole house, the reminders of this terrible night and morning would disappear. They confirmed a 3 PM arrival. They had a key to the house, so Jack could escape the stench by getting out fast, get in his car and back to the hospital.

Many thoughts raced through his mind. First of all, he couldn't believe that Molly had reappeared. It had been ten years pretty much to the day. She looked strangely different, but not particularly very beautiful at this time. An oxygen mask covered her nose and mouth, an IV was left in her arm and some other gismo was strapped around her right wrist, whatever for. Though they had successfully scraped, cleaned and washed off all the vomit, her hair was still a mess and her face looked awfully pained and discolored. But Jack also saw something else, something that disturbed him a little. He quietly pushed it away and for now it was gone – but only for now.

Fielder picked up the rest of his stowed away money, bought some coke and was on his way to Washington D.C. in a used car he had just purchased. The fake ID told those who were interested, that his name was Victor Moore from Houston, Texas. Fielder had always wanted to be from Texas, so why not. He decided to take it easy and figured that a leisurely drive would have him in D.C. within the next three or four days. But he needed to get laid first and knew where some very professional women would be more than willing to supply what he wanted – and he had plenty of cash and coke to support those naughty girls. Straight sex was okay, but years in prison, he needed to be knocked around a bit and the more the better. He smiled in his excitement as he traveled east on the busy freeway. Washington D.C. – 820 miles.

Her face had slowly shifted to a healthier color. Jack had been by her side the whole time and in between his dozing off, made sure all was well. Every time she moved he jumped, like he was attached to her in some mysterious way. The nurse had suggested he should go home and get a good night's sleep in his own bed and then come back in the morning; but he declined every time. She had brought him a toothbrush and paste, which he put to use very quickly.

His thoughts went back to the many years with Molly around; her being part of the Millers. He recalled so many moments of excitement for Caroline, Michael and Jasper, as well as for Sara and himself. Molly had carved her way into their hearts so fast, and she got stuck there, certainly in Jack's case. He had truly believed that her disappearance was finally out of his mind and heart, but seeing her there in the bed in front of him this very moment, he knew that she had just been hibernating in some corner of him and was now back in full force. He was sure that everybody would have the same feeling and same reaction. He especially hoped that Caroline would forgive and forget, as her disappointment was vast and deep. He wished when Caroline reconnected with Molly again that only the presence and the future counted, not the past. But where had Molly been?

Jack decided that he would talk with her first before telling anybody that she was in town. He didn't know if it was just for a short time or if it was for good or whatever, but he was sure Molly would let him know and then she could decide how to handle the reunion if any was going to take place. He quietly hoped she would stick around; in some gentle way he felt that she needed him and that he needed her. She seemed as miserable as he was, so maybe they could help each other. But then again, maybe not – only time would tell.

She was pretty much out for over 24 hours straight. The doctor had asked Jack if there was anybody who could look after her the next day or so. She was probably in D.C. alone, he figured. He hadn't seen her grandparents for many years, actually for longer than Molly had been gone. But he could take care of her. She could stay with him and if he needed help, he'd find it. The doctor said that if a nurse was needed, to give him a call and he'd arrange for one. He also realized that he had been unfair. Now Mr. Miller looked much more like a concerned parent than that dirty old man image he had wrongfully seen at first.

Molly woke up only for moments at a time. She recognized Jack and met the sight of him with a brave and exhausted little smile. At least she had acknowledged who he was and that was good, he thought. He found her hand every time and comforted her that all was fine and they would get out of the hospital soon. She whispered thanks and went back to sleep.

She was waiting on the couch in OR scrubs and a large hospital blanket wrapped around her. The soiled pajamas and even the bunny slippers had been discarded; had actually been burned – Molly had insisted. Jack was busy preparing the upstairs guestroom. Nobody had stayed there since Molly had disappeared. It was untouched, but kept nice and clean and fresh at all times; same as the rest of the house. On one of the nightstands, the heavy brass-framed photo of Caroline and Molly standing in front of their favorite library at Georgetown University was one of his favorites. Sara had taken the photo and caught those best pals laughing and looking extremely happy, arms solidly locked together the way they always did. The other photos in the room were of their own kids; but most of them included Molly.

As Jack returned to the living room he found her fast asleep. 48 hours ago she had looked and acted like a wild and crazy person, but now she looked peaceful and calm. He carefully picked her up and though she was not petite, she seemed to weigh nothing in his arms. Her head found a natural resting place in the nook between his shoulder and neck, with her arms and hands gently holding on. He felt a deep sigh and thought he saw a smile.

He removed the blanket and figured the scrubs would play the part of pajamas tonight. After he tucked the comforter around her, he as naturally as anything, kissed her forehead; *that's what parents do,* he thought. The small lamp was left on and the door slightly ajar. His bedroom was next to the guestroom, so if Molly needed anything, he would be by her side in seconds.

His head finally rested on the pillow and thoughts about the last 48 disturbing hours tumbled around in his brain. He had been torn down and finally left for good by people he loved and they had in clear and stern voices told him how they felt. They would consider coming back if he found himself again at any point – but no guarantees and certainly not for sure. It had been horrific and depressing, but he finally understood how utterly pathetic and retarded his behavior had been. He wondered how he could have done this to them for so blooming long – ten years? That was insane; he was insane. All the values he had preached and lived by until Sara's death had been flushed down the toilet. He had abandoned his precious children, pushed everybody away from him, probably screwed up his job and partnership with Nora and CR as well as lost his father and Colleen. He was ashamed that he had not attended Charles' funeral as he felt his own misery took priority. His father had given him a solid scolding about it and demanded he begged for Colleen's forgiveness; she would think about it, was her response. George had screamed at his son as he had never screamed at him before, and Jack, in his dismal state of mind, had cried and uttered thousands of *I'm sorry*. George told him that it was too little and too blooming late and pushed Jack out the door; they had not talked much since.

Nora left in total frustration with the ultimatum that pretty much read *either shit or get off the pot* – (her words). Otherwise sweet and adorable Karen had been vicious in her attack. She had clearly expressed grave disappointment and extreme anger, because *he didn't bloody get it* – (her words). Victoria had finally given up, and the last he had seen of William was when his best friend walked away shaking his head and rolling his eyes. Frank and Nicole had also joined the *get it together Jack or else* society.

In spite of trying desperately not to feel sorry for himself, he still desperately did. But he finally felt a tiny glimmer of hope that maybe he would be able to dig himself out of this deep hole – a vague hope that he eventually would be able to move forward, might squeeze out some progress – maybe. He was now more willing to give it a go, which was nearly for sure. Desperation was talking, but did Jack listen? He decided that very moment that to save his own pathetic and sorry ass he had to act now – this very moment. But in spite of this decision (for the millionth time), Jack felt utterly alone and he knew that it would take miracles to make him a Happy Jack again. But now with Molly back, was he really all that alone? Well, nobody else really gave a shit about him anymore, so why would she. Only time would tell.

That Molly had all of a sudden showed up, gave Jack many confusing thoughts. Was it a sign? Had she come to fix it all? Was she also on the bottom of the pit-of-her-life at this time? Looked like it. Were they supposed to help each other? Whatever had happened in his bed was so utterly weird, but what did it mean; if anything? His sweet fantasies about Sara and then finding Molly in bed with him, and so intimate could not be good; just the thought of it made him uncomfortable as it was so wrong. He really had to talk with her about that – and as soon as possible. He believed that nothing happened, but he wasn't positively sure at all, as his lovemaking dreams about Sara were always so vivid and intense and seemed so real. He did not find any physical proof on his body, so he felt all was fine; but he still had to talk with Molly – and fast. The fact that he had actually been so awfully close to Molly in Sara's and his bed was a huge *Yuk*. These eerie thoughts kept haunting him.

It started with the painful sliver-opening of one eye and then the considerate risk of opening the other one - but only if the first one succeeded. Watching the world around her through nearly closed shutters was not fun. First of all she had absolutely no idea where she was, why she was and even if she was still alive. As her eyes opened more and more, a few of her still slightly alcohol soaked brain cells started, resentfully, to turn fog in to specks of information. The space she was in looked familiar in a confusing way. Was that a picture of her with…; that was Caroline! They looked goofy, but in a good way, she thought. Closing her eyes again gave her brains a rest, but her curiosity was stubborn. A few minutes later she tried the sliver-opening thing again. More of the room came into focus and she realized that she had been here before. Trying to move her head was stupid, she found, as needles, arrows and spears rammed through her eyes by the slightest motion. The decision to close up and wait for better times was the much wiser plan. Molly fell back into the comatose level where she felt no pain – all she felt was nothing, and for now, nothing was the ultimate of good.

At first light Jack slowly got out of bed. He tiptoed to the guestroom door and pushed it a bit more open; he was met by loud, but consistent, snoring. Molly was lying on her back, her head to the side, half off the pillow. Her eyes were semi open, but Jack felt that she didn't see a thing. It was not a pretty sight - that was for sure. He quietly closed the door, went downstairs and headed for the kitchen; the much needed caffeine was ready within minutes.

He felt different, it was hard to pinpoint how, but it was in a curiously good way. Out of very old habit, one he had not activated for nearly ten years, he grabbed the steno pad that was sitting next to the kitchen phone for notes and messages. These steno pads had been his faithful companions since childhood, through school and work - until Sara died. He must have gone through hundreds upon hundreds of them over the years. He had used them to write down thoughts, ideas, things to remember, short and long-term goals. He would write down problems that needed to be solved, dissecting what the problem was and notes about possible solutions. His father had always called those steno pads Jack's 3rd brain – Jack had always agreed.

With steaming coffee in front of him and pen in hand, he was met by a very empty page. It seemed to be smiling at him encouragingly to get started; or was it a smug smirk predicting failure? His hand wanted to get going, but his thoughts were not at all organized at this point – far from. A few sips of coffee would do, he thought, but that didn't do it either. After several moments, he finally wrote on the top line: *Michael, Jasper and Caroline*. Then he thought for a minute longer and wrote: *Reconnect*. From just writing that simple word, he finally and truly realized what he had done, and tears streamed down his face. How could he have been so selfish and so self-centered all these years? Had he pushed them all off the cliff because they were in the way of *his* misery, *his* mourning, *his* utter idiotic self-imposed need to self-destruct? Was it already too late to reconcile? It wasn't that he had only lost his Sara; he now fully realized that he had also lost his children.

And the list continued: George, Colleen, Nora, Karen, Victoria, William, Linda, Ella, Nicole and Frank. As tears fell to the paper as he wrote, he continued with the people at CR, people who had trusted and relied on him for years. He had also failed them as well as their families. He was supposed to be there for them as a leader and as a friend.

When he was done writing he put the pen down and read the list again and again. Finally he pushed the pad to the middle of the table and got up; he found himself at the foot of the mountain and looking up he knew the climb to the top would be very difficult and hard. But through tears and realizing the harsh realities, he decided to crawl to the top, no matter what it took, no matter what he needed and had to do. Another chapter of Jack Winston Miller's life had just begun.

Fielder was lying naked and spent on the large bed. He had been knocked around by two very effective professionals, supported by alcohol and cocaine. They were far from being beauty queens, but after so many years in prison, being able to only reach satisfaction on his own, he was not going to be choosy at this point. Some of the better looking sluts did not want to beat him up as they thought it was disgusting, so it had been the two older worn-out, boozed up and wrinkled women he'd ended up with. They had done everything he had ordered them to – harder and harder. It had been an expensive night, but it had been worth it. Bruises, cuts and blood had sprung up fast and the handcuffs they had spread him out with had nearly cut to the bones on wrists and ankles. But it had felt so good – all night long. Blood still dribbled from his nose and mouth as he smiled. He'd soon get up, shower and get dressed, have a bit of breakfast and continue his quest eastward; the bitch he was getting together with there was not ugly to any extent – she was the one he had fantasized about all through the time in prison. It was going to be the greatest time ever. He had even convinced himself that it would be the greatest time for her as well. He would bring her so close to full satisfaction and then keep her hanging there as she would be screaming for more; at that very moment he would snuff her away while telling her that nobody screws with Fielder without getting punished - nobody.

Michael was at his desk when the phone rang.
"Detective Miller, Homicide." A slight giggle came from the other end.

"Big bloody deal; Mr. Detective my ass!" Michael smiled at once.
"Wow, Richard bloody Palmer. How the heck are you?"
"Just fine; and you?"
"Couldn't be happier." Richard Palmer had been Michael's classmate through the years at the police academy. They had instantly hooked up when they met and had thoroughly enjoyed their close friendship in the classroom and during training. Michael had from the start wanted to become a homicide detective and Richard focused on a title of FBI agent – they had both achieved their goals. A few days after graduation, Richard was off to FBI *kindergarten* as he called it. The special FBI program that catered to highly intelligent, talented and promising young recruits fresh out of police academies as well as stand-outs from military intelligence units. Richard was very high in the IQ department and had an uncanny sense of solving problems – any problem; the FBI had caught those talents early on. Michael did his beat-time in the streets of D.C. and as quickly as possible worked his way into the homicide unit. They were both very happy campers; Michael in Camp D.C. and Richard in Camp Chicago.

After the academy they hadn't communicated much other than professionally at times and the sporadic calls of *how the heck are you?* But no matter how far between calls, they never missed a beat in their friendship.
"So what's up, Special Agent Palmer?" Richard giggled as he always heard that slight tone of good natured sarcasm when Michael called him that.
"Well, Detective Miller," he teased back and then his voice turned serious. "We might have a bit of a situation. You recall the case of a certain Mr. Fielder some years back?"
Michael froze immediately. Of course he remembered that case. He was not sure if he'd like what Richard was going to say next.
"Go on," he urged his friend.
"I got a call this morning and it confirmed that Fielder escaped a couple of days ago."
"A couple of days ago? Why the hell haven't we been informed earlier?"
"I really don't know, Michael. It was a screw up from the get go."

"How many days precisely does he have?"

"I estimate 72 hours give and take."

"I'm sure we all know where he's heading?"

"Yeah Michael, I'm sure it's east."

"Did you call George?"

"Just before I called you."

"And his reaction?"

"Well, you know he's not active anymore, but he would make some calls to his former department at once."

"Yeah, that's my 80 year old Grandpa for you. I'll call him after we are done. I'll call Victoria as well, of course; anything else?"

"I was told that a laundry truck driver was found shot in the head 15 miles from the prison. We believe that might be the work of Fielder or maybe some cohorts of his. We are not sure. I also got a call from a colleague of mine this morning. She felt that I would find it interesting that they discovered two male bodies in a motel room off Interstate 66, both with big holes between their eyes, which no doubt caused their untimely death."

"Why would she assume a connection?"

"She figured three dead bodies within hours and geographic feasibility, literally and seemingly caused by the same caliber bullet, .45. They are doing the forensics as we speak."

"Any obvious evidence?"

"The truck was clean, they tell me; no bullet, no prints, no nothing. The motel room as well; except for one bullet that for some mysterious reason didn't make it all the way through one of the victim's otherwise thin skull. No witnesses of any kind, other than the motel manager recognized the smaller of the two dead ones to be the one who checked in and paid in cash."

"Not much, but enough to see where this is going, huh?" There was a pause. Richard's voice had changed again – it was more serious now.

"Listen Michael: I'm not far away. I had a few things to deal with in Virginia and though I'm not fully done, I'll be in D.C. within hours, okay?" Michael appreciated that.

"Thanks Richard. I'll get things rolling here and will call Victoria right away. I'll go over there myself and also check with George and see what he has come up with. Thanks again, and I'll see you in a bit." And the line went dead.

Michael looked at the clock on the wall and decided to call Victoria's office first. He was told that she had left for the day. He asked if she had any inclinations as to where she was heading and was told that she probably headed straight home as she had been very tired from a long week of work. Next Michael reached George. He informed Michael that four active colleagues of his were already on their way to Victoria and William's apartment. He had also called the doorman's desk, but no answer so he had left a message. He figured that his buddies would reach the apartment building within 20 minutes.

"I'm going over there myself in a minute."

"No Grandpa, you stay precisely where you are, and that's an order from the detective in charge." George smiled a bit; he was preparing for a lie.

"Yeah Michael, you're right, I guess this 80 year old fossil should stand back. But keep me informed, okay?" After the end of the call, George was quickly on his way to the garage, his trusted Magnum 357 strapped to his belt. *Just like the good old days,* he thought as he started his car. But this was not just like the good old days, far from; this was too close and way too personal.

Next Michael speed-dialed Victoria and William's number. It rang several times and the answer machine came on with Victoria's voice. Michael hung up and dialed again. 4 to 5 rings later the machine came on. After the beep Michael started his message:

"Hi Aunt Vicky and Uncle Billy; got some bad news that we urgently need to address. Give me a call at..." The line suddenly died - just like that. He redialed, and nothing – and once more with the same lack of result. He tried both Vicky's and William's mobile phones several times; those lines were also very dead. He did not like this at all. He called nearby cruisers to rush to the apartment building to check on Victoria and William. Then he grabbed his sidearm, clipped the holster to his belt and was out the door. Two colleagues quickly followed him as he had asked for their back-up. They were soon racing down 15th Street NW, lights flaring and sirens blaring. Detective Miller had that really bad feeling in his guts – a sign that rarely failed him;

unfortunately in this case though, it was an even more horrid feeling.

As the snoring had subsided to near silence, he checked for vital signs by observing the comforter moving up and down with her breathing; it did. Jack quietly closed the door. Climbing that mountain had to be done in small steps and one step at a time. He would first *cleanse* himself physically by taking a long, hot and relaxing shower. He turned on the stereo in the bedroom and Stan Getz helped with instant serenity. He splurged with 20 minute of water massaging beams, scrubbed and rinsed like never before. After a life-renovating dry-down he was finally standing clean and naked in front of the closet door mirror. With steno pad and pen in hand he started from the top and worked his way down: Haircut, eyes checked, new glasses, dentist appointment, fitness club schedule, full physical check up by Doctor Jennifer Bowles. He started to dress and kept writing: Go through closet, throw out old and sentimental clothes and shoes; get fresh stuff – revitalize and renew, was the topic of the day. He contemplated making the dentist and doctor's appointments on Monday, but caught himself procrastinating. It was Friday and still a few hours left of the workday. *Do it now*, he urged himself. A few moments later he had both appointments on the kitchen calendar for Monday. *That's the ticket, Jack, that's the way to start climbing that mountain.* He tightened his bathrobe belt and was on his way upstairs to get dressed. Passing the first window on the way, he noticed something going on in the driveway. He didn't recognize the car that had just swung around and was now parked near the front door; he stopped and stared. The young woman popping out of the driver's side looked a bit familiar, but didn't register instantly. *Oh yeah, one of Caroline's schoolmates,* he thought. *OH NO, NOT CAROLINE!* She appeared on the passenger side and the two young women were now by the open trunk, pulling out backpacks and small suitcases. *OH MY GOD*, Jack thought out loud. *I totally forgot that Caroline was coming home – but that was not before tomorrow, not today, Saturday not Friday*. Jack's mind flew a million miles an hour. *What about Molly upstairs?* He hadn't even talked with her about anything, though he had spent the last 48 hours with her, uh, around her. He didn't even know what was going on in her life, what she wanted, where she'd been, where she was going – whatever. And here comes Caroline, *OH MY GOD*. Jack raced upstairs as fast as he could, but was stopped in his tracks halfway.

"Hi Dad," Caroline's voice was cheery and happy as ever. Jack turned around and there she was. So it hadn't been a bad dream after all; he really wished it had, just for this once. He cleared his throat – several times.

"Hi Sweetheart, nice to see you," he turned and tried to reach second floor again.

"Dad, what are you doing?" Her voice was surprised. "What happened to the welcome home *kiss & hug*?" Now her voice was pleading as well as pouting.

"Can we do that in a few minutes?"

"What's the matter with you, aren't you glad to see me?" She started to walk up the stairs. "Well, I guess I have to come after you to get that hug, huh?"

"Oh no, Caroline, I'll come down there, don't come up here, no I'll come down there, just wait." His voice was not normal to any extent; even he could hear that. Caroline was laughing.

"You are acting so weird; anything going on around here? And you are in your bathrobe at five in the afternoon." She looked directly into her father's eyes as she stood on her toes and demanded that kiss and hug. Jack wrapped his arms around her and held her for the longest time. She kissed him and tried wriggling away.

"It's great to see you, Caroline, it really is. Welcome home, Sweetheart." He returned her kiss and held her in arms length. "And as beautiful as ever; how long has it been?" Caroline laughed.

"Two weeks."

"Well, seems like a lifetime." He gave her another hug and kiss.

"Dad, you remember Nancy Wilson."

"Of course I do, welcome Nancy." He reached out for a hug and got one; Nancy smiled wide.

"That was random, Mr. Miller, but thank you." Caroline looked a bit puzzled at her father. He never hugged her girlfriends, especially not in his bathrobe.

"Yeah, that was random, Dad." He realized that it *was* rather random and maybe a bit awkward. He quickly tried to smooth it out.

"Why don't you sit down and relax and we'll have a glass of wine, maybe?" Caroline was not at all sure what was going on. Her father seldom drank alcohol and certainly not this early in the day. She slowly uttered:

"Okay if that's what you want. Nancy, would you like some wine or perhaps something else?"

"After that long trip a glass of wine would certainly be nice." Jack got up, picked a bottle from the wine rack, opened it and came back with three glasses. His mind was still rumbling around like crazy. Molly was upstairs – in bed, and Caroline had come home too early.

"Say, weren't you supposed to come home tomorrow; not today?"

"Yeah; you sound a bit disappointed, Dear Father."

"Oh no, not at all; it's really great to see you – and you too, Nancy."

"So it's okay that Nancy stays here tonight?" Jack couldn't remember any of the Nancy stuff, but it didn't matter.

"Yes of course it is. There's plenty of room down here – or upstairs or…" Caroline looked at Nancy.

"You'll have the guestroom. It has its own bathroom and all – very comfy." Jack looked panicky and Caroline picked it up right away.

"What *is* the matter with you, Dad? You have been all frazzled since I got here. What's the matter?"

"Oh, nothing - stuff – you know."

"No I don't know, so why don't you tell me." Jack desperately tried to save face *and* the situation. He saw Caroline eye his steno pad, but reacted too late as she swiftly picked it up.

"Wow, Dad. I haven't seen you use this thing for the longest time. You haven't used it since Mom died, have you?" Jack's face turned a bit reddish.

"No, that's right."

"When did you start?" she asked as she started turning the pages. She raised her eyebrows as she read. Jack nervously tried to snap it out of her hands.

"Come on, Caroline, that's personal stuff." She pulled a bit away from him, smiling.

"What's going on here, Dad?" She closed the pad and put it back on the sofa table.

"Stuff!"

"What kind of stuff? What's with the names and all that *stuff*?" Jack shifted uncomfortable in his seat.

"Can we talk about this a bit later, Sweetheart? I mean, Nancy is visiting and it's kind of personal." He reached for the pad and placed it next to him on the sofa. "So Nancy, how have things been plucking along?" He tried to say in a normal voice.

"Fine, Mr. Miller."

"*Jack,* please; just call me Jack, otherwise I feel my age a bit much." Nancy smiled. She had met Caroline's father a couple of times and really liked him. Caroline had told her how her father had not been able to handle the death of her mother well at all; actually he hadn't been able to handle it what-so-ever. But the times she had spent with him when he visited Caroline at MSU, he was charming, funny and seemingly an intelligent man. She liked that very much in men; intelligence and humor. But she had not told Caroline about that part. She giggled every time she thought that maybe she had a little crush on her girlfriend's father. But it was not the same Jack who sat in front of her this afternoon. He seemed nervous and pre-occupied; fidgeting, would be the word.

There was something really strange about her father, Caroline thought. He was most certainly not his own self, though that would have been fine as the old self had been disturbing the last many years, to say the least. He seemed a bit more energetic, but not totally on track. It was weird, but in a much better way than that idiotic *mourning* mode he had been living in for so long.

"Well Nancy, let's get you settled upstairs and…" Jack jumped.

"No…, I mean let me make sure the guestroom is all clear - I mean clean. Here, let me take your bag, suitcase…, that thing." He jumped up and reached for the luggage Nancy had brought in.

"Don't be silly Dad. We'll take care of it." Caroline headed for the stairs with Nancy in tow. "We'll be down in a few." Jack was very desperate at this time so he ran to the stairs and hurriedly passed Nancy and Caroline by taking two steps at a time. He was soon in front of the closed door to the guestroom and in dramatic fashion, trying to be funny, blogged the passage.

"Why don't you use Jasper's room, Nancy? It's all set up for visitors, just like this one." Nancy smiled and was still curious concerning his behavior.

"No problem, Jack;" and she headed down the hall. Caroline stood in front of her father and suddenly a light came on.

"Now wait a blooming minute here. Is there somebody in there?" She tried to get past her father; he clumsily blocked her. He couldn't let her meet Molly again, not this way; that would be fatal and extremely awkward.

"Now listen young Lady; I have nobody here, so there. It's just that the room has not been cleaned lately and…" She looked into her father's eyes.

"You are not a very good liar, Dad; and there is still that bathrobe thing in the afternoon. Ah, now I get it - you do have somebody in there – let me see." Jack held her off for a moment, but he felt it was futile and hopeless. He maturely closed his eyes as Caroline opened the door.

"Honey, let me explain…" Caroline was already inside the room next to the ruffled up bed. He kept his eyes closed as he expected the worse. She pulled the comforter back and found the bed empty.

"Oh Daddy Oh; who has slept in the big bear's bed?" She smiled slyly as her father was twisting on the hook. "Somebody we know?" Caroline had for the longest time hoped that her father would start to do something outside the house, socialize - do anything to snap out of these 10 years of self inflicted misery. So if he had had a girlfriend staying overnight, she would fully approve – anybody, anytime. "So do tell, Dear Father."

"Nobody, yeah nobody stayed over."

"So why is the bed all messy?"

"I couldn't sleep so I tried the guestroom." His lying was amateurish and naïve. Caroline looked at the floor and picked up the greenish set of scrubs, pants and top.

"And you are going to tell me that these are yours as well?"

"Yeah, I like sleeping in scrubs at times." That didn't come out well either.

"A bit small for a big man like you, aren't they?"

"I like them tight. Let's just get out of here and leave my doings alone, shall we?" Caroline smiled happily.

"You played doctor last night?" Jack shook his head too eagerly. "Wow, Dad, way to go."

"No I didn't…, I mean it was a friend who needed a place to crash, so she.., he, I mean she did just that – end of story." Caroline went into the bathroom.

"So she didn't shower while she was here, did she Dad?" She suddenly saw the picture. "Oh I see, you showered together in *your* bathroom." She giggled and turned towards her father: "I'm so happy for you, Dad, I really am – very happy."

"Nothing happened, really - nothing to be *happy* about."

"Doesn't matter, you had a woman over – good for you; really, really good for you, Dad." She hugged her father and kissed his confused face.

"But nothing happened." He pleaded.

"Whatever, Dad; I'm happy for you whatever." She turned towards Nancy who had followed the silly drama with a smile on her face. "So Nancy, as my father had company last night, you'll have Jasper's room." Nancy giggled, and Caroline continued on her father: "So who is she?"

"Just leave me alone, Caroline, okay?" He blushed slightly and she knew it was enough already.

"Okay for now, sweet Lover Boy, okay for now." As the girls went giggling down the hall, Jack raced into the guestroom searching everywhere. Molly could not be found and he even looked under the bed, no matter how stupid he thought *that* was.

Victor Moore from Texas, also known as escaped Inmate 56634 Richard Fielder, was sitting on the sofa with the telephone cable between his crippled fingers. He was a bit surprised how easy it had been to disconnect communication to the outside world. He was actually surprised how easy this whole thing had turned out to be. Getting rid of Gordon was quick and clinical. Eliminating the *cousin* and the *attorney* had been easy, but not as satisfying as he had hoped. The three of them were drinking heavily and snorting long lines of cocaine in the motel room. He had pulled out his gun with the silencer still attached to show them how he had popped Gordon – just for laughs.

First he put the gun to his own forehead, and spat out a *BANG*. Then he pointed it at the *cousin's* forehead and *BANG*. They had all laughed drunkenly, especially as he kept repeating *BANG - BANG* over and over. Then he pointed it back at his own forehead again, screamed a louder *BANG* and fell onto the bed, mimicking a dying man. The two other men had laughed hard and uncontrollable. He struggled getting back up, but finally made it. The *cousin* painted an invisible bulls-eye on his forehead. Fielder laughed and faked an unsteady hand, pressing the muzzle hard against the intoxicated man's skull. He made sure to watch the *attorney's* face when he pulled the trigger. The large caliber bullet blew the back of the *cousin's* head out, spraying brain mass and bone fragments all over the curtains and the small window. The expression on the *attorney's* face hurried from laughter to utter horror in a split second; it was priceless to watch. So there he was, totally frozen in disbelief, with his stupid mouth wide open. It had been too easy to swing the weapon around and blast that second asshole out of the water – no fun at all, really.

Getting into the apartment building had been a piece of cake. The doorman was not going to guard any more doors; maybe the gates to Heaven or Hell, but not on Earth; Fielder had made sure of that. The only hiccup had been that the bitch's husband was home. He had been very polite as he opened the door, but horrified as he suddenly looked at the large gun pointing at him – that was a fun transition to watch. Interesting how the emotions are so different on the two sides of a loaded weapon: cockiness and horror; *hmm, I should write that down some day,* Fielder thought with a smile. Victoria and her husband didn't smile at all – quite the opposite. They looked scared for some reason. Maybe because he had tied up the husband and strapped several layers of duct tape over his mouth. He had considered taping his eyes shot, but he wanted him to be able to see what he was going to do to his wife – he might even get excited watching, he thought. But at the moment he looked rather fragile; *you were in the wrong place at the wrong time, jerk.*

She still looked beautiful. What he could see from the way she was dressed, she still packed an exciting body. Her tits were bigger now, they seemed; her legs as long as he had ever fantasized about them, curved behind his neck. Her hips wide and waist narrow. Yeah, she was not a disappointment to him; even after all those many years. She was hot as hell and she was soon gonna have the time of her life with him; he was very sure of that. Just thinking about it aroused him no end, and there was no reason to hurry.

"Keeping yourself pretty for Fielder, haven't you?" She didn't look at him but kept fiddling with the silver duct tape around her wrists behind her back. Her ankles were already numb; he had been vicious in taping them and she had fought with all her might. It was when he had threatened to kill her husband that she had stopped. But now she couldn't feel any form of circulation in her feet – things could be worse, she thought; and they most certainly would.

As Detective Miller's car screeched to a halt in front of the apartment building, he felt his heart stop. The ambulance sat silently with lights flashing as many people stuffed the gurney in place and closed the door.

"It's the doorman, Sir." The uniformed officer looked sorry as he faced Michael.

"What's the situation?"

"It looks like some bloke was let in and then shot the doorman and went upstairs, we think."

"What's the injury?"

"Shut through the upper left part of his chest, I hear; one shot only."

"Is he gonna make it?"

"I don't know, Sir. The medics arrived a few minutes after we called them. No time for talking, I guess."

"What else?"

"We are not clear about the situation, but..." Michael looked tense as he cleared his throat and interrupted.

"I believe it's in reference to apartment 606, listed under Grant and Baxter. Acting on that as the case, have the apartments evacuated on floor 5, 7 and the rest of 6, please. Then report back to me."

"Yes Sir; consider it done." The officer twirled around on his heels and was gone. Michael for some reason looked up on the outside of the building. Aunt Vicky's and William's apartment was facing towards the river. By counting up and down, left and right, he figured where the apartment was. He couldn't see any lights. Nothing happened when he pressed the 606 button. He held it there for a while, but no answer. He tried the landline again, as well as the two mobile phones – nothing. This smelled like a hostage situation, so he blared out orders with that assumption.

Soon residents from the apartments on floor 5, 6 and 7 quietly started to trickle out the front door. SWAT team members arrived and placed themselves according to the situation. Michael had handed over the command to the strategic leaders. Then a hand rested on his shoulder and a welcomed voice followed.

"How are you holding up, Michael?" It was Special Agent Richard Palmer, FBI.

"Thanks for coming." Michael quickly filled Richard in on the situation. He was suddenly occupied with something he saw over Michael's shoulder.

"Wow, see what the cat brought out." He said with a big grin. Michael turned his head and saw his grandfather coming towards them fast.

"What the hell; I asked him to stay away." Richard laughed.

"Like asking that same cat to stay away from an open can of tuna, huh?"

"What's the scoop, gentlemen?" George was a bit breathless. "Oh hi Richard; thanks for coming."

"What are you doing here, Grandpa?"

"Let's just solve this thing and then we can discuss what the hell I'm doing here later, okay?" Michael quickly got his grandfather up to speed.

"A few of my still active colleagues should either be here now or arrive shortly."

"I think they are here. But they can't just run around and do their own God damn thing, George."

"I know and they won't – much." The last bit he said quietly. "Listen, I need to get to the doorman's station. Some years back I had a security system installed in Vicky's apartment, including a couple of tiny eyes. Let's see if they still function."

"Why wouldn't they?" They quickly moved towards the lobby.

"After Vicky married Baxter she didn't feel that she needed them and with Fielder tucked away for life, she didn't see the reason to keep running it. I agreed, but I never had it dismantled. I told her I did, but left all the stuff in place.

Some of my people did the new installation while pretending to remove the equipment; they actually replaced it with newer technology – just in case." He paused and looked at Michael's disapproving expressions. "What? I think we can consider this *just in case* situation, huh?"

"You are a piece of work – just so everybody knows, it might not be legal to turn the system on." Michael looked at his grandfather and continued: "But what I'm concerned, I really don't give a shit if it's legal or not. We have a situation we need to solve. We have people who need to be rescued through whatever bloody way we can eliminate that bastard, that's the way we'll do it." George looked at his grandson with pride – he clearly saw the bloodline coming from him, but it had totally missed his son. Jack didn't have fire in the guts like Michael – not even close. "So let's get going."

A second later they had entered the lobby and headed for the doorman's area. The monitor was not on, so George sat down and turned some knobs, pressed some buttons and worked the keyboard. Several screens popped up but disappeared as fast as George's fingers could move. The password screen came on and twelve asterisks later the image of Victoria and William's bedroom appeared in black and white; it was empty.

"Bingo, Gentlemen, we are in." George was getting excited. He didn't feel his 80 years at all; he just felt good being this kind of active, using stuff from his old bag of tricks. When he was on top in this line of work, he had been one of the best in the world. Not only had he been *invited* to the USA back in 1943, but several other nations had since flirted with him. But America had been it from he was a child and was going to be it till death do us part – it was a decision he never regretted, not for a second.

The next image was the kitchen – empty. The bathroom was also empty.

"What are we looking for?" Richard asked.

"Wanna see if the target is alone, nobody else, friend or foe, maybe hiding somewhere." The office was also empty; same with the guestroom. Finally the image of the living room came up.

"Bingo, gentlemen; target in sight." Several police officers were now watching the monitor. The two SWAT Team sergeants were taking notes. The direct image of Fielder was disturbing to George. He felt he had failed Vicky. He was convinced that he should have finished him off when he had the chance; he was so close, but instead of gut reaction, he hesitated that one split second, something he had never done before. In his heart he immediately promised Vicky that he would rectify the mistake and tonight would be the time he would do just that. It sure felt good to be here, he thought with a determined face; revenge would be sweet, but there was still a lot of work to be done.

Michael looked up as he saw Linda rushing in. She showed her badge to the guarding uniforms and was quickly by his side. She smirked as she acknowledged George's presence.

"What do you know; the whole Miller gang is here. What's the situation?"

"The situation is that you shouldn't be here, Linda, it's not your department." Michael sounded frustrated.

"I heard Victoria and William were in trouble and I consider that my department as much as its George's and yours." Michael shook his head.

"Well, please try to stay out of the way, okay." Linda looked at the monitor and observed Fielder. His was obviously talking.

"George, can we listen in?" Linda had put her hand on George's shoulder.

"Yeah, let me check a few things; can't fully recall how to bring it up." His fingers flew over the keyboard and through several screens; no sound. Linda smirked again.

"How about turning the speakers on?" She noted as she pushed the on button on the left unit. George smiled sheepishly.

"Yeah, that should do it. Thanks Linda." The audio was not very clear but clear enough to understand what was said in apartment 606, six floors above. Everybody who listened in cringed as the eerie voice cut through their heads. If the urgency of action had not been prevalent up to this point, what was being hissed and spat out the targets mouth, cemented the extreme importance of quick action. Lives were at risk and at a huge risk at that.

Richard produced blueprints of apartment number 606 as well as of the apartments next to, over and under. In this otherwise secure building, all front doors were steel enforced. He explained the near impossibility of blowing the door open without hurting or killing somebody. Fielder was sitting in a big sofa with his back towards the door. The sofa might protect his body from the neck down, but could possibly blow his head off. Richard was fine with that, but Victoria and William were sitting across from Fielder facing the door, so that would be too risky. Fielder also had a sidearm in his right hand. Considering how crippled his hands were, Richard was amazed that he would actually be able to pull the trigger. He was sure that if Fielder felt threatened to any extend, he would not hesitate to kill Victoria and William – he wouldn't even think twice. He had killed before and at this point it didn't matter how many more he would bring down with him. He could only assume that Fielder knew that he was caught and done with, so that realization would make him even more dangerous and unpredictable. He pulled Michael and the two SWAT sergeants over to the desk.

"My suggestion at this point would be to divert Fielder's attention. Not in a big way, but just enough so he doesn't overreact and does something stupid, but something enough to make him curious; maybe something that might even pull him out of the sofa to investigate." Michael's brain was swirling.

"What about some loud music from one of the next door apartments, or a TV running?" He looked at his friend.

"Yeah, something like that. See, this wall here between 604 and 606? That's the master bedroom and you have the walk-in closet full of clothes right here. We have the master bedroom the farthest from the living room, so if we can keep some of Fielder's attention occupied with sounds from the apartment on the opposite side, we might have a chance to open a hole big enough to get some people into the apartment."

"Wouldn't that be too noisy to cut out?" One of the sergeants asked.

"I have used this method a few times, and the success lingers on how we can direct and divert the target's attention while we cut the hole. The noise level is minimal; any suggestions concerning diversion?" Linda's face suddenly lit up.

"What about a loud argument between the neighbors, you know a verbal fight, some plates and china throwing contest and loud music. It seems we are all somewhat attracted to other people's fights and miseries, no?" Richard laughed.

"You know, you might actually have something there." Linda stepped over to Michael's side.

"I always wanted to fight it out with my husband, so if this is what we are going to do, we both volunteer." Michael looked at Linda.

"We do?"

"Yes dear; do you have a problem with that?" Michael shook his head.

"We've never had a fight before. I wouldn't even know if I could do that." Linda smiled slyly and looked at Michael.

"Just follow my lead and you'll be fine." Richard pointed at the front door on the blue-print. "Get your people in place with the hole-cutting – take this with you" He handed him the blue-print. "And one last thing: cut quietly but fast and don't start before we notify you. We need to get Linda and Michael in place in 608, okay?"

"Roger that." All of a sudden there was a lot of movement with people running in and out quietly. Equipment was brought up to sixth floor. George had listened, but also stayed on what was happening in the apartment. He didn't see Fielder being aware of any of the activity outside the apartment. But he must know or was he just that totally stupid? Richard whispered an *okay go* into his handheld radio.

The scene hasn't changed. Fielder sat with his back to the camera as Victoria and William was facing the camera and the door.

"Linda and Michael, start on my signal. Consider that Fielder does not like women as far as we know. 604, start operating on my signal." Linda already had a stack of dinner plates in front of her on the table; she was quietly hoping they were neither heirlooms nor irreplaceable. Never the less, she was as ready as could be and was hoping that this would all work. With a slight nervous giggle she looked at Michael who seemed a bit tense and then she thought that this was the weirdest action in-the-line-of-duty she had ever been involved in. Everybody was in place.

"So Mr. Baxter, you ended up with the bitch here, huh? I haven't banged her yet, but some time back I was damn close. As you see, I'm back and ready to pick up where we left off. She's still pretty, wouldn't you say?" William didn't move a muscle. "Now, since Victoria and I are going to be intimate, is there a position she's real excellent at, one you would recommend?" William stayed calm and controlled; didn't react one bit, though he was erupting inside. "Excuse me, but are you fucking deaf or something? I'm talking to you, asshole." He held up the sidearm with both crippled hands and aimed at William's head. "Bang-bang and you will be dead." He grinned as he thought it funny and did another line. "But anyway Victoria, you've kept yourself in good shape I see. Looks like you got some new tits, huh? They look bigger than last time you showed them to me – I'm sorry, you probably don't remember that, do you?" Victoria was also frozen. "You were somewhat out of it, as I recall." Though she was tied up, her mind was busy killing Fielder. She was scared and furious, but she found her thinking to be organized and calm, no matter the violent direction it was all heading. Fielder started to get out of the sofa. "Well, we can't sit here all day, so Mr. Baxter, I'm going to take you wife into the bedroom and give her a good time. Is that okay with you?" William didn't move. "But first I want Victoria to do a little striptease for us, huh Baxter? Wouldn't that be a hoot?" Fielder went out in the kitchen and picked up a knife, came back and cut the tape on Victoria's ankles and wrists. She cringed as the knife cut into the skin and bleeding started. She didn't feel the pain; she only saw the blood.

"Here's the deal Victoria." The pistol was aimed directly at William. "Since you fucked up my life so many years ago from the day you entered the doors of Anchor till my *unscheduled* release from federal prison a few days ago, I have thought of nothing else than getting a bit of revenge. I have banged you over and over and then snuffed you out like an irritating rodent, again and again. My anger became vile and nasty and as I diligently worked on making these crippled hands and fingers function over the years, that anger grew more and more violent. And I was not a violent man to begin with, Victoria, but you created what you see here today – your stupid actions totally fucked me up and brought me to a point where I don't give a shit about anybody anymore and especially you. I lost my life, my wife, two children who dismissed me, my family and friends. I have nothing else to lose. So I'll have one last roll in the hay and then *BANG* you'll be gone as well." His trying smile was just that. "So the deal is that you remove your clothes piece by piece and very slowly - we have plenty of time. If you at any point stop or refuse to get naked, I'll put a bullet into lover boy over there, just like this." The pop from the gun could barely be heard, but William's muffled scream of severe pain could. The .45 caliber bullet had torn its way through his left shoulder. Victoria's scream was loud and horrific. She was getting out of the sofa, but immediately Fielder had the gun in her face.

"That would be a stupid move, bitch. Just shut the hell up." William kept twisting in pain. "Okay start to undress." Victoria's fingers were shaking violently as they desperately tried to unbutton her blouse. Fielder was quickly fixated on the undressing. He had waited so long and here it was, right in front of him. As the last button was done, she put her hands down her side as she looked at William. He was breathing noisily now as the blood kept rolling down his white shirt. Half of it was already soaked and Victoria knew he needed help fast or he would bleed to death.

"Concentrate, bitch, concentrate. Get going - skirt next." Victoria slowly stood up again and unzipped her skirt on the back. She soon stood in quiet rage with the skirt on the floor and her blouse open. Fielder's breathing could now be heard loud and clear. Victoria's laced bra barely held her breasts in place. This was more than he had ever been able to imagine. She was a bloody bitch, but she was bloody beautiful. He was looking forward to have her, he drooled. "Continue." He whispered out loud. Hesitantly Victoria slowly pulled down her pantyhose; Fielder got more and more focused and soon lost track of anything else in that twisted world of his. William fought hard to stay conscious. He wanted to attack Fielder, but with his hands and legs tied as well as the weakening from the loss of blood, he didn't see any way of succeeding. He hopelessly watched Victoria struggle and felt he was betraying her. Fielder didn't pay attention to William anymore, so maybe he could find a way to distract him enough for Victoria to escape. He had to try something – anything.

Fielder was visually salivating at this time. The black laced panties were also more than he could have imagined. For a fifty year old, she was gorgeously curved and utterly sexy; his mind was spinning faster and faster. He looked forward to have her, to be on top of her. All these years of waiting and finally the moment had arrived. He would have her for momentary pleasure and when he was done, he would kill her for all the pain he had suffered and for screwing up his life; that was the plan.

The crash of china hitting the wall was loud and direct. Fielder's head snapped up with an irritating look. He stared at the wall for a second and turned towards Victoria as another crash was heard. Victoria had stopped moving as she herself had been stunned a little from the noise. Fielder's head turned towards the wall again.

"What the fuck is that?" He more or less asked himself. Suddenly a very loud female voice appeared above the music and noise.

"What the hell do you think you are doing? How dare you even think about doing that, you asshole?" A shaky male voice answered.

"What do you mean *what am I doing*? It's not any of your bloody business you dumb broad." The crash of yet another piece of China hitting the wall was heard; this time with force. Fielder's face looked puzzled.

"What the hell is going on? Your neighbors?" He looked like a question mark. Victoria swallowed.

"Yeah, they fight all the time." She had no clue what was going on. She had never heard a single sound from any of the apartments around her. Didn't even know who lived there, but she kept mum and played along with whatever it was.

The fight grew louder and louder and more China found its demise against the wall. Fielder got more and more involved and a small lingering smile appeared on his face. Looking at the wall he thought: *Give the bitch what she deserves, asshole.* The male voice was getting more aggressive and much louder and the language was just what

Fielder wanted to hear. Suddenly the woman screamed in pain: *Don't hit me you jerk*, and then she screamed again. Another plate hit the wall and another scream pierced through the apartments. Fielder could only imagine what was going on and as long as the bitch got what she no doubt deserved, he felt eerily good and more and more excited.

Victoria watched Fielder as he got involved with the ongoing fight. He finally stood up and was now leaning against the wall, listening closer. But the pistol never left its aim on William; Fielder was distracted but not unaware. It was when the woman had screamed *Micky, don't hit me; please don't hit me, Micky*, that she all of a sudden recognized the voice. Could that be Linda; and maybe Michael? Victoria concentrated on the voices as they kept fighting, screaming at each other. Fielder was smiling louder now as he begged *Micky* to beat the crap out of the bitch.

During the noise and distraction, nobody had noticed the black clad trained body in a kneeling position observing the living room from the hallway. His riffle with the 9 inch scope was aimed at the target leaning against the wall at the far end of the space. His partner was flat on the floor right behind him. The man with the riffle whispered into his microphone: "Target in clear sight; no obstructions - ready and in place." The small explosive that was now draped around the lock on the front door was at the ready as well; the screaming from next door continued. The SWAT Team commander said a quick prayer and whispered with stern authority into his handheld: "Let it rip."

What happened next was all in fast slow motion. The enormous sound of the explosion was louder than the damage. It had done its work and several SWAT members rushed into the apartment, weapons ready. But that was slightly after the rifleman in the apartment had commanded Fielder to drop his weapon. As Fielder had been shocked and certainly distracted by the explosion, he had automatically dropped to the floor; that action the rifleman had not expected. All of the sudden the target was out of sight. The inrushing SWAT members didn't have a clear shot either and made the mistake of stopping their movement.

"Drop your weapon, and do it now." Fielder responded with a shot in the direction of the rifleman. Victoria had dropped herself on top of William to protect him. One of the inrushing SWAT members finally got up and approached Fielder weapon ready. Fielder turned towards him, but had to raise his head a few inches to get a shot off. That was enough for the rifleman to catch him in his scope and pull the trigger – but not calmly enough. The shot only cut a line in Fielder's scalp and snapped his head back. He twirled around towards Victoria and William and aimed his pistol at them. He managed to pull one more shot off just before the second bullet from the rifleman tore through his head killing him instantly. The dead body dropped to the floor like a sack of pudding. Two SWAT members swiftly secured the scene.

Michael and Linda had rushed in after the shooting and were both evaluating the situation concerning Victoria and William. None of them moved. As the medics carefully lifted Victoria off William, they noted extensive bleeding from a large hole in Victoria's lower back. As they gently turned her over and moved her to the gurney in the hallway, they found that the bullet had torn all the way through her body and into William's. The exit wound in his lower abdomen was massive; he was barely breathing. The first shot that had smashed his left shoulder, also exposed a huge exit wound; again, there was blood everywhere. It was obvious that both victims could become fatal cases if not treated at once, so the race to the emergency room was on.

George had tears in his eyes as he saw Victoria and William being rolled by and hurriedly placed in the two ready ambulances. He had thanked everybody for a job well done, but was not so sure if it had been done that well. The next few hours would expose the result. Michael and Linda had embraced him and thanked him for his help. They had also been tearful as the three of them walked to Linda's car to get to the hospital. Michael drove and they were soon sitting in the emergency room waiting for news. George did not have his usual optimistic attitude. He was quiet and sat on the chair like a stiff board. Linda was holding his hands as Michael was tearing up the floor by the opposite wall. Finally a male nurse appeared.
"Are you next of kin?" Michael nodded eagerly.
"Yeah, what's up?"
"I can't say at this point other than we need blood. Mr. Baxter has lost a lot of blood as well as Miss Grant. We have

enough blood for her here and can get more, but we need donors with O-negative; any of you?" Michael jumped up.

"I'm O-negative, my father is and my brother and sister." The nurse looked bewildered.

"Are you sure? Because that's extremely rare."

"Of course I'm sure; my Mother was O-negative and my Dad is for sure." The nurse smiled quickly.

"Can you get hold of your brother and sister and father real fast?"

"Consider it done." Michael followed the nurse as they left the waiting room. He was already rolling up his left sleeve. Linda was on her mobile and soon had Jasper on the line. She expressed no time for chatting and explanations, just *come to the hospital at once.* Soon after, she also commanded Jack to get to the hospital as fast as possible; on the way he got hold of Caroline, who was just getting ready to dive into dinner at Nonna's; she was quickly on the way to the hospital.

The surgeons stabilized Victoria somewhat. She was far from out of danger. They would wait a bit before heading into her abdomen again; have her body recuperate some strength. The bullet had certainly done some major damage, but it looked like she would survive – *looked like* was the key term.

William was not that well off. His loss of blood was frightening. He had slumped in the sofa for too long and no pressure had been applied to the wound and therefore the blood had freely drained out of his body. One thing that was somewhat positive was that he had slumped to the extent where the blood had actually flowed a bit slower than if he had sat upright. When they tested for blood type they had all cringed when it came up O-negative. They needed lots of O-negative blood besides what they had on site. They made quick calls to all nearby blood banks for emergency deliveries, as well as they contacted two employees with this blood type. As luck would have it, they had found four family members who could make a huge difference. The first one was already donating and the other three would be in shortly. Everybody was ready and as soon as the blood had gone through the general checks and declared useable, the patient would benefit right away. Four donors, four pints, plus what else was on the way; it looked better now, but nothing was for sure – he was not doing great, but hope was still floating around, though nervously so.

Hours later they were all together in the emergency room's waiting area. Everybody had heard about the dreaded events and sat around in quiet silence. Caroline was sitting next to her father with her arm over his shoulders; Nancy had towed along from Nonna's and was holding Caroline's hand. Michael and Linda sat on each side of George, Linda still holding on to him. Jasper had arrived in a hurry and Ella had showed up minutes later. Nora and Karen had arrived as soon as they heard. Attempts on conversation were feeble at best and nervous for the most.
"Where are the kids?" Jack asked Linda.
"Neighbors got them." Jack nodded. He realized that it was at least the third time, he had asked.
"Oh good;" Michael was looking at Caroline.
"Just home for the weekend?" She turned towards him.
"Actually we don't have to be back before next Thursday."
"Good, let's get together then."
"Of course, Michael; we'll do that." The silence raced on. Every time a door opened or closed, they all jumped; for the most for no reason. The waiting was long and worrisome. The doctors, who came out very few times, had suggested that they should all go home and get some sleep. At the moment there was nothing they could do to help and both patients were under constant observation; but they all stayed in place.

It was around midnight when two of the surgeons appeared in the waiting room. They both looked worn-out tired. Everybody turned as they both cleared their throats at the same time. The taller one looked around at everybody and cleared his throat yet again.
"Victoria Grant is now in a stable and satisfying condition. We are positive about her recovery, though it will no doubt take some time to recover 100%. We did not find any major issues, issues we in the beginning thought we would be forced to deal with. No major arteries were severed, so the blood loss was not extensive." He paused; it sounded as everybody in the room finally could exhale and did, all at the same time. There were glances of relief exchanged, but the

attention quickly went back to the surgeons who were obviously not done. They both cleared their throats and looked down. The shorter of the two started to talk.

"When Mr. Baxter was brought in we found the injury to his shoulder extensive, as well as the secondary injury was equally damaging; he lost massive quantities of blood. We supplied him with as much additional blood as we possibly could get our hands on, but the damage had already taken affect and additional blood would not have made a difference. We tried everything possible to save his life, but Mr. Baxter went into cardiac arrest and we were not able to resuscitate him." He paused and cleared his throat again; this time his voice was shaking: "I'm terribly sorry to inform you that Mr. William Baxter passed away approximately 15 minutes ago."

The shock in the room was devastating. The surreal reality of the horrifying news that William had died, did not immediately register. Tears were flowing as questions were asked to nobody specifically, as nobody specifically had any answers. George had fallen physically ill and was now in a hospital bed with an IV and calming medication. He kept blaming himself for what he thought was his fault from the start. He should have blown that piece of shit to pieces when had had the chance. He felt that he would never be able to face Victoria again and he kept begging for William's forgiveness. Nobody could comfort him, so the doctors felt that due to his age, though his overall health was good, a night in the hospital would help him rest and calm down.

Jack had found a corner where he was shaking and crying. There were so many questions, but only few answers. The massive guilt concerning how his relationship with William had deteriorated due to his pathetic mourning, till this very final day, smashed his heart and could never be rectified. But this was not about him; this was all about William whose life had been cut short. He had told Jack how much happiness he had found with Victoria, how he felt that he finally had won her over. Sure he knew she still lingered on her obsession with Jack, but it had finally been treated with tongue in cheek and she had at last realized the silliness she had gone through for so many years. But she also regretted and had a hard time dealing with the whole Fielder issue that stemmed from her obsessive determination of revenging Jack for his rejection of her. She had often cried in William's arms and begged forgiveness from him and from Jack. William had always comforted her and assured that all was forgiven. But now he had paid the highest price for her weakness.

Caroline and Nancy brought Jack home, and after a few moments of reflection, he headed for bed, but didn't sleep.

It was some time after Jack's 48 hour incident with Molly. He tried to get hold of her, but the house had been dark and empty. This mysterious disappearing act, yet again, made the whole Molly thing even more surreal. If it hadn't been for the scrubs he was holding on to, he would be tempted to file it all as a weird dream. He hadn't told a soul about Molly's momentary resurrection; he kept that to himself for now.

He had started his own resurrection, step by little step, though William's death had been a huge setback. He felt a strong urge to comfort his father, and also found comfort *from* his father. George's health took a toll from William's death and his guilt not being able to protect Victoria. Medication and weekly check-ups were part of his daily life; at least for now. Colleen, who had lived with George for some years, had moved to Key West, Florida for health reasons. George visited her often, but started to find the trips too draining, so they had stopped. Colleen also found a new friend, so her life had taken a different direction. George was happy for her, though admittedly a bit jealous of the lucky guy. They often talked on the phone, which turned to not so often and then stopped. George had resigned to the reality that he would not find another companion at his age and he was okay with that. He kept busy with the family and friends and was never one to just sit back and wait for them to call. He especially enjoyed Nicole and Frank and saw them often. Caroline, Jasper and Ella as well as Linda and Michael would stop by unannounced or by appointment, but either way they showed up, they always had a grand and fun time. Of course George had missed Jack, but it had gotten to the point in his self-inflicted misery that George simply couldn't stand it anymore. Sure he loved his son, that was never a question, but being dragged down constantly in his company was nothing neither he nor anybody else could face anymore.

But then Jack had showed up unannounced a few weeks after William's death. He had been compassionate and supporting and George realized that Jack was there for *him*, not for *himself*. He had made them some lunch and proved that those early cooking skills Colleen taught him were still intact. They enjoyed a bottle of wine and it was late afternoon when they sat in the living room with after-lunch drinks, both slightly tipsy at this point. The conversation had circled around many fun memories of William, but had also turned to *what's next* with respect to Jack. No, it was not brought up by Jack, but by a question from his father. Jack had told him about the revelation that had opened his eyes some weeks ago, how he had felt such confusion concerning William's death, but that he felt strength more so than misery, when he realized that William was not going to come back. He set out on a mission of recovery and he was not going to screw it up this time, no Sir. George's heart soared as he listened and he felt that his son was finally focused; he felt that he would succeed and he would help him along as much as he could.

Jasper and Ella had stopped by after work so George asked them to stay for dinner. Jack quickly hijacked Ella and they were soon deeply involved in creating a meal using whatever they could find in a bachelor's kitchen. The conversation was lively and spiced with lots of laughter. Jack loved Ella; she was well suited for Jasper and it was obvious that they were in big love with each other. She had both feet firmly planted on solid ground and guided their relationship in so many directions. Jasper had always been the loner as a child and as a young adult, and though the relationship with his mother had been exceptional, socializing with anybody other than family and very few friends, was not his forte, far from. But Ella constantly pulled him out from under the shadows and forced stuff-to-do on him – and he loved every moment of it. If she was there, Jasper wanted to be there as well – really bad. It was a joy for Jack to watch Jasper as he at times were so much like his mother; the way he laughed and the dry comments with that sly sense of intelligent humor – just a joy and so much

Sara. As Ella and Jasper left that evening, George followed them out to their car. Ella kissed him goodnight and as Jasper hugged his grandfather, he said:
"Looks like Dad Is back?" George smiled big time.
"Yeah Jasper, I think that Jack is back; and I hope he is back for good."

Jack stayed with his father that night – a thing about not mixing drinking and driving. George felt happy having his son in the room a couple of doors down – somewhat like the good old days. Then there was the delightful breakfast he whipped up the next morning. George was used to coffee and cereal, but with Jack in charge of the stove, it was magic feeding time. Their conversation was energetic and positive, fun and entertaining. After Jack cleaned up, they shared the last of the coffee as they scanned through the daily papers; just like those many mornings, so many years ago.
"Well Dad, gotta go. Have a get-together with Nora and Karen this morning and lunch with them at Nonna's." Jack smiled: "Haven't seen Romano for the longest time, by the way." His father looked at him and smiled.
"Good having you back, Son." He paused and looked into Jack's eyes: "I know how hard it is for you not to talk and think about Sara. I struggled with my loss of your mother for so many years and I still cry for her. I tried so hard to keep that sorrow to myself and it has been a struggle. So trust me, Jack, I've been there and done that – and I am actually still doing it. You will never forget Sara and what you had, but you can learn to live with it without making your life a total nothing."
"I made it a *nothing* for ten years, Dad. But it wasn't just my loss; I made it everybody else's misery and in the process pushed them all out of my life." He paused as he got slightly emotional: "I *am* finally going to try to pick up the pieces, pick up my life, friends and family, hopefully. It's going to be tough, but I'm willing to do whatever it takes and no matter how long it takes. I know Sara has been waiting a very long time for me to grow up." George smiled again.
"Not only Sara, Dear Boy, also the rest of us – everybody who loves you." They embraced and Jack was on his way.

As he drove towards the offices of CR Constructions he couldn't recall when he had been there last. As he got closer, the reality of what he had done, more so *not done*, became even more apparent. He wondered what kind of role he would have with the business in the future and also considered that Nora might want him out for good. He would fully understand that, as he had done close to nothing for ten years. In that span of time, he had still cashed paychecks and bonuses, though the last five years, he did return the bonus checks, guided by sheer guilt.

And he was wondering if he could pick up his friendship with Nora again. If she wanted him out, could they still save their friendship? And what about Karen? She had been the angriest of them all. He felt very uncomfortable just thinking about it. He was sweating a bit as he parked the car in one of the visitor parking spaces and a bit hesitantly walked towards the entrance.

The building looked sharp. The red bricks made it stoic and gave it a solid appearance. On the way up the wide stairway towards the lobby a few people passed him, people he didn't know or didn't recognize. He said quiet *good mornings,* but most of them didn't hear him; they just glanced at him with a small *hello* nod; at least he thought that was what it was. The young woman at the lobby counter greeted him with a big smile.

"Good morning, Sir. How may I help you?'

"My name is Jack Miller and I have a 10 o'clock with Nora." She smiled again and looked at a list on her computer monitor.

"Please be seated, Mr. Miller and I'll let Miss Clark know you have arrived." Jack awkwardly walked over to the group of chairs and sofas by the large window facing the little park-like area behind the building. He all of a sudden had very violent fears that this was not going to be a good day at all. He felt intimidated and extremely uncomfortable. He was the little naughty schoolboy waiting to see the principal for something bad he had done; the extreme urge to get up and run away was real. He was sweating some more and his vision got slightly blurry. He saw the young woman on the phone and she had suddenly popped into a standing position and finished with *Yes Nora, right away.* She hung up and came over towards Jack in a hurry. Her face was red and she started talking before she reached the waiting area.

"Mr. Miller, I am so terribly sorry. I had no idea who you were - who you are. I'm really terribly sorry." Jack smiled nervously.

"Don't worry about it; miss?"

"Warner, Sir. Erica Warner. Oh my, am I ever going to get it from Nora now." Jack kept smiling.

"I'll make sure that doesn't happen; okay Erica?" Now it was her turn to smile nervously.

"I hope you know her better than I do. She can be a tough one at times. Please come with me, Mr. Miller."

"And Erica, it's Jack, okay?" She took a deep breath and looked more relaxed now.

"Thanks, Jack."

Erica knocked on the door with the brass sign: *Nora Clark, President, CR Constructions*. The front office was bright and lively. Karen got up from behind her desk and greeted Jack with a handshake.

"Good morning, Jack." He greeted her back as she turned to Erica.

"Thanks sweetheart," Erica blushed.

"I'm so sorry about the mix-up," she pointed at Jack behind his back; Karen smiled.

"Not your fault, Erica. I should have told you, but I forgot. I'm sure Jack will forgive you." Jack smiled nervously.

"Already done," he said, and Erica disappeared.

"You look better, Jack." Never being one to sugar-coat anything, Jack took her observation as a statement, not a compliment. "Let's go and chinwag a bit with the boss," She stopped herself in the tracks, but let it slide. She realized that statement was a bit insensitive, but what the heck, we're trying to resolve a situation, she thought.

"Let's go see the boss," Jack played along.

Nora looked great. Her business suit fit exquisitely, her hair beautifully styled and her smile was as wide, dimples and all, as ever. She came towards Jack with outstretched arms as he entered her large office. The embrace felt good for both of them and lasted longer than normal.

"It is sure good to see you again and sorry about the mix-up in the lobby. I'll fire Erica right away." She laughed. "It was actually Karen's fault." Karen smirked and walked over to the large conference table.

"Come and sit down, Jack; coffee, tea, water, anything?"
"Coffee would be nice, cream and sugar, please." Karen talked into the intercom and coffee for Jack and water for both Karen and Nora arrived within moments.

The two women sat next to each other with an empty chair between them; Jack was on the opposite side of the large oval mahogany table. He felt he was going to be interrogated, which of course he was; he did not feel comfortable at all. Thoughts of leaving this room without a job, without these two *former* friends scared him no end. But he tried to stay calm and controlled. Nora pushed a folder with several sheets of papers towards him; he didn't really want to open it to find out what it said, as he felt rather sure it was his final will and testament, as well as the freshly signed death-certificate. He refused to look, which was the way Jack had dealt so *maturely* with issues of conflict during the last ten years. The school principal started to talk. First it was a bit about the loss of William and how they were slowly trying to find somebody else for the job he left behind.

"You know Jack, it's like when we were kids and we believed that if we covered our eyes nobody could see us. As adults we figured out that was not really true, but we do it anyway. Karen and I have been procrastinating because we naively believe that if we keep our eyes closed, William will eventually walk through that door with that stupid grin of his and say that same stupid thing he said every bloody time *What's up, Doc?*" Nora paused. "And I miss that terribly. But we must return to reality and the real world. We must take care of business to honor William and his work and the enormous friendship he gave all of us. He'll never walk through that door again ever; and we know that." Nora shook her head to shake off the tears pushing on. After a bit more reminiscing about William, Nora straightened up, folded her hands in front of her and looked directly into Jack's eyes. *Here it comes*, he nervously feared.

"Jack, you and I need to resolve our partnership." The fears were being answered; he was a dead man. "The last ten years have not been pleasant for me concerning our relationship. The business part I can deal with; but it's been harder to accept the way our friendship slowly but surely has spiraled down to a level of deep resentment on my part. I can only find sadness in that loss." Jack felt his own deep sadness by that true statement. "I don't know how or if our friendship can be rekindled, but if there is the slightest possibility that we could make it work again, I'll most certainly try to do my share. There will also be certain conditions I need in place if any *salvaging* is in the cards." She paused. "I do hope that you at some point would like to see us be friends again." Jack nodded quietly; she did the same. There was a moment of uncomfortable silence before Nora continued. "Now, the business part of this might be more complicated then re-establishing a friendship. Karen and I have come up with several scenarios, ideas and thoughts that we want to discuss with you. We have *our* wish-list, but we will not expose that before we know what *you* would like to see happen." He nodded and mumbled:

"From where I'm sitting and from what I have done, or more so, what I have *not* done through the last ten years, I can't see that my opinions or what I would like to see in my future has any validation or relevance." Nora and Karen acknowledged what he had said.

"We both figured that would be your attitude and your honesty is of course appreciated." She continued by opening the folder in front of her; Karen did the same. "The different scenarios we came up with are not in any specific order numerically, alphabetically or stacked in any form of preference; please be aware of that." Jack nodded in understanding. "Again, also understand that Karen and I have our version, a big picture we *must* materialize, and hopefully that is where you want to go as well." Nora paused for a moment and cleared her throat. "Karen has been with CR for many years and she has done a fantastic job. She is talented and aggressive and extremely assertive and everybody in this company simply adores her and follows whatever *suggestions* she barks out. Not to make her head get too big, but she is utterly essential to the success we are riding on right now and have for the last eight years. I'm considering a promotion; just so you know." Neither Karen nor Nora looked away from Jack. He felt he should say something in response.

"That doesn't surprise me at all. You were on a mission from the very day we hired you." He smiled nervously as Karen nodded as thanks.

"The top page is a statement of the salary-total you have received during your absence. As you already know, you returned the last five year's annual partnership bonus payments. We didn't bother you by trying to make you *accept* these payments, so we opened an account in your name. The money is yours and whatever is decided this morning, those funds belong to you." Jack looked at the balance and couldn't believe his eyes.

"Wow, business has been good." He shook his head and pushed the folder a bit away from him. "But I can't take this, Nora. We have an agreement, actually we *had* a contractual agreement and I faltered big time. The partnership clause clearly stated that if one of the partners ceased participating in the daily mechanics and development of the business for a period of twelve months plus, the active partner can sever the relationship by dismissal of the non-active partner; either that or offer a buy-out, based on the business' P & L based on the last 12 months." He cleared his throat nervously. "I'm of course willing to accept the intention of that clause…" Jack kept shaking his head in disbelief: "Wow, you guys have done really great." Karen cleared her throat.

"We haven't done great, Jack, we have done outrageously fantastic. Our bottom line, as you no doubt have noted as you, as a partner have signed CR's monthly reports the last ten years, is the best in the industry. We now have over 75 fulltime employees who earn the highest wages in the nation for the job and responsibilities they have. 42 employees are related and when needed, we have a bank of employees from families and friends connected to our current staff." Jack looked puzzled; Karen continued: "Meaning that at a moment's notice we can add bodies to any project to make sure we get things done in time. Furthermore, our benefit package is unheard of as well as the bonuses on many levels of the work we do – they do. We have had 5 employees leave the company in 8 years – five people. Two were pregnant and wanted to stay home, the others found management positions in other companies, not related to what we do. All our managers are home-grown. We have totally negated hiring people from the outside. So as you can see, we are not just doing great, we are doing fantastic." Karen leaned back in her chair a bit; he could see how proud she was of their accomplishments. "And as you can see on page three, we have guaranteed projects in the books for an estimated 2-1/2 years with the staff we have now." Jack was utterly impressed. He mumbled the next sentence.

"You have actually brought CR to the place we wanted it to be in." He looked up at Nora: "You have done an amazing job." Karen looked a bit puzzled; Nora saw it and continued, looking at Karen.

"Before we bought CR, Jack and I had these long drawn-out discussions of what we wanted to do. We came up with many horrific scenarios, but as we sifted through everything we talked about, dreams we had, goals and silly ambitions we wanted to implement, we pretty much came up with this." Nora giggled: "The last session we had was in Jack's old room, away from Sara, kids and all. It lasted three days and three nights, catered by the local Pizza joint and our host, George Miller." She looked at Jack: "Remember that?" Jack nodded and smiled, and continued.

"And we didn't shower for three days and three nights." Now Karen had to laugh. "But as long as that session was, we did produce the map that pretty much consisted of what you guys have done – that is so impressive." Nora smiled and shook her head.

"I guess we did."

"You most certainly did." Jack felt a little better by that exchange, but he also saw Nora and Karen quickly getting back to business at hand; Nora started off again.

"Back to the partnership contract: As you, I'm fully aware of what the contract says. Sara was adamant about covering all bases and all possible scenarios. As I recall, both of us giggled loudly when some of these *unrealistic* scenarios were brought up. But the fact is that one of those *unrealistic* scenarios unfortunately became a reality. We don't have to go through the list of *whys* and *why-not's*. We have all been in your face often, so that's history now." Nora sipped some water: "All these years, Jack, I have kept this built-up resentment to myself. I did not want it to influence my relationship with you, personal or business-wise, but it got to a point where I couldn't hold back and I simply gave up on you." At this point Karen nodded in agreement. "So it became a matter of doing something for *me* and not for you. I looked at the contractual responsibilities and sought advice from Karen, Jasper and William. I found that I could kick your butt out of CR in a second and it wouldn't cost me a dime. That's how much Sara made sure we could protect our assets. Of course she didn't have any way to foresee the last ten years." Nora drank a bit more water, cleared her throat and continued: "I mulled it over and over, talked with several legal eagles, finance geniuses, business consultants and pretty much anybody who would listen. They all said *dump him and move on*. Jasper and your father were some of the eager ones." Jack looked down at the table. If he hadn't felt shitty before, this certainly brought it down a few notches. Jasper and his father had taken Nora's side, or was it CR's side? Either way they had not been happy with Jack and he did understand why and he did understand it fully. Nora watched Jack and she saw a beaten man with a slumping body and *remorse* written all over his face. He was pale and shaking. She felt like running over and give him a hug, but she had to do what she had to do, no matter how much she loved him.

"So even with all this outside advice, *Karen* was the one who asked *me* the right question, the one question nobody else had asked me: *What do you think Jack would do if the situation was reverse?* I remember that I quickly sat up straight as she brought that one on, and I knew immediately that whatever my answer, that would be the solution." Jack's shaky hands fumbled with the pen on the table in front of him; Nora continued: "I have no doubts that you would have ignored that part of the contract. You would have carried me as I have carried you. I have absolutely no doubts in my heart about that. So all of a sudden I found peace within myself and I could finally move forward." Nora smiled: "That was a great moment – thanks to Karen." Karen smiled. "You are welcome," she mumbled.

"So we conspired to hacking on you no end. You would end up hating us, but we felt strongly that the only way we could get you off your otherwise cute ass, was to give you hell; and that we did." Jack looked at Nora as if this was not real. "We involved everybody who loves you and decided that ten bloody years was enough, so it was either getting Jack back or he could go to hell with his miserable life – we wouldn't bother with him anymore, seriously. And we were all okay with that."

"I'm confused."

"Well you should be." Karen snarled.

"So what are we doing here?"

"Whatever you came for, Jack; whatever you decide about your personal life has nothing to do with what we decide here concerning your part in this company's future or not."

"So what are we doing next?" He mumbled nervously.

"Turn to page four." Karen answered; Nora continued.

"This is a buy-out proposal. As you can see, you will be paid handsomely, more than your fair share of the business' present market value. The property my father left me in Houston has reached a formidable dollar value. I have two serious buyers waiting to sign the checks. So with that money and some contribution from CR's coffers, you do not have to worry about us or this offer draining funds from CR. Though the amount is big, it will not make enough of a dent to get us off track." Nora paused; Karen continued.

"By accepting this buy-out, you must obviously be aware of its fairness. After signing on the proverbial dotted line, you'll have the funds deposited in your bank in a matter of thirty days and you are then fully disconnected from CR Constructions." She paused: "On top of that you also have a nice amount of bonus money in the account we established for you." She looked up at Jack, and continued. "This proposal should leave you without any financial concerns for the rest of your life." Jack looked at the figures, and again things went slightly blurry. Automatically he was going to ask for time to think about it, but instinctively he knew that would be a waste. He looked at the bottom line again and his amazement continued; it was a lot of money. After a long and silent pause, he had made up his mind. He glanced up at Nora and Karen and slowly closed the folder. It was an extraordinary offer and only an imbecile would turn it down. They had made it easy for Jack to decide; then he cleared his throat. The words came out very slow, calculated and hard.

"If you to any bloody extent think or believe or even *hope* that you can get rid of me with a stupid, cheap and insulting monetary offer like this, you must be out of your blooming skulls." Both Nora and Karen's mouths fell open. Jack evilly continued: "Sure I have gone through shit the last ten bloody years, been depressed, lost my children, my family and my friends, but if you in spite of all that still believe you can just discard and erase me like this, you are both pathetically mistaken. And if you think I have completely lost my mind or my edge, you couldn't be more wrong. *Yes* I did lose my mind for ten years, and my edge became as dull as could be." The chair flew back and fell to the floor with a large *bang* as he suddenly stood up. "No bloody edge, no initiative, no desire, nothing at all to do anything constructive – nothing." He raised his pointy finger at Nora and Karen; they recoiled into their chairs: "But don't you ever get me wrong again, Ladies, because now I can feel that edge coming back sharper than ever, cutting its way through every fiber, every muscle, every nerve and every cell of my being. I can feel that immense power of energy and positive attitude oozing from my brains, spreading back into my body. Read my luscious lips, fair ladies *JACK IS BACK*." He grabbed the buy-out proposal, violently tore it to shreds and threw the pieces high up in the air. Nora and Karen sat shocked and stunned, as they watched the pieces land on the top of the table. Calmly and in full control, he picked up the chair, sat down, looked serenely at Nora and Karen and smiled as he sweetly asked: "What else have you got?"

The silence in the room was loud and majestic. Nervously Nora and Karen started with silly giggles, but it soon erupted into the loudest laughter. Jack soon joined in and the group-hug that followed was warm and confirming. All three had tears running – and finally, after all these years, it was tears of pure joy and relief. Nora whispered in Jack's ear:
"You bastard…" He took that as a compliment.

It was one of the biggest revelations in Jack's life. He felt that he had finally figured it out – and most certainly with a lot of help from his friends and family. The next couple of hours Nora, Karen and Jack went through the options for an adjusted reinstatement to reactivate his partnership. They agreed he would work closely with Karen the first six months. As operational manager, she knew more about the mechanics of the business than did Nora. As Jack had been absent both physically and mentally, he needed to get up to speed before functioning in his old administrative capacity as a partner; Jack was more than fine with that. Karen had looked at him with a bit of concern.

"I work a lot," she told him. Jack had smiled and nodded. "No Jack, I mean I work a *LOT*," he nodded again. "A real big lot; something like 60 to 80 hours weekly." He smiled overbearingly. "And during weekends as well; and then there are the traveling to trade-shows, visiting out-of-town clients and all that stuff."

"I know Karen and I'll do my utmost to keep up with you - seriously." Karen wasn't completely convinced, but she smiled anyway.

He still did not want to accept the bonuses they had kept for him. He wanted the money ear-marked for scholarship funds benefitting children of the employees, in remembrance of William and Sara. Nora and Karen agreed. Then Nora asked Karen to step outside for a moment. Nora and Jack quickly agreed to offer Karen a junior partnership and percentages of business ownership. She had tearfully accepted her new title and office. The lunch at Nonna's had been fun and energetic. Romano Rossi finally recognized good old Jack he knew so many years ago; it was nice to have him back - so very nice indeed.

Victoria received support from everybody. Her recuperation had dragged out due to complications through her recovery, but she had certainly not lacked company. Jack had been very attentive and though Victoria slept through most of the first many visits, she slowly got to the point where she could communicate a bit and then finally talk. She was thankful of all the support and especially thankful for Jack's caring concern. They had long conversations, had talked about their friendship as *kids;* they talked about life after that, how much they missed Sara and William. And what was next for Victoria? Mr. Richards from Anchor had visited her often. He would talk about business and talked about it in a way where she felt connected; he wanted her to come back whenever she wanted. She told Jack that she was considering a change, something not as hectic, but she was not sure what it would be or if it would be at all.

When Victoria was told about William's death, she refused to believe it. It had been hell and back; her denial lasted for days. She was suffering tremendously from her own wounds, but dealing with the thought and the reality of her best friend's death was insurmountable. She felt she was being punished to the extreme, but also conceded that this was not about her at all, this was all about William and the life he didn't get to live. With a saddened heart she often thought about what he had said so many times: *Vicky, I have never been afraid of dying, but since I met you, I'm afraid of not living*. And this sweet, sweet man had died way before his time; for this she felt a horrendous guilt. She was totally devastated – for him.

She did not want to go back home. Her assistant from Anchor had helped listing the apartment for sale, as well as he had looked around for another place for her to move into. A few days after the hospital released her, she was in her new home. It had been heart-breaking to dispose of William's clothes and personal items. She had broken down again and again, but Jack had been there with the shoulder to cry on, helping to ease the pain.

He had brought Nora and Karen back to CR from Nonna's and was now sitting exhausted on the couch in the living-room, sipping a glass of chilled white wine. What a day it had been. His mind was still spinning, trying to inventory what had happened. After a quick run-through and another glass of wine, he ended up with a small satisfied smile as the phone rang. It was Michael; he wanted to know what was going on and had heard rumors that things had happened, good things. Jack confirmed and then they talked about this and that – just basic stuff, like the good old days. Linda got on the phone after Michael; she had been laughing and smiling and happy. Then it was Frank's and Nicole's turn. Frank was still a bit suspicious, but he let it ride.
"So the real Jack is back?"
"So Frank; Jack is back." There had been a slight pause and then:
"Good to hear Jack. See you real soon, okay?"
"You bet Frank." And the line went silent.

As he put the phone down, he absentmindedly looked at the couch across from him, hoping to find a sleeping Molly; of course she wasn't there. But where the heck was she? He hadn't seen her, heard from her, nothing, since those strange 48 hours. He knocked on the door to her house, taped a note to it, left phone messages and kept lookout. It was a mystery to him the way she had suddenly shown up, and as suddenly disappeared. He hoped she was okay; but he also hoped for more than that.

The first month back at work was hectic. Karen had been correct about her working hours, but it wasn't just that she worked a lot of hours; it had to do with what she was doing during those hours. Though Jack was out of shape work-wise, he quickly figured that he had never worked even close to the level of intensity as Karen did. She rarely paused and every time Jack figured they were finally done for the day, Karen would have a few more issues to finish up and Jack stayed on, every time - without blinking.

Business was good, but Karen and Nora had expressed a bit of concern with respect to the Virginia Project's future possibilities. It wasn't something that had been dealt with *on the table*, but a strong feeling they both had. Jack suggested to simply ask Virginia's owners, but Karen and Nora thought it was a bit premature – they had to think about it some more and look for any signs. The last 8 to 10 years they had exclusively handled Virginia's business and though they always felt it was dangerous to do so, the *all eggs in one basket* syndrome, they also felt secure as Virginia Projects was a rich and well-run business – but still, you should never feel too sure. Victoria had helped out researching the intimates of Virginia Projects and had come up with a suggestion, based on what she had found: they should probably start to look for additional business. Her last comment had been: *you never know these days*. Nora, Karen and Jack considered the possible situation, agreed and decided to start reeling in supplementary business. They could hire additional labor, train them and apply them to whatever projects they could land. It would be somewhat of a balancing act, but so far they had done well in that area.

Jack energetically approached many new business prospects and possibilities. Several developers had promised that when CR had time available, they would submit projects to them. Jack started the process contacting those developers, trying to log more work in the books, establishing a least a safety bumper. One of those potential clients had their main office in New York City.

The meeting had gone well. *Selling* had never been Jack's strong side at all, but he had learned to handle the weak areas and reached a point where he felt comfortable. Nora refused to do that part of the business, no matter how essential she knew it was. Karen was too direct, so Nora and Jack held her back dealing with prospects. She was excellent with active clients as they had already been sold and were only interested in hard facts and reality – that she could give them night and day and they respected her for it. So the selling bit was up to Jack.

The three client representatives and Jack were in the middle of an enjoyable dinner rounding out a good day of work. The Madison Avenue restaurant was full of chatter and laughter. Jack realized he had really missed out these last ten years. The woman of the three had been delightful and funny. Her balance between business and now *time to relax* had been remarkable. Both men sat back during the day-long meeting while she had done the talking. It was mentioned during dinner that she was the owner's daughter; her father had retired. Considering her probable age, as she couldn't be more than in her mid-twenties, she had been the ultimate negotiator; Jack was very impressed. It was also very nice to communicate with an *outside* female again, he thought with a smile.

As more after-dinner drinks were served, a tall and elegant woman entered the restaurant. She had two suited gentlemen following her, both carrying briefcases. They were lead to a table behind Jack and his guests. Jack couldn't take his eyes off her; nobody could. The way she carried herself was intriguing. There was a confidence oozing from the whole person; for most, it was an intimidating look. She walked right by him with her entourage, but suddenly stopped, paused and turned around. Her smile was bright and wide.

"Jack Winston Miller." Her voice was loud and clear. Many guests turned to look as well as the people at Jack's table did. She walked towards him, still smiling. "Well, if it isn't Jack Miller." Jack looked puzzled as he didn't recognize her. She stopped just a few feet from Jack, with a question mark on her face. "You don't remember me, do you? That really hurts, Dear Jack." He still didn't know who she was; confusion blurred his mind, but then there was her voice.

She made a pouting face, then smiled and looked at the people at the table.

"Last time Jack saw me, I threw up all over him *and* his bed; unfortunately that is the only thing I remember from that night..." She giggled teasingly.

"Oh my God, Molly!" He jumped up and was soon in a warm embrace. She kissed his lips and cuddled into his hug, "Molly where the heck have you been?" She whispered into his ear:

"Lost, so very lost." She was holding on to him tight. "It's so incredibly good to see you again." They released the embrace and Molly said out louder: "Where are you staying?"

"The Plaza."

"I have a few lose ends to tie up tonight, but I'll ring you later, okay?"

"You better." She kissed him again and walked away. The people at Jack's table stared at him as he sat back down.

"Who was *that*?" Everyone asked.

"It's a very long story," was Jack's flustered answer.

"We have plenty of time." They all responded with laughter. So Jack gave them the short, edited version, while holding on to the business card she had placed in his hand.

Molly West, CEO. The West Foundation and a Madison Avenue, New York City address. He had returned to the hotel and the card was now standing in front of him leaning against the phone. He had changed into his pajama and the oversized hotel robe, not expecting to go out any more that evening. It had been a long and exhausting day, but overall successful. It was also nice that it was over. The West Foundation logo was simple; a few colorful lines weaved together. His fingers touched the raised letters and thought about the short seconds with Molly in the restaurant. She had looked great, especially compared to the 48 hours image of sheer sickness that still lingered in his memory and was hard to shake lose. He giggled as he wasn't totally sure who the real Molly was; maybe he would find out some day or maybe he wouldn't.

Nora and Karen, still in the office at this late hour, were excited when he had told them about the day's developments. It looked like they were going to get the business they were after and it would come at a perfect time, just in case Virginia Projects seized operations with CR. But that was still just a *feeling* that the three of them had – nothing had come from their client. He didn't mention Molly – nobody at all knew that he had seen her. He wanted Molly to make the call, when or if she wanted anybody else to know.

The bottle of Zinfandel was more than half empty and the finger sandwiches nearly gone. He decided to stay in the room and eat just in case Molly actually decided to call – which he somewhat doubted she would. It was close to eleven-thirty, when the door was knocked on; room-service with another bottle of Zinfandel, he thought. As he opened the door he found Molly. He had hoped for her call, but this was so much better. She was wearing comfy clothes; sweat–pants and a fluffy sweater. She had the bottle of Zinfandel in her hands.

"What about a nightcap, Mr. Miller?" She smiled, though tired.

"If you promise not to throw up on me, I wouldn't mind at all." Molly laughed.

"I promise." She slid by Jack and headed for the corkscrew on the table next to Jack's empty wine glass.

"With the alcohol experience you had not so long ago, don't you think a visit to the local AA chapter would be more appropriate than being here drinking?" Molly giggled.

"Luckily, I have no memory of what you are talking about, young lad, none what-so-ever. Only that we slept together." She laughed teasingly.

"Let's underline *slept*, Shall we!"

"We shall – but do we really know?" Molly giggled as she knew she was making him uncomfortable. He changed the subject by lifting his glass towards her.

"Would it be reasonable to toast your return to earth or are you just passing by again, hurling and all?" Now Molly became a bit uncomfortable.

"That's what I want you to help me decide, Jack. I was going to ask your advice last time, but gin and tonic, Johnny and Jack got in the way as you no doubt acknowledged." She looked at the floor for a moment. Jack sat in silence and then cleared his throat:

"So what's the story, Molly? One day you were here and then you were gone for ten years. No calls, no notes, no letters, not any form of communication. You simply disappeared. Quite honestly, we all took it very personal. Caroline was especially heartbroken. First she lost her mother and a few days later her best friend disappeared without a goodbye, without absolutely anything. She was sad and depressed about it for years. She never wanted to talk about you or have anybody mention your name. Then it turned to a milder form of hate for the ignorance you had shown and now she doesn't care anymore. She has moved on and done very well with new friends and all." Molly's eyes were moist with tears. She had grabbed a napkin and made good use of it.

"I'm so sorry, Jack, really sorry." He continued:

"I missed you as much as anybody did. But the sorrow of losing you was nothing compared to the pathetic ten years I mourned over the loss of Sara. But I believe I'm over that now and have finally moved on – bloody finally, ten bloody years later."

"What happened?" She asked.

"I fell to so many pieces, though I always preached that the true character of any person shines through by the way we handle adversity. I didn't shine through one bit; not even the smallest speck of light. I turned egocentric, self-centered and ignorant. I pushed everybody away from me, as they didn't mourn Sara, didn't miss her the way I did; at least that was what I thought. But I was so wrong and so stupid and so totally pathetic – and it took me ten years to figure out that I had to *continue life*, not *mourning death*." He got his own napkin. Molly got up and was on the couch next to him.

"She was a wonderful person, Jack; there was a lot of mourning to be done."

"Yeah, but not ten bloody years worth; including the loss of your children, family and friends. That *is* pathetic." She nodded.

"I agree, that was a bit extensive – but I shouldn't talk. I was not better than you, Jack, not one bit." Jack smiled concerning the *extensive* remark and was now looking at Molly's face. Tears had moistened her cheeks, but in spite of her tired look and red eyes, he found that she had turned into a beautiful young woman; just like Caroline; he poured more wine.

"So what is *your* story, Molly?" She got up and fell back into the big chair in front of him.

"My story is long and complicated. Are you sure you want to hear it?"

"Does it have a happy ending?" Molly smiled bravely, paused and looked into Jack's eyes.

"I think so; I mean I'm finally sitting in front of you again," she dried her cheeks: "To me, that is a *very* happy ending so far, with a lot to be continued, hopefully." She smiled bravely and Jack's heart soared; he knew Molly was coming back to them, at least he had a strong feeling that she was on her way.

She had felt an unusual resilient sense of something being wrong, something was going to hurt Sara that day over ten years ago; she had desperately tried to get hold of her and had raced into D.C. from Georgetown like a mad person. She was afraid and terrified for Sara's life. Something she had never been able to fully understand and probably never would. It was just a crazy feeling she had, and tried hard to discard, throw it out of her mind; but she was not able to. Later that day she was told Sara had died, and she simply blacked out. She could not believe the tragedy, could not believe that she had not been assertive enough to follow through with her warning that something was terribly wrong; Sara had needed help immediately. Jack interrupted her.

"There was absolutely nothing that could be done; there was no time to bring her to a hospital; nobody could have saved her. It was a non-detectable time-bomb that exploded without warning. It was nobody's fault – nobody's, and certainly not yours, Molly."

"It took me years to finally understand that it wasn't my fault. But that never eased the guilt I felt; the guilt I still feel." She continued her story.

Her grandparents had been busy in Africa establishing daycare facilities, schools and health centers through The West Foundation. She had never felt abandoned by them, though she had more so lived with the Millers. Immediately after Sara's death she went into a mode of severe depression and anger; running away and hide, was her *mature* way of dealing with that. She wanted to see if she could survive life in Africa with her grandparents; that could make for her hiding-place. That night she packed and was on a plane to Frankfurt the following morning. She wrote a letter to her grandparent's attorney in New York to let him know what she was doing, to keep her whereabouts a secret and expect further instructions within a week.

Her depression and anger was blinding to the extent that she couldn't face *goodbyes* to the Millers, the few friends she had, classmates or professors; she simply wanted to get away as fast as possible. She cried many hours straight in First Class, dried her eyes in Frankfurt International Airport and picked up crying again the few hours it took to finally reach Casablanca in northwest Africa. Her grandparents were *home*, so they picked her up as she arrived.

It took many weeks before she could function to any extent. Though her grandparents tried their best, they also had a horrid schedule, so being *home* in Casablanca where their offices were, was a rare treat. At first Molly didn't want to fly around with them in that little 6-seater plane owned by the Foundation; she preferred to mope around and do next to nothing – and even less if possible.

Though she promised her grandparents to contact the Millers about her whereabouts, she kept procrastinating and the more she procrastinated the harder it got and she realized that too much time had passed, so finally she couldn't do it at all. That was something that had gnawed at her ever since. She had never been like that, but she had become like that – and by her own doing. She had become somebody other than the Molly she knew a long time ago. She did not like the new Molly to any extend; she ended up despising herself.

As the next year rolled by, her grandfather had finally persuaded, actually *demanded*, that Molly get off her butt and do something. Helping out with the Foundation seemed a logical solution, so she started in the mail-room. He told her that getting to know *any* business well, it was essential to follow the paper trail from the bottom and then slowly apply what you learned from that knowledge up through the different departments. In the beginning it was tedious and boring paper shuffling that she performed with an attitude. But as she started to learn what it was she handled: contracts, agreements, invoices, buying and selling, soliciting donations and reports of all sorts, she started to realize that there were actually real people behind all this, people who wanted to make a difference and unfortunate people who desperately needed those differences to be filled with all the help they could get. It started to become an issue of lives and deaths for her, an issue of enormous importance, and she finally acknowledged her calling, something she had decided when she was so young – it was all crystal clear now, and time to roll up her sleeves. She had smiled when she realized what her grandfather had done – and for that she would be forever grateful.

At first she did not realize the enormity of it all; she ignorantly treated it as some numbers in front of issues. She still had to learn the connection between the human beings involved; their lives and their deaths were depending on her part of the equation. When Molly moved to an office, she was an intern observing the many aspects of statistics, negotiations, food and medical supplies, building equipment, supplies for the schools and the list was horridly long. She quickly advanced beyond intern-status and began dealing with suppliers, donors, volunteers, hire staff and everything in between. She found that she was better than good concerning organizing and negotiating. Though The West Foundation was based on her grandparent's wealth, it also relied heavily on the charitable contributions from the private and corporate sector in America as well as from European and Asian contributors. She soon felt comfortable and worked with utter efficiency and long hours; the impressive results showed accordingly. The West Foundation doubled contribution collections every 18 months through the following 8 years and the massive donations collected, were put to good use immediately.

As the offices grew with staff, paid and volunteers, Molly was finally encourage to go on trips with her grandparents and their assistants. They were looking for new areas to develop. Schools and nurseries, medical care centers, food distribution centers; there was a lot to be done. Her grandparents never tired and most of the time Molly had a hard time keeping up. The work at the office was nothing compared with the field-work, she quickly found out; but she hung in there.

The thousands of children she got in contact with within a few weeks simply stole her heart; her calling was confirmed again and again. She cried herself to sleep every night, though sleeping was sporadic at best. She felt that if she didn't work herself to the bones, she had not worked hard enough for these utterly lovely children; they needed everything, needed it yesterday and they needed love on top of that. Molly, like so many other people involved, could only do so much, but they all kept doing more. For every child that died, Molly become more devastated and then worked even harder. So when she had CEO's and other donors on the phone, whatever nationality, she could sincerely transmit the pain these children were in, to solicit massive contributions to ease that pain and help save lives. Every Dollar, Euro, Franc, Deutschmark, Lira, Yen, made an immediate difference; Molly rarely hung up before an amount was committed.

But the emotions she went through were harsh; bit by bit it ate up her insides. She tried to keep a brave face, but flying out of Casablanca to visit camps and villages, damaged her as nothing had ever done. She struggled dealing with the tasks at hand, and seeing the faces of all these children, looking at her with pleading eyes filled with pain and hunger and the question *why?* finally did her in. The guilt she felt for this admission was devastating. Alcohol started to help ease some of that pain, however short that *ease* was; but then more alcohol was applied – and not only in the evening.

She traveled Europe as well as the USA and Asia to visit private individuals and corporations with big wallets. She dined with the top executives of the world and got things taken care of. Donations from China, Japan and South Korea started to materialize. But she admittedly traveled beyond extensively as an escape from the reality she feared to face.

Molly had worked with the foundation for over six years. It was late evening when one of her assistants, Hugh Walker, had entered her office. He looked rather somber and as if he was crying. The call he asked her to take, tumbled her whole world in a flash of a second; it was the worst of news.

Nora and Karen high-fived after the conference call from New York. It was not because the prospect of accumulating more business was unimportant, but it was more so the euphoria of having Jack back in the saddle. Karen should have been with him on this trip, but she had *dishonestly* mentioned other commitments, so Jack was doing it solo; it had worked out beyond their hopes. They were sitting on the couch in Karen's office, heads resting on pillows. Karen had felt fantastic, though rather exhausted. Life had been good to her and in her late twenties she had to admit that in spite of her lack of academic education she had reached higher than she ever thought possible. She had a job she adored. There was nothing else in her life that had the same meaning to her as work. The people she worked with, no matter what level they were on, were all *her* people, a responsibility she was very serious about. Sure she had lost Jack on the way, but she patiently awaited his rebirth. She never felt that she was a reason or even some of the reason for his recovery, but no matter what, she was happy, actually utterly thrilled, having him back next to her. The *relearning* period they agreed to, had been exciting. Though she could teach him a few tricks of the trade, he slowly but surely started to show her, by his sheer natural ability, some of the reasons he could be a rather smooth and effective producer.

During their trips together, they had separate hotel rooms. But for the most, they ended up sleeping in the same room, not the same bed, though. There was never any hanky-panky, not even a hint; *sex* was never part of Jack's thinking, Karen was positive about that. So these *sleepovers* had been as natural as if she was his daughter. Sure there were many years between them, but Karen had at times some rather *interesting* dreams about Jack Miller; she also knew he didn't have a clue. In some areas he was as sharp as could be, but some of all that *other stuff*, he was adorably innocent.

Then there was Nora. She was Karen's role-model from the day she had left her controlling father to join CR. Nora was the ultimate leader. She ruled with an iron fist, but you would never know. She was stubborn and tireless and after exhausting meetings were over, there would always be that one more thing to be done. But she got it done, took care of it in her way and at that very moment, if not before. She vested all her confidence in Karen; she trusted her more than she trusted herself. She also expected a lot from Karen, but never more than she would expect from herself.

Karen looked at Nora, buried in the soft couch, wineglass in hand. Her skin looked beautifully black and smooth. Her lips were full and colored red and her facial features soft and strong. Nora suddenly smirked; the odd question made Karen laugh.

"You'll never guess who I had a *sex-thing* with?" She smirked even more. Karen was giggling as she had no idea where this was coming from. Had she read her mind?

"Jack?"

"Oh, God no - not him."

"Why not?"

"Wouldn't be right – in some way."

"So who was the lucky stud?"

"William Baxter." Karen's mouth dropped open.

"Get out of here; you and William? You gotta be kidding."

"Not kidding; the sex was terrific and especially the conversation before and after - even better. You know I'm a sucker for tight brains." Nora giggled, but her face soon turned thoughtful." I miss him a lot, Dear William." Karen nodded; they sat in silence for a moment.

"Why not Jack?"

"I don't know. He was so dedicated to Sara and then he went weird for ten bloody years. What about you and Jack?"

"When we travel we normally end up sleeping in the same room, separate beds, of course. But nothing of *that* nature has ever happened."

"Why not?"

"I don't know. At times I find him very exciting and sexy, and other times he's a bit of a bore – especially when he starts his Sara references."

"I know what you mean." There was a pause. "But would you like to - you know!"

"I'm not sure, not sure at all." Karen took a deep breath. "God, I got to find myself a good man, don't I?" She laughed; Nora quickly joined in.

"Yeah, me too." She paused and held up her glass towards Karen.

"You know, if we weren't such devout heterosexuals, you *would* be the woman for me – really." Karen laughed as she lifted her glass.

"Same goes for you – God, we must find some men, and quick, huh?" Now they both laughed and the glasses clanged lightly together.

"Cheers – and let's get back to work…" They agreed in unison.

It had been a busy day in the offices of The West Foundation. Molly was wearing a thin sleeveless cotton dress, sandals and a lot of sweat. Though the air conditioners were working overtime, cooler moments were rare. Casablanca was enveloped in a breathtaking heat wave, literally. The last meeting of the day had ended and Molly's assistant fixed ice cold gin and tonics, topped with thinly sliced lime.

"I think we can safely leave the bottles and ice out this evening – don't you?" Hugh nodded and fell into a chair, hoping she wouldn't get on one of her binges. She was as nasty as could be when intoxicated.

He was a sharp dresser with a slight build, padded with softly pronounced muscles; his deep tan was very unusual for a member of the British Isles. His hair was blond, but Molly was near certain that it was not the color nature had blessed him with – but she really didn't care. But she did care that he was an efficient worker. Her grandparents had brought him to Casablanca as a favor to one of the bigger contributors from Manchester; it had worked out great. They had worked together for over four years now, and Hugh seemed solid and dependable.

They had chatted away through Molly's four, large drinks; it was finally decided to close up shop and go home. She put some documents in her briefcase, locked the safe in the outer office and as she turned the lights off, the phone in Hugh's office had broken the late evening's silence. She heard him pick up, state his name – and then that ghastly scream – he was back in her office within seconds.

Jack was staring at Molly as she told the story. She had moved on to his bed, leaning against the headboard with pillows for comfort. He was sitting in a large armchair, facing her. It was obvious that she was becoming emotional. So far she had used a calm and matter-of-fact voice; but he could see that wouldn't continue.

Hugh's scream had been eerily sharp and painful. Standing in front of her, his tanned face was now pale-white; he pointed at the phone on the desk - Molly picked it up. All she did was nodding at times and utter feeble and near-silent *yes'* and *no*'s. Then she scribbled a few lines on a pad Hugh handed her, nodded again, said a shaky *thank you* and hung up. If Hugh had not been there, she would have smashed her face against the tile floor as she fainted and fell down fast.

A couple of days earlier, Anna and Harry West had flown to Luanda, Angola. It was for an important strategy meeting with local volunteer organizations. Molly had been adamant about her grandparents not going, as she saw them worn-out and exhausted; she would make the trip in place of them, which she would do from time to time. But they had insisted in spite of Molly's pleading protests. They were in the helicopter for the short ride to their meetings in a village about 60 kilometers east of Luanda. It was just the two of them, the pilot and many cartons of medical supplies; a routine flight they had done hundreds of times.

Flight conditions had been superb. It was warm and dry and barely a wind. But something had gone terribly wrong; one of the rotor blades had apparently worked itself loose from the rotor mast and was later found over 200 meters from where the helicopter had swirled down, crashed and exploded. The deafening sound had been horrific, witnesses told government investigators. After the crash itself came a moment of severe silence, and then the screamingly loud explosion which pulverized the aircraft and everything in it. People from the small village nearby, arrived within minutes. There was nothing they could do other than pray; and that they did.

Molly was crying openly. Jack had brought her some more tissues and was sitting on the bed holding her hands. He did not know what to do, did not know how to comfort her, what to say. After a while she continued her story.

The helicopter had been identified, as well as the names of the pilot and the passengers were confirmed; shortly after, the officials had called the offices of The West Foundation. A couple of days later the authorities contacted Molly again to explain that it had been impossible to salvage and sort out individual remains and asked her what she wanted them to do. After she had talked with the pilot's wife and his parents, it was agreed that one memorial gravesite be dedicated to all three in Casablanca. So the combined remains and ashes were buried together and their names etched into a large block of marble.

The following weeks were hectic. Her grandparent's attorneys had been helpful as well as patient and said that the legal issues could wait till Molly felt up to it. As they were located in London, she decided that maybe a bit of an escape would do her good. Hugh and her personal assistant, Liz, would tend to business while she was gone. So she packed a few things and was soon settled in her grandparent's apartment in Kensington, London. The attorney's made sure the arrival would be smooth and her stay comfortable; the fridge was full, so after the flight and the drive from Heathrow, a couple of gin and tonics would feel good. But as of lately, her drinking never stopped with *just a couple;* far from.

The next morning she took a cab to the attorney's office. The furniture was large and dark and heavy; the employees stiff, as well as boring in their demeanor. But they were nice and kind to Molly and she was a little bit puzzled why. She soon sat in Sir Robert Annett's office. He was about her grandfather's age, she thought. He had several assistants and other legal experts present; most of them younger than him and some about Molly's age. The clearing of many throats started the meeting; everybody sat up a bit straighter.

The quantity of paperwork Molly was presented with was enormous. The many institutions, schools, health clinics and the list went on, all needed to be handled and carried forward – if that was what Molly wanted. Several companies in the USA were owned by Molly's grandparents and handled by the American attorney located in New York City.

"I'm a bit confused here, Sir. You are giving me all this information, all these hundreds of forms and I'm not sure I fully understand what you are trying to do." Sir Robert smiled embarrassed and looked at Molly.

"I am so terribly sorry Miss West. I simply jumped ahead with what needs to be looked after and decided without confirming, without *informing* you, Miss West, that you are the sole recipient of Anna and Harry West's estate. I assumed you knew." Molly's head spun fast. Sure she had been like a daughter to her grandparents, but she assumed that whatever money they had was poured into their passion of giving, to The West Foundation.

"You look puzzled, Miss West;" Sir Robert Annett seemed genuinely concerned; his small smile was warm. "Is something wrong?"

"Not other than I arrive here and expect that my grandparents wanted me to continue their work with The West Foundation – which of course I will, no question about that. And now you shove all these documents and things under my nose. That's what I'm a bit confused about. I run the operation in Africa and I know what kind of money we can play with – for the most donations from nice people and businesses. So this whole trip to London and all you guys here is puzzling." He smiled in an apologetic way.

"From that point of view I can see where the confusion comes in. Did your grandparents ever talk to you about any of their financial doings, their portfolio, so to speak, and especially about leaving it all to you?" Molly was silent for a moment.

"Every time they brought it up I shot the conversation down. Both my parents died when I was 6 – car accident. I refused to talk *death* with my grandparents ever since; maybe in the naïve hope that if I didn't talk about it, it would never happen. I can see now that I was wrong." The last part she said more to herself. Sir Robert Annett showed a sad smile.

"Your grandfather told me this many times; many, many times." He cleared his throat a couple of times. "Miss West, your grandparents loved you more than anything on this earth. You were the spark in their eyes and the beat of their hearts; and those are their words." Molly all of a sudden felt overwhelmed. "You created a wonderful life for them and with them and though they hated being away from you, you were always with them – in their hearts. When you all of a sudden showed up in Casablanca some years back, you made your grandparents the happiest people on earth." He placed a box of tissues in front of Molly. "I worked with your grandparents for over fifty years and not one day did I ever consider them clients. They were the kindest and warmest people I have ever met – will ever meet. And they were smart people, very smart with money, both your grandmother and your grandfather. They liked to compete – for fun." Molly smiled. He had obviously known them very well. "They didn't want to die, Molly. They wanted to live so much, and all because of you." Several of the other people in the office sniffled a bit. He pulled out a folder, opened it and placed it in front of Molly. "This is your grandparent's Last Will and Testament. You are the sole recipient of all they owned. By signing on the bottom of the last page, you will make them both extremely proud and very happy."

"Do I need to read it through?" Molly said through tearful eyes.

"That is your choice. Your grandmother read it through many times to make sure that you would get everything, precisely everything." Molly's hand was shaking as she signed *Molly West* and drew a little heart after the *t*.

Jack had moved back into his arm chair by the bed. Molly was talking with a smooth voice now and to him it felt like she had really wanted to tell this to somebody – he felt honored that she had chosen him.

She attended several meetings with the attorney's and though she considered herself smart, she was still left a bit foggy concerning many of the business deals her grandparent's had engaged in. Their *financial portfolio* was something she had never really fully understood. She asked if it was okay to sent copies of the documents to her New York attorney; it was done at once. She was familiar with the New York attorney as he, his wife and their teenage son had visited them in Africa several times. It had been business and pleasure. She liked his sense of humor as well as his energetic way of handling the business. He seemed dead honest and always spoke his mind, just like she did; and she felt he knew her well.

It had been around bedtime for Molly in London when he called her. He had received the package with the copies and several of his staff sorted things out. Everything was on the up and up, understood that everything in the portfolio was showing a profit; but that was only the businesses part. The financial *paper* portfolio showed a very different picture. The stocks and bonds purchased over the last fifty years had a huge value. There were also bank accounts showing liquid cash just sitting there. On top of that the apartment in London; fully paid for. The house in Washington D.C., the large beach villa and the office building in Casablanca as well as an ocean view villa in the Virgin Islands – all paid in full. Molly's head was spinning.

"Are you still there, Sweetheart?" Molly mumbled *yes*. "You signed the papers?"

"Yeah, about a week ago."

"Good. So Molly, you are a very rich woman; you know that by now, don't you?"

"I'm getting there. But I'm not interested in that; all I want is my grandparents back." There was a paused on the line; his voice was soft and honest.

"I know, Molly, that's what we all want." And the line went very quiet.

Jack looked at Molly. He knew that whatever Molly could do to get her grandparents back, she would do. He felt the same about Sara. But back in the real world, all they could do was to live lives in their honor – every single minute of every single day.

"Do you want to know how much money I'm worth?" Jack smirked and shook his head.

"Not important; I really don't want to know." She half smiled to his answer.

"Jack, the irony is that I am not into money or wealth or stuff like that. I like working, I like building; I like reaching goals beyond money and wealth. I want to see sick and hungry children getting better by feeding them and loving them. I want to help them get a better life; that's really all I want to do. That is *my* life and I will die doing precisely that, just like my grandparents did." Jack was sitting on the bed again, holding hands.

"I know, Molly. I think I have always known. You have consistently been a determined bugger, no matter what you did. I always liked that in you; and you carry it very well." Molly finally exposed a smile.

"Thanks Jack." He smiled back.

"You are welcome. Oh, I'll get us a bottle of gin and a load of tonic. Would that be okay?"

"That would be lovely. And we have a lot more story left."

"... And I can still expect a happy ending?"

"You old softy; I think it might be up to you if it's going to end happily." She smiled. Room service brought the gin, tonic and ice cubes. He poured a couple of drinks.

"So you don't want to know?" She continued.

"Know what?"

"About that money thing."

"Not really; seriously..." Molly smiled; Jack didn't.

"... I'll tell you anyway." Jack looked at her with a puzzled face. "With all the properties, investment portfolios and liquid cash, I have about 550 million dollars – of my grandparent's money, that is; and it's growing a lot every day, all by itself." Jack shook his head. " All profits from this money go to The West Foundation and over the last 15 years it's been more than 160 million dollars..." She smiled. "And I will continue to give, and even more..." Jack shook his head and smiled.

"As I said, I really didn't want to know that."

"You didn't want to know that I'm a rich broad?" She tried to laugh, but it sounded strained. Jack didn't find it funny at all.

"No Molly, what I meant is that there are certain sides to people, friends or family I really do not wish to know anything about. Certain knowledge changes things, changes the perspective of what is real and what is not; at least it does for me." He paused. "It might sound rather naïve, but my image of you is the one of you as a vibrant and interesting teenager; the best friend to my children, to me and my wife. You were Miss Molly *No Bullshit* West."

"That was a long time ago, Jack. We all change."

"Yeah, I know, but sometimes I don't want change. I want things to stay the same."

"So it'll fit into your world?"

"Yeah, so it'll fit into my world or my limited mold. I told you it's a bit naive." He moved uneasy in the chair. "It's not *you* per say, it's an issue *I* have to deal with, *I* have to be able to handle. You see, every time you were in my thoughts, it was the image from when you disappeared, not the updated version of a well-off and radiant woman. You were still a girl to me, though a teenage girl admittedly and in my memory you didn't age those ten years. Then you suddenly appear out of nowhere, all grown up, very woman-like and beautiful, so for me to accept that you are not the image I have carried around for so long is a bit tough."

"You think I'm beautiful?"

"You have always been beautiful to me – in your own special way; but that's not the point, not the point at all." He took another sip of his drink. "I think we all have a tendency to claw ourselves too tight to how we want the story to read. But that's impossible to do; for the most we will be way off track and disappointed when we find that it's only in very few cases that we hit it spot-on."

"So I'm not *spot-on*?" Jack showed a small smile.

"I haven't decided yet, Molly. First of all I'm working on getting used to the fact that it is actually you sitting here in front of me, and not some gorgeous imposter. Then I hope that you'll stay around and not disappear again. Then I also hope that the rest of the gang will embrace your return with forgiveness."

"Do you want me around?"

"Of course I do, I just said so, but I will use great caution until I feel safe. I'm more so thinking about Caroline's reaction, Jasper's and Michael's; how they are going to handle it." Molly sat quietly fiddling with the ice in her glass. Jack was ready to drop the conversation, but he continued anyway. "You know, it's like we met for the first time a few hours ago. There are some similarities that reminds me of this fascinating girl who used to hang around with my family so many years back. We all loved her and she brought so much additional energy and fun into our little world. Now you are telling me that you were that girl, and *yes* life changes us physically and mentally, but the sheer reality of that does not automatically adjust our full acceptance of those changes; we all react differently."

"You don't seem to have changed much, Jack." He smiled with a chuckle.

"Oh I have; actually, I have in a big way, and in other ways I have not."

"You still look great physically."

"Thanks, but luckily you can't see the inside inventory of Jack Miller. It has been a mess, a really big mess, but I'm working on getting back to whatever was normal so many years ago – at least I'm trying real hard." He took another sip.

"Did you ever imagine what I would be like if and when I returned?"

"Not really; as I said, you pretty much stayed the same. But it has been a long time since I last thought about that. Maybe I pondered an older version of the younger Molly. That seemed to be the most logical and of course, the most naïve wish in a feeble mind."

"Are you disappointed?"

"Not that you are back, are you kidding me? It's the *getting used to* that will be a bit harder, but it'll no doubt swing by at some point – I'm sure of that. But disappointed? No, that I am not, far from." He giggled and continued: "Now it's the return of some Molly imposter with cash in her pocket and a life story to tell. To me it seems like Molly with the millions is not the Molly I pathetically envisioned would show up. Now I associate you with some wealth you have wrapped yourself in. Not that it's wrong, but that's how I see you now and that's also what I need to get used to – respect and accept."

"I'm the same person, Jack. The same I was before, the same bloody confused and pathetic person I was before – nothing changed."

"You were never pathetic; eccentric for sure, but never pathetic. For me a lot has changed, but as I said, that's *my* problem, not yours. I'll come around, I thoroughly believe that. At least I truly hope so."

"Do you feel we'll be able to do some repairs and make our relationship work?"

"I'll definitely do my part – if you stay around long enough this time; I still love you, Molly, so that's not the problem that needs repairing."

"You still love me?" Jack didn't get the real question she asked.

"Yeah, I've always loved you. We all love you and I know that will never change." She looked a long moment at Jack. She was not going to lose him or them again; that was not going to happen. And her story continued.

The news of Mr. and Mrs. West fatal accident spread like wildfire and jungle drums. The funeral ceremony escalated into an event attended by many thousands; among them politicians, business moguls, entertainers and a huge crowd of volunteers who had worked with Molly's grandparents through the years. High up executives from the United Nations and UNICEF had flown in from all over the world, as well as so many other charitable organizations had been represented. Molly was stunned by the sheer fact that so many people had loved and respected her grandparent's work. To her they had always only been grandmother and grandfather – her sole family.

The huge arena was at *standing room only* capacity; the massive quantity of flowers and telegrams and wishes and condolences was breathtaking. Molly had a very hard time grasping it all. Donations in her grandparents honor flooded The West Foundation's offices, donations from all over, and it didn't seem it was going to stop any time soon.

The speeches had been many and the praise of her grandparent's work honored in tears and appreciation. A young girl, so perfectly black and beautiful, delivered a touching story about how these two Americans had come to her village nine years earlier and organized a school-room and a small healthcare facility. She had been suspicious of them at first, but Mrs. West had sat down and talked with her and finally she felt she could trust them and went to the health-clinic for a check-up; many other children followed her. She was found HIV Positive, but she had received treatment and medication and she was alive to talk about it, eight years later. She finished her speech saying very loud, that she was planning on living a full life. While the standing ovation had sounded for many minutes, she was in a warm embrace with Molly.

Many hours later, Molly was in the middle of the reception. So many people had thanked her for the work she was doing and told her that Anna and Harry could not have found a better successor. So many people had introduced themselves and the evening was long and exhausting. Several of Casablanca's hotels and restaurants supplied the food, beverages and servants, as their contribution for all the business The West Foundation had brought to them through many years. And the large and strong gin and tonics kept coming Molly's way.

Through it all, Hugh had been an extraordinary help. He stood by her side constantly, took notes, introduced and looked after Molly with all his might. Half through the evening Molly knew that she had to stop toasting all the guests constantly – with alcohol. But at that point she had reached the stage of wasted, not obviously, but none-the-less wasted. Hugh applied damage-control when needed. As the evening, or more so the night was winding down, Molly conferred with Hugh and Liz, if it would be acceptable for her to retire as in, head home, throw up and go to bed. Hugh asked for a few more moments as a food contributor from Denmark had just arrived. She sighed and stayed for a few more handshakes and toasts.

In spite of her blurry vision, sponsored by too much gin and not enough tonic, he looked like a Nordic god, the warrior prince without the white horse; never the less, exquisitely handsome. His blond hair was golden, his icy blue eyes warm and clear, the whitest teeth exposing the warmest and most charming smile and a body that simply wouldn't quit – at least that was what Molly saw through drunken eyes. His voice was soft and strong and the slight foreign accent so utterly adorable; his vocabulary was without a fault and his humor a mixture of intelligence and sarcasm. After a few moments, Hugh informed Molly that it would be okay to close her mouth – which she did. His handshake was like lightning, all the way to her heart – and beyond.

"Molly West, it is an exquisite pleasure to finally meet you. My name is Sven Nordgren and I'm with ScandiFood International." Molly couldn't reply. Hugh stepped in and grabbed his hand.

"I'm Molly's assistant Hugh. It's so good to meet you as well and thanks so much for coming." Sven and Hugh held the grip for a moment and both smiled.

"Thanks so much, Hugh." The smiling Dane said. "And it's good to meet you as well, I'm sure." Molly was still frozen – and very intoxicated, now in more ways than one. She saw Sven move further into the partying crowd, shaking hands with everybody, and kissing most of the women. Molly couldn't take her eyes off him, watching his every move.

"Molly, I think it's time for you to do that *go home and throw up* thing, huh?" She answered without taking her eyes of the Viking prince.

"What?"

"I think it is wise that we take you home, okay?" She nodded.

"Okay, take me home, please." She pointed at the Dane. "Where does he stay?"

"I'm not sure, but I'll find out. We do have a meeting with him and his people tomorrow afternoon, by the way." She nodded slowly.

"Okay, let's go home."

As Molly and Hugh worked their way through the crowd, Sven Nordgren followed them with his smiling eyes. Molly was waiting for Hugh to bring the car around when she suddenly heard that voice again.

"I'm sorry we arrived so late; got caught up in a meeting in Frankfurt." She looked at him and he was still beautiful and charming and oh so... "Can we go somewhere and have a quiet drink, perhaps?" Molly nodded eagerly.

"My place?" Sven smiled.

"Does it have a view?"

"Of me or something else?" Her drunken voice responded; Sven laughed.

"Either way would work." Hugh drove up and Molly went over and chatted with him for a second. He was fully against her taking that person home with her, but she insisted.

"Listen Molly, you are drunk; no let me rephrase that: You are royally shitfaced as the Queen of Skunk and you shouldn't be alone with some person you don't know." She smiled drunkenly at her friend and assistant.

"I'll be fine, I promise you, dear." So Hugh drove Molly and Sven to her villa by the Atlantic and didn't see her again for a long time – weeks, actually.

The whirlwind romance was precisely that and more. Molly and Sven had laughed and loved and laughed and loved and flown off to the Virgin Islands to the remote villa on the beach, the private strip of secluded sand and crystal clear water. But they had spent most of the time in bed, making love and sleeping and eating and most certainly drinking. Molly cocooned herself in lust and love and she didn't let up. Euphoria went from utterly satisfying orgasms to the deepest sorrows and depressions from the loss of her grandparents and the heavy guilt she carried for their demise; it should have been her, not them. It had not fully registered, so her emotions swung from one end of the emotional spectrum to the other. Alcohol was her sole support system, mixed with the attention from her Nordic God; and he lavished her with attention. After the dizzy days and nights in the Virgin Islands, they stopped in London and got married. Molly's New York attorney had screamed *NO NO NO* over the phone and had insisted a prenuptial agreement should be in place, sealed, signed and activated. Molly hung up on him, turned to Sven and with slurry speech announced: *Let's go do it.*

On their return, Hugh and Liz nearly fainted when Molly introduced Sven as her husband; they did not want to believe it. It was with tears held back that they finally forced themselves to congratulate the couple; they both questioned Molly's flippant response: *Yeah, whatever...* And Sven's remark: *Hugh, you look rather yummy today.* The next morning Liz had been in Molly's face screaming hell and high water – she even threatened to quit.
"Watch my lips, Molly. He is a sleazebag and you'll be so sorry... He's going to screw you on more than one level, trust me on that..." She had turned on her heals and stormed out of the office. Molly just rolled her eyes and giggled, pouring herself a second gin and tonic – at 9 AM...

Sven moved some of his stuff into Molly's house and quickly returned to Denmark and work, supposedly. He would see if he could conduct business in Denmark from Casablanca; but he didn't seem to be in any hurry about it. Molly was fine with him coming by for a few days and nights at a time until other plans could be implemented. Those days and nights were filled with lust and laughter and Molly's two trusted friends, gin and tonic. Accordingly,

Mondays became Molly's sleep-it-off days and though she did come in on Tuesdays, she was in no condition to conduct any form of effective business. Hugh and Liz had more or less taken over the major responsibilities, but the foundation needed Molly's personality to thrive. The unfortunate reality of Molly's *personality* those days oozed from a mix of bad liquor breath, and a naïve attempt to cover it up with mouthwash. Her otherwise sharp mind was as dull and confused as could be. Liz often found Molly slumped over in her office sofa with a drink in hand, crying violently. She would comfort her as much as possible, but these days, the only comfort for Molly came in a bottle. Liz was a good person, a caring soul and the best co-worker anybody could have – Molly considered her a best friend – actually her *only* friend. Liz stayed Molly's personal assistant, but only hesitantly so. What she was concerned, her friendship with Molly was in a state of probation; so these days Liz was all about work, which now included massive damage control.

"I'm so alone again." She would whimper. "My parents left me, Sara left me, my grandparents left me; I'm so alone - I have nobody." Liz pulled her into an embrace.

"You have me and the hundreds of people around here who loves you." Molly would take another sip of her alcoholic beverage and sniffle some more.

"I know, but I still feel so alone," she would cry. And that was how the days would go, one after another. The roller-coaster ride of sad emotions was only interrupted by the fleeting moments of passionate, but soon more mechanical lust with her Viking stud. But Molly loved him and the times together were for the most fun and exciting; something she looked forward to. She thought she had been lucky, as she felt happy with her arms and legs wrapped around Sven – but in semi-sober moments, she wasn't so sure at all.

Days became weeks and weeks became months. Sven's trips to his *office* in Denmark became longer and the time in bed with Molly shorter. She compensated for that discrepancy with - what else? Alcohol. So Liz had to drive her home, make her throw up and put her in bed, for the most in the middle of the day.

Hugh had at one time suggested that he should visit the food supplier Sven worked for in Denmark as he thought it would be good business as they were such a great source of helping supply the foundation's warehouses in Africa. Molly didn't really care, so she gave the okay. Hugh left with Sven a few days later and were gone 5 days – Molly barely made it to the office any of those days.

Her New York attorney in was in Zurich on business so he decided to swing by Molly in Casablanca. He hadn't heard from her since she told him she was getting married. Several of her trusted staff had called him with scared voices, informing him of Molly's overall condition, lack of work and erratic behavior. Not in so many words, they also expressed deep concern with respect to Sven Nordgren and his obvious devastating influence on Molly; Liz had made most of the calls.

The moment he entered Molly's office that early morning, he could clearly smell the alcohol. Molly was sitting behind her desk and he nearly fell backwards by the sight of her; she looked beyond a mess. Her hair was unkempt, her eyes blurry, red and tired. The pronounced bags under her eyes, guided by gravity, were blue and black. She was dressed in a wrinkled dress, no sleeves and low cut. It was obvious that she wasn't wearing much underneath. Parts of her breasts were exposed any time she moved, as the sleeve openings were large and deep. She looked up and didn't recognize him, while he took a long and deep breath.

"You look like a pile of shit, Molly, what the hell is going on?" She looked at him again as she tried to pull up information from her alcohol soaked brains that would make him become somebody she knew; nothing appeared. She pushed the gin bottle towards him.

"Let's start with a welcome toast," she giggled. He didn't react. Her eyes finally focused on his face. "Now I got it, you are that guy from New York." She laughed out loud.

"Jeremy Novak, yes, and you are in deep shit." He left the office and found Liz.

"Where's Hugh?" He asked after a few *hellos*.

"He's in Denmark with Mr. Nordgren."

"When will he be back? And when will Nordgren be back for that matter?"

"Hugh called this morning and told us they'd be back within a few days."

"Does Molly have contact with Nordgren?"

"I doubt it. He rarely calls her when he's out of town."
"Could you help me with Molly, like for the rest of the day and probably all night?" She looked puzzled, but nodded. "We need to get her dry and clean and very sober, okay." Liz smiled; somebody had finally come to the rescue.
"I'll go home and get a few things and then meet you at the house as soon as I can." Jeremy thanked her and went back to Molly's office. He grabbed her arm and pulled her out of the chair. She giggled and looked at him with question marks in her blurry eyes. He unceremoniously dragged her seemingly boneless body out to her car, pulled the keys out of her purse and strapped her into the passenger seat; shortly after they arrived at the villa. The housemaid opened the door and helped him carry Molly's lifeless body to the downstairs bathroom; Liz arrived moments later.
"So what are we doing?" She asked as she sat down her small bag.
"We are going to empty her stomach."
"Shouldn't we call a doctor?"
"Let's do this thing ourselves. Molly doesn't need the publicity." He smiled at Liz, as she agreed. "I lived with a father who was a big time alcoholic, so I know a few tricks that might help; at least they helped my father." Jeremy, Liz and the housemaid lifted Molly's body into the large bathtub. She looked up at them a few times, with wasted and saddened eyes.
"Okay ladies, if you are faint at heart, you might want to wait outside." Both women stayed. Jeremy turned on the faucet, found an acceptable temperature, tilted Molly's upper body forward so her face pointed downwards towards her slightly spread legs; then he jammed two fingers down her throat. Molly tried to fight him off at first, but Liz held her in place. Her face started to get very red. Liz looked concerned at Jeremy and pointed at Molly's face; he smiled a little. "We are fine. Her system is fighting back at first and when it realizes it can't anymore, things will develop." He had barely finished the sentence, when *things* developed. A projectile of Molly's stomach contents splashed all the way to the other end of the tub. Her body convulsed in spastic jerks, over and over. She didn't need help from anybody's fingers anymore, as the continuous vomiting was now on automatic. After five or six expulsions, her body slumped

over and her breathing was labored and loud. The housemaid was ready with drinking water and several towels. The stench that filled the room was horrific. Sure Jeremy had been exposed to the same situation at home, helping his mother with his father – night after night, but the smell of this kind of sickness, he never got used to. Liz was still holding on to Molly's shoulders as she was going through the aftermath of gagging. Nothing solid came up, actually nothing solid had come up at all, which told Jeremy that Molly had been on a liquid diet at least three to four days. He looked at her and she was not a pretty sight; she was an extremely sick person at the moment, but he'd get her well again; but of course keeping her well would be the tricky part. Finally the post-gagging stopped. Jeremy looked at Liz and smiled.

"Well Liz, I think the tank is empty; time to clean her up." They pulled off her soiled dress and found that she had only bothered with panties underneath. Liz looked at Jeremy a bit puzzled as she nodded towards the housemaid.

"Shouldn't *we* be doing this?" Jeremy smiled back.

"Don't worry I have known Molly from a little girl and I have actually seen a few naked women in my life."

"Okay then," Liz answered as Jeremy continued.

"But if you feel better, the two of you should wash her down; no problem. I'll go check her bedroom and get it ready." He got up and left. Liz and the housemaid proceeded to scrub Molly down real good – and then they did it again and again.

Half an hour later Molly was in bed, clean from head to toe, with an empty stomach and a full headache; but she didn't know as she was already snoring loudly. Jeremy had advised against pain-killers or other relieving medications, *from experience,* he explained. The housemaid stayed for the first two hour watch, bucket and cool moist washcloth at the ready. Jeremy took a quick shower and Liz followed suit. Soon after, they were both sitting on the deck with a glass of wine, enjoying the view and light conversation. They agreed on a plan of action concerning Molly's husband; Liz informed Jeremy that she had already been planning for *eventualities.* He had laughed out loud as she told him what it was; it had been quite a day.

Jack was staring mesmerized at Molly. He was confused as to how she could have gotten herself into a situation like that. She was an intelligent person who obviously had done an extremely stupid thing. She had underlined, but not as an excuse, the painful loss of her parents as well as the loss of Sara and then of her grandparents. And then, all of a sudden that combined massive realization of those brutal losses and her guilt, had hit her hard. That was something she had not been able to handle in her otherwise levelheaded and rational ways. It had been very *non-Molly*. And here she was in front of him, all flesh and blood, exposing her insides without blinking.
"Should we be drinking this stuff?" He asked as he raised his glass. She smiled.
"Don't worry, I'm cured and I do like a drink once in a while; I can handle it."
"Those are not just some famous last words?" She giggled.
"No Jack, they are not." And she continued her story.

Jeremy and Liz stayed with her four days and four nights. Both housemaids had been a tremendous help, so Jeremy had suggested that they take a break and as many days off as they wanted, with pay, of course; they returned two days later helping out with meals and comfort. Liz and Jeremy had found that they liked each other and had many interests in common in spite of the differences in their ages. He had for the most talked about his wife and son, how he loved them and how he missed them. Liz had talked about daily life at the office, working with Molly, especially when she was the real Molly. She also spread some light on what had happened since Molly's grandparents had died; the deep depressions, the marriage to that Danish guy and her massive intake of alcohol. Liz and Jeremy also spent hours in The West Foundation's offices with accountants and legal advisors.

Molly had slept hours on end. The few moments she was awake, she'd ask for water and short bathroom visits. She had finished vomiting after the first night of being horizontal, but certainly didn't feel good to any extent of the imagination; she had actually never felt as bad as she had those last few days of drinking and then the violent cleansing. But she got better every day. Liz and Jeremy would often find her crying in her sleep, but they were okay with that. *Let it all come out,* they agreed. During the nights, Liz stayed in the bed with Molly, watching over her and getting a bit of sleep herself. The third night Molly woke up, looked at Liz and smiled bravely. *Thank you*, was all she said and went back to sleep.

Jeremy and Molly spent a couple of hours together talking before he left for the airport and the flight back to New York. He told her that he felt comfortable with how she looked and concluded that she was at least sober and clean, inside out. Now it was up to her to stay that way. He couldn't babysit her; nobody could and nobody should. They embraced warmly and through tears she thanked him for all his help, for his concern, for his love and for rescuing her pathetic ass. Jeremy was not good with compliments, so he just kissed her and got in the taxi.

"Anything you need, you know where I am." She waved until the back of the taxi disappeared around the first corner. Liz was standing on the steps to the entrance and felt good. Molly still looked tired, but she had gotten some of that old Molly spark back in her eyes; not all of it yet, but she felt it was just a matter of time. Molly grabbed Liz' hand as they walked into the house.

"Do we know when Mr. Nordgren will show up?" Liz was surprised. Molly had not mentioned her husband at all the last many days. Liz was more than okay with that, as she had never liked him at all. He had flirted with her several times and had clearly made very inappropriate suggestions, all of which had been sexual in nature. Liz also knew other females in the office had been approached by him. As far as she knew, none of them had gotten involved and nobody had mentioned it to Molly as they saw her so overly happy and so much in love – or lust? And constantly *oh-so drunk*.

"I do believe he's supposed to return in a few days; I'll double check with Hugh."

"Okay," Molly said quietly and they soon sat on the deck with a cold glass of ice-tea and a light salad lunch coming up. Liz looked at Molly and smiled; Molly caught her.

"What?"

"What *what*?"

"That smile-thing *what*," Liz grinned broader and giggled.

"Good to have you back, boss." Molly laughed.
"Good to be back, my dear friend."

Molly had stayed at home another week, being very busy. She started exercising again in her small home-gym as well as jogging with Liz on the beach. Liz had brought work from the office to the house, documents to be signed, plans to be considered, decisions to be made. She went through the last four months financial statements, found a few *adjustments* to be dealt with, but otherwise acknowledged that things had run rather smoothly during her self-inflicted absence. She was looking very much forward to get back in the saddle.

Her office was clean and looked very organized. Several vases had huge bouquets of colorful flowers; none of them from Sven. Her formerly well-stocked liquor cabinet was very empty with only a few bottles of gin and many bottles of tonic. Liz had laughed when Molly had ordered the last remnants of her past to be disposed of.
"Nah, boss, it's a test for your determination; you can handle it." She smiled at Liz, but wasn't so sure yet if she actually could handle it. But she did appreciate Liz' trust in her assumed abilities to say *no*. Every employee came by Molly's office during that first morning with lot of wishes, welcome back and warm embraces. She was overly touched and so many tears had flowed. She was soon back-on-track and it didn't take long to get on the phone again; a lot of good people she had ignored too long needed a call.

A few days later Sven Nordgren finally returned and stood in front of Molly in all his Viking godliness. She had to admit that he was still a very handsome specimen and as far as she could remember, he had been a passionate, wild and satisfying lover. His smile was dashing and charming, but when he tried to embrace her, he was utterly surprised when she gently, but firmly pushed him away; nobody had ever rejected him before. Molly asked her husband to sit down. Liz had quietly entered the office and stood against the wall by the door behind Nordgren; she was not about to miss this one.

"We need a bit of a talk, you know, chat about things and settle matters," Molly said with a small satisfied smile; he quickly looked puzzled and confused, but inside he knew that there was nothing this woman could throw at him that he wouldn't be able to handle. She was so much in love with him and she didn't have a clue who she was dealing with. But for once, Sven Nordgren was wrong in his assumptions.

"For the most I have had a really good time with you, Sven," she started. "But lately, actually the whole time, I could never figure out why I had to marry you. Maybe I had always wanted to be scooped up, married and bedded the way it happened – with somebody like you. I was extremely vulnerable at the time and you took advantage of that. Granted, I was stupid enough to *let* you do that. But now it will all end." He was shocked by her words, but also didn't believe that she meant what she just said; how could she?

"But darling, what are you saying?" He tried his most pleading look, which he hadn't had much practice with, but he was so sure it would work magic; but it didn't.

"I'm saying that the ride is over and we are getting a divorce. I have arranged for the paperwork to be signed and filed, so all you have to do is put your signature on the bottom line and initial those cute little highlighted boxes." Now he not only looked stunned, he *was* stunned and very much so.

"You can't mean that, Molly. You love me and of course I love you." She giggled her response.

"You are so much in love with yourself, dear Sven and that love affair will go on till the day you die; I'm sure of that."

"No, you are wrong, I love you more than anything," he kept pleading.

"No *you* are wrong as you are incapable of loving anybody else but yourself." She pushed a document across her desk. "Just sign and we can get on with our lives, okay?" He picked up the folder and started to scan it with his trained eyes. He started to shake his head and giggled a bit.

"Molly, what the hell is this? You are kicking me out with nothing. Sorry, but you can't do that." His voice suddenly turned nasty. "There was no prenuptial, so yours are mine and mine is yours; that's the law."

"Well, dear uninformed person, the situation is that you didn't bring anything in to our relationship other than a large personal debt, which I paid off for you, some clean underwear and that adorable smile of yours. I investigated you further, and found that you have no secret accounts hanging around or any other financial inventory. So I realized that you were, and that you are, as utterly broke as a person can be." His mouth fell open; how could she know that?

"But I still get half of yours, Molly." His tone of voice had turned cold and business-like. She looked into his eyes, with a faint smile. Her tone of voice was calm and collected.

"Listen to me very carefully: Sven, you will get nothing, not a bit, now or ever, understood?" He was starting to sweat a little, but recovered quickly.

"Sorry Molly, but the law says that in case of divorce, I have the legal right to half of your money, your wealth; that's how it is." Molly smiled and continued in a condescending voice.

"I know that, but you are not listening, Sven; here's the deal," she said as she pushed another folder across the table. "Why don't you take a gander at this and tell me if you are willing to go to court fighting and screaming about what you think your rights are or what they should be and we'll let the jury decide the outcome. Are you ready for that?" Sven was scrambling through the pages in the second folder. First page showed many copies of Molly's personal checks that he had forged with her signature. The amounts were high; copies of credit card statements with highlighted postings of additional huge numbers. Now Sven seriously started to sweat; the hands holding the papers went shaking. But he was battling for an out, for something he could use against her.

"You agreed to all this, you know," he said as he held up the folder; Molly giggled.

"No I didn't. I would never have *agreed* for you to fraudulently milk me out of over $250,000 in such a short time. I gave you permission to spend according to *our* lifestyle, not yours – which obviously is much more extravagant than mine. You stole from me, Sven; plain and simple." He moved nervously in the chair.

"You can't prove I stole that money – which of course I didn't do, at all." He quickly added.

"Don't you worry Sven; further down in the stack of papers you'll find the forensic writing expert's report on the forged signatures you used on the checks as well as on credit card receipts. He has no doubt that you did them."

"It'll never hold up in court Molly, you know that." He smirked and looked at her with disgust; he was not going to let her get away with this. He wanted what he had the right to, what he had planned to get. Molly continued:

"It will hold up very well, thank you. If I'm not mistaking, the next few pages coming up in the folder in front of you, show just a few samples of other s*ituations*, if you like, and this time in visual form." Molly had a hard time holding back yet another satisfied smile. Sven looked at the photos and his heart and soul sank to the bottom. Liz was fighting hard to stay calm and not laugh out loud.

"You had me followed? You had somebody spy on me?" He slowly flipped through each page. It wasn't just revealing photos of his adulteries around Casablanca, but also from Frankfurt, Copenhagen and other places. How the hell had she done that?

"I never trusted you, Sven. You were too bloody perfect, too smooth. So why did I marry you? Not to blame the liquor manufactures of the world, but I do believe that my better judgment, as well as being utterly vulnerable at the time you showed up, mixed with parts of gin and tonic *made me do it*, as they say." She started to see Sven Nordgren slump into the chair, becoming part of the chair; she liked what she saw. "I truly enjoyed your company even after I learned who you really were; which I pretty much found out a few days after the honeymoon was over – literally. You were charming, funny, attentive and quite the stud-muffin. Admittedly, that was the best sex I had ever had – so far." Now Molly smirked a bit. "But now you are sitting here like somebody I don't know, somebody I would never hook up with and the sad part is, that I'm married to you; but not for much longer."

"But Molly dear, we can make it all happen again, really."

"Not in a million years, as it is ending right now."

"But I can explain…"

"You can explain shit, Sven. As an example, try to explain this: how could you even in your sickest of imagination think that any of my employees would have anything to do with you? Are you really that shallow or are you just legally that stupid?" He looked puzzled.

"What do you mean?" He knew precisely what she meant, but he hoped she didn't know.

"*Sexual harassment*, does that ring a bell? I know it's new around here, but really." Now he squirmed in his chair.

"You can't prove that." He heard the little click and saw the small digital recorder in Molly's hand. What the tiny speaker exposed, was finally enough for Mr. Nordgren to concede defeat. So she had been a bitch after all; but she was obviously not a stupid bitch. How could he have been so wrong! He felt totally deflated. But he was quickly planning to have the last laugh – he hoped.

At that moment two of Molly's Casablanca attorneys entered her office, now joined by Liz and Hugh. They introduced themselves to Sven, quietly explaining the legal process and pointed at the different places to sign and initial the divorce papers; he did it slowly as in a trance. Liz and Hugh signed as witnesses. Then Molly faced Sven across her desk:

"We have packed your personal items from the house. Those few boxes are now waiting for you in a van by the front entrance and you will be transported to the airport. Your one-way ticket is for Copenhagen as I assumed you'd like to at least get that far. Now all you have to do is hand my attorneys the checkbook you removed from my cabinet, as well as the two credit cards you misused. This is of course only a formality, as all three accounts have been closed." He did as she asked him to, and Molly wrapped it all up. "I consider this a fair settlement because I am not dragging you into court. And I do call it a settlement and so will you. And please be aware that I have filed a restraining order against you, so don't even think of looking me up or call or communicate with me in any way, shape or form. If you do any of the above, we'll come after you." She smiled lightly and finished. "So you are free to go. Copies of the papers will be mailed to you as soon as the divorce is final, and that shouldn't take long. Goodbye Sven." He got up and slowly walked out of the office between two security guards. As he walked through the offices, sporadic applauds followed him. He was soon on the plane heading north, a broken man – at least for the moment...

It was just a few weeks later that Hugh left Casablanca and The West Foundation. He hooked up with Sven in Denmark soon after and they quickly started living together. Hugh was ecstatic and in love, but Molly had warned him that the minute he ran out of money, Sven would be done with him, drop him like a bag of garbage. Hugh had held on to the misconception that Sven was now his friend and would be his hot lover forever; but unfortunately Hugh was sadly wrong.

A month after Sven dumped Hugh, Mr. Nordgren got fired from his executive position at ScandiFood. They had received an anonymous package that exposed many of the unethical things Mr. Nordgren had participated in. They never suspected Molly West or The West Foundation to have supplied them with this information; they never even considered it. In the matter of fact, they never figured out who had submitted this for Mr. Nordgren fatal disclosure. But back in Casablanca cash-poor Hugh had finally gotten his revenge – with a little help from the copy machine in his office, at his new job at The West Foundation - with Molly.

"So what happened after that?" Jack was curious.
"I received several threatening and fairly nasty calls from Sven. I was advised to record any communication with him which we did; and then it suddenly stopped."
"Do you think he is out for any form of revenge?"
"I doubt it. He's too stupid to figure anything out and I have all bases covered, so I'm fine." Molly held out her empty glass; Jack took it and made a fresh drink. It was past midnight at this point and she was tired, Jack thought. She looked at him with a small smile. "Would it be okay if I sleep here tonight?" Jack wasn't surprised.
"Of course; you take the bed and I'll camp out on the floor. There're plenty of pillows and blankets; that'll be fine." She smiled at him.
"Thanks Jack."
"Can we talk about your possible return to the Miller and friends again?"
"Of course Jack; can we do that in the morning?"
"During breakfast." She had turned in to a beautiful young woman, he thought. The more she had talked, the more she

had started to act and sound like Molly of the past; just a more mature model; he was satisfied with what he saw.

Victoria had mourned for the longest time. It was a combination of the loss of William and her slow and painful recovery from the damages to her body as well as to her mind. It was later on assumed that she might not recover fully. Besides the physical damage, the trauma of the situation itself had of course been difficult to heal mentally. The vicious nightmares that occurred after the first attack, had quadrupled after the second attack; she pretty much couldn't sleep at all. But she did return to Anchor and soon after started to somewhat function in her previous work capacity. Even applying a huge workload and long hours, trying to desperately drown herself at the office, didn't change much; she still couldn't sleep.

Jack had been a sweetheart for her. He was very supportive, caring and a true friend. Victoria often saw flashes of him as that young and sweet boy she met so many years ago. He was the epitome of friendship and why she had caused him all her vengeance from being a jilted lover, she could now only think about with shame.

Her new apartment did not have much from the old one. She had discarded most of the stuff; Salvation Army had been the sole benefactor of her vast donations. It was a much smaller place, but it was adequate and all she wanted – for now. Jack had helped her choose new stuff and acted as her advisor. She was restless and not able to decide, so Jack had stepped in. The funny thing about it was that now she felt so much of Jack in her new place. She recalled why the dining room table was what it was; the modern dishes, the sofa, the TV-set and so forth. She was especially impressed with the way he had put together the bar and her wine selection, racks, glasses and all. The only depressing thing was that too often he brought up Sara. It was Sara this and Sara that; she would like this and hate that and so on. Victoria felt it was pathetic and she really didn't want to feel that way about Jack. It was like he had lived in this hole of what the heck it was for so long – had it been ten years? It made him weak and *yes* rather pitiable. But after a long day of shopping and decorating and chatting about this and that, they would sit here in her new living room and have the nicest time. Through a few glasses of wine she saw this charming man and then she wanted him to make love to her – but it was a longing that did not materialize, no matter how much incredibly *sexy* she turned on – he did not respond. At times Victoria smiled about her lingering obsession with Jack; she did feel she had matured enough to move on, so she felt in full control again. But many times, whatever maturity she thought she had gained, flew out the window. She would again and again lie in bed, fantasizing and bringing herself to the most explosive fulfillments. It was rarely William who appeared as that experienced lover who knew precisely what she needed – it was for the most Imaginary Lover Jack, again and again.

"Good morning, Mr. Miller." Her voice was sleepy. She was standing in the doorway to the bathroom wrapped in one of the hotel's robes. He turned towards the sound and tried to smile.
"Yeah; same to you."
"I gotta get going. Should go home and change clothes, you know, they might get a bit suspicious seeing me in comfy treads, don't you think?"
"I also think breakfast."
"I don't have time – I really got to go." Jack sat up in his makeshift floor bed, clearing his throat.
"What about that little chat we were going to continue?"
"Jack, I'm sorry but it has to wait. I'm flying to Casa this…"
"… *Casa* as in Casablanca?" She smiled.
"Oops sorry - an ingrown habit; anyway, I'm heading back to *Casablanca* this evening and have a couple of weeks of work to finish up. So I was thinking that if it would fit with you, I'll come to D.C. when I'm done and then we'll do the reunion thing." Jack looked at her with a small smile.
"You're not that keen on that *reunion thing*, are you?"
"No, but it's utterly essential. I really want to explain and then plead for forgiveness."
"I think the boys are going to be fine. Caroline will probably be your toughest customer. She loved you so much and even after all these years, she feels that you betrayed her – she hasn't been able to put it to rest."

"I did betray our friendship *and* Caroline," her face turned sad as she said that. "I just hope she is not going to hate me forever."

"I'm sure that with your charm and sincerity, Caroline will understand and apply her emotions accordingly."

"I hope so." They both did.

"What's next?"

"I'm heading back to D.C. for an afternoon meeting, hoping to catch a plane to Europe tonight and then Morocco… And you?"

"Heading back to D.C. this noon."

"How?"

"On the old track 'n train."

"How fun and then what?"

"My dad wants a chat with me this afternoon."

"Things are going well with the two of you?"

"Things are going really well - finally." Jack smiled as Molly moved off the bed. She didn't feel shy in front of him; not at all. When she had finished getting dressed, they hugged and kissed.

"Oh by the way, Miss West. So you literally dropped by my house some time back; rather intoxicated and all. And I never got an explanation why and why so tipsy. You informed me last night that you had the intake of such chemicals under control. So what gives?" Molly laughed with a tone of embarrassment.

"I had a slight relapse. You see, at times I do get into these deep depressions when I think of my grandparents, then of my parents and of Sara. I had some stuff I needed to pick up at the house, and most of Anna and Harry's things are still in place, believe it or not. The memories on the walls sparked it - and you paid dearly for that." She giggled as she shook her head. "There is still an overwhelming feeling of guilt riding on me and for the life of me, I cannot shake it off."

"Tried any professional help?"

"Lots of help, but no solutions – I have tried way beyond the call of duty."

"So you go wacko with the drink once in a while, and then you throw up on close friends…"

"… I'm normally alone when I go wacko; your case was the exception to the rule, you lucky dog."

"I know I shouldn't say this, but in a somewhat perverted way, I do feel honored..." Molly laughed, kissed him again and was out the door. They agreed to keep *Molly* a secret a bit longer; she wanted to *un-secret* it herself, when the time was right.

"I'm home," Jack shouted in a TV series voice as he entered. George slowly got up from the chair by the desk. He looked frail, Jack thought fleetingly, but the big smile was the same.
"What's up Dad?" The hug was a bit longer than normal.
"I want to ask you a favor, Jack."
"Go ahead, ask away," he smiled cheerfully and sat down.
"You remember Saint Paul-de-Vence?" Jack smiled.
"Sure do – South of France, north of Cannes and east of Nice; remember the stories rather well; and passed by with Caroline."
"Good; I want to go there for a couple of weeks or so, you know, to relax and enjoy."
"Sounds great to me; I'll take care of whatever things you want me to take care of in your absence." George smiled.
"That's nice, but the thing is that I want you to come with me." Jack's eyebrows lifted to capacity.
"You want *me* to come along? Why?" George giggled.
"Why not? I like your company; you are back to that old Jack again and did I mention that I like your company?"
"Twice; wow Dad, that's random."
"So is that a *yes* or what?" Jack giggled.
"Well, there is some of that *work* stuff I'm involved with, so I would have to look at my schedule, run it by Karen and Nora and ..." George was holding up a hand.
"You are fully cleared for take-off. I got the go-ahead from both Karen and Nora a couple of days ago. They'll gladly cover for you; actually they wanted to come along, but I said no; you know, in a nice way. It's a bonding trip, the father/son stuff."
"Didn't know we needed bonding," George smiled as he looked at the expression on his son's face.
"No we don't; I need the company, and you were the one I thought I could get along with the best."
"Thanks for the vote of confidence, George." They both giggled. "And when are we flying out of here?"

"Go home and pack; we are on Air France 08.00, Dulles, and tomorrow morning."
"What about tickets?"
"As far as I know we are sitting next to each other."
"What if I couldn't go with you?"
"I never considered that an option." He looked rather satisfied with himself.
"Shoot; I better get the hell home and do that packing thing."
"Yes you better. We don't want to miss *this* flight, do we?"
"We sure don't." And off he went.

George gently walked back to his chair. A moment later he drew his felt tipped pen through the third line of the *Last things to do* list next to him; he did so with a tearful and sad smile.

Jack swung by the office and spent the next two hours chatting with Nora and Karen, as well as he organized what needed organized for this sudden time off. He didn't ponder the reasons for the trip, so for now, he filed it as one of those whims of his father's; he was more than satisfied with this kind of whim.

"Isn't this the life?" Irene was wearing a light summer dress with the biggest and most colorful flower pattern available in the little store near the promenade in Nice. George had some months earlier kiddingly suggested a second honeymoon and this time in the South of France; when the war was all finished, of course. Irene had not forgotten about it, so the very moment it was possible to travel freely again, they had packed their suitcases. George was cleared by Hamilton, as well as the government head of the department had okayed the trip. They wanted to secure George's safety when traveling outside the USA this soon; it was finally deemed safe – Hamilton had given his word.

They spent four glorious days and four exciting nights in Paris. The days they spent in galleries and museums, only interrupted by breaks in sidewalk cafés and eateries. Two full days in the Musee de Louvre had not been enough, but they promised each other that they would return – which they never did. At night they walked and walked. The sounds, the smells and the noises of the busy city were intoxicating and life reviving. George often thought that it had been worth it all, being part of the solution, his participation in securing democratic freedom; now they walked in the middle of it. The evenings and nights had consisted of late dinners in small restaurants few meters from main avenues; it had been utterly romantic. Irene had physically held on to George the whole time. It was as if she wanted to make sure that this was as wonderful and real as she deeply felt it was, hoped it was. George couldn't stop smiling from all the enthusiasm Irene exposed; but then again, he was very much in love.

After a long day, they showered and rested naked on their narrow bed, thin cotton sheets covering their bodies. The windows left wide open to catch the cool breeze and the lingering night sounds from the *City of Love*, as they called their Paris. Hours later they would finally fall asleep in each other's arms with satisfied smiles on their glowing faces.

Even the long, tedious and bumpy train ride, heading south from Paris to Montpellier, involving many stops on the way, excited Irene no end. Her nose was glued to the window the whole time and only detached when she in eager voices wanted to make sure George saw the many oohs and aahs. The compartment was small, but to Irene it was her kingdom on wheels. They stocked up on several bottles of wine, bought bread, cheeses, grapes and fruit from the many vendors soliciting their products from the platforms. They had tried to make love during the train ride, but found the bed too narrow as well as too short and the constant movement of the train too silly. Irene laughed and laughed as they had tried and tried, but they finally gave up. Lying close together, holding hands with soft kisses had been as good and a lot easier to accomplish.

The many hills of Montpellier crafted a beautiful city. They walked the streets and avenues, fully enjoying the 19th century architecture off Rue Foch and many hours spent just sitting around on Place de la Comedie, getting intoxicated by it all. They found themselves peaceful for long moments inside the Saint Pierre Cathedral. The coolness and the vibrant silence recharged their batteries. It had not been easy, but they finally found a place where they could rent a car. With the two suitcases on the backseat of this rather small vehicle, they drove the ten or so kilometers south and soon had their feet cooling off in the Mediterranean Ocean. Irene had cried from joy and her grip of George's hand had been near painful – but he didn't care. Irene was happy and that made George happy.

The trip east had for the most been with grand vistas of the blue ocean. The landscape didn't change much, but it still fascinated both of them. They'd stop and find small hole-in-the-wall shops, buy bread and cheese and wine and then find that perfect spot in the middle of a vineyard or on a rock with a view. They would eat, nap or rest and be in love.

It was actually more by chance they found Saint Paul-de-Vence. After a short visit to Cannes, they had for some reason headed north. When they first saw this beautiful medieval fortified village, perched up high between two long valleys, they knew why they had chosen north; they were also fully convinced deep in their beings, that the sole reason they had journeyed this far at all, had obviously been to find this very special place.

After approaching the village on narrow and crooked roads with steep drops off the shoulders, they finally parked outside the walls. They hesitantly walked through the portal entrance and found themselves in another world; their world. The streets were narrow and cobblestoned alleys. The buildings hundreds of years old, with the original architecture kept alive. They started by slowly walking the circumference of the village, guided by the inside of the walls. Then they explored everything in the center, from the small artisan stores, the few art galleries, to the small tourist shop. Irene and George had not said a word since they entered Saint Paul-de-Vence; there was no reason to.

They saw it at the same time. The hotel was small with a narrow front; barely enough to fit the skinny glass-paned double-doors suggesting an entrance. Both doors squeaked as they opened, pleading for any kind of grease. The moment the doors closed, a unique silence embraced them. The old woman did not smile as she appeared from a side room. But when she learned they were Americans, her face lit up and she expressed a lot in French with *pardon* and *merci-merci* being the repeated words.

Using universal sign-language, they were guided to the top floor. Several rooms were located on the ground floor, fewer rooms on the first, only two on the second and finally one room on the very top. It had a small double paned window pointing south, a tiny bathroom with a handheld shower head, a small bidet and a toilet. The beds were narrow and short, leaving little room for a couple of worn-out armchairs, separated by a small wobbly table. The floor was wood and bare and the curtains certainly needed some help; but for Irene and George, they had arrived in paradise.

They stayed in Saint Paul-de-Vence for longer than three weeks. The whole area around the village had been thoroughly investigated; numerous picnics and trips to the edge of the Mediterranean, to Cannes and Nice had made the experience busy, fun and constantly romantic. Madame Clague, the owner of the small hotel, had insisted that they joined her for many meals. With her limited English mixed with French, she told of the loss of her husband and her only son to the war, and though she didn't talk much about this, it was clear to Irene and George that a solemn sadness filled the place, rightfully so. Socializing improved dramatically when her daughter-in-law arrived for a couple of weeks. Bernadette Clague had studied English beyond school and was eager to test it out. She was a true lifeline for Madame Clague, who lit up the moment she arrived. The four of them spent many hours together over dinners, picnics and afternoon bottles of wine in the small courtyard behind the hotel.

It was with utter sadness in their hearts they finally had to head back to the States. From the Cagnes-Vence Road going west, they stopped for moments to inhale that last vision of their paradise. It was a beautiful sunny day with the deepest blue sky. The vineyards on the hillsides had been lush in green and the aroma of this part of the world quickly carved its way euphorically into their hearts. Irene and George traveled back to Saint Paul-de-Vence many more times during the unfortunately few years they had left together. They kept in contact with Bernadette, as well as Madame Clague, with the help of her daughter-in-law. After Madame Clague died a few years later, Bernadette moved in for good and had been the proprietor since.

As they settled in their First Class seats, a glass of champagne was served. The cabin seemed only one third full and the flow of boarding passengers had by now subsided; it was near departure time. George occupied the window seat and Jack was next to him on his right.

"Here's to a grand trip, my son," he said lifting his glass for the clang.

"A very grand trip indeed Dad." And they sipped some champagne. At that very moment their collective eyes observed the same image. She was dressed in casual elegance, comfy but stylish. Her hair was in a ponytail with a thin, red ribbon, designer sneakers and a face smooth and strong. George's mind spun fast as he processed the information he was fed; Jack knew immediately who she was. He realized they both said her name out loud at the same time, *Molly*! She responded at once by turning around. Her face exploded into a huge smile and as she dropped her briefcase in the aisle, she was quickly in a warm embrace with both of them. It lasted long and loving, actually until the flight attendant suggested it was time to break up, find their respective seats and fasten the seatbelts as they were ready to leave the gate. The third seat in the row Jack and George occupied was empty, but only till Molly claimed it. One more switch and she sat between her two stunned friends. Molly was soon all over George, holding his hands as she eagerly told her story, a shorter version of the one she had told Jack some 36 hours earlier. Jack listened to her eager voice and his father's responses; the smile on Jack's face was good; actually, it was really good. She told Jack that she missed last evening's flight, stayed with a colleague of hers and had found a seat on the 0800 Air France. She was beaming big smiles of happiness and fortune having two such fabulous travel companions; Jack fully concurred.

There was something about Jack that Molly hadn't seen so clearly before; something she had not noticed when she was younger, she thought. He was a nice looking man in good shape. He wasn't the handsome catalog man, but his charm and that wit of his made up for that. He was smart and considered and so brutally honest. As a father he had brought up three fine adults who adored and respected him no doubt, as they had as kids. He had always showed affection for the people around him. Of course there was the relationship he had with Sara. It was out of this world and no other woman would ever be able to live up to that performance – nobody. She kind of understood the way he had tried to handle that, no matter how long it had taken. The tenderness he exposed still talking about her was loving and respectful. She wondered if he had actually had any relationships with other women after Sara's death, but laughed it off as unrealistic. But of course he must have; women around Jack, for the most, wanted Jack. This she had observed back when he was happily married; the way they would flirt with him, try their best to entice him, though they knew they didn't stand a chance. And then of course there had been Victoria's quest for Jack's attention. To Molly it had been laughable and every time she mentioned it to Michael, Jasper and Caroline, they had in an irritated manner scoffed it off. *You're insane*, they would say. Maybe they did not want to believe that Aunt Vicky was hot for their father. *Oh well*, Molly had smiled.

Finally sitting next to Jack again after all these years, she felt some rules had changed. No, it was not that she found him a love-interest, she giggled. *Really, he had been like the best father to me*, though she had never expressed that to anybody in any direct or indirect way. But he had always been that solid-as-a-rock role model she looked up to and more or less lived by. Her mother and father had been role models for her, but had vanished in a car accident. Sara was her loving friend, and she had vanished. Her grandmother and grandfather had been there for her, but had also perished. But Jack was still standing and he had always supported her with love and respect, no matter what. He could have rejected her when she all of a sudden showed up after all those years. He could have been angry, bitter and disappointed; he could have turned his back and she would have understood. But instead he had listened and he *had* understood - that's how solid he was and that was why she respected and loved him.

She turned her head and found Jack sleeping with eyes closed and a small smile. She tilted her seat back, pulled on a blanket for the both of them. Underneath, her hand found his and she was soon far away. This was the first time for so long that she actually fell asleep; she had finally found peace in a very safe place - at least for now.

Paris arrived too soon, they all thought. There had been a lot of laughter, some tears and many hugs and kisses. George had listened and asked questions as well as he told his own story to Molly. It was great to have her back, his eyes said as his heart soared. The few times George had gotten tired he got a blanket tucked around him, fluffed pillows, a kiss from Molly and wishes for sweet dreams. Then Molly and Jack moved to some empty seats and chatted away, catching up on so much time passed.

"Yeah, I'll be in Paris a few days and then finally back in Casablanca. It'll be nice to be back in the office, really." Jack had an idea.

"Why don't you come and visit us in Saint Paul? I mean, it's just across the water for heaven's sake." She smiled and giggled a bit.

"That would be nice, but I do have a lot to straighten out in the office."

"Come on Molly, just for a few days. George would like that very much, I know he would."

"What about you?"

"What about me *what*?"

"Would you like it too?"

"Of course I would – that's not a fair question." She looked down and giggled some more.

"I'll see what I can do."

"You better…"

George woke up from his nap and saw Molly and Jack chatting away on the other side of the aisle. They were laughing and smiling and gesturing. It had been wonderful to see her again, something he had not even dared hope for. His people from work had done their best to find her, but for some reason they had not been able to; not even going after her grandparents, had helped. They had not been visible at all. But that was of no importance now that she was sitting just a few feet from him. He mentally drew a line through her name on his *Last Things to Do* list.

For a girl at 75, she looked good, George thought. She was all over him with kisses and hugs from the moment they arrived at the hotel inside the walls of Saint Paul-de-Vence. Jack was finally introduced to the famous Bernadette, famous in respect to the many stories George had told him about this place, about these people and especially about her. He had looked tired after the long trip, so after Bernadette and Jack had settled him into a bigger room on the ground floor due to his decreased mobility, he had leaned back in the bed and after a long deep breath, felt at home again – back in paradise with Irene lying next to him. The peace he felt was overwhelming and the tears slowly started to run down the sides of his face, gently landing on the pillow. He was really back home; for the last time.

Early next morning the sun was up and the Mediterranean sky was as blue as could be. Jack opened the small windows, and by leaning to the right he could see beyond the walls and take in the view of the hillsides filled with green vineyards. The smells were euphoric, just as his father had told him they would be. The quiet was filled with a soft humming and the occasional human sounds. The aroma from downstairs was a mix of freshly brewed coffee, newly baked bread and the distinct scent of fresh fruit – it was overwhelming. Jack took a quick shower in the very small space dedicated for that function and tried to catch as many of the few streaks coming out of the tiny shower head. He got dressed and headed down the two flights of narrow wooden stairs. He didn't get an answer when he knocked on his father's door, so he quietly pushed it open. He went over to the bed – it was empty. There was no other place George could be in this small room other than in the tiny bathroom – but that was empty as well. Both beds had been slept in, he noticed with a smile.

"Good morning Jack and welcome to paradise." The small courtyard behind the hotel building consisted of many varieties of flowers and plants in old terra cotta pots of all sizes. Three small tables with checkered tablecloths sat close together. You had to watch out for the many hanging pots as well as walking carefully on the uneven cobblestones. George was wearing a white shirt and pants, topped with a large-brimmed straw-hat. Jack smiled as he realized how perfect his father looked in this spot.

"Sit down and enjoy life." He gestured towards the chair across from him. The table was covered with the reasons of all the wonderful smells he had encountered just a few moments ago. He did what his father asked him to; he sat down and enjoyed life.

All through breakfast they briefed through smaller things in life. George wanted to know about his grandchildren, how were they were doing and Jack's version of it. He told Jack that they all kept in contact with him and had especially done so during Jack's ten years of *self-inflicted* absence. It was still painful for Jack to be reminded, but he accepted it as part of the punishment for his stupidity; he had never asked for forgiveness because he felt he did not deserve it.

Jasper had gotten married to Ella and they worked together in the law-firm; children were not an option at this time, but Jack smiled and added: *But what do **they** know!* Michael and Linda were fully engaged and employed with solving major crimes. They had filled out applications to become partners, but their superiors had laughed and responded *in your dreams*. It was against departmental policies. But they had been granted access to each other's minds in the office, getting together to solve cases. It was a working relationship that had and did produce surprisingly good results and solved many cases other detectives had struggled with. At times loud communication across their desks expressed frustration and anger, like *Are you that legally blind? Why don't you understand? Your argument does not make any sense at all* or *have you fully lost your mind?* Just to name a few. But the second Linda and Michael's workday was over, they walked out of the department hand in hand, acting like newlyweds and very much in love; they had successfully defined work as being work and off work was another animal altogether. *Off work* was for them, their home and the kids – and at home, work was rarely mentioned.

Jack and George had some good laughs talking about Nicole and Frank. They were such great kicks to have around. Frank and his apparent photographic memory, as well as his total disregard for what people and peers said and thought about him, was beyond his age in maturity, common sense and academic levels. It was clearly evident that they were best friends. As twins they had the advantage, in their case at least, to be in the same classes in school. When teachers tried to separate them in the classroom, they revolted. They wanted to sit together and it was always Frank on the right with Nicole to his left; no matter where or when, it was always the same thing. When meeting them for the first time, one would get the feeling that Frank was far ahead of Nicole in most matters, but they didn't know what the people who knew them knew. Frank was the outgoing one, at times a bit too outgoing perhaps, so he appeared smarter and brighter than Nicole; but it was quickly apparent that Nicole was as sharp and intelligent as Frank – she just had to work for her results where information and academic knowledge was something Frank obtained with ease – some would say he was gifted. Frank had his own explanation, and *gifted* was not one of them. Frank adored his sister and she was the only one who fully understood him and loved him for who he was, as their parents did. He found a balance between the two and he had learned a lot from her over the years, more than anybody would ever know – because they wouldn't understand; it was something only this set of twins would get.

Jack listened to stories about Frank and Nicole his father told with laughter and tears of joy. Bernadette had joined them after more coffee was supplied – a lot more. The way she looked at George, Jack could tell she really cared for him; there was such sweet tenderness, a relaxed calmness in her smiles and so much life in her laughter.

Caroline was up next and Jack talked about her with pride and joy. She had a few more years of forensic science studies at MSU and it was the determination and stubbornness that made her special. At times Jack would tell her there was another life besides microscopes and DNA; Caroline always responded that she didn't think so. She had dated a couple of fellow students, but quickly found that it was a waste of time, compared to the enormous joy she got from hanging around specimen samples, bodily fluids, bones and their challenging mysteries.

During Jack's ten dismal years, Caroline had been supportive to the extent that it didn't bother her. After her mother's death she had been hand-holding and hugging and kissing her father, but as she, even as a young girl, didn't see any improvement, but only saw her father staying in the dark cellars of despair and self-pity, she backed away and concentrated on herself and her brothers. She had accepted her mother's departure within a year; she had passed the time of grieving with maturity and with eagerness to go on with her life – to strive to make her mother proud of her. Obviously her father had other things to do and being supportive and proud of his daughter was not one of them. It had only been a few months ago that Jack had *returned* and his few meetings with Caroline after that had been pleasant, but hesitant on her side. She obviously did not want to put herself in a situation where she would end up disappointed again; the careful approach seemed the way to go. She had not come home to spent moments alone with Jack for the longest time; she had always had a girlfriend with her and had always gone out evenings and days at a time. But Jack felt things were finally going in the right direction.

"You sure fucked things up, Jack." Which Jack of course, admitted to - for the millionth time.

"That's for sure and I'm still paying for it – as I should."

"They'll all come around, son."

"You think so?"

"Well, look at me, I've made the turn."

"You're my father – you *should* make that turn."

"No can do, son. I do not believe there is such a rule that just because the same blood is streaming through two bodies promotes automatic forgiveness and understanding." George smiled. "Didn't I teach you that a long time ago?"

"I must have conveniently forgotten," he said with a smile; Bernadette laughed.

"Maybe I shouldn't be here. Maybe I should get more coffee." She attempted to get up, but George's hand rested on her arm as he smiled.

"No my dear, we are done with the silly talk. Understand that I love that boy of mine and he has been the blood to my heart from the day he was born. Sure he was *absent* for some years, but I didn't love him less for that; I just felt pity for him and I was disappointed that I couldn't help him – but then nobody could." Jack looked at his father. He had never told him this, but hearing it now, even told to a third person was still warm and loving. George had always been there for him as a friend and as a father. It was Jack himself who had made *help* impossible.

"Thanks dad," he said quietly.

"You are welcome, son. Always remember that my love for you has never been in doubt – ever."

They made a day-trip out of a visit to the beaches of Cannes. Le Promenade behind them was humming with strolling tourists of all nationalities. In front of them the scantily clad sun-worshippers, with tanned and fit bodies, seemed to give a lot of ammunition to good old George's full enjoyment. Jack had to admit that if this was what one was interested in, this was definitely the place to be. Bernadette had packed a picnic and with a big smile rolled her eyes every time George uttered *oh-la-la,* which was often. Jack would just laugh, but secretly agree – with his father.

He had fallen asleep a couple of times, so Bernadette and Jack used that time to talk. It was pleasant and comfortable. He especially paid attention when she talked about the times she met George *and* Irene. She immediately fell in love with both of them, and being a young woman at the time, she soon found she had a crush on George. But through the many times Irene and George returned to Saint Paul-de-Vence, she realized she also had a crush on Irene. They brought her along on picnics and excursions, first as an English speaking guide, but soon as their good friend. Bernadette was devastated when she heard Irene had died, but sadly happy for him that they had a son; George had a boy. It was years later that George finally visited the South of France again and again. In between they communicated by letters and phone calls. She had remarried but then her husband had died; but George had never left her heart – he had always been a true friend of hers.

When George called some weeks back and announced this visit, she had been ecstatic. It had been four years since they had last been together. When he told her Jack was coming along, she had gone berserk; but in a good way. The hotel was turned upside down, cleaned and painted and washed and scrubbed. Not that it really needed it, but simply as therapy for Bernadette's jubilant mood.

"But he didn't know if I was coming." Bernadette laughed as she poured more wine.

"He knew, Dear Jack, he knew you would. For him it was not a question at all." Jack had to smile. "And it is so wonderful to see you and finally get to know you." Her eyes were tearing up. "You know, you have this beautiful glow as your mother as I remember her. Your eyes have that same lovely tenderness and there is something gentle about you, not that it makes you weak or something like that, but just underlining kindness; so much like your mother. She was lovely and I felt blessed being her friend." Jack blushed as he took her hand and gently squeezed it.

"Thanks Bernadette; I really needed to hear that."

It was another lovely morning in the small yard behind the hotel. They were entertained by the early day chit-chat and had exchanged pleasantries with a young couple that had so far kept to themselves. *Honeymoon* they thought or perhaps *an adulterous affair?* But George and Jack were too busy and not that interested. Bernadette had kept the coffee coming and as she had picked up some empty plates, a big smile had formed on her face, as she looked at Jack:

"Has George ever told you about his friendship with Marc Chagall?" Jack looked puzzled.

"Not that I recall and I would have remembered if he had ever told me." George was shaking his head.

"It's no biggie. I met him by chance in Paris a few years after the war – at an exhibition he had, a one-man show I believe." Now Jack was very interested.

"And?" George giggled at Jack's reaction.

"There's really not much to talk about. Marc was a Russian, actually French-Russian to be precise and a superb artist – well at least I thought so, but obviously many other millions thought the same later on. We just got to chat a bit, him being from East Russia and me from Moscow, well, Kazan, actually. We spoke Russian whenever we got together and…" Jack interrupted:

"How many times did you see him?" George smiled.

"It wasn't like I kept score. But pretty much every time I was in Paris we found time to get together. Strange relationship when I think of it. He didn't talk much about his work and I didn't talk much about what I was occupied with. It was more about marriage, family, traditions, you know, that kind of stuff – a lot of Russian stuff."

"Chit-chat!"

"Exactly; just two fellow Russians doing some chitsky-chatsky over a cup of coffee, sidewalk café, you know that kind of thing." He looked thoughtful all of a sudden, and smiled.

"I actually told him a lot about the South of France, the French Riviera and especially about Saint Paul-de-Vence. I wonder if that's why he moved away from Paris!" He smiled again: "He lived around here till he died some years back," George said as an afterthought. He looked a bit sad with the thought of the death of a person he had known so well, but known so little. His face lit up. "You know Jack, let's go say goodbye to Marc. He's buried not far from here, actually." Jack looked at his father and nodded his head.

"Of course we will." And they did.

It was a solemn ride to the cemetery where George for once had not spoken a word. Bernadette sat next to him in the backseat, holding his hands. He stood in full silence by the gravesite for the longest time, hands folded in front of him. Before he turned to leave, he spoke a few sentences in Russian and blew a kiss towards the grave. He quietly walked away and thought with a sad mind, that this was an addition to the list he called: *Last Things to Do*. He mentally drew a loving line over his friend Marc's name.

They had been stationary in Vence for nearly two weeks. The wonderful weather was certainly cooperating with their plans. They visited Musee National Marc Chagall and the mighty Foundation Maeght. There had been other excursions, especially of the Bernadette catered kinds. She was a delight and all three got along well. This morning George felt better, not as tired as the other days, though he more or less successfully had disguised his fatigue. When Jack got a bit concerned about the many naps, George underlined his age, now past eighty. The loss of weight he thanked his new diet for. Jack had seen that as something more recent; but he left it alone, for now.

"Are you okay boss?" Liz was going through the 3 inch deep stack of documents and forms that needed Molly's attention; she looked up and smiled at Liz.

"I'm fine, sweetheart. What was that again?" She tried to focus on the piece of paper in front of her. "Do I sign anywhere?" Liz was laughing out loud.

"What's wrong with you? Since you got back you've been weird - like very weird."

"Approximately on what level of very weird do you see me?"

"Top shelf extremely very weird."

"Oh; but I'm fine." Molly pushed the thought aside and tried again to concentrate. "Okay, so I sign for what and where?" Liz shook her head, pointed and Molly signed.

Liz was suspicious by the way Molly had acted since her return a few weeks ago. She told her how she had hooked up with Jack again; this time without the vomiting, and how they had spent time in a New York hotel room together, talking all night. It had been great therapy for her and she felt that it had also helped Jack. Then the chance run-in on the plane to Paris and the reconnection with Jack's dad; the wonderful hours spent in the air with two of her most favorite men in her world. But for Liz it hadn't been what she heard, it had been the way Molly told it. There was a sweet gentleness to it, but she couldn't nail it down precisely. She couldn't be in love with either of these men, the age difference and the status they had in her life – so Liz dropped that thought and was just happy that Molly was in such a good mood. It had taken her a long time to get over her Danish Viking God, but now it seemed as she had fully recovered. Molly signed a few more documents, put her pen down and sat back in her chair. She smiled at Liz.

"Do you think you know me well?" Liz was slightly puzzled by the question; hesitantly she responded:

"I believe so; I mean you have always been extremely open with me and the employer – employee thing quickly became friendship. At least what I'm concerned." Molly nodded in agreement.

"That's correct. You have helped me beyond the job description, that's for sure; like a true friend." She giggled a bit: "Are we paying you enough?" Liz giggled back.

"I'm fine, Molly."

"So since you know me so well, explain what's weird about me these days." Liz laughed.

"We don't have time for that; gotta lot of work to do."

"No seriously; give it a try."

"Why?"

"Because *I'm* not sure what's going on with me."

"Meaning what?"

"You know, there's this feeling hanging around me that I can't explain."

"Feeling of what precisely?"

"See that's the point. I'm not so sure."

"Could it be love? Could it be hate? Or possibly gas?" Liz mocked as Molly laughed.

"I really don't know what it is." She pulled a couple of reports from the stack. "Oh well, let's do some signing, shall we?" Liz looked at Molly as she started reading; yes, there was something – she could see it now.

"But you look like you have a plan, boss person." Molly looked up and smiled.

"I think I do, my dear friend, I think I do." and she did.

"This would be a good time for you to tell me what's going on, Dad." George looked up from the breakfast table.

"Meaning what?"

"Well, you wanted me to come with you to spend some quality bonding time. I'm happy you did and I'm happy to be here – bonding with you and all. But what is *also* the reason, please?" George shifted uncomfortably in his chair.

"Meaning what?" Now Jack looked irritated.

"Listen here old chum; have you ever lied to me and I mean *ever*?"

"No," was his short answer. "But there were things I didn't tell you about."

"Okay, I'm your fifty year old child and though some still consider me more on the immature side, I'm still sensitive to untruths – just so you know." George smiled a bit.

"I know that Jack." Bernadette appeared with another pot of freshly brewed coffee. George gestured for her to sit down, which she did quietly. She knew immediately what was coming next. George cleared his throat and looked straight into his son's eyes; his son also knew what was coming.

"Some time back I was diagnosed with cancer. At first we tried several treatments, chemo, you know, those sorts of things. We tried some experimental options, some solely based on medication, but nothing helped or even gave us any hope for remission." Jack sat frozen. He heard what his father had just said, but he hadn't heard it, as it did not register. Bernadette's hands were on his and tears worked their way down her face. She must have known all the time, Jack thought.

"Chemotherapy didn't work?" He whispered.

"I went through some, but it was not doing a thing." George tried to smile bravely, comforting his child.

"Why didn't you tell me?" George swallowed and put his hand on Jack's, while fighting tears. His broken voice could barely be heard in the silence of the morning.

"I really couldn't, Jack. You were getting out of your stupid absence and I didn't want to drive you back into it." He dried his eyes: "Jack, I have loved you so much your entire life no matter what. You have never disappointed me, as you have always followed your heart and your emotions. Sure those ten years of nothingness and mourning could have been handled better, but you did what your heart told you to. I didn't want to bring on *my* situation to make matters worse." Jack was stunned. His father had always been there for him and now he was told that he was dying and he had not wanted to tell him because of his pathetic behavior. He looked at his father and grabbed his hands.

"What now, Dad?" George tried to smile again.

"Now we'll have a bit more coffee and enjoy the day."

"You know what I mean. What's the prognosis?"

"You mean time-wise?"

"Yes, I mean time-wise." George looked at Bernadette; she looked at Jack.

"According to the last visit, two days before you flew over here, they gave him anywhere from three to five weeks; it could vary either way – they can't tell for sure, of course."

"Have *you* known about this all the time?" Bernadette nodded her head.

"My mother-in-law died from cancer and I was by her side the whole time. My husband also died from cancer. George called me the day he was diagnosed." George looked at her with loving eyes.

"Jack, Bernadette has been such a rock for me. I would have gone bunkers without her."

"That's wonderful Dad, but I could also have been there for you."

"I know you could and now you are. I really didn't want to bother you with this on top of all the other stuff you were dealing with at the time."

"How can a dying father be a bother?"

"I know, Jack, and I'm sorry. But now you are doing what I really wanted you to do, spending time with me; some really good time." George squeezed is son's hands. "Let's keep enjoying, okay?" Jack nodded his heavy head slowly.

"Okay," was his answer, but it would take a long time for all this to sink in to where it would make any sense, where he could apply comfort and support and where he would one day find acceptance to this dreaded reality. But to George, his son had given him the biggest comfort and sweetest gift by spending these last days of his life with him; Jack would never know how much that meant to his father.

The next few days were a bit strange. Jack found that he was more careful in his relationship with George, where George and Bernadette had continued as nothing had been mentioned, as if everything was normal. They had both been kidding Jack about his all of a sudden more sensitive approach, and he realized that it was wrong. Knowing your father was dying right in front of you, *acting normal* was a bit of a stretch to accomplish. But little by little he helped himself by applying humor, no matter how sarcastic or cynical. Bernadette and George were laughing and having a great time, so Jack slowly but surely got back to that *normal* bit. But he did cry at night as he felt very sad and so utterly helpless.

The trip had been quick and uneventful. She had struggled with the *why* issue the whole way, but finally decided that she would just keep pursuing what her guts told her; more or less to see what would happen. After the driver was paid, she rolled her carry-on over the uneven pavement and was soon standing in front of the hotel. The narrow double-doors covering the entrance to the lobby opened without a sound. As it was late evening, she didn't expect anybody there except perhaps a night porter. She gently rattled the small bell and moments later an older woman appeared down the stairs. She was fiddling with her hair as she approached her.

"Bonsoir, mademoiselle" She didn't exactly smile.

"Bonsoir madam; je suis Molly West avec Casablanca." She paused, trying to pull any French she had learned to the surface; not much showed up. "I'm sorry, my French is awful. Do you speak English by any chance?" Now Bernadette smiled.

"I do, I do. How can I help you, mademoiselle?"

"I'd like a room if possible." All of a sudden Bernadette looked sad.

"I'm so sorry; this is a very small hotel, only a few rooms and all are occupied." Now Molly looked sad.

"Are there any hotels nearby?" Bernadette nodded.

"Yes, but not nearby so much." She started looking at a list. "This one will be fine. Not that far away; are you interested? I'll call right away to see if they have a room for you." Molly smiled.

"Thanks that would be nice." Bernadette dialed and started to speak French into the phone. She then turned to Molly.

"What is your name again?"

"Molly West." Bernadette abruptly stopped what she was doing.

"You are *Molly*?"

"Molly West." Bernadette uttered a *pardon* into the phone and hung up.

"You are Molly from Casablanca. You are Molly who is a friend of Jack and George Miller?" Now Bernadette was smiling big time.

"The one and only." Molly answered with a giggle. Bernadette embraced her at once and wouldn't let go.

"They will be so happy to see you, Molly. They will be, how you say it: ecstatic?"

"That would be one way to say it. And you are?"

"I'm so sorry; I'm a friend of George, very old friend as you can see. My name is Bernadette." Now Molly had to laugh.

"Of course it is. George told me a lot about you on the plane; you know we flew together from Washington to Paris. It is so nice to meet you, Bernadette." And they hugged again, the way those French always do.

After a few moments of chit-chat Bernadette rushed up the stairs; w*ait here,* she told Molly. The reunion of Molly and George was happy and wonderful. Bernadette had not seen George this energetic for a long time. As they didn't want to wake Jack, the three of them soon sat in Bernadette's living room and a bottle of wine was opened. George eagerly told Molly about all the things they had done so far, and how great it was to have Jack along. Then George had solemnly told her about the limited time he had left. Molly had sobbed uncontrollably in his embrace as Bernadette held her hands and stroked her hair. It was about an hour later that she had calmed down and conversation had entered other areas, but only to bypass what was really on their minds. Finally Molly felt exhausted and needed to sleep. Bernadette prepared her large sofa for the night and would figure something else out for Molly in the morning.

Molly's sleep was restless; the thought of losing yet another friend, like another father, a role model, was a terrifying reality she yet again had to deal with. And how was Jack taking all this? Finally getting on with life after the loss of Sara; and now this?

"So great to hear from you," Nora's voice was loud and happy. "So how have you been, Caroline?" She gestured Karen to pick up an extension which she did.
"Hey Caroline, it's Karen." They chatted fast and furious and quickly decided to meet for lunch at Nonna's; things had to be discussed - things about Jack.

"Now that dad is out of the woods, so to speak, concerning that damn lengthy mourning period, I wanted to see if you could help me find some female companion for him. He really needs to move on, be happy again." Both Nora and Karen nodded as they sipped Chianti and waited for their spaghetti and meatballs to arrive. Nonna's was busy as usual and Romano Rossi was happy to see the three girls together again. It had been some time since the whole Miller family and friends had been in the restaurant, so Romano enjoyed any combination of them showing up. He had known Caroline from she was born and sitting on her parent's laps. And here she was all grown up and beautiful. Nora and Karen came by on a regular basis for lunches and dinners.

But seeing the three together made that big Italian's smile even bigger.

"I'll try to come home from MSU as much as I can, but your help is essential. Do you know anybody who might be interested and that Dad would be interested in?" Nora giggled.

"How about Aunt Vicky; she's always had the hots for Jack." Caroline shook her head.

"How about *not*?" She snarled. Nora looked at Karen; Karen stared back.

"Don't you even go there Dear Nora or you are in deep do-do." Caroline looked puzzled.

"What?"

"Oh it's just that Karen has expressed her interest in your father beyond work and overall friendship." Now Caroline looked even more puzzled.

"What are you talking about?" Nora smiled.

"Just that Karen once told me that she wouldn't mind..."

"...Okay Nora, that's enough. I don't think Caroline wants to hear silly stuff."

"You had the hots for my father?" Caroline looked shocked.

"In a way, kind of; but this is totally taken out of context. We were just chatting away through bottles of Merlot; just for fun, you know."

"So you had an interest in my father?" Karen cleared her throat.

"Nora and I just talked about men we wouldn't mind, you know, be intimate with..." Now Caroline was holding her hands firmly pressed against her ears.

"I don't want to hear this. My dad is about a million years older than you, so how could you even think like that..." Karen smiled at Nora, pointing at Caroline.

"She's really matured a lot over the years, hasn't she?" Nora was laughing.

"Jack was also *my* choice, by the way." Caroline shook her head harder.

"I am not listening at all." Nora was in a teasing mood.

"Jack and I did try out some of that stuff years ago." Now Caroline looked at Nora even more shocked.

"What do you mean *tried out some stuff*?"

"We were just curious to see if there was any physical attraction between us, so we went through a few heavy duty kisses just to check it out." Nora laughed as well as Karen did. Caroline didn't find any humor in this at all.

"That's disgusting."

"What do you mean *that's disgusting*? We were adults doing adult things."

"No, disgusting things, that's what you did."

"Now this is not a racial issue I assume?"

"Don't be stupid, Nora; you know better than that. I mean, you are best friends doing stupid things."

"Now wait a minute," Karen interrupted. "You sit here and ask our help to get your father laid, right? So are you going to judge and evaluate every prospect we dish up for Jack? Because if you are not letting Jack choose, I am not playing along. Hookers would be the choice for your father's physical entertainment, but I'm not sticking my neck or my friend's necks out for you to make an initial judgment *yes* or *no*; that must come from your father." Nora nodded.

"Caroline, we'd be happy to help out and I'm sure we are as eager to see him move on as you are. I have a couple of female friends I think your father would like and if we can hold Karen back from jumping your father first, I'm sure she has some prospects as well. But let us leave it to your father to make the choices, okay?" Caroline nodded hesitantly.

"Well, okay, I will, of course. You know his taste somewhat."

"I think we'll know who would fit and who would not. And just another issue, Caroline, do not expect your father will choose another Sara, okay? That would be wrong, especially for your father. So don't even look in that direction.

They continued their lunch, chatting and laughing and Romano was grinning from ear to ear. He had heard the part about finding a companion for Jack and had offered his help. Several of the restaurant's female regulars had often asked about Jack's availability.

"Okay Rossi, but nobody young. Must be around his own age and maybe a year or so younger at the most," Caroline had advised. Romano had smiled and was impressed with Caroline's concern about her father's romantic wellbeing. He had somebody in mind – his wife's younger sister Angela. She wasn't a raving beauty, but she was fun-loving and charming, he thought. Jack was a nice man and had recently returned to earth from his long journey of excessive self pity. When Nora and Karen returned to the office, they did a quick list of prospects.

"So according to Caroline we should remove ourselves from contention?" Nora laughed; she looked at Karen with a sly smile.
"Are you removing yourself?" Karen smiled slyly back.
"Are you kidding? Shit no, I'll still try to seduce him, you know, at least once; why not give it a shot." Nora laughed harder.
"Yeah, I'd go for him as well." Karen looked a bit speculative.
"Will he bite?"
"Not in a million years, my dear." And then they wrote a few names on the list they had marked: *Getting Jack Physically Involved.*

As Caroline left Nonna's and drove home she tried to shake off the notion of Nora and Karen and a relationship with her dad. It felt creepy to her and especially that Karen, being so much younger, had wanted her father; how sick was that?

Molly could not sleep. The devastating news about George's condition tore through her again and again. He had told her straight forward and though he tried his old *I can handle anything* attitude, the sadness in his eyes was heartbreaking. Sure he had tried to convince her that he had accepted the terms of the situation, but she also knew he wanted to live more than he wanted to die. But the illness was eating his life away bite by bite and there was nothing he could do about it.

Her tears flowed freely; she went to the bathroom to blow her nose and wash her face. How was Jack taking all this? Finally out of the loss of Sara and then this. Molly felt an urge to be with him, to comfort him and for him to comfort her. She went out in the courtyard at the back of the hotel, found a chair and wrapped the blanket around her legs. Then she inhaled the cool night air and closed her eyes. The sounds at this time at night were so different from the day's busy humming. The sky was dark, blue, she imagined. The smells were calming, but not enough to keep her away from thinking about George. Sometimes life sucked, she thought; right now was one of those times.

Sara was wearing an oversized T-shirt; she often slept in T-shirts on cool nights. Jack liked the T-shirts better than nightgowns and didn't like the fancy laced things at all; a pajama top would also do well. But no matter what Sara wore to bed or anywhere else for that matter, he always found her utterly sexy.
"What are looking at, Big Boy?" She was standing by the open window and the moonlight shone through the thin T-shirt and clearly outlined her naked body underneath; she fully knew what Jack was staring at. He probably had his mouth hanging open, she thought with a teasing smile. "Cat got your tongue?" She slowly turned around to take in the mighty view of the vineyards on the moonlit hillsides; Jack was busy taking in the mighty view Sara offered him. He smiled, all satisfied and happy.
"I think I'll go to sleep," he said as he slowly turned in the bed and invitingly fluffed the pillows. Sara giggled and turned around to face Jack in the bed.
"I'm sure you will, but first you have some unfinished business you need to finish." She quietly slid across the floor while dropping the T-shirt on the way and soon her naked body was gently pressed against Jack's back. "Still want to sleep?" He smiled and Sara knew he did. "I didn't think so – at least not yet." Her hands caressed his back and his front, so Jack reached behind him and caressed whatever he could get hold of; soon the small French hotel room was filled with noises of pleasure and love – sleeping was for later.

"So you are basically saying that you want Dad to get laid!" Jasper looked at Michael across the table and smiled. "Sounds weird to even say that with respect to ones father, huh?"
"Well, as I see it, he seems to be back on track; seems to be back to whatever normal condition he used to be in." Michael answered; Linda nodded. "When I talked with him a couple of weeks ago, he was very energetic and looked like he was on a roll. Now, if that is a small roll or one of the longer ones, at least he's heading in the right direction." Linda sipped from her glass. Ella was cleaning up the dinner

table with the help of Nicole and Frank. Nicole looked at Frank in the kitchen and whispered:

"*Get laid*, what does that really mean?" Frank was going to explain this to his sister as their mother's stern voice was heard from the dining room.

"Don't even go there, Frank." The other three adults looked at Linda and laughed.

"She has good ears, doesn't she?" Nicole was shaking her head. Frank looked at her with a small smile.

"Don't you know that by now?" He held on to Nicole and whispered directly into her ear: "I'll tell you later."

"No you won't Frank. That's your father's job." Linda's voice was calm but firm, and even Frank was impressed.

"What's my job?" Michael questioned.

"That sex-thing-talk job you have successfully postponed for ages." Michael smiled sheepishly.

"Oh that one; yeah I'll do that soon."

"I know you will and I also believe that talk might take place after they each have their third child or something like that." Linda looked at Ella.

"And what about the two of you making three?" Jasper laughed as Ella smiled.

"Linda, come on, we have visited that question so many times. Jasper and I are fine trying making babies, but we do not want any; and if you tell me one more time that the clock is ticking, I'll have to hurt your husband." Linda laughed.

"Sorry Ella, I'll keep my mouth shut."

"Mission impossible, I believe." Was Michael's response, he continued: "But back to getting Dad laid!" Linda swatted her husband.

"Michael, come on – the kids." Nicole was standing next to her mother.

"Don't mind us, Mom. Frank has explained that *laid* thing to me already." Linda turned towards her son.

"What did I tell you, Frank?"

"But Mom, she has to know and since Dad is not telling her, I felt it my civil duty to inform her." Ella laughed and grabbed hold of Frank.

"How old are you and Nicole now?" Michael answered.

"12 going on 42 – and I mean both of them." Frank shook his head.

"So how do you and Nicole know so much at this tender age?"

"Reading books and stuff; it just sticks, I guess." Linda smiled.

"And a lot of it is just empty knowledge if you ask me."

"Like what?" Ella asked.

"Like how many times does Buddy Holly use the name Peggy Sue from the same song from whenever?" Frank jumped in with a monotone voice:

"Charles Hardin Holley also known as Buddy Holly used *Peggy Sue* 24 times in the song of the same name. He died in an airplane crash at the age of 22."

"How do you know all that?"

"I listened when Mom played an old 45 on that turntable-thing and was singing and dancing like crazy; she played it a couple of times."

"That was it?"

"Nicole looked up the additional information on the Internet, just to see who it was that made Mom go wild."

"The dancing bit?"

"Precisely," Ella laughed and shook her head; Linda smiled.

"See what we have to deal with?"

"Anyway, let's get back to the evenings topic," Jasper interrupted: "Getting Dad romantically involved or at least interested." Nicole looked at Frank with a question mark.

"Same thing," he answered her. "They are desperately trying to protect our not yet fully developed minds." The adults ignored him.

"What about Aunt Vicky?" Nicole added: "She has the hots for Granddad." Michael looked at his daughter.

"Where did that come from?" Frank answered.

"Dad, even a blind person can see that she has been after him at least as long as I have understood what it was that people were after." Jasper laughed.

"Good answer, Frank, very good."

"Thanks Uncle Jasp."

"Jack wouldn't look at her as a prospect; she's Sara's sister for crying out loud." Linda shook her head: "I must admit for a 50-something older person she is hot as hell." Michael laughed and then smiled.

"Tell it like it is, Dear wife of mine."

"Don't you think she's gorgeous?" The all nodded. Frank's voice was soft.

"Especially with those new knockers of hers." Linda turned fast.

"Watch it buster or you'll be… whatever," and she laughed.

"Why did she get new breasts? I didn't see anything wrong with the old ones." Michael asked.

"So you looked, didn't you?" Linda tried to look stern, but it didn't work.

"I'm sure we all did." Frank raised his hand.

"I did and I thought they were beautiful."

"Shut up, Frank," they all responded.

"Let's leave Aunt Vicky's breasts alone and move on: does anybody have any form of prospects befitting Jack?" Deep into the night a short list had been assembled.

    She did this often. Sure she had tried to dissect precisely why and the only explanation was that it gave her at least a sense of physical security. What she had between her ears had never been an issue concerning quantity. Her IQ was above average, but there had of course been a few times too many when she had not explored and implemented what she had with neither great sense nor logic. But what was done could not be undone; so rationally and automatically she moved forward – having learned her lessons on the way.

    Standing in her utter nakedness in front of the mirror again, she saw a tall and well-shaped woman. Her legs were long and pleasantly muscular, with smoothly rounded thighs followed by classic curved hips. Her stomach was flat and strong and the new implants had done more for her sense of self than she had ever hoped for. Sure she initially thought of this enhancement with Jack in mind, or was that: the *pursuit* of Jack in mind? But she also rationed that her fight for Jack was still a tough mountain to climb, maybe even impossible; she still hoped that this new set might tip Jack in her direction. If not emotionally then at least physically, which would also be okay – for a while. But the scar running from her ear to her jaw had unfortunately not diminished with time; it had gone the other way. She had been advised that it could be corrected to some extent, but advised with a caution. She was not interested and in a peculiar way she had finally succumbed to the reality that this horrifying mark, at least horrifying to her, would stay the constant physical reminder of the attacks on her and the death of her beloved William. There was nothing that would change that; it had been the hardest thing to accept.

But it wasn't the reminder from the physical branding that was the issue; it was the terrifying nightmares, the many times waking up screaming and crying from constantly being raped again and again, beaten, stabbed, kicked and smothered. She was physically and mentally drained from these recurring horrors and didn't dare go back to sleep, as she knew they were waiting for her, waiting every night to finish her off. Medication had been suggested, but Victoria was not going there. She had always been cautious about stuffing any form of pills into her body; breast implants were okay, but no pills - go figure. The doctor urged her to at least try once, which she did. *Take this and you'll get a good night's sleep*, she was told. Victoria had stayed with it for two weeks, but she didn't get any more sleep than before; it was still nightmares galore.

After she finally had accepted and rationalized William's death, she buried herself in work at Anchor. Times had been tough for the industry the last few years; everybody was struggling. But Victoria had not noticed as it had been the total opposite for her. Her production accumulating business was far beyond average and Mr. Richards had mentioned several times, though Victoria didn't care, that she was probably the highest project grossing producer in the industry - for sure in the USA. *Why can't anybody else produce as well as you do?* Richards would ask. Victoria's tart answer was always: *They don't work hard enough.*

And she kept working harder and harder and days ran into evenings and evenings into nights. It seemed she could at least get a few hours of uninterrupted sleep if she started out totally exhausted. She hired a trainer for her physical up-keep and worked out with him in the fitness center at the office – six times weekly, two hours each session – her first trainer quit after two weeks; he had not been able to keep up. The nutritionist she had on contract took care of food and supplements; so she was in top shape inside and out. But there was of course something missing in her heart.

Victoria refused to see any shrinks for her mental anguishes. Work drowned out most of what she did not want to deal with and if something came to the surface and needed to be addressed, she just worked harder and longer hours – that normally cured it, at least for the time being. It would never go away and she knew that at some point in the future it had to be solved; she was certainly not ignorant.

She had not had any sexual encounters after the loss of William, other than what she provided for herself by herself. It was satisfying in a momentary physical way, releasing stress and giving her a few relaxed moments in the aftermath. But emotionally there was a huge void. She was a giving person sexually as well as emotionally, but for the longest time, nobody had given anything back to her – she longed for that feeling of body to body, mind to mind and heart to heart. She had those life-giving essentials for a short time with William and many years ago she had had the same feelings in her relationship with Jack. But that was it. She took one more look in the mirror. *For an old broad she wasn't that bad looking*, she thought with a satisfied but sad smile – all alone and by herself.

Sara and Jack were side by side in the narrow French bed; she was on her back, Jack on his side facing her. She glowed as she always glowed after making love. It was the most beautiful she could be, he thought. When she was pregnant with Michael, Jasper and Caroline, she had also been utterly sexy and Jack had a hard time keeping his hands as well as his eyes off her. She had fully inhaled and appreciated all the additional attention and though she felt flabby, floppy and fat, and at times irritated and ornery, Jack's constant love had made her pregnancies bearable; actually a happier time than she had expected. Sara had closed her eyes, but he knew she was still awake.
"George is dying." He said it quietly and soft.
"I know and I'm so sorry; so very sad for him and for you." Her right hand found his. "But you'll be okay, honey, just as you finally accepted that I died, you will also accept that your father will be gone."
"It took me a while with you, Sara. I couldn't help it. I miss you so much and though I have been *reborn* and feel better, looking forward instead of back; I miss you." Tears found

their way down the side of Jack's face. She wiped them off tenderly. "And now my Father; he looks so sad and fragile and he used to be so strong minded and assertive – he has always been my role-model. Now he can barely smile without an effort; barely walk without pain. He wants to live, Sara, he doesn't want to die – not now." Jack's body started to shake from the emotions. "And I can't do anything for him, absolutely nothing, other than trying to act normal around him – he knows I'm trying hard, but he doesn't say anything."

"He also knows you love him Jack and that you are here for him. That is important, very important and not only to your father, but also for you. Why do you think your father wanted you to come along? He loves you and he knew that the best gift you could give him and that he could give you was some weeks together in his most favorite spot here on earth; think about that."

"You are right; I know you are right." He gave her a kiss and rolled unto his back and stared at the low ceiling. The darkness was soothing and the light breeze coming through the small window had the smells of soil and vineyards; the moisture in the air was brought in by the Mediterranean Ocean. He took a deep breath and rolled over on his side to embrace Sara, to give her a kiss *goodnight* and tell her that he loved her– but Sara had never been there.

"Oh! What about Rachel Moore by the way?" Linda was all of a sudden excited. She was weaving through morning traffic, heading for work; Michael giggled.

"What about her? You mean for me?" Linda swapped at her husband.

"Way too old and way too experienced for you, dear boy. I was thinking for your father. She has the age, what about 45-50 something like that. She has a job and she's good looking…"

"…For an old broad that is..." Michael got swapped again. "I mean, isn't she?" She glanced towards Michael. "I'm not sure what we are looking for, but Rachel does come with the four B's."

"I'm afraid to ask, but pathetic curiosity is forcing me: What do the four B's stand for?" Michael smirked satisfied.

"*Beauty, brains, breasts and buttocks.*"

"Does it *have* to be in alphabetical order?"
"Oh how very observant. But the question is if my beloved father is seeking the whole set, or if he can discard one or two items and still be happy. But you have to admit that Rachel have all the B's." Linda laughed and nodded.
"…And overflowing a bit on the third B indeed."
"Never knew my father to be a breast-fan; but maybe he's secretly into those things."
"What about you?"
"I'll never tell, dear wife."
"No need, I acknowledge from vast experiences where your interests are."
"I don't hear any complaints."
"No, since none are forthcoming." Linda turned right and they both flashed their ID's to the guard by the gate and were waved through.

Linda talked with Rachel later that day. She was a colleague, detective in homicide and both Linda and Michael respected her work ethics and energy. It seemed that smiles of different sizes were on her face constantly. The only time you wouldn't see any of her smiles was when she was facing proven criminals. She had absolutely no mercy for them. Neither Linda nor Michael had any idea how she would response to Jack or Jack to her, but they did feel it could possibly, maybe, perhaps, nearly for sure, be a match – only time would tell. Rachel's single response was: "I hope he has balls." Linda nodded: "I think he does, but let me check on that and get back to you." She giggled as knew fully what Rachel meant. Linda wasn't sure if he actually had enough balls to handle Rachel. It proved later on that he did not; one down and many more to go.

Caroline made dinner for Karen and Nora. After the fun time they had spent at Nonna's a few days earlier they all wanted to get together again and as soon as possible. She also invited Victoria, but she was in Los Angeles. Caroline was concerned about her aunt and had done some lunches and dinners with her whenever she was home from MSU. She liked Victoria as she found her funny, in her own sarcastic style. Victoria had admitted she freely used sarcasm as a support mode. That way she could actually tell people what she thought of them, without being utterly blunt. They would only laugh and think it to be in fun and Victoria had had her say; it worked very well. But what Caroline really liked about Aunt Vicky was her brains. She had so much knowledge and wisdom, she was sensitive in a hardcore way and she did not have time for bullshit. She was fascinating to listen to and was herself a terrific listener, patient and concerned. By the pointed questions she would ask, you knew she listened to what you said.

Caroline was a fitness nut, and that was initially inspired by Molly so many years ago, but since Molly had disappeared, it was somewhat her father who had kept her running. But it was Victoria who was her main mentor now. After the horrific attacks and terrifying circumstances she had been through, one thing she never gave up, was her innate dedication to fitness; it was a drug to her as it had become a drug for Caroline and they were both big time addicts. Whenever possible she would go to Victoria's office where they used the gym together, with a trainer or without. Jogging was also something they found time to do whenever possible. The 27 or so age difference between them was not apparent, looking at Victoria's older body compared to Caroline's younger one. Victoria's stamina came from her love of competing, in business as well as in anything else; Caroline often found herself in second place. And Victoria competed with no mercy what so ever. She never made excuses for this part of her character as well as Caroline had never heard her brag about any of her victories.

After her father had come back to the real world again, so to speak, Caroline entertained thoughts getting him hooked up with somebody he could enjoy, have fun with and then possibly fall in love. Everybody agreed that he was a terrible bachelor, as he was a bit on the shy side going out seeking new female companions. He had met Sara and that was that; then the ten years or so of pathetic stupidity. But he had finally emerged, though empty-handed in the love department and a bit on the older side - if fifty-something could be called that.

The first time she had thought about Victoria as a prospect for her father, she had quickly disposed of the idea as being so close to the issue of incest that it made her slightly nauseated. After all, Victoria was his deceased wife's sister, his sister-in-law and an aunt to his children.

But as she thought about it bit by bit and was spending more and more time with Victoria, she found her to be a person so different from her mother. If she hadn't known, she would never have guessed they were sisters; but that was not an excuse she used to substantiate the way she finally thought about her father and Victoria *that way* – not at all.

Her father was not the most assertively aggressive person she knew; her opinion was of course very biased, but never the less true. He was charming and funny and a delightful person to be around. He had been and was, the most significant father anybody could have wished for. But it had been the many visits he made to MSU, trips and travels they had been on together that had exposed another side of him that she found fascinating and loved dearly. He was caring and thoughtful and a terrific friend, besides the father bit. She giggled as she recalled her and Molly talking about her father so many years ago. Molly had only been around for a while, when she had said something like: *Your father is such a nice man.* Caroline had quickly claimed that when *she* was old enough *she* was going to marry him. Molly had just smiled and said: *You can't do that; he's your father*. And she had continued: *But I can, because he is not **my** father*. Just by that short remembrance, Caroline realized how much she still missed Molly. She had tried hard to push her away, but she kept lingering in her heart, as she always had; she finally concluded, that it would always be like that.

So considering her father's personality, he needed somebody with energy who could drag him out of his cave and get him going with life and living. Aunt Vicky might just be that person. Sure there had been some issues in the past, but that was just that: the past. Michael, Linda, Jasper and Ella were against Victoria as a prospect, but Granddad of all people, was very much for it. He had always liked Victoria and at times Caroline was wondering if Sneaky George from Russia had something else on his mind concerning Aunt Vicky. Caroline laughed and made a mental note to ask that old charmer about his inner secret desires. She would do that when he returned from Europe.

During the dinner with Nora and Karen several prospect possibilities were discussed. After emptying a few bottles of wine, the conversation turned silly. Nora had told many stories from CR and times with Jack; Caroline obviously influenced by the wine, asked Nora:

"Okay, tell me about that time you and Dad tried, you know…" Nora giggled.

"Are you sure you want to hear it?"

"Yeah, why not – I can always cover my ears if it gets, you know…" Nora smiled.

"Well, help yourself…" Caroline and Karen were all ears, so Nora began her story:

"There was this time, I think about 3 years ago; I sat here in this very house having dinner with Jack. It was one of those many days when I thought he'd finally emerge from his depression. Sure a bit of wine and adult beverages after dinner supported that inclination; but that's not an excuse, by the way. The conversation had turned to finding a companion for Jack." Nora giggled: "Then he asked me if I had ever had thoughts about him and me, you know, that companion bit." Caroline's mouth dropped, and Karen grinned.

"You're kidding?" Caroline stuttered. "Doesn't sound like my father…"

"Anyway, so we realized that we had had a few fantasies about each other, which I guess would be fairly normal…"

"What kind of fantasies?" Caroline asked. Nora smiled and shook her head.

"How old are you again?"

"I'm sorry; please continue."

"So we talked about some of these fantasies and the more we talked the weirder it got. Our fantasies were pretty much about sex, with just a few other situations involved; but for the most it was about us, you know…"

"Fornicating?" Karen quipped with a laugh.

"That wasn't the term I was going to use, but essentially *yes*. So we are sitting there slightly intoxicated and find that we had actually always been attracted to each other from the day we met back in '63. Sure we became good buddies and business partners, but it was the physical, okay the *sexual* attraction that we had never acted on. So that evening we decided to give it a go." Caroline's eyes nearly fell out of the sockets, and Karen was laughing loud and happy.

"Oh my God, you and Jack did the old humpy-dumpy thing?" Caroline was holding her hands over her ears.

"I don't think I want to hear this." Nora laughed.

"Yes, I think you want to." Karen raised her hand.

"I do, I do, please continue."

"So we decided to see if there was any sexual attraction between us, other than in those juicy fantasies of ours. Like they do in films and books, you know, we'd first try to kiss to see if anything would register, you know..."

"That's a rather unromantic approach." Caroline mumbled, hands still covering her ears.

"I know, but that was the charm of it. Okay, so we get up and face each other, arms length. As we try to get a bit more *in the mood* or *romantic* as you want it to be, we started by desperately trying to relax, but we could not stop laughing. To tell you the truth, I was actually getting excited about the prospect of kissing Jack and the possibility of maybe, you know…"

"Fornicating?"

"Thanks Karen," Nora laughed: "Anyway, so we finally stop laughing and begin with holding hands. I tell you, to me it was electrifying. Then we prepared for that first kiss."

Jack put his hands on Nora's waist; all of a sudden he had turned serious. She looked lovely, he thought. They slowly leaned towards each other and finally their lips met. They were perfect kissing partners and as they kept kissing, their bodies touched and the embrace got stronger and tighter. But they had suddenly stopped. Caroline and Karen were paying full attention now.

"And then what?" Karen asked; her voice laced with curiosity. In dramatic fashion Nora continued:

"Our lips parted and the kiss was over. Then Jack said…"

"In spite that I'm a bit tipsy – did it feel right to you?"

"Being drunk?"

"No, the kissing thing; kissing each other."

"Anything personal?"

"Of course not Nora, you know that."

"Is it a color issue?"

"Most likely – I'm a bit green and out of practice."

"Have you ever kissed a black woman before?"

"Before what?"

"You know what I mean."

"Yes I do and no I haven't – not as far as I can recall." Now they were both laughing slightly nervous, but never the less laughing. Nora had grabbed Jack's hands.

"Just one more time – to make sure, you know." The second kiss lasted longer and this time they stopped with a warm and loving embrace.

"You know Jack, I'm actually really sorry that it doesn't work for either of us, but I'm glad it doesn't work for either of us, if you know what I mean?" Jack looked a bit disappointed.

"Yes, I know what you mean. Looking at you I can't see why I shouldn't be in love with you. You are intelligent, have a lovely personality, you're fun to be with and all that stuff and now I also know you are a superb kisser. So why doesn't it click?"

"We are best friends and I think that's what this is about. Neither of us wants to take a chance that a failed relationship would possibly ruin a perfect friendship." Jack had nodded.

"So adding it all up, I'm not getting laid tonight?"

"Me neither, but we can of course still go back and enjoy some of those wild fantasies about each other, if needed."

"There's a positive thought." Caroline was relieved.

"So nothing happened?" Nora smiled.

"No Caroline, we didn't *fornicate* that night or since. But at least we gave it a shot. I seriously think we could have made a good couple, good partnership; we do have a lot in common." Karen nodded eagerly.

"The way the two of you communicate I thought in the beginning that you were actually having a thing going."

"Well you were wrong, weren't you?" Karen smiled. Caroline suddenly looked at Karen.

"What about you?"

"What about me *what*?"

"You know; you and my dad." Now Karen was smirking. She was not going to tell Jack's daughter that she had had the hots for her father from the day she met him. Her fantasies about Jack were more so romantic than sexual. Those thoughts she had only shared with Nora and she knew Nora was not going to say anything about it to anybody; not a word – and she never did.

"Too old," was her short brush off. Caroline didn't quite buy in, but dropped the subject immediately. They finished the evening by discussing a few actual prospects and felt that the plan to get Jack romantically involved was ready to be implemented and would begin the second he returned from Europe.

He woke up a few hours after he was finally able to fall asleep. The dreams about Sara had again been vivid. He wanted so much to be able to handle not having her around, but it seemed the images wouldn't go away. Sure he had *officially* returned to the real world, but no matter how hard he tried, there was still that lingering link to Sara through his dreams, his fantasies and so many other constant reminders during the routines of his everyday life. It wasn't that he didn't love her anymore, but it had to stop, it really had to end; he had to move on before he went totally insane.

Family and friends had been tremendous in their support and they all believed that he was fully cured and had moved on; luckily they couldn't look inside him, where he was still clouded by deep and dark mourning. He was sure they would drop him in a second or less, if they knew the real truth about Jack. The knock on the door swiped those thoughts off his mind – for now.

"Room service;" he didn't recognize the voice and another thing was that he had not previously had any form of room service in this hotel. He rolled out of bed and opened the door. A sight for sore eyes met him and he was quickly in a long and warm embrace.
"It is so wonderful to see you again. Thanks for coming."
"I'm glad I did."
"When did you arrive?"
"Last night. You were already in bed, so I got to chat with George and that wonderful woman, Bernadette." He held her out in arms length.
"So you know about my dad?" She dried her eyes with the sleeve of her blouse.
"Yes I do," she fell into his arms again: "I'm so sorry, Jack, really so very sorry."
"Yeah I know. Shit happens, but it's supposed to happen to other people, not me or you or Dad."
"How are you getting along?"
"I really don't know; and I wish I knew."

"With you finally coming back and then this; that got to be tough."

"But I'll handle it okay I think; after all I've had a few years of experience," he said with cynicism.

"That's not the point, Jack; it's about how you are going to deal with George these last weeks..." She started to sob: "My God, that is so awful to even have to consider."

"That's okay; I talked with Dad and we have found a way to deal with it so it doesn't interfere with how we normally get along – at least we'll try." Jack went over to the bed and sat down. "What room did you get? – I thought Bernadette had a full house." Molly smiled.

"Last night I slept on her sofa of all places. She's going to see what she can figure out. She knows all the nearby hotels, so she'll look around." Jack pointed at the narrow bed on the other side of the room.

"You can use that one till Bernadette finds you something else, if you like."

"Seriously?"

"Why not - we're family; kind of."

"Thanks Jack; that would be great. I like this charming little hotel and can see why George has returned so many times with Irene – and now with you."

"How long are you able to stay?"

"For however long is needed."

"Thanks Molly; I know that you being here means the world to my Dad, really."

"It means the world to me too."

The rest of the time in the South of France was spent exchanging stories and anecdotes, filled with laughter, tears of sadness and tears of joy. Bernadette didn't leave George's side for a minute – day or night. Jack and Molly were thrilled that he felt such comfort in her friendship; it was obviously that this warm and loving relationship had developed over many years – so good, though sad, to see how it was confirmed these last weeks of George Miller's life.

They picnicked, ate at home where all four helped out and frequented an array of local restaurants. Slowly life was ebbing out inside of George, which was clear to anybody who spent time with him. But his spirits soared on any occasion and you quickly forgot how sick he was. Bernadette told Molly and Jack about the nights, and tears were hard to hold back. The medication George was taking did create some comfort and a few hours of uninterrupted sleep, but that was about all it did.

Molly and Jack were getting along just fine in Jack's small room. Bernadette had found several rooms in local hotels, but had told Molly that there wasn't anything available. Bernadette didn't like the lying, but George had pleaded with her not to tell Molly the truth - so she hadn't. She felt George was up to something, but he didn't tell her what it was. From her own observation of Molly and Jack, she did feel what she thought George felt; there was such compatibility between the two. The only thing was that Jack was so much older and Molly should in Bernadette's opinion settle for somebody her own age; but Molly stayed in Jack's room, just like George wanted her to.

Most of the nights, with each in their own narrow bed, in that tiny room on the third floor, were spent talking. Molly was listening to Jack, as he was listening to her. Respecting each other's privacy, they had managed to shower and change clothes without awkward moments. Jack was surprised by the oversized pajama Molly used. At first she looked funny, with sleeves too long, covering her hands and pant legs dragging the floor. But she felt utterly comfortable, obviously – just like Sara had.

Explaining ten years of misery, mourning and depression in less than a few nights should normally produce a rather concentrated, though full of holes, story. Jack had often tried to explain it all to himself and understand what it had been, what it was and what it was not, that he had gone through. He often questioned why he had let it happen and for so long. As a husband, a father and also as a business partner with Nora before Sara's death, he had been the ultimate solution finder, not just for himself, but for Sara and the children and even more aggressively so with his business partner. He would analyze any situation in seconds, ad up the options, find the correct route out of the problem, implement the decision and it was solved; he had been very good at that.

But there was something else with those ten years. It had been like a trance, staying on a destructive track he couldn't get off, no matter how much he wanted to. Molly had listened, agreed and disagreed. *Maybe you didn't want to get back to normal. Maybe you felt that living a full life without Sara by your side was treason, to some extent. Maybe you felt that you shouldn't have what she couldn't have.* It had been an interesting way to look at it and so sweet of Molly to consider. But she had not been all sweet; she had actually attacked some of Jack's decisions, reasoning that he was, after all, an adult who had proved to the people around him before Sara's departure, that he was pretty much in control of his life, even with major setbacks. But then Sara died and he went comatose; a short time of grieving would have been accepted by all, and fully understood; but ten bloody years? Wow, that *was* really pathetic.

She was quick to bring parallels from her own Nordic God incident and her own withdrawal after Sara's death. Though the situations were not particular fully compatible, many of the feelings were alike. Though her husband hadn't exactly died, the feelings of loss, betrayal and dishonesty hurt her bad. Sure she had handled some of the issues with the help of alcohol, the aftermath of which Jack had witnessed firsthand not so long ago. But she had taken control and soberly faced the many challenges to get herself back on track. The funny thing was that she never felt stupid about the choice she had made marrying into such predicament; she fully knew what the situation was all about, but did it anyway. She took full responsibility for her actions and more importantly, she only blamed herself. Nobody had pointed fingers; the people around her felt they understood: grandparent's untimely death, alone in the world kind of feeling and then that Danish knight in shiny armor, with good looks and charm arrived. She had been very vulnerable, but she never used that as an excuse.

They found themselves opening up more than ever, though Jack did not tell Molly about his occurring dreams about Sara, the tender moments of lovemaking and his reaction to the images of her. In a restaurant not long ago, he had dinner with the daughter of one of Bernadette's friends, about his own age. She was in building construction out of

Cannes, so Bernadette had thought it would be interesting for them to chat over dinner some evening. It had been a lovely time, at least some of it. She had been entertaining, fun and utterly charming. They had gone through some delicious local wine and Jack felt a bit lightheaded. It was then that he noticed she kept pulling her hair beyond her right ear using her right hand – just like Sara used to do. Then he noticed another thing; when she talked she constantly looked directly into his eyes, like she was reading his soul to find out what he was thinking. Sara had always done that, from the first time they met, by the pool, about a million years ago. But it was that first casual touch by her hand that had sent sparks through him. He was immediately very confused about these feelings, but decided to let it ride. He knew that she was probably not interested in him *that way*; after all she was married and hadn't shown any signs of interest otherwise. She was just one of those touchy-feely people which Jack for the most felt slightly uncomfortable with.

But then it had happened again. He had talked about his father and his father's situation. Her eyes had moistened and her touch of his hand across the table had been tender and caring. It was then he saw Sara – right there in front of him, with tears in her eyes. He had reached across the table and caressed her cheek. *Don't cry, Dear Sara, please don't cry.* At first he didn't hear it himself, but the immediate change from sympathy to startled surprise, told him that he had done it again. *Jack, my name is Michelle.* The sad thing was that she had really liked him, cared for his misery about Sara and now his father. She thought that they felt something for each other, and she had actually considered the possibility of spending the night with him, husband or no husband. Of course Jack didn't know all this, so as she suddenly felt insignificant as he had called her by his dead wife's name, it was natural for her to gather her purse, throw some money on the table and leave. It left Jack sitting there, stunned in disbelief, in disbelief that he could have been so insensitive, so utterly dumb and ignorant. He looked sheepishly at Molly and giggled:
"It's situations like that where stupidity actually sounds rather fascinating." Molly didn't laugh nor did she smile – there was nothing funny about it at all; the only thing that

came to her mind was *pathetic*. She cleared her throat and sat up in her bed.

"Listen Jack, I'm not your guardian angel, your common sense or sense of logic. I'm just a friend, that's all. But I think I know you well and I believe it was good that I did not see you those ten years or so. I sadly believe that I would have either tried to help you as much as I could, and if that hadn't worked, I probably wouldn't have stayed around and wait for the real Jack to show up. I would no doubt have dumped you and gone on to better things. But that's me, Jack and that has always been me." Her voice got angrier. "I got married and I got screwed on so many levels; a genuine fuck-up overall, but I came out of it smelling like a rose. You know why?" Jack shook his head slowly. "Because I wanted to, that's why. Looking at you and listening to your stories, I have not heard a single beep about Jack wanting to fix it and move on. It is all about sad me-me-me-me and honestly, that is pathetic to listen to and it must have been even more pathetic to live through. How you did this crap for over ten years is unbelievable in so many sad ways. Okay, so Sara died many years ago and with her some of you died as well. Sara came out of it dead, but you were still alive; only technically, I admit. But you know what, life continues; no matter how much we screw it up – it keeps churning along, second by second, minute by minute and so forth. But we have options, many options. We can either give up and get off, or we can actively participate in this, the only bloody life we are so privileged to have been given. Remember every second you don't fully enjoy life is a second that is wasted. It's gone, it's out of here and you'll never get a chance to redo those seconds and minutes and hours, days and months and in your case some ten bloody years. What a waste, what a bloody waste." Jack was now sitting uneasy on the edge of his bed and was ready to flee whenever the possibility opened up. "So my suggestion is that you snap out of it for the health of yourself and for those who loves you. And I do think the list is dwindling to just a few. Snap out of your Sara obsession, if not for you, then for her and her memory. The way you have carried on, you have seriously tarnished her name, soiled what she stood for and dirtied all the good things she did here on earth. If that was your plan, you have succeeded; if not, then you have royally fucked up." Molly couldn't stop now. She felt that she would either reach him or lose him. Either way she would have spoken her heart and that was very important to her. "Jack, you have placed Sara on a pedestal so high where nobody would ever be able to reach her, to live up to the utterly insane expectations you have applied. She wasn't like that, I know that and you must know that too. But you keep comparing Sara with anybody, anything what-so-ever, and the way you have built her up, made her goddess-like, nobody and nothing will ever compare to her; you singlehandedly raised the bar so far out of reach. You have screwed yourself out of the enjoyment of life, a life you should have lived with pride in Sara's honor. Instead you have been pissing on her memory from the day she died. You keep asking *why did you leave me, Sara?* For your information, she never left you; dying or not dying wasn't an option she had; but living or not living was the option you had, but you fucked it up. You never thought about it that way, did you? No, it was all about *her* leaving *you*. Feeling so sorry for yourself and for so bloody long is eerily pathetic. So take that to the mirror and open your eyes – if you dare." Molly dried her eyes with the sleeve, got up and started to pack her small suitcase. Jack's head snapped up.

"What are you doing?" Without turning towards Jack she responded.

"I'm getting out of here. This is way more than I bargained for."

"But I thought you were staying for a few more days."

"That won't work. I gotta go say goodbye to George and Bernie and get a taxi." She quickly changed clothes, gathered the few toiletries and was out the door. But before she left, she turned around in the doorway. "You know Jack, I listened to your chat about how you have returned to life, how things were better now and all that shit; but be honest and admit that you are lying to yourself and even worse, you are lying to the people who loves you. How bloody heartbreaking do you think your father would find it, if you told him that nothing had changed? Be honest with yourself and don't give anybody any of all the bullshit you have poured on me the last few days and nights."

"But I am over it, Molly."

"Don't go there, Jack. You are so far from over it as you were ten years ago. So don't make yourself believe that you are cured, because you are not. Maybe you haven't noticed, but every bloody night I spent in this room, you cried and twisted and turned and I haven't a clue how many times you screamed or mumbled or cried out *Sara, Sara, why did you leave me, I love you* and an assortment of other self-pitying expressions. I bought in on your self-proclaimed return, but spending a couple of nights with you quickly told me that I had been had. One thing I will not accept are people lying to me – and you knew you were lying to me. My true friends would never dream of doing that as I would never lie to them. So I'm getting my butt out of here and heading home. I truly hope you'll seek professional help, because you are a very sick man. I truly loved Sara; she was my mother amongst mothers, my truest friend and the most intelligent person and the sweetest human being anybody could ever dream of – and she was real. I honored her in life and I most certainly honor her in death. Your self-pity will never stain the image I have of Sara – I will never let you do that; it will never happen." She turned quickly and went down the stairs. Jack sat frozen on the edge of the bed; he could barely breathe, but he didn't really care. Reality for Jack had finally caught up with him and he was hurting bad; he was back to square one. He was wondering if he would actually ever return – at this moment he had very deep doubts about that – again. He admitted that Molly had struggled through some long years, but at least she had gotten back on track and moved forward; while he hadn't moved a single inch.

George tried to stay in control of his emotions, but with Molly holding his hands and weeping, he simply couldn't hold back.
"I've always loved you, George, and I'm so sorry that I ran away and never contacted you. If I had contacted anybody during those years it would have been you." She kissed his hands. "You accepted me so fast when I was a little frightened girl. You were the only one who could see how scared I was. Remember how you picked me up all the time?" George nodded. "You were the only one I felt good about picking me up. And then you gave me those noisy blowing kisses on my neck, Sara would watch and shake her

head; remember how she always smiled?" George kept nodding while Molly whimpered more. She looked deep into his eyes and felt she hit his soul. That was where she wanted to go; she wanted to leave a part of her in there, something of her that would stay with George wherever he was going. The spark in his eyes was nearly extinct, but he tried bravely to keep them glowing, just for his sweet Molly. She saw the sadness in his eyes, and for once she knew why.

"Thank you for coming, Molly, it has really meant the world to me."

"Me too George; yeah, me too." Bernadette was now holding both Molly's and George's hands. She had been crying the whole time and even though George had sent her silly faces to cheer her up, the short giggles quickly turned back to crying.

"You better get going, Molly, the taxi is waiting." Her body was now shaking and tears flowed freely. Her embrace was warm and tender and filled with unconditional love. She didn't know what to say, what to part with, but George's smile and embrace did it all. Bernadette and Molly hugged while George dried tears off his face; his, Bernadette's and Molly's. She grabbed her purse and luggage on the way out the door.

"Molly," she turned immediately.

"Yes George."

"Promise me something; it's something you can do for me."

"Anything, George."

"Help Jack if you can." She was surprised by his request.

"What do you mean?"

"He needs to stop lying and he needs to get cured." Molly tried to look puzzled but she didn't do a good job.

"I'm not sure I understand."

"I know you understand, Molly, you of anybody. And you are the only one I think can help him." She paused.

"What makes you say that?" George smiled as he realized that she didn't know.

"Because he loves you, Molly; he loves you very much."

"I love him too." George smiled again.

"No Molly, you don't understand. Jack loves you beyond your typical *love*, the kind we use with friends and family. Jack truly loves you in that old-fashioned romantic way."

"I'm sure you are mistaken, George. Why haven't he told me if that's what it is?"

"Because he doesn't know it yet," Molly shook her head.

"That's crazy." Bernadette smiled as she looked at Molly.

"You love him too, don't you?"

"Yeah I love him, but not *that* way." She said making a face of disbelief. Bernadette looked at George.

"See what I told you, George, they really don't know." George nodded.

"But will you promise to try to help him get back to real life, for me?"

"I'll think about it and give you a call or E-mail or something." George knew what the score was, but didn't bring it up so he just smiled. "When are you heading back to D.C.?"

"In three days." Molly paused.

"I'll call you and let you know."

"Thanks Molly; I'll look forward to hearing from you." She walked back and kissed him, then kissed Bernadette and soon after she was in the taxi on the way to Nice and the airport. After a while she finally calmed down, but not before she had used up all the driver's napkins. Liz answered her mobile call.

"You are not okay, are you?" She asked.

"No, I'm not okay at all; but Liz, I'm coming home. Will you be there for me?"

"As always, my friend; call me with airline and arrival. I'll pick you up." At this point, a fatigued *thanks* was all Molly could muster.

The First Class cabin from Nice to Paris was fairly empty. George and Jack had not spoken many words. There was somberness between them, with emotions raging on their minds and in their hearts. The goodbyes to Bernadette had been painful and touching and as George waved leaving the parking area outside the walls of his beloved Saint Paul-de-Vence, he had physically been shaking. His expressions of grief were filled with sobs and many tears. Bernadette finally disappeared as they rolled away from this hilltop paradise and George had slumped back in the seat and nothing was said on the way to the airport.

He requested help with his father as they checked in and George had quietly accepted the wheelchair. The formalities were handled quickly, while a porter looked after George.

At Charles de Gaulle Airport outside Paris, help was waiting at the gate and they were guided into the First Class lounge area. Departure to Washington D.C. was about two hours away, so they settled in for a while. Small talk was all they could do, as sadness was hanging over them as the darkest cloud.

A female porter picked them up and they were soon in their seats. This First Class cabin was also near empty. They declined the champagne and soon George was asleep; Jack quietly tucked him in with a blanket and fluffed the pillows. Take-off was smooth and they soon cruised at 35,000 feet heading west.

Liz was a sight for sore eyes; in Molly's case, sore *and* red eyes. The flight to Casablanca had been uneventful as she had slept most of the time. The porter placed the luggage in the trunk of Liz's car and after a warm *nice to see you again* and *welcome home* embrace they were soon at the villa.

Liz set up a table with fruit, cheese and a bottle of chilled white out on the deck, while Molly spent time in a long and relaxing shower. It was a pleasant early evening and the sunset would yet again be a spectacle of colors. As Molly walked out on the deck, wrapped in her comfy bathrobe, a small smile appeared.

"How can you not love this; I mean how can you stay sad and depressed and confused when you have this?" She gestured towards the ocean and the sky. "I think the correct academic and scientific expression that fully covers this majestic view we are so privileged to experience is *WOW;* don't you agree?" Liz nodded and smiled.

"Nice to have you back, Boss."

"Nice to be back again Liz; and thanks for being my friend." So they drank some wine, ate some fruit and cheese, enjoyed the view and Molly's head started to clear up a bit. After talking with Liz an hour longer, it cleared up even more.

What a pathetic idiot he was. He had crawled out of this deep hole, telling everybody he was back. He fooled everybody and had lied till his nose couldn't get any longer; that's what he had done. Some said that lying to one self was even worse, but that was not true – everybody else had an importance far superior to his own little pathetic world of lies. Jack had always lived an honest life where lying was considered ignorant and disrespectful. He had jumped on his children the second they even got close to avoiding the truth. He would scold them and preach the gospel of truthfulness. They had listened and learned and applied. Jack could not recall a single incident where his children had been caught in a full lie, and he was very proud of that. But here he was, the biggest fake, the biggest deceiver of them all; he was utterly ashamed and again, depressingly so. He had to find a way to get it all back on track, find himself and as Molly had said, seek the professional help he desperately needed but had avoided. It was either that or find a way to leave it all. But he hoped it wouldn't come to that.

She was so right; he had singlehandedly soiled Sara's memory by feeling sorry for himself, not for what Sara had missed. He had to reunite with his children and with his friends, the few left – if they were still his children and his friends. He had his work cut out, and he had to do it. This would be his last chance and it wasn't going to be easy. He had to tell everybody that he had duped them, tell them where he is at that moment emotionally, ask for help and set some goals. Maybe they would understand, but he seriously doubted it.

He felt certain that he had lost Molly. It was a devastating thought. Luckily, if any luck could be found in this situation, he hadn't announced her return; but on the other hand, maybe he had successfully pushed her away for good. It seemed she had a full and exciting life in Africa as it was, so it probably wouldn't be a loss not to reconnect. His father's hand suddenly reached out. He gently caressed the old fingers and turned his head.
"Nice nap, Pop?" George tried to smile.
"Not bad, Son; can I get some water or something?"
"I'll get you some; anything to eat?" George shook his head. Jack pressed the button on the armrest and a flight attendant showed up right away. He asked for water for his father as

well as a gin and tonic for himself – *make it a double, please.* Moments later they both sipped from their glasses and all that could be heard was the humming from the big jet engines. Jack cleared his throat a couple of times and turned towards his father; his smile was sheepish and embarrassed.

"I really fucked up, didn't I?" George didn't turn his head.

"You have to ask?" Jack knew he was not going to get any sympathy from the man sitting next to him and that was fair enough. They had talked about the whole situation at length the last day in Vence. George had been on a tirade of sorts and it was Bernadette who finally had to break it up and ask them to literally shut up and behave like mature adults. Jack had never seen his father so agitated and would never see him like that again. But he had fully understood and accepted his opinions. Many new issues were brought up, new to Jack and they made a lot of sense – definitely something to work on and fast. The dinner that evening had been cozy, fun and very emotional for the three of them. Not a word more about Jack's predicament and what he had to do next to salvage any little speck of his previous life. They decided to get a good night's sleep before the long trip home. George had just one more thing to say.

"Jack, you have to fix your relationship with Molly and you have to do that fast."

"I don't have a relationship with her anymore."

"That's why you have to fix it so you do. This is important and I ask you to promise me this one wish before I expire: Fix the damn thing, okay? Promise me." Jack was a little miffed why this was so important to him. George did not mention what he had asked Molly to do and nothing about that his son was in love with her. Some things Jack had to figure out himself; he was after all an adult, he reasoned with a smirk of occasional doubt.

"I promise, Dad." He paused for a second. "You know what; I think it would be a fair deal if you tell me a bit about what you did in Russia before you arrived in D.C., and come to think about it, what about telling me what you really worked with all those years with the U.S. government?" Now it was George's turn to look miffed and smiled in the process.

"You gotta be kidding."

"No Dad, I'm not even close to kidding." After a moment George spoke.

"I don't even know where to begin."

"Well, any beginning is a good starting point, wouldn't you say?"

"I need more water for that one."

"Coming up;" moments later they had a new serving of water, gin and tonic.

George talked about his childhood in the Soviet Union, about his mother and father, his language skills and uncanny sense reading and dissecting documents of all sorts. He told Jack about his work with Stalin inside the Kremlin and his close friendship with Vadim, the Russian-German translator.

"Weren't you afraid of the Stalin regime?"

"Vadim and I were scared shitless twenty-four hours a day, seven days a week. We had to be extremely careful who we talked to, how we talked to them, body language – anything. They would shoot you in a second if your tie had the wrong color. We traveled on very narrow roads and what Vadim and I did could have brought a death sentence in a flash."

"But you did make it out."

"Obviously, but only narrowly and by a lot of luck."

"What about Vadim?" George laughed.

"That was the screwy thing. I found out later that he was working for the CIA, can you believe that? I never ever suspected that he was anything else than a true Russian, not a communist, just a genuine Russian who loved his homeland enough to hang in there even under a terrorist dictatorship. So he's a blooming CIA agent." George was laughing, followed by a dry cough. "You see Jack, and I have never told anybody about this, Vadim and I did not just translate documents, we were also part of a hidden entity of the secret police, directed by Stalin and a few other morons. We were *encouraged* to join them, meaning that if we didn't, we would be on a lifelong vacation in Siberia – and that only if we were lucky."

"What kind of work was it?"

"Typical Josef Stalin work. Somebody sneezed? Kill the bugger and it couldn't happen fast enough."

"No arrests, no court appearance, anything like that?"

"Track them down and eliminate was the fastest and less complicated way for the regime to fix things. Load gun, pull trigger, problem solved." Jack was hesitant with his next question.

"Did you, you know, *eliminate* anybody?" George smiled and padded Jack's hand.

"No I didn't *eliminate* anybody in Russia; at least not directly."

"What do you mean?" George smiled and giggled.

"I can smile and giggle these days because it's such a long time ago and seemingly so far away. Vadim and I had made a pact, an agreement, that with our combined brain power and overall smarts, we would figure something out where we would not be involved in any innocent Russian's death, torture or imprisonment. Now remember we were young and on some levels extremely naïve. This was a very delicate life or death balance act; we had to cover our own butts, to help save others. You must understand that we worked smack in the middle of the Kremlin and had all these secret agencies and their staff around us constantly. Not only did we forge documents, obscure interpretation of documents, but we also negated forwarding certain messages we felt would not help our purpose or be dangerous to innocent bystanders. Most of the people within the Kremlin walls were ignorant morons, solely surviving on the power they were given. So we used a lot of fancy words in our reports. They would just sit there and agree to about anything because they didn't understand a word of it; stupid bastards." George paused: "You remember that Hans Christian Andersen story *The Emperor's New Clothes*?" Jack smiled.

"You read it to me a million times."

"I guess I did. So it's about these tailors who are conning the emperor to believe that if he can't see the *nonexistent* gold threaded cloth they weaved, then he must be stupid. So as not to look stupid, he said he saw it. Well, there's Stalin's Kremlin for you; with Vadim and George your conning tailors."

"You said you didn't kill anybody directly?"

"I never did, but the assassins we had to *employ* had to go do the work, any work, actually. We had to find a way where they eliminated somebody for the record, without eliminating anybody. They were never told who they were sent after and who they were shooting, or the reason these people had to disappear. They were like puppets, really stupid puppets, I might add."

"So what did you do?" George took a sip of water and continued.

"We covered our form of operation by sheer deception and we ran this process for nearly 22 months before I finally had a chance to get the hell out; and guess who gave me the opportunity to a one-way ticket? Josef bloody Stalin, can you believe that?" George was smiling to himself as the memories evolved. He hadn't thought much about his life in the Soviet Union since he left. Though he had done okay, there were too many disturbing images he wanted to shake off but couldn't; it also felt like somebody else had lived that life and then told him about it. He felt that thought to be more of an excuse for what he had been involved in, for what he had done. Suddenly his face went from a smile to concern.

"Are you okay Dad?"

"I'll manage."

"You want to stop talking about this?"

"No I'm fine Jack," he cleared his throat again and sipped some more water. Then he continued. "I'll give you the shorter version, okay?" Jack nodded.

"Of course Dad."

"My department was given specific *advice* concerning targets from Stalin's office, supposedly, subjects they wanted us to deal with. I also thought that many of the assignments had a personal touch; a commander who wanted to get rid of his neighbor, somebody who had insulted him, had screwed his wife or whatever. The supposedly non-traceable orders were simple by stating name, last known address and a time frame within which we had to *deal* with the situation. At times we got a photo as well."

"Did they give you any training in these matters?"

"Vadim and I were sent to some kind of elite school, elite elimination school, I suppose. I tell you, neither one of us wanted to do this; we just wanted to handle documents, do some translations and basically be kept in peace till we could flee the hell out. But we were good at that translation stuff, so the morons felt that we would be good at anything. Another reason was that the assistant to the top general of this secret faction really liked me for some reason, so he had recommended me for the job and since I couldn't refuse, I asked Vadim to help me out. I knew from the start that I was not going to kill anybody what-so-ever; that was not going to happen."

"…And you didn't?" George paused as he thoughtfully analyzed the question. Then he slowly said:

"…I was close twice; finger on the trigger and ready. Luckily somebody else shot first both times," his body slumped more into the seat.

"Are you okay?" George nodded. "You prefer not to talk about it?"

"I'm fine."

"Stop any time you want to, okay?" George nodded his head and sipped some water and continued.

"Most of the targets were in our estimation good Russians. So the dilemma was that Stalin wanted to rid the world of individuals who actually were good, so you see that we had an enormous problem, since we did not want to eliminate those guys at all. And we never did; we were actually that cheeky, that bloody lucky and I must say extremely clever. We knew we were skating on very thin ice all 22 long and scary months and when I was offered the way out – by Stalin more or less, I grabbed it with both hands."

"But how did you survive?"

"Our assigned assassins were fanatics; totally bunkers. They only functioned when told what to do; I mean they were stupid, really stupid. We had them do stuff that would get themselves eliminated if they as much as hinted what they had done and what they were doing. We had 14 of these goons in the show, so you'd think you'd at least have one with a brain; but that was luckily not the case. We kept them close to us, by supplying them with booze and willing women. As long as we did that, they did precisely what we told them to do. Vadim and I often had a good laugh with respect to some of the stuff they would do and especially some of the stuff they would say. You see, after an *elimination* they had to write a report before the final file could be discarded. Some of the stuff they wrote was hilarious, really moronic stupid. So Vadim and I suggested that we would help writing the reports for them; they quickly agreed. So from that day forward, Vadim and I wrote the assassin's reports and wrote what we wanted. That was very essential to our cover and just a lifesaving lucky break for us. All the goons had to do was sign and date; they never read what they signed – ever."

"But how did you get away with it, I mean how many did you have to take care of in those 22 months?"

"Our department was assigned 32 cases and we solved 28; solved them our way. I really don't know what happened to the four we missed – I'm afraid they were probably assigned to other departments." George was looking frail and tired. "We wanted to do it all, Jack, really wanted to help the good guys, but we missed those four and we were doing so well, really. We felt we had nailed the system and nothing could stop us," he smirked: "except a bullet, of course; we were constantly aware of that." Jack called for more water and another set of gin and tonic. George smiled at his son. He was a good guy, he knew that; but he had to figure it out himself, again. "Vadim was a pal, Jack, a real pal. He was so funny and dealt with many situations using his terrific sense of humor. To me he was the glue that kept our sanity together, as I tended to be easily frazzled and hyper. Vadim would just say something funny and I would come back down. So what we did when we got an assignment was locating the target. Vadim and I did that before we even brought the assignment up with the goons. Normally we were given 5-6 days to take care of the problem, so we acted quickly. We met up with the target, sat down and had a bit of a chin-whack, placed the cards on the table and got their attention rather quickly. By the time we got to the chat about possibilities and outs, we knew all about these people: marital status, how many children, their ages, if they had mistresses or any kind of homosexual relationships we should worry about that they might try to contact after they *disappeared*, their work, colleagues, you know, all the essentials. They were cooperating very quickly and even though some of the information we had on them sent shock and at times anger through the wife or kids or the target himself, they had enough sense to choose life and not the option of death."

"So what did you do?"

"After they decided they wanted to continue living, we took their photos, double checked all the information we already had on them and told them to sit tight for a few days.

Somebody would contact them and would lead them away from their home."

"Wow! This sounds like a real spy-story." George smiled.

"You are not listening are you Jack? This *was* the real stuff – and very scary. Anyway, we also told them to live their normal lives the next few days with no changes at all. We told them not to take any money out of their bank accounts other than what they would normally do. No packing of anything, no departure-like actions. No chats with neighbors and no *it has been nice knowing you* stuff. They would be given what they needed for the trip – that would be all. We had identification cards made and we didn't even have to forge the papers, as the legitimate ID department was just a few blocks from the Kremlin. We knew how to fill out the applications, which of course was forged and had nothing to do with reality, but since we had some massive clout in the sandbox, they took our word as guarantee. A day later we had the papers and visited the target one last time, handed over their new ID's and collected the old ones. That same night a couple of our good people, not working in the department, and who were basically working against the state, kind of a resistance movement, anti communism, picked up the target and whatever family was going. They went with them and left everything behind. Many times they staged a massacre, fake blood and all, and took pictures for the file – just in case. We even used bodies from the local morgue; bodies that had not been identified. Through a network of safe-houses pretty much all over Russia, they easily disappeared without a trace. They would be settled in areas far away from Moscow and Stalin's henchmen, settle in and lived a fairly normal life, with new names and all."

"Didn't you have to prove the… eliminations?"

"You sound like a diplomatic assassin now," George laughed. "See, that was the lucky break we exploited big time. What Stalin's officers were concerned, the targets should be killed. That was their *intellectual* way of solving problems. So when we submitted the corresponding report with all the identification papers we gathered from the target and possible family, as well as photos of the slaughter, they were utterly impressed. They never asked if the whole family had been erased, or killed, as they didn't want to know. I never figured out the reason they didn't ask, but I can only assume that it's the old thing about covering your eyes and nobody can see you – maybe."

"What were the goons, the assassin's jobs, you know the ones working in your department?"

"The exterminators, you mean?" George said with a smile. "We sent them to the target's address after we had received notification from the resistance that the coast was clear. They were very good at that and as far as I know, they never got caught; I can't figure out how they avoided that. But anyway, our goon-squad would go to the targets home and we would give them free range to take whatever they wanted; the old *steal and plunder.* Then the orders were for them to burn down the house, including those bodies from the morgue that another faction of our department had placed ahead of the goon's final visit. They would stay on site till it was all burned down and in case the fire department got a bit too eager, they kept them away; by force if necessary. When the fire was out they would take photos of the damage, the burned bodies and whatever was left."

"Nobody ever tried to identify the bodies?" George smiled.

"When you saw the photos there was no need to ask. The assumption was that these poor saps had succumbed in a horrendous fire, pity for them and *they were such nice neighbors*. You see, back in those times you refrained from asking questions. You never knew who the snitch was, just like Nazi Germany with the Gestapo, the SS and so forth. You would be stupid to trust anybody. Vadim's and my positions within the Kremlin were perfect for what we could do and what we did. We had great intellectual power with our language knowledge and document interpretations. Most of the people we dealt with were ignorant…"

"*The Emperor's New Clothes* syndrome…?"

"… Precisely; so most of them really didn't know how much or how little power we had, who we palled with up on top, who we knew and what we knew. I spent time with Stalin on many occasions, and just that made me a much more powerful person, even though I wasn't. But nobody would dare take a chance on me, or Vadim, for that matter. Of course we never exposed what kind of power we really had, as it would have killed our little undercover operation – and us, no doubts." George sipped more water.

"So Vadim was a CIA agent all this time?" Now George laughed.

"Yeah, that bugger worked for the Americans all that time. He was already an agent for them when I hooked up with him at MSU." Jack looked momentarily puzzled. "No Jack, not Michigan but Moscow State University. But the point is that I never figured that out. I considered myself a rather expert self-made agent. Kremlin, actually the NKVD, had me followed and tapped 24 hours a day, 7 days a week. That's how much they trusted the director of their foreign document translation department. But I knew they kept an eye on me and on Vadim, of course. They even sent female agents to squeeze information out of us by the cunning use of sex. We didn't mind that part at all." George was laughing out loud and dry. "It was actually very funny and I really don't think they thought they'd get anything out of us other than an orgasm or two." He shook his head with a smile.

"Wow, that's a long time ago." Jack was giggling in amazement of his father's exploits. He had never heard anything about his life in Russia and even about how he got out. George had kept that fully to himself; something about covering one's eyes and it had not happened as he was not overtly proud of that part of his existence.

"But you finally got out?"

"I sure did, and luckily so." And George told his son about how he had attended the conference in Casablanca in 1943, met and actually chatted with both Roosevelt and his all-time hero Winston Churchill. In detail he described the approach by the Americans and his first meeting with Hamilton and how they had stayed close friends till this very day. Then it was the dramatic *escape* by plane and when he first laid eyes on his Irene. His eyes soon got moist and his voice became less forceful and less energetic.

"Jack, the very second I saw your mother, I knew that I had found the right partner for life. In my eyes she was stunningly beautiful, military uniform and all. I knew that was it for George. We both knew before we landed in London on the way to America that we would be it – we had no doubts what-so-ever."

"Like when I saw Sara for the first time."

"Precisely; and I don't know what it was or what it is, but the feeling was immensely strong, with no apparent explanation."

"Do we need an explanation?" George giggled.

"You know me Jack; I worked for explanations all my life; situation-evaluation was my strength. That's why I was paid the big bucks, because I was extremely good at it. So feeling the way I felt and how I reacted when I saw Irene the first time had since been a mystery to me – but not a bad one, not at all. And I'll soon see her again…" George paused for a moment: "The rest of the story you know, I guess." Jack looked at his father and shook his head slowly. Even now he was not willing to tell him what he had worked with for the U.S. Government since he arrived in America. All Jack knew was that his father had an office in the Pentagon as well as somewhere else. Jack had never been to either of his offices and though he had asked a few times through the years, his father had always been very protective about what, when, where and why. But one thing Jack knew, his father had never brought work home. He was always there for Jack and in that respect, for Jack and himself. The traveling had been extensive, but then again when his father was home, it had been all about Jack. Luckily Colleen and Charles had also been there and had done a bang-up job in the process. That extra set of parents, had worked out very well. But Jack decided to ask one more time.

"So what did you do with all the time you worked for the government?" George looked at Jack with tired eyes. It wasn't just his eyes, but his whole body that seemed exhausted.

"Jack, I cannot reveal a single minute of what I worked with, what I did, how I did it, my responsibilities and the lot. I signed that guarantee of trust with my honor and in my blood. That is a promise I will never break."

"Not even a hint?"

"The only hint I can give you is, that my department made life more secure in the United States of America and in many other friendly nations. That's about it."

"Was your life ever in danger?" This time a tired George had to laugh; the laughter petered out to a giggle and then a smile.

"All the time, Son; all the time." He looked contemplating and sadness showed on his face.

"Was I ever in any danger?" George took a while answering. "I implemented and secured the safety of your mother until her death. I received several death-threats against myself and your mother. When you were born it was against me and then threats that harm could be applied to my son in way of kidnapping or death. But the people I worked with were exceptional. They would never have anybody hurt anything of mine, my own life included – and they did a terrific job." George frowned: "I even had some of those friends of mine look out for Victoria. Unfortunately William became a victim as an innocent bystander, and for that I'm eternally saddened by and utmost sorry." Jack caressed his father's hand.

"You did what you could. We can't be blamed for any misfortune as long as we do our best." George shrugged.

"Obviously it wasn't good enough."

"I'm sure Victoria feels otherwise."

"I hope so" He paused. "Son, I need to nap a bit. I don't really feel too well at the moment." Jack picked up the blanket and pillows from another seat and tucked his tired father in. George was soon sleeping deeply; his breaths had started out a bit inconsistent, but soon settled in a more fluent rhythm.

The plane was humming along and it would be another few hours before they arrived at Dulles. Jack asked for another gin and tonic. His father's life had been amazing and he felt an urge to visit Russia and the places his father had told him about, where he had lived, worked and where his parent, Jack's grandparents were laid to rest in Kazan. He quietly promised his father that he would do precisely that.

Then his thoughts turned inward again. He had a lot of work to do, and first and foremost he had to come clean with himself, seek professional help as Molly had suggested and fess up to his children, grandchildren and friends, business and otherwise. He had to find a solution to his problem, one that he could implement with the goal of success. He knew he was not allowed to fail this time around; failing was not an option anymore, honesty was the only road for him to travel, now or forever hold your peace.

Then there was that whole Molly thing. He would hate to have lost her, hate to have missed the opportunity to get her back for all to reunite. She had been such a spark in everybody's life as a girl and he could see from the time they had spent together lately, that her eagerness and her energy for a good life had not diminished, it had only increased. Okay, so the whole vomit incident wasn't something to write home about, but it had at least been Molly and in a sense that was a good thing – all considered. But only time would tell, however much a cliché that was.
After an hour of napping, George moved a bit. He turned and smiled.
"Hello there, dear boy."
"Hi Dad. Got a bit of good rest?"
"Yeah, a bit; thanks." Jack held the water for his father to drink as his hands were still under the blanket. "That was good; still on the gin and tonics?"
"Yup; want some?"
"Trying to cut down." He sat up in the seat very gently and looked out the window. The sky was majestic in its colors and the clouds far down reflected the sun's last rays. "We'll be home soon, huh?"
"In a few hours..."
"Good; as usual I can't wait for my own bed. The fact of getting home to you and my bed; yeah that was pretty much all I was thinking about when I traveled, couldn't wait to get home." He kept looking out the small window as he talked. "I liked traveling and where it brought me, but I loved heading home, home to Irene, and later home to you..."
"... and your bed..."
"Yeah, and in that order..."
"I appreciate that, Dad." Jack giggled. Even as an adult he always looked forward to see his father again, but especially when he lived at home or stayed with Colleen and Charles. They always made sure Jack was home when his father arrived.
"So Jack, please promise me to work hard on getting your life in order, okay?"
"I promise and it's my last chance; I know that."

"Knowing the problem is half the solution; just stick to it and you'll get it done."

"I promise."

"And that thing about Molly, Jack: fix it, okay? Promise me that you'll fix it."

"I've promised you twice already."

"Just want to make sure." George felt he had gotten things in order with Jack. It had actually felt good to finally talk about Russia. He thought his son should know at least where his roots were. He really wanted to take Jack on a trip to Kazan and Moscow, but the few times he had brought it up with Hamilton and the department, he had been advised against it – security reasons. Even though the Russians had dropped communism, Hamilton loved his friend too much to send him into situations they could not fully control. He didn't think that the *new* Russians would allow George & Son travel around in their lands, followed by a slew of CIA and other operative agencies fully loaded and ready for action to protect one of their finest; especially when he had been one of *their* agents a few years back. Maybe they would forgive, but Hamilton wasn't sure about the *forget* part; so they never went. Still looking out the window, George mumbled a few words; Jack looked up.

"What was that again?" George turned and looked at his son.

"I said that I have had a terrific life; I have been extremely lucky, Jack. I have been extremely lucky and privileged to be your father."

"Which I assume you still are," Jack said with a smirk.

"You are a good person and you will find the way back – because you promised me - isn't that true?" Jack had to smile.

"That is very true."

"And I have always loved you Jack, no matter what."

"I know that as well and I have always loved you."

"I know you have – and I have always known that. We are good pals, aren't we?" Jack laughed.

"The very best, Pop; the very best."

George had felt some vague muscle-pulls in his chest; at least that was what he thought it was. A sharp pain was running just below his heart and down his chest; he didn't mention it to Jack as he had experienced it before - but now it was back in force.

"Could you get me some water, please?"

"Coming up;" this time Jack got out of the seat and returned moments later with a big glass of cold water. George looked as he was asleep, so Jack gently woke him up.

"Here's your water, Dad."

"Thanks," and George took some careful sips and handed the glass back to Jack.

"I think I'll take another nap," and his head settled back on the pillows. Jack adjusted the seat to a more horizontal position and soon his father was resting comfortably. Jack looked at his watch; a bit longer and they'd be home again.

Liz had been all ears during Molly's telling of her visit to Saint Paul-de-Vence. She expressed her utter sadness concerning George's condition. She had deflated as she talked about his life, their relationship from when she had been six and all the way through her teens. She talked about his kindness towards her and the respect and love she had always felt from him. She was distraught that she had reconnected with him at a moment when he didn't have much time left on earth. She felt guilty for Sara's untimely death and now she felt some unsubstantiated guilt for George's demise as well.

"Maybe I'm simply not good for that family!" She more so questioned herself. Liz had smiled to cheer her up.

"Silly person; that has no merit what-so-ever, and you know that." Molly nodded.

"I guess I do," and then she talked about Jack. Liz quickly detected frustration in her voice. She had sipped a little more wine and sat up a bit straighter. "You know, it's so bloody impossible that this otherwise strong man, this man who used to be the beacon for his family, wife and children, totally fell apart after Sara's death. Of course I understand your *basic* grief and a period of mourning, but ten years doesn't make any sense at all."

"We all react differently to death and dying and we have no idea how we are going to react to it. When we tell people who are mourning that we know how they feel, we really don't have a clue."

"I know, but ten bloody years, for crying out loud – that's *sick* in my book of references. I mean, you have a mentally healthy individual, balanced and strong, fair and logical and very funny as well, I might add, who decides to go bunkers over an extended period of time – to me that does not make any sense of all; to me it shows weakness and no backbone." Liz looked at Molly with a pause.

"And you are frustrated because you don't want to feel that way about Jack?"

"Of course I'm frustrated. Wouldn't you be?" Liz looked a bit perplexed.

"What's the core of your frustration?" Molly looked puzzled.

"What do you mean *core*? What I just told you." Her voice was a bit defensive, Liz thought.

"I don't think you told me the full reason, Molly. So why don't you tell me about the real reason, huh?" Molly felt like snapping back at Liz, but refrained from doing so.

"I'm not sure I fully get your drift here."

"Okay, let me see if I can express this in a somewhat diplomatic way: Are you in love with Jack?" Molly reacted shocked and irritated.

"What is it with you people? *NO* I am *NOT* in love with Jack and I really don't understand where the hell you guys are getting that from."

"So I'm not the only one who's noticed, huh?"

"What do you mean?"

"Didn't George kind of mention something similar?"

"Yeah, but what does *he* know?" Molly was a bit uneasy. "I mean I've been totally in Jack's face; I have torn apart whatever he had left of interior hope with respect to reconnecting with the real world; to get back to normal. I told him he was pathetic and that he wasted his as well my time with his stupid behavior and I finished my tirade by telling him that he was a bloody liar. Now you tell me how that sounds like I'm *in love* with the man." Molly stood up and went out to the railing between the deck and the beach. She spoke more so to herself again: "Yeah, you tell me…" Liz got up as well, stood next to Molly and put her arm around her waist. "… And he's a million years older than me, for crying out loud." Liz was giggling.

"That *is* a big difference, really; a million years! Now who would have guessed?" Molly had to smile.

"Yeah, who would?" The two women embraced as the good friends they were. Nothing had ever come between them the many years they had worked together and they both felt that nothing ever would. Their friendship had soon taken over from their working relationship and it had been as natural as anything.

"It's just the way you defend him, Molly; that's what gives you away." Molly pushed Liz out of the embrace.

"Now wait a minute you little twerp; how the hell can you say that?"

"Well, that's what I hear. Sure you're frustrated with Jack and all, but it sounds more like a disappointed bitterness and disappointed because you want to have Jack be his old normal self so you can build a relationship from that; not wasting time digging him out of a deep hole first."

"You're insane, my little misguided psychiatrist. There are no thoughts like that. Liz, you know me, I'm probably the most rational person you have ever met in your young life, right?"

"Guilty as charged."

"So try *rational* for once by putting two and two together and what do you get?"

"That you love Jack?" Now Molly had to laugh.

"You are terrifyingly impossible; but I wouldn't have you any other way."

They finished the rest of the white wine and went to bed. Liz often stayed over and had turned one of the guestrooms into her home away from home. Molly always felt comfortable with somebody else in the house; especially Liz. At times they would chat and laugh and then chat again some more in Molly's huge bed and then they would fall asleep. They would wake up the next morning and quickly continue the chatting and laughing, just like two silly girls; and the closest of friends.

Molly was alone in her bed. It had been a long and complicated day, but the evening with Liz had been precisely what the doctor would have ordered; rclaxing and cieansing. She loved Liz; she absolutely adored her. She respected her opinions and her common sense in business as well as in their friendship. Her logical mind was fiercely calculating and worked in an abnormal speed. Molly considered herself intelligent with a superb mind and a big nose for business; the continuing success The West Foundation enjoyed, certainly proved that point. But she always had to be on her toes working with Liz as well as vice versa. A relationship made in heaven, actually.

But how could brainy Liz be so wrong in her assumption that Molly could be the slightest romantically interested in Jack? It was the silliest notion ever. Sure he was, and emphasizing *was* a great guy and a good person, but not now? He was like a wet dishrag and seemingly not reparable. Of course there was also the age difference – and that would always be there.

Just before Molly slipped into a fast sleep from total exhaustion, her slight tears were from the image of George sitting in the chair in Bernadette's living room. He had looked frail; he had sounded even frailer. She knew he was dying and she didn't like that at all; she felt helpless as she wanted to do anything to negate his destiny as she knew he loved to live. Just before she reached deep sleep, she could clearly hear George's voice ringing in her ears: *Promise me to help Jack, please; promise me that*. Liz was soon at Molly's bedside. She caressed her hair and wiped the tears and then she kissed her goodnight. The door between the two rooms was open so she would be able to hear if Molly needed help during the night. *Promise me to help Jack, please; promise me that,* the voice kept churning.

Jack had never been able to sleep on planes; oddly enough he had no problem falling asleep on trains. For him the option of flying or taking the train between Washington D.C. and New York was easy. After a long day or days in New York, getting on that four hour train ride to D.C. was the same as getting four hours of solid Z's. Interesting enough, he would even get on the train in Washington early morning after a good night's sleep, be heading for New York and a minute or so after departure, he was fast asleep again. But plane rides had never been an extension of his bed. He turned and looked at his father and smiled. Of all the traveling he had done with him, there had never been a problem for good old George to turn off the light, tip the seat back and head for the Z's.

The time in Saint Paul-de-Vence had been lovely – for the most. The basic theme of his father's reason to invite his son along was sadly morbid in a not very charming way. They had leisure traveled together through the years, so the request from his father for Jack to accompany him didn't surprise him that much. Though his father had given up on his son the last four or five years, it still didn't ring any bells with him, other than it was going to be a grand time in the South of France. But now he knew the score, the reason why they traveled together this time; this last time. Jack had switched to plain tonic and his mind kept wandering.

As George settled in for yet another nap, his mind was traveling to many parts and corners of his life. Though he was dazed and not as coherent as he would have liked to be, blaming the medication, he did see many images of a life well lived. He remembered with a smile when he was lying next to Irene, both of them with glowing faces; he often said that if he died that very moment, he could only look back and say that he had lived life to the fullest. Irene would turn towards him and declare that it was far from over; he always agreed.

The death of Irene after the birth of Jack had been so ironic in a terrifying way. It didn't feel ironic at the time, but looking back, his life with Irene had taken a turn so dramatic, that he was not able to function for the longest time. Hamilton had been his true friend, not just his boss, but the truest friend one could find. *Take all the time off you need* he offered George. But George couldn't do that, so he concentrated on work and on his new child; his and Irene's son.

It had taken years regaining balance and zest for life. It had also been years of confusion, the pain of not having Irene around and the feeling that he was failing as a father as well as failing at work. But he did a grand job bringing up a great kid and Hamilton's constant acknowledgements of George's results at work told a story of success, not failure. George found that he was trying to punish himself for living when Irene couldn't. He never thought it to be fair on any level of fairness. He never took chances with his son, but at work he started to take on missions with a determination and irrational attitude that other agents saw as a form of determined death wish. They thought that George would be gratified and substantiated, if he died in the line of duty. It would be the ultimate excuse for dying, one he didn't have to explain to his child and his family; and he would finally be with Irene again.

George knew what Jack had gone through and was still going through. He had been there, he had suffered no matter how much self-inflicted punishment that it was. So his frustrated aggression towards Jack was because he knew and he didn't want Jack to suffer anymore. George never felt that he could advice his son to recovery as he himself had struggled for years to find his own wheels again. He was not the one to give advice – the blind leading the blind. When Jack had declared his rebirth, George knew at once that he was lying, but he didn't address that issue at the time. He was naively hoping that Jack would get on track and off lying. But it had not happened. He was finally able to tell his son what he really felt and he saw only devastation in Jack's eyes. Would it have been possible that Jack was swimming in the sea of denial? Could he really be that ignorant? And then his thoughts turned to his own experiences and the flow of advice dried up immediately.

The time in the South of France had been wonderful and on top of it all, Molly had showed up. It had been absolutely thrilling to see her again. And what a beautiful woman she had turned out to be. Just thinking about her again was exhilarating for George. As he smiled to himself, caused by other pleasant thoughts, he acknowledged yet again that he had lived a full and satisfying life. He did not like the fact that it was cut a bit short; he didn't like that at all. Sure he was up there in age, but his zest for living was extremely far away from taking that final step. And then his mind skipped a few moments, as the pain in his chest increased. By trying hard to ignore it, he hadn't felt much of it the last hour or so. But now it was back and more painful than he had ever felt any pain before. It was a fist-tightening and increasing pain, lingering for short moments on one level and then it came back with greater intensity on another. Compared with the pain he had experienced the few times he had taken a bullet to his body, this was excruciatingly real pain; the bullets had been nothing. He felt his mind skipping a few thoughts again; drowsiness started hovering around inside him. *Am I dying*? He asked himself, his mind surrounded by dense fog. *Is that what I'm doing?* He wanted to reach for his son, wanted to tell him that it was okay; he wanted to hold his hand to comfort him. But he found that he couldn't move, couldn't speak, and couldn't reach out that very last time. His mind was still functioning somewhat, but only enough to make him aware what was happening to him; nothing else worked. So in his mind he turned towards his son, caressed his hand and looked into his eyes. From there he looked deep into his heart and deep into his soul. *I love you, Jack; I love you so very much,* he whispered again and again. That was his last moment of clarity. He felt something he had never felt before and would never feel again; it was the sensation in his heart as his soul flowed into his child's body. It was a dizzying and surreal experience, as he felt his body deflate and his lungs slowly collapse; his being was finding tranquility. The pumping of his big and warm heart ebbed out beat by slower beat – and then it gracefully stopped. Silence and darkness enclosed on George Winston Miller; he was finally resting in the arms of his Irene.

The scream was loud and piercing. She had stayed with Molly the last few days and was by Molly's side in seconds. She sat rigidly on her bed covered in sweat. Her eyes were wild and her hands could not stay still.
"He died," she screamed again. "Oh my God, he died."
"Who died?"
"George died – on the plane."
"What do you mean? It was just a nightmare, sweetie." Liz was on the bed holding her frightened friend.
"No it was too real to be a nightmare. Oh my God, I should have been there; I should have been there with George." Her shoulders shook from her accelerated breathing and whimpering cries. It took a long time for Liz to calm her down. She stayed in the bed with her and called George's home in Washington D.C.; no answer other than the recorded announcement. Then she dialed Jack's home number as well as his mobile – no answer on either. Those were the only numbers on the note Molly had given her the night before to enter in her address book. She kept holding on to Molly who was now sleeping without getting any rest.

Jack was in deep thoughts and suddenly realized that his father had slept longer than his normal naps. He noticed that his hand had fallen down in the crack between the two seats, hanging there in an obvious uncomfortable way. Jack gently pulled his father's hand up and placed it under the blanket on his chest. It was then he realized that his father's hand was uncommonly cold. First he reasoned that it had been hanging on the side from under the blanket for God knows how long, but then he froze as he felt an urge to check the other hand. He gently reached under the blanket and soon found that hand was cold as well; Jack realized what had happened. In a sudden move he turned his whole body to face his father; he quickly grabbed his left wrist searching for a pulse. There was none. He tried the other wrist with the same result. He gently shook his father while peacefully calling his name.

"George, wake up." No reaction: "Dad, please wake up." Still nothing. Jack leaned over and put his ear close to his father's mouth. He thought he felt a breath, but realized that his right hand was leaning on his father's chest – maybe that caused it. He tried again and again, but now he knew that his father had died – right there next to him. As reality sunk in, Jack convulsed into deep sobs as he held on to his father's hands.

"Oh my God, my dear father." He had to bend over to be able to breathe and the convulsions grew bigger. "My dearest, dearest father," he kept saying again and again, holding and kissing his father's lifeless hand again and again. The next moment one of the flight attendants was in front of Jack.

"Is everything okay, Sir?" Now she could see Jack's face and realized that nothing was okay at all. She quickly checked George's pulse and found that none existed. She bent down facing Jack with a hand on his shoulder and told him that she would be right back. A few moments later the captain was communicating with Jack as the flight attendant was using a stethoscope on his father. In quick order and following airline protocol in these situations, they tried resuscitating George, but finally had to stop as nothing helped.

"I'm so sorry, Sir; I am really so sorry," he touched Jack's hands as comfort; he paused, and looked slightly uncomfortable and continued softly. "I'm sorry that I have to ask you, but your father is George Winston Miller, right?" Jack nodded. "Would it be possible for you to find his government ID card?" Jack thought it a strange question. "I'm sorry, but it's a request I have to follow; it's a request from his former employer – I hope you understand." Jack knew where his father kept his wallet and quickly found the ID card. He had never seen it before.

"Is this what you are looking for?"

"I'll bring it back in a moment." As the captain left, two flight attendants had tended to Jack and to his father. They had pulled a larger blanket over George's head, which appeared utterly surreal to Jack. There weren't many passengers in the First Class cabin and the few present were asked to move to the seats in the front. Partitions were quickly in place which gave Jack and George full privacy. The Captain returned and gave the card back to Jack as he sat down.

"I have notified the authorities in Dulles and they got back to me immediately confirming that everything will be ready when we land. I understand your father had some friends high up in government, and they informed me that all will be in place and everything will be taken care of." Jack nodded *thanks,* but had no idea what he was talking about. *Friends high up – government*? No information at all.

The moment the plane reached the gate, a man in a dark suit, about Jack's age and two other gentlemen entered the cabin. The fellow travelers were politely ushered off the plane. The man in the dark suit came towards him with an outstretched hand; Jack grabbed it.

"Jack Miller?" Jack nodded a yes. "My name is Brandon Hamilton; my deepest condolences. I'm a friend, sorry, I was a friend of your father." Jack looked puzzled and Brandon picked it up right away with a small smile: "… and my father and your father were very close friends for many years, starting back in 1943." Jack got the connection.

"I met him a few times; John Hamilton. He was a very nice man; my father loved him as a brother." Brandon smiled at Jack's comment.

"He is still a nice man, but very retired. He's older than your father and doesn't go dancing anymore. You should go visit him one of these days; he would enjoy that." Suddenly Brandon got back on track. "I'm very sorry about your father, Jack. He was a trooper and highly respected; the very best in the business." He gestured to the two gentlemen, who were waiting a few rows down. "With your permission we want to take care of all the details. We have many people available who would find it an honor if you let them help out." He paused. "The second the sad news arrived at headquarters, everybody called in to help."

"I don't know what to say..." Jack was still confused. Brandon had gently guided Jack away from his father and the gurney that was brought on board. The two gentlemen were carefully placing his father's body on the gurney and covered him with white sheets.

"Just say *yes* and we'll take it from here. We have transportation by the gate. It will get your father and you to the hospital where they will fill out the pertinent documents and forms. We'll then take him to our morgue and prepare him for the funeral. If you allow us to, we would very much like to celebrate your father with a funeral reception."

"Okay, if you feel this is all something my father would have wanted. He never got around talking about these matters; not even after he received the last prognosis." Brandon nodded.

"We'll do what we feel your father wanted; I promise." Brandon had made a slight hand signal to the two gentlemen and they proceeded to carry the body of George Winston Miller out of the plane.

It had been a hectic, emotional and confusing day for Jack. When Brandon said he would take care of everything that was precisely what he did. Luggage had been retrieved, passports checked and hurried through on the tarmac before they took off for the hospital. At the morgue Jack finally found strength to call his children, Nora and Karen as well as Victoria. He had been guided into an office where there was solemn peace away from the stormy action. Brandon sent cars and drivers to everybody and within two hours all were gathered in the main reception area. They were soon embracing each other with tears of crying. The loss of the family patriarch was devastating.

Nicole and Frank immediately hooked up with Jack and didn't leave his side. They held on to him for dear life and were adamant about comforting their grandfather as much as they possibly could. Brandon and his people were busy; everything was handled with quiet and respectful efficiency. John Hamilton had called Jack to extent his condolences. He made Jack promise to visit him real soon; he had some stories about his father he wanted to share with him; Jack agreed.

"George was one of a kind, one of those people who come by every hundred years. I know he hasn't told you much about what he did for this country and I think you must know at least some of the things he bravely executed through the years. He was a patriot to the fullest, and I want you to know that, okay?" Jack thanked Mr. Hamilton and looked forward to seeing him.

After a few hours, everybody had left and Brandon was driving Jack home. Nicole and Frank came along and had decided that their grandfather shouldn't be alone tonight. Caroline was in deep sorrow and had so far been impossible to console. Nicole also stayed close to her in the car, holding her hands.

"Can I ask you somewhat of a personal question, kind of?" Brandon asked; Jack nodded.

"Of course."

"Did your father ever talk about the work he was doing?" Jack smiled a little.

"Not a single word other than *I'm off to work* and the more popular one *honey I'm home*." Brandon had to laugh as that had also been the routine with his father. "What?" Jack asked. "Sounds familiar?" Brandon turned his head and smiled at him.

"Very much so;" now they both giggled. "The only way I could find out what my father did was to join the party; so I became an agent as well."

"And agent of what?"

"Wow, you really don't know do you?"

"Not a thing. So are you going to tell me?"

"No-can-do, Jack; I'll leave that to my father and what he doesn't tell you I'm sure I can't tell you either - if you get my drift."

"The secret agent code & handshake deal, I assume."

"Something like that." They both smiled; after a moment Brandon spoke again. "One thing I can tell you, though. Your father was the most decorated agent in the country; but I guess you already know that." Now Jack looked even more confused.

"Decorated? What do you mean? He never told me about any *decorations*." Brandon smiled.

"Just like my father; never talked about it until a few years back. He got a few pieces of hardware himself - but George beat them all, combined."

"Meaning what?"

"He got two Purple Hearts, one Distinguished Service Cross, and was one of very few who received two Medal-of-Honors."

"Wow," was all Jack could say. "I didn't know that." He really thought that he knew his father well, but found that he hadn't known him at all; except in the more important department of parenthood, where he had been a terrific father; and tears pressed forward yet again.

Six days later, George Winston Miller was buried in Arlington National Cemetery with full military honors; only the family was present as requested. Over eight hundred friends and colleagues, politicians and government officials, foreign dignitaries and ambassadors, as well as a short visit by the President of the United States of America, attended the memorial reception which had followed the funeral.

Molly had finally reached Jack and they had stayed in contact by mobile since. She wanted to know how things were going, how he was doing; all in a very cordial manner. She had wanted to come to the funeral, but felt it was neither the time nor the place to reconnect with everybody. He fully understood and agreed. They would wait for a more appropriate time; but Jack doubted that it would ever happen.

In the following months things went back to whatever normal was normal. Brandon Hamilton had been a caring and compassionate support for Jack. The realization that his father was no longer around took weeks to emotionally settle; but then mourning and grief showed up in force. To Jack's surprise it was the sadness that his father didn't live anymore that was dominating; not his own loss – nothing like his longtime grieving loss of Sara; Sara who *had left him*, he thought with embarrassment. Everybody had been right, and he had been so very wrong.

He enjoyed Brandon's friendship and had also spent some time with John Hamilton. He told stories about his father that were exciting and fascinating, but elegantly negated anything that was top secret and clearly related to national security. But what his father had done according to Mr. Hamilton was so opposite of the person Jack had known: the loving, gentle father and friend.

"And remember where he came from, you know, deep inside the Soviet Union." Mr. Hamilton smiled.

"Yeah, another part of his life he never told me that much about." Mr. Hamilton smiled.

"You know, it was hard for him to leave, no matter how much he disliked the communist system. He was Russian at heart and that never diminished. There were certain situations, you know work wise that he refrained from doing – some of the things that had to do with the Soviet Union, except document analysis; that he was always willing to do – one of the major reasons we wanted him to come over here in the first place. And he was damn good at it; the best I ever worked with."

"What was the major reason you approached him?"

"Young, smart, fearless and utterly intelligent."

"No, I mean work wise; what was the major reason?" Mr. Hamilton smiled.

"Sorry Jack, I cannot give you any information about that. But he never disappointed us, quite the opposite." At least the hours Jack spent with Mr. Hamilton had given him somewhat of a look at the other side of his father and for that he was grateful. Mr. Hamilton had added: "Some time back George told me that he had always wanted to take you to Russia to show you where he came from. But due to circumstances of diplomatic rules and assumptions, we didn't feel it would have been safe; didn't want him to take the chance, you know, of possibly being detained."

"Even after all these years?"
"Some people hold grudges for a very long time," Mr. Hamilton smiled. "But Jack, he really wanted you to see Russia, visit Kazan and Moscow. We know where your grandparents are buried, just in case you are going." Jack had smiled at this sweet old man. It was impossible to imagine the business he had been in, sitting there in his comfortable chair looking like the ultimate grandfather – kind, gentle and peaceful; very much like George.

Jack worked hard concerning crawling back to a balanced life. His dreams about Sara were now further and far between. At a dinner with everybody gathered, he had opened up and explained himself about his lying, about how he had lied to himself in his naïve assumption that it would all automatically adjust and make him better. But it had all been an act of futility and, yet again, was betraying the people he loved – for that he despised himself. After the deepest apologies he also told his family and friends that even though he had *tried* before, he had never really tried. It was as if he wanted to be miserable, wanted to grieve and through that get attention in the process. The time with his father in Saint Paul-de-Vence had been refreshing and sobering. George held nothing back and for Jack it had been devastatingly eye-opening. He announced that for him to move forward, he had been seeing a psychiatrist twice weekly for the last six weeks. Everybody in the dining room applauded and approved. They had been waiting for this for such a long time.
"Thanks; I know I should have done this many years ago," a small smirk showed up on his face: "It's somewhat ironic though – the psychiatrist, she looks so much like Sara." The room went eerily silent. He smirked: "*What*? - In a good way, I promise you," he smiled and the room finally exhaled. "Really; we talked about it the moment I sat down with her, and the way she dissected it, we agreed that we could make it a good thing; would make reality more prevalent, make me work harder on moving forward. And no, I have never called her Sara." Now the room was giggling. "But I did ask her out for a date;" now the room went eerily silent again. "Only kidding;" and the room exhaled one last time.

"What's with Victoria?" Brandon asked.

"Meaning what?"

"You know, is she available?"

"Available for what?"

"Come on Jack, you know what?"

"I've been out of circulation for some time as you know, so I'm not sure I know what *what* is anymore."

"You are not going to make this easy for your new pal, are you?" Jack smiled.

"New pal? I like that. Anyhow, if you are asking if she is dating anybody, is attached and/or committed in any relationships, I will have to say that I don't think so."

"That was the gist of my question."

"But am I going to ask her if she would be interested to get to know you? That answer is: *not in a million years*. You are a man of the world; you speak the language fairly fluent and you know words with more than six letters in a row, some which you can actually pronounce. So based on that, I'll say go for it and good luck, young lad." Brandon laughed.

"Were you always this cocky and sarcastic?"

"Yes and charmingly so, dear friend."

"So that's a sure sign of recovery?"

"One would hope so – and here is Victoria's mobile number. I'm sure she will not be against you calling her. Just tell her that I gave you the number, okay?"

"Thanks," Brandon paused for a moment: "Is there anything I should know about Victoria?" Jack laughed.

"A lot, but that must come from Victoria, not from me."

Brandon, who lost his wife many years ago – to another man, had since neither been dating nor tried to get into other relationships. He had simply buried himself in work to make up for this void in his life – the romantic bit, that is. Sure he had been out here and there with women pushed upon him by well-meaning friends, but no bites. Even his ex-wife had submitted prospects. No, he wasn't pining away for his ex to return, far from; it was his awkwardness in the romantic *dating* department that made it easy for him to negate confrontations with the opposite sex. Jack had laughed by the explanation, as he mentioned that Brandon was dealing with a heck of a lot more dangerous situations at work.

"Yeah, even driving to the office in the morning is more dangerous," he laughed out loud.

He finally gathered enough courage and called Victoria. They had done the traditional dinner at Nonna's. Romano Rossi had been beside himself seeing lovely Victoria with a handsome and charming man. He had always been in love with her, but due to circumstances under his control, Romano was also a happily married man; it was only innocent fantasies of Victoria being his daughter. Seeing her with this man had been wonderful. He seemed to be able to make Victoria laugh and though he had looked very nervous in the beginning, three hours later, he was relaxed and very much alive. Jack had called earlier to get a report about how things were going with Victoria and Brandon. Romano had laughed and told him *great*.

"But mio amico, I do believe it is your turn to have dinner with someone lovely, somebody to love – amore, you know."

"That sounds like me eating alone." Romano giggled.

"Not the same, my friend, not the same at all." But in reality, time had come for Jack to spread his wings, find somebody to spend time with and enjoy. He felt he was getting ready. Anna Kirch, his Sara look-alike psychiatrist, underlined that no matter how *not* ready he was, he needed to get his butt out there and the sooner the better. Procrastination was no longer the convenient, however pathetic, option for him.

Anna Kirch had actually been close to suggesting a couple of her single and divorced girlfriends as suitable candidates; but Anna and Jack agreed that it would be a really weird situation if it didn't work out and even more weird if it did. She would feel responsible from beginning to end and she also saw it as somewhat unprofessional.

"So you and I trying it out, you know, that date thing, would therefore also be out of the question?" Anna had laughed.

"Not only professionally; also impossible on the personal level."

"Meaning what?"

"Jack, you are still so screwed up and you carry a lot of baggage we need to get rid of; so, on that *personal* level you are far too complicated for me. And professionally it's a huge *no-no*."

"Thanks for the vote of confidence Dear Doctor." Anna smiled as she looked at Jack's pretend pouting face. She liked him fine, but she was honest and fair; besides he wasn't really her type, at least not what she imagined he would end up like; but she liked him just fine in spite of that.

"Dad!" Caroline was eating cereal at the table in front of him.
"Yes?"
"I know a couple of women I want you to meet." Jack's head snapped up. It was just a few days ago he had the same conversation with Anna Kirch.
"Did you talk with Anna?"
"Anna who?"
"My shrink lady."
"Noooo; why?"
"She suggested the same thing."
"Well I guess we all think it's time."
"All who? Time for what?"
"You know: *everybody*."
"Oh, I see; *everybody* who? Should I consider this a conspiracy, a confused emotional support group, a plot to get me laid or an issue of *you-have-nothing-else-to-do*?" Caroline paused; then she pretty much smiled.
"Just about all of the above." Jack grabbed her free hand.
"But the *getting laid* part is not the essential one?"
"Dad, be serious and *no* it's not and don't use that term, please. But you need to go out and meet people, you know *women* people, built relationships, friendships…"
"… and then get, you know…?"
"Dad, stop it – not funny when I'm trying to be serious."
"I'm sorry sweetheart; now let's be serious. So who's unsuspecting victim number one?" This time Caroline ignored the sarcasm. She pulled out a sheet from a legal pad; Jack was impressed. "So we actually have a list – how impressive is that? By the way, do we know the other conspirators?"
"Everybody except Victoria."
"Wow, that's impressive – and why not Aunt Vicky?"
"She still has the hots for you. She wouldn't be able to come up with rational suggestions – other than offering herself, I guess"

"I thought I was the only one who knew."

"It was Nicole and Frank who told us."

"I'll be darn; my own grandchildren: the dating experts." Caroline laughed.

"But is it true?" She asked with big eyes.

"I'm sorry to say, I do believe it is; that Vicky thing."

"Do you have any interest in her?"

"Oh, I love her dearly, but not *that* way, if you know what I mean."

"Well, she's not on the list, so there. But we have a really fun and intelligent prospect; her name is Maria Fletcher. She's divorced, about your age, she likes fitness and looks like it too; one adult child, two grandchildren, own home and is an attorney. She likes walks…"

"… on the beach, reading books in front of the fireplace, long drooling conversations about life, blah, blah, blah…"

"Dad listen," Caroline said without laughing. "We are trying to help."

"Sorry my little matchmaker, if you are trying to help, I'll try to behave." Then Jack paused: "I'll even do better than that, let me swing Maria Fletcher by Nonna's, that way we can get going with the selection process. What's her number, my little social administrator?" While rolling her eyes Caroline gave the yellow sheet to Jack as he got up to get the phone. Sitting back down he dialed Maria Fletcher's number; Caroline watched with positive hopes for her father's first attempt of setting up a date; he looked at his daughter and winked.

"Maria Fletcher?" He listened for a second: "Yeah hi, I'm Jack Miller. My utterly confused daughter Caroline has asked me to call you to see if we can get together for some unconditional and wild sex, you know to see if we are fiercely compatible in bed or wherever you want to do it." He paused for a moment while Caroline was busy trying to understand what she was hearing – she did, and her face showed utmost horror. "My truly misguided daughter also told me you have a great set of melons and legs that never end and you are more than willing to use that sex-machine shaped body of yours for anything naughty, and certainly nothing nice. Is that true?" Jack paused again; now Caroline was hiding her face in her hands. "Oh me? I'm pretty much shaped as an Adonis kind of stud-muffin, can stay up all

night, if you know what I mean, and morning breath is not something I'm familiar with." He paused: "Friday at Nonna's sound good. I'll pick you up around six and maybe we can do a quickie trial-run before dinner. Sounds good Toots; see you." Jack put the phone on the table as Caroline pointed an infuriating loaded finger at his face; Jack smiled.
"What do you know; I have a date on Friday. That was easy, so who's next?" All of a sudden Caroline got to her senses and realized she had been had.
"She was not on the phone, was she?" Jack looked puzzled.
"You mean I did all that for nothing? No sweetheart, Maria was not on the phone; but I do have a date with the person who answered - but I didn't get his name…"
"You bastard, you had me going there for a second," she said rather relieved: "Now try one more time and this time get it right, okay?" Jack made a face and picked up the phone. A few minutes later, he had a date with Maria Fletcher - she sounded very nice.

And that was the first of many dates he went on; *practice-dates* as Jack called them. At first it had been awkward and nerve-wracking, but the more he found himself listening instead of talking, the more interesting and fun it was. Karen, Nora and Caroline called him in succession after each date to find out what happened, what he felt about the previous night's prospect and so forth. After several dates the questions became rather direct; to save time it seemed.
"Did you, you know?"
"Me know what?" He would tease back their innate curiosity: "Nothing very sacred anymore, huh?" But they kept calling, especially when it was about somebody they had suggested themselves.

Jack did feel he was on the way forward. Visits with Anna Kirch twice weekly had been a tremendous help. She was brutally honest, very straight forward and constantly called it as she saw it. The 45 minute sessions were purposely scheduled late afternoon. Anna Kirch told Jack it would be better for him to finish his workday and then come to the sessions. But she more so herself wanted the sessions in the latter part of the day. This way they often ended up with time together after the sessions were officially over, shared a glass of wine and each other's company in a more relaxed way. But it wasn't very professional at all, she blushed. Jack liked her beyond the professional help she administered and she seemingly enjoyed his company and attention. She found improvements in his attitude and felt that he was moving forward faster than expected; but she didn't tell him that. She kept calling him on his feeble tries of showing happiness and *I'm cured,* when he was not. She was actually the only one who could read him that well. She also liked to stay after work, as she didn't fancy going home to her husband of 16 years. If Jack thought *he* had problems, it was nothing compared to the problems Anna Kirch had in her marriage; but she never mentioned that to Jack either.

He took all his dates to Nonna's. Romano was in seventh heaven seeing his good friend Jack out on the dating scene. He had pretty much given up on ever seeing that, but here it was. The cooks and waitresses kept a score-board in the kitchen and small bets were constantly being exchanged; the excitement never ceased. For the most Jack would plan dates for Fridays, just in case he would get lucky. By that he meant that the date and he might ooze some kind of common sexual chemistry that would lead to, well, *you know what*; *getting lucky* is another term. For the most Jack enjoyed himself and it seemed that the women he spent time with were enjoyed as well. In most cases they would all want to see him again and again, which was fine with Jack as he needed the practice and did savor their company. But he had yet to experience that *physical* thing, going beyond chat and laughter. He slowly accepted status quo; it was probably never going to happen. He felt the importance of it all was overrated; and he was actually fine with that. One of the sessions with Anna had started with her asking:
"So have you been intimate with anybody yet?" Jack laughed at first, as she had smiled.
"Can I assume that's the professional term?" Anna shook her head.
"It's a serious term, Jack and I think it's utterly important that you consider why it's not happening?"
"It doesn't matter, really," he sheepishly mumbled.

"Don't lie to yourself; you know you are trying to figure out what it is, but you can't put a finger on it, can you?" He thought for a moment.

"Most of these women are intelligent; my biggest turn-on after a sense of humor. Most of them have very pleasing and chauvinistically speaking, well-shaped physical features - rather sexy in some cases. So I'm confused. Sure I haven't had sex with anybody else for so many years…"

"Ten?" Jack looked teasingly annoyed.

"Thanks for bringing up that sad number; very much appreciated." Anna smiled.

"You are welcome. Do you have anxieties about having sex again?" He looked thoughtful.

"Not really; I figure it's just like biking, you know, get in the seat and start pedaling; something you never forget."

"So what's the problem?" He giggled and looked thoughtful.

"What if I have a flat tire?" Now Anna had to laugh.

"I think you'll find that it will not be an issue. You jog; you do a lot of fitness stuff, you don't smoke and you eat fairly healthy. If it's a matter of..." Jack quickly interrupted.

"No, that is not the problem, trust me." She smiled.

"Okay, I trust you. I know a very efficient sex-therapist, actually a personal friend of mine and I'm sure she could guide you along if it's either a mental or a physical issue – or both." Jack shook his head.

"I really appreciate your interest, but Anna, let me do the dating thing a bit more and maybe we can get back to this issue on a need-to basis, okay?" Anna was fine with that, as she had also begun to fantasize about helping Jack solve his *physical* problems herself – after hours, of course. The situation at home was not getting better; why couldn't her husband be a bit more like Jack?

According to Romano and the staff at Nonna's, Debbie Sullivan was Jack's date number 13. That itself should be a true sign of disaster, if superstition ruled. Romano laughed it off; he felt this was going to be a good one. Many of Jack's dates came back, but none of them seemed to be moving to the next level. Romano began to get a bit jittery about it as many dollars were on the line and the score-board was running out of space.

Date number 13 was five years younger than Jack. She had called him at work and Jack never got to ask her how she got his number; that wasn't really the thing to ask anyway. She was well-kept, self-assured and physically in good shape – at least with clothes on, of which she wore without hiding too many of her curvy features and all that with brains to match. All men and most women would turn their heads several times when she passed by, as there was an awareness about her that was intoxicating. Romano was positive she was just going to chew Jack up and spit him out; he didn't feel Jack was even close to be in her league. But body and brains and straight forwardness were the only cards she could put on the table, according to Jack. Her sense of humor was very limited to none and Jack's expert sarcasm and humorous remarks rarely registered with her at all. But she did have something she wanted to share with Jack; she knew that from the second she met him.

They had been at Nonna's a couple of hours and were enjoying philosophical conversation. The coffee and after-dinner drinks were served and it had actually been an interesting evening so far. The way she looked at Jack was dizzying and he couldn't explain what it was. She was a great listener and made Jack talk without interruptions. She'd ask pertinent questions which told him that she was actually hearing what she was listening to. She talked about traveling, the places she'd visited and the out of body experiences (her words) she had had traveling especially in the South of France. They had both talked excitedly about Saint Paul-de-Vence, Nice and Cannes and she smiled as Jack told her about his own time there. She sipped some more brandy, licked her lips and looked at Jack.

"I've had a terrific evening with you; really terrific." He was nervously waiting for the *but;* when it came it proved to be a good one: "I don't know, but would you consider coming home with me so that we can continue the evening?" Jack was somewhat shocked, but what he had gotten to know about her these few hours, it did seem like the most natural thing to do next.

"I would be honored indeed." Without a word they got up, Jack grabbed her jacket and his coat and a taxi was waiting outside, courtesy of Romano. He had very convenient connections, especially for friends like Jack Miller. Seconds later Romano and his staff were all doing high-fives and paying off the winner.

Debbie Sullivan's place was an interior decorators nightmare. No matter where you looked it was balanced in colors and design. On top of that it oozed of personality and individual taste that few would find within their own walls. She excused herself after handing two chilled glasses and a bottle of champagne for Jack to open. Moments later she showed up in a man's pajamas. For a split second Jack saw the image of Molly wearing the same.
"Talking about slipping into something utterly comfy…" She smiled.
"Of all the clothes I have, this is seriously my favorite. It has three promises: one: that I'll be in bed soon; two: that I might end up having some great sex before I go to bed; three: a cozy evening reading in front of the fireplace all by myself. Yes, I actually seriously do that –as well as the walk on the beach." Jack was laughing as Debbie had actually said something humorous – for once.
"Very funny, Debbie." They snuggled up on the huge sofa in front of the fireplace and soon they were exploring each other's bodies. They quickly found that their kissing compatibility was top notch perfect. She was very responsive to Jack's touches and he quickly found that sex *was* just like bicycling; and he didn't have a flat tire.

When Jack was taking a shower the next morning in Debbie's huge marble covered bathroom, he saw Sara in front of him. At first it was a fairly clear image, but as he kept denying her presence, just as Anna Kirch begged him to, Sara evaporated, but only slowly. He felt a sharp pain of guilt in his gut, but as he tried to talk himself out of it, the pain subsided bit by bit, but didn't fully disappear.

The feelings he felt as they said goodbye that morning were confusing. He really liked her as she was deliciously yummy, but unfortunately not very funny. The sex had been wonderful, really, and not because he had not experienced bodily satisfactions with another person for so many years. It was just a good physical fit and he wouldn't mind seeing Debbie again to make sure that it was really that good. As she embraced him in her nakedness, he really wanted to stay, but he also wanted to see what he felt leaving – tough decision as it was, he did leave.

Debbie and Jack did not plan anything after that night together. He was eager to find out what she wanted, what she expected and then he could decide if he was on the same track. He went jogging with Caroline that morning, but not before she grilled him for juicy tidbits from the night before. He finally caved in, and soon after she was covering her ears going *WAH WAH WAH*.
"Okay my snooping daughter; *yes* I did it last night, if you really want to know." Caroline was in shock, but also happy. She felt her father was moving forward, no matter how much she did not want to hear the details.
"Do you like her?"
"I do to a certain extent. She's actually rather yummy, but lacks a sense of humor. But she makes up for that with…" Caroline was now covering her ears again.
"I don't want to hear about it *WAH WAH WAH…*" Jack laughed.
"How old are you again?"
"I can't hear you; I'm not listening." But she had listened and that same afternoon everybody who knew Jack also knew that Jack had, oh well – not exactly those words, but the meaning was clear. And they were all happy for him. But Jack seriously didn't see how important this could be – for anybody else…

Jack and Debbie began seeing each other regularly. Their planning was more so based on spur-of-the-moment efforts like *Want to come over?* Or *Doing anything tonight?* However casual this may sound, that was pretty much their relationship. They liked their intellectual communication, but most of their time together was spent in bed. Some might say that's an empty proposition, but for Debbie and Jack it was convenient; it was actually very fine indeed, for now.

"So how's your sex-life, Jack?" He had been with Debbie several times when Anna asked him.
"Well, in the matter of fact I met a terrific woman, very intelligent and somewhat interesting to spend time with…"
"Somewhat?"

"She's lacking a good sense of humor; but don't get me wrong, she's very exciting."

"In bed?" Jack giggled and blushed.

"Yes, and I really don't want to chat about it, seriously" Anna's face froze a bit; she felt jealousy sneaking up on her, more than she thought it would. "But if you do need to know, the intimacy seemingly drives the relationship so far."

"Well it should…" she mumbled. His head snapped up.

"Meaning what?" Now Anna blushed.

"Nothing - just nothing, other than it was the intimacy you needed to explore to balance with the dating and, you know…" Jack looked directly into Anna's eyes.

"Is there something you need to tell me or am I getting a wrong sense of things here?" Anna looked flustered: "Listen Anna, I am not known as a very good liar and you are not even close to being in the same zip-code of good, so what's up?" So Anna had to confess.

"Remember the sex-therapist I mentioned, you know my good friend?" Jack's mind added it all up.

"You got to be kidding me. This is bloody therapy you have tricked me into? I was wondering where the heck she had gotten my number from, but after I met her I didn't care. And I have been intimate with a professional?" Anna squirmed in her chair.

"Jack, please understand. I really want to help you. I've grown to like you very much, which to some extent is not professional at all. You are a terrific guy, but *you* don't know that yet; but you are. When we are done here, I know you'll go on having a terrific life, happy and fulfilled. You have all the tools and all we have to do is simply sharpen some of them, and trust me, we are getting there." Jack looked at Anna; she looked vulnerable and fragile and not as confident as she looked during their first few sessions. He was wondering what was going on.

"I know, Anna, and I'm okay with what you say. I really trust your judgment and so far I have done everything you've asked me to do. But you have attached a sex-therapeutic friend to me and now I'm confused about what I *should* feel. I like Debbie, but now it turns out that she was a professional courtesy. I feel very bad about that; bad and disappointed." Anna looked as she was going to cry. Jack continued: "And come to think about it, the only reference to her work was *consultant*, not what kind…"

"I'm so sorry. It was a bad call." She paused: "If it is of any comfort, Debbie likes you a lot. She finds you funny, entertaining and a good partner. And please trust me; she never entered this with therapeutic overtones to any extent. I told her about you for the longest time, though nothing clinical of course, and she was the one who took the initiative." She paused: "And I was the one supplying your phone number." They sat in silence for a moment: "Will you forgive me?" Jack looked at his friend, no matter how professional or not their relationship was.

"Of course; but only if Debbie is not conducting experiments and statistics about my overall performance." Anna laughed relieved and happy again.

"She likes you too much to do those things." Jack got out of his chair and pulled Anna out of hers. The embrace was long and warm; she inhaled it all. According to what Debbie had told her, Jack was a warm and considered lover. If the embrace she was in was any indication, she fully believed what Debbie had told her. Jack did not confront Debbie with the Anna Kirch connection – there was never a reason to do so.

"So are you coming?" Molly was gathering the last folders filled with reports and statistics for her trip to New York; Liz looked up.

"I would really love to, you know that; but somebody has to stay back and control the chaos you are leaving us." Molly giggled as she placed the folders in her briefcase.

"There's no chaos here. You are in control as you have always been and I'm just the usual pawn in your game of international chess; I will not be missed."

"Fishing for assurance of importance, aren't we?" Molly laughed.

"As usual I'll miss you, very much so." The car was ready for her with the luggage in the trunk and the driver by the open door. Liz walked with Molly to the front of the building and they soon embraced warmly for the longest time. Molly giggled loudly.

"*What?*" Liz asked. Molly held her in arms length and looked straight into her eyes. She paused for a moment and then smiled.

"Nothing – I just love you lots... really." They kissed cheeks and she was on her way to New York and Washington D.C. Anxiety filled Jack was waiting thousands of miles away.

Victoria was in the shower. As she dried off she looked at her image in the mirror. For a woman her age she *was* rather good looking. Brandon kept telling her she was the sexiest woman he had ever met. Meeting and getting acquainted with him had been a Godsend. He was precisely what the therapist had ordered. Sure she was still thinking about Jack, the impossible mountain she wanted so badly to climb. But she somewhat seriously doubted it would ever happen; Brandon was good, but was he *that* good?

"Dinner is ready." Jack was done with his shower. Caroline was home and had prepared dinner together with Debbie. They were getting along fine, though Caroline kept seeing disturbing images of Debbie having *yummy sex* with her father. *Yummy* was an expression her father had promoted to tease her – and it worked. She found Debbie to be utterly intelligent, though lacking that sense of humor. But when Caroline had talked DNA and MSU, Debbie had many interesting questions, so Caroline was on a rampage to inform and chat. She liked Debbie more and more and thought, in spite of the missing humor bit, that Debbie was a possible match for her father.

"Looks awesome," Jack said as he picked up the glass of wine offered to him by Caroline. He kissed his daughter as well as he kissed Debbie. "Does it taste as good as it looks?"

"We certainly hope so," was Debbie's response.

Debbie had met everybody associated with Jack: all his children, their partners and kids as well as friends and business relations. Jack and Debbie spent most of their spare time together. The overall *judgment* was that she was liked by all and loved by some. Those who knew Jack considered it a good match for him. He had finally found that new life partner – they thought. Jack was not as convinced; but for now, he kept that thought to himself.

It was Saturday morning; Michael and Jasper were waiting in the kitchen for their father to go jogging with them; Caroline came down the stairs in her robe at the same time as Jack. He looked a bit frazzled while folding his mobile. He was not fully sure how to handle this matter, but it had to be handled without everybody ending up hating him or rejecting her. Caroline looked at her father's face and saw concern.

"What's up Pop?" She tried; Jack took a deep breath.

"There *is* actually something *up* and I need to talk with you about it; and now would be a very good time, really.

Michael, Jasper and Caroline sat down around the kitchen table. It was the same table they had occupied thousands of times from the time they were born. Not much had changed around the house except some of the more technological components like computers, Hi-Fi's and flat screen TV's. But the rest had pretty much stayed the same; and this kitchen table had always been the central point for family meetings. Their father looked uncomfortable and was the last one to find his seat – at the west end of the table, as usual. He cleared his throat and had a hard time looking at his children. Jasper broke the silence.

"Okay, so you are pregnant, have to marry Debbie or you won the lottery? Am I close?" It loosened up the air a bit and Jack tried to smile.

"None of the above," he answered and cleared his throat yet again. "I have been in a bit of an uncomfortable situation and uncomfortable because I couldn't tell you about it as the person involved wanted it done this way." He looked up for a second and caught Caroline's facial expression. She sat frozen and wide eyed; he knew immediately that she knew. Her voice was shaking.

"It's about Molly, isn't it?" Both Jasper and Michael's heads snapped towards their sister.

"Molly?" They said in unison. "Where did that come from?" Jack looked at Caroline and quickly realized that she thought more about Molly than she had ever admitted.

"She's right – it's about Molly". Caroline's face was still frozen.

"She's okay, isn't she?" Her voice was now shaking loudly; Jack put his hand on Caroline's and smiled.

"Yes Honey, she is just fine; really fine, actually." Caroline's face lit up and she gasped for air. "She's good, really good." Jack took a deep breath himself and braced for the many questions already hanging in the air.

"I think that when I tell you how all this came together, most of your questions will be answered." He looked around at three open faces. "To make matters easier I'll do it in chronological order; the whole thing makes more sense that way." Michael and Jasper were staring at their father as Caroline moved closer.

"And she's fine, isn't she Dad?" He padded her hand again and nodded.

"Yes, sweetheart, very much so."

So Jack told his children about the sudden disappearance of their good friend Molly. He told his children about how she had always felt an enormous guilt about her parent's death, always felt it had been her fault. She had felt an even more enormous guilt concerning Sara's death as she believed that she could have warned her. She felt guilty about her grandparent's plane crash. She had told them it was important to get to that village that very morning and if they did not feel like going, she would go there herself and bring Liz along and take care of matters. But they had insisted on going and they had died. All these feelings of guilt had accelerated and accumulated over the years and though she externally looked fine and balanced, the guilt kept eating her up on the insides.

He told them about her failed and insane marriage. He told them about Molly's 48 hour visit during a drunken stupor that could have caused her life. He didn't tell them about her financial status after her grandparent's had died. But he did tell them about the chance meeting New York City; the night they spent together talking and the chance run-in on the same flight and the days in the South of France. And now she was on her way to see them in a few days; she wanted to reconnect and she wanted it with all her heart.

"We have communicated by phone and E-mail since Dad's death and she has since been asking me if it would be okay to come home to us; she is tremendously nervous about it, but I can tell you, that she wants very much to reconnect with everybody; especially with the three of you. You are her only *family*, so to speak." There was a moment of silence. Caroline was drying off her moist eyes.

"When is she coming home?" Jack was touched by the tender sound in her voice.

"She is on her way, sweetheart."

"Wow," came from Jasper, "After all these years, and here she comes." His face lit up. "Imagine that, Molly is coming home." Michael had his mobile out and Linda on the line in seconds.

"Molly is finally coming back," was all he said. He smiled at the response and said: "Thanks Linda; yes it is wonderful – love you." Caroline got up from the table, flew up the stairs two steps at a time and was back in the kitchen in a flash. She unfolded her mobile and eagerly looked at her father.

"What's her number?"

Molly was on the phone with Liz for their daily update. It was at the end of the workday in Casablanca and late-morning in New York City. The chat had been productive, but there was an undertone in Liz's voice that did not gel with her normal self. Molly had picked it up from the *hi sweets*, but had filed it for later in the conversation.

"So all is well in America?" Molly smiled.

"Yes, all is swell here," and she paused. "But is all swell in Casa, huh?"

"What do you mean?"

"Liz, remember who you are dealing with, okay?" Now it was Liz' turn to pause; the next sentence stung Molly.

"Sven Nordgren called yesterday," she informed Molly matter-of-factly. The connection went silent for a long moment. "Are you still there?"

"Yeah I heard you. What did he want?"

"He wanted to get in contact with you."

"Why?"

"He didn't say."

"Was that all he said?"

"No. I told him that contacting you or me or the Foundation broke of the restraining order as well as of the divorce settlement. I told him that we would activate immediate prosecution in response to any violation of the agreement. I advised him to refrain from any contact in the future."

"How did he react to that?"

"If you want it word for word: *Just shut up you stupid bitch*. Then he pretty much laughed and told me that he had something *the major bitch* no doubt wanted to pay the utmost attention to."

"And did Mr. Nordgren elaborate on what that possibly is?"

"Not directly; but you know, in the movies it would be something like photos of some sort. You know this asshole, Molly; he'd do stupid stuff like that."

"Yes he would; but you and I know that the insignificant size of his brain have little chance of concocting anything more than slightly irritating, don't we?"

"I agree, but you and I also know that stupid people can do very stupid things." Molly nodded; after a moment of silence, Liz continued: "By the way, if photos *are* involved, would you know of any such that could be used to any length of embarrassment for you?" Molly giggled.

"I doubt it; but of course I wasn't a member of the *sober-club* around the time Mr. Nordgren was here, if you recall. I have no idea if he took photos or had anybody take photos or whatever. But let's not start fretting before we know what to fret about;" now it was Liz' time to giggle.

"Okay sweetie; if by any chance there are some exciting photos of you floating around, could I have a set, please?"

"Of course you can – choice of frames and all, but for a price, of course."

"Meaning what?"

"That's for later." Molly giggled some more. "But anyway, let me know if he communicates back and in that case see what it is he is hoping to achieve." Molly grinned as she already knew the answer to her next question. "You have the call recorded?"

"I do, Boss."

"Good girl. Hey, I'll call Jeremy here in New York so he knows what's going on, and if any more crap from Nordgren, let him know, and Dr. Watson, please keep the recorder on at all times."

"Okay Sherlock, we'll do…"

"Thanks my little sneaky detective person; talk with you tomorrow and call if anything else exciting happens – love you."

Molly folded her mobile and sat back in the armchair. The room service breakfast was still sitting on the table, but she had lost her appetite. *Now what was that jerk up to?* She thought. He had gotten a fair and uncomplicated settlement, meaning she had not prosecuted him for the many forgeries and unauthorized spending of her money, extramarital affairs or for any other reason. Last she heard anything about her ex-husband, was that he had lost his job in Denmark, by some stealth intervention of jilted short-term boyfriend Hugh. The money Mr. Nordgren stole from Hugh ran dry really fast and Mr. Nordgren had dismissed Hugh at that very moment. Since then he found that nobody wanted to employ him as he was considered a huge liability; damaged goods as he was. The few business' that had considered employing him, based on falsified background information, had by anonymous means received communications about Mr. Nordgren's true employment history, laced with juicy hints why his marriage to Miss Molly West had been dissolved. Nobody really knew who supplied this damaging information, though most people involved, other than Mr. Nordgren, certainly had their suspicions. Mr. Nordgren stayed unemployable on a very black list.

Molly slipped out of her robe and was soon trying to enjoy a warm and long shower. Though she was pushing away thoughts of what Sven was up to, they would be lingering in the back of her mind. She rationed that whatever he could bring to the table, she'd be more than able to deal with – swift and efficiently. With that confidence in mind, she got dressed and was soon ready for the day.

Half an hour later the chauffeur stopped in front of the UNICEF building. She had always been impressed with the marble façade, but more so with the diversity of people by nationalities, colors, cultures and languages, milling in and out. He was holding the door as her mobile rang. She looked at her watch and realized she was running late, but when she saw the caller ID, she instantly lost track of everything around her and fell back into the limousine's comfortable seat. This was the call she had been yearning to receive for over ten long years. With already moist eyes she pressed *talk*.

Sven Nordgren was sweating. The hot sun hanging over Mallorca mixed with the humid winds from the Mediterranean Ocean made people sweat like that. But his type of sweating stemmed more so from the photos he was staring at on the monitor in front of him. Lennart, pretty much Sven's last chance of a friend, had been stupid enough to let him into his small and cramped apartment in the middle of Palma, the largest city on this beautiful Spanish island. Lennart was not the smartest bloke on the block, so it had been a piece of cake for Sven to talk himself inside and stay for awhile; initially just two weeks. Well, the *for awhile* two weeks, was already on its fifth; Lennart couldn't see the end of it. Sven had more or less been forced out of Denmark with no friends, loss of connections and no work; so he had sold the few belongings he had and with a few thousand Euros in his pocket he *borrowed* his uncle's car. That car was now collecting dust in a parking lot by the ferry terminal in Valencia, Spain; a long way from Sven's uncle who didn't have a clue. The ferry ride to Palma had been boring, but at least Lennart had been home. He was devastatingly horrified and extremely unhappy to see this ex-friend from high school show up on his doorstep. He thought he had gotten rid of Sven many years ago, but here he was – yet again, asking for another free ride.

Lennart had to admit that the photos on the monitor were awesome. The digital sharpness showed every dirty detail and the colors were superb. But it was the nakedness of the people in the photos that admittedly turned him on, which he desperately tried to hide.
"Where the hell did you get these from?" Sven smirked and took another sip of his rum and Coke.
"That bitch is my ex," he casually pointed. "Pretty good body for a wife, wouldn't you say?" Lennart would say that much indeed. She looked hot, sweaty and either extremely drunk or coked out; her eyes were red and her face slurry.
"What do you want to do with them?" Sven looked at his stupid roommate.
"What do you think I wanna do with them, dummy?" Lennart had no idea. "The bitch is filthy rich; I mean, we are talking millions, Dear Friend." Lennart's mouth fell open.

"Really?"

"Yeah, fucking really." They went through all 22 photos stored in Sven's digital camera. He had forgotten all about them and it was only because Lennart had a computer and some computer smarts, that he even thought of looking at what was on the camera's memory card. At first he had been saddened by what he saw, the opportunities he had missed; but then a second chance reared its ugly, but possibly very profitable head. He knew instantly what to do; just like in the movies, he'd blackmail the shit out of the bitch - piece of cake.

"So where are these pictures now?" Sven asked; Lennart looked puzzled.

"What do you mean?"

"Are they in your computer now?" Lennart's slow mind suddenly worked a bit faster.

"No," he lied, "they are securely stored on the memory card in your camera." Sven was nodding eagerly.

"Good, let us keep them there for now, okay?"

"Whatever you say; so what's next?"

"Can we change things in the pictures?"

"Depending on what you want to change; I could - why?"

"I want her to be with somebody else; not me, in the pictures." Lennart was thinking that he wouldn't have minded being in the pictures himself – she was really hot. He hadn't had a woman for a very long time and the last one was old and drunk and smelled really bad. He was desperate at the time and didn't care. But the one in front of him was supreme.

"Oh I see, like she was unfaithful to you or something?"

"No you bloody idiot, so I don't get personally implicated in the photos. I want to have photos that will embarrass her enough so she wants to keep them off the market; which of course will cost her dearly" Lennart finally got what it was Sven was aiming at; but he also saw an opening that could possibly help his own bank account – if he had one.

"So what do you want me to do?"

"Change my face to somebody else's face, you know."

"What's in it for me?" Sven had of course thought that his idiot friend would ask for a cut.

"What about 30% of whatever I get?" Lennart thought for a moment.

"How much are you gonna ask for?" Sven smirked.
"Let's start with a cool million American dollars and then work our way up; how about that?" Lennart smiled and quickly made his own plans. "So are the photos back in the camera now?" Lennart giggled inside.
"No, but let me transfer them; I can do that real quick..." His fingers slid over the keyboard a few times and in the process he simply turned off the monitor. When Sven saw the dark screen he asked:
"All back in the camera?" Lennart nodded *yes*– still giggling.

Sven and his camera went out that afternoon. The moment the door closed behind him, Lennart made many copies of the photos, placed them in different files and folders all over the place. He continued his work on the keyboard for a moment and finally finished by pressing *Enter*. The many files, folders and photos of Sven and his ex-wife was now stored on distant servers protected by firewalls, ID codes and a multitude of case and time-sensitive passwords. He was sure nobody could ever get in due to the way he had stacked the files. He felt proud of himself at that very moment. One thing he knew he was good at was computers – but that was sadly enough the only thing he was any good at.

"Caroline?" Her voice was shaking with so much emotion.
"Molly?" Caroline's voice was soft but scared. "It's really you, isn't it?"
"Yeah and it's really you too," Molly smiled through tears. "Do you hate me?"
"Of course I don't hate you, but I sure missed you a lot, a very big lot."
"Same here sweetie," she took a deep breath.
"Where are you?" Molly thought it a funny question, but then she understood.
"In New York; and where are you?"
"D.C.; when are you coming to see us?"
"I have some meetings, a conference and that kind of stuff the next few days here in New York and then I was planning on coming visit you guys – if Jack told me it would be okay – with nobody hating me or something."

"Silly person, nobody hates you; listen to *these* weird people. Does that sound like hate to you?"
"Hi Molly – welcome home." It was Michael and Jasper screaming in the background.
"I missed you too," Molly screamed back, tears running faster. Suddenly she had an idea.
"Listen sweetie, what are you doing the next few days?" Caroline thought for a moment.
"Not really a lot; why?"
"Come to New York and spend time with me here. Perfect chance for us to catch up on a lot of stuff…"
"Ten years worth and then some; but what about the meetings and all you have to do?"
"That's the good part, I'll sign you up as another attendee; it will be fun – please come?"
"Hold on…" Molly could hear Caroline talk with Jack and was back on the phone quickly.
"I'll come; so what's next?" She screamed eagerly. Molly's mind swirled around; she figured it out fast.
"Listen, here's what you do: Pack only a carry-on and quickly," she looked at her watch and then at the screen on her phone. "There's a United leaving Dulles around 2:20. You should be able to catch that. I'll have a ticket waiting for you at the First Class check-in counter. You'll arrive at La Guardia around 3:40, and be met there by a limo-driver, he's actually very cute; you know your last name on a piece of cardboard and all. He'll drive you to the Plaza and you tell them who you are and they'll get you to our room, okay? I should be there around 6 o'clock. You got all that?"
Caroline repeated what Molly had just said and added:
"But what should I bring to wear?"
"Don't worry about it. We'll go shopping - my treat."
"Molly this is really you?"
"You'll see when you get to New York; I missed you."
"See you later, Molly, I gotta run – we don't want to miss *this* flight, do we?"
"No we don't." Both Molly and Caroline folded their mobiles with huge smiles and many tears. Caroline turned to her brothers and her father.
"It was really her, really."

In New York City, Molly's face was teary and smiling and the little make-up she used showed the signs of her emotions. As she arrived to the meeting fifteen minutes late looking the way she did, somebody softly asked: *Are you okay?* Molly looked at her with the biggest smile. *Life can't get much better than this, thank you.* She sat down by her place-sign, opened her briefcase and pulled out a pen and a pad.

"I'm sorry I'm late, but it was worth it; trust me. Should we get started?" Any remnants of Sven Nordgren's existents had been erased for now; only sweet Caroline was on her mind.

On the other side of the world Sven was looking at the images of his ex-wife in compromising positions; not much was left to the imagination. He found that he was getting slightly excited just looking at the pictures. Lennart had done a good job erasing the images of him and placed another man's face in the photos with his ex-wife. Though Lennart was basically stupid and slow, he was good with this computer stuff, as far as Sven knew.

Lennart ended up with six useable photos and Sven had agreed. He asked him if he should delete the other pictures and he agreed again. Lennart deleted those files in front of Sven, which didn't matter as he had several sets Sven didn't know about. Sven was very animated as he had showed him the final clear images.

"Good job Lenn, really good." He hated it when Sven called him Lenn, but then again he pretty much hated everything about Sven, except for the possibility of making some easy money.

"What's next?" Sven handed him a wrinkled piece of paper; it had an E-mail address written in shaky handwriting.

"Can you find out if this is active?" Lennart looked at him and wondered if he was legally that stupid.

"I'll try," he sarcastically responded. After a few keystrokes, he turned to Sven.

"Yeah, it's *alive*."

"Can you send them one of the photos, like without them finding out where it's coming from?"

"I can do that," he said; but it'll cost you, he thought. "I have several layers to cover my butt and if anybody can find a way through, they have to be very experienced hackers or extremely lucky." Sven didn't know what a hacker could actually do; he actually didn't know what a hacker was, but he nodded anyway.

"Send that one, okay?" He pointed at a thumbnail.

"Want to write something to go with it?" Sven thought for a second.

"How about: *If you like what you see, this is for sale*. And don't sign it." Sven felt a cool thrill down his spine. This was more fun than he thought it would be. It had been a good move to look up Lennart. He promised him 30%, but his plan was that Lennart would get nothing.

He created a bogus E-mail sender address, entered the E-dress Sven had given him, attached the photo, added the message and pressed Enter.

"It's sent," he said without turning his head. "Now what?"

"We'll wait for a response, that's what." The smirk was evident; Sven was pretty proud of himself. He felt sure the bitch would bite.

"Oh shit, here we go," Liz said to herself. The image of Molly all naked and boozed up was as digitally sharp as could be. She giggled for a second, as she admired Molly's nicely shaped body. But the giggling quickly stopped and she turned her effort into immediate action; she dialed Jeremy Novak's number in New York.

"Sorry about the hour, but Nordgren E-mailed a photo of a naked Molly. Not one for the wallet, I must add." The attorney's sleepy voice responded.

"Let it sit on your computer. No need to E-mail it to me or to Molly. She's here in New York, so I'll call her later, okay? Just sit on it for now until you hear from me. Any demands other than the image?"

"Just hinting it's for sale. Seems like he would have more than one, huh?"

"I'm sure he does. Liz, we'll get out of this, so let's not panic to any extent, okay?"

"I'm not panicking. He's too stupid to get away with this." The giggle on the other end of the line confirmed her statement. "The male-person in the picture is not Nordgren. It's a sad try at replacing somebody with somebody – really bad work."

"I'm not worried about that at all. Just tells us what idiots we are dealing with..." Liz nodded in agreement and the call ended.

So far Caroline's day was utterly hectic. Everything happened in a blur, but in a good blur. The limo-driver *was* cute as Molly had said, so she sat in the front passenger seat next to him on the way from La Guardia to The Plaza Hotel. From the second she stepped out of the limousine, she was fully catered to and was soon on one of the top floors and in the biggest hotel suite she'd ever seen; it was fantastically beautiful, with a matching view through the floor-to-ceiling windows. The hotel manager herself brought Caroline to the suite and had offered any help and any services; *just give me a call* she'd said handing Caroline a business card - *night or day*, she added. She had been genuinely friendly and very professional. Caroline was snooping around the huge space as her mobile rang.

"Welcome to New York City I hear."

"Molly, this is awesome; can we afford it?" Molly laughed.

"Yes we can. I guess Jack hasn't told you."

"Told me what?"

"That's for later. Have to make one stop and then I'll be on my way; I should see you in about 30 minutes, okay?"

"Can't wait."

"Hey Molly; it's Jeremy." She was sitting in the back of the limo finally headed for the hotel.

"What's up, Mr. Novak?"

"Oh just a little hiccup with that ex-husband of yours; seems like he's attempting playing big-bully the blackmailer."

"So he does have some photos?"

"Apparently; Liz received an E-mail with an attachment."

"Have you seen them?"

"No, but Liz said it was not something for the wallet."

"Okay, so now what?"

"We won't respond; we'll just wait and see what his next move is."

"What a jerk, huh?"

"I agree. Well, Molly, we'll chat later; I'll keep you posted." There was a small pause.

"Jeremy, are you still there?"

"Yup."

"I just want to say that I really don't care about those photos. If they are plastered all over newspapers, the Internet or what have you, I really don't care – seriously. And I don't think they'll ruin any of the projects we are involved with. When they know the story behind that whole stupid marriage thing, etc. they'll all hate Nordgren, and not point nasty little fingers at me. And another thing, I have a pretty good looking body, so I don't feel I must hide it for anything this jerk might be asking." Jeremy laughed.

"As your attorney I can respect that, but as your friend I suggest that we don't let this jerk get away with anything at all. Off the record, I would be geared more so to ruin whatever life he has left. You know he's out of money so it's not a revenge issue; it's purely a monetary opportunity. But he really doesn't know what he's up against, so he's skating on thin ice."

"Thanks Jeremy; I appreciate that."

The last half hour had been the longest half hour in Caroline's life. But finally the sound of the key-card-click was loud and welcome. The door opened slowly and she ran into the arms of her best friend ever. They were both crying tears of joy and their embrace was long and warm. Finally they were whole again – as they had safely returned into each other's lives; they released after a while and Molly picked up two big gift-wrapped packages.

"This is for you and this one's for me." Quickly they tore the ribbons and paper off like two excited little girls Christmas morning. Out came oversized, big checkered PJ tops and bottoms, as well as pairs of big fluffy bunny slippers; Caroline's face shone.

"Perfect – and so utterly mature," she laughed.

"Screw mature; this is girlfriend's night at the Plaza. I don't know about you, but I need to take a quick shower; you can do the same in your room, and then we'll get something to drink and some silly food; whatever we want – fine with you?" Caroline nodded and ran into the additional room. Ten minutes later they were on the phone in their PJ's and bunny slippers, ordering drinks and silly food.

They had eaten and emptied a bottle of wine and were now sitting across each other on Molly's big bed.

Besides the interrupting sips of wine and eating of food, the conversation had gone full speed. There was laughter and tears and more laughter and each of these two best friends told their life stories of the last ten years to each other all night. It was 5 AM before they finally succumbed to total fatigue and sleep. They stayed together in Molly's bed and went into dreamland with smiles on their faces. They were together again and nothing else mattered.

"So what about boyfriends?" Molly was buttering some whole-wheat toast the next morning. Caroline smiled.
"Haven't really had time. MSU and my responsibilities there have been enormous. When I approached that whole forensic science thing, social time soon became a rare species. I've had a few lose relationships, but nobody to bring home."
"But you've gotten, you know…"
"If you are *you knowing* what I think you are *you knowing* I have had some of that, thank you; nothing exceptional, but enough to keep me going." Caroline didn't particular like talking about her sex life or lack of same; Molly knew it right away.
"I'm sorry sweetie; I'll close the file on that subject. And besides my short marriage, I haven't really been out there at all, but that has also been okay. I think it has a lot to do with time and trust. But I'm also sure that someday it will happen; we'll see.
"But besides that short *incident* of marriage, have you met some other guys on the way?"
"Like you, I pretty much buried myself in work. At times I felt it was to negate the whole issue of looking for love. But I do travel a bit, a lot actually, and the many meetings and conferences somewhat create possibilities of all sorts, but so far I have not been that interested."
"Why do you think that is?" Molly giggled.
"First of all I think my overall attitude rejects many possible suitors; they think failure before they try – I guess." She paused for a second. "Maybe I'm not as beautiful and charming as I think I am!" Caroline smiled and shook her head.
"You know that's not the reason…"
"Thanks sweetie, I appreciate that. I don't know, really."
"Do you at least know what you are looking for?"

"As I said I'm not looking and if I was it would be in my own pathetic and very organized way. I would create…"

"…a list of negatives and positives; yeah, I remember you taught me that some million years ago."

"Well, my dear, it works for me…"

"…and it's working for me too – in a lot of situations." Caroline giggled. "Some of my science professors laughed in the beginning when I literally drew that fat line down the middle of the legal pad. Then I painted a big N on the left top and a big P on the right; most of them are now using the same system, I believe," she giggled. "But anyway…"

"I haven't really taken the time to even do a pre-evaluation with respect to what I want in a man." Molly showed a small smile. "Maybe since you and I are back together it could possibly inspire me; and inspire you as well?"

"I'm fine for now. I'm twenty-two so you must be…"

"…28, thank you. So you are saying that I'm six years more desperate than you; is that it?" Caroline laughed as she poured more coffee in both cups.

"Pretty much," Molly faked facial concern.

"Well I guess I better get going with that thing, then…" Now Caroline laughed more.

"Let's spend some time together first before we start spending time away from each other due to boys or men or whatever." They clanked their juice glasses and in unison said: *"hear hear"*. Molly looked thoughtful.

"But since you brought it up, I would be looking for somebody who is mature, but not boringly mature; I want somebody who's older then I, but that wouldn't really matter; looks are fairly optional, but within the limits of basic attractiveness and bodily hygiene is a must; a good communicator, for sure, including the art of verbalizing as well as having the patience to listen. But foremost, he must have a great sense of silly as well as intelligent humor – that part is a top shelf item." Molly paused and made a smiley face. "And he has to be hot in the sack, a certified stud-muffin and able to bring me to the highest points of…" Immediately Caroline's hands settled over her ears, *WAH WAH WAH WAH*. Molly laughed as she now knew how much Caroline hated this specific item.

"Have you stopped?" She screamed and Molly laughed out loud.

"Well sweetie, at least you know what I'm ready to track down and nail to the floor." She said as she kept laughing; Caroline was still shaking her head.

They showered and dressed and 30 minutes later they were walking down Fifth Avenue arm in arm – just like in the good old days. Molly had told Caroline that they were going shopping and that's what they did, having the time of their lives – together, again.

Across the Atlantic on a small island in the Mediterranean Ocean sat Lennart in his little dirty apartment, sweating in front of his computer's monitor, having a good time as well, but for very different reasons. Old food wrappers and containers were strewn in no particular pattern on the small sofa table and on the floor. The kitchenette sink or at least it used to be, was full of filthy plates and odd sox utensils he had lifted from various cheap eating places near the Plaza in Palma; and all the filth had a matching foul smell. But for the moment, Lennart didn't have interior decorating on his mind; he was deeply enthralled in the images of Molly West. He worked on all 22 pictures he downloaded from Sven's camera. The backgrounds were deleted and he filled that space with dreamlike patterns of colored clouds, sunsets and quiet oceans. He was thrilled by the effects, as he made her naked body even more so the focal point. She was so beautiful, he thought and he had already reached many levels of satisfaction, just fantasizing about her willingness to make him happy, to satisfy his urges as he would fully satisfy hers; and all this in his small twisted mind. Suddenly the door sprung open and Sven was by his side.

"What are you doing, Lennart?" He had been fast enough to turn off the monitor so Sven couldn't see what he was doing.

"Nothin'; just rebooting the damn thing; what have you been up to?" Sven smirked.

"I've been doing a couple of German Frauleins all night," he said as he threw some money on the table in front of Lennart. "I told you I'd pay my share of the rent."

"What did you do to them; kill them?" Sven laughed at his stupid friend.

"No, but I did bring them closer to heaven - several times."

"You did?"

"… And got paid in the process – lots of cash."
"You robbed them?"
"No Lennart, I work for a living. I do my job and get paid." Lennart wasn't sure if he should get sick or be jealous. In his feeble mind he would not be against getting paid for sexual services. In the matter of fact, he wouldn't mind paying for sex – but he didn't have the money. "So here's what we do next," and Sven told Lennart that the next move would be to start squeezing money out of Molly.

Liz opened the attachment and another photo of Molly appeared. This one showed a very involved naked woman with a non-distinct male. The first photo was acceptable to a certain point; this new one was pornographic in nature and would not be acceptable if exposed in any form of media. This was not what she had hoped would be Sven Nordgren's next move; she quickly had Jeremy on the phone.
"This is not good," was her first comment. "This is not good at all, Jeremy."
"Any monetary demands?"
"The only thing the E-mail said was *enjoy*; nothing else. Want me to forward the E-mail to you?"
"Heavens no; not secure enough. Fax the E-mail, but no pictures, and I'll chat with some people I know around here – some of them have experience in these matters and could possibly help us out." So immediately Liz sent a fax to Jeremy and Jeremy called Molly's mobile at once.

They were both wearing the oversized pajamas and fluffy bunny slippers, sitting on Molly's bed watching TV, eating popcorn. She picked up the phone, checked who called and answered. Caroline soon watched in horror as Molly's face went white as the sheets they were sitting on. She answered with nods and *okay's*, but for the most she listened intensely. Her whole body had slumped into the bed and there was a sense of defeat in the few words she spoke.
"Thanks Jeremy; so we'll wait for his next communication and decide from that what we need to do, okay? Thanks again," and she slowly folded her mobile, staring straight ahead.

"What's up?" Caroline asked apprehensively; and Molly told her precisely what was up. When she was done Caroline was in her arms.

"I'm so sorry – that's terrible." They sat like that for the longest time, both with tears of fear running down their faces.

"I really don't care about me; but this kind of exposure could set the Foundation back and possibly ruin everything we have built over the years, all the people we have been able to help get started on life, fed and kept healthy. It can all be erased because of this."

"So what can be done?"

"I guess we'll just have to pay – I mean I have the money, but as Jeremy says, if we pay he'll keep coming back for more and we'll never know if the photos have been deleted or if they are already flying around out there – we'll never know."

"So it's a bottomless hole, pretty much."

"That was random, Caroline, and rather dramatic; but thanks for the image." Molly smiled a little. She looked at her friend and grabbed her hand. "I'm glad you are here, really happy; but sorry that this mess suddenly popped up." Caroline smiled; she grabbed her mobile and pressed a couple of keys.

"I have an idea..." she said and winked at Molly.

"Oh, hi Caroline; so what's up?" And Caroline told her all about Molly's predicament.

"So I thought that maybe you know of somebody at work who might have some computer forensic or IT experience in these matters." Linda thought for a second.

"Why don't you put Molly on the horn, okay? I have a few questions to clear up a thing or two." Molly was on the phone at once. "Great to have you back, but let's do that thing later. Seems like you have an item on your plate we need to deal with." Linda and Molly talked for a while and then the call ended. Molly looked a little less stressed, but that was only on the exterior.

"Linda said that since the communication from Nordgren so far has been through E-mails, she wants to pursue that avenue by back-tracking and find out where it's coming from and who owns the account and possibly a geographic location." Caroline smiled bravely. "She'll call Jeremy right away as well as Liz at the office. I'll call them all in a few minutes."

A few moments later, Caroline's phone was ringing. "Hi sweetheart," Michael's voice sounded cheerful. "We have talked with our IT guy here at the office and he wants to get a copy of the two E-mails sent to Liz, if that's okay. He has friends in computer forensics at the FBI."

"Molly already talked with Liz in Casablanca. You can call and ask her anything and she'll help you out with whatever you need."

"Good, I'll do that right away." Caroline suddenly had a thought.

"Are you home?"

"No, why?"

"Never mind." She ended the call and speed-dialed yet another number, waited a moment and then smiled big.

"How are my favorite twins doing?" Frank was in seventh heaven when Caroline called them or visited; soon Nicole was by his side, eagerly listening in on her own phone. Caroline talked and talked and talked and when she was done it was Frank's turn. He asked for specifics, but found that what information he needed was not coming from her. Nicole had some questions as well and then Caroline turned to Molly. She quickly explained her idea and Molly agreed by nodding eagerly.

Molly was on the phone with Liz the next minute and five minutes later Liz received the call from Nicole and Frank. He asked specific questions, but most of them beyond her capability of understanding Internet, computers and the like. So Nicole and Frank narrowed it down to a short list of things, information and actions she should be able to supply. Liz didn't fully know who Nicole and Frank were, other than the nephew and niece of Caroline's.

"I'm sorry, but I have to ask: How old are you?"

"Going on 14."

"... And Nicole?"

"We are twins, so you figure it out; and how old are you?" The question made Liz laugh.

"30."

"Married?"

"No."

"You sound like you should be," Frank added; Liz smiled.
"So what's with all this computer knowledge you obviously have?"
"Just basic interest; we'll see what we can do. Sometimes it's hard to hack into accounts when they are hiding behind a lot of walls, passwords and stuff, but we'll give it a try."
"Will all this be legal?" Frank smiled shyly.
"It was nice talking with you," he responded, smoothly avoiding an answer. Half an hour later Nicole and Frank had the information they needed from Liz to at least give it a go. Their computers were sitting next to each other and the battery of four monitors glaring at them with colorful desktop images, always ready for action. Liz talked with Frank about the one photo attachment and wanted to make sure if he needed it. She was not going to E-mail the second photo – that was not going to happen; not to two kids. But Frank had told her that they needed both and complete files, to be able to try and find out where it came from to be able to destroy it – if that would be possible. Nicole gave Liz an E-mail address; Liz had never seen an E-dress like that before.
"Don't worry about the way it's put together. We are working with many layers and stuff to protect what we communicate and look at and especially to protect our own computers from hackers." Liz wrote the E-dress down and had one more question.
"Isn't that what *you* are doing?" Nicole knew what she meant, and turned off the phone with:
"We'll let you know what we find and you'll let us know if and when you hear from that guy again, okay?" And the line went dead. "This should be fun, huh?" Nicole said with her arm over Frank's shoulder as he was already working the keyboard with great fluency; he looked up and smiled at his sister.
"It'll be so much fun that some of the stuff we can't tell Mom and Dad about it; only loosely." Nicole smiled back. If their parents were aware to even the smallest extent what their twins were capable of, and had already done computerwise, there would be hell to pay; they high-fived, giggled and raced forward.

Lennart was contemplating what to do next. He could either partner up with Sven for some money that he might get, but somewhat doubted he would, or he could hide the photos and ask for money directly from Sven's ex-wife to delete the images – of course he'd still keep a set way off on a distant server for his own pleasurable entertainment; she would never know. He felt that she might be more willing to cough up money to him than to her ex-husband. He thought about how he could make that happen, when Sven pressed for the next step.

"Ask for a million U.S. dollars in the next E-mail, okay?" Sven was getting too eager and Lennart felt that when you got too eager, you would lose track and make mistakes.

"Okay – wanna send more photos?"

"No I'm sure the bitch got the idea already." Then he paused, fished the digital camera out of his pocket and handed it to Lennart. "Let's take another gander at the action, just to make sure we have a quality product to sell." Lennart took the camera and stuck an already connected USB cable into the camera's socket. Now he had the chance to permanently remove all the images from the camera's memory disc; Sven didn't understand what he was doing, so it should be easy. He switched between several screens four or five times to confuse him. He finally stopped and opened the cover-up folder named *Nordgren*. The images they had decided to keep as negotiation pieces popped up as thumbnails. Lennart had the programs slide-show format open each image. Sven drooled and Lennart did too, but for slightly different reasons. "Looks bloody good; so send that million dollar request, okay?" Lennart nodded, switched to another screen and typed fast, using all ten fingers.

"You want the pleasure?" He gestured towards the *Enter* key and Sven was more than willing to let it rip. A few seconds later in Casablanca, Liz acknowledged the new mail and this time without an attachment; she quickly referred to the directions Nicole and Frank had given her, by forwarding the mail to them unopened, as well as she left the same E-mail on her computer unopened. All she had to do now was wait; something she was not good at – at all.

"Liz tells me she talked with the twins about helping out concerning finding some information from those Nordgren

E-mails. What is it I don't get – aren't they like, what 13 or something?" Caroline smiled.

"14; listen, Michael said that he and Linda will call several of their colleagues as well as they will talk with the departments IT group – real sharp nerdy computer geeks, like really sharp ones. One of Michael's friends from the police academy is an FBI Special Agent and Michael tells me that the two of them always help each other out when need be. So lots of support is being applied. They also asked about your IT people in Casablanca."

"We are using an outside company."

"So they need to communicate with them as soon as possible. I assume that Liz will have contact numbers and that stuff." Molly nodded.

"But what about Nicole and Frank? What can *they* possibly do?" Caroline smirked.

"They can do everything else and more than most computer experts and hackers. They started fiddling with computers when they were only 5 and have become very good at it. When they were barely ten, Michael had a problem with a PC Linda and he used at home. They are both okay with computers, but like most of us, just okay. They had two other PC's that were outdated and just sitting in the garage. Michael had tried everything, but couldn't get the darn thing to work. So one day when he got home from work, Nicole and Frank sat there with this computer and the biggest smiles on their faces. They asked Michael to boot up the old thing to see what would happen. It came to life in seconds and was now working faster and smoother than ever before. The kids had worked their magical computer skills. They also had a list of a few hardware changes that would make the unit beyond up-to-date, speed and memory wise; and the rest is history."

"But still, they are only 14."

"…But going on 32; remember they both have rather perceptive memories between their ears and all they read and see and hear pretty much sticks around. They both jumped up two grades in school, but they are still bored – very much so. Just wait to you meet them; they are rather unique and very humble about their *talent*, I guess we could call it." Caroline smirked. "In many ways they keep reminding me of you, you know, when you were their age…"

"Eccentric or pathetic?"

"Neither, Miss Insecurity; smart…"

"Do they always do stuff together?"

"Only since they were born; actually, maybe even before. They tried to split them up in school, but they wanted to be together – next to each other and the same classes, side by side, all the way through."

"Wow; isn't that a bit weird?"

"A bit weird in what way?"

"Won't this get in the way later on?" Caroline smiled again and caressed Molly's hand.

"Why don't you ask them when you get to know them; you see, when you get to know them, you probably don't even think about asking them; it won't come up, really." Molly shook her head with a smile.

"So do they *hack* as well?" Caroline laughed.

"Do they *hack*? I don't know if anybody has ever asked them directly. I know their parents *advise* them not to do anything illegal, so I guess they *probably* don't. Michael once told me that Nicole tried to explain to him how they cover themselves with different layers on several levels – I can't remember how, but she explained it to let her parents know that whatever they did on-line or otherwise could never be traced. They feel that their security set-up is fail-proof."

"But don't these fail-proof systems become outdated?"

"They constantly upgrade their security." Molly shook her head again; "at least that's what I remember them telling me; I really don't know much about it."

"Well most of this is rather foggy to me too. I can do E-mails; write letters and a few other things; otherwise I'm a dingbat blindly flopping around in the sky of high tech."

"How very poetic…"

"Thanks sweetie – we'll hope it all gets straightened out and the sooner the better."

Sven spent another night with the German Frauleins. Sure they were not spring-chickens, far from, but they paid well and he desperately needed the money. His needs involved overseas travel expenses and he couldn't charm his way to a ticket, so the next best thing would be to screw his way to airfare – so that's what he was doing. At first he was repulsed by the sight of these two older women, but they wanted him as they wanted each other as they wanted the three of them to be together – and they had lots of cash. So to dim the image of them, massive quantities of alcohol came to the rescue. Sven had of course taken photos of the action just in case their husbands back in Dresden would like to see what their wives were doing in summer camp; of course the Frauleins would be offered a chance to pay for the photos to disappear.

Lennart saw those photos as well, but couldn't get excited at all; *nauseated* was more the feeling that went through his body. But of course any woman at this time... He dropped the thought and concentrated on his plan. He had to be very careful making sure his tracks were covered over and over. One of his loser friends worked in a small local bank in Palma-de-Mallorca and always talked about schemes of milking his employer a little here and a lot there. But it had always just been talk. He contacted him and hypothetically suggested a situation where someone had large funds transferred from anywhere in the world and how could such transfers be done without any trace possibilities what-so-ever; it should appear that it had never happened. His loser friend had told him that it could be done, but also that he wouldn't suggest a Spanish bank, but a bank in some obscure smaller nation somewhere off-shore, as it was called. It all sounded very exciting to Lennart and he immediately started to spend the blackmail money – in his mind.

24 hours had passed and still not a word concerning the million dollar request. Sven told Lennart to send another request, this time sterner and more specifically demanding.

"Time is running out. As you haven't responded to the first demand as of yet, an additional one hundred thousand U.S dollars has been added to the principal amount. So the total to be paid now is $1,100,000.00 and for every 24 hour delay, another hundred thousand dollars will be added on. Stay tuned as transfer information will be submitted to you momentarily." Sven was perversely satisfied with the wording; he had actually used the lines from a book he had read by accident.

He decided that Lennart's bank connection idea could be feasible; but then again, Sven wasn't fluent in blackmail. But in his ignorance he felt this was the way to do it. Lennart's friend had given him some numbers he should use, being routing number, password access code and an account number; in all 36 numbers and 12 letters, case sensitive. Sven was excited as Lennart put all this in the next E-mail and pressed Enter. They both stared at the monitor as if the response would be immediate; but it was not *immediate* at all.

Liz made all the appropriate calls to Jeremy, Molly, their IT group in Casablanca, Michael and his people as well as to Nicole and Frank; Michael contacted his FBI buddy. The initial reaction by all had been *be patient* and *don't do anything yet.* Nicole and Frank looked at the two unopened E-mails Liz had forwarded; they had both smiled in eagerness facing the challenge.

"What are you doing?"

"I want to check that number thing; see if it dissolves after use."

"But we don't have any money to test it with."

"I know, but there got to be another way to find out without actually transferring money, you know, or information." Nicole rolled her black desk-chair next to Frank's.

"Okay so what would we do?" Frank smiled at his sister. She was as evil as they came, but in a sweet way. He didn't want to do anything their parents didn't want them to do, but sweet sister Nicole would always be balancing on the edge of what needed to be done and what they were not allowed to do. There had to be a way, he thought.

"Call Dad and see what's up."

"Meaning what?"

"See if they are going to pay that money or what." Nicole was on speed dial at once. After the call she shook her head.

"He doesn't know; he said it's too early, whatever." Frank kept his fingers running over the keyboard.

"So what he wants them to do is transfer money to this account. It has a routing number, a password access code and an account number, just like a real bank accept the access code. But why give us a password access code?" Nicole smiled,

"... Because right after you transfer the money, the whole thing will dissolve, like *poof*. No way to trace the transaction, where it went..."

"Yeah, wouldn't that make sense?"

"So how can we test to see if that's it?"

"Let's think a bit." And they did that by looking for clues in their vast quantity of computer related books and journals and on the Internet.

"Okay you have the money and we can transfer the funds right away. But we have absolutely no way of knowing if the photos will be erased and I'm sure they will be floating around somewhere; even if they are technically deleted they still sit on the hard drive in bits and pieces till something else needs the space. We have no way of knowing."

"So we shouldn't pay?" Molly's voice was calm.

"At this time no; we need to see how tech-good this jerk is or whoever he works with..."

"He doesn't know much about computers, that I'm sure of..."

"... Okay, so he must have somebody there who might be a bit more inclined to pull off something like this; do you know of any he talked about?"

"Not a one; he was too busy ripping me off, remember?" Molly's laughter sounded forced.

"Okay, we'll pluck along...oh by the way; Michael called and asked if we were contemplating responding to the last two E-mails. I told him that we had not decided. Then he mentioned something his kids had said and that was actually interesting. They think perhaps the transfer information is disposable."

"Meaning what?"

"That any trace of the transfer would simply disappear after you press *send*."

"Could that be true?"

"I think so. It makes sense. But anyway, the kids are looking into it and I gave that tidbit to the IT people I know here in New York. I'll let you know."

"Let's see what the photo consist of," Nicole suggested. The file with the photo of a naked woman and naked man appeared on the monitor. They didn't even as much as glance at the image; they went straight to the file's properties. Adding more power, hitting it from many sides at the same time, their digging went deeper and deeper. Frank had his nose on the left monitor when he finally smiled.

"Look what we have here." Nicole looked and knew immediately what he was talking about.

"Good work, Brother Frank. That was too easy, wasn't it?"

"Yeah, no fun at all; please call Dear Dad, Sister Nicky." She was on the phone right away, and as Michael answered she handed the phone to Frank.

"What's up Frank?"

"Besides that we think the bank stuff number will dissolve after use and make it near impossible to trace, we also found that maybe we can delete the photos. To do that, we need the dude to E-mail all the files for us to try to do that. If we just did one, it would warn him and he'd hide the rest…"

"How do you guys figure that?"

"Deep down in this one file's property we cracked a small hole big enough to see that he has kicked this image up through three servers and assigned each new level server with an entrance password; very cryptic, no doubt – at least if I was him."

"Three servers; isn't that a bit much?"

"Not if you want to hide something from somebody."

"Do we know where the servers are?"

"We haven't gotten that far yet. If we are lucky, we'll only be able to locate the first server; the other two will be nearly impossible to find without luck and a lot of work. But if we locate the first one, we have a much better chance to find the other two; but it all depends on how good this guy is. If he hasn't protected himself well enough, we should be able to find all three and depending on how they are set up, we might be able to erase whatever we want." Michael took notes.

"There are a lot of maybe's and might's, huh?"

"Yeah; sorry about that."

"No problem; I'll get this out to everybody else and maybe we can all contribute and take care of it this way. How much time do you need to come up with something?" Frank looked at Nicole.

"I'd say six to eight hours?"

"What about school?" Frank held his breath. "Okay stay home and I'll explain with a note, okay?"

"Thanks Dad, we'll work really hard and hopefully come up with something." After the call Nicole and Frank high-fived again and went to work. Many other friends and associates of Molly's had their noses in the keyboards soon after.

"How are you holding up Molly?" She was sitting in the big armchair by the window; Caroline was napping on Molly's bed.

"Okay I guess. How are you?" Jack was in his office at CR.

"Rolling along and working harder than ever. How's Caroline doing?"

"Fine; we are in spite of this little hiccup having a great time. It is so wonderful to see her again; really great. I think we have worn each other out and will be ready to either fly or take the train to D.C. tomorrow afternoon. Either way, we'll call and tell you what time we'll arrive."

"Sounds good; we'll all be ready for you - that's for sure."

"Can't wait, Jack; so how's *your* social life?" Jack giggled. He had told Molly about Debbie and some of the other dates he had been on. They talked about Molly also finding somebody and get out in the dating world. It was a fun conversation and Molly had laughed long hours listening to Jack's stories. *Just wait till it's your turn, Toots*, and she laughed some more. They kiddingly promised to inform each other how their dating was progressing and everything between.

"Debbie is okay and it's more like a friendship – nice lady and utterly independent. Let's go for more details later." Molly smiled.

"But what can I tell *you* about?"

"No hot dates lately, Miss West?"

"Not that I recall. Maybe I'll make up some stories instead, huh?"

"As long as they are exciting and utterly naughty…"

"Yeah, you would no doubt enjoy that."

"Kisses and love to that daughter of mine; see you both tomorrow."

"Looking forward to it, Jack;" she got out of the chair and went over to the large bed. "Kisses and love from Daddy and get your cute butt out of bed – it's our last night here in vibrant New York City, so let's not sleep it away; it's party time, girlfriend." Lingering images of Jack stayed with her the rest of the evening.

Jack and Debbie's relationship was cozy. The combination of jogging and fitness, mixed with dinners and quiet evenings at home, was spiced up with intimacy; but that part was now slowly decreasing. What had begun with satisfying sex had fizzled to an automated physical *just-something-to-do* thing. But they still found their friendship interesting enough to seek each other's company a few times weekly. *Something is definitely missing* Jack would often think and acknowledged that any chance of a real love connection between them was between slim and impossible; Debbie felt the same, but they never told each other. So far the friendship was beyond that, it seemed; for now it was convenient, which they both had accepted.

Caroline, as well as her brothers, their significant others and friends, kept plucking along, looking for prospects and setting up chance meetings, arranged unsuspected run-ins as well as regular dates for Jack. He did appreciate the efforts, he really did, but he had not experienced a single date or evening or moment where he felt that *ping* in his heart – not even close.

He still tried hard to get the memory of Sara out of his mind, out of his dreams and out of his sight. Too often, actually most of the time, when sitting across from a woman in the spirit of dating, getting to know her, he kept measuring and comparing and judging from the big picture to the smallest detail, mannerisms and anything else possible; consistently, Sara came up a clear winner. When he incoherently kept calling his dates *Sara*, not just once but several times during the few hours he would be in the company of these dates, several of same otherwise well-meaning females got up, grabbed their purses and left in a huff, never to be heard from again – at least Jack never did.

Caroline, being his dating-service coordinator, started to have prospects kindly pass the chance to meet Jack. For the most the main reason started with *didn't he take Helen out the other night?* And Caroline knew right away there was a problem. Helen had got up and left in the middle of the entrée, as well as Fran, Charlotte, Ann, Annette, Mindy – well, you get the picture. Caroline did not know where to look, as she pretty much had exhausted her own resources. There was also the situation where people who knew her and liked her, started to reject *her* a bit after they had been on a date with her father and in most cases just that one time – but obviously one time too many – and Caroline was blamed.

Jack rarely had a second date; but when he did, he was sure that there was something utterly wrong with that woman; *why would she try this again?* He would think. But these *give-it-a-second-go* women quickly figured how wrong they had been and several *second-timers* had even left during the appetizers – and all this action or lack of, was followed on the board in Romano's kitchen.

Caroline, as well as other well-meaning family members and friends had finally reached a dead-end. Not because they ran out of prospects, but because they ran out of *willing* prospects. Rumors of Jack's dating skills had unwittingly become a giggling factor in certain circles; and we all know how rumors can spread rather quickly. Jack's main problem was his constant obsessive obsession with Sara – *dead Sara.* He had achieved a high level of concealment of his true thoughts and feelings about his dead wife that all around him finally believed that he had moved forward and was not haunted by her memory anymore. What Molly had screamed at him in Saint Paul-de-Vence had of course been true and correct, so it had made him try much harder so he wouldn't lose family and friends - again. Molly and his father had looked straight through him, so when they had verbally expressed their anger towards him for lying about his feelings, he most definitely knew he had to make drastic changes – and he had done that. Unfortunately one of those changes involved better concealment of his true feelings, enough to maybe finally have his family and friends believe he was saved and had moved forward. To Jack, this whole dating thing had been one long and tedious process. Sure he had found a few of those otherwise lovely women attractive on many levels, but none of them measured up to his Sara – none. But he dated to the tune of make-believe, to satisfy the people around him.

Anna Kirch, his Sara look-alike psychiatrist had funny enough been somebody Jack had learned to find attractive and exciting. He acknowledged that her looks was somewhat of a factor in the beginning, but the more time, therapy or not, he spent with her, the more he enjoyed her company. She was intelligent, good sense of humor and a great listener. Of course Jack was paying for her listening skills, but he found that their after-session chats were moments of well-being and great entertainment, seemingly for both of them.

Anna was sitting on a sharp edge. In Jack's case her professional ethics were getting in the way of her personal wishes – desires, actually. The relationship with her husband had started deteriorating long before Jack showed up in her office. Just after a few sessions and especially the after-session moments with this patient, her home life turned unbearable in comparison. She knew she wanted out of the marriage and spending time with Jack, she realized how badly she wanted out. Was there a Jack and Anna chance? At least she could fantasize about it and that she did – rather often. He was not the hot stud-muffin look-alike, but he was in good shape for his age, funny, charming and very compassionate about his family, his work and his life – but that *Sara* obsession thing constantly got in the way and also blocked bringing Anna Kirsch's dreamy fantasies into passionate reality. But she was working him hard to cure that. She knew his dead wife was the toughest competition, but she also felt that it could be done – Anna Kirch had never been a quitter and she was not going to start quitting now.

"Any response at all?" Lennart shook his head as Sven returned from a night with the German Frauleins and more Euros to prove it.
"I'll check again, but I don't think so."
"Doesn't she know that I can ruin her lovely reputation if she doesn't pay?" Lennart agreed.
"Could you sell this shit to papers and stuff?"
"My dimwitted friend, what do *you* think?"
"I guess you could." Lennart was checking his second server's E-mail account. All he found was a Spam message; he hated Spam. Suddenly his head snapped back as he had

no idea how that could have gotten there. This E-mail account was virgin and only used for… His face suddenly froze… Unless they had found a way; no that would… There is no way in bloody hell anybody could send anything to this account. The response would arrive on the first server… Lennart was confused. Sven looked at him.
"So did we?"
"Not that I can see," he nervously shook his head.
"Well, keep checking, okay? Oh, and I have the info on my German client's husbands. All it took was a lot of alcohol and the wives yodeled like there was no end," he smirked. "We'll do something about that tomorrow, okay? More dough bro;" Lennart nodded okay and went back trying to figure out what was going on.

He checked the 16 images of Sven's ex-wife. All the thumbnails were still showed up and that file was tucked away in a distant folder protected in layers of multiple access codes, walls and passwords. So what was the problem? He spent the rest of the day working on the uncomfortable feeling that something was amiss – but then again, maybe it wasn't.

"Call Dad and tell him that we traced the one E-dress to a second server – located in Germany, it looks like – but we'll get that narrowed down." Nicole picked up the phone and speed-dialed Michael.
"How did you guys do that?" Nicole knew precisely what to tell her father.
"We forgot," and she quickly hung up. Frank turned towards her.
"Sister Nicky, you did well," they both giggled and went back to work.

Molly and Caroline's last evening in New York consisted of dinner in a Greek restaurant and a last arm-in-arm stroll down Fifth Avenue back to the hotel. They were both tired from the hectic nights and days together, so they were in the mood for relaxing more so than dancing. Soon they were flopping around on Molly's bed, dressed in their matching oversized PJ's and fluffy bunnies, of course.
"You know what I was thinking?" Molly laughed.
"Am I a psychic now?" Caroline continued.

"You have talked a lot about work, you know, you doing the long hours, the traveling, the conferences, you know all that stuff. But you've never really told me about how it's like out there…"

"Out where?"

"You know, out there in the villages and those areas where you guys are involved and helping out." Molly's face immediately turned sad and thoughtful. She looked into Caroline's eyes as if she was looking for some kind of way to tell her, but she ended up in the same predicament as she always did even thinking about it. But maybe trying to explain it to her best friend would bring some sense to the surface. She had talked with Liz about it often and it had always helped her cope, though she felt it would never make it better – ever; no matter how much she tried. She took a deep breath and cleared her throat.

"I have only talked about this with Liz;" Caroline sat up and was leaning against the headboard.

"Okay;" was all she said; and Molly labored through her emotions the next hour or so.

He checked again and all sixteen images of Sven's ex-wife were still present in the designated folders; running a properties test didn't reveal anything abnormal. Lennart knew he was good at what he did on the computer – but a small fear had sneaked inside his head; he had no clue yet as to what it was.

"How are you guys doing?" Michael casually asked.

"Okay; what about on your end? Anything we need to know?"

"They ran the course you suggested, but didn't get much farther. Overall we believe that it could be possible to delete the files the way you said it could be done. What about hacking into the senders main computer and crash it?" Frank was giggling as he was listening in on the speaker-phone.

"Isn't that known to be illegal?" Now it was their father's turn to laugh sheepishly. "And Dad, it wouldn't eliminate the photos – they'll still be hanging around out there, somewhere."

"Can you hack without a trace?"

"The trace part is not the problem, but finding the main source of this whole thing is the biggest problem."

"And guys, we feel it's getting to the point of a time issue. If we are not eliminating this situation rather quickly, it might not matter at all."

"We are doing the best we can, Dad."

"I know Nicole and it's appreciated. Everybody is trying their best, so let's forge ahead. Later, Kids." Frank clicked the phone off and his face lit up a tiny bit.

"Sister Nicky; I was thinking that if we try to delete the two images available at the server level, they would know what we can do and not send any more, however many there are. The original files will probably still be on the main computer – wherever that is." Nicole smiled.

"So we need to make them send all the images to us, but we would not know if they *are* all the images…"

"So we *have* to find the originating hard-drive on the main computer where the images are sitting and do some deleting… or crashing as our father calls it… Let's call that Liz person again."

"But it's late evening in Africa."

"She'll be fine; she has to answer the phone anyway…" Liz was very awake, listened to Frank and Nicole and took notes.

"I'll get hold of them right away. Good work, guys." And the line went dead.

"But even if we delete the original files the will still have copies hanging around on other servers, wouldn't they?" Frank asked his sister.

"Okay, I got an idea. When we figure out how to find the files on the servers or just one server and a way to delete, why don't we delete it on that server?"

"… And Dear Sister, your point being?"

"First of all, wouldn't you be concerned that it's not sitting out there as safe as you thought it would be?"

"Yeah; and?"

"So if you found that your files were not safe out there, what would you do?"

"Oh my wicked sibling, I would get the heck out of there…"

"And where would you go?"

"I would probably go home…"

"Bingo; and that's a probability we can work with…" So the kids went back to work yet again.

Molly and Caroline decided to take the train to Washington D.C. They made the noon departure out of New York and arrived at D.C.'s Union Station within four hours. Jack picked them up and immediately saw the happiness in both girls; just from that he was sure the reunion had been wonderful and rewarding. They looked as they did in the good old days – just a slightly older version.

That evening they all gathered at Jack's house for dinner. Michael and Linda, Jasper and Ella, Karen and Nora and even Victoria and Brandon showed up. Debbie had worked on the meal all day, with help from Karen and Ella and the additional potluck dishes made for a terrific spread. But it was the wonderful realization that Molly had returned that made the evening so very special. Lots of tears, laughter and catching up filled the hours deep into the night.

"Thanks for all your help, Debbie." She rolled unto her side and caressed Jack's chest.
"You're welcome," she smiled tiredly. "You have a wonderful family, Jack. Your friends are not bad either," she giggled.
"I know and I do feel very fortunate… also that you are lying here next to me."
"So what are you going to do about that?"
"But you look tired..."
"That never seems to hold you back, big boy…" Jack was smirking now.
"All-righty then…" and the lights went off.

It was strange to be back in her grandparent's old house again. Jeremy had over the years taken care of upkeep and bill-paying. He had made sure the house was newly cleaned and the fridge and cupboards filled with a few necessities. She was lying on her own bed, kind of own bed away from home – or was this home, really? Caroline had asked if she wanted to spend the night together either place, but Molly decided it was time for recharging, gather some thoughts and get some practical matters out the way. She had business to do in D.C., had to return to New York City for a couple of days, would swing by D.C. again and then head back to Casablanca. Fortunately, Liz and her gang were doing a superb job. They had been good at finding new hires to cover the constant need of more hands and minds as the Foundation grew bigger and bigger. So with that kind of coverage, Molly seriously felt very comfortable being away.

But one thing did frighten her now, as she had time to think about it in private. If those photos would actually come out, it would no doubt course a huge set-back for the efforts made by the Foundation. She really did not care about her own reputation or the finger-pointing that would come with the disclosure, but it was her reputation in connection with the Foundation that would no doubt do immense damage; even non-repairable damage.

During the dinner at Jack's, Michael told her that Nicole and Frank were at home working hard to find a solution to the problem. They had come up with a basic idea that others involved also found might be the way to go. Now it was all about finding the actual way to do it. He felt that with that many eager minds to help out, it was only a matter of time before they could implement a sound way of execution. That had comforted her a bit, but the threat was still looming out there, nasty and big.

"So this will tell us if they get scared or have other options or will pull home." The phone rang.
"They have a total of 22 images." Liz's voice was excited.
"How did you find out?"
"I got an E-mail this morning."
"So trusting that the idiot told you the truth, we'll…" Frank paused. "So let's say that it's true, with the two we know of, there are twenty left. That means that we should try to delete the two we have from the next level server they are sitting on – and which has been found…"
"Did you guys find it?"
"Can't take the blame for that one; actually it was your IT people in Casablanca who got to it first."
"So now what?"
"We'll do some stuff here and hopefully we can delete those two files and then see what the dude will do next, and then watch what he does with the rest of the files…"
"What would that be?"

"Hopefully pull the files off the server and get them home."
"…And?"
"Then hopefully we can sneak in and smash the main computer into many pieces, totally erasing everything…"
"...And we can do that?"
"Yes *we* can do that… I hope…" Nicole giggled. After thirty minutes and a lot of keyboard tapping, Nicole and Frank crossed their fingers and pressed *Enter*. It was now up to the Gods of Bytes to do their part.

"What the hell was that?" Lennart stared in disbelief at the monitor. His fingers rolled as fast as they could. The folder on the next-level server only showed twenty images, not twenty-two. He restored the thumbtacks and counted. *Shit, only twenty. What the hell is going on?* He frantically tried to restore, find, and search. *Did I do something stupid?* He checked a few more things and threw his arms up in the air. *Wow; this is not good…* Lennart frantically realized that the folder on that server obviously was not as safe as he thought it would be. Nobody should be able to get in there – nobody; at least that's what he had assumed. Tearing at his long and greasy hair for a moment, he finally knew what he had to do. *I got to delete that folder 100%; get rid of the damn thing.* As it was only copies with the originals still sitting on his own machine, it wouldn't be a big deal - he thought… But he didn't feel good about the new situation at all. Everything on the exterior server was erased within minutes. He wasn't aware of the domino effect he incoherently had started. Server two and three had automatically deleted as well; but that he didn't know. His quick action made him feel a bit better and he felt that he had just saved his own sorry ass – but that was of course very far from the truth.

"Liz, we got him." The IT guy sounded eager and happy. Liz smiled really big.
"Where is he?"
"Palm de Mallorca, *Espana*. He is wide open, really. If he considers himself a computer genius, he is very wrong."
"What's next?"
"We'll talk with the people in Washington and see how they want to handle it. What has to be done next is a bit on the

not-so-legal side. I'm not sure if a judge needs to be invited to the party; I'll let the guys in D.C. make that call."

"Hi Dad; what's up?"
"They found him..."
"We know…" It didn't really surprise Michael.
"What's next?"
"You tell us."
"Can you still do that thing, you know, with no trace back to you at all?"
"That's illegal, Dad." Michael giggled quietly and also knew his son was being charmingly sarcastic. "But *yes* we can."
"How fast?"
"How about 30 minutes?"
"Sounds good to me… You have my blessings this time only."
"Dad?"
"Yeah, Nicole."
"Please say that thing, you know, the thing they say in the movies." Michael laughed and knew what she meant. He changed his voice to a detective-like movie character, making it deep, husky and slow.
"You listen up Kids; for the record, this conversation never took place, you hear?"
"Thanks, Dad." And the connection died.

Thousands of miles east, Lennart died as well. He had just opened the E-mail Sven said would come from that ex-wife of his. Just to make pretty damn sure, he compared the E-dress sitting in the inbox with the note from Sven. It was the same he had used to send the demands for payment. But Lennart was so terribly wrong. It should have read: mwtwf2000@----. The E-dress in the inbox had read: mwtwf2ooo@----. He mistakenly read the four o's as four zeros. Somebody had tricked him, but now it was all too late; he turned horrified as he recognized his mistake the very second he clicked on the attachment. There was no way back. His crappy and pathetic world exploded around him, as his computer dissolved in front of his eyes. Sure he had dealt with viruses and other irritating shit, stuff he could easily fix and quickly bring back on track, but what had just transpired right in front of him, he would never know what was. It had just taken a few moments and the monitor went eerily black. He desperately tried rebooting again and again, but nothing popped up – nothing at all.

"Can't even light up the OS; what the hell is going on. Oh shit, the photos, the German women photos." He had uploaded all the files from Sven's camera and then deleted everything on the memory card – just to have some leverage negotiating with Sven. *Oh my God, Sven! He'll kill me...* He would soon enough find out what Sven was capable of when angry – in Lennart's case Sven went ballistic.

"We double-checked everything again and again and we believe that your problem is solved." Molly had taken the call deep into the night.

"Thanks so much, Michael, thanks for all your help."

"No need for thanks; that's was brothers do for their sisters." Molly smiled; she still had a bit of trouble concerning the *brother/sister* thing.

"Well, thanks anyway. I hope to finally meet the twins one of these days. I want to thank them in person."

"They are looking forward to meet you as well; dinner here this coming evening?"

"Sounds lovely; I'll bring some wine; see you around six?"

"Looking forward to it." There was a small pause.

"Molly, the only concern we have left is that the pictures might still be on the camera's memory card and if they want to use them for any form of financial harvest, they could try to sell them to newspapers and magazines, ask you for money again, post them on the Internet and what have you." Molly sighed.

"So it's not really over, is it?"

"Not a hundred percent, no. As I said, there is that possibility. Now, if they approach you again with those pictures, we still have a chance to do something about it. But let's hope for some reason they erased them..." Michael felt the possibility of that was slim, but of course he was allowed to hope – and for once he wished *fate* would smile kindly in Molly's direction, just this one time.

The detectives went through the smashed up tiny apartment on top of the small garage. They canvassed the nearby houses and businesses with no apparent witnesses willing to talk. For the most, people in this neighborhood kept to themselves, didn't get involved and continued conducting whatever legal or illegal trade they were involved in. They all agreed they hated the constant interference of the local police; today was no exception. The detectives knew the score, so they pretty much ignored the human garbage milling around.

The landlady was huge, smelling of sweat from severe lack of hygiene; her near toothless mouth was foul and she could only inform the two detectives that her tenant had lived in the apartment, as she shamelessly called it, for a couple of years. She didn't know if he had a job or not, but he had for the most paid his rent on time. When he couldn't pay, he'd work the rent off painting some other properties she owned. That was all they got. Nobody had seen the tall, tanned and blond Viking God walk in earlier that day, spending about 30 minutes in the tiny place and then come out, his white jeans visibly stained with splatters of red.

The body had been rushed to the emergency room, but the medics had more so acted that out as a dramatic formality. He was pretty much gone as they scraped him off the dirty apartment floor. Nobody could have survived the severe beating that eventually killed him.

Sven Nordgren spent one more night with the German women. He had just lost all his blackmail material and wouldn't be able to get anything from that Molly bitch, at least not this way. But there was other ways, he scoffed. So he decided to spend time with the horny Germans, actually doing them a favor, he prided himself, take some more revealing photos and make a few hundred Euros in the process. But it was not at all Mr. Nordgren's day today, which infuriated him. He had gone to the hotel's large pool and found the two women sitting together with two men about their own age having drinks, chatting away, laughing. Sven pulled a waiter aside and asked if he knew who the men were. *The husbands,* was the short answer. The two women saw Sven and waved wildly; the two men waved as well, laughing - Sven didn't wave back. He thought he heard something like: ...*nur ein kleiner Schwanz* followed by more laughter. He furiously turned around and immediately headed for Plan B. He hailed a cab outside the hotel, drove by the bus depot, picked up the few items he had left in a locker, as well as the cash, rolled into a pair of socks for some reason; he was back in the cab within minutes.

"Aeropuerto;" he directed the driver. The eight kilometers didn't take long, and soon Mr. Nordgren was using all his charm bargaining for low airfare to New York or Washington D.C. His passport would expire within four weeks, so unfortunately the ticket had to be roundtrip within that time. But that was more than enough time to do what he needed to do; so that didn't set him back too far. But the price of the ticket did and left him with very little cash to spare. All he had to do now was hang around the airport until the following day's afternoon departure; but he had all the time in the world to do what he had decided to do – he was determined and ready. This time nobody was going to screw things up for him; he would do everything himself and do it his way, he grinned.

"So how old are you again?" The twins laughed. They had spent about an hour with Molly and really liked her. Frank had whispered something in Molly's ear as he pointed at two small thumbnails sitting innocently on the desktop. He highlighted both of them and looked at Molly. She grabbed the hands of both kids and together they ceremoniously pressed *Delete*, *Yes* and *Enter*. In that split of a second the thumbnails were no more. Molly high-fived both of them and smiled.

"In reality you could bring them back, huh?"

"In reality you should be able to. But we put a program together that pretty much blow the file to so many fragmented pieces that it would be difficult to impossible to bring them together ever again, even for expert computer forensics."

"But you could do that?" Nicole smiled.

"Of course *we* can because we know the secret handshake – but of course we won't." Now Molly smiled back.

"Thanks." They told her about the computer system they had set up and for the most constructed themselves. They talked about hardware pieces they were saving money for to make their machines work even faster and better. Molly casually fished for brands and model numbers and memorized what she needed to memorize. Two days later a UPS package arrived for Miss Nicole Miller and Mr. Frank Miller. The hardware was precisely what they had wanted, but even faster and better. A little note said *MERRY XMAS* – in the middle of June…..

The evening at Linda and Michael's had been lovely and entertaining. Jack and his *friend* Debbie, as Molly preferred to call her, had joined them and the conversation was animated and a lot of fun. Nicole and Frank had been an extremely pleasant experience for her. They were intelligent beyond their years and they participated in the conversation like adults and at times more logical than the average *grown-ups*. The endless quantities of information their brains held was mind-bugling, but they used it only as reference and certainly not with bragging rights. It was interesting how their parents communicated with them as adults, but mixed with the proverbially silly kids/parents stuff. They were pleasant and helpful and did everything in unison. Frank got up to clear the table – Nicole followed suit. Nicole made the coffee after dinner – Frank set the table with cups, cookies, cream and sugar. They had arrived to dinner *together* and they left after dinner *together*. Molly thought it was fun to watch such camaraderie between these two siblings – just awesome; it had to be experienced to be appreciated – Caroline was right.

It was somewhat interesting observing Jack and Debbie, listening to them, their physical interaction and the way they verbally communicated with each other. At first it had been weird to see Jack without Sara. That was the image from the old days still hanging around, but to Molly's surprise, it had quickly disappeared. Debbie seemed to be a nice lady. She carried herself with great confidence; she certainly *dressed* with great confidence. The outfit she was wearing simply couldn't fit any better. Molly felt a bit of disdain as she had to admit that Debbie's beautifully curved body was just that and therefore sensuous as well as sexy. But she also comforted herself by quickly finding that Debbie missed a major part of a personality: she didn't have a sense of humor. Sure she would laugh when everybody else laughed, but there was no response in kind; Molly felt strangely satisfied with that, which in itself puzzled her. Overall she didn't find Debbie right for Jack – not the least.

And Jack, well Jack was old Jack again, as far as she could tell. He was funny in that charming and sarcastic way of his, a good listener, sensitive and passionate about his opinions. It was amazing to Molly that he hadn't hooked up with someone yet, anybody who fully could appreciate what this man had. Caroline had told stories, rather funny ones, about his many dates and especially the way he himself retraced the events to Caroline the next morning or in most cases the same evening, as most of the dates ended faster than planned. Caroline had been in tears laughing just trying to get through these adventures.

Molly started to think in terms of who she knew that could possibly be good dating material for Jack. Through her many connections in New York and Washington she was sure that there had to be at least, well, several; she decided to work on a list the next morning.

She left Linda and Michael's place before Jack and Debbie. As she got out of the cab she saw lights on in the Miller house and went to the kitchen door, knocked a few times before unlocking and entered – just like in the good old days.

"Honey I'm home," she shouted.

"Come on in," Caroline's voice shouted back. As Molly entered the living room, Caroline came down the stairs in her PJs and bunny slippers.

"Time for a nightcap?" Molly nodded *yes please*.

"I'll be right back," and she rushed out the kitchen door towards her own house and quickly returned. Five minutes later the two best friends sat on the huge couch in the living room with glasses filled with gin, tonic and slices of lime, chatting away in identical outfits.

That was the sight Debbie and Jack met as they returned from Linda and Michael's hours later; Caroline was already in a giggle mode.

"The kids are home; we can finally lock up and go to bed." Her father smiled.

"You shouldn't have waited up – but thanks anyway." They said their goodnights and ascended the stairs. Both girls were watching in awe as Debbie seemingly glided above the steps, her body swaying softly from side to side. They giggled as quietly as they could. Molly whispered first:

"Is that a body or is that a body?" Caroline nodded eagerly.

"Her chest could easily make bigger sets for the both of us, huh?" They looked down their own fronts and laughed out loud.

"And then some," and they laughed and giggled some more. There was a tiny feeling of something uncomfortable as she had watched Jack and Debbie walk upstairs. She couldn't place the feeling, so as she usually did, she simply discarded it as nothing– and it was gone, she thought.

"Earth to Mr. Miller…" Karen's voice was teasingly loud. Jack's head snapped up.

"I'm sorry, did I miss anything?" It had been a longer morning conference at the office.

"Too much dating for Jack?" Nora didn't look up, but you knew she was smiling in that smirk-like way. "Late night candle-dinners, sweet nothings whispered in your ear, those longing glances across the table of lust and sweaty eyebrows and then those proverbial five words: *My place or your car?*" Nora looked up at Jack. "That's how it is, isn't it, Jack?"

"You've obviously been there, huh?" She looked at him mimicking a sweet begging face.

"I'm patiently waiting my turn, Lover Boy."

"We tried once, remember? So I don't think your turn is coming up – and certainly not with *this* Lover Boy, thank you." Nora's face went into a pouting mode.

"But what about me, Mr. Miller; when is it my turn to be wooed?" Karen's voice was mockingly sexy. "What about some young meat, Big Boy?"

"That's precisely why not – that *young meat* factor. How old are you?" Jack asked, well knowing how old Karen was, as well as her answer.

"As old as you want me to be." He shook his head with a laugh, gathered some papers and got up.

"Look around in the sandbox and find some kids your own age to play with, okay?" Now Karen was mockingly pouting.

"But I want to play with the *big* boys…" Nora shook her head on the way out.

"Okay boys and girls; let's see if we can get some work done…"

A few minutes later Nora entered Jack's office, closed the door behind her, sat down on the couch and patted the spot next to her.

"Now come here, sit down and tell mamma all about it." Jack looked up with a curious smile, but didn't move.

"What? I'm busy."

"Just get your butt over here and spill the beans, boy." So Jack got up and was soon sitting next to Nora. "That's much better; so what's the score?" The next half hour Jack was running a monolog. He told her all about how his relationship with Debbie was declining, especially the physical part. He told her how much he was looking for that *ping* to happen – he really wanted it so bad. He told Nora about his thoughts with respect to Anna Kirch, his therapist, how he felt that if he pressed her to see him outside the office, she would probably say yes. He also mentioned that he knew she was in a bad situation with her husband, so she was no doubt in a vulnerable position and would make decisions on shaky grounds. Jack didn't want that to happen. But he liked her as she was intelligent, sharp as a knife, great sense of humor, charming and entertaining; but it was too complicated.

"How old is she?"

"About 45."

"So on the younger side of Jack."

"Yeah, that's okay." He told Nora about his many dates and how they all ended on a *going-home-alone* note.

"So what is it? You are not attracted to any off them on any level or what?" She asked.

"See that's the deal; some I like because of their brains; some for their bodies which of course is a bit shallow; some for their sense of humor, you know, but not all in the same package."

"Thanks for generalizing the female species as *packages*," Nora sprouted and Jack laughed.

"See? Why can't I find that in any of the many lovely women I have had the privilege to meet? Why can't they be more like you?" Nora smiled.

"You mean *black and beautiful*? We've been there and done that Jack; besides I really don't have the answer." She looked speculative and smirked. "We *would* make a dynamic couple, you know. Don't you think?" He nodded and patted her hand.

"We most certainly would. You are as hot as they get, Dear Friend; but it would be devastating if we screwed up that friendship of ours."

"We would never let that happen."

"Another set of famous last words." He leaned over and gave Nora a kiss. "I love you dearly and I respect you more than you will ever know, but I think I'll like to keep our friendship where it is and not challenging it with physical activities – how about you?" Nora nodded *me too*, but her heart didn't agree – never had.

"So what *are* your future dating plans?"

"I think I'll play it a bit more by ear. Molly told me about a friend of hers she wants me to meet; so I might do that."

"And what about Debbie?"

"Oh, she's fine with that; we have a pretty open relationship. Seeing other people is part of it."

"Does it bother you when she sees other men?"

"Well, she either doesn't or she's not telling me about it; I don't really know." He paused for a moment. "You know, it's kind of sad that it's like this, sad that we don't have more compassion than that, can't find a better partner to spend time with – I mean, she's nice and all that and we are very compatible in, you know... But besides that it's more a relationship of convenience. She's pleasant - I'm pleasant, so we eat and talk, exercise and sleep together – literally, for the most; all very convenient."

"But convenient as in *boring*?"

"Yeah – and isn't that kind of sad?" Nora nodded.

"To some extent yes, but on the other hand it seems to work."

"Yeah, but no *pings;* I want *pings,* any kind of *pings.*"

"No *pings* – and we want *pings*..."

"Yes we do," Jack laughed. "So let's see if we can at least achieve a few *pings* from the simple joy of going back to work, shall we?" And they got up.

Debbie was looking out on the Potomac River from her office window. She had always liked the view; it gave her time to take breaths, to think and ponder. Jack Miller had been on her mind a lot the last few days. Their relationship was nice, and nice was nice for a few months, but nice hadn't turned to nicer or beyond – at all. She enjoyed his company. He was sweet, gentle, attentive and obviously funny; at least other people thought so. He had a family who loved him and accepted her; and that was another reason she didn't feel she fit in like she would like to fit in. She had been by herself for about 4 years now. The business was rolling along and kept her busy, but now she felt an urge to see her personal life roll along as well and into something more permanent than what Jack Miller could offer at this time. She was not low on offers, but she was low on good offers. The end had arrived concerning the brief and casual encounters; now the search for a long-term relationship and perhaps marriage had begun. Jack Miller was not a candidate anymore, no matter how convenient their agreement was; it was time to break it off and move along. With that decided Debbie sat down with a sad smile and quickly dived into the day's schedule.

"Are you alone?" Molly's face was barely visible. Jack looked up from the morning paper and gestured for her to come in.
"All by my lonely little self; the coffee's ready – help yourself," he smirked, "like I have to tell you." She was already pouring, grabbed a piece of toast and spread some strawberry jam on it.
"What's up?" she asked as she sat down across from him. She was dressed for jogging and he refrained from asking the obvious.
"Not much; what's up with you?" She moved her face a bit closer towards him as if she was going to reveal a secret.
"I have a date for you. Her name is Sharon Beck; she is very nice inside and out…"
"Nice; like in *personality* nice or what?"
"The whole deal; I think the two of you will get along splendidly."
"Sounds like an assumption if I have ever heard one."
"Well Mister Miller, it doesn't seem to me that you should be too choosy these days; what do you think?"
"I guess not. How old is Sharon Beck?"
"I'll guess around 40..."
"Too young…"

"Well, tell me about that part after your first date…"

"By *first date* you assume a second date is imminent…"

"That's what I do – I'm the eternal optimist. More toast?" She pointed at his empty plate.

"Please.., and by the *dating* way, how are *you* doing in that department?" She was standing with her back towards him making two pieces of strawberry jammed toast.

"I actually have a date tomorrow evening at the same time you and Sharon will be enjoying each other…" Jack smiled, but didn't look up.

"That was rather conceded of you to assume I would be available…"

"There are lots of assumptions flying around this morning..."

"You started it…," Molly giggled.

"So are you coming jogging with me?" Jack still didn't look up.

"Let me finish this gourmet breakfast, brush all my pearliest, and then dress accordingly..."

"So that's a *yes* - Swell!" And she started to read the business pages while Jack got up to get ready to run.

Both Molly and Jack's upcoming dates got cancelled the following morning; the official reason: *busy schedules.*

Sven Nordgren stood up as the row calls started. It was going to be a packed plane, which he hated, especially now that he could only fly economy class – *surrounded by smelly and noisy peasants*, he grieved. Of course a loud baby and its ignorant mother were sitting next to him in the side row of three and of course he was trapped in the window seat; this was going to be a long, bloody flight. But with a smirk he knew it would all be worth it – big time.

He had picked up a paper in the Palma-de-Majorca Airport where he read about the unfortunate mishap to a Lennart Gregersen. Mr. Gregersen had met his Maker by the way of a severe beating which had been rather fatal – no suspects were detained. Thinking back, Sven realized with some disparagement that he had actually felt surprisingly okay beating the shit out of that jerk. The swings of the two by two piece of wood were exhilarating, but it was when they landed on the poor sap that he had felt an overwhelming rush – however disturbing that was. He soon found that he couldn't stop swinging and hitting; it was when Lennart had stopped moving for awhile that he finally ended the hammering. When he checked for signs of life and didn't find any, he found himself shaking uncontrollably, sweating and float into a daze. He seriously couldn't fathom what he had just done; it had felt sexually arousing which scared him tremendously and made him sick all over the place. So he pulled himself together, showered, changed his clothes, rushed out and ran away. He had unfortunately splattered his pants with blood on the way out through the tiny space. The image of Lennart's mutilated body was forever burned onto his mind; the sight of massive blood pools and stains, as well as brain tissue spread all over the floor and the walls.

They had jogged silently together for about an hour when they stopped at the foot of the Washington Monument. It was a glorious morning with the bluest sky. Molly walked over and rested the front of her sweaty body against the cold morning surface of the obelisk, tilting her face towards the top with her arms winged up and out, totally flat to the cooling stones.
"I used to do this as a kid." She smiled as she turned to Jack. "Try it; it's quite a sight." Jack was hesitant and didn't want to look silly in front of the many sightseers already gathered around this gigantic symbol. "Come on, nobody knows you – and it's worth it." Jack finally went over to Molly's left side, gently leaned the front of his sweaty body against the stones, arms hesitantly out to the side and his face pointing upwards. In this single vision was the full height of the 555 feet tall structure as well as its total width from the bottom to the very top; a magnificent image against the perfectly blue morning sky. In one swell sweep he had the whole monument in a triangular sight he'd never considered before; it was breathtaking.

Two small children stood and watched Molly and Jack flat against the stones. Molly smiled at the parents and gestured to the children. The parents smiled and Molly gently guided the kids towards the monument. Jack was still enjoying the view and they mimicked his position with some guidance from Molly. When they were both flat against the rocks and looked up, all they could say was *wow,* while their parents snapped photos.

"Isn't this just so cool?" She asked them. Without turning towards her, they both nodded eagerly. "Well, take care," she told them, patted them on their backs and walked away from the monument; Jack followed moments later.

"That was rather random, huh?" Molly smiled and nodded.

"Yeah;" she grabbed Jack's hand and started jogging towards home. "Come on; I gotta get home and get going." They were soon in a rhythmic trot and home within an hour. As Molly walked towards her house she turned towards Jack.

"Haven't been to Nonna's for the longest time; interested in some lunch there today?'

"If we can make it no earlier than two, you're on"

"See you at two…" as she walked through the door, smiling.

Sven Nordgren found that with the sponsorship of alcohol, the baby's consistent bawling and the mother consistently ignoring same, it was just barely possible to get through the trip. The flight attendant had already served the limit according to the serving rules, but she fully understood his predicament, and quietly kept the booze flowing. He was actually a very handsome man and charming to boot. He kept making funny remarks during the short moments of her drinks deliveries that made her laugh and had seriously picked up her mood. Sure he was getting intoxicated, but he carried it well – at least *she* thought so.

He got out of his seat a few times to stretch his legs and stood in the rear of the plane to do so. She had *casually* been nearby and at one of those *all the other passengers are sleeping* moments, she had started chatting with him. His accent was cute and he sounded intelligent. She didn't notice a wedding band, which she found nice, though she didn't have reasons to make that an issue. Fraternizing with passengers was against the rules, but she knew that many of her colleagues didn't particularly follow that rule to the letter; yeah, he was definitely cute.

"I really don't like to talk about it." Molly's voice had turned hard and emotional. Jack looked at her across the table.

"I'm sorry, but…"

"You see, Jack, it's the only side of what we do, what I do that I can't cope with. When I see those children looking into my eyes and I realize that no matter how hard I try to help every single one of them as we are trying to help their siblings, their parents, their families and their friends, it is only so little we can do." Her eyes were getting moist. "I simply cannot face them – I'm a bloody coward hiding in my office trying to forget these faces, those big beautiful eyes, pleading eyes for help. I simply cannot do it."

"But you are doing so much more besides that…"

"Yeah, but it will never be enough." She took a sip of her water. "In the office I have asked everybody to remove photos and posters of these kids. That's how paranoid I have become about it."

"But Molly, you are so strong in so many other areas. You can't expect to be strong all around – nobody expects that from you or from us. We are all perfect to a certain limit, but our lesser perfect sides take over once in a while. It's actually rather human I'd say..." Molly smiled a little.

"What's *your* less than perfect side?"

"That would be *sides,* as in *plural."* Molly giggled.

"Okay *sides*." Jack's face turned serious.

"That whole Sara ten year mourning crap; that was rather *less than perfect* as in *pathetic."* Molly nodded in agreement. "And of course the slew of crap that carried with it; well you know the whole thing many times over." Molly nodded again.

"And you'll never leave that alone, will you?"

"I don't really find it a matter of choice; not something I can just turn off and forget. It's actually okay as a constant reminder not to do it again – ever. But it does pain my heart at times as I sit and chat with Caroline, Michael or Linda, or Jasper and Ella or Nicole and Frank. The times I didn't spent at work with Karen and Nora; I wasn't as supportive and participating in the business as I should have been. I despise the many moments I should have spent with my father, but didn't; the times I should have spent with William, and surprisingly, the support and times where I should have been with Victoria. I was just so wound up in *me*, in *my* situation, in my own little pathetic screwed up world."

"Wow, you are really hard on yourself."

"Well, we all are to some extent?" Molly nodded.

"You're right – me too."

"I wasn't hacking on you, Molly. I meant people in general."

"But now you are over all that?"

"Over what?"

"The Sara stuff."

"I believe I am." Still a semi lie, he thought; but then he thought better of it. "I'm never going to lie to you or anybody again, so the deal is that at times I still see Sara in other women." Molly was pleased with the honesty, though momentarily set back a step or two.

"Including me?" She smiled as Jack smiled back.

"Not including you. You are more like *family* than a date or *that other woman*. It's the poor lovely women I abuse by not being totally on track – and I really hate myself for that."

"I'm not family to you – I'm a family friend; there's a huge difference."

"And your point is?"

"Never mind… Coffee?" Jack smiled and nodded. Romano was at the table in seconds with the coffee.

It had been *fantastico* to see Molly again. He was still in awe watching her. He remembered that funky looking red-haired and freckled–faced kid from so many years ago and here she was as this beautiful and vibrant woman.

"What happened to your freckles?" He asked her. Molly giggled as she looked at Romano.

"Disappeared, unfortunately; I really liked them a lot. Jack do you remember when I painted freckles on Caroline's face? That was really hilarious as she didn't want to wash them off and Sara was okay with that. But of course they rubbed off the pillows overnight." Molly laughed. Romano smiled and left. She was something else – had always been.

"What are you guys doing here in the middle of the afternoon?" It was Caroline who had entered the restaurant together with her friend Nancy. Both Molly's and Jack's faces lit up. Embraces and kisses were exchanged, and the two women joined them at the table. Soon they were all involved in chit-chat and laughter. It turned out to be a terrific afternoon at Nonna's and Romano was left with a puzzling thought on his mind. He was rarely wrong about this, but it was also so, well, very *impossibile*.

Caroline and Nancy drove back from the restaurant, full and exhausted.

"I like Molly..." Nancy stated. "She is something else, isn't she?" Caroline nodded. "And all that stuff she's doing in Africa and all – very impressive."

"And it's a lot more than she tells you it is. There are things she has told me that I still cannot understand how she can do and how she has been able to pull so many of these things off. I mean the stuff she went through of meetings and things in New York is unbelievable."

"She believes in what she's doing, huh?"

"Big time and then some; I don't understand how she can do all that stuff. She's asked me to come to Casablanca and visit for a while; you wanna come?"

"I can't afford that – I'm a struggling student, remember?"

"She told me I can bring a friend if I like."

"Like in paying for it?"

"Yeah; she has a big house on the beach, so we would room with her."

"Is she loaded or something?"

"Loaded big time…" They continued in silence for a few minutes.

"Maybe I'm just seeing things, but is there something going on between your dad and Molly?" Immediately Caroline's face froze in disbelief.

"Are you totally out of your bloody mind? She's like my sister, you know family and besides that, she's 28 and my dad is like a million years older – are you crazy?" Her voice was now on a level of highly increased volume while shaking her head frantically from side to side. "You *ARE* crazy…" and then she laughed. "*My* dad and Molly? That's the stupidest thing I have ever heard – ever." But in reality she wasn't so sure if Nancy was wrong or right; just in case, she mentally held her hands pressed over her ears refusing to deal with it – it was simply too horrendous of a picture to even consider.

Molly was deep into meetings and work in D.C. the next five days. Her schedule was packed and her agenda long and demanding; it was all necessities and responsibilities that needed tended to before she returned to Casablanca. Still, every single morning she popped over to

Jack's house and they went jogging for an hour or so, finishing off with a light breakfast and coffee. For Molly, each workday ended with drawn out fundraising dinners or busy cocktail parties – or both. Shaking hands, smiling, embracing, explaining and pleading her case, made for a very tired Molly returning home very late every night.

"Honey I'm home…" Jack grinned as he heard her voice. It was a bit after eleven and he had worked all evening on an estimate for one of CR's clients.

"Gin and tonic, I assume?" After giving him a kiss on the cheek, Molly landed heavily in the armchair in front of him.

"Could we make that a quadruple? Oh man, what a day."

"Good or bad?" Jack asked as he got up to fix the drinks.

"Both – no actually more good than bad. But it's those dinners and stuff afterwards – it's killing me; and my shoulders are so blooming sore…" She tried to rub her left shoulder herself but gave up. Jack returned with the drinks.

"Come over and sit her on the floor and lean up against the sofa; I'll see what I can do." Molly sat on the floor with her back towards Jack. He gently started to massage her shoulders and she immediately began the oohs and aahs.

"Oh yeah; that feels so good – and a little harder if you don't mind…" Molly pulled the top of her dress off her shoulders so Jack could massage with no hindrance. "Wow, you are good at this; how about becoming a professional – I'll hire you on the spot…" Jack smiled.

"Just shut up for now and enjoy, okay?"

"Okay boss…" she said, shutting up, but still doing the oohs and aahs. Ten minutes later, massaged and half a drink down, Molly yawned and got up. "Thanks Jack – I'm sorry to drink and run, but I really need to get some rest; I'm pretty beat up and a woman my age needs that beauty sleep, you know…" She moved into to Jack's arms and embraced him long and close; Jack was holding on to her in a way he suddenly felt slightly uncomfortable with – in spite that it was a nice feeling. She was a good friend, he substantiated – a very good friend.

"Needs tucking in?" Molly smiled and kissed him on the lips.

"I'm fine – see you in the morning." He watched her from the kitchen window until she was safe and sound behind her own closed and locked door. Jack was smiling as he cleaned up for the night, turned off the lights and went upstairs. "Such a good friend," he thought as he was brushing his teethes and headed for bed. *If she'd only been more my age,* he thought, followed by *what the heck am I thinking?*

Majestic in its mass, the ocean's calmness was still eerily threatening. She was frightened, standing by the edge of the falling cliff; she could not move. Her body felt out of control by numbness - disconnected from her mind. Her spine begged to change position, but was not acknowledged. The long night had turned longer and solutions were not reaching the surface as she had wanted them to. She was stuck; could not shake the thoughts off - could not find the track leading back to normality and options - did not see the flicker of light at the end of the gruesome, narrow and seemingly endless tunnel in front of her. *Why?* She repeated: *Why?* Her mind was struggling to get back in control - she felt helpless and desperate, reaching for something, somebody to save her, to rescue her – simply grab hold of her hand. She did not want to be here – all she wanted was this nightmare to finish and go away. She wanted to wake up and realize it had all been a misunderstanding, just a mix-up in words and meanings and feelings exposed - but it was not so; the reality was horrifically brutal.

It was down to the last step, the last move - this very last decision that could throw her into eternity. *Nobody would care*, she thought, *nobody at all. Why would they abandon me? What did I do?* Dying should not be an option, not now. It was too early and there were too many loose ends that needed tying up. It was not that she was afraid of dying; it was all about not living. The wind got colder and harder - the darkness of the night suffocated and strangled anything, anybody alive. The ocean was begging her to come and play in its cruel and unforgiving embrace – longing for her soul. The edge between life and death was narrow - the will to fight against it weakened as the rain's razor sharp knives made deep cuts into her determination of fighting back to her very last breath – cutting, never giving up. *I want to die!* She screamed. *I don't want to die!* She screamed even louder.

She closed her eyes and grabbed on to that last piece of strength, from deep, deep inside. For a moment, her determination got hold of something. It was not much, but it was a handle to something. Bright flashes in her mind – her hands untied – some strength reborn. Did she feel her father's grasp of comfort! Did she see her mother's smile, begging her into an embrace? It was all about that first small step back; dragging away from the edge. *Pull yourself away - do it, Molly! Do it!* The howling wind fought against her motions. The rain was relentless in its search for hell. One foot scraped back an inch as her mind kept screaming. *Come on, Molly!* She tightened up, leaning against nature's forces and its will to conquer her. *Don't let go, Molly!* A voice encouraged. *You can do it, Molly!* It begged repeatedly. Was it her father's voice - her mother's whisper! Her left foot scraped back over the wind-shaped rock; one inch at a time! It seemed like hours, but suddenly Molly felt her heels on more solid ground, not so threatened by unbalance and eternity. She hurried backwards in slow motion, slower and further. Her heels stopped suddenly and she slipped and fell.

From the moment the back of her skull hit the protruding rock, she evolved into a beautiful darkness, sprinkled with sporadic colors and sounds of harmony. It was a soothing and floating feeling until no light was visible, no thoughts exposed - seemingly no life living. Molly was finally resting in soft arms. She had reached what she had wanted for years. The wind, the rain and the ocean were furiously trying to keep up the battle, but as reality struck and the loss was eminent, it all faded to lazy windy blows, a softer rain and a calmer sea.

Molly's body was battered and soaked and cold, so very cold; but her heart was slowly building strength beat by beat – her blood pumping through. She had won again for the millionth time. She had been strong again, stronger than nature, determined and not willing to die, not now – not for a long time.

Her father's eyes were moist from saddened tears. His gentle touch gave her calmness and warmth. Her mother was holding on to Molly's hands, filling them with hope. Sara was caressing her hair, and her grandparents were smiling forgiveness and love; George was by her side, speaking in a softened voice. Molly felt safe and secure. But she felt the tears of joy were mixed with fading guilt, streaming from her eyes. *Are you here? Are you really here? Are you watching me? Am I safe with you? Where have you been? Why did you leave? I missed you so much. I wanted you so much. I felt alone all these years. Why did you go? Why did you leave me?* Molly's parents, her grandparents, George and Sara sat around her, smiling sadly as they reached for their child. But their hands could not be felt anymore as they slowly clouded further and further away. *We love you, Molly – we have always loved you, Molly – we will always love you Molly.* Their voices could barely be heard and soon Molly's eyes closed as she cried softly. She was exhausted and in despair again, for the millionth time. She had been down this road before, again and again, and no matter which way she turned, it would be the same over and over; it would never end.

The French doors to the master-bedroom balcony were half open and the long white cotton curtains flowed softly with the breeze, gently carrying into her space, as the morning's coolness reached her side.

She was soaked in sweat, and more tired now than she had been when she went to bed so few hours ago. She was afraid of closing her eyes again and struggled in pain to begin the day. She slowly left the bed and spent a long time in the hot shower; she was so utterly exhausted.

"You look terrible this morning." Jack was getting ready for the jog; Molly didn't even try to smile.
"Yeah and good morning to you too, buster..." and off they went. At mid-jog they found themselves pausing with the view of the Potomac River.
"Well, one more day and it's heading back home..." Molly said as if only to herself.
"Home? I thought this was home for you." Jack said without turning his head. Molly showed a tired smile.
"Yeah I know; I'm rather confused myself. It's like when I'm here, Casa is home and when in Casa, this is home..."
"Seems like you can't make up your mind, huh?" Molly giggled.
"Something like that." They sipped from their water bottles and in unison got up and headed back. They were soon

sitting in Jack's kitchen inhaling breakfast while glancing at the paper's headlines.

"What are plans tonight?" Molly looked up.

"A late afternoon cocktail-something reception; there's a dinner afterwards, but I declined. Some people from the office in New York will do the honors in my place – luckily. Wanna come with me?"

"Where?"

"That cocktail thing – free drinks and horsy-dewers…" Jack smiled.

"I'll decline, but thank you. I was thinking that if you have time tonight I'll get a dinner together and Caroline and the boys and whoever can make it – would that be something you won't decline?" Molly got up, gave Jack a kiss on the lips and headed for the kitchen door.

"You're a sweetheart and that would be lovely. I'll help when I get home."

"Don't worry, Debbie and Caroline and I think Nancy will be here; but I'll probably have the feast catered if that's okay with you…" Molly smiled the okay and was gone.

As she came out of the shower her thoughts were on *Debbie*. She had again felt a bit different when Jack said her name and again she dismissed the inclination and quickly discarded it – at least for now.

It had been a lovely evening at Jack's house. Everybody had showed up and the lively conversation, laughter and merriness carried deep into the night. As Debbie and Jack were cleaning up, Molly and Caroline were deep into planning Caroline's and Nancy's visit to Casablanca. Jack enjoyed listening to those close friends chatting away, but also with somewhat of a saddened heart that Molly was leaving. She was a good friend and he liked her company, very much, he had to admit; *if only!*

They went for the longer jog the next morning, didn't talk much and silently agreed to skip the midway recovery break. They quietly ate their breakfast and it was now time for Molly to shower, get dressed, pack and head for Dulles. Jack had volunteered to drive her. The time it took to get to the airport was only sporadically interrupted with basic remarks and common tidbits. There was an apprehension in the air that neither of them understood.

Jack lifted the two suitcases out of the SUV, and then he just stood there like he didn't know what to do next. His mind was swirling with thoughts and feelings as Molly was getting her ticket and passport out of her briefcase. Finally she was done fiddling nervously with the documents and looked up at Jack's face. She could not hide the tears and Jack was confused as to what they meant – very confused. She finally smiled bravely and soon they were in a warm embrace. Molly pressed her body close to Jack's, reached for his lips and they kissed gently and politely as friends do. But there was something a bit more different than that. She looked into his eyes and smiled; then she whispered silently:

"I love you Jack." His heart stopped by the way she had said it.

"I love you too, Molly," and she smiled more.

"No Jack, I *really* love you – very much." And she wiped more tears with her sleeve. Jack was not sure what was happening, not fully sure about what she was saying. He suddenly knew what he wanted to hear her say, but what he also would be terrified to react to. What if she didn't really mean it the way he only dared to hope that she meant? Maybe… "This last week here has been wonderful. You make me relax and rest and laugh and now this – crying. Thanks for being so absolutely great..."

"Any time, Molly," and that he meant with all his heart, as well as he was frightened to admit it.

"I'll take you up on that, trust me." She wiped the last tears off her face, kissed him again, grabbed the luggage and soon disappeared inside the terminal. Jack was left in pure confusion and a huge argument had quickly started between his heart, common sense and a lot of other inconvenient entities that he didn't want to listen to. The sound of the nasty car horn brought him back to earth; he smiled and waved to the impatient driver, got in his car and headed towards the office. He only drove a few miles when he felt it; he knew it was a real *ping*. And then he felt it again and again. But this he couldn't tell anybody about – and telling Molly would only happen once in a million years, as in *never*.

Molly settled in her window seat and was quickly in deep and confusing thoughts. She tried desperately to make sense of the feelings raging inside her that very moment. As rationally and ruthlessly she handled business situations, these new feelings came out of the blue and certainly surprised her. She didn't think at any moment that she couldn't handle it or be able to reach a sensible solution, but on the other hand – maybe she couldn't, at least right away. *Stay focused and realistic, Molly*, she encouraged herself over and over.

As she had done most of her life, something her grandfather had taught her, something she had taught Caroline and something Jack had also been doing since a little boy, she made two columns on her yellow legal pad. On the top she wrote *negative* and *positive,* left and right. Then she thought hard and calculating about the feelings she had developed for Jack as well as the utmost important ramification involved; she had to think hard and calculate the pros and cons – but doing so with feelings massively occupying her heart, was something she had never had to deal with before – it was indeed all new.

He watched her coming out of the bathroom wrapped in a towel, drying her hair. It had been easy persuading her to bring him along to the hotel where she was staying the next few days. Sven didn't have much money left and certainly not enough for a hotel room in New York City. So it had been an effortless *two birds with one stroke* deal. He had a place to sleep for a couple of nights and she was being treated to grand satisfactions for her hospitality; *fair enough*, he thought. She wanted him to come with her to the Metropolitan for the day and as long as she was treating, he was okay with that. All he was waiting for was a way to get to D.C. within the next few days. Sure he didn't know where the hell Molly was, but he would be patient and play his cards by ear and eventually it would all end up in his favor – he would finally hit the big-time Royal Flush, no doubt about that. And the flight attendant was actually rather exciting in bed, though one to only ravish with the lights off. *Oh well, the sacrifices he had to make*, he thought grinning. But she was hot to trot and Sven only found breaks from the action when they were either sleeping or eating. All in all it was fine with him and of course an experience she'd never forget; at least that was what Sven thought as he was lying totally exhausted on the bed recharging his batteries – watching her.

Caroline and Nancy were feasting on their First Class travel experience. Being good friends they could be silent together in enjoyment as well as they could chat up a storm. Molly had insisted they stop over in Paris for a few nights. So from Charles de Gaulle they were picked up by a small SUV-like limousine and transported to Hotel George V a few steps off Champs-Elysees. From they exited the limo till they finally stood on the small balcony with a glass of champagne, enjoying the tremendous view from the suite, their collective mouths had been hanging open – being in utter awe was the understatement of the century. The flowers and the fruit basket with the particular bottle of California Merlot that Molly knew as Caroline's favorite, was sitting on the sofa table. *That Molly is something else*, Caroline thought of her best friend.

The next days and evenings were filled with entertainment and sightseeing tours. It had all been such fun and as sudden as it had started, as sudden they found themselves back on a plane heading south. A short while later they were greeted by Molly and Liz in the airport outside Casablanca.

This part of the world was rather different from anything they had ever experienced. After a few days recuperating from the flights and Paris, the four of them strapped themselves into a six-seater two prop and headed into *the bush*, as Liz called it. After a few hours flight they landed, visited a small village and the healthcare center established by The West Foundation. They were immediately surrounded by hundreds of children and many adults and Caroline was quickly overwhelmed. Soon after the small plane had refueled, they were off yet again and soon in another village, healthcare center and hundreds of children. That was how the next many days evolved – rich on exhaustion and images. When they finally returned to Casablanca, both Caroline and Nancy were totally beat; it wasn't just physically, but more so mentally and emotionally.

The Atlantic Ocean looked calm and gentle as all four sat on the huge deck which connected the house to the wide sandy beach. Molly's housekeepers were two young black women and Caroline had to laugh about the way Molly treated them. She more or less participated in everything and helped wherever she could. The two women ate all their meals with them and everybody helped clean up afterwards. As soon as they had served after dinner drinks on the deck, they joined them and though they were not that fluent in English, they seemingly had a ball. It created a very pleasant environment that everybody enjoyed and appreciated.

"I can't have another human being *serve* me – never gonna happen." Molly explained. "Sure cleaning and keeping house is a job, but serving other than in hotels and restaurants – I can't accept that – ever." The two women laughed as if they knew what she was talking about. Molly responded: "And as you can see, they are also very weird..." And the two women laughed even more, got up and hugged Molly. *Time bed, okay?* Molly smiled: "See what I mean, just weird..." and to the women she said: "See you in the morning and thanks for all." They nodded their heads, smiled and left.

After twelve exiting days, evenings and nights, it was unfortunately time to get home. Liz, Nancy and Caroline had quickly forged a friendship, which made it even harder to leave. Many tears and hugs and kisses were exchanged and it had finally been time to let go and check in. Both Nancy and Caroline were still sobbing as they were sipping their pre-flight champagne, then soon up in the air and deep into sleep. From de Gaulle it had been a quick change of planes and then off to the U.S.A. It was about 30 minutes before landing at Dulles that Nancy looked at Caroline smirking.

"You know what?"

"No, *what*?

"Of all the wonderful times, hours, days and nights together with Molly, she never ever mentioned your father – did you notice that?" She *had* noticed that, but had tried desperately to ignore the connotations that could possibly have.

"Oh shut up Nancy. There is nothing going on – bloody well not be." But she was in serious doubts at this point.

After Molly's departure, it had been strangely odd around Jack; at least that's what he felt. He could not substantiate his feelings of romantic involvement with respect to Molly. It was a thought so far off the register that it would never become a realization based on common sense. He quickly rationalized that it had absolutely nothing to do with physical attraction. That he was sure of. Just the thought made him feel rather confused – again. So what the heck was it? He dove into long and hard hours at work, cascading anything else than *Molly* on his plate. But he also found that doing it that way, didn't really serve the intended purpose – at all. So he brought out his legal pad and drew a line down the middle. *NEG* and *POS* he wrote on top of the page.

Nora and Karen exchanged many glances during meetings and the days of work, trying to figure out what this new energy ball, formerly known as Jack, was all about. He came in extremely early every day, seven days a week so far, and worked long hours – way beyond dinner time. They were certainly not complaining as he coughed up one good result after another. Nora was especially baffled – as well as rather confused. She was standing in front of Jack's desk; it was about 9 PM and she was ready to head home.

"So what the heck is the matter with you?" Jack didn't look up.

"Meaning what?"

"Meaning, why the heck are you not communicating with your pals around here, explaining, asking for help, you know, stuff like that…"

"Why are you angry?"

"I'm not bloody angry, I'm just utterly concerned."

"Haven't I produced to your expectations?"

"Jack get off that shit horse and talk to me, okay?" Jack finally leaned back in his desk-chair.

"I do fancy the way you talk dirty to me."

"Screw that, Jack. Spill the beans…" Nora was more so frustrated than angry and Jack knew it. He looked at his friend and smirked.

"I really, seriously don't know. If I had any sense of what is going on, I would seriously bother you with it, seriously."

"So…?"

"So I can't because I'm so confused and screwed up about it, that even *I* don't know where to begin and where to end… kind of."
"*Kind of*, meaning what?"
"Shit do I know – I just told you."
"You told me nothing; but will you tell me when you know?"
"You know I will…" But Jack wasn't sure at all if he would – ever. How could he?

It had been utterly delightful having Caroline and Nancy visiting. The time had raced by and it seemed from the arrival to departure only a few hours had passed. She absolutely loved Caroline. She was so, well, so how a best friend should be. Liz loved her as well and Molly was so happy the way they had all enjoyed each other. It had been a success, though she had expected nothing less.

But it was the thought of her negating even the mentioning of Jack while his daughter was here. She felt that it ended up awkward that they never talked about him to any extend – perhaps rather weird. But it wasn't because she didn't think about him all this time – that would have been the furthest from the truth possible. She thought about him every waking moment and in her sleep the fantasizing took over. She would wake up in the middle of the night covered in sweat, but not from nightmares anymore, but from dreams of love and intimacy. Most often she was exhausted, but with a satisfied and relaxed smile on her face – and still very confused.

Liz was in her office and Molly was in front of her laptop staring and agonizing. She wanted to write an E-mail to Jack, tell him how and what she felt, but didn't have the writing capacity; it had to be face to face. But what if she was totally wrong about her assumptions concerning his feelings? Wouldn't that kill a future relationship? It seemed such a huge chance to take and she did not think she had enough evidence to build on – far from. She had to be careful, extremely careful. Or should she try to forget it all? But she already knew she couldn't do that.

Her next scheduled trip to New York was a long time out and she agonizingly despaired about it. She wracked her brain to find any form of legit excuse to leave earlier, but she knew Liz would question why. She already had the longest to-do list for the next many weeks of things that needed to be accomplished in Casablanca – only things Molly could do and sign for. But was this so important? Scrutinizing the situation, she found it all insane. What the heck was she thinking? She finally shook her head, giggled and returned to Earth. *Take a deep breath and be rational;* this advice had for the most kept Molly West sane and on an even keel. She was begging herself to make it happen again. *Molly & Jack* was simply way too complicated - how could she even have thought for a moment that… But she had and it was not going away.

"Call line 2, sweetie," it was Liz' voice on the intercom that shook Molly out of her disturbing dreamland.
""Who's calling?"
"Somebody Garcia somebody…" Molly giggled. She picked up the phone and pressed 2.
"Molly West," was her short greeting.
"Miss West, my name is Carlos Garcia and I'm a homicide detective from the Forensic Crime Division, Barcelona…" Molly was already lost.
"I'm sorry, but you are a Spanish detective calling me… and why is that?"
"Is it correct that you have been married to a Sven Leo Nordgren?" Molly was still puzzled.
"That is correct and divorced as well, very happily so." Detective Garcia cleared his throat.
"Did he, to your knowledge commit any criminal acts against you; that would be physically, financially – anything at all that you know about?"
"He forged signatures on some documents and many checks, misused credit cards, that sort of stuff; but it was discovered and I kicked him out – why?"
"Did he ever physically harm you?"
"No; he wouldn't dare…"
"Do you have any idea where Mr. Nordgren is at this time?"
"No; why?"
"Has he contacted you in any capacity after the divorce?"
Molly told Garcia about the failed extortion attempt and that she had not heard from him since.

"Why?" she tried again.

"Well, my partner and I went to Palma de Majorca on a homicide case and from our investigation and crime-scene evidence, we found many fingerprints belonging to Mr. Nordgren." Molly was puzzled.

"Are you sure about that?"

"Very sure; Mr. Nordgren's prints has been part of Interpol's permanent collection for over fifteen years…" Molly was flabbergasted.

"I beg your pardon – you are saying what again?"

"There is only so much I can actually tell you, but Interpol, you know the International Criminal Police Organization…"

"I'm aware of what that is..."

"…Well, Interpol would like a chance to talk to Mr. Nordgren, or Mr. Johansen…"

"What do you mean *Mr. Johansen*?"

"His legal name; you didn't know?"

"No I didn't know…" Molly was now sitting straight up in her chair; Liz was standing by the door with big eyes. Molly gestured her to listen in which she did by picking up an extension. "I'm having my assistant listen in, okay?"

"Well, initially Mr. Nordgren, let's stick with *Nordgren* for now, was sought by the police in Norway for fraud and possible homicide…" Molly's face turned white. "…It was a complicated case. The victim had been married to Nordgren for a year or so; she always kept her finances very tight to the extent that the criminal investigators couldn't fully unravel a picture of fraud to gather enough evidence to charge Nordgren. Furthermore, there were so many questionable issues concerning her untimely death. The coroner finally had to apply cause of death as: *accidental drowning* and the case was left at that. Nordgren ended up with the life-insurance pay-off of over $500,000. Her children pretty much got everything else which was quite a huge estate. She had not changed her will after she married Nordgren…" Molly's ear couldn't be pressed harder to the phone.

"But you called her a victim!"

"The Norwegian detectives were fully sure that it was the work of Nordgren, but couldn't prove it without reasonable doubt. They only had some circumstantial evidence that the prosecutors couldn't make stick in court; they had to let him go. So they filed the case with Interpol to at least keep an eye on Nordgren – or Johansen, as he called himself back then. Nordgren left Norway and pretty much disappeared. Norway kept checking with Interpol, but he was gone. It was assumed that he switched citizenship from Norwegian to Danish..."

"He was Norwegian?"

"Yeah, he still is, but is no doubt traveling with forged documents, you know ID cards, driver licenses, passports, birth certificate – the whole lot of what is needed. Obviously of excellent quality as nobody has detected him – yet."

"Did he ever become a Danish citizen?"

"Interpol believes he's still Norwegian." Molly was shaking her head.

"So now you want to find him with respect to what?" Detective Garcia continued.

"Well, there are a few more cases Interpol is convinced he has been involved in. He had a relationship with an older woman in Frankfurt..."

"... Let me guess *accidental drowning*?" Molly had started to shake.

"Correct. The German detectives ran into the same predicament of not having enough evidence, but again they were sure it was Nordgren's doing. He got away with another big insurance settlement and then..."

"...disappeared."

"Correct. The thing is that Interpol was not notified quickly enough to get involved. For once German efficiency unfortunately failed. Then a case from ..."

"...You are not done yet! – oh my God, there's more?"

"Sorry Miss West, but it's important that you know what has gone on to be able to hopefully help us along in apprehending Nordgren. He is a very unstable and dangerous individual and he needs to be stopped as fast as possible. So a case from northern Italy shows up and Interpol was brought in from the start. The modus operandi was very similar, but parallels concerning Johansen and Nordgren was unfortunately never detected or investigated; though the MO was blatantly the same, nobody picked it up until he had, yet again, disappeared."

"He worked with a Danish company when I met him, didn't he? Or was that not true?"

"He eventually ended up in Denmark and a childhood friend of his hired him. The Danish police investigating the case found that he had given his friend some money as a token buy-in concerning some business deal. That was the only way he could get a legit job-title. But he had an affair with his friend's wife and when Nordgren also went after his friend's sixteen year old daughter, he got beaten up and kicked out. That was about the time they also exposed that Nordgren had drained money out of the business and pretty much brought it to bankruptcy. For some reason we don't know how he landed the last known legit job. I believe the company was ScandiFood International…"

"…and that's where I came in as the biggest sap on earth…" Molly had tears in her eyes and Liz was already by her side holding her hand; Garcia continued.

"Miss West, please understand that Nordgren or Johansen is a ruthlessly calculating individual. Unfortunately he is smooth as silk and can talk just anybody into anything he wants to profit from. Don't be hard on yourself, but consider how lucky you are having survived. Other women didn't have that luck – probably more of them that we know of at this time…" Molly took a deep breath; this was way too surreal.

"What can I help you with?" She finally asked.

"We are sure that Nordgren worked from Palma de Mallorca when he tried to sell those photos you mentioned. We feel certain that he worked with a murder victim and we assume something didn't go as Nordgren wanted it to go. Maybe the victim tried to make his own money by double-crossing Nordgren – at this point we don't know for sure. All the computer equipment was smashed to pieces and forensic cannot put much together at all – hard drives fully eliminated…" He paused and cleared his throat. "We believe that Nordgren killed Lennart Gregersen in Palma. We are positive about his fingerprints as well as Forensics found some blood splatters with somebody other than Gregersen's DNA. We can only assume it will show up to be Nordgren's – another reason we want to talk with him." Garcia cleared his throat again. "I think that Nordgren might still be interested in you," Molly froze in place. "Since the failed extortion he might have decided to confront you to be paid off. We have no clue as to how he would approach that, so that is why we are calling you to make sure that you, from now on and till we tell you otherwise, stay safe and guarded. This is extremely important Miss West, utterly important. So if you…" Liz interrupted him.

"… Consider it done. We are working with a security firm here in Casablanca and we'll have somebody on it first thing tomorrow morning…"

"No, tomorrow morning won't work. Get it in place now – this very moment. We do not know where Nordgren is – have no idea at all. He might still be in Palma, but he could be anywhere – we simply don't know and do not want to take any chances, okay?" Liz left Molly's office and made the necessary calls.

"Do you think he would be heading this way?"

"He could be, but we don't know. Do you have a home in America?" Molly's answer was hesitant.

"In Washington D.C."

"Okay, we'll have the local authorities look into that. Could you please fax us the address?"

"Why don't I just tell you what it is?"

"Safer by fax…" After a few more minutes the call ended. Molly was stunned and speechless as she sat alone in her office. This couldn't be true – had she been that stupid, so totally bloody dumb and pathetic. She shook her head and hoped she would wake up from this bad dream. But she was very much stuck with the reality of the situation; how utterly stupid she had been.

"What's his number?" Liz asked.

"Who's number?"

"Garcia?"

"I want to call back and confirm that it was really him…" Molly tried to smile while Liz dialed Garcia's number. After a few rings it was picked up.

"Policia…"

"Carlos Garcia, please."

"One moment…"

"Carlos Garcia," Liz smiled.

"This is Liz, Molly West's assistant; and we were just checking…" Garcia giggled.

"I fully understand – let's keep in contact, okay?"

"We'll do…" and the line went dead.

The flight attendant slowly woke up. Her head was near exploding and as she tried to roll out of bed she found the floor and bed soiled with vomit, blood and bodily fluids. She had no clue what had happened and didn't have much recollection of anything. All she could concentrate on was the severe cramps in her abdomen and the distinct blurry sense of floating; she barely finished the call when she lost consciousness.

The emergency room staff knew that if she had not been able to call for help, she would have been dead on arrival. They quickly started treatment for alcohol poisoning and the prognosis looked promising. The black, blue and red bruises on her face and body were horrendous; she had been a victim of a terrifying beating, but she would seemingly survive.

The detectives found all her valuables missing and the room had been wiped clean – no prints available. She told them that Mr. Johansen had stayed with her for a few days and nights; he had used condoms during sex with her and she distinctively remember that he had flushed all of them down the toilet, which left forensic with little chance of picking up any DNA from that source. She eventually recuperated, and lost her job with the airlines.

He used one of her credit cards to purchase a one-way ticket to Washington D.C. and was now waiting for the train to get moving. The dumb broad had written the ATM card PIN on a small note in her wallet; he'd tapped the account for her daily max and had $600 cash in his pocket. Tomorrow he was planning on doubling that, and then dispose of the card, just in case they were catching up – which he actually doubted they would; they were all so bloody stupid.

In about five hours he would be in D.C. and soon in Molly's house. In case she wasn't there, he would just patiently wait, no matter how long it would take. A long time ago she had told him where the spare key was hidden – just another dumb broad, he thought as the landscape flew by outside the window.

"Sergeant Miller speaking."

"This is FBI Special Agent Richard Palmer," Michael's face lit up.
"Hey Richard old pal - what a pleasant surprise. What's on the menu?"
"Well, we got a communication from Interpol concerning a man named Sven Nordgren or could go under *Johansen*. I believe he was once married to Molly West, your family friend…"
"That's right – what's up with him?"
"He has been a naughty boy and he's believed to be coming after Molly…" and Special Agent Palmer filled Michael in on all the known details.
"What can I do from here?"
"Just be aware what's going on. We have already contacted the local office. They are keeping an eye open."
"Do we know if he's here or on the way?"
"We are doing our usual stuff and have notified the port authorities, airports, etc. The ball is rolling, so we should catch him before he does anything silly again." Palmer sounded confident.
"He could also be on his way to Casablanca, huh?"
"That area is covered by the local police and Interpol. I understand that Molly is in the care of a couple of security people; she should be alright."
"Thanks for the call, Richard. I appreciate you thinking of me. Keep me posted, okay?" Richard promised he would and the call ended.

Michael went into Linda's office and told her everything he had talked with Richard about. She took some notes and looked disappointed when Michael informed her that the FBI was on the case and didn't need any help at this point. Maybe later if the problem moved into their jurisdiction. Michael smiled and kissed his wife's forehead. *Sorry Honey, orders from the Feds…*" was his only consolation; but he was going to try something anyway - just in case.

"Hi Dad," it was Nicole's energetic voice answering his call. "What's up?"
"Please get your brother on the speaker-phone." A few clicks later Frank had joined them. Michael continued.

"Now, I have a hypothetical question for you..." Nicole looked at Frank.

"By hypothetical Dad means what?"

"*Being or involving a hypothesis*, like blah blah blah: - *for the sake of argument*."

"Thanks Frank. Okay Dad, do that hypothetical question thing."

"Okay, so for the sake of argument; would it be possible to check who and when people are entering this country?" Frank didn't flinch.

"Yeah!"

"Is it easy?"

"No," was the curt answer.

"Would it be traceable to somebody's computer?"

"Depending on *whom* you are; and a minor detail..." Frank stated with Nicole continuing.

"... It would be very illegal..."

"I was afraid of that." Michael paused. "But it could be done?"

"Are you asking if we can do it?" Nicole calmly questioned.

"Hypothetically, yes..." Frank continued.

"We can, but those Web-sites we are not too keen visiting."

"But you could, hypothetically that is; do it without being caught?"

"You make it sound like a real crime, Dear Father," said Nicole with a bit of irony attached. Michael paused for a moment.

"I know it's a bad idea. It has something to do with Molly and a man that might want to harm her."

"The failed blackmailer dude?"

"Yeah; he has seemingly done something real bad and might be on his way over here, but we don't know..."

"He might be here already?"

"Could be; it would be good if we knew – that would help tremendously."

"Are you fishing, Dad?"

"Yes I am. But I can't ask you to do anything illegal..."

"... Haven't held you back before..."

"Yeah, but this *Sven Nordgren* might not even be on his way..." Michael continued as Nicole wrote down the name; Frank continued.

"He could also travel under another name, couldn't he?"

"You are right and perhaps that would be *Johansen* – or something like that." And Nicole wrote that down as well.
"Well, Dad, *hypothetically*, our hands are legally tied…"
"Yeah I know; sorry to have bothered you..." and the line went silent. Frank looked at Nicole and shook his head.
"That man is not the smoothest dude on the block, is he?"
"He sure isn't," Nicole answered and they went to work.

Michael's mobile vibrated during his daily staff meeting two hours later. The text message read: "Within the last 72 hrs no such names entered through the following airports: LGA – IAD – EWK." So no luck with New York, Washington and Newark; he quickly responded: "Txs – keep checking"

Roland Gentle; he looked at the photo in the forged passport as the train rolled south. Choosing that last name had been fun and *Gentle* was so related to his basic personality, he scoffed. Things were going well and soon he would be hiding out in his ex-wife's house. He seriously needed to lie low and be off the face of the earth for a long while – Molly's house would be the last place those assholes would look for him; that was the last thought he had before he closed his eyes.

Molly, Liz and the two body-guard's movements were like synchronized swimming. The women found great giggle factors in what they were doing, and the body-guards had finally given in, but not lost track of their responsibilities; but at times they giggled as well. Molly and Liz felt secure with them around 24/7. It had not changed much concerning their everyday routine; only that two huge and armed shadows were hovering over them - constantly.

He tried to erase certain thoughts from reappearing, certain voices, visions, and fantasizes; everything about his assumed feelings of confusion with regards to Molly had to be straightened out, dealt with or discarded. At this point he was going for the first part and not the latter. Well, life went on – no matter how awkward.
He survived several days and nights, had clumsily avoided getting together with Debbie, and just one more date

planned with Anna Kirch; the therapist he now felt seriously needed a therapist herself. But who was he to talk. He was still concerned that she looked so much like Sara; but he was a big boy now and felt in full control – at least he had convinced himself he was.

The evening was pleasant, so many weeks ago. Dinner at Nonna's was entertaining. Romano's head had spun as Anna Kirch had entered the restaurant. He truly believed that he had seen the live ghost of Sara Miller. It hadn't helped that she had Jack in tow. How often he had seen them enter like that in the past – as much as he wanted to see them enter like that again. So here *they* were, but unfortunately only an illusion. Romano had a bad feeling about this, involving the term *disaster*.

Anna constantly tucked her hair behind her ears and she looked straight into Jack's eyes; just like Sara. He quickly found that Anna was one person in the office and a total different person outside the office. She was soft-spoken, though in a clear way. She was a bit frazzled in the beginning, but started to relax after a few moments and was then charming and relaxed. At times Jack struggled with her conversation, but found that he actually could catch up by asking more questions in the process to finally fully understand and then participate. Romano had stayed close as if he was trying to warn Jack. He was sure this was all a bad choice and wanted it to go away – *molto veloce*.

They had ended up in her bed and that itself tempted disaster. From the restaurant to her apartment they had suddenly conversed awkwardly and turned very confused. In spite of that, they felt that if they got intimate, it could evolve into some kind of friendly romance; but how wrong they both had been. Anna had not been intimate with anybody since the last time she had sex with her soon-to-be ex-husband over fourteen months ago. Jack seemed like the nicest option at this time; and she felt she was ever so lightly in love with him. Very unprofessional, she kept telling herself; but here he was, undressing shyly and entering her bed. She quickly turned the lights off as she concentrated better in the dark – an old habit of hers. But disaster appeared as predicted. The excitement from fantasies about each other didn't translate into the intimacy they had hoped for. All they could do was acknowledging the lack of physical chemistry between them. So it had ended up in one long and uncomfortable hug before Jack finally got dressed and went home. His dreams about Sara had not materialized with the body of Anna; and Anna was left in bed embarrassed by her decision and saddened that Jack wasn't the one. Jack never saw Anna Kirch again, neither professionally or socially.

As he drove his car into the garage, his heart skipped as he thought he saw a sparkle of light inside Molly's house. *Was she home?* He thought hopefully. *Why hadn't she told him?* From the kitchen window he had the whole west-side of her house in view, but now there weren't any signs of light at all; must have been the headlight's reflection or something. He was soon done brushing his teethes and fast asleep, dreaming about Sara and Molly.

With a stroke of fortunate luck, Molly was summoned by one of her UNICEF administrative groups to an emergency meeting in New York City three days out. She had Liz confirm and make the usual plane and hotel reservations. She would handle things in Casablanca, guarded by their shadows and Molly would travel with one body-guard and two other guards would take over in New York.
"It's a two-day meeting; anything else you want to do in New York?"
"I wouldn't mind a few days in D.C… Get together with Caroline." She added a bit too fast.
"I believe she's back at MSU…"
"Oh, I forgot… But there are a couple of things I need to take care of with the house…"
"Jeremy has everything under control… As far as I know everything is up-to-date…"
"So I could get together with the Millers – that would be nice…" Liz was not stupid and knew Molly better than anybody.
"Anyone of the Miller's specifically?" Molly blushed and felt caught in a lie that hadn't even been told yet.
"What do you mean?"

"Molly, who the heck do you think you are dealing with? You are my best friend and you know I know you better than anybody on this globe…"

"… And probably better than myself, no doubt…"

"In some areas that is probably correct – so what's going on?"

"What do you think is going on?" Liz sat down in front of Molly's desk.

"A guessing game, it seems." She paused and scoffed. "I can only *assume* and I do really hope that I am so blooming off track." She took a deep breath. "Well, here it goes: You have the hots for Jack Miller – is that it?"

"It's that obvious - oh my God." Molly said while deflating.

"Yeah, but I hope it's only me who can see through you, otherwise you'll be in deep shit, really…"

"Meaning what?"

"Don't you get it? You are so much not his age – not even close. You are what? Twenty-eight and he is like a million years older. He has a daughter slightly younger than you and you are her best friend ever; and now you want to be her step-mother too? Besides that, she is immensely protective of her father, as you've so often told me; her brothers are your age and they vigorously consider you their blood sister, have treated you like a blood-sister and will protect and serve you as a blood-sister with their lives and beyond… And now you want to bed their father; *your own* father, as *they* see it?" Liz shook her head. "So you tell me how that will all work out, because I cannot see it and I don't care if you can make pigs fly, make hell freeze over or fully explain why turning right can be wrong…" Liz was breathing heavily. "You are totally nuts, that's what you are…" Molly slumped further down in her chair.

"It's that complicated, isn't it?"

"Only if you don't drop that stupid, inane and retarded notion this very second…"

"But I can't – I love him…" Liz covered her ears.

"I can't hear you – I can't hear what you are saying – *WAH WAH WAH WAH*…" Liz imitated Caroline.

"It is insane, isn't it? But I think he loves me…"

"He loves you the same way he loves Caroline and Michael and Jasper, jogging and French toast. He is so close to being a real father to you that would make some real father's blush in shame as they are not as real a father as Jack is a real father to you – his close-to-real biological daughter..." Now Liz slumbered into the couch.

"But I never considered him my father nor Sara my mother – my *real* parents died a long time ago."

"Molly darling, don't give me that crap – not now. What you think and what you feel in this case is so not important – it's what you are going to *do* with it that will have devastating consequences – consequences nobody will be happy with, trust me." Molly was now petrified as she knew Liz was right, no matter how much she didn't want her to be right this time around. She paused thoughtfully for a moment.

"What about just two – maybe three days in D.C.; to straighten things out?" Liz got out of her chair and shook her head.

"You are the boss of your own life – I have given you my opinion and told you precisely where I think you'll make one of the biggest mistakes in your life…"

"…Where were you when Sven Nordgren showed up?" Molly uttered coldly. Liz looked up, shocked and deeply hurt by the vicious remark; Molly immediately knew how terribly wrong it had sounded. Liz stared angrily into Molly's eyes, burning her way deep inside; she spoke through her teeth.

"That was totally uncalled for… You personally disregarded any advice I gave you about that fucking asshole; I was the only one who saw through him from the moment we met – everybody else went soft and stupid. So don't fly in here on your mighty white horse and be rude like that. I have always supported your choices and have always told you precisely how I saw things for you. And now you feel you have this ignorant right to ask me where I was with respect to that asshole? That's some kind of nerve – I never ever expected that from you; even for you to think that, less saying it is very disturbing. In this case: fuck you!" She left Molly's office in a hurry, raced into her own office, closed her briefcase, picked up her jacket and was soon in the car on the way home – guard in tow. Tears were running fast as she was hurt to the bottom of her heart; hurt by her best friend - a hurt that was unbearable.

Molly, left alone in her office, kept mumbling *I'm sorry* – and suddenly as alone as she had ever felt. She was stunned by her ignorant, arrogant and devastating remark and it had been totally unlike her. Of course Liz had always been there for her – always; but had she always been there for Liz? She worked as hard as and even harder than herself and had no doubt sacrificed her personal life in the process. She was a true friend and she knew that without Liz she wouldn't be where she was today and The West Foundation would not even be close to the results achieved so far without her. What had caused her to say what she said? Was it because she didn't like Liz' interpretation of her feelings for Jack and what a situation like that would cause if implemented? That was the only thing Molly could find that made any kind of sense – but it most certainly wasn't a valid excuse; not even close. She was embarrassed, devastated and shocked by her stupidity – and she was at a loss as what to do next. Liz was more important than anything, so losing her was not an option – not in a million years.

Getting into the house had been a piece of cake. In one of Molly's many drunken stupors back then, she had told him where the spare-key was hidden and that the security code was her birth date - backwards; what a stupid bitch, he thought. Now the tricky part was to get comfortable and lie very low as in *not-getting-caught*. If he only knew when Molly would show up; he knew how to find out - tomorrow. After exploring the contents of cupboards and pantries, he found enough alcohol to keep him happy for months and enough canned food to last him even longer. So he settled in and would do a few things around the house - starting tomorrow. When she arrived all would be ready for their very special reunion. He had turned on the lights in the kitchen for a moment, but realized his mistake and quickly turned them off.

Jack glanced towards Molly's house as he was cleaning up the kitchen after dinner. That slight bit of light he thought he saw earlier, was not repeated. It must have been the headlight's reflection as he drove up, he reasoned with himself yet again.

Liz was in no mood to talk with Molly, but the banging on her front door continued as she heard her pleading voice.

"Liz, please let me in – I really need to talk with you, please." But Liz didn't answer. After a few minutes of the same, Molly used the key Liz had given her, unlocked the door and walked in. She found her on the deck in the large swing facing the ocean.

"I am so sorry for being so utterly ignorant. I have absolutely no idea why I said what I said; it was uncalled for and rude and…" Liz' face was moist with tears and she looked lost and distant. Molly tried to embrace her but was pushed away. "Liz, I don't know what I would do without you in my life. You are one of my two best friends and I cannot see how I would have survived without you this far or how I will survive without you in the future. You know me better than I do…"

"… Well obviously not well enough, huh?"

"… Yes you do and you know that what I blurted out earlier was not me – not me at all. I love you dearly, Liz, with all my heart and I beg you to please forgive me. I don't often make boo-boo's, so can't you forgive this for once?" Liz tried not to smile.

"*Boo-boo's*, there's a description if I ever heard one." Molly's eyes were tearing up.

"Please Liz, friends again?" There was an awkward silence of anticipation. Finally Liz spoke.

"It's going to cost you…" Molly smiled through her tears.

"Anything – name your price…"

"A million dollars…" Molly went over to her purse and got her checkbook out.

"… No problem…" Her face was serious and firm. Liz looked on in disbelief.

"You would do that?"

"If that's what you want, that's what you get. I'd be happy to give the money to you – and not just because of this situation; mind you, I'm not buying your friendship, I'm only granting you a wish – because I love you, Liz…"

"You really would?"

"Yup…"

"But I was only kidding…"

"Well, I'm not..." and she wrote the check. "Here you go," and she handed it to Liz. "Remember that this is what you want and I gladly give it to you, but it doesn't make up for anything I said to you..."

"Forget it Molly; it just hurt so much that you would even say that kind of thing. But I do know you very well and it was just the oddest thing. Let's kiss and make up, okay?" Liz looked at Molly with a smile and they soon embraced.

"See what a million dollars can do, huh? The power of the mighty buck." Molly's voice had turned sarcastic. Liz giggled.

"Nah, you are wrong there, Moneybag Molly – it has nothing to do with money, only something to do with friendship..." she said as she tore up the check; and they were back on track.

The call to The West Foundation's New York City office confirmed that Molly West would be in Washington D.C. in a few days. How convenient, he thought. He was ready for her arrival and she would no doubt be so pleasantly surprised. The small storage-room in the basement would keep her screaming mute to the surrounding areas. He had built a major locking mechanism, however crude and simple, though effective no doubt, with what he could find on the workbench that must have been left intact after Molly's grandfather's death. There would be no way she could get out, especially with the tape and rope he would wrap around her. A chair and an old mattress was all she would get. The simple toilet across the way would be safe and convenient – though he didn't really care if she didn't make it when needed.

The big revolver he had found in a locked cabinet during his earlier exploration of the house was in excellent condition. It was already loaded with six rounds and the cylinder turned like a dream – not that Sven knew handguns or other kinds of weapons, but it felt right and ready; he was looking forward to use it – if he needed to. He had never killed anybody *this* way, but with a smirk he thought that there was always a first time for everything. Yes, he was ready for action; *come on down, Good Golly Miss Molly,* he said as he aimed at a small spot on the wall. *BANG* he spat through his teeth – revenge would certainly be sweet.

"So far no luck, huh?" Nicole and Frank looked dejected as their father asked yet again. They hacked into the airlines a few times more, but *Nordgren* or *Johansen* were not names that had entered the country the last 96 hours.

"I'll see what my FBI friend has found out. At least they can legally get the INS information. But thanks for trying, guys." Michael was far from comfortable with this Molly and her ex-husband thing. The report Richard had been able to supply him with had been eerie at best. Was this man a consistent killer; how had Molly survived and why. What would this man do next? Where the hell could he be at this point; what would his next move involve? To Michael it was all about keeping Molly safe by neutralizing this horrid little bastard. He had talked with Liz earlier and was informed that Molly was on her way to D.C. for a few days. She was traveling with a bodyguard so that was good. Michael was considering taking over the guard thing in his spare time as the captain probably would not allow full time guardianship. Linda had been all ears concerning the whole ordeal and she was now quietly processing that information. Michael was in awe as to how consistently Linda's visions, predictions and assumptions unfolded to near perfection during her time in homicide. It was uncanny how she singlehandedly could blow new life into dead-end investigations and especially heat up ice-cold cases. This Molly situation had not created her response yet, but Michael kept waiting – he knew better than putting pressure on her line of thinking. Richard had supplied all the FBI files he could without getting in trouble and Linda had read every single statement and report over and over. Now it was just a matter of patiently waiting; something Detective Miller was not that good at.

Molly insisted keeping the guard from Casablanca. Thirty minutes after landing they were in a limousine and on the way out of Dulles International Airport towards the city. He had actually been a very entertaining travel companion. He was well read and had a passion for classical music – Brahms being his utmost favorite. She had shared pieces of music by the way of his iPod and they had discussed their individual interpretations – it had been a lot of fun, and made the trip much shorter.

Looking out on the passing landscape going through parts of Virginia had now brought the very specific reason why she was here to the forefront. She had not been able to get Jack out of her mind and the many rather confusing thoughts and strong feelings still didn't make sense. He was a lot older than her, but that was not a problem she shared. It came down to what she felt for Jack and what Jack felt for her. The horrific part was that she might fully have misinterpreted his feelings and was setting herself up to be ridiculed and only met with total embarrassment and an even bigger disappointment. It was a huge risk, but as determined as she had been all her life, as determined she was to find out what was going on – it was that important and worth the risk.

It was late evening when the limo stopped in front of her house. Before she entered, she would see if Jack was around. There were no lights on, but that had never held her back from visiting and it was not a problem for Jack; she asked the guard and the driver to wait a few minutes as she unlocked the kitchen door to the Jack's house.

"Honey I'm home..." she uttered as her normal greeting; no answer. She looked around in the kitchen and other than two wineglasses in the sink, it was clean and shiny as Jack normally kept it. She picked up the glass with the smutch along the rim – yes, it was lipstick for sure. Just the thought of lipstick on a glass sitting in the sink in Jack's house was disturbing to Molly; now, *how silly was that?* She thought.

He very carefully lifted his eyes to the level of the front parlor bay-window where he could observe what had caused the sound of a stopping vehicle. He nearly fainted as he saw the chauffeur open the door and Molly stepping out. Then he had nearly fainted as he saw a huge muscular man stepping out on the other side immediately looking around. *Now what the hell was that all about*, he hissed. The grip on the revolver tightened even more, as he slid down on the floor and crawled into his planned position. So far so good – except for the added gorilla...

"Jack?" Molly uttered on the way up the stairs. "Are you home, Jack?" But no response at all; the house was silent.

She took a deep breath in front of the closed bedroom door, turned the handle and quietly walked in.

Jack was sleeping; he was lying on his right side facing her. She stopped in her tracks and many thoughts went through her mind. Her initial idea was to get undressed (to some extent) and slip under the covers with him. That was part of her fantasies which to no extent was associated with reality. So plan B had Molly sit down in the side-chair and she simply watched Jack's sleeping face. He was not precisely that handsome of a man in a way, but there was something else about him that she was attracted to. He was fun and kind and smart and gentle, mixed with a slew of other redeeming factors. It was hard to explain and even at this point, she had not combined any sensible justification why she loved him – *that* way. He started to stir a bit and slowly opened his sleepy eyes.

"Molly?" He uttered in surprise; "what's up? When did you get in?" He was rather confused, but in a way happy to see her.

"It has been an awful time, Jack…"

"What has been awful?"

"Being apart from you…"

"Apart from me meaning what?"

"You know…" All of the sudden something moved on the other side of the bed. Molly's heart started pounding wildly.

"Who the heck is that?"

"What *that*?" Molly pointed.

"*That* that…" Jack turned a bit to his side.

"Oh *that* that; that's…" The *that* answered for Jack.

"Debbie…"

"That's right; that's Debbie. You have met, I believe…"

"What is she doing here?" Now Molly's voice had changed to semi hysterical.

"Desperately trying to get some sleep; thank you." Debbie responded.

"Jack, what is she doing in your bed?"

"As she said, trying to get some sleep…" His voice was calm and collected. From under the covers on the other side of the bed Debbie asked:

"So she *is* as weird as you said, huh?" Debbie was now giggling, still talking under the covers with her back towards Molly. Molly realized that she *did* know Debbie. "Well Dear

Molly, Jack must have told me everything about you by now – over and over, all evening… and *yes* we have actually met before." He looked at the alarm-clock on the nightstand.

"Molly, it's very late and I have a job to go to tomorrow; and by the way what are you doing here?"

"Did you do, you know, that thing with her?"

"Molly please…"

"Well did you?"

"Now, it isn't really any of your business, is it?"

"I didn't think you were going to have, you know, with anybody – not now, I mean, you know, what's going on…"

"Are we getting to some kind of clarification soon?"

'I thought there was something… you know, between us…"
Molly was sweating now. She had never been this confused and insecure.

"So did you have sex with… that?" Debbie couldn't stop giggling.

"*That* would be *Debbie* and *yes* Jack and I *did it* and due to overall physical exhaustion, we need to sleep a bit before dawn – okay with you?" Molly couldn't believe her ears.

"So you did fornicate with this – woman, didn't you?"

"I guess *fornicating* would cover it; now leave so I can get some sleep and we'll get together tomorrow, okay? Jogging? 7 AM?"

"How could you?"

"Meaning ethically, physically or morally?"

"How could you at all?" Debbie stirred a bit and looked at Jack.

"Yeah, how could you?" She uttered sarcastically, mocking Molly.

"Thanks Debbie; I appreciate that…" Molly was steaming now; she huffed in Jack's general direction and raced out the door, down the stairs and out in front where she ran into her bodyguard and the driver chatting. He grabbed her before she could go any further.

Debbie had turned towards Jack.

"That was rather eccentric, wouldn't you say?" She leaned over and kissed his face.

"Yeah, that *was* eccentric…" He smiled big. "She was pretty much like this when she was a girl. Kind of nice to have that part of her back…" He turned and kissed Debbie. After the short kiss, Debbie pulled away from him a bit and looked into his eyes. Her face was relaxed and her small smile sweet and sad at the same time.

"Besides being utterly eccentric, she's obviously deeply in love with you." The statement was hanging heavily in the silence. Jack's smile all of a sudden froze; but the massive *ping* in his heart felt good. An eerie but heavenly feeling ran through his body as he realized what was happening – what had happened. He had been calm and collected in the short confrontation with Molly a few minutes ago and now he knew why. Before, he had been confused and concerned about his feelings for her; but those feelings were now settled and established, therefore he knew what direction he was headed – they were headed. He finally knew and was calm and confident in the process; it was really that simple.

His head rested calmly on the pillow and the smile was broader than ever. Debbie could feel her intimate friendship with Jack ending that very moment. The way Molly had looked at Jack and Jack had responded in kind, was enough for her to realize that they were in love – with neither really knowing. Jack's last words that evening confirmed she was right.

"Yeah, I know she is in love with me and I'm in love with her as well." He turned the light off and sighed. "I think I'll tell her in the morning…" And he closed his eyes.

"Men are stupid and ignorant," Molly was rambling on as the bodyguard tried to calm her down in the back of the limo. She was very confused and out of the kind of control she had always been able to manage so well. But this was different; very different indeed. After a few minutes she collected herself and rolled her suitcase up to the front door of the house. The driver and bodyguard moved to help.

"No, you guys just go and get something to eat. I'll be fine and I'll see you later, okay? Just take your time."

"Let me check the house first and then we'll run out and eat, okay? At least it'll make me feel better." Molly tried to smile and agreed.

The key slid into the lock and then the deadbolt snapped open. As he stepped inside he quickly turned towards the security pad and keyed in the numbers Molly had given him. The six sharp beeps seemingly declared the system off, but to him it had not sounded right. He checked and realized that the system was on, so he did it all again and finally, security was off; he must have keyed it incorrectly, he thought. He helped Molly with the suitcase and after he had checked all the rooms on first and second floor, he deemed the premises clear and safe. Later on he never understood how he had missed checking the basement. He told her that he would be back in an hour or so, and asked if she wanted a burger as well. She declined and went upstairs to shower and get those big old PJ's on with the matching bunny slippers – she couldn't wait.

It was much later the bodyguard suddenly realized that when he had first looked at the security pad's LCD screen it had spelled *ALL CLEAR*. He flipped out his mobile and speed-dialed Molly's number. It was ringing and ringing and finally a voice-mail announcement came on. He ended the call and tried the landline number. Not even an answer machine kicked in; it didn't even ring.

"Gotta go," he screamed and soon the limo was screeching out of the parking lot full speed. He called Detective Michael Miller's number that Molly's attorney had given him. At least he got a connection. In a minute or less he explained the possible situation and Michael was on his way and called the units and the people he needed. Just as Michael was taking off, Linda had jumped into the passenger seat, all out of breath.

"I know where he is…" Michael grinned.

"I think I know as well…" and he explained to Linda what was going on.

"I called Molly's mobile and landline and no answer." Linda continued. "I called the security company covering Molly's house and the alarm has been off for over three days."

"Do you think he's been there all those days?"

"Seems like a thing to do if you're on the run and hiding from everybody. And if he wanted to hurt Molly, she would eventually show up at some point; in her own house, how about that?" Michael was speeding up, lights blasting away.

Jack could not sleep to any extent. This new revelation was too much to just hang back and act on later.

He had to tell her now – it couldn't wait till the morning and why should it?

He grabbed the keys from the mirror table in the hallway and went out through the kitchen door. For a brief second he felt it was strange that no lights were on. She must have been inside for what, thirty minutes or so? Maybe she was taking a shower, but then he should be able to see the light from the upstairs bathroom. But it was only a fleeting thought and nothing alarming. First he knocked several times; nothing happened. Then he unlocked the lower lock as well as the deadbolt; he could only open the door as far as the security chain would let him. It was a huge chain and he would not be able to force it open, which of course he didn't have a need for at this time.

"Hey Molly," he shouted loudly. "Please open the door…" There wasn't a response. He rang the doorbell and waited a few moments; still nothing. "Molly, come on, I know you are in there. We need to talk – I need to talk." He tried the doorbell again, but nothing happened for a few seconds. Then suddenly he heard an eerily scraping voice from behind the door.

"Well, well; if it isn't the good neighbor himself. Good evening Mr. Miller, I believe it is?" Jack stood frozen for a second not comprehending the situation at all, not being able to figure out who the voice belonged to.

"Who the hell are you and open the bloody door…" He pushed the chain to its full length but it didn't budge. "You tell Molly to let me in…" The voice scraped on.

"Oh Mr. Miller, but I can let you in…" The chain was unfastened and fell heavy on the doorframe. The door opened slowly, as slowly as the barrel of a large revolver was placed under Jack's nose. He had no time to react as the door banged shut behind him.

"What the hell is going on?"

"All in good time, Mr. Miller – why don't you lead the way down to the basement?" The big revolver was buried deep into Jack's back. He could feel sweat coming off his face as he walked down the stairs. In the small space he found Molly sitting on a chair in the middle of the room. Her oversized PJ's and pink fluffy slippers looked totally out of place. Though Jack didn't know what he would have expected in a situation like this, this was not the sight he would have imagined.

Molly's ankles were taped tightly to the legs of the chair, as well as her chest was taped below and above her breasts. Her wrists were not in view as her arms were gathered behind the chair and were no doubt taped as well. Her mouth was also taped shut; her face red and moist from tears. Her eyes were pleading with him, he thought.

Jack felt surprisingly calm as Sven Nordgren asked him to sit on the floor. He watched closely what this bastard was doing, how he moved around, now having to cover Jack at all times until he could tape him up as well. And taping Jack up would be a problem. For him to hold the revolver and do the taping at the same time would be a tricky challenge. In some weird way Jack was looking forward to see how he would handle that. Another thing was that Sven Nordgren smelled like a distillery. It wasn't just his breath, but it seemed as his whole body had floated in alcohol for many days and nights. He had never heard him talk before, but he was sure that the blurriness was not part of his normal speech. So Jack added another positive to Molly's and his situation. Of course there was that big revolver issue which could cause a fatal problem. It was an older model and though Jack didn't know one gun from another, this one *did* look familiar. Sven Nordgren was busy trying to figure out what to do with Jack. The easiest would be to shoot him first and then get rid of Molly, the bloody bitch who had ruined his life.

"Under the circumstances are you okay Molly?" Nordgren turned around swiftly and hit Jack with the revolver across his face.

"Shut the fuck up or I'll smash your ugly face…" Jack went dizzy and couldn't move his hands up to estimate the damage. They were now tied behind his back in an awkward and painful position. He felt the blood stream down his face from cuts on his lips and a wide opening just above his left eyebrow.

"What the hell is the matter with you?" He screamed and the second blow hit just below his right eye again cutting open the skin. Molly looked on in horror and shook her head as much as she could.

"Okay everybody calm down…" his drunken voice squeaked. "Let's get this over with before the cavalry arrives. I assume the fuckers will be here in a few moments…" He giggled incoherently.

"What do you want?" Jack found his voice calm, but commanding. Sven Nordgren looked at him with disdain and tapped the revolver on Jack's chest.

"I'll tell you what the fuck I want; one simple word: *revenge*, that's what I want…"

"Revenge for what?" He got caught in the moment and looked at Jack with tired and drunken red eyes.

"You see the bitch over there? She caused me to do things I should never have done. Sure I have been a naughty boy all through my fucking life, but that killing shit was not something that should have happened, you see?" Jack just looked squarely into his beady eyes. "But the bitch ruined it all for me. She had all the fucking money in the world, but would she throw me a bone; me, the husband? Never in a fucking forever; stupid bitch. So I have eliminated a few people to get to her, but now I find that I pretty much painted myself into a corner and I figure that there is no bloody way for me to get out alive – isn't that a shame Mr. Miller?" Jack didn't react. "So I thought that I would do the revenge thing by getting rid of the bitch and then bring myself to Forever-Land. Does that sound like a good sensible plan to you?" Jack spat out some blood.

"You are a bloody loony, that's what I think…"

"So here you come to the rescue and get your own ass kicked. The fate of fucked up planning… And why that is, you may ask? Because you got in front of this big gun and now I have to kill you as well; how about them apples?" He turned and grabbed a bottle off the floor and took a big gulp. "Want some?" he said as he poured the alcohol on Jack's open wounds. The sting was frightening, but he found himself to be holding on to his exterior calmness.

"Why don't you just kill me and leave Molly alone?"

"Just shut up, you stupid man. You mean shit to me and I'm gonna go anyway and if that's with one or two additional bodies coming with me means nothing… So just shut up…"

Jack could hear a small sound from the living room upstairs. Neither Molly nor Sven Nordgren had heard anything – so far. He spoke in a somewhat louder voice now.

"That revolver looks familiar… Did you find it here in the house – in the chest of drawers in the guestroom?" Sven Nordgren looked at him in disgust.

"Yeah and what it's to you, asshole?" Jack tried to smile through the blood that had been flowing steadily. The front of his T-Shirt was soaked by now. He desperately tried to get the bastard's attention as he had seen a slight shadow outside the wide narrow blinded glass on the top of the wall. He knew it was facing towards the back yard. With the sound from upstairs and now the vague shadow passing by twice outside, he was praying for Molly's immediate rescue. Though he wasn't a man of any religion, praying seemed to be the right thing to do. At this point Jack had absolutely no concerns about his own wellbeing or life – it was all about Molly's; he mentally already discarded himself.

What happened next happened in fast slow-motion. The noise was horrific and excruciatingly loud; there was quickly blood and bodies everywhere – and then it went quiet, extremely quiet.

Michael and Linda were racing through the city, lights flashing and sirens at its highest volume. They had summoned several other units and issued a warning that the suspect was dangerous and possibly armed. As they approached the neighborhood, sirens came off, but the speed stayed the same. When they finally turned into the tree-lined street in this otherwise calm and gentle neighborhood, they slowed and came to a stop. Both were out of the car in seconds and grabbed heavier weapons out of the trunk. The limousine was crawling away from the front of the house and uniforms were already in place. The SWAT team had been summoned, but Michael couldn't see them get in place fast enough.

"What's the situation?" He whispered to the officer in charge of the uniforms.

"As far as we can tell Molly West is in the house. We are not sure if anybody else is."

"Did you check that house?" Michael pointed at his father's home. The officer nodded.

"We have evacuated across the street, the back of the house and on both sides three houses deep." Michael was impressed; they had responded so fast and efficient. He thought his dad should be home; that was when Linda showed up.

"Talked with Debbie, she's safe a few blocks from here. She said Jack had gotten out of bed; something about he needed to talk with Molly…"

"When?"

"About half an hour ago…"

"And he didn't come back?"

"No…" Michael did not like what he heard.

"So we figure that Molly and Dad are in there with Nordgren?"

"Well either that or they are having a chit-chat and a glass of wine by themselves…" Michael grinned at Linda's typically sarcastic comments. "I told you that the security company informed me that the alarm has been off for some time. So ergo, somebody has been in there and didn't deactivate the system when leaving or because they are still in there. Molly's attorney who is the main caretaker when she is not here says nobody has been in there that he has authorized. Somebody from his office normally comes around and opens the house when needed; you know maintenance, janitors, repairs…"

"I get the idea. So you were right about Nordgren staying here several days."

"Of course I was right," Linda responded shaking her head. "What's next?"

"We need to get somebody around the house. Right now we got to find out where in the house they are."

"They are in the basement."

"How do you know?" Linda pointed to a small area on the ground off the foundation by the back corner of the house. There was a vaguely lighter area that could be a light coming from the inside. A uniform quickly and quietly slipped over and confirmed *lights on* in that part of the basement. Michael looked at Linda.

"Right again, huh?"

"Yeah, and then what?" Linda tapped Michael on the shoulder, pointed and moved towards the back of the house. Michael sent a uniform with her. The lights from the street lit the way they were they were going. Michael shook his head as he observed how smoothly his wife moved. A second later she was in his ear again, whispering:

"We are in place; the back of the structure is covered." Suddenly a hand grabbed his shoulder. He turned and found a familiar face.

"Wow; that was fast…"

"You call – we come. What's the situation?" Michael's friend from SWAT had arrived with his team. In less than a minute he was brought up to date. Thirty seconds later the locks on the front door clicked open and the first three team members quietly searched and cleared the first and second floor. A tiny, though exceptionally strong microphone was attached to the small basement window and audio contact was established. It was soon confirmed that Jack Miller as well as Sven Nordgren was in the target space. It was only a few moments later that Molly's name was mentioned in a way that somewhat confirmed that she was also present. Michael wanted to listen in, but his SWAT friend's voice came through his ear-bud said otherwise.

"This is my game now, Detective Miller. You are too close to the hostages, so let me do my job, okay? We are in place and we'll make a big bang and hopefully stun the suspect. It's a very small space, so let's get going before we regret not reacting. See you in a few."

"What about negotiating with Nordgren?"

"Negative. I believe he feels at the end of his rope and probably know he'll either get caught or killed."

"My father and my sister are in there…"

"… And that's precisely why you are not – gotta go…" and the ear-bud went silent.

"So you see, at this point I really don't give a shit if I die. I'm not going to do prison time, so my options are rather fucking limited wouldn't you say?" He took another deep hit from the bottle of vodka; some ran down his chin and dripped onto the floor. Jack had raised himself up to lean against the wall. It felt better and he would be able to get up fast if needed. His hands were hurting and his wrists were dead. Molly's face was wet from tears and sweat and her eyes as scared as ever. Nordgren got over in front of her.

"You bloody bitch; you really fucked up my life, didn't you?" He slapped her hard across the face; then he paused as her head fell down towards her chest. He took a short step back and slapped her again. Blood started out of both her nostrils and landed on the front of her PJ top. She kept her head down; Jack thought perhaps she was unconscious.

"You are such a bloody bastard, Nordgren," he screamed to get his attention away from Molly. "You are just a bloody piece of garbage, aren't you?" Nordgren was biting. "Is that all you can handle, beating up women; you bloody ignorant idiot." The barrel of the revolver hit Jack's mid-section deep, hard and painful.

"Only women you say? Okay so let's add a man to the list, shall we?" The next blow came as a surprise as it hit hard in Jack's mid chest. It made his heart stop for several seconds until the pain fully registered. His scream of agony was loud and long. Sven Nordgren laughed even louder. "Hey, let's try that again…" and he did and Jack felt that he was on his way to dying. This time his heart stopped and his lungs momentarily collapsed. Nordgren laughed hysterically and turned towards Molly. Her head was up as she watched the blows hitting Jack. She was horrified watching such incredible violence and things went blurry as tears streamed down and salty sweat hit her eyes. *If you kill him, then kill me too* she quietly begged.

"I believe it's time to party. Everybody knows what to do and do it fast and efficient; any last questions?" He paused: "Well, good luck ladies and gentleman. On three… one – two – three."

Nordgren aimed the big revolver directly at Molly's chest. He was only standing six feet away, swaying from the massive overdose of alcohol.

"Well, my Dear; this is it. First I'll shoot you dead and then that asshole over there will get a taste of the same," he stammered, using the gun pointing in Jack's direction. That was the moment Jack decided that enough had already been enough. He gathered all his might and threw his body forward, expanding all the muscles in his strong jogging legs. A split second later he had his back against Molly and his full body between her and Nordgren. In the immediate confusion the big revolver swung up and quickly pointed directly at Jack's chest; a distance of less than three feet. The noise from the weapon was horrendous; the second shot was even louder if possible. Jack was thrown backwards as the shots sounded and landed on Molly; caused by his weight, Molly and the chair crashed sideways with Jack's bloody body landing on top. Nordgren stopped everything for a split second, shocked by what he had actually done; what he felt next was even more shocking. First it was the loud BANG and then watching his right hand splinter into bloody threads and pieces of crushed bones and muscles. He stared in disbelief at the end of his arm that a second ago had held the big revolver – neither the hand nor the revolver was there anymore. And then the pain arrived and he could think of nothing else than scream – so that's what he did. The sniper already had a second round ready in the chamber, but at this time two SWAT members had crashed Sven Nordgren to the floor and in seconds he was double cuffed above the elbows and dragged out to a waiting ambulance under very tight security.

Three medics were immediately tending to Jack and Molly. After they carefully turned Jack's body around and placed him back down on the ground, their initial assessment was that it did not look good what-so-ever; his chest was soaked in blood and his face was a terrible mess. SWAT personnel swiftly removed the tape from Molly that freed her from the chair. Initially it looked as the damage to her face was extensive and needed immediate medical attention. Her body was shaking and she couldn't utter anything other than raspy gurgling sounds. She pushed herself towards Jack's lifeless body, but two sets of strong arms firmly dragged her upstairs and out to one of the waiting ambulances. The last she saw of Jack was soon etched on her mind and tearing her heart apart.

Out in the street she saw Nordgren being tended to. He kept screaming in obvious agony. The medics had stopped the bleeding from the area where his right hand used to be. She pulled herself towards him and asked the SWAT members who otherwise had a good grip on her, if she could just say one thing to Nordgren. She was soon in front of him, speaking while spitting blood and saliva in his face.
"You killed Jack, you miserable asshole. If you don't get the death penalty I will personally make sure you die one way or another. All the money you wanted to steal from me I can now use to kill you, you miserably bastard." Nordgren

listened with a smirk on his face. "And that charm of yours will get you fucked over and over in prison by big hairy sweaty guys; you'll be everybody's new bitch again and again. So I don't think you'll need this…" Her knee smashed into his groin with the most terrifying power created through her strong legs. His testicles were smothered in an utterly painful way and would never recover; the nerve damage to his genitals was beyond repair. The pain was impossible to measure and it forced his body to immediately bend over; and that wasn't good either. Molly's right knee quickly came up again, this time harder and faster and landed with excruciating force on his nose. The specific angle and the applied power pushed the tougher cartilage and the bone supporting the ridge of his nose towards his brain on the way to crack his skull. Two millimeter further and Sven Nordgren would have been dead. Instead he screamed and screamed and as the two SWAT members pulled Molly away, she had smiled through sadness, pain and a perverse feeling of satisfaction. But Jack was dead and there was nothing she could do about that; she couldn't even see her life continue. Everybody she had ever loved had died – and now the one she had loved the most was gone.

Though Michael was frantic and hysterical on the inside, he was calm and in control on the exterior. He efficiently called the action after the initial ordeal was dealt with. The ambulances had rushed towards the hospital, sirens and lights blaring. He asked the medics about his father, but they had shaken their heads and said *sorry, we gotta go.* So at this point he didn't know if his father was dead or alive. He saw Molly's confrontation with Nordgren and the strong SWAT team members dragging her kicking and screaming into the ambulance that took off as soon as the doors closed. He quickly engaged Linda's help in the crime scene formalities; then he speed dialed Jasper and talked solemnly with him for a few moments. Next he got Caroline on the phone in her apartment near MSU. She had screamed and cried and would get on the first plane the next morning. Michael asked her to call when she had her flight information and he would arrange for somebody to pick her up at the airport. Then he called Nora and Karen and Victoria. He had the hardest time trying to summarize what

had happened in a not so dramatic and scary way to his children. Both Nicole and Frank had been on the phone and Nicole had immediately broken down in tears. Michael wanted them at the hospital right away and decided that he himself would pick them up. The sitter would make sure they would be ready. As Michael took off, Linda showed up teary-eyed in the passenger seat.
"Talked with everybody?" Michael nodded. "What about Molly's friend Liz or Molly's attorney in New York, Jeremy Novak?"
"No I didn't get to them…"
"I'll call them – you drive. Picking up the kids?" Michael nodded again and they were on their way.

As Liz slowly put the phone down, the on duty bodyguard looked at her with big eyes.
"What happened?"
"They caught Nordgren in Washington – he might have killed Jack…" Her eyes were focused on nothing. "Jack might be dead – she really loved him; now I know that she really did." The big guard came over and embraced Liz.
"I am so sorry – that's all so terrible. What are your plans? Whatever you want to do, I'm here to help you, okay?" Liz nodded towards the big gentle man.
"Thanks, right now I really don't know."

Molly was rushed into the emergency room and received immediate attention. She sobbed uncontrollably and shook from head to toes. She kept asking about Jack, wanted to see Jack, asking for any news about him. Then she recovered that last image of his lifeless body and broke down again. The nurses quickly cleaned off the blood covering her face, hair and chest. They had removed all her clothing to check for further damage. It had looked like a mess at the first assessment, but the cleaning exposed only a large bruise and a deep cut on the left side of her face. Her nose had taken some of the blow, but though it was very swollen, it wasn't broken. Her left eye was nearly closed and the black bruising under it rather severe. Her lips were cracked, cut and swollen as well. Molly didn't feel much pain as her mind was on Jack. After the nurses thorough work, the on-duty ER physician agreed that a sedative would be the next step; Molly was rolled into a private room for further observation and was soon in a deep and restful sleep.

"We have a pulse, not much, but some...," the medics reported to the ER nurses and the doctor who all helped push the gurney with Jack Miller's body into the emergency room. From there he was quickly moved to an operating room and placed on the table; two nurses cut his clothes off and other nurses had quickly started to clean off the immense quantity of blood found in his hair, on his face and chest. IV's were attached; blood pressure, pulse, pupils and heart beat constantly monitored.

"Pulse the same," the nurse noted. The surgeon was getting ready; she was a gunshot specialist.

"Whatta we got, ladies and gentlemen?" Her mask was now in place as she moved towards to the table.

"Two shots to the chest; supposedly a big caliber handgun."

"Vital signs?" The nurses communicated that information in rapid fire format. They were still examining and cleaning the body, with two of them concentrating on the chest area. One of the nurses suddenly stopped, wiped even more frantically and stopped again; the second nurse caught on.

"Doctor Saleno; we don't seem to have any entry wounds..."

"What?" She quickly leaned over the table to take a look. Her hands ran over the chest and as most of the blood had been cleaned off, it was soon clear that there actually were no entry wounds.

"Let's check the left upper back, shall we?" She quickly ordered. A moment later it was discovered that exit wounds were also missing. When the chest was finally all clean, they found two severe and bleeding circular burn-marks of six and a half centimeters in diameter. They overlapped each other by two centimeters and were located on the upper left part of the chest – exactly on top of the heart.

Michael and Linda sat as calmly as they could with Nicole and Frank by their side. Ella and Jasper had arrived shortly after Michael's call and later on Karen arrived. Victoria and Brandon showed up as soon as Brandon could get off his work assignment. Nora was in Florida and would be on a plane as soon as possible. Every time a door opened or closed they were all on the edge of their chairs. The first report was about Molly and to everybody's relief, she would pull through okay – she should actually make it back to normal – given some time.

At first the report from the OR was disturbing. The surgeon initially explained what they were going to do, as they had found a very vague pulse; one she thought they could work with. The damage to his face and skull alone had cost a lot of blood, but he was already hooked up and taking in replacement. They had quickly stopped the bleedings, so that area of the damage was under control. Somebody would come out when they knew more about the severity of the gunshot wounds. She had turned around and walked away quickly, leaving many anxious questions hanging in the air.

"So Doc, what the heck *is* this?" They all looked and examined the two large burn marks on Jack's chest. She ran her experienced gloved fingers over the raised edges and looked up.
"Where are the clothes he wore – Shirt, T-Shirt; whatever?" One of the nurses showed her the bloodied T-Shirt. The holes in the shirt matched the burn-marks on the chest; suddenly she smiled and nodded her head. "I'll be damned. I've only seen this once before – some years ago. I was treating a Confederate Soldier…" She immediately had everybody's attention; by the looks she knew they needed more of an explanation; she giggled and looked around. "Come on, I'm not *that* old. It was a Civil War reenactment and one of the riffles went off accidentally about ten inches from this poor soldier's thigh. It had the same pattern as this… I clearly remember how the edges of the burn stood up more than normal and the redness in the center - very dark." She checked the wounds again.
"Treat it as burns; I'll be right back," and she left in a hurry, leaving behind the OR staff smiling in relief. When she spotted Michael in the visitor's area she gestured for him to come over. She grabbed his arm and pulled him into another room – within seconds Linda was with them. Doctor Saleno looked at her with a question mark.
"Linda is my wife and she's also with the police department." She nodded okay.

"Do you know where the weapon is that was used in this shooting?"
"As evidence and at the station I assume – why?"
"Let's also assume the unspent ammo is still there; please, have the ammo checked immediately; this is very important, okay?" Michael and Linda nodded in unison.
"Is he going to be okay?" She grabbed his hand and smiled.
"I think we'll be able to get him back…" she winked and was gone.

Michael knocked on the door to the OR and a nurse's head popped up.
"I have the information Saleno asked for…" She was there at once.
"So?" Michael showed a giggly smile.
"I don't know what *you* think it could be, but…"
"… I know what it is, Michael; your father was shot with blanks."
"That's what they told me it could be. The unspent ammo *was* blanks and the two spent cartridges had the same characteristics." His face was one big smile. "How did you know?" Now she laughed.
"I once treated a Confederate Soldier for the same type of burns – but that's a long story. Let's go rescue daddy…" Michael and Linda looked at each other with big eyes.
"A Confederate Soldier?" They laughed in unison and their embrace was tender, happy and full of relief. Now it was time to report the good news to all of Jack's family and friends.

"So what's the deal?" Michael's voice was searching for answers.
"Well, this Smith & Wesson 629 44 Magnum is something else; it held up pretty well being blown out of the guy's shooting hand. It's registered to a Harry West some time back. I assume that…"
"…would be Molly's grandfather. I wonder if Nordgren was aware it was loaded with blanks…"
"…maybe he never checked; possibly just saw the bullets in the cylinder and assumed it was ready to go." Michael cringed.

"I wonder if my father knew!" He thanked for the info and hung up.

Caroline looked at Molly as she was fast asleep. There were not so many IV's stuck into her now, and she had started to regain somewhat of a healthier color. Her face looked horrible and her lips were still puffy and swollen. But she looked restful and was still on sedatives. Caroline had been able to get on a plane early and travel time had been quick. It had been some devastating 24 hours, but from what started as a tragedy, had turned to hope. Molly was coming around well, but her father was still out. The surgical corrections had been minor though the trauma had been severe. She saw the two circular burn-marks on his chest as the nurses had changed the dressing. It didn't look grand, but dad was alive. She was told that he would recuperate, but that it would possibly take some time. She decided that she would be there for her father during his time of healing – no matter how long it was going to take.

Molly finally started to come around. At first she was confused and dazed, but she improved and as she was getting more aware, her first concern was Jack. Before she could even ask, the doctor attending her awakening, had gently told her that Jack had survived and was healing, however slowly; but he was alive. Tears had started rolling down her face and her body reacted accordingly. One of the nurses had called for Caroline to come in and be with her. They sat in peace holding hands and Caroline stayed as Molly quietly dozed off again.
"I really love your father," Molly had said over and over. "I would have died if anything had happened to him – you know; if he had... He saved my life, you know." Caroline had responded in agreement that she also loved her father and it would have been terrible if anything had happened beyond... she didn't even want to go there, not even in thought.

The next day Jack had regained some strength and could finally look around. The room had been empty, but he quickly realized where he was. Some blurry pictures of the small basement with that horrid little man, Molly strapped unto a chair and then the big noise. He remembered that he had jumped in between Molly and the revolver, but could not recall anything after that. He tired quickly and was soon back in empty space. A couple of hours later he felt a familiar hand touching his. Caroline was sitting faithfully by his side and she was a beautiful sight. He softly caressed her hand and she quickly sat up with the biggest smile.

"Welcome back, Dad." He squeezed her hand a bit more.

"Thanks Honey. Aren't you supposed to be in school? How have you been?"

"From the deepest despair all the way to paradise;" she stood up, leaned over and gave her father a gentle kiss.

"How's Molly doing?" He anxiously asked.

"She'll be fine. She's actually up now in a wheelchair, roaming the hallways, getting impatience, ordering everybody around and spending endless hours on the phone with Liz and business…" Jack smiled.

"Sounds like something Molly would do. Can she come and visit?"

"I think she'll like that very much. She's asked about you a million times every bloody day. I'll go and get her." A few moments later Molly was rolled into his room. As he saw her, emotions were too strong and tears flowed down his face. Molly's eyes were moist as she grabbed his hand and kissed it. She looked at him tenderly and smiled.

"You look like shit, don't you Mr. Miller?"

"Welcome in the club. Those lips of yours make you look like; what's her name?"

"Don't go there or else…" She giggled. "How do you feel?"

"… Like going bowling… How do you think I feel?"

"Thanks for saving my life…Thanks so much," and she sobbed a bit more. They sat in quiet peace for a while, just looking at each other. Caroline excused herself to go and make some calls about her father's recovery. The second she was out of the room, Molly slowly stood up and leaned over Jack. The embrace was a bit awkward, but she finally had her mouth next to his ear.

"I was so saddened when I thought you were dead, when I saw you lie there on the floor – all that blood everywhere. But here you are and now I am as happy as can be." She gave him a soft kiss on his cheek. "I love you Jack as I have never loved anybody else." His weakened arms came up and pulled her close as much as his strength could muster. He smiled and closed his eyes. This didn't feel real, but if it was a dream he would milk it for whatever it would give him. She was gentle not to touch his battered face. Her kisses on his neck and his ear felt like butterflies with extraordinary sweet powers. He clearly felt the *pings* in his heart and was dazed from what he felt in his banged up body. He finally uttered what he had wanted to say for the longest time.

"I love you too, Molly; I love you more than you will ever know." By those simple words, Molly's body softened and relaxed; a feeling she had missed all her life. She was finally home and it felt more right than she could have ever imagined. She sat back in the wheelchair, but held on to Jack's hand; finally she broke the silence.

"Not to change the subject," she giggled, "but what happened down in that basement?" Jack looked and smiled.

"Meaning what?"

"You know, you being a bloody hero…"

"… And utterly stupid, out of my mind, insane and severely dim-witted?"

"Yeah, any of the above would describe it well." Jack paused for a second.

"Didn't that gun look familiar to you?" Molly shook her head *no*. "Well it did to me and I realized that he must have found it in your house."

"There wasn't a gun in the house – at least that I knew of."

"You see, I remembered a long time ago Harry mentioned he had bought a big revolver because of a couple of burglaries in the neighborhood; it was to protect you and Anna."

"My grandfather could never hurt a fly. He tried to avoid stepping on ants in the garden, for crying out loud; shooting at somebody would not be his style." Jack laughed carefully.

"You see, that was the beauty of it; no matter how stupid. He bought this huge, shiny canon - and then he loaded it with *blanks*. He had no intention killing or hurting anybody; he just wanted to scare them away."

"That is so like my grandfather," Molly said with a smile. "So in the intense mess we were in, you remembered that?" Jack looked somewhat proud of himself.

"I sure did and that was why I asked Nordgren if he had found the gun in the house."

"So you figured that if he had found it in the house that you could play hero for a day and get away with it?"

"You're good; you're very good, Dear Watson. But don't you see, by the slight noise upstairs and the shadows passing by the basement window a few times, help was on the way; at least I hoped it was. So I figured it was time to act."

"I didn't notice a thing – I was busy being scared and horrified and utterly uncomfortable…" she grinned sarcastically. After a short pause, she continued. "But you didn't really know, did you?"

"Know what?"

"If the bullets were real or just blanks – the jerk could have put some real ones in there." Jack looked thoughtful for a second.

"Yeah you are right, he could have. But I didn't think about that. In retrospect I didn't know for sure," he paused. "But it was worth, you know, taking a chance." Molly sat back stunned in her chair. "Maybe a bit naively I thought I could save the fairy princess."

"But you did – risking your own life in the process." Jack tried to sit up in the bed, looking a bit agitated.

"Now listen Molly, let's get one thing totally straight and out of the way right now. Don't you ever let what happened in that basement guide your feelings for me or even be a part of the feelings we have for each other. I do *NOT* want to believe that you are crazy about me because you think I saved your life. I do *NOT* want that to be a factor at all. Do you fully understand that?" Molly giggled.

"Oh Big Boy, I get rather warm all over with that type of assertiveness; my life-saving hero…" She laughed.

"See? That is precisely what I do not want to happen, not even in fun." And his face turned into a pout for a second. Molly raised herself out of the chair and kissed his sore lips.

"I'll remember that, Big Boy – at least I'll give it a go." And she sat back down, her face turning serious. "But you know we have bigger problems than that." Jack nodded in agreement.

"Yeah – all of the above was a piece of cake compared to what's next. Here comes the tricky part, as they say." The door to the room opened and Caroline came in.

They were all getting back to normal and life would return to sanity and daily routines, she thought. But Caroline didn't know the half of it. Nothing after today would get even close to normal; she would soon be in for the biggest shock ever.

A week later Molly and Jack were discharged from the hospital; for post-care, all they needed were a few follow-up appointments. Besides their healing faces, bruised bones and Jack's new set of circular chest scars, they survived. They both agreed that what they felt for each other was not to any extend based on what they had gone through in that little basement. Their feelings had opened up before that, though never verbally been expressed between them.

They rationalized, planned, discussed, organized and desperately tried to find a way to substantiate their relationship to the people around them; the people they loved so dearly. But even more importantly, try to make sense of their relationship themselves, make fully sure that this was it, no matter the background status of who they were, how they had so far been conceived by everybody around them through all these many years. Jack's situation was clear as the husband and father and grandfather. Molly's situation to some extend was a bit blurry; was she a sister to Jack's children or considered such? Michael and Jasper had always treated and protected her as an equal sibling; she never had. Caroline saw a best friend in Molly and Molly saw that in Caroline as well. But at times Caroline, without admitting so, treated Molly as the big sister she could look up to and full-heartedly trust. But Molly had never treated Caroline as a sister to any extend. When somebody mentioned they looked like sisters, she was the one who for the most corrected the wrong assumptions; Caroline would simply glow and never deny the mistake – she wanted so bad that Molly was her real sister, then as well as now.

They had more or less spent every moment together in secret. They were far from ready to announce their intentions as so many issues had to be solved. There were upcoming emotional aspects to deal with and they found that the art of procrastination came in rather convenient; but down the road it had to be faced.

"Okay so let's talk about the issue of age-difference." Jack started.

"What do you mean?" Molly responded with a semi puzzled look.

"I'm surprised you seem surprised. Don't you think that's an issue we need to address?"

"Okay; so the *issue* is what again?" Now Jack look puzzled.

"You are what?"

"28…"

"And I'm 52 – so that makes for a fluffy cushion of 24 years between us," he said with a grin. "So how do you want to deal with that?"

"I'm not sure what you mean. Is it a problem for you?"

"No it's not; well only to a certain extent…"

"Meaning what?"

"Well, when you hit 50 I'll be 74."

"I'm still not convinced that we have a problem. Anyway, when we get to 50 and 74, such age gap is null and void. I mean the male gender do not age as fast on the exterior as the female gender." Molly smiled and looked at Jack. "And, anyway, you are rather well preserved; you jog daily, you have a solid fitness routine and you don't drink excessively or do drugs. As far as I know you don't smoke and you eat sensibly covering most of the major food-groups."

"So I pass the physical?"

"Well yeah…"

"Well, *yeah* what?"

"There is of course that mental fracture, the time of obsession and basic insanity we need to address."

"It only lasted ten years, for crying out loud; or are you referring to my unbalanced choice of new wife?"

"The first part of course; the second part is a hopeful sign of pure genius and recovery." Molly sipped from her drink. "So you see that all in all we have pretty much scraped away most of those 24 years that are bothering you. Of course if I was 4 and you were 28 we might run into some legal issues – but anyway. So what was the question again?" He sighed.

"You know it also has something to do with how our relationship will be received and accepted by Caroline, Michael and Jasper and the rest of the gang."

"I understand all that Sweetie, and my initial response is that Michael, Linda, Jasper and Ella will embrace that their father is happy again; they just need a bit of time to swallow the idea that he is happy again with Miss Molly. The boys will struggle with going from the sister image to call me *Mother*;" she snickered.

"Not funny," Jack responded, "and Caroline?" Molly's face went serious.

"I'm afraid that she will not have the same understanding as her brothers and everybody else. I would be floored if she responded with *Oh jolly grand and so keen; may I call you mother?* And continue with *Oh jolly good Sweetie, please hurry up and make me some more sisters and brothers, would you darling? I just adore the image of you, oh bloody well, **fornicate** with my father…* Yeah I can hear that."

"You really think so?"

"I really hope not, but I'm also realistic and you should be too."

"And talking about making sisters and brothers; is that part of your overall scheme of things; you know *kids*?"

"Not unless *we* are scheming that sort of thing together; but *yes* it's in the cards."

"Well, fair warning…"

"Do you want more kids?" Jack smiled as she asked; he had suddenly come to yet another revelation in his life.

"If you do I do – seriously. But my biological stopwatch is ticking away, so sooner is better than later, huh?" Molly leaned over and kissed him.

"I know; and there will only be time for very few practice runs, Big Boy. So be ready for action on that wedding night of ours." Now it was Jack's turn to giggle. "Okay, so that side of the equation is agreed upon;" and Molly put a line through an imaginary word on the legal pad in front of her. "By the way, you need to promise me something…"

"…what?"

"That you stay alive and well till at least the ripe age of 80." Jack smiled.

"That should be feasible as long as you don't have more friends like you-know-who show up unannounced…" Molly smirked.

"Let it go Jack, okay?" He nodded. "What else you got concerning that age-gap thing?"

"How about: *Dirty old man seeking very rich, very beautiful and utterly young woman*?"

"Okay, now you just described the basics of our relationship; been there, done that. What else you got?"

"24 years is still a big difference…"

"You are hacking at this over and over. One last time: *your point is?*"

"Well…"

"…Is it because I knew Madonna when she was like a virgin and you remember when the Bill of Rights was signed?"

"Not funny… I didn't grow up with Madonna; but I grew up with the Beatles and I'm proud of that."

"I'm sure they are too. Still sounds ancient to me." Molly was teasing.

"Well it's not like the Beatles arrived on board the Santa Maria, you know." Molly laughed as Jack looked a bit ticked off.

"Let's drop it," she then looked more serious. "But I know what you mean; it's not the two of us who has to accept this gap in the age department…"

"…It's breaking the news to Caroline, Michael, Jasper and all." Jack's face lit up; he looked at Molly across the table. "I got an idea: *YOU* tell them…" Molly giggled.

"Not even close, Buster. When the time is right, *WE'LL* tell them."

"And the time is right when exactly?"

"When we are fully sponsored and supported by an immense quantity of high octane alcohol; that's when." And they tabled the announcement to take place as soon as other things and decisions was dealt with first; many practical things.

"So this will be the second marriage for both of us…" Jack stated.

"The first one for me;" Molly responded.

"You were married before…"

"… I was drunk, so it doesn't count."

"You don't call me anymore – no more love left?" Caroline was teasing Molly on the other end of the line. She did feel rather guilty as she had not found a way to feel comfortable communication with Caroline since hers and Jack's plans for a future together had been decided on, but so far had stayed a secret. She could not give anything away prematurely, not before they knew how to present this slight predicament.

"I have bunches of love left for you, Sweetie; don't you ever forget that…" and they chatted away. Caroline was back at MSU and Molly was still in Casablanca slaving away to get things up to speed.

Though Jack and Molly had been rather organizational, maybe in other peoples view very coldly so, they fully knew how their lives together would function, had to function, and how they wanted it to function. They had explored the ups and downs, negatives and positives over and over; the same result came up again and again: They *were* it. With that established they moved on to other issues like where to live as in one place or two? They decided on two, as Molly was not going to give up her involvement with The West Foundation and all the work needed done; things were not slowing down but more so speeding up. She would not consider retirement. Liz was a fabulous administrator, so Molly felt she could spend less time in Casablanca and the rest on trips, leisure as well as business and time in Washington D.C. They would sell both their houses in D.C. and buy something somewhere else in the area, Georgetown or nearby Virginia.

Jack was adamant about his job and his responsibilities concerning CR Constructions; so their individual work situations were understood and fully respected. But that didn't mean they couldn't spend time together – which they would and a lot of it. That was a priority and they would stick to it. Molly softly suggested, with great hesitance, that with her money they could easily retire and just travel and do stuff together. Jack realized that he had forgotten that whole money-thing, but also acknowledged that he had a responsibility to his partners Nora and Karen. Yes, Karen had inherited a nice sum of money and some property and had bought a third of the interest in CR, with Nora and Jack as the other two thirds. But there were responsibilities that had to be effectuated by Jack – for now, at least. Molly also acknowledged the important part she had concerning her work for The West Foundation. It was nothing she could just drop like that. So they were both on the same track also understanding and respecting each other concerning their many outside commitments.

Then there was the thing about the intimate part of their relationship. During the time they had spent together since their acknowledgement of commitment to each other, for now and for the rest of their lives, it had just been cozy evenings and nights holding hands and kissing. Sure they had spent time in bed, lying close and warm together, but it had only had a very slight hint of physical intimacy. There was a very relaxed and comfortable aura about that whole issue and no urgency towards consummating their love. They were never guided by lust to any extend, in trying to find out if they were *also* compatible in the lovemaking department; or as they called it *romantic physical intimacy.* They were sure that it would not be a problem that couldn't be solved – just another part of the big romantic picture. They had agreed to make their wedding-night that *first time* thing and it would therefore be even more special. Oh, and by the way, they were planning getting married as soon as humanly possible; well, so much for waiting patiently!

But even immense and thorough planning, even by expert planners, can run into unforeseen snafus; especially when the planning involves human beings and the proverbial emotions of same. When secrets are parts of plans to avoid premature excitement, (or despair), parts of these same plans can screw up and backfire. It was not any different concerning Molly and Jack's schedule.

Molly was back in Washington D.C. and it was soon time to officially disclose the intentions concerning their relationship. Were they seeking everybody's blessing and understanding? Of course they were. Did they expect everybody to be happy for them? Of course they didn't – but they were hoping so.

Caroline was in town and had made a date with Molly for their usual girlfriend lunch. Molly didn't have a good feeling about this, as she was struggling to hold back what she really wanted to tell Caroline; she hoped by God when she finally could tell her, that she would embrace the whole thing and… But she was far from sure how Caroline would react. The night before Molly had dinner at Jack's place together with Caroline, Linda and Michael. She had acted as normal as she could under the circumstances, but she was not a talented actress to any extend, so it had been a very frustrating evening.

Now she was sitting at Nonna's waiting for Caroline. She normally didn't drink wine or any other form of alcohol during the day, but for some reason Romano had offered her a glass of Campari. *Did he know her fears?* All Romano knew was a slight feeling of something amiss…

Lunch had been fair, but Molly struggled as she thought she would. There was no doubt that Caroline had sensed something not on track. They were in the middle of the shared dessert when the girlfriend's world started to crumble. Caroline cleared her throat and looked directly into Molly's eyes; and then she looked down.

"This is really awkward and I hope you'll forgive me, but I have to ask; I have to be assured that I'm *so* wrong…"

"… So wrong about what?" Molly asked, well knowing what was coming next.

"What's going on between you and my Dad?" Though Molly knew it would come, she was still stung by its clearness. She was an expert negotiator and a charmingly effective business woman; but this was a very different ballgame.

"What do you mean *going on*?" She asked, but fully knew what it meant. This was right away utmost uncomfortable for both of them.

"All last evening, the way the two of you looked at each other, those hidden glances, those nervous giggles and the way you slightly touched each other like nobody would notice. That's what I mean by *going on*…"

"So what is it that you think is going on?"

"I hope what seems somewhat obvious is *NOT* going on, that's what I think." She hesitated for a moment. "Okay, are there anything going on between you and my father that I should be concerned about?" Again it stung Molly as she knew she had to tell Caroline; this was not according to the overall plan, but she could not see any way to avoid it anymore. She took the deepest breath ever and tried to hold the tears back. In a shaky voice she told the truth as friends must.

"Your father and I are in love with each other…" Caroline's whole being froze within a split second; her eyes nearly popped out of her face. "We found out some time back and it kind of began to become obvious when we were in the South of France with George…"

"I'm sorry, could you go back a couple of sentences and say *what* again…" Caroline's voice was shaking and weak.

"Caroline, your father and I are in love and we want to get married and spend the rest of our lives together, with you, the boys…" Caroline's face turned eerie red.

"Are you out of your fucking mind?" She exploded and her voice got louder. "You and my father getting married? Are both of you totally insane? What the hell is the matter with you?" She gasped for air. "It will never happen, ever. You and my father will only happen over my dead body. Are you crazy or something? He's a million years older than you and you are supposed to be my best friend and like a sister to me."

"I am your best friend, but I am not your sister; never was…" Molly stuttered.

"Michael and Jasper have always treated you like a sister…"

"That's sweet of them, but I have never been and I never will be their sister…" Caroline pushed her chair back and grabbed her purse.

"Best friends don't marry best friend's fathers. But then again we are not best friends anymore. You just shut that to hell by bedding my father…"

"We haven't…"

"… Just shut up Molly – I'll make damn sure that you and my father will not happen and I want you out of my life and I want you out of my family's life and that cannot happen fast enough." She scuffed. "What kind of a friend you turned out to be; and after all these years…"

"Sweetie, please listen…" Molly pleaded; but Caroline had made up her mind.

"… Don't bloody *sweetie* me. You and I are as done as you and my father are. And don't think I cannot talk some common sense into him – because that I can. So blow away Miss West and don't come back because you will never be welcome again ever – I'll make so bloody sure of that…" then she turned on her heels and stormed out of the restaurant leaving behind a sobbing and devastated Molly.

Caroline spent a long time in her car crying before she was able to drive. Everything in her world had turned confused and crazy. Just the thought of Molly and her father together infuriated her no end. How could they even think this would be possible? How could they have double-crossed her like that? The many thoughts flew blurredly around in her head, but she clearly knew her first step of action; she had to confront her father immediately. He had to be told to drop anything *Molly* now and forever; *they* were never going to be an item - ever.

Romano had observed the exchange between Molly and Caroline and Caroline's swift and angered exit. He brought a bottle of Chianti and two glasses to Molly's table and sat down. She was sobbing and shaking her head and only looked up when he gently caressed her hand.
"Have a little vino – it only helps, okay?" Molly tried to smile but couldn't.
"Thanks…" and she emptied the glass in one gulp; Romano giggled.
"That's my girl – anything you want to talk about?" For some reason Molly wanted to tell her longtime friend and so she did. After half an hour and halfway through the second bottle of Chianti, Romano pretty much knew what had happened; he smiled at Molly and spoke softly.
"You know, some time back you and Jack were having lunch here, you know, before you knew that you were in love with each other. I said to myself *Romano, there is the perfect couple.* At first it appeared a strange thought as I have seen you since you were what six or something, a little girl, you know. Jack at times would carry you in to Nonna's on his shoulders for fun, or you would sit on his lap and talk with him; he would always listen and laugh. And you grew into a beautiful mature woman and Jack, well, he's a mature man, and I see no reason why you shouldn't connect, you know, be together." Molly looked at this big sweet man with love in her eyes. "And you of all people know what a good man Jack is. He and Sara welcomed you into their hearts in seconds. They were both proud of you and loved you with no conditions, you know," he paused and smiled at Molly; "…and now we are all much older."

Molly felt comforted by the words and for his acceptance of her and Jack. He was close like family and a true friend for so many years; his support was immense. Later he drove Molly to her hotel; she didn't stay in her own house after the incident with Nordgren – also the reason she had put the house on the market immediately. She considered calling Jack, but decided to wait. Instead she took a long warm shower; soon wearing her large PJ's and was fast asleep. Though it was in the middle of the day, it had never-the-less already been excruciatingly exhausting. On the other end of town, another storm burst open.

Caroline's car came to a screeching halt in the reserved parking area in front of the building. Several people milling around outside as well as inside, turned and saw a furious young woman racing towards the entrance, ripped the doors open and disappeared. Jack was deep in thought in front of his computer, working on a proposal when he heard the commotion in the front office. He didn't get time to give it any thoughts as the door swung open and banged against the wall. Caroline stood in the middle of the floor with a red face and moist cheeks; Jack only looked up for a split second. He had seen her like this so many times when she was a little girl, not so often as a teenager and so far never as an adult; but that was in the process of changing. His attention went back to his monitor again.
"How could you?" She more or less screamed.
"I'm sorry; I'll never do it again…"
"Are you out of your bloody mind?"
"I'm sure that must be it…"
"Were you ever going to tell me?"
"Probably not…
"It is never gonna happen – ever."
"Sounds good to me…" Jack finally looked up at his furious daughter. "Sorry, just for reference: What the heck are you talking about?"
"You and Molly, that's what I'm talking about," she made a short pause. "Are you totally insane?"
"I thought we already established that." His mind shorted for a second. This was not the way they had planned the announcement; that was for tomorrow evening. His response was automatic. "Who told you?"

"Well guess who; Molly of course. We just had lunch and she admitted that you and her are *in love*." The last bit came out cynical and derogatory. "Is that true?"

"I wasn't there…"

"Just stop it Dad. This is serious and it will not happen."

"I know it's serious that we love each other; and what is it that will not happen, Caroline?"

"You and Molly, that's what." Jack finally looked up, put his pen on the desk and leaned back in the chair. He had thought many times about what to say next, but it wasn't easy.

"Molly and I will happen, Caroline. We love each other and after we found out, we have discussed all the intricate reasons why, how will it work, what do we do, what do we want, is it right, is it wrong… and the last bit, also an utterly important one was: How are they going to react? With you storming in here, I can say that was not one of the reactions we were looking for."

"What the hell did you expect?"

"We expected…"

"… Drop that *we* stuff; as I said it will not happen…"

"… We expected at least respect, if not love and acceptance. Your respect is very important to us, but as strongly as we feel about each other, it's not essential. We will be saddened if you do not accept this relationship, Caroline; we will be very saddened, but it's not going to refrain us for a life together."

"You are not going to get my blooming blessing – ever. You guys are sick and irresponsible – I mean just look at the age difference, the fact that Molly was like a sister to me…"

"… She was never your sister…"

"… The way Michael and Jasper always treated her as a sister…"

"…. She was never a sister to them either…"

"… The way Mom loved her as a daughter…"

"… Wrong, Caroline; your mother always treated Molly as a true friend – age difference aside – never as a daughter."

"Molly is 28 and you are like a million years older…"

"We talked about the implications of that; many times over. It's not quite a million years, but close… "

"I can't sit around and look at my former best friend and my immature father make total fools of themselves – never ever." Jack looked at his daughter's rage.

"What is it precisely that you can't accept? That we are in love, that we like spending time together, that we are compatible on so many levels, that in spite of a few years between us we still see a fascinating future together? What precisely is it that aggravates you so much? Why can't you just be happy for us?"

"Because it is so wrong - you and her."

"Oh, it's the sex thing that bothers you?"

"Don't even go there. Just thinking about that makes me sick. She was my best friend and sister and my father wants to be with her – that's so sick; don't you get it?"

"Obviously I don't – but you don't get it either, do you? Are you so blinded by *what was* that you cannot see *what is*?" Jack paused. This was not turning out well. He most certainly did not want to lose Caroline if could be avoided.

"No it's not me, Dad; you are the one being delusional. Are you being guided by your genitals and that whole *much younger woman* thing?

"Wow, Caroline. *No* to both. Not that's it's any of your business, but we have not had sex. Secondly, the age-gap thing did not appear before the by-the-way issues came up for discussion; it has absolutely no meaning to us, but we realize of course that it might be an issue for others; case-in-point, you being here screaming at me – not what I had hoped for."

"My blessings will only be in your dreams – trust me on that one." Jack watched his daughter's anger; he leaned further back in the chair.

"Now let's be fair; you were the one who wanted me to go out and date, find somebody. You even used the term *get laid*. I did everything you asked me to do; I dated every single woman who had the courage to spend time with me. Then I finally found somebody and you find it all wrong. What am I missing here?"

"I never suggested Molly – it would be like dating your own daughter…"

"No it's not. We have been there and talked about that so many times; let's not grind it into the dirt again." Caroline stood silently for a moment and then she looked straight into her father's eyes for one last time.

"Well, you have a nice life. I'm not going to stand here and bless this totally insane relationship of yours – that is not

going to happen in a million years. If you want to make a fool of yourself, it's not going to be with me on the sideline." With that she turned around and raced out of the office. Jack got out of his chair and followed her.
"Caroline, come on; let's talk about it…" But Caroline was too furious and down the stairs, in her car, screeching through the parking lot, out into the street – and gone.

"What was that all about?" Nora was in Jack's office.
"Nothing…"
"… Rather loud *nothing*, wouldn't you say?" Jack looked up at Nora as he picked up the phone; he tried to smile.
"Can we please do this later?" Nora nodded and left. What she thought she heard of the *conversation* had been eye-opening; unless she had misunderstood what she heard. In a way she hoped for the misunderstanding.

Molly picked up on the fourth ring; she sounded exhausted. Jack gave her the short version of his confrontation with Caroline and Molly gave him her version of the scenario that took place at Nonna's.
"What do you think will happen next?" Jack carefully asked.
"She will come around and be part of our lives; that she will at least respect our decision." She paused. "Do you think she will?"
"You know how stubborn she is…"
"…from Sara."
"Yeah, from Sara for the most," Jack giggled, "but I'm not sure what she is planning. My initial thought is that she'll come around after a few days, you know. She'll get the picture when we all get together tomorrow evening." Molly nodded in agreement, but was far from convinced that would happen; Jack didn't believe it either. After a short pause he continued. "Okay, I don't really believe that, do you?"
"Not for a second…" and the line went dead.

Linda, Michael, Nicole and Frank had arrived a bit early. The twins were immediately hanging around their grandfather; he would have been disappointed if they didn't. Ella and Jasper showed up a bit later together with Karen and Nora. Finally Victoria and Brandon arrived. Molly and Jack had opted for Nonna's to cater the simple spaghetti feast, so two of Romano's people were there to make that part fluent and easy. There were a few things to be brought up, so being involved in food preparation was not ideal.

Jack had several times sneaked into his study and dialed Caroline's number, but she didn't pick up. He left messages on her voice-mail; he had called her three times within forty minutes. Finally he asked everybody to sit down and they started dinner.

Conversation was as usual brisk, noisy and fun. Jack was sitting nervously at one end of the table and Molly was sandwiched between Nicole and Frank on one side, as they had demanded. When dessert was being served Jack cleared his throat; this was the moment he had both feared and looked forward to – but mostly feared. He tapped the glass with his fork and everybody stopped talking and looked at him. *Formality* had never been part of the socializing within this group, so it took all by surprise.

"There is an alternative motive to bring you all here tonight. It's something I have been thinking about to such depth and heights that I am sure of what I feel and what I have decided is honest, logical and very real." He had everybody's attention as they all felt the seriousness in his voice. Frank turned towards Molly for one second and had figured it out. His hand grabbed hers under the table and as soon as that had happened, Nicole's hand held on to Molly as well. She felt a rush through her body as she glanced at these two *old* children. *How could they know already?* She thought; Jack continued.

"Before you react to what is next, I do want to tell you about the process I went through, that *we* went through to make sure that what we felt, what we wanted, what we needed, were thoroughly discussed, agreed to and settled. The many levels of practicality, logic and the big one: *reality,* had to be handled without having the *being in love part* blind us and make us believe that all would be well." The room was as silent as rooms can get. Nicole and Frank kept holding on to Molly's hands. It was a warm and wonderful feeling for the three of them, and Jack went on. "As all the practical and emotional matters had cleared our deepest concerns, we felt very good about what we were going to do next. But there was that last and very important bit, one very dear to our hearts: the respect, understanding and acceptance of our union by the people we love, the people we adore and that *people* is you." Several glances had started heading Molly's way and as she became aware of that, her body froze and she held on to Nicole and Frank's hands even tighter. Jack cleared his throat once again; with a shaky voice he continued. "Molly and I have decided to get married, as we want to spend the rest of our lives together…" Jack stopped breathing as the room went even more silent. Molly was sure her heart had stopped, but the squeezing of her hands made her realize that she was still alive. Everybody's eyes were now glued on her, but still no response. Jack was looking for any sign of reaction, but none came quickly. Brandon Hamilton was the first to break the silence.

"Well well, Dear Jack and Molly. That one was not expected – at least what I'm concerned. Wow, that's – exciting. I guess congratulation is in place…" Both Jasper and Michael were staring at their father. Linda and Ella were smiling and Victoria's mouth had been open for a while.

"I'm sorry, but isn't this weird to you guys?" Michael gestured around the table. "Molly, you've been like a sister to me, to Jasper and Caroline. I mean, come on, you guys; this is insane…" Linda put her hand on his under the table; Jack looked at Michael.

"I have never considered Molly a daughter of mine nor did your mother. She has since she was a small girl been adamant about not being your sister…" Molly's voice finally appeared.

"Michael, I am not your sister; I have never been and will never be. I tried to find out why I was concerned about that and found that the simple reason was I did not want to be totally glued and committed to you or Jasper or Caroline or Sara or Jack. I lost my parents and that was hard. I didn't want to lose a brother or sister or mother or father again." Michael smirked.

"So now you'll be my stepmother," he cynically stated. Linda looked at him in a flash and he quickly knew better. "I'm sorry, that was not necessary," he said looking at Molly. "But you must understand how this relationship will be perceived, what other people will think; what *we* will think about it."

"Michael," Jack responded, "we have no illusions about instant acceptance, none at all. Trust me, that when Molly and I had the slightest feeling for each other, it was not communicated for a long long time. I wanted to know how I really felt and would not to any extent jeopardize whatever relationship we had at the time by blurting out that I loved her. What if she didn't feel the same way? That whole process alone, gave me a lot of thinking time and trust me, I did an awful lot of that." Molly cleared her throat.

"I was going through the same process and it was very weird. I felt like I was a big time traitor and had a horrible time being around all of you as I had this secret even Jack didn't know about." She paused for a moment and looked around the table. "All we are asking is that you give it some time. Whatever judgment or decision you come up with, we will both fully understand and respect; and whatever it is, we will always love you – very much." Ella looked at Molly with a small smile.

"This might be off track but I'm sure you have been there: how about the age difference – what is it?" Frank sat up.

"It's 24 years…" Molly turned and looked at him with a puzzled look as if saying: How the heck do *you* know? Nicole smiled and squeezed Molly's hand.

"Frank pretty much knows everything…"

"Nicole does too…" he responded and a smirk formed on his face. "Do any of you know that when Grover Cleveland married Frances Folsom in 1886 she was 21 and he was 49?" Everybody turned towards Frank; Jasper spoke first.

"And your point is?"

"They lived rather happily together and the 28 years difference seemingly didn't interfere in *their* union." Jasper shook his head.

"Whatever, Frank." Now it was Linda's turn.

"Initially I am just so stunned. With all the dating you have done so many months and then this… I'll take you up on taking some time to think about it. Now don't get me wrong, I'm pretty much for it, for your relationship and all, but it's just this thing about Molly being your wife and you being Molly's husband that needs some adjusting to." Jack nodded and Molly's eyes turned moist.

"Thanks Linda," she whispered.

"I'm with Linda," Ella expressed. "This is so coming out of the blue and I'm still a bit numb, but again, I'm on track with Linda; so please give me some time, okay?" Both Molly and Jack nodded in appreciation.

"Wow, and I thought you girls would be all over them with reasons why it won't work, is insane and stupid and so forth – but then this? Wow." Jasper shook his head. Ella kissed Jasper on the cheek.

"I'm glad we can still surprise you, dear." Jasper turned and smiled back. Michael looked at Victoria and she was still sitting with her mouth slightly open.

"And what does Aunt Vicky have to say about this newsflash?" She startled a little and looked at Michael, her open mouth closing and turning into a smile.

"I think it is wonderful, I really do. I have been in love with Jack many years and somewhat obsessed with him – only God knows why, but Molly and Jack? Yes that is so wonderful. I always thought the best couple I ever had the privilege to know was Sara and Jack, but you know what? Molly and Jack will no doubt be of the same quality. Since Molly showed up again, I have seen a huge change in Jack, a very positive one and I tried to figure out what it was. Finally I knew; it was because Molly was around, was part of all our lives again. This is not in retrospect, but Jack started to look at Molly as he used to look at Sara. But this time around he didn't *see* Sara, he only saw Molly." Victoria's smile was big and warm. "Sure I wanted that cute body of his and become his girlfriend or wife; but not lately – and nothing personal, Jack. I have everything I ever wanted here next to me," she said as she leaned over and kissed Brandon. "I can only wish you both the best ever and I fully respect and accept your relationship. You are a very lucky couple." Victoria got up and was soon embracing both Jack and Molly.

Nora and Karen also gave their full support, though both struggled with the age-gap fact. But with time it disappeared as they experienced Molly and Jack together as a couple; most times they couldn't see who was the younger and who was the older.

Jasper and Michael were hesitant in their full support and both felt that maybe time would tell. The issue was the sister becoming their father's wife, but they were both mature enough to acknowledge that legally there were no fences to stop them from a future together. But there was still that image to deal with – and that would take some time to fade and disappear into acceptance and respect. But nobody had heard from Caroline; she had not showed up nor had she returned calls.

It had all been a blur; tears mixed with disbelief. She felt utterly betrayed by both her father and her *former* best friend. How could they even think a union of the two was sane and acceptable to any extend? Were they totally stupid and ignorant? But it was the feeling of treachery that was tearing Caroline's insides apart. She had stopped by her father's house, grabbed a few items, stuffed them into a suitcase and got back in the waiting taxi and off to the airport. She knew she had to stop and think, but she got a quick departure, had to hurry through security and onboard the plane, so thinking before take-off had been impossible. One of the items she had hurriedly grabbed was the framed photo of her and Molly, arm in arm, in front of the library.

As the plane was humming away, she pulled out her legal pad and divided the top page with a line, creating two columns: negative and positive. But she quickly found that she was too emotional to be rational, so she put the pen down. After a few minutes the soft movements of the plane lulled her to sleep, something she had needed for a long time. When she was rested and back at MSU, she would decide what to do. At this moment she knew what she wanted to happen, but she was aware that those wishes would not come true. She had seen that in both Molly's and her father's eyes.

There had also been this calmness about her father as she was screaming at him; the same calmness she enjoyed all the years as a girl at home, when her mother was alive. He was so calm and happy and nothing could knock him over. He handled everything with stoic control and made everybody around him feel safe and comfortable. But that had all changed when mother died, she thought tearfully. Just those few minutes in his office seemed as her *old* dad *was* back for real. He could have screamed and yelled or rolled over and played dead, but he didn't. He listened to her ranting and yelling and had tried to reason, even making a joke or two, but she had been too enraged to acknowledge that maybe she was wrong, maybe they were right in their decision. But for now she was not going to stand around and applaud their effort. It was so totally wrong and immoral.

Caroline decided to make changes, as she would not have any more contact with her father and certainly not with Molly. Her very best friend in the world had yet again betrayed her – this time teaming up with her father.

The wedding was lovely. The guest list had been short; only family and close friends. Michael and Jasper did the best man bit; Linda and Ella the bridesmaids. Molly missed Caroline and had wanted her to *give her away* to her father; at least that had been the initial plan. But nobody had heard from Caroline and nobody had been able to find her. She had moved out of the apartment she shared with two roommates; they did not know where she had disappeared to. MSU admission could only say that Caroline Miller had not signed up for the upcoming semester and had not attended school the last several weeks. Michael was devastated when he received that information. Both he and Jasper didn't feel that *they* should be punished for what she felt was wrong, as it didn't have anything to do with them. Michael and Linda took a couple of days off and flew to MSU, looked around, asked around, but found no signs of Caroline. Her mobile phone was deactivated and no new number available. Even Nicole and Frank tried their Internet magic, but it would bring them into dangerous and illegal areas to obtain the information they wanted; for once their parents said *no*.

Even though the ceremony was romantic and fun, Caroline's absence had put a damper on the festivities. The reception was intimate and warm; Molly and Jack had received many wishes for happiness and as they retired to their little get-away place, they had been exhausted, though so utterly happy. The wedding night had not disappointed and was worth waiting for. Warmness and patience had been the dominant factors and as they glowed in the aftermath, they both smiled with relaxed and sweaty faces. Their life together had started – on a very good note.

"So I take it this means that we'll never do that thing, huh Jack?" Victoria had looked stunning. She had always looked stunning, but on this night at the wedding reception, there had been something beyond stunning about her, which Jack couldn't put a finger on.

"I believe that all bets are off," he smiled as he kissed her cheek.

"You know I always wanted you to make love to me..."

"I know you did and seriously I have always been flattered; I mean why me? You can choose any man alive, so why me?" Victoria smiled.

"I believe it's that obsession thing; that impossible dream."

"So it's not due to my stud-muffin looks and sex appeal?"

"Sorry Jack, never been because the lack of that. Just something that was never wired correctly inside my feeble brain..." Jack laughed.

"Well, if you are trying to make me feel good, you failed." Now it was Victoria's turn to smile.

"Sorry Jack," she leaned close to him and planted a big wet kiss on his lips. "That was for being such a good sport and a terrific friend all these years. Remember that I will love you my own silly way till the day I die." Jack kissed her back.

"I love you too, Vicky, I really do." It was at that point Molly was next to them.

"So what's up? Still trying to ravage my husband?" Molly said teasingly; Victoria grabbed Molly's hand.

"No, those days are over. But I'll hold on to the rights of still fantasizing about him." She teased back. Molly embraced Victoria and whispered into her ear.

"Just so you know, Miss Vicky, you touch you die; understood?" Victoria nodded and squeezed Molly lovingly. She felt warm happiness for both Jack and Molly. She had to admit that it was a union that was meant to be. She walked away from them swinging her lower extremities a bit more than usual: she knew Jack was watching - all men did.

"I mean, look at that body..." Molly looked straight at Jack.

"Now, don't turn into a dirty old man on me – not on our wedding night." Jack looked up and down Molly's body.

"What is it they say: why have hamburgers when you can have...?"

"Thanks for the analogy. I'll stick to basic compliments, if you don't mind." Jack looked up and down again.

"Your curves rock my socks off..." Molly laughed.

"Much better – you're catching on."

That was the last communication between Jack and Victoria concerning *that thing*. A few months later Victoria married Brandon Hamilton, and her beaming substitute father, Romano Rossi, proudly gave her away. Their lives were full of work and fun; but mostly work - that was how they liked it. They stayed good friends with Molly and Jack.

"So what do we call Molly?" Nicole was curious about the legal term of their grandfather's new wife.
"You could call her *Molly*, maybe..." Frank smiled at his grandfather's silly remark.
"So it's not going to be step-grandmother?" Molly's face was quickly two inches in front of Frank's; she whispered through her teethes.
"Now listen buster, if you ever even think in those terms, you will regret it for the rest of your miserable life, got it?" Frank stepped back and looked at Jack.
"She's a feisty one, isn't she?"
"Yeah and I decided to keep her for myself, so hands off, boy."

Nicole and Frank had presented the rings to Molly and Jack, though Frank was against it. He thought it stupid and non-practical and something small girls in frilly dresses should do. But as Molly's big beautiful eyes had begged him to, he sacrificed his male ego. Of course he had attached a condition; so Nicole and Frank wore black suits, ties and hats, as well as really cool dark sunglasses as they strolled down the aisle. They adored Molly and though they had visited their grandfather often through the years, their visits to Molly and Jack's new house increased. And with their own fully equipped computer room there, they spent many nights at their *grandparents*. They also went on trips with them and often stayed in Casablanca. The times they all spent in Saint Paul-de-Vence were especially wonderful; Bernadette cried joyfully every time.

Michael and Linda found many ways to work together. Not to break any rules and regulations, they would compare notes, cases, evidence, suspects; pretty much anything they could do to help each other solve their cases. In many instances they also helped out their colleagues. Though they were breaking the rules *in secret* at home, everybody including their superiors knew what was going on. But due to the overall positive rate of solving crimes, nobody complained. Nicole and Frank kept helping out with research on their computers – at times borderline legal, but nobody neither watched nor cared – really. The results were that convincing. As they were also married to their jobs, having Molly and Jack look after the twins when in town, was a blessing. But when they were off work, it had for the most something to do with Nicole and Frank.

Ella and Jasper stayed childless. Ella had become a partner of the firm and Jasper was in seventh heaven every single day as he could get out of his chair and walk next door for a kiss and a hug – which he often took advantage of. She finally asked Jasper if he would marry her and his simple response was: "What took you so long?"

Nora finally gave up finding the one and only and then he walked into her office and asked for a job. He didn't get the job, but he got Nora.

Karen was as busy as ever in her partnership with Jack and Nora. She took business classes at Georgetown University, flew around the world participating in conferences related to anything *building*. She was still considered young in her position, but had obtained a vast quantity of experience which of course benefitted CR very well. Her next move would be to buy Jack out of his third of the partnership together with Nora. Nora was all for it, as Jack's interests started to switch to his relationship and life with Molly. It was understandable, especially now, since Molly was eight months pregnant. And then their world fell apart.

The excruciating pains going through Molly's entire body had happened at a time when Nicole and Frank were visiting. They had spent the night and were now enjoying breakfast. Jack had left early for work and as Nicole and Frank heard the piercing screams from the second floor bedroom, they had rushed upstairs as fast as they could. The second they saw Molly on the floor, Nicole was on the phone dialing 911. After that call, she called her grandfather's number and he would meet them at the hospital. The ambulance arrived within minutes and the looks on the medic's faces as they brought Molly out didn't look encouraging, Frank thought.

As they arrived at the emergency room, several nurses and doctors were waiting and ready for immediate action. Nicole and Frank were more or less pushed aside as the gurney rolled into OR. Jack arrived a few minutes later and hooked up with the twins. He quickly found a doctor attached to the situation and what he told Jack was not what Jack wanted to hear – not in a million years.

Nancy Wilson had never lied beyond the convenience of the proverbial white ones now and then; everybody did it, so guilt was, not surprisingly, really a factor. But keeping Caroline's whereabouts a secret had become horrifyingly uncomfortable. First Nancy didn't fully get why Caroline was so defiantly against her father's marriage to Molly. Sure it was her father and her best friend; that made it understandably extremely awkward, but they were both adults and obviously loved each other in spite of the many levels of concerns they and others may have had. But they had figured it out and forged ahead with their lives. So why Caroline couldn't respect that, was a mystery; kind of a mystery.

She had never known a more stubborn person than Caroline. In one of their forensic classes, the instructor adamantly claimed that a certain chemical applied to two slightly different materials, showed the exact same reaction. Caroline had calculated and recalculated again and again and had finally confronted the instructor with her results; the instructor's test-results were wrong, she stated. The other students had giggled as she battled it out with the instructor. By her calculations one of the materials should have a tiny fraction more of an acidy reaction. The instructor had laughed and explained that it had been proven over and over that the reactions were precisely the same. He finally had to ask Caroline to drop the subject so the class could move on; but she didn't want to drop it. The next four days Caroline spent most of her waking hours in the lab; Nancy had played along with her, but with the attitude that she was wrong. But four days later and after many tests and retests, Caroline plainly stated: *I was right and he was wrong.* She had proven without a doubt that under certain conditions you would see a more acidy reaction; just as she had stated to begin with. Her stubbornness had worked overtime. After the instructor admitted to the class that she had been right, she never ever talked about it again. Bragging rights were never Caroline's beef; but she sure was stubborn.

So maybe her stubbornness was working overtime concerning her reaction to her father and Molly's marriage? Had it gone to the point where she felt she couldn't go back because of stupid pride? Did she desperately try to find a reason for her to embrace their union? Or did she really hate them that much? And if she did: *WHY*? Michael had called Nancy so many times and it hurt her more and more listening to his pleadings for help. She felt he knew she had contact with his sister, so he knew she was lying. It was time to talk with Caroline yet again.

"At this time we are not sure what we are dealing with," the physician was sitting behind his desk in front of a distraught Jack. It had been two horrible days already and Molly was obviously not getting better. "But your wife is kept stable and the baby is closely monitored as well. We are running all possible tests for all possible reasons and if this is a known entity, we will find it." Jack sat rigid in the chair, racing through his brain for ideas, questions, solutions; just about anything. "One of our concerns is that perhaps at some point your wife picked up some form of germs in Africa; some virus or invasion of some form of unknown bacteria stemming from that. Taking that into consideration we have been in contact with several hospitals in South Africa, Kenya and the Ivory Coast. We have supplied them with every minute detail we are faced with here; the condition of the pregnancy, your wife's symptoms and background, your health and health history. Hopefully they can find relative cases and treatments and will advise us accordingly."

"Do anything and everything you can; money is not a problem. I want Molly and the baby to get well and healthy again and fast is not fast enough." He paused. "What else can I do?"

"Be by your wife's bedside, talk with her the few moments she is coherent and also when she is resting or at sleep. Read to her, touch her and comfort her in any way you can. Just like you have been doing; it's a great help and she gets a lot of strength and energy from you that way; we are very sure of that." He got up from the chair and Jack did too. He looked into Jack's eyes as he spoke slowly. "We are doing the very best we can, and as long as we can buy time keeping everything level, I'm sure we'll get to a solution; so hang in there with us, okay?" Jack nodded. The doctor smiled. "So what are you going to name the baby-boy?" He asked optimistically; Jack smiled a little.

"George – we'll name him George; that was my father's name…" The doctor smiled as he walked away. He suddenly turned towards Jack as they were leaving the office.

"By the way, who is *Caroline*?" Jack stopped in confusion.

"That would be my daughter. Why?"

"Your wife has called out her name several times in her sleep – haven't she done that while you were in the room?" Jack shook his head.

"Sounding like?"

"Kind of pleading, I don't know, like she wants her to be here, perhaps? Has she been around for visits?" Jack shook his head again.

"No; we actually can't get hold of her – a long and sad story."

"Oh well, just wanted you to know…"

Molly didn't get better the following 24 hours – quite the opposite. The medical staff was running desperate as none of the treatments showed the results and improvements they were hoping for. Jack stayed in the room all the time, pleading and begging and praying. He recalled again and again his father's farewells to his wife, the mother Jack never met. He saw images of the same here, but he did not want to acknowledge the severity of the situation. There would be no reason for him to continue life without Molly or the baby. He had struggled so many years trying to handle one terrible loss; he was sure he could not survive another and he was positive he didn't even want to. But this was all about Molly now, all about baby-George. She was so young and vibrant and had so much life to live and life to give. And she was so close to become a mother and Jack was sure that she would be exceptional in that department as well. But as the situation darkened every hour, the future looked dim and uncertain; Jack felt horrified that he could do nothing to help.

"Caroline?" Molly's voice was barely audible. Jack immediately moved closer, wiped the sweat off her forehead and kissed her.

"What sweetheart – what can I do?" He asked with moist eyes looking lovingly at his fatigued wife.

"Is Caroline here?"

"No sweetheart; do you want her to be here?" Her tired eyes looked pleading at Jack.

"She ran away, didn't she?" Jack nodded.

"Yes she did and we have not been able to find her."

"She hates me, doesn't she?" Jack shook his head.

"No, she doesn't hate you, Molly. She is just very confused." A vague smile formed on Molly's lips.

"Can we try to *un*-confuse her, Jack?" He smiled back – she still had her sense of humor - a bit.

"Yeah, of course we can try to *un*-confuse her," he squeezed her hand and instantly a determined look showed on his face.

"Stay where you are, okay?" He got up as she tried to smile again.

"I'll stay put…" but Jack was out the door as Nicole and Frank walked in.

"Is she awake?" Nicole asked. Jack smiled and nodded.

"Go right in guys – thanks for being here; perfect timing." And he quickly disappeared down the hallway.

After his father yet again had explained the utmost necessity to locate Caroline and get her back to D.C. immediately, Michael made a decision that could cost him his job. He was on the phone at once. Nancy picked up on the second ring. He quickly told her the situation Molly was in and that she had called out for Caroline again and again. It was essential for him to get in contact with his sister right away. But Nancy stuck to her own stupid stubbornness, as she repeated that she did not have any contact with Caroline; then Michael went livid.

"Nancy, this is a matter of life and death. This is not a fucking game about who knows what and *why am I protecting my pathetic friend?* shit; friend or no friend. I have been around long enough to know that you are lying for her, but this is not the time to do so anymore." He abruptly hung up and dialed yet another number.

"I need a favor, please."
"*Personal,* as in: *not an authorized search*?"
"Precisely."
"Well, Michael, I do owe you and as long as my name stays out of this: what do you need?" Michael gave his friend the number and five minutes later a one page fax buzzed through. Looking at the bottom of the page it showed that Nancy had made a call within 30 seconds after his call with her had ended. He looked at the rest of the page and noticed that same number twelve times. There could be no doubt and he dialed the number as fast as he could.

Caroline picked up the phone from the desk and looked at the LCD screen. No caller ID, so she didn't answer. A moment later it rang again and then again and again. Finally there was a pause and the phone vibrated with a short ringtone which told her a voice message had been recorded. Very hesitantly she flipped open the phone and speed-dialed her mail-box.

As she listened to the message she slowly sat down, her face expressing fright and horror. As the recording ended she couldn't move as she was frozen stiff and all she could do was barely dealing with the thoughts racing through her head, thoughts of terrifying proportions as she now felt guilt amass and sensed strong embarrassment taking over. She knew her stubbornness had brought her out of control, as it had taken over at a point where she had not been able to find a way back. Now she understood how her father could have gone through such a long time of depression; he simply had not been able to find a way out of that deep hole called stubbornness. And now, when Molly needed her the most, she was hiding and staying away; Caroline was doing the same thing Molly had done, but Molly had come back. She looked at the phone with tears of guilt running down her face. She had missed her father so much for so long and Molly, she couldn't even express how much she had missed her best friend ever. What had she done? Was it time to pay?
It only rang once.
"Michael?"

"Where are you?"

"I'm so sorry…"

"… We don't have time for that crap now; again, where are you?"

"Chicago…"

"Get to O'Hare as fast as you can. How long will that take you to get there?"

"Less than an hour…"

"Go to United's counter and they'll have a ticket ready for the first flight available to Dulles. When you get to Dulles, either I will be there or Linda; somebody will pick you up"

"Okay…" she whimpered.

"And Caroline – *DO THIS RIGHT NOW*." He screamed and hung up. Moments later Caroline had stuffed a few things into her backpack and was on the way to O'Hare.

After reading the text message on his phone, Jack smiled while holding on to Molly's hand as he read it for her.

"Caroline will be here soon…" Though her eyes were closed, she smiled a tired and brave smile and mumbled:

"Good – very good," and she went back to sleep.

Linda had always wanted to do this, but had never in all her time with the police department or at the academy, been behind the wheel in emergencies or done car chases. The negative aspect of her finally getting a chance to feel what it was like, the great adrenalin rush that she had only heard about, was that she could very possibly lose her job – and quickly. Michael had addressed her concern with *screw it* and that was good enough for her.

Caroline had only waited a few minutes by the curb when the flashing police cruiser arrived. Linda popped out, embraced Caroline for a second, mumbled welcome back and shoved her into the front passenger seat. Belts securely fastened, she started up the powerful engine, flipped a couple of switches and was off in a blur of flashing lights and ear-piercing sirens. Any vehicle in front quickly scurried to the side of the road and it wasn't before they reached the hospital that the lights and sirens were turned off. Linda's face was red from excitement and wet from sweat - and Caroline could finally exhale.

"Wow; that was so cool, don't you think?" Caroline couldn't move any parts of her body if she wanted to. "That was so unreal…" She could only nod in agreement – her vocal cords not functioning quite yet. "Okay, let's go see Molly…" And within seconds they were in the lobby and by the elevator.

Riding up to third floor, Caroline's body suddenly went from rigid to shaky. The feelings she had felt when she heard from Michael in Chicago game back even stronger. She feared the reunion with Molly and her father. She was also overwhelmed with the importance given her to be here - for Molly's sake. It was never a question of yes or no concerning returning; it had only been a question about how she could fight and escape her controlling stubbornness and then get back; she had a lot of explaining to do and a lot of apologies to hand out. As the elevator doors opened she took a deep breath. Linda was down the hall before she turned around to see why Caroline wasn't following her; she was still standing by the closing elevator doors. She smiled as she felt she knew what her sister-in-law was going through; she walked back towards Caroline.

"Trust me, everything will be fine again. Nobody's going to hate you, despise you or discard you. We all love you and have been worried sick, but you are back and that makes us all happy, okay?" Caroline smiled a little and nodded *thanks*. Linda grabbed her hand. "Now, let's go make Molly better…"

"I'm so sorry, Dad." Their embrace had been long and warm. "I'm so sorry about what I did, but I…" Her father looked at her face.

"It's all forgotten; you are back and that's all that matters, okay? So enough of that; now go to Molly…" Caroline walked over to the hospital bed as Jack left the room for the two girls to be alone. Molly was sleeping so Caroline sat down and started caressing her hand. She wiped some sweat off her face and tucked the covers under her. So there she was, all married, all big and pregnant. She only imagined how beautiful she must have been at the wedding and so happy. But she also knew that by running away, she had no doubt caused some sadness. It had been such an utterly stupid thing to do, because she had done it to punish not just Molly and her father but for some reason everybody – how pathetic was that and how would they ever forgive her. She really didn't expect forgiveness at all.

It was getting dark outside as she had dozed off a bit. The slight movement of Molly's fingers had awakened her. She sat up in anticipation, but nothing else happened. Then slowly a small smile appeared on Molly's face, her eyes still closed; in a slight voice she mumbled:

"I would recognize that hand anywhere. So soft and warm and furry – Kong, is that you?" Caroline giggled.

"So why don't you get well, Sweetie, or you thrive on the attention you are getting?"

"You know how it is; we run away and nothing changes and we come back and it's actually all the same. So are you here to stay or are you heading back under the rock you have been under lately?"

"The rock next to yours, perhaps?"

"Touché, Sweetie." She giggled. "And of course my husband, *AKA* your *father,* also knows about under-the-rock living, huh? What a trio we are."

"Yeah, and you are done with the *husband, your father* bit?" Molly smiled.

"It's all taken care of and out of my system," she pulled Caroline closer. "Good to have you back; so give your stepmother a hug and a kiss, okay?" Caroline shook her head.

"Will I get sick or something?"

"I hope so; then we can lie here in bed together and do nothing…"

"Okay then… Let's do a trial-run." Caroline swung her legs up in the bed and managed to lie next to Molly. "I miss my PJ's and bunnies, though…" Molly giggled.

"So how the hell have you been, Sweetie?"

Molly and Caroline chatted and chatted for hours on end, only interrupted by nurses and doctors entering the room for check-ups, deliverance of food and drinks. Caroline would sit by the bed while Molly was sleeping and resting the many times in between and up in the bed again when she was not.

Jack would guard the door so the girls could do their re-bonding in peace, no matter how loud the chatting got at times. He visited the cafeteria when hungry and went outside to connect with the office and the rest of the world by mobile. In his heart he was happy watching Molly and Caroline, but in reality also scared and worried about what could happen next. He couldn't fathom ever losing his young bride or the baby; he became dizzy and confused just thinking about it. He had found a secluded bench in the little park on the west-side of the main building where he would shed tears of sadness and fear. He begged for help and hope from nobody specific – over and over; he didn't know what else to do.

Caroline was napping from exhaustion in the chair by the bed. Her father had sneaked in and kissed his wife and lifted his daughter's legs up on another chair. He tugged the thin blanket around her and tiptoed back out of the room.

The gurgling sound from the bed woke her up immediately. She jumped up from the chair and had Molly's hands in hers in an instance. Molly's eyes were closed and her mouth half open. The gurgling sounded again and this time it woke her up.

"You okay, Sweetie?" At first Molly's eyes didn't focus, but quickly they found Caroline's face. She coughed again and pointed at her mouth. Caroline quickly brought a bowl under her face and the hacking and spitting took a few moments. Caroline dried off her face when she seemed done. "Feeling better now?" But Molly was asleep again already.

Two nurses arrived seconds after she pressed the button. She told them what had happened and they quickly did what needed done. Caroline was anxious as to what they found. The male nurse smiled at her and winked.

"She looks better today… Really." Caroline's heart soared and followed him out of the room.

"What do you mean – how?"

"Her color has improved dramatically and her blood pressure is stabilizing, getting back to normal, it looks like." He smiled as he turned down the hall. The female nurse had come out and padded Caroline on her back.

"I don't know what you do, but keep doing it; she's improved reasonably well since you arrived…" and she went down the hall. She raised her thumb in the air without turning. "Good job…" Caroline looked for her father and found him in the visitor's lounge. As he heard the news he

raced into Molly's room. She turned her head as he entered with Caroline in tow. Her smile was wide and refreshing.
"So what's up?" She quipped.
"What's up with you?"
"I think I feel better and George has been kicking so many times the last hour." Both Jack's hands rested on her size eight month tummy. He gently put his ear close to her stomach – and waited. A few moments later he looked at Molly and Caroline.
"He sounds alive and well, if you ask my expert opinion," he happily expressed. "Good future soccer player or ballroom dancer, I suspect." He bent down and whispered in Molly's ear. "Thanks so much Molly; thanks so very much.

Caroline could see the caring between them, how tender and lovingly they communicated. The next few days grew better and better and finally Molly had been released from the hospital, but only to return in a hurry two weeks later. George was born a healthy baby and seemingly didn't have any problems from what had been deemed a virus that they had both survived.

Michael and Linda were put on unpaid leave until results of the internal investigations would be available. Unauthorized use of a department vehicle as well as driving in a state of non-department emergency and breaking many traffic laws in the process, were the headline accusations against Detective Linda Miller. Use of department resources for personal gain, were the lesser charge against Detective Michael Miller. Most of their colleagues believed that superiors would look through fingers in both cases, but a certain captain within the Washington D.C. Police Department had always had a thorn in his side concerning the *overrated* successes of these two homicide investigators; he felt the department had consistently been too lenient with their methods of operation, no matter the results. Too often they had been allowed to work outside department policies and rules. He saw his chance to punish them once and for all.

During the forced leave from their jobs, Linda and Michael became the Godparents to George Jr., vacationed with the twins and had begun to talk about the future, as in *what's next?* They had for a long time for fun more so, dabbled within the idea of working as private investigators. The possibilities in this city were huge and with their police department track record and experience behind them, they should be able to make a living from that – they thought. As they mentioned it to Molly and Jack, they had both enthusiastically asked many questions and the more Linda and Michael had answered the more they thought about the many possibilities. Alone with Linda, Molly had whispered: "With all there's going on, you know, maybe losing your jobs and what not, please know that Jack and I; well I'm not good at this, but what I'm trying to say is that you don't have to worry about, you know, money and stuff..." She was blushing a bit due to uneasiness. Linda had smiled big and said:

"It's okay Molly; I think we are fine, at least for now..."

"Yeah I know, but you know, we are here if and when you need us to help out, okay?" Linda okayed the offer with a big hug.

"Thanks Molly – I really appreciate it, *we* really appreciate the offer. I'll let you know how things are going."

After the investigation, Linda was the first to stand in front of the board and its decision. She was being discharged according to the policies, ethics and rules of the department. Michael was furious when she told him she was out. He was still fuming as he finally stood in front of the board and its members. For his deed he was given a warning and a probationary period of six months and could return to work immediately. He thought about it for a second, but had already made up his mind.

"You have no idea what you are doing and what you'll be missing. My wife is one of the best investigators the department has ever had and in your innate wisdom you are getting rid of her? And you give me bloody probation? Linda and I solved more cases for this department than any partnership ever did and due to your stupidity and ignorance, I resign as of this very moment." He turned on his heel and was gone in a second. It took a long time for him to wipe the satisfied smile off his face. Linda laughed as he approached her outside the building; she knew precisely what he had done. Michael embraced her for a long time.

"So you resigned, didn't you?" Michael laughed even louder.

"I sure did and it just feels so bloody good. They are never gonna treat you like that." She looked up at him and smiled.

"Oh, you are such an incredible stud-muffin, aren't you? Let's go home and get tipsy. Are the kids home?" Michael laughed.

"I certainly hope not…" And they weren't – and they did.

*****

"Wow, so this is where it all started, huh? About a hundred years ago?" Nicole was sitting in the window seat with her nose pressed against the Plexiglas. Jack was leaning over her a bit to get a look as the plane approached Kazan Airport. It was a clear day and the flight from Moscow had been comfortable. The sights down under instantly refreshed everybody. The outline of the city with its over one million inhabitants looked lovely from a few thousand feet above, with streets and avenues making interesting patterns. Molly was holding on to baby George and Caroline was sitting across the aisle with Frank in the window seat, expressing a lot of *wow*'s. The *fasten seatbelt* sign lit up, chairs went upright and trays disappeared. Jack leaned over and gave George and Molly a kiss.

"Thanks for coming along…" Molly smiled and George Jr. drooled.

After eating dinner and spending a full night of ultimate sleep in their big luxurious rooms at the Mirage Hotel on Moskovskaya Str., everybody showed up for breakfast, rested and ready for adventure. The day was about sightseeing around town and the nearby surroundings. Their driver, John Flemming was British, who had gladly settled in Kazan after marrying a Russian named Alina; in the same breath he explained that the name meant *beautiful*. When they met her at dinner the following night they all fully agreed; she was very *Alina*. John's knowledge of the city's vast history of over one thousand years was fascinating and his love for the Russian people extraordinary.

They had finally reached the latter part of the afternoon on their last day in Russia and were heading north on Sibirskiy Trakt, turned west on Prospekt Yamasheva, across Reka Kazanka and then south of Ulitsa Debabristov. The cemetery was not big and grand, but a gently sloping piece of land, grazed with orthodox symbols, crosses and stones of so many denominations. After John had pointed them in the direction the needed to follow, they all somberly and peacefully headed towards the small corner on the north side. Jack saw it first and quietly sat down on the stone bench. Molly with a sleeping George silently placed herself next to him; Caroline soon after arrived arm in arm with Nicole and Frank.

The carvings on the headstone had worn over the many years; weather permitted. The names were readable if you knew what to look for and the years of birth and the years of death were just faintly clear. Jack read the stone again and again. The more he read the more he became aware of where he was from. The understanding of what his father had tried to explain over the years about his blood background, his lifeline from Russia finally overwhelmed him; the full understanding of who he was, where he was from and what had influenced his whole life and the people around him, came to a crashing display of fireworks. This was it. This was what his father had wanted him to know; this was what his father had wanted him to see; it had all started here.

Jack's grandparents were buried in front of him; grandparents he never met. They had accepted that their only son wanted out of the Soviet Union for a better life. They had respected their child's wishes and had come to terms never to see him again. To Jack it was the ultimate sacrifice a parent could make; he could not to any extend understand how it was possible to come to such peace.

His father had told him all about his own father's shallow life that had turned to love for the woman who had always loved him no matter what. He had talked about his own mother, the strongest woman he had ever known besides the strong sides of Jack's mother. He had told stories with tears of joy and tears of longing, wanting to go back, at least for a few moments, just to embrace the father and the mother living in his heart.

Jack thought about his father and wondered about the strong feelings he must have suppressed and then the strong feelings he had acted upon. From he was a young boy he always had America in his sights, in his future. It was a somber and opening feeling no matter how you looked at it. Jack felt relieved and peaceful the longer he sat here on the cool marble bench, in Kazan, in the middle of Russia. He felt he had come full circle what his father and his grandparents were concerned. He felt them reaching out of the ground and into his heart; he felt their smiles, respect, love and understanding.

Molly silently sat next to Jack with George Jr. sleeping in the Baby-Bjorn carrier on her back; her hand gently folded into Jack's as she saw the tears.

"Imagine that, Jack." She said as she looked at the stone in front of them. "They died within two weeks of each other." Jack nodded and wiped his cheeks. "It can't get more romantic than that, can it?" Jack caressed Molly's hand and smiled bravely.

"No it can't…" Caroline was now standing behind her father, her arms around his shoulders. Nicole and Frank joined them after they had placed the many flowers on the graves. Nicole snugged in between Jack's legs with her back leaning against the bench.

"This is so beautiful," she whispered softly. "Here lie our great-great grandparents." Frank hooked his arm into Caroline's and rested his head on her upper arm. She turned and kissed him and he squeezed her arm a bit.

"So it went from Milkovich to Miller…" Frank pondered quietly. "I could have been a Milkovich, huh?" Jack giggled.

"Part of you is Russian; I'm not sure how much of a part or what part." Frank felt some pride in that statement, being related to a country with so much tradition and history. Caroline looked at Frank.

"That *is* actually pretty cool, isn't it?"

"Da Karolinsky; it is very coolsky…" Nicole automatically rolled her eyes listening to Frank. He paused and tugged closer to his aunt. "You know I have a special place in my heart for you Russian women, Da?"

They stayed around the gravesite of Mr. and Mrs. Milkovich for the longest time. Conversation was soft and thoughtful. The cemetery's majestic silence was only broken by the slightly dancing wind. As the day turned into evening and as the sun was heading down in the west, memories and reflections brought this moment in their lives a richness they had never experienced before. George Jr. had awoken, but he kept quiet as if he also sensed how special this moment was; a moment of tranquility and somber understanding. They were all touched by spirits they had never felt before; it was a fine and overwhelming feeling, a feeling each of them would carry in their hearts for the rest of their lives.

They had connected the hundred year circle, by returning to where it had all started. Wiping the last tears off his face, Jack slowly stood up. His hand holding on to Molly's; a glance and a loving smile from his young son. Caroline's arm in his and with Nicole and Frank in front, they slowly walked back towards the south gate.

He looked around in wonder. The people he had been so privileged to know, to have in his life, to love and to be loved by. It wasn't a question of deserving such blessing; it had been all about respect and acceptance flowing to and from. He had not been perfect, but his imperfections had been accepted. He had turned into a gentle man living a gentle life and that realization had now fully revealed itself in front of these graves. He felt cleansed and refreshed and saw nothing other than happiness in his future. For Jack, this happiness had come with a price, but it had been worth fighting for; he knew that for certain.

*****

The glow of fairytale had lingered, but always with the mixture of reality, raw emotions and a bit of luck as well as fate. Had he been naïve when he was counting on too much luck? His father told him that *nothing comes from nothing*, that *to make your dreams come true, you really have to get out of bed*. But Jack had at times closed his eyes and ignorantly trusted fate; an entity that he now knew should never be relied upon. But luck and happiness had prevailed, had stubbornly given Jack more of a fairytale life – of that he was convinced as he looked around this early evening in his life.

The sun was almost gone, gently packed in volcanic red. As they drove back towards Kazan they sat as close and as silent as they possibly could. The togetherness was unique and utterly restful - they all felt richer and harmoniously blessed; a feeling one might only experience once in a million years. And *yes*, they did live happily ever after – as far as we know...

The End

Made in the USA
Charleston, SC
15 June 2011